THE PRECIPICE

ELUDING DESTINY
BOOK FOUR

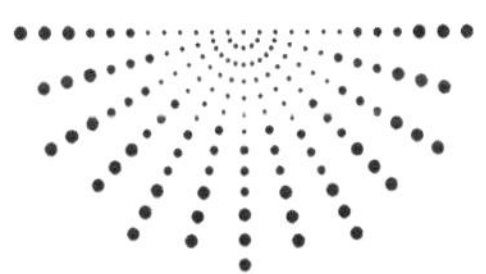

CHARLIE NOTTINGHAM

LIQUID MIND PUBLISHING

THE ELUDING DESTINEY SERIES

Eluding Destiny

The Horrors That Created Us

Aftershocks

The Precipice

Land of Light

The Quiet Army

Sacred Sins

Flash Back

The Shift

Lost to Time

Gods Among Us

The Cover Up

Blank Slate

Sign up for Charlie's newsletter and receive a free copy of the Eluding Destiny prequel, Blood Bar:

https://liquidmind.media/eluding-destiny-prequel/

CONTENT WARNING

For everyone who's wanted a baby and hasn't been lucky enough to have one.

PROLOGUE

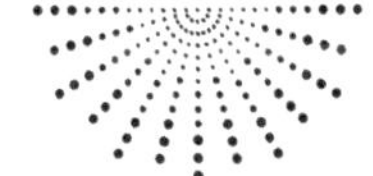

DECEMBER 22, 2020

"Oh, would you stop?" the man murmured to the crying child in his arms. His eyes met those big, glowing blue irises. Such a beautiful thing, how their eyes lit up that way. One of the few things he enjoyed about the Fae. "You liked me once. Don't you remember, Micah?"

He tickled his armpit. Micah giggled, pulling back and rubbing his fist against his big eyes. The man smiled. "There we are, esiasch. Will you please hush for just a few minutes now?"

Micah pointed to his uncle unconscious on the ground. "Cis."

"Chris, I know." He fought an eyeroll. "He'll be back soon, it's alright."

He pointed still. "Huwt."

"He's not hurt, he's sleeping. We have to be quiet." The man lifted his finger over his lips. "Let Uncle Chris sleep, esiasch."

Micah rubbed his eye again. The glow in them receded.

The man smiled. "Good job." He lowered him back into the crib. "I'm glad you can talk a bit now. You can tell me what you want to bring the most."

Still, for a child of his age, he could verbalize remarkably well. Not full sentences just yet, but he was sure he'd get there soon. All the time he and his uncle had together, surely they had nothing to do but talk.

If Micah were anything like the first version of him had been, he'd never shut up once he did. The man smiled at the memory. That child.

Sweeter than a bee's nectar, that's what he'd always said. With a soul like his, he supposed he'd have to be. All that power in there.

But always so chatty. His mother had been too. Never knew how to keep her damn mouth shut. Not then, not now. In any life, that bitch didn't know a damn thing about being quiet.

He doubted he would get his father's silence. If there was anything to say about that child's father, it was that he knew how to keep a secret.

The man clenched his jaw at the memory. He dropped the bag onto the changing table. Diapers, they'd surely need those. The next place wouldn't have a toilet; they might need some for Chris over there too.

He tossed some into the bag and pulled open the drawer below, tossing the bathing necessities into the sack. Didn't want to have to make any stops at grocery stores. He supposed he could—they didn't have his face set up on any facial recognition algorithms—but he had no desire. It was time he got back to the few years he had left to enjoy in this place.

His mission here was simple. Pack the child's bag, take him to the next location, watch over him until Peterson was done with Chris, and then get back to his life. Let his three miniscule cohorts handle the rest.

He picked up a yellow onesie and held it out in front of the child. "Do you like this one?"

Micah smiled, nodding fast.

The man gave a smile back. He dropped it to the bag. Most of this wouldn't fit the boy for much longer. But—now that he thought about it— he'd better take it all. Perhaps if they had enough of the child's possessions, they'd finally get one of those locator spells to work.

He dumped them all inside.

Couldn't have that.

Micah pointed to a photo on the wall. "Mama?"

The man glanced up.

His jaw tightened again. "We'll get some more."

The child clutched the bar of the crib. He bounced, lips pouting down. He pointed with his other hand. "Mama!"

He huffed. Then he leaned over the bag and took the photo off the wall. He stared down at it for a moment.

Those bright green eyes. So similar to what they'd been all those years ago. Her face was prettier now too. Those plump lips perfectly proportioned beneath her small nose, the dainty roundness of her cheeks, the dark locks against her fair skin. So pretty.

His hand tightened on the frame.

But then he looked down at her neck. That scar. That big, ugly scar.
The man passed Micah the photo. The child smiled big.
He pointed to the picture and looked up. "Mama."
The man sighed. "Yes, esiasch. Your fucking mother."
But the child just smiled and looked down at the photo.

PART I

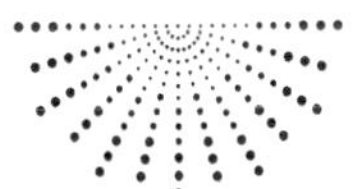

THE WORST OF TIMES, AND THE BEST OF TIMES

CHAPTER ONE

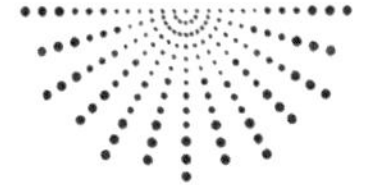

JANUARY, 2020 - LAILA

I glanced up at the ticking clock. Half past ten. I needed to get to bed soon. I was opening tomorrow.

I was almost done though. I just needed to check the note Sophie had left me. She said she couldn't work Tuesday. Or maybe it was Wednesday. Damn it, I couldn't remember. I reached for my notebook on the edge of the desk.

But just as my hands touched it, the strangest sensation I'd ever felt dropped in my chest. A sudden, collapsing gape. Like the air was siphoning from my lungs. It stretched from my heart down into the pit of my stomach. I heaved in an audible gasp. The book fell from my palm, hand raising to my heart.

A loud bang vibrated the light fixtures from our apartment upstairs, and I reached into Jeremy's mind. But I found nothing.

There were no thoughts. There was no vision through his eyes. It was just... Empty.

My heart raced as my stomach sunk. I teleported upstairs.

"Jeremy?" I stood in the living room and looked around. "Baby, where are you?" I hurried down the hall to our bedroom. My gaze traveled over the recently cleaned empty room and I furrowed my brows in confusion.

"Jeremy." I walked to the guest room and pulled the door open. The empty nursery stared back at me. I yanked the door shut.

"Baby, are you okay?" I yelled.

That's when I saw the bathroom light peeking from beneath the door. I grasped the handle, swung it in, and nearly hit him in the head.

Jeremy lay on his side against the tile. His lips were purple on his pale white skin. His eyes were closed. His leg was crooked in an odd contortion, foot caught against the edge of the toilet beneath the other. One of his arms laid lifelessly next to his body while the other was awkwardly tucked beneath his side.

My heart hammered against my ribs.

I dropped to the ground beside him and began struggling him onto his back.

"Baby, wake up." My hand flew to his neck, fingers searching for a pulse. I moved it around but couldn't find one. I had to be wrong. He had to have a pulse. He had to.

But he didn't.

His skin was warm to the touch but there was no pulse.

Tears poured from my eyes, head shaking. I grasped his shoulders and shook him again. "Jeremy." I climbed on top of him and pushed my fists into his chest. "Jeremy, wake up. Wake up, baby, wake up."

There was nothing lying around to explain it. There was no blood, no weapons, no other person. There was nothing for me to heal. He had no wounds. He was seemingly dead without a cause.

I didn't even think to look at the granite counter where grayish white powder laid loosely next to his driver's license.

I held onto him tightly and teleported to the house.

"Hannah!" I pumped my fists into Jeremy's chest. "Help! Hannah!"

"Laila?" Adam called from the kitchen.

I kept pushing into his chest, tears pouring down my cheeks. "Help! Somebody help me!"

It couldn't be happening. Not after everything we'd been through. That wasn't a death fit for him. If he was going to go, it had to be because a Demon or Werewolf or Vampire took him out. Not just sitting in the bathroom.

"Shit." Adam teleported beside me. "What the hell happened?"

"I don't know!" I pumped my fists into his chest without missing a beat. "He was upstairs and I was in the diner and I heard a thump and I went upstairs and he—He was on the floor."

Adam gritted his teeth. "God damn it, Jeremy." He disappeared.

Leah ran in from the kitchen. "What's going on?!"

"He's not breathing." I stared down at his pale face and blue lips. His chest wheezed a loud sound as I pumped, like a balloon that hadn't been tied and air escaped from. I heard his ribs crunching like a bag of chips beneath my tight fists. "He's not breathing. He's—He's not breathing."

"What happened?"

I continued thrusting my fists into his chest. "Get Hannah."

"Hannah doesn't need to see this—" she began.

I looked up at her with glowing green eyes, still pumping his heart with my fists. "Fucking get Hannah! *Now!*"

She gave me a look like I was crazy, but scurried to her feet and started up the steps.

Adam appeared beside me. He dropped to the ground and fiddled with a small white bottle. His shaking hands ripped off the seal and pushed it up Jeremy's nose.

"What the fuck is that?" I said.

"Just keep doing CPR." He squeezed the bottle up his nostril.

Then I saw the label.

Naloxone.

I glanced at it in confusion, still pumping my fists against his dead heart. Everyone in western Pennsylvania knew what naloxone was, even those who don't use drugs. We were in the midst of a heroin epidemic. And naloxone was the only thing that could save someone from an overdose.

He'd used.

And he hadn't told me.

But that didn't matter. I didn't even have the chance to think about how much that hurt, I just had to keep him alive. I couldn't lose him too. Everything was finally okay again. If I didn't have him, I didn't have a reason to keep living.

"C'mon, dude." Adam smacked Jeremy's face. "Wake up, Jeremy. Fucking wake up."

I continued pumping, but nothing changed. Adam was saying something I couldn't hear over the thumping of my heart in my ears and the horrible wheeze coming from Jeremy's lips.

Brody came down the steps, yelling something, but I couldn't hear him either. I couldn't hear anything.

I don't know how long I sat on top of him, furiously slamming my fists into his chest. It could have been only a minute, but it felt like a year. A year of watching his beautiful lips turned blue. A year of hearing the wheeze in his chest as I broke his ribs in a desperate attempt to keep oxygen to his brain until Hannah arrived.

"Laila." Leah gripped my shoulder. I could hear the sadness in her voice. Her eyes overflowed with tears. "Sweetie, he's gone."

"No." I pushed her hand away. "Get Hannah."

Adam gripped my face and turned it to meet his. Tears rushed down his cheeks like mine and landed on Jeremy's face. "Hannah can't help, Lai—"

"Yes, she can!" I screamed. "Get Hannah."

Adam bit his curling lip. I turned to Brody with a trembling jaw, continuing to pump my fists into Jeremy's chest. Even if he were dead, I had to keep as much oxygen going to his brain as possible until Hannah could heal him. I had to keep his body worth returning to. "Brody, please. Please get Hannah."

He had tears pouring down his cheeks too. "He's dead, Laila."

"You don't think I know that?!" I screamed. "I need Hannah. Please. Please, just bring her here."

"I don't see what good that's going to do—" he began.

"*Just fucking get Hannah!*" I screamed again.

He stared at me for a moment. Then he disappeared.

My arms grew so tired. I grasped his cheeks, lip quivering. I just wanted those eyes to open. "Baby," I whispered. "I need you, please wake up."

But his face remained still.

A loud sob left my lips.

I collapsed to his cold, dead chest. It was still beneath my ear. For the first time, there was no rise and fall inside those ribs. And as that realization dawned on me, my weeps turned to loud, painful sobs.

"Please come back to me, baby. Don't leave me," I murmured through trembling lips. "Not like this. Not yet."

It felt so different to lie on his chest without hearing his heart beating away against my ear. It hurt more than anything to think about never hearing that sound again.

It hurt like nothing else. There was this sudden emptiness lined with agony inside of me, like half of me was gone. Like I was literally half of myself. And the half that remained ached in a slow, dull throb.

He had to wake up. He couldn't leave me like this. He had to wake up. He had to explain it to me. He had to live.

We had so much more to do. We had to find Chris. We had to start a family. We had to *live*. We were only twenty-one and twenty-four. We had our whole lives ahead of us. We were too young to die.

"Baby." I returned my hands to his chest and began pushing again. "Baby, please wake up. Don't leave me here. I need you, Jeremy. I fucking need you. Wake up. Please. Please, just open your eyes."

"Oh my god," I heard Hannah say from a few feet away.

I abruptly sat forward and wiped my cheeks. "Bring him back," I said between sobs. "Please bring him back, Han."

She dropped to the ground beside us. Her eyes closed and her fingers found his.

I sat there anxiously for what felt like a decade. Every second that ticked by felt like months. It had to work. He couldn't die. He had to wake up.

"What's happening?" Leah said beside me.

"Shh," Hannah hushed, brows creased in focus.

My hands shook as I took Jeremy's in mine. As I unclenched his fingers, a rolled-up dollar bill fell to the wood floor.

It immediately brought me back to tears.

But I couldn't think about that right now.

I pulled his cool hand to my lips and kissed his knuckles. I had to push every other thought from my mind.

All I could think about was him waking up. He had to wake up.

After a few moments, Jeremy's eyes flung open. A deep grasp heaved into his lips.

My heart jumped with excitement for a fraction of a second.

Then his eyes rolled back, and his body began to convulse.

"Get him to the hospital." Hannah fell backward. "His soul's back but he's going to code again."

I gripped his shaking body and teleported to our closest facility. We landed on the ground. I called for help, trying to prevent his writhing head from hitting the wall.

In seconds, three nurses came trudging toward us. "What happened?"

My lips quivered. "I—I think he overdosed."

"Did you give him narcan?" another asked.

The last one wheeled a gurney toward us.

"He—He died and I kept giving CPR." As the bed drew closer, I teleported Jeremy's writhing body onto it.

"Good," the nurse said. "That's good. We'll take care of him, alright?"

I bit my trembling lip. "Please don't let him die."

CHAPTER TWO

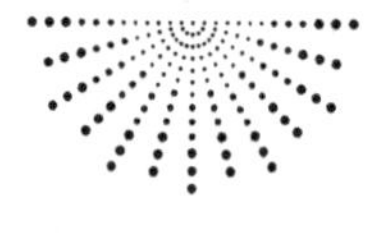

LAILA

I sat on one of the couches in the waiting room with my knees pulled up to my face. I'm sure I looked a bit crazy rocking back and forth the way that I was, but I could care less.

How could I not have known?

Nothing happened recently that would have led him to a relapse so it must have been going on for a while. But he seemed so normal. I couldn't understand how I hadn't seen it. How I thought everything was fine. How I thought everything was better.

We were so happy. We were lying in bed for hours every day, laughing together as we played with each other's hands. We were going on dates again. We were having sex a million times a week.

We were happy.

Why did he relapse?

When did he relapse?

But most importantly, why didn't he *tell me* that he relapsed?

We told each other everything. Or at least, that's what I thought. But I hardly knew a drop in the ocean that had been his life recently.

"Laila," a voice pulled me from my thoughts.

I looked up. Olivia's soft blue eyes looked down at me behind her glasses. She gave a gentle smile. It wasn't particularly shocking to see her. I knew she volunteered here, but I certainly wasn't expecting it.

"Oh, hi." I wiped my cheeks and brought myself to my feet. "How are you?"

"I'm alright," she muttered. "I saw Jeremy back there, what's going on? They won't give me any information because he isn't my patient and I'm not family."

I wiped my cheeks. Perhaps I shouldn't have told his business to his ex, but it just fell from my mouth. I didn't even think. "He overdosed."

I'm not sure what I expected her response to be, but her annoyed expression definitely wasn't it. "Jesus Christ. I thought he'd learned after last time."

"Last time?" I asked. "What do you mean?"

"A few weeks before the wedding. He ODed at my house. Adam came to take him home," she said. "He told me he told you everything."

Those four sentences hit me in the chest like an asteroid plummeting to earth. It took everything in me not to appear breathless. I had to remind myself to breathe.

Before my wedding. Almost four months prior. That's how long he'd been using. That was how long it'd been since the last time his heart stopped beating because of this shit. And he was doing it at *her* house. He was with *her*.

She knew. He lied and kept it from me, but she knew.

That's what hurt the most.

"You said 'everything.' That he said he told me everything. What else was he supposed to tell me?"

Her eyes widened, and she shook her head. "Uh—His relapse, I meant. And his, um, you know. The depression and everything."

Her expression said it all. She was lying. She was scared of me, so she was lying.

"Is there something else I should know?"

"Oh, um." She looked like a deer in headlights. "No. No, it's all good."

I crossed my arms against my chest. "Why do I get the feeling that you're not being honest with me?"

"Laila Callidy?" a voice said from the hallway to my right.

I turned to meet the doctor's gaze. "That's me."

"I'll see you later." Olivia was already halfway down the hall. "Give Jeremy my best."

"How are you today, Mrs. Callidy?"

I shook it off. I needed to know how my husband was.

"Is he okay?"

"He will be. We're not sure why he was seizing, that's not a typical sign of opioid overdose."

He probably seized because his soul was thrust back into a dead corpse.

"We had to give him a sedative to stop the seizures. He's in and out of consciousness now, but it looks like he's going to be fine. He doesn't seem to have any brain damage from lack of oxygen which makes sense since you started CPR immediately."

"When can I see him?" I asked.

"You can go in now if you'd like. He's going to be groggy for a few hours though. We're going to monitor him until he wakes up to make sure his respiration is at a normal pace."

"Do you know which room he's in?"

She looked down at her clipboard. "Looks like he just got moved to room two-O-six."

I ran my fingers through my messy hair and rubbed the bridge of my nose. "Is that on this floor? Or downstairs?"

She gave a bare smile. "It's right through those doors there. Here, follow me."

"Thank you. This place is confusing," I muttered, following behind her.

"Yeah, it took me a while to get used to," she murmured. "I hate to be so insensitive, but if you don't mind my asking..."

"What?"

She swiped a card at the double door. They opened inward. I blinked, remembering a similar beep and click that still haunts my dreams.

"You're *the* Laila Callidy, aren't you?"

"What do you mean?"

"Back in June," she muttered. "All those people, the ones in that torture chamber. You're the girl who saved everyone, aren't you?"

"I didn't do it alone."

"But you did do most of it."

"I wouldn't say that."

She turned and met my gaze with a loving smile. "My niece is one of the survivors. She says that you saved her life. All of their lives."

I forced a smile. "Not all of them. But I'm glad she's home now. Wish her well for me please."

"I certainly will. But thank you. For saving her. We thought she was dead for over two years, but then the hospital called and... Just thank you."

"Thank you for saving my husband."

Still smiling, she pointed to the door on my left. "He's in this room here."

I headed inside. As I looked at him, my stomach dropped.

He looked better than he had. Alive at least, but still incredibly weak. Although maybe he didn't look all that weak. Maybe that's just what I saw when I looked at him after what I learned today.

He'd always been my rock. He was the stable one. He was the sober, calm voice of reason ninety percent of the time. I was the mess. I was the unstable, rollercoaster of emotions and thoughtless actions.

But seeing him lie there, I realized how little I really knew him. He was broken too. And I hadn't noticed until his body was strewn out on my bathroom floor.

His eyes were closed. Greasy black hair laid on either side of his face. I pushed the door shut behind me and headed toward the bed. I sat on it beside him and wiped the damp hair from his face. Then I cupped his cheek in my hand. He didn't wake up, but he nuzzled his face closer to my palm.

Tears welled in my eyes then. How could he keep it from me? He died because he didn't tell me the truth. He fucking died.

It hurt more and more the longer I thought about it.

All of that time, I thought we were in a good place. I thought he was happy. But he couldn't be, not if he were still using. Olivia said he was depressed, and he never told me that either.

That's when I began to rerun our conversation in my head.

Everything. *He said he'd told you everything.*

She was lying about something. I didn't know what, but she was lying.

I heard Jeremy's phone vibrate on the counter in his bag of possessions. Never in our four years together had I gone through his phone. It just wasn't my thing. It wasn't even the fact that I could read his mind. I just trusted him. I never thought he would do me dirty.

But now, I had an impending suspicion that he had.

It was almost unwilling. My feet moved beneath me until I was at the counter pulling his phone from the clear bag.

A smile, and a tinge of guilt, came over me as I clicked the home button to reveal one of my more recent selfies. But I looked past it and opened his text messages. It took a few moments to find his conversation with Olivia, but when I did, I scrolled back to the beginning. He got that phone last year so I couldn't go further back than that.

The first message was in regard to Daniel. Jeremy asking Olivia to give him a brief physical. Then a few texts later, about his autopsy. I shuddered as I scrolled past them.

I read further down. Then it became a little suspicious.

Jeremy. 2:33 p.m. on May 26. *Can I come over later?*

Olivia. 2:46 p.m. *Sure, I get off work at 5:30.*

Jeremy. 3:06 p.m. *Cool. I'll be there around 6 then?*

Olivia. 3:07 p.m. *Sounds good.*

Not too weird, I guess. A little shady considering it was his ex but whatever.

As I got further down, there were a lot of conversations like that. Clearly, he had spent a good bit of time with her while I was in captivity. None of which he mentioned to me.

Then, a date stuck out to me clear as day.

June 22nd.

The day Micah was born.

The day Micah died.

Olivia. 7:14 a.m. *Hey, can we get together?*

Jeremy. 7:18 a.m. *No. I'm busy.*

Olivia. 7:19 a.m. *Oh, shit. Sorry. Can you still pick me up so I can grab my car from your place?*

So I can grab my car from your place. The bitch was at my house?

Jeremy.7:35 a.m. *No. Brody can though. I gave him your number.*

Olivia. 7:36 a.m. *Alright. Thanks*

He didn't reply.

Olivia. 9:48 a.m. *Could you call me when you get a second? I really want to talk about last night.*

My heart ached and my legs grew heavy as I read that one. My hands even started to shake.

Jeremy. 10:15 a.m. *No, Liv. I can't. Last night shouldn't have happened. Leave it at that.*

Olivia. 10:16 a.m. *Damn, alright. Got it. Point taken.*

Again, he didn't reply.

Olivia. 10:32 a.m. *It was a mistake. I know you're taken. I know we're never going to be together.*

Jeremy 10:34 a.m. *I'm busy.*

Olivia. 10:35 a.m. *Geesh, sorry. I'll leave you alone.*

I cupped my hand over my mouth.

Can we talk about last night?

Can I still grab my car from your place?

Last night shouldn't have happened.

The night I was in labor with our son, Jeremy was talking to his ex-girl-friend about "what happened" the night before.

My chest was heavy, my hands were shaking, and my stomach ached. But their conversations didn't end there.

I continued scrolling until I was in late July. Right around the time I started getting better. Just when I was starting to be as close to myself as I would ever be.

Laila's going to bed soon, can I come by?

My stomach clenched.

She thinks I'm with Adam. Is it alright if I drop in?

There were more than ten conversations that started out like that.

It brought tears to my eyes and made my stomach tighten.

All that time, I thought things were great. And he was lying to me. He was sneaking around with her. He was getting high with her.

No.

I couldn't forgive that.

After as much as I had been through, there was no way in hell I was going to let my partner make me feel like I didn't matter. Sneaking around to see your ex behind your wife's back while you're using heavy drugs and lying about it aren't things that can be easily moved past. Those are divorce worthy situations.

I had to leave him before he could leave me. Because he just had. What that did to me, I could never feel again.

It had to be me. I had to be the one to end it before I could ever hurt like I did in that moment again.

CHAPTER THREE

JEREMY

I blinked in confusion, blinding fluorescent lights shining in my eyes. The sickly smell of hospital settled in my lungs. I heard beeping from the machine beside my bed. I struggled to look around.

I turned my head. Laila sat in a hospital chair with my phone in her hands. She gazed down at it like she was reading a page turning novel.

"Baby." I struggled to sit up. She looked up from my phone and met my gaze. "What happened?"

She ran her tongue along her teeth. "What do you remember?"

"I—I don't know. I was at the apartment."

I lied and she knew it. The last thing I remembered was sniffing a couple oxies and sitting down on the toilet. Then I was wrapped up in that warm blanket. The snow was drifting to the ground outside the window. I was beside a fire, and I had a little ball of warmth wrapped in my arms.

Then I was here.

She licked her teeth. She slid her hand through her hair and pushed it to the opposite side of her head. Her hand moved from her head to her face. She rubbed her black, mascara smeared eyes and gritted her teeth. "You overdosed. And then you died."

The beeping on the monitors got faster. My heart picked up in my chest. I met her furious gaze.

I should've told her. I had a thousand opportunities. And I hadn't. Why didn't I just fucking tell her?

No words left my lips. I didn't know what to say. I fucked up.

I fucked up bad.

"Are you going to say something?"

"I'm so sorry."

Her eyes were against the linoleum. "I bet you are."

"Baby—" I began.

"When did you relapse, Jeremy?" She looked up with a piercing gaze.

I considered lying. I considered saying just last week. But lying seemed like a bad idea right about then. "The day we got into that big fight."

"That was months ago." Her brows knitted together above her watering green eyes. "That was before we got married."

I struggled to hold her heartbroken gaze.

Laila huffed again. She wiped a tear from the corner of her eye. "Were you going to tell me?"

I remained quiet. A lump started to form in my throat.

"So, no then."

"I wanted to, but I just... I just didn't know how," I murmured. "I'm so sorry, Laila. I—I didn't want to hurt you, I just..."

"You just had to get high, huh?" she asked. "You promised you would tell me if you wanted to use again. You *promised* me, Jeremy."

The most I could make out was, "I know."

"And you didn't," she said. "You lied."

"I thought I would at the time." I licked my dry lips. "But you were in a bad place, and I couldn't burden you with—"

"Okay, but what about when I got out of that place?" she snapped. "What about before we got married? What about when you fucking over-dosed before the wedding and had Adam cover your ass?"

My stomach sunk and my hands got sweaty.

She knew. Fuck. She knew everything.

What the fuck had I done?

"What—Didn't think I'd find out?"

"I wanted to tell you, baby—"

"Don't." Laila's teeth began to chatter in anger. Or maybe pain. I couldn't be sure. "Don't fucking call me baby like nothing's wrong. I found your corpse on the bathroom floor six hours ago, Jeremy. I had no clue what was wrong with you. But Adam knew the second he saw you."

"Don't be mad at him, I asked him not to—"

"Oh, I am. I'm mad at him, I'm mad at you." She curled her lip up in disgust. "I'm mad at Olivia."

I felt my hands begin to tremble and tightened them to fists. Licking my lips, I quietly said, "So you know?"

The next several months of my life may have gone much, much different if I hadn't phrased it that way.

She gritted her teeth. "Yeah, Jeremy. I fucking know."

"I'm so sorry, Laila. I'm so sorry."

Her jaw was still tight. "Is it still happening?"

"What?"

"I told you I know, Jeremy. Just answer the question."

"Baby, I would but I don't know what you're asking."

Her eyes grew a brighter green. "You and Olivia. Are you still fucking her?"

Obviously, I should've seen what she was saying, but I was barely conscious, and I hadn't seen Olivia in months. "What?"

She lifted my phone to her hand and began reading. "'Laila just went to bed. Can I come by?' 'I need somewhere to go, can I come over?' 'She thinks I'm with Adam.' 'I'm going to tell her. I am, really.' 'She's out with Leah, do you want to hang out?' 'I'm really tired but I'm still down to chill if you are.'"

Laila looked up at me with tears in her glowing green eyes. "Oh, my personal favorite. 'Last night shouldn't have happened. Leave it at that.' Or, oh wait, maybe this one's better. 'Can you still pick me up so I can grab my car from your place?'" Her nose curled in disgust. She looked back up and met my gaze with a quivering lip. "You had that bitch at my house while I was giving birth to your child in fucking prison."

"No." I shot up in the bed. "No, I swear. It wasn't like that. It wasn't at all, we never slept together, I promise—"

"Your promises mean nothing, Jeremy." Tears began to silently stream from her eyes. She tossed the phone to my lap. "You lie, and you lie, and you lie. Our entire marriage has been built on a foundation of fucking lies."

My heart rate on the monitor beside the bed started going crazy. I knew how those messages looked. But it never was how it sounded. I never cheated. I never wanted to. I got high at her house, that was it.

"No, that isn't true." I turned and lifted my feet off of the bed.

Her brows pulled together and downward. I couldn't tell if in anger or pain. "I could have gotten past the relapse, Jeremy. You know I could. But this? Cheating on me with your ex?"

My head shook violently. I rushed toward her. The IV yanked out of my arm, but I hardly felt it. The pulse oximeter fell off and the beeping stopped. I dropped to my knees before her. "I didn't cheat, Laila. I love you, I'd never cheat on you. I swear, I didn't—"

"This?" She gestured to the phone. "This is fucking cheating, Jeremy. Lying to me about where you are? Who you're with?" she snapped. "I thought we were good. I thought we were great. I've been happy. I've been in a good place. I thought *we* were in a good place."

"We are," I said. "We are, we're great."

"Great?!" Her voice raised, eyes widening. "This is great? You fucking lying to me about almost every detail of your life? That's great?"

"Baby—"

"Don't fucking call me that!" she yelled.

I didn't know what to do. I didn't know what to say. I knew I'd fucked up, I knew that. I knew I'd just broken her heart. That was never what I wanted. I wanted to get high, but I didn't want to hurt her. I just wanted to escape.

She rubbed her eyes. "Were you high at our wedding?"

Maybe I should have lied that time. "Not really."

"But kind of?" Her tone was like ice. "You *kind of* did heroin before our wedding."

"I haven't done heroin since I was seventeen," I murmured.

"Well, congratu-fucking-lations, Jeremy," she said. "I'm so glad that you didn't touch the bad stuff on the streets. You still overdosed though. Twice in a year. Actually, in five months. You overdosed twice in five months. But I'm so proud that you didn't do heroin. And let's not forget how you've kept it from me. Did a damn good job at it too."

"I'm sorry." My irises stung with tears. "I'm so sorry."

Her head turned to the ground. She closed her eyes. "Me too."

"I'll get clean." I leaned closer to her. I placed my hands on hers in her lap. "I will, I swear. I won't touch it again, I promise. I know that doesn't mean much, but I will, Laila. I will."

She looked down. "I'm leaving, Jeremy."

"No, please stay. Please, Laila. I love you. I can fix this. I will, I'll—"

"It's too late." She did everything in her power to keep her tone flat. "You hurt me, Jeremy. You *fucking* hurt me."

My heart started to fall through my chest. My stomach twisted and spun. My hands shook and so did my head.

Her jaw trembled as she spoke. "I held your dead body in my arms. I heard your ribs crack while I gave you CPR to keep you alive. I laid my head on your chest and I didn't hear your heartbeat. I didn't feel your breath move in and out of your lungs." Her lip quivered. "You left me."

"I'm so sorry—" I began.

"No. No, you don't get to apologize and make this all disappear." Tears pearled her cheeks. "I'm going away. I'm going to travel for a while. I talked to Max; he's going to handle the diner. I should be gone for about a month. That should be enough time for you to find somewhere else to go but if not, I can stay at Mom's until you figure it out."

It was like the ground fell out beneath me. My stomach sunk. My breath caught. My heart pounded like a drum in my ears. There was a sudden hole punched into my gut that hurt more than any real punch ever had.

"No, Laila. Please. Don't say that. I love you, I love you more than anything—"

"Not more than getting high." She wiped her cheeks. "Not more than seeing your ex."

"I'll never talk to her again. I'll get clean and I'll stay clean. I will, Laila, I will." Tears slid from the corners of my eyes. "Let me fix this."

"We need a break. We both need time to think about what we really want—"

"I want *you*." I grasped either arm of her chair and tried to find her gaze. "I want my wife."

She stared at the ground beside my knees. "You can take money from the account to get yourself started out. A month should be long enough to find a job and an apartment, but you can use our joint account to help you get on your feet. Just let me know if you're gonna use any large amount of money before you do so I can make sure there's enough in the spend account. I'm not just kicking you to the curb. But I can't be with you, Jeremy. Not right now."

I reached out to take her hand and she ripped it back. "Please don't do this. Please, Laila. You're my whole world. Don't leave me. I'll do anything, I swear I will. I love you, I love you, Lai."

She met my gaze with watery, pain filled eyes. "You left me, Jeremy." She paused. "You can take whatever furniture you want. I can get new stuff. I know you love that coffee pot so you can take it too if you want."

I tried to meet her gaze, but she kept avoiding it. I wanted to look at her. I needed her to see that I was being honest. I wasn't lying, I wanted her to know that.

"Laila, please." I took her hands in mine. "Please don't do this. I'll do better. I promise, I will. I'll make this right. I love you; I love you more than anything. Just please. Please don't do this."

She didn't pull away that time. Instead, she began to cry. Her head shook back and forth and her lips quivered. "I don't want to. But I have to."

"No. No, you don't. We can work through this," I said hopefully. She turned her gaze to mine. Black mascara water dripped to her chin. I lifted my hands to her cheeks, wiping the tears away and cradling her face. "We can go to counseling. I know a few psychiatrists that are connected to our world, they can help. We can make it work. We can fix this. *I* can fix this. Just please. Please give me a chance. Let me fix this."

Her hands made their way to my face. She continued to cry. They felt so warm, they felt like home. Her voice sounded so broken, but it felt like home too. "I love you so much."

"I love you too," I whispered.

"You have to get clean. And you have to do it for you." She wiped my tears. Her head shook and her lip quivered. "You won't stick to it if you do it for me."

Tears overflowed my eyes. "Please, baby. Please. Just stay. I mean, go and travel by yourself if you need that, but just... Stay with me. I know we can get past this. I know we can, but we have to stay together. Please don't leave me, baby."

"Maybe. Maybe one day. But..." Tears rushed from her eyes and she fought the urge to sob. "But not right now."

My shaking hands held her trembling jaw. My chest felt like a hole had just been punched through it. My legs were quivering. Everything hurt, the withdrawals may have played a part in that, and it was all my fault. All I had to do was tell her the truth and I just kept lying.

"Are you going to divorce me?" I whispered.

"I don't know. Not today or anything." I nodded to that glimmer of hope. "But for now, we aren't together. We're single unless one of us decides to file the papers. We'll live separate lives, we can see other people..."

"No," I said. "Baby, no. I don't want to be single. I'm married, I'm married to my best friend. I don't want to lose you. Please, Laila. Don't say that."

"I don't want to end on bad terms. We can still be friends."

"I don't want to end at all," I whispered. "Don't do this, Lai."

She leaned forward and pushed her lips to mine. I moved my hand from her face to her neck and held her as close to me as I could get.

I'll never forget the way that kiss felt. Not just emotionally but physically. Our lips quivered, allowing an entrance for that salty water to enter our mouths. Our lips nearly vibrated as they opened against each other's. Our hands shook just as furiously. Both of our hearts were breaking behind our ribcages. She wasn't just ripping mine from my chest but hers too.

Neither of us wanted it. It wasn't one of those situations that you look back on and think, 'It was a hard decision, but I know I made the right one.' It just fucking hurt. At least, that's how I'd always see it.

As she pulled back a bit, she rested her forehead against mine.

"Please, Laila. Please, let me make this right. Just don't leave, baby." My voice was nearly a whisper because if it were any louder, I wasn't sure I could keep from sobbing. "I can make this right. I can do better too, I can. Just give me a chance. Please, Lai. I love you so much. Please don't do this."

"I'm sorry, baby," she murmured.

Then she disappeared.

Suddenly I was staring at a wall behind an empty chair. My mouth fell open. My chest grew so tight that it was hard to breathe.

The tears in my eyes overflowed. I collapsed onto my ass. I cradled my head in my hands and squeezed my temples.

What the fuck did I do?

After a moment of weeping, I heard my phone vibrate on the bed. I stood, grasped it and slammed it across the room. It hit the wall and fell to the ground in broken chunks.

"Fuck."

CHAPTER FOUR

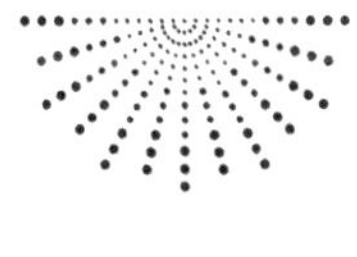

JEREMY

A quiet knock tapped at the door before it slowly creaked open. I turned around and wiped my cheek. Hannah made it through the threshold.

"Hey." She gave a sad smile. "Can I come in?"

I ran my hand along my face and lowered myself to the bed. She drew closer, sat beside me. and wrapped her arms around my shoulders.

I laid my head against hers and bit my shaking lip. "Have you talked to Laila?"

"Yeah, I have."

"Does she hate me?" I asked.

She frowned. "She'll never hate you."

"I—I..." My eyes stung with tears again. "I don't know."

"It'll be okay," Hannah murmured.

I was quiet for a moment. "She broke up with me. She said we're single until one of us decides to file for a divorce."

Hannah squeezed my shoulder a bit tighter for a moment. She pulled away. "She's hurt right now. She'll come around."

"This is different, Han."

"Damn right it's different," Leah said in the doorway. "You fucking died."

I looked up and met her gaze. Her teeth were gritted, she had black lines of mascara beneath her eyes, and her lips were quivering.

And I braced.

She hadn't been kind to me when I overdosed as a teenager either. Not that I expected her to be. She'd almost lost me, she was scared. She was hurt, and she had every right to be. It's hard to lose a sibling, we all knew that.

"Come here, shit head." She made her way across the room and extended her arms.

The tightness in my chest softened a touch. I stood and put my arms around her shoulders. She tucked hers around my waist and rested her head against my chest.

"I'm sorry," I murmured.

She stayed quiet for a moment. "Why didn't you just tell us?"

I wiped my eyes. "I don't know. Because I wasn't ready to get clean. And I knew you'd tell her."

"Are you ready now?" she asked.

If Laila wouldn't have broken up with me, the answer would have been yes. But in that moment, there was nothing I wanted more than a needle in my arm.

"I don't know."

"Well, you know you're always welcome to come home. Your room's open."

A nod was the most response I could give.

"Look, Jeremy. I'm angry with you. You brought Laila into our lives and she became my best friend. Then you hurt her and that makes me furious. After all the shit she's been through this year, you pile this on top? It's fucked up, and it's selfish, and I completely support her decision to leave you." I looked away. She grabbed my chin. "But I don't want you to leave us."

She looked more sad than angry now.

"I'm not happy that you're on drugs. I'm not happy about the shit you did with Liv. I'm very disappointed. More than anything, I'm hurt. It pisses me off that you hurt her like that. And it pisses me off that we had to see you like that. But you were dead, and that's the scariest thing I've ever seen, and we've all seen some horrible shit." Tears welled in her eyes, but her face remained steady. She used her thumb to motherly wipe a tear from my cheek. "And as angry as I am, I'm not going to tell you what to do with your life. You're a grown man. You know what you're doing. You make your own decisions. And even if I'm not pleased with them, you're still my little brother. And I love you. If you're going to use, you're going to use. That doesn't mean we don't want to see you. That doesn't mean we don't want you around. We just don't want you to die." I nodded slowly. "Just don't block us out, okay? Talk to me. Talk to Adam, or Hannah, or Brody. Just don't think that we don't care because we do. We fucking love you. We've already lost a brother. We can't lose another."

That hurt. It hurt so bad. But it was so relieving at the same time. Because I was gonna need her. I was gonna need them all. If I didn't have my wife, I needed some other reason to live.

"I'm sorry you guys had to see that," I murmured.

"If we hadn't, you'd still be dead." Leah glanced at Hannah. "If it weren't for *Hannah*, you'd still be dead."

I turned to Hannah and cocked my head to the side. "What?"

"Hannah's a necromancer," Leah said. "She brought you back."

"What?"

Hannah swallowed. "I never told anyone..." She shook her head. "You know what they say about necromancers."

That I did. Everyone did. Dark magic that should never, *ever* be used. It was a Guardian ability, but even we turned against them. A few hundred years ago, there'd been something of a genocide to wipe them all out. The Chambers killed every bloodline where the gene remained. I didn't know any survived. And it surely wasn't a Skoulda gene. Two of us wouldn't be on the Chambers if so. It must have come from Mom's side.

That would explain why Annie hated the Chambers so badly. Always thought it was because she was just progressive, but maybe it wasn't. Maybe it was because her and Mom were necromancers.

I continued to blink in confusion. "But... How did you... I mean, you..." Daniel crossed my mind. She was with him when he died. And he was still dead. I didn't deserve to live any more than he did. "But Daniel..."

She looked down. "I tried. I brought his soul back, but his body was so... He came back, and he was just screaming. Trapped inside a body that would never work again. Fae can't heal paralysis. And I..." Her frown was so deep. "I let him go."

A lightbulb flicked on over my head. "At the hospital when Laila got out. That's why you didn't leave. Because she kept coding."

"I couldn't let her die."

"Also how Laila survived when Adrian stabbed her," Leah muttered.

I smiled at Hannah. "You're our own little guardian angel, huh?"

She smiled, giving a shrug. "I don't know."

"And Laila knew?" I asked. "About what you are?"

"She was the first person I brought back," Hannah said. "She heard me in the abyss. I've gotten better now. That's why you didn't see me when I ripped you back."

"She can only bring you back if you just died," Leah said. "Otherwise, it uses a huge amount of energy. Then people could figure out what she is."

"I don't really know how to anyway," Hannah said. "It's all kind of been self taught."

"We can't have that," I murmured.

"Only our family knows, and it has to stay that way."

"Yeah. Yeah, just us. And Laila."

"And Kai," Hannah said. "Kai knows."

If it were anyone else, I'd have said we needed to wipe their memory or kill them. But it was Kai. And I trusted Kai with everything I had. He'd never tell a soul.

Leah cleared her throat. "So, what are you going to do, Jeremy?"

"What do you mean?" I asked.

"With your life," Leah said. "What are you going to do?"

I looked away. Then I lowered myself to the bed. "I guess I'm going to leave like she asked. I don't know what I'm going to do about a job, but I'll figure it out. Maybe I'll work on cars. I'm not certified but maybe a shop will take me on. Or maybe I can work out of the garage if that's okay? I don't know. I'll figure it out." I glanced at my broken phone. "Can we go to T-Mobile?"

"As soon as they let you out," Leah said.

"And can you make sure she knows I didn't cheat? She doesn't believe me, but nothing ever happened with Olivia. I was just going there to get high and bullshit. Nothing happened."

"Jeremy..." Leah murmured.

"You can read my mind, Leah. I never did anything with her. I didn't want to. I just want Laila." My eyes glimmered with tears. "I was just using Liv. She wouldn't let me die and I knew she wouldn't tell Laila. I-I never did anything with her, I never would. I love my wife, you know I do."

"Once she calms down, I'll tell her that. But she showed me the texts, Jeremy. They don't read well for you."

CHAPTER FIVE

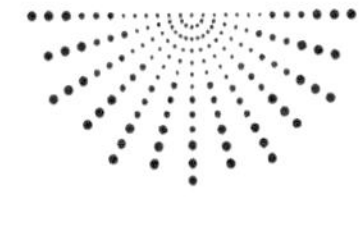

LAILA

I folded a pair of shorts and set them into my pink suitcase, slow breath easing from my nostrils. My eyes caught at my wedding ring on my left hand. But I couldn't bring myself to take it off.

It hurt. It hurt so bad. But he was still my husband. I was still his wife. I didn't want to change that.

I just wanted it all to go away.

But it wouldn't. So I figured I'd go away instead.

Shaking my head again, I grabbed my glass of whiskey from the side table and took a long sip. When the sip wasn't enough, I tilted my head back and gulped up what remained in the glass.

"Hey," Adam said in my bedroom doorway.

I glanced at him and rolled my eyes.

"Can we talk?" he asked.

"I don't have anything to say to you, Adam." I teleported the bottle of whiskey to my hand from the dresser, twisted off the cap, and raised the bottle to my lips. After a long chug, I set it down on the bedside table.

He walked toward me. He reached past me to the bottle on the table. He raised it to his mouth, guzzled for a moment, and set it back down.

"He loves you, Laila."

"Fuck off."

"I didn't want to be Brody," he said. "It wasn't my place to interfere."

My brows furrowed as I looked up at him. "At least Brody was honest with me. But you were part of the conspiracy. You were my friend before I loved him, you should have been my friend through it too."

His sincere blue eyes moved between mine. He looked so much like Jeremy, and it hurt. "I am your friend."

"Friends don't lie." Tears stung my eyes. "Friends don't let each other think that everything is fine when it's not. He died, Adam. And if he would have stayed dead, that would have been on you. I could have watched out for him if I knew but you kept me in the dark and he fucking died."

He placed a hand on my shoulder. I pushed it away.

"You knew, Adam." Tears began to stream down my face. "You knew he wasn't sober, and you let me marry him. You knew he was lying to me and you didn't fucking tell me."

"He told me he was clean," Adam said. "He swore he wasn't going to use again, Laila."

"You knew." I raised my hands to his chest and pushed him back a bit. "You picked him up from her fucking house when he overdosed. You *knew*."

I pushed him again as tears began to pour from my eyes. "You knew he was fucking her and you let me marry him anyway." I pushed his unmoving body again. My glistening tears turned to a loud, ugly cry. Then my pushes turned to smacks. He gazed down at me and let me go on hitting him. "You knew. You fucking *knew* and you kept it from me. You helped him lie to me."

He placed his arms around my waist and hauled my crying body to his chest. I wanted to pull away, but I wanted that hug more.

"You fucking *knew*," I said between gasping tears.

"I'm sorry, Lai." He squeezed me tight against him. "I'm so sorry."

I don't know how long we stayed like that. All I know is that he let me cry. He comforted me just as he had a thousand times before.

At the end of the day, it wasn't Adam's fault. In his shoes, I would have done the same thing. How could he ruin his brother's marriage? How could he be expected to interfere like that?

Ultimately, none of it matters now. The whole ordeal is so far in the past, it feels like a different person lived it entirely.

It was just another page.

Another chapter in the story of our lives.

It was far from the end.

CHAPTER SIX

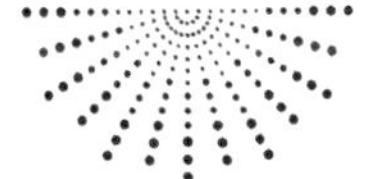

JULY 10, 2020 - LAILA

6 MONTHS LATER

Fuck, I hated it here. Not the women, they were all nice. I just didn't like it. Doctor Williams, my therapist, insisted it would be good for me. I was trying to give it a chance, but it hadn't helped a damn thing. In fact, it did the opposite.

A sexual assault survivor's support group.

Her other advice hadn't been so bad. Journaling was soothing. Meditation was okay. I liked the hot baths. And her blessing on covering my scars with tattoos had been best of all, part of why I liked her so much, in fact.

But this sucked.

Listening to all of these women cry over the men we should have killed before they had the chance to hold us down and stick their dicks inside of us fueled a fire inside of me, I was desperately trying to extinguish. Each time I heard another woman tell their story, my heart hurt for a moment, then it ignited aflame.

My ass throbbed against the freezing, fold-up metal chair. I sipped my iced Irish coffee—the only thing that made this bearable—and enjoyed the burn as it settled in my stomach. My gaze shifted over the circle of women murmuring amongst themselves. It smelled old. There was really no other word I could think of to describe it, just old. It wasn't that it smelled like old people, it just had an odd, elder scent to it. Although, I supposed the church above us probably was.

"Hi, everyone." A young girl wrung her hands together and gazed between us, cutting off the conversations around the room. She pushed a long, curly lock of blond behind her ear. Her light brown eyes were bloodshot, standing out from the dark circles beneath them. She struggled to steady her trembling hands as she spoke. And judging by her round cheeks and jaw, she couldn't have been more than sixteen. "My name's Tori. This is my first time here so I'm not really sure where to start."

The side of my neck stung a bit when I craned up to look at her. My tattoo there was fresh, I just had it done this afternoon. But I sipped my spiked coffee. It helped to lighten the sting.

"Just talk about whatever you're comfortable with." The therapist gave a reassuring smile.

"Well, um." She cleared her throat. "I just turned sixteen two months ago. That was exciting." She twirled a piece of hair beside her face around her fingers. "My friend told me I should try coming to one of these groups because I don't really feel like I can talk to anyone else. And I just really need someone to talk to."

Looking up at her, all that I saw was a baby. Just a little girl.

"You came to the right place," a girl beside me said.

Tori strained a smile. "Well, um. About three months ago, I... I, um..." She paused and wiped the corner of her eye. "I was raped. And two weeks ago, I went to Planned Parenthood. Monday, I got my test results back. Thankfully, I'm not pregnant. And that's good." She gave a sad smile, tears forming in her eyes. Then she bit her lower lip before pressing them together. "But now I'm HIV positive."

Others moved their hand to their mouths. Some even got tears in their eyes.

But me? That fire ignited. I felt it burn in my chest then slide down to the pit of my stomach. I had to chug a few sips of my coffee just to put it out and keep my eyes from glowing like traffic lights.

"And that's not so good." She sniffled and wiped her eyes. After a moment, she regained her composure. "Now I have to tell my parents about what happened, and I know they aren't going to believe me. I'm really scared they're going to hate me because they're super strict. And they're... They're friends with him. I, um..." She blinked some tears away. "I don't know what to do."

I wanted to kill the fucker that hurt her. I wanted to chop off his dick and shove it down his throat.

Come to think of it, not just him. I wanted to kill her parents too. They were blessed enough to have a baby, and she couldn't even confide the worst thing that had happened to her in them? To protect a rapist? They didn't deserve a kid.

"Are you looking for advice?" the therapist asked.

"Yeah, I think so."

"Well, maybe a good idea would be to talk to your school guidance counselor," the therapist said. "Maybe they could sit down with you when you tell your parents."

"I'm home schooled," she muttered.

"Would your parents be willing to take you to a counselor?" she asked.

"They say therapy is pseudoscience. They're strict protestants, it's hard to get them to hear a word unless it's in the bible. My dad's the senior pastor at our church. He says that there isn't a problem that God can't solve."

Ah, so they were probably the same type of people that would say it was her fault. That she seduced him with her wilding beauty. That she was the one to blame, not the man who'd done it.

A huff of a laugh left my lips, and I sipped my spiked coffee. The therapist turned to me. "Is there some advice you'd like to give, Laila?"

"I'm sorry, hon, I wasn't laughing at you," I said quickly. "Just the God comment."

"Yeah, God doesn't seem to have an answer for this one."

"Because there isn't one. God wasn't watching over you when the bastard hurt you, he surely isn't watching over you now." I felt darting gazes on me but held Tori's. "I take it you didn't get a rape kit."

"I didn't really have the opportunity."

"Do you have any dirt on the guy?" I asked.

"Laila," the therapist interjected.

"Hey, I'm just saying. If you can't get him for the rape, get him for something else," I said. "Probably get a longer sentence anyway."

"No," Tori muttered. "No, he's clean as a whistle. A pillar in the community."

Damn. I thought for a moment. "But is it known that he's HIV positive? That might be enough evidence in court."

"You don't understand. He'll never be charged," she said. "My parents wouldn't let me go to the police if I wanted to."

"We'll go over some options after the meeting, Tori," the therapist said before turning to me. "You seem pretty chatty today, Laila. Would you like to share something with the group?"

"Sure," I muttered. As Tori sat, I stood.

"Good afternoon again, everyone. How are we all today?" I said in my typical ironic fashion. There were a few shrugs and chuckles as I went on. "Well, good I hope. My life's pretty good right now. Got the bite scar on my neck covered today so that's cool. I like that you see the art and not the assault now, ya know? But life's kind of weird too. I went on a date last week. It didn't go well."

"What happened?" the therapist asked.

Well, he'd been a prick. He was a 'social media influencer;' he'd announced that with pride. Then he kept asking when we were gonna go back to his place. My final straw had been when our server spilled his drink on the table, and he called her a cunt.

Then I told him to go fuck himself and ate dinner on my own. He was a human anyway.

"I don't know. Just wasn't my type." I drew in a deep breath and slowly let it out. "The only guy I've been with since I was raped was my husband. And he was super careful, and he asked me if I was okay all the time. He didn't squeeze too hard, he didn't try to hold me down, he was gentle. I haven't been with anyone since he left and now, even just going out with a guy I don't know makes me kind of uncomfortable. What if he grabs me too hard? What if he doesn't know how to be with someone who's been raped? What if things start getting heavy and he doesn't stop when I tell him to?"

Of course, I knew what would happen if a guy did anything like that to me. I'd kill him. I wouldn't even give him the chance to hurt me. But those thoughts did linger.

Still, I did want to get back out there. Jeremy had. I'd felt another bitch's nails sliding down his back the week before.

Okay, that's not fair, I shouldn't call her a bitch. She probably didn't know he was married. And even so, I told him it was okay for him to see other people. At least he hadn't brought any girls back to the family.

The fact remained though. I'd gone the last six months without sex. And I missed it. Not that I wanted a relationship or anything, but I missed fucking.

Really, I missed fucking my husband. But I wasn't ready to go down that road.

I just wanted sex.

"It's just weird. Like, I know my husband's out there fucking other girls, so I shouldn't feel guilty for considering it with someone else. But like, I don't know how to go out. I don't know how to date any more. I was in a monogamous relationship all of my adult life. I don't know how this shit works. And I don't even really want to date. I don't know. I'm a mess. End rant." I plopped back into my seat.

Daisy—one of the girls I'd formed something of a friendship with over the past few weeks in this group—laughed. Then she lifted my coffee to her lips. She took a sip from the straw and quickly widened her eyes. I chuckled as she shivered and handed it back to me. "Damn, girl."

"It's medicinal," I muttered. "This tattoo hurts like a bitch."

It didn't. Well, as it was getting done, it had. But now, it was barely a dull throb. I sure did feel that whiskey burning in my belly though.

⁂

Once the group ended, everyone sat around talking for a while. There was a snack table by the back door. I usually booked it the second everyone stopped talking, but I felt bad. I wasn't exactly as kind as I could have been to that young girl. I owed her an apology.

That, and I wanted more information. I wanted to help her in any way that I could.

"Tori, right?" I asked.

She looked up from the cookie tray. A sweet smile lifted into her round cheeks. "And you're... Laila?"

I gave a friendly grin. "That's me."

"Nice to meet you." She extended her hand.

"Yeah, you too." I shook it. "Hey, I'm sorry about laughing. It really wasn't about you, just the irony. As girls, we're constantly told to stay pure and be careful. We're continually told that every man in our life is going to want to rape us, and then when they do, everyone says we're liars. And if you tell someone in a church, they'll say, 'What were you wearing? Did you lead him on? Did you even say no? Maybe he didn't hear you.' It's just ironic."

"Yeah. Yeah, you're right. The funny thing is that before this, my entire life was dedicated to the church. I thought God loved me. But if he does, why would he put me through something like this?" She paused. "I don't even think he's real anymore. And if he is, he's a dick."

"If he's real, he's a fucking asshole."

She laughed.

"Do you have a ride home?" I asked.

"We're a few blocks from my house. My parents think I'm at the park with my friends."

"I'm walking too," I said. "Mind if I keep you company?"

She smiled. "Yeah, that sounds nice. Thanks."

I lifted my purse over my other shoulder so it laid across my body like a postal bag. "I could use the company too."

Truthfully, it wasn't about keeping the girl company. Her story moved me in a way most of the stories didn't. They were all devastating; they all made my stomach turn. But hers did something to me that no other had.

She was the first kid I'd seen at one of these. Whoever hurt her damaged her body for the rest of her life. Her life could never be close to normal again.

It hit me hard. And when I get hit, my instinct tells me to hit back.

We spoke as we walked. Mostly about menial things. Her favorite subject in school, the type of music she liked, the sweet boy at her church who asked her to go with him to his high school dance. Her overprotective parents said that she was too young to go out with a boy. Little did they realize that the biggest threat to their daughter's virtue had already come and passed. And he was right beneath their noses.

As we approached her house, I saw her pulse thump hard at her neck. Her light skin grew even paler with a tinge of green to her cheeks, looking at the black Mercedes in the driveway. Her gaze traveled to the bay window where a few middle-aged people stood around a living room holding glasses of scotch and wine. I sipped my coffee, glancing at her hands that began to shake when she stared at the man in the black dress shirt.

He was middle aged. He had a friendly, relatable smile as he spoke and swirled his drink. He was on the heavier side but not overweight. Just an overall bigger guy.

I looked at the tiny, five foot tall sixteen-year-old girl beside me. Her hands traveled down her thin, chilled biceps, trying to wipe away the goosebumps that bubbled against her flesh.

"Is that him?" I asked.

She blinked a few times, trying not to let me see the tears in her eyes. Then she gave a slow nod. "He's the youth pastor at our church. Him and Dad have been friends since before I was born."

"That's why you think they won't believe you?" I asked.

"There's been allegations in the past," she said quietly. "One girl was kicked out of the church, sent to boarding school, and the case was brushed under the rug. The same story with the other one. No one believed her. Not her parents, not the church. Not even me. They won't believe me either."

I was a few shots in at that point, and the longer I stared at him, the faster my heart hammered. I could see it. The young, tiny girl fighting against that bulky man without a chance in hell.

My therapist would say it was projection. But I hated that man. I didn't know him, but I knew I hated him.

"Thank you for walking me home, Laila. I'll see you at group next week if I can make it," Tori said.

Then she started toward the house. I usually stayed to see if someone made it inside safely because I was afraid of what would happen to them before they made it through the door. But the biggest threat to Tori was already inside for cocktail hour.

So, I found a bush nearby where I could still watch through the window without being seen and had a seat. At first, I thought I was just staying until I saw him leave. But the longer I sat there sipping from the flask in my purse, the hotter the blood in my veins began to boil.

She sat in that living room for two hours.

The only thing that separated him from her was the center couch cushion. I could see the general discomfort all over her. She tilted her knees the opposite direction, she twirled her hair, she nibbled the nail of her thumb.

She was forced to sit there with her rapist and act like it hadn't happened.

I couldn't let her be in that position again.

When I saw him give his goodbyes and start to his car, I stumbled to my feet. I watched him slowly back out of the driveway and start off.

I began teleporting through the brush beside him as he drove. I didn't even know why I was following him until he started down a dark and deserted, tree canopied road. When the opportunity was there, I took it.

As he made a bend a little too tight, I used the wind like a tunnel of sorts and flew his Mercedes off the road. It spiraled, flipping through the air before rolling onto the roof.

No one was around. So, fuck it. I'd make sure he never hurt anyone again.

I teleported beside the car and looked inside the broken window. The man cried out in pain. He hung upside down, blood drizzling from a cut in his forehead. His eyes were wide, trembling hands frantically reaching for his phone. His brows were pulled together, his forehead wrinkled, and his mouth was open.

He was terrified.

Good. He fucking should be. For once in his god damned life, he should be terrified.

I wanted him to know what it felt like to fear for his fucking life.

Then our gazes locked.

"Oh, thank God." Tears ran to his bloody forehead. "Oh, thank you, Jesus. I don't know what happened, I just lost control. Did you call 911?"

I watched blood stream from his lip toward his nose. "God's got nothing to do with it."

"What?" he asked. "Please, just call 911. My back really hurts. I need help."

I wanted to make it hurt.

But I also knew he was HIV positive, and I didn't want to run the risk of getting it. So, I contemplated for a moment.

I squatted to get a better look at him. "I will in a minute."

"What?" he repeated, going back to looking for his phone. He found it on the roof.

I reached inside, grabbed it from his hand, and threw it to the other side of the car. He swatted me away. He began crying for help again. But I spoke over his pleas.

"You raped a fifteen-year-old girl and gave her AIDS," I said behind gritted teeth. "You're the worst type of scum on this godforsaken planet."

He widened his eyes. "No. No, I would never—"

"I believe her." I siphoned the air from his lungs for a moment and watched him gasp. "You don't have to admit it because I know she wasn't lying. But you know what? If your God exists, maybe you'll get the judgment you deserve."

I let the air enter his lungs.

He struggled to get a full breath. Then I spun the air near his face and quickly twisted the wind upward. His neck snapped in the opposite direction.

His head fell down in an odd contortion. His cold, dead eyes stared at me. I reached into the car and checked his neck to make sure he was dead. When I didn't feel a pulse, I stood and began walking through the grass onto the road.

He wasn't the one I really wanted to kill. But he deserved it just as much. And with his death came a wave of relief.

Tori was safe. He couldn't hurt her again. He couldn't hurt any more young girls in his youth group. They were all safe because that man was dead.

I pulled my phone from my pocket, blocked my number, and dialed.

"Nine-one-one, what's your emergency?"

"There's an accident on route thirty-one. Please send an ambulance." I ended the call and dropped my phone back to my purse.

I chugged what remained in my flask as I sauntered down the warm, humid Pennsylvania back road.

After everything that happened last year, they called me a hero. A savior. But I wasn't. If I had to put a label on myself, I guess I'd say I was an antihero.

CHAPTER SEVEN

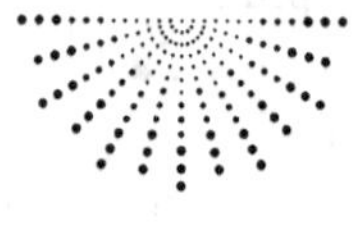

LAILA

I stumbled drunkenly into my usual bar and sat in my seat by the jukebox that should have had a plaque with my name on it by now. The smell of cigarettes and the faintest hint of vomit touched my nose. Cool, relaxing air whooshed around me. I looked up at the blue rope lights that framed the bar. They were pretty. *Maybe I should get some of those for the basement at the diner.*

Sure, I'd drunk plenty throughout the night. But I wasn't passed out, so it wasn't enough. I lifted my flask and shook the last few drops to my tongue.

"What are you drinking tonight, Laila?" Candy leaned over the bar in front of me, blond locks falling to her cleavage. "The usual?"

"Yeah, but make it a double."

She laughed. "Your usual is a double."

I grinned. "Alright, well, pass me the first double and pour me the second while I chug the first."

With a laugh, she shook her head. "You're wild, girl."

I laughed, then heard a familiar voice behind me. "Hey, stranger."

I turned, smile tugging up my lips. My gaze met Ray's warm brown eyes. "Long time no see, my man."

"Yeah, well. Between work, and Lydia's therapy, and all the extracurricular activities. I haven't had much time to myself."

"But you love it." I grinned.

His smile widened. "But I love it." I smiled back. He gestured to the seat beside me. "Mind if I sit?"

"No, please do."

"Thanks." He pulled off his jacket and placed it over the back of the stool.

As Candy set my whiskey in front of me, she said, "What can I get for ya, Ray?"

"Whatever she's having." He gestured toward me.

She huffed. "You're usually a beer guy, pal. Sure you want whiskey?"

I laughed. "Oh, c'mon, Candy. Give the guy some credit, he's not a total lightweight."

"Alright, whatever you say. But if he pukes, you can clean it up, Laila." She wagged a finger my way.

"You're not going to puke, right?" I asked Ray.

He chuckled. "I can handle a little whiskey, guys. Relax."

"Mhmm," Candy mumbled, starting across the bar.

"Where's Lydia tonight?" I sipped my drink, basking in the burn down my throat. "I'm sure you didn't bring her here."

He laughed. "No, she's at a sleepover. Her second one this month."

"Wow." I smiled. "So she's adjusting?"

"Not really. Her friend's a little weird. She likes to go on hikes, find dead animal bones, and try to reassemble them into freestanding skeletons."

"That's more than a little weird."

"I guess her grandpa was some famous archeologist?" He rubbed his eyes. "I don't know, man. It's weird. But Lydia's weird so I can't really expect her to befriend the cheerleaders and jocks. And most kids are real dicks about her scars." He paused, then met my gaze with a smile. "Oh, and thanks, by the way. Lydia saw the picture of your tattoos on Instagram and now she wants to cover her scars too."

I laughed. "Well, can't say I blame her. She is a little young though. But there are other options. Her skin's dark, you might be able to get some flesh-colored tattoos to cover them. My artist said I was too light; it'd be close to impossible to cover mine without using a dark pigment."

"Maybe in a couple years. But she's only twelve, I want her to think on it a while longer."

Maybe so. But if she were my kid, I'd let her. However, I knew what it was like to be gawked at over something I had no control over. He didn't. Still, not my kid.

"Eh. Well, you've got to do what you think is right."

He smiled, eyes shifting between mine. "But how are you? You look stressed."

Actually, I felt pretty damn good. Relieved. Killing that bastard felt like the right thing. I was fairly certain I wouldn't be going to one of those survivor groups again, but I was still riding the high of the adrenaline rush.

Candy set my second drink beside my first. I muttered a thanks and lifted it to my lips. "That's what a lady likes to hear."

"I didn't mean it like that." He smiled. "You look great. You always look great. Your heart just looks kind of heavy today."

"That's a better way to put it."

"What's on your mind?"

I glanced around to make sure no one was close enough to hear me. Then I leaned a bit closer. "I killed someone an hour ago."

"Oh," he murmured. "Did they deserve it?"

"Yeah." I lifted my glass to my lips and tilted my head back. I guzzled until it was empty and set it back to the bar. "He fucking deserved it."

"What did he do?" he asked.

I lowered my voice and gave him the quick rundown.

Then he raised his cup to mine. "Well, thanks for your service to humanity."

My glass clanged off of his. I smiled. "To murder."

He laughed, we tilted our heads back, and chugged.

As we set our glasses down, Ray met my gaze. "Since you're here, I should probably tell you something. I wanted to tell you sooner, but I just came to this decision a week or so ago and we've both been pretty busy."

"Uh-oh," I muttered. "Bad news, huh? It's always bad news when it starts out that way."

"Kind of. Not really, but, um... Well, you know things have been difficult here. Lydia's doing alright I guess, but it's lonely. I only moved here because the opportunity for detective was available. But my sister just told me there's an opening for chief of police in my hometown. I called the department, and the current chief was ecstatic when I called. He wants to personally appoint me."

"Oh, wow," I said. "That's great. You must have been one hell of a cop up there."

"Yeah. Yeah, I was. I left when me and Amy got married and we went to the city, but I've wanted to go back for a while. I think I've had enough of Pennsylvania. Some good times, I guess, but a lot of shitty ones too. I have my sister up there. She's got kids so Lydia will be around family. It just seems like the best option for us."

Wasn't gonna argue with him. If I were in his shoes, I'd do it too. Kids need family around; it would be good for Lydia. It's not like we were all that close anyway. He was a friend, a good one, but not exactly family. We hung out from time to time. But not enough that I'd be devastated he didn't live down the road anymore. Plus, I could always teleport up to New York to see them if I wanted to.

"Yeah, it probably is. Kids need a family support system."

A soft smile lifted his lips. "But I want you to know how happy I am that I met you, Laila. You gave me back my reason to live."

I tried to smile back. I really did. But honestly? Part of me wished I'd never met Ray. If I hadn't, I wouldn't have lost Micah. Jeremy wouldn't have spiraled. I'd be at home with my husband and son right now, and life would be perfect.

Although, we would've never known Chris was alive either, but it wasn't like he was home either way.

A knot stiffened in my throat, and I cleared it away. "I'm just glad she's home. No kid should be in a place like that. Nobody should, but especially not a kid."

Ray's eyes washed over me. "Nobody should."

"Don't look at me like that, Ray."

"Like what?"

"Pitifully." I gestured to Candy for another round of drinks. "I'm no victim."

"That's not how I was looking at you."

"No?" I asked.

"No," he said. "No, I was thinking about how much you've changed since we met. Feels like you were just a kid yourself then."

Candy set my drink in front of me. "Yeah, I kind of was. I didn't know it but..." I lifted my glass and took a sip. "I had a lot to learn. Probably still do, ya know?"

"Well, you've come a long way."

"Yeah, you could say that."

"Is that new?" He gestured to the tattoo above my collar bone and gingerly pushed hair from my neck behind my shoulder.

"Yeah." I tilted my head to the side, moving the hair further back to give him a better look. "I just got it done today. Does it cover well?"

I hadn't even gotten a good look at it yet. But my artist had done amazing on the rest. The orange lily on my wrist, the vines ascending my forearms and thighs, the sunflowers and roses on my back. I was sure the blue and purple butterfly on my neck would be gorgeous too.

"Yeah." He moved in a bit closer to examine it. I felt his breath against my neck and chills slid over my skin. "Yeah, you can't see the scar at all. It's pretty, I like it."

"Thanks." I pulled the hair back in front of my shoulder and swiveled to meet his gaze.

"Any time." He smiled, eyes gently resting against mine. "You look good, Laila."

I smiled and arched a brow. Then my eyes shifted over him for a moment. The clean shaved, strong jaw. Those big brown eyes. That warm brown skin. His mature, manly smile. And those toned, strong arms.

Some part of me had always been attracted to him. And hey, I'd been looking for a way to get back out there.

I took another sip from my drink, and my grin widened. "Ya know, if I didn't know better, I'd think you were flirting with me, detective."

"Me?" He bit his grinning lip. "No, I wouldn't do that."

"No?" I rested my elbow on the counter and placed my chin in my palm. "Never even crossed your mind?" He laughed, raised his glass to his lips, and chugged. "I'm not gonna lie, it's come across mine a time or two."

"Oh?" He set his glass back to the counter. Then his brow raised, smile against his lips.

"All I'm saying is that if you *were* flirting with me, now would be a good time to shoot your shot."

Ray's gaze traveled from my eyes to my lips. Then he gently moved forward, tilted his head slightly to the side, and delicately put his mouth to mine.

Fuck, it'd been so long since I'd been kissed. Granted, it wasn't who I really wanted to be kissing. But it still sent warm goosebumps over my skin, a spin to my stomach, and a flood between my thighs.

I'm still not sure what it was about Ray that I liked. He'd been a real asshole from time to time, but the two of us had become friends since our awkward meeting almost two years prior. Despite his attitude in certain situations, he was a pretty soft guy.

He was a great dad. He was attractive. He was a little damaged too. He was moving so I didn't have to worry about things getting awkward if Jeremy and I got back together.

We were already friends so I wasn't anxious like I would have been with anyone else. He seemed like a good steppingstone to get back out there.

He was a way better kisser than I'd expected. His rough lips caressed mine with just the right amount of moisture. His hand gently cupped the side of my face. He smelled like Old Spice and cigarettes which was, for whatever reason, extremely arousing.

My hand made its way to the denim over his thigh. He tugged my face a bit closer to his. My fingertips slid to his neck, feeling his heart racing beneath them.

"Do you want to get out of here?" I asked.

"Seriously?"

"I mean, yeah. If you want to." I inched my fingers closer up his leg.

"I mean, if *you* want to."

I grinned. "Let's do it."

He reached into his wallet as I fumbled for mine. "I got it." He tossed two twenties on the counter.

"Thanks." I stood and started toward the door, glancing at him over my shoulder with a grin.

Ray smiled back. Then he finished off his drink and trailed behind me. As we stepped outside and made it to the concrete landing, Ray said, "Are you okay to drive? I think I had one too many."

"I am definitely not." I took his hand and pulled him into the alley beside the building.

I pushed him into the wall and reached onto the tips of my toes. My lips pressed into his. My hands rested on his hard, strong chest. His went around my waist. One grasped my hip and the other slid down my lower back to my ass. He gripped it, and I laughed.

With my lips still on his, I murmured, "My place or yours?"

"Mine's good," he muttered.

That was perfect. I didn't particularly want to fuck another man in mine and my husband's bed.

He moved his lips to my jaw and down my neck. His hand at my waist coasted downward until it was on my ass too. He lifted me to his hips. I giggled. Then I looked around to make sure no one was nearby. I glanced up to check for security cameras.

Then I teleported us to his living room.

I felt his lips smiling against mine as he lowered us to the couch. I swiveled my knees until they rested on either side of his thighs. Then I began to fiddle with the button on his jeans. His hand found the button of mine, pulled it open, and tugged the zipper down.

I bit my lip, pulling at the edge of his shirt. He leaned forward. I raised it up his body and over his head. My fingers slid over the firm lines of his chest. Damn, he had abs. Really thick, firmly defined abs.

Jeremy did not. The last time I touched strong, defined abs, I was seventeen. And it was really fucking hot.

His hands were gentle as they slid over my skin. It reminded me of Jeremy. I tried to push the thought from my mind but the image of him turned me on even more. Even if he did *not* have abs.

I teleported my pants to the ground behind me.

His eyes widened. "How did you do that?"

"Like this." I did the same with his.

"Damn."

Ray pulled his shirt over his head. "Was that a good damn? Or a bad damn?"

"Definitely a good damn." Grinning, I pulled my jeans to my hips and buttoned the clasp. "Didn't know you had those tongue capabilities, detective."

He chuckled and tugged his pants around his ankles. "I'm a little rusty, don't flatter me."

"Yeah, well, not as rusty as you think." Lifting my shirt over my head, I said, "You know this was a onetime thing, right?"

"Yeah, kind of figured. I'm moving, and you're obviously in love with Jeremy."

I placed my hands on my hips. "What makes you say that?"

"Aside from when you called out his name?"

My cheeks burned hot. "I did that?"

"You did. But it's alright. The two of you always bragged about your sex life. I was pretty flattered."

That was super fucking awkward. But hey, at least I got laid. And it wasn't as scary as I'd thought it'd be. It was pretty damn great, actually.

I laughed. "Well, sorry about that. But I should probably head out. I have to open in the morning."

"Right." He stood and pulled his pants up.

"But when are you guys leaving?" I asked.

"A couple weeks. Hey, if you wouldn't mind helping me move some big stuff so I don't need to rent an extra U-Haul, that'd be really awesome. I can pay you if you want."

"Yeah, I'm sure Adam or Brody wouldn't mind helping too."

"Great." He smiled. "Thanks again, Laila. For everything."

"Thanks for the orgasms." Three of them, in fact. "It's been a while. I needed that."

Another laugh. "Any time."

"See ya later, Ray," I said.

Then I flashed to my living room.

Alone again. Don't get me wrong, I enjoyed the peace. But I was so tired of being alone all the time.

I walked to the kitchen and opened the fridge. A jug of rotten milk sat on the top shelf. There was a box of chicken tenders though; Max had whipped them up for me before I headed out for my tattoo appointment that afternoon. I grabbed it out and set it on the counter. But I was starving, chicken tenders wouldn't be enough.

My gaze shifted back inside. A bottle of ranch sat beside the milk. Hadn't I bought a head of lettuce? I was sure that I had.

I pulled open the bottom drawer. *Ah-ha, there it is.* Bagged spring mix though, even better. I lifted it to my chest. Then I saw a cucumber below. A smile came to my lips. Cool shit. Chicken tenders and salad it was.

I flicked on the light switch, grabbed a salad bowl, and made my way to the counter. Mindlessly, I filled the dish with greens. After washing my hands, I set the cucumber on the cutting board and began chopping away.

As I was finishing up the end, the knife slipped and sliced through the edge of my palm.

"Fuck." I dropped the knife and lifted my hand to examine the cut. It didn't hurt too bad, but it was gushing. I hurried to the sink and ran cold water over it. Then I grabbed a dish towel from beneath and held it to my bleeding palm.

I felt my phone vibrating in my back pocket. My hands were too full to get ahold of it, so I ignored it. Struggling a bit, I eventually managed to tie the rag around my hand. By the time I finished up, my phone was vibrating again.

With an annoyed huff, I slid it from my pocket. Jeremy's picture looked up at me. My stomach involuntarily flipped. He felt the cut. And if I didn't answer, he was gonna show up and say, 'You were hurt, I had to check on you.'

"Hey." I held the phone to my ear against my shoulder. My free hand wiped the blood from the counter with another dish rag.

"Hey, beautiful," he said. "You alright?"

My stomach flipped again. Jesus, I hated that. He called me beautiful, and that was it. One word. That's all it took to make my knees weak. It was exactly why I couldn't see him. If his voice uttering that one word made me feel like this, seeing his smile would do so much more.

"Yeah. Yeah, I'm good. Just making a salad," I said. "Thanks for checking though."

"Yeah, sure," he said. "But how are you? I haven't talked to you in a while."

"I'm good," I said. "Things are good. Pretty boring, but good. I like boring."

He laughed. "That's not even close to true."

I leaned against the counter, smile edging up my lips. I wasn't sure why, it's not like I really wanted to talk to him. But there was just something about that man that always made me smile. Even if he was a few hundred miles away, his voice alone made me feel less alone.

"How are you? What've you been up to?" I asked.

"I've been alright. Just performing a lot, traveling and everything," he said. "Nothing too exciting."

"Yeah, I saw that on Facebook," I said. "That's awesome though, following your dreams like that. You sound really good."

"Eh, I'm alright," he muttered. "It's income, ya know? Not necessarily what I want to be doing."

"What do you want to be doing?"

He laughed. Then he paused for a moment. "You know what I want to do and where I want to be, Lai."

I fell silent. I raised my hand to my forehead and pushed the tips deep into my temple. My eyes closed.

It's not like it wasn't what I wanted too. It was. I wanted my partner back. But there were a million reasons I wasn't ready for that. He was still using. I was a shit show. And there was a lot of bad blood.

That, and I'd just fucked our mutual friend.

"I'm sorry. I probably shouldn't have said that."

"No. It's okay," I murmured. "Can't say things are exactly as I'd pictured them either."

His lips vibrated in a trill. "So have you gotten any new information recently? About Chris and everything, I mean."

"Not really. We thought we got a lead on Leah's facial recognition algorithm, but it wasn't Peterson. So that was disappointing. We're looking into documents now. Cross checking aliases, seeing if we can find the names being used anywhere else. Mostly just chasing our tail. But he's a genius, coming up with a new identity is a piece of cake compared to the rest of the shit he's pulled off." I paused. "I don't know. But we aren't giving up."

"Yeah. Well, if you guys need anything, or if you just want to bounce ideas, I'm always here. You know I want to help."

"Yeah. Yeah, I know. I'll keep you updated if we find anything."

"Thanks," he murmured. A long silence crept up on us. "Would you want to get together sometime soon? Maybe get lunch or something? The world's back to normal now—we could go out somewhere."

I cleared my throat and closed my eyes. "I have to go. But thanks for checking in on me, I appreciate it."

Another heartbeat of silence. "Yeah, of course."

The disappointment riddled his voice. But he knew there wasn't any use in pushing. It was better I didn't respond than say no. No hurt more than no response.

"I'll talk to you later, alright?"

"Sure. Let me know if you need anything."

"Yeah. Likewise," I muttered. Just as I started to pull the phone from my cheek, he spoke again.

"I love you, Laila," his deep voice said. It sounded so soft, yet still so strong. It made my stomach flip and goosebumps pulse over my skin.

"I love you too, Jeremy," I whispered.

"Bye, baby."

"Bye." I pulled the phone from my ear and clicked the end call button. As I slid it into my back pocket, I rubbed my eyes.

I really wasn't sure how I felt about everything with Jeremy. He lied to me about relapsing. He lied to me about everything, and just kept pretending like it was okay. But at the end of the day, when I sat on the couch we picked out together and lay in the bed we waited weeks to come in, some part of me wanted to beg him to come home.

The thing about it all was that I didn't blame him for relapsing. He was going through a lot of shit too, and it's not like I was any stranger to substance abuse.

I wasn't exactly easy to love after what happened to me. I didn't treat him like my fiancé; I treated him like my personal servant. He was running my business. He was taking care of the drunken desolate disaster

I'd become. He was trying to make sure I didn't kill myself. I put him through some shit.

Despite understanding, it didn't make it hurt any less. It didn't make me magically forgive him. Not only did I feel betrayed, but it hurt my ego. He was comfortable enough with Olivia to get high in front of her. She knew everything that he couldn't bring himself to tell me, and it fucking hurt.

But that wasn't the part I couldn't get past. The thing that really did it was the fact that he had that girl at my house while I was birthing our baby in a cell by myself. If that wasn't a slap to the face, I didn't know what was.

The blood at my palm began to drip down my arm and pulled me from my thoughts. I grabbed another rag and wrapped it around my hand. Once it was tied up tight enough, I sprayed the counter down with bleach and wiped it with some paper towels. I went to throw the bloodied cloths and cucumbers away when I noticed it was overflowing.

I fiddled with the bag, pulled it from the can, and started out the door. Then I walked down the stairs, flicked up the lock on the back door, and started outside. I mindlessly tossed the bag into the dumpster.

Then a rustling sounded behind it.

I brought a flame to my hand. Then I tiptoed to the edge and peeked around the corner.

A large white dog leaned over a paper to-go container munching away on some stale fries and a burger. Its fur was long and fluffy, matted to its hollowed ribs and stomach like it hadn't been combed in ages.

"Hey, buddy." I lowered myself toward it.

It looked up at me and bared its teeth. A growl barreled from its snout, staring up at me like a demon. I laughed and extended my hand.

"You're a feisty little shit, huh?"

Its nose curled back, snarl leaving its snout.

"Shh, it's alright." I extended my hand for it to smell.

Nose still crinkled in fear, it reached forward and sniffed my hand. Its teeth were still bared. But its tongue slipped between its canines and licked my palm.

I laughed, bringing myself to my knees. "Are you hungry, dude? I can make you your own burger. You don't have to eat somebody's trash."

It drew a bit closer as if it knew what I was saying. It studied me hard for a moment. Then its head shifted beneath my palm. A smile edged up my lips. I slid my hand along its head and down the back of its neck.

"You look like you could use a friend," I murmured. "I'm kind of lonely too. Want to keep me company?"

Then its tail started to wag. Its tongue lapped through its teeth, leaning toward my face. It licked and licked away at my cheeks. I laughed, stumbling back a bit.

After a moment of puppy kisses, I struggled my way onto my feet. From that angle, I got a glimpse underneath, noting her sex. Girl for sure. I started toward the door and smiled back at her. "C'mon, buddy. Let's go get you some real dinner."

She was just a dog, but she chose me when I needed something to take care of. She could have run away that night, but she followed me inside.

She found me at a time when I deeply needed someone. I didn't need a boyfriend or another person to get drinks with. I needed someone to take care of. Someone who would always be there for me and wouldn't hurt me.

That's the best part about loving a dog. They never betray you.

CHAPTER EIGHT

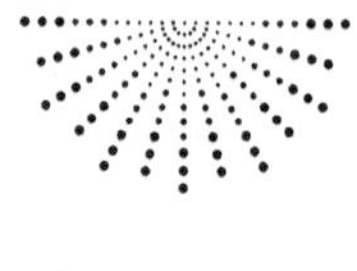

JEREMY

The scent of cheap perfume drifted into my nose. Cool air from the register whooshed against my bare skin. I glanced at the clock on the hotel nightstand. 10:46. Yeah, time to go. Wasn't about to spend the night.

Fucking other people felt dirty enough. Lying there with another woman made my stomach churn. Not that there was anything wrong with her. I'm sure she was a really nice girl. But there was only one person I wanted to cuddle in a warm bed with. Cuddling and one-night stands weren't it for me.

"Who was that?" the girl asked.

I pulled my jeans up to my hips. I fought the button of my pants and pulled up the zipper. "My wife."

"You're married?"

I grabbed my T-shirt from the floor and pulled it over my head. "Yeah, but we're seeing other people so."

"Oh. Are you, like, polyamorous or something?"

If we were actually in a relationship, I could say that. But polyamory implies actually seeing the person you're with. Which she hadn't let me do in months.

"No, she just hates me." I adjusted my shirt. "Kind of fucked her over last year. She told me to leave so here I am."

"Damn. Are you getting divorced?" she asked.

"I hope not," I said. "But I had a lot of fun tonight. I've got to get to work in the morning though so I'm gonna head out."

"Right," she muttered. "Can I get your number?"

"No. Sorry, I don't do that."

"Don't do what?" she asked.

"Ya know, date." I grabbed my jacket off the armchair. "Sex is fun but I'm not looking for a girlfriend. I love my wife."

For the purpose of the story, I wish I could remember her name. Although in hindsight, I'm not sure we even exchanged names. She was cute though, I remember that. Long dark hair, light eyes, and skin. Petite with small boobs and a bubbly ass. I guess one could say I have a type.

"You just fucked me like you haven't had sex in years. And you love your wife?"

"You're gorgeous so no offense or anything. But I wasn't really thinking about you."

Her smile widened as she sucked her teeth. "None taken. I wasn't really thinking about you either. But listen dude, I'm not looking for a boyfriend either. But I haven't had sex like that in a really long time. It'd be great if we could do that again."

"Sorry, just not my thing. Fuck the same person too many times and one of us is bound to get feelings. I'm not interested in that."

"Well, if you have to head out, it was nice knowing you. But if you have a few more minutes..." She dropped the blanket from her chest to the bed.

I laughed. "Thanks, but I really have to go."

She bit her smiling lip. "Well, nice meeting you. Have a nice life."

"Probably not, but got to live it anyway, right?" I grabbed my phone and car keys from the dresser. "But you too."

I headed toward the door, swiping my phone up and leafing through my notifications. I cleared a few on social media before making my way to the missed calls. Adam called twice and Leah called once.

I dialed Adam's number, pressing the down button to the elevator.

"It's alive," Adam answered.

I rolled my eyes. "What's up, man?"

"Leah said you were coming over tomorrow," Adam said. "What time are you coming by?"

"Uh, I don't know. I was gonna start driving now. I'm in Maryland so I'll probably get there around one or two." The elevator doors opened, and I stepped inside. "But is everything good?"

"Yeah. Yeah, everything's fine," Adam said. "Just making sure."

I clicked the button for the first floor while the doors closed. "Got to warn Laila so she doesn't come by while I'm there, right?"

"I don't want to get in the middle of anything, man."

"There's not really anything to get in the middle of," I muttered. "I don't get it. She said we could be friends, but I've seen her once since the breakup."

"I don't know, dude. But hey, could you help me do the brakes on the jeep while you're here? The rotors are good, but the pads are getting pretty low."

Of course. Couldn't exactly talk to my brother about this shit because Laila's sister was probably sitting beside him. If he said the wrong thing, he'd be sleeping alone too.

"Yeah, sure," I said. "Do you know what Leah wanted?"

"She was also going to ask about the brakes. I'll pay you, by the way," Adam said. "But how long are you going to stay?"

"I don't know. A couple days. I have a show on Saturday so no more than a week. Why?" I asked.

"Jenna's car's making a weird sound. I was hoping you could look at it. I thought it was her tires, but she got them changed and it sounds the same."

Did I particularly want to see Jenna knowing how everyone felt about what had happened? Not really. But family's family. And hey, maybe it'd give me an in with her. Jenna did a have a way of convincing Laila to do things she didn't really want to.

"Yeah, that's fine. Do you know if Lai's got her car in for an oil change? It's probably getting to that time. I could take care of it while I'm there."

"I don't know, I can ask her," he murmured.

He knew what I knew. Laila wouldn't ask me to work on her car because that'd remind her that I existed. She liked pretending that I didn't.

I walked out into the lobby. "Alright, well I'm leaving now. If you're asleep when I get there, I'll see you in the morning."

"Alright, cool. Drive safe," he said.

"Will do. See ya later."

The call ended as I made my way to the car. I unlocked the door and plopped myself inside. Reaching into the glove compartment, I pulled out a pre-rolled joint and a lighter. I sparked it and cracked the windows. Then I plugged my phone into the AUX cord, put on some Beatles, went to my GPS, and typed in "Navigate home."

It was ironic because home wasn't really home any more. For the past six months, I hadn't really had a home. I could have stayed at the house; it had always been home before Laila. But I hated being there now. There were too many memories. Mostly good ones but even the good memories were disappointing when I came to terms with the fact that they were only that now. Just glimpses into a life that wasn't mine anymore.

Since the breakup, I kind of disappeared. I stayed at the house during the shutdowns, and it was miserable. When they lifted, I packed a bag and got back on the road. I just didn't want to be in PA. I didn't want to accidentally bump into her somewhere and make things more awkward than they already were.

So, I took off. I'd been all over the country booking little gigs in shitty bars and lame cafes. I didn't like performing all that much before, and I still didn't love it, but I felt more comfortable on stage when I wasn't clean and serene. It was easier to be confident with a drink in my hand or a couple pills in my veins.

I hadn't made an attempt to get clean since the breakup. She'd made it abundantly clear that I didn't have a chance either way so why not be high? I hadn't gone back to dope, primarily because it was too hard to find, but also because of the whole fentanyl thing that had been sweeping the country. I stuck to pills. Usually just a couple Percocets but snorting them wasn't doing the trick anymore so I'd gone back to needles. I was still careful; I didn't share needles or anything like that. Not like I'd made any friends to share a needle with anyway.

Since December, I'd been alone. Maybe not physically, but even when I was surrounded by people, I was alone. I wished I could say I liked it that way, but I fucking hated it.

CHAPTER NINE

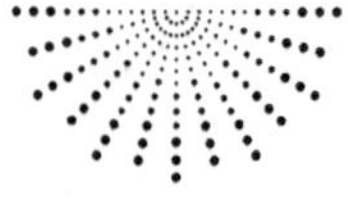

JEREMY

Bright sunlight shined in my eyes, hot summer air coasting against my bare chest. I lifted my water and took a long, refreshing gulp. Wiping sweat from my brow with my shoulder, I twisted the lid back on and set it to the cement. Then I turned back to Jenna's Honda and lifted the hood. As I put the hood strut into place, Jenna cleared her throat.

"Thanks for doing this, Jeremy. How much are you going to want? I can have Adam run me to the bank."

"That's okay. Just buy the parts and I'll take care of it."

"I have to give you something," she said.

"Nah. You're family, don't worry about it."

A smile came to her lips. She pushed blond hair behind her ear. "Well, thank you. I'm a little strapped at the moment so I appreciate it. How have you been though? It's been a while."

"Yeah, it has, huh?" I asked. "I've been alright. Just playing a lot of shows."

"Anywhere cool?" She leaned against the right fender.

"Not really. Bars, cheap clubs. Nothing special. But what about you? How have you been?"

"Pretty good." She smiled. "School let out so I'm off until August. That's a good feeling."

"Yeah, I bet. So you and Adam are getting pretty serious, huh?"

Her cheeks reddened. "Yeah, kind of. Who would've thought, ya know?"

"I didn't see it coming, but hey, life's full of the unexpected. You seem really good together. He's happy. That makes me happy."

Jenna smiled, lowering herself to the step into the house. "Yeah, not exactly as I pictured life going either. When I met Adam, he was dating my sixteen-year-old sister's best friend."

"Kind of creepy." I lifted the dipstick and wiped it on a paper towel.

"Yeah, but in all fairness, Adrian was seventeen and she told him she was eighteen," Jenna said.

"Probably should have asked for ID." I dipped it inside and lifted it back up. The sloped section had no liquid in it whatsoever. There was a speck of dark black oil on the very tip, but that was the extent of it. "Do you ever check your oil? Because you're almost bone dry in here."

"Is that bad?" she asked.

"Yeah, that's bad. When was the last time you changed it?"

"I don't know, a year or two ago."

"Jesus." My eyes widened. "No wonder it's breaking down on you. Oil is like blood to a car. You'll blow your motor if you don't have any in there."

It didn't surprise me that she didn't check on stuff like that, but Adam knew a thing or two about cars. He definitely knew how to do an oil change. At some point, he could've at least checked it. But then again, my brother was pretty well known for being lazy.

"Oh, shit. I didn't know."

I turned from the car to the old work bench, grabbed a gallon of 5w30, and a funnel. "I'll do an oil change while I'm working on it, but I need to put some in before I drive it around. What did you say it sounded like?"

"I dunno, it just goes like, 'clunk, clunk, clunk' sometimes," she said.

That sounded exactly like something Laila would say. As if 'clunk, clunk, clunk' was a description that could point me in any direction.

"Is it when you turn the wheel? Or when you go straight too?" I asked.

"It's not constant, but it doesn't matter if I'm turning the wheel or not."

"Alright. Could be anything. I'll take it for a drive and see what sound you're talking about." I placed the funnel into the oil hole and poured about half the gallon in. I screwed the lid back on, set it on the ground, tightened the cap on the bottle, and let the hood fall back to its place. I cleared my throat and turned to meet her gaze. "So, how's Lai?"

"She's good. Or so she says. I don't know, she's gotten pretty good at hiding how she feels."

"Doesn't sound like Laila."

Jenna handed me the keys. "I don't know. She's changed a lot in the past couple years."

That was accurate. She didn't resemble the girl I'd met five years ago by a long shot. I guessed I was far from the guy I was then, too.

I pulled a joint from my pocket and lit it. "I guess trauma does that to you."

"And break ups," she murmured.

I took a long drag off the joint. "Yeah, that too."

"She feels bad, you know," Jenna said. "Not about ending things, but the way that she did. She doesn't talk about it much, but..."

Hurting as I may have been, and as much as I wished I had her back, I'd done her dirty. I knew that. She did the only thing that she could to keep from getting hurt again. I didn't blame her for that.

"She shouldn't. I lied to her for months. She went through a lot, and then I put her through more. She doesn't have anything to feel sorry for."

"Yeah, I know. But..." She paused. "I don't know, Jeremy. She loves you. I don't think this is permanent."

It was a nice thought. I prayed that one day she'd give me a chance again. But after that day in March when she asked me to leave again, I came to terms with the fact that it'd take a miracle to move past what happened.

I chuckled as I rubbed the back of my neck. "I don't think there'll ever be a time that we don't love each other. But she won't even meet up for coffee so... I don't know. Seems pretty permanent."

"She hasn't filed for divorce, has she?" she asked.

"Not that I know of."

She looked back up to meet my gaze. "Then it's probably not permanent."

I forced a smile. "Guess I can hope."

She smiled back. "I'm going to go get a drink. Do you need anything?"

"Nah, I'm gonna take your car for a drive." I lowered myself to the ground and put the joint out on the cement. "Thanks though."

"Sure." She started past me to the man door that led to the kitchen. "Jeremy?"

"Yeah?" I glanced over my shoulder as I stood.

"Just don't quit trying. We're all rooting for you." She smiled.

A quiet chuckle left my lips. "Yeah, well. I'm not giving up, but I'm not going to harass her either. She wants time, she can have it."

CHAPTER TEN

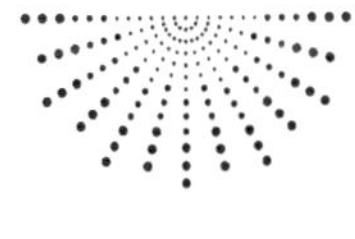

LAILA

The smell of greasy burgers mixed with the coffee brewing behind me. *Hey Jude* played over the speakers in the corners, vibrating to my ears. Cool air fell from the register above, casting a shiver up my arms. I looked back up to the customer at the other end of the register, smiling as I passed them their receipt.

"Have a good one," I said.

"Yeah, you too," the man said. He turned toward the door, holding it open for a moment. Then a familiar blond bobbed through the doorway. Her blue eyes met mine behind her glasses, smiling wide.

"Hey." Jenna sat at the counter with an awkward, almost pained smile.

I arched a brow. "Hey, what's up?"

"Nothing really. Can I get a burger?" she asked.

I pulled my tablet from my apron and scribbled her usual on it. "Fries too?"

"I think I'm in the mood for onion rings today," she said.

"Well, we're almost out of onion rings, so you're getting fries," I muttered.

"Wow, okay, bitch." She smiled.

I laughed, grabbed a glass from beneath the bar, and dumped some ice in it. Holding it beneath the pop dispenser beside the register, I felt her gaze on me.

I looked up. "What?"

"Okay, so something is up."

"Alright." I set her cup in front of her. "What is it?"

She scratched her head. "Your husband's working on my car."

"Oh," I murmured. He was in town then. Guess I wasn't meeting up with Hannah for drinks later after all. "Oh, I see."

"It's not a big deal, is it?" she asked.

"No, that's fine. That's his primary source of income right now."

"He told me not to pay him," she muttered.

"No, you definitely have to pay him. If you don't have any money, I'll give it to you to give to him."

She creased her brows. "Really, Laila?"

"Yes, really." I placed my hands on my hips. "He's working. He deserves to be paid."

"Even if it's from the same account he's already been using?" She raised brow.

"Yeah, even then."

I knew it didn't actually make sense. But I didn't want him to think that doing favors for my family would somehow give him rights to waltz back into my life. Granted, I also knew he wasn't doing that. He was genuinely a kind person who would work on his friends and family's cars for free. But the fact remained.

She rolled her eyes. "You're crazy."

"No, I just feel like he deserves compensation for the time he spends working," I said. "He's too nice. He needs to stop doing so much for other people and take care of himself."

If he'd cared a little more about himself last year, maybe we wouldn't be where we were. If he'd have said that he was struggling, that he needed help, life would be a lot different. But no, he hid it. He was so worried about what his relapse would do to me that he wouldn't come forward with it.

Jenna laughed. "You're too much. But alright, give me some cash and I'll give it to him. School's out so I'm a little broke at the moment."

"I'll PayPal it to you when I can get a break." I turned to clip the order note to the wheel that led to the kitchen when I heard a voice behind me near Jenna at the bar.

"Excuse me," he said, tone formal and polite. "Do you know where I can find the owner of this place?"

I turned with a raised brow. "That'd be me. How can I help you?"

He was an attractive guy, probably a few years older than me. His tight black curls were cropped close to his scalp. He stood around six foot tall with a medium, but muscular, build. A light blue button up rested on his shoulders, covered by a gray sweater vest. Dark washed blue jeans lined his legs. He wore thick black glasses over his warm chocolate eyes. His skin was a light, ebony color.

Seemed a little suspicious. People that looked as clean cut as he did didn't usually walk into my bunk little diner. And when they had, they were journalists asking me to tell them my story—offering me a book deal. That'd happened twice since the shutdowns ended. And both times, I told them to piss up a rope and get the fuck out of my business.

What happened last year was no one's business but mine and the other survivors. I had no desire to tell the world my sob story. Maybe it'd make a good book, but if it would, I'd write it myself.

His full lips worked into a smile. He reached out his hand. "You're Laila Callidy?"

I shook his palm. "I am. And you are...?"

"I'm Liam. Liam Moore. It's a pleasure to meet you." He stared at me for a moment. "I'm sorry, I thought you were a brunette for some reason."

"I was." I glanced at the cherry red pieces around my face that hadn't made it into the ponytail. "But I needed a change so here we are. Do I know you? That name sounds familiar."

"No." He gave a polite smile before it fell a bit. "No, we've never formally met. You may have seen me the night..." He cleared his throat. "My little sister's a survivor. We never actually met, but, ya know."

Ah, that was it. I remembered from a roster I'd looked over with Leah. We were tracking all the survivors to see if there were any patterns. That name stuck out because she lived close, just on the other side of the city. A little girl, if memory served. Early teens? Around Lydia's age. I couldn't remember her first name to save my life though.

"Oh," I said. "Oh, I see. I expected you to be a journalist or something with the way you're dressed."

He chuckled. "No, I'm a nurse actually. But that's not why I'm here."

I glanced around the mostly empty diner. Only two tables were taken aside from Jenna at the counter. "Why are you here then?"

He cleared his throat and straightened his broad shoulders. "Could we talk somewhere more private? Outside or something?"

"Sure. I have to take my dog out anyway. I'll have one of my waitresses take over my tables, and I'll meet you outside. Give me ten minutes?"

He smiled. "Sure, of course. Thanks for making time for me."

I breathed in the hot, humid air. It was so thick, I could practically taste it the pollen and moisture. Cars rushed by on the road ahead, scent of exhaust touching my nose.

I pulled on Tinkerbell's leash to get her further into the grass. Or rather, Tinkerbell pulled me. "Liam you said, right?"

He nodded.

"So what's this about, Liam?" I reached into my back pocket, lifted out a pack of cigarettes, and struggled with the lighter as Tinkerbell pulled. Then he brought a flame to his fingertip and held it out to me. I leaned toward it, lit the end, and muttered, "Thanks."

He smiled. "Those things'll kill you, ya know."

"That's kind of the idea." I smiled. "But what's up? Why'd you come here?"

He cleared his throat. "Rumor has it that you and your clan are still looking for the remaining survivors. Is that true?"

"Much to our dismay. But yeah, we're digging."

"Well, I should probably give you some back story first. Until last year, my family and I all thought my brother and sister died three years ago. But then we heard the rumors about Chris Skoulda while you were missing. Then my mom got a call from your Angel, your Mom, if memory serves."

"Biologically." I took a drag off my cigarette and flicked the ashes to the ground. "She's not really my Angel anymore, but I follow. Go on."

"Right," he muttered. "Mary, she asked if any of us were willing to help. We didn't have much information, and we figured they were probably dead, but their bodies were never recovered. Mom was sick. She wasn't willing to risk her life on such a short chance, but I figured even if my siblings weren't there, someone else's were."

"Admirable of you," I said. "So, you were there?"

"Yeah, I was. I didn't do much though, you handled most of it. You were a hero back there."

A hero. I was no hero. An antihero, maybe. But I was no hero.

"Hardly. But still, thanks. Couldn't have done it alone."

He smiled. "My sister's home, and she's safe, and that's great. But they still have my brother. I've been compiling my own research. And I don't know if it's as much as you guys have, but it's something. I just want to find my brother, but I know I can't do it alone. I think that if we all put our heads together, we can come up with something. At the very least, my abilities might come in handy."

Another person in our arsenal wouldn't be a bad thing when we did find a lead. Especially one that was immune to my fire. But Fae weren't the only ones who could control fire, and I wasn't getting the gentle vibe from his aura that I typically got from Fae.

I took another hit off my cigarette. "What are you?"

"I'm a hybrid," he said. "Half Demon, half wolf."

Huh. Well, my fire might be able to kill him after all. I knew it could kill wolves. It couldn't kill an Angel though, and that's essentially what Demons were, just not quite as powerful.

Not what I'd been anticipating, exactly, but not necessarily a bad thing. It was kinda cool to meet other hybrids. There weren't many of us out there.

"Oh, a half Demon," I said. "You're the first I've met. Not as scary as I expected."

He smirked. "Yeah, well. We aren't our parents, ya know?"

"Ain't that the truth," I muttered. "Bitten or born?"

"Born," he said. "Eighth generation."

"And your abilities. What can you do?"

"Aside from standard wolf stuff, fire and invisibility. Some telekinesis, and I'm working on teleporting but I'm not great at it."

"So lower-level guy." I smiled. "Invisibility might come in handy though."

He chuckled. "We can't all be Laila Callidy."

I laughed and took another hit off my cigarette. "Thank God for that."

An awkward, almost sad smile came to his lips. Guess my dark humor wasn't for everyone. "Could we get together some time and go over our findings? See if one of us has some information that the other doesn't?" he asked. "We could all have coffee or something. I'd love to meet your family. And your husband, he's the one that opened my sister's cell door."

"Uh," I muttered. "Yeah, Jeremy's not really in the picture these days. But yeah, I'm sure that could be arranged."

"Oh, alright," he said. "So, the rumors are true then."

"What rumors?"

"About you and Jeremy. You know, breaking up, I mean."

"Ah. There are rumors."

I could practically hear it. *"Oh, did you hear? The legendary soulmates? Must not have been true after all, they split in one nasty breakup. He's living hotel to hotel and she's getting shitfaced drunk four times a week. I knew the whole 'par animo' thing was just a bunch of hoopla."*

The par animarum myths were far from just stories. We were incredibly real. But we weren't as romanticized as the stories made us out to be. Soulmates aren't just characters in a fairytale. They're people. Real, genuine people with faults and shortcomings.

But the glossed over, sugarcoated version makes for a better story to tell kids before bed each night. Definitely prettier than the story of a scar covered captivity survivor and drug addict's very complicated, very trivial marriage.

"Yeah. Yeah, there are."

"Well, give me your number. We'll figure out a day and all sit down together."

He handed me a small slip of paper. "Great. Just let me know and I'll be there."

"Sure," I said. "Thanks for coming by."

"Yeah, thanks for talking with me. I'll see you soon," he said.

I gave a smile, and he turned away. As I took another hit off my cigarette and flicked it to the ground, he swiveled back to me.

"This might be a little presumptuous." He gave a geeky grin with an arched brow. "But would you like to get a drink some time?"

I laughed. My brows raised when I realized he was serious.

He was a good-looking guy. He had nice eyes, and big shoulders, and from what Celena had told me, sex with a Werewolf seemed like a damn good time. And I had enjoyed last night with Ray.

Plus, he was kind of my type. Maybe not the skinny white boy portion, but he definitely had the kind, awkwardness down.

"Maybe. But I've got to get back to work. We'll talk soon."

He smiled back. "Alright. Well, you've got my number so... Just hit me up some time."

"Yeah. Yeah, I will."

As the day went on, I got shit done around the diner. I cleaned, I finished paperwork, I arranged next week's schedule. Once I finished closing up, I locked the doors and set the alarm. Then I started upstairs.

I kept thinking about that Liam guy. How badly I wanted to get back out there. How cute he was. How thick those lips were. What they'd feel like against mine...

Then I felt guilty for thinking about him. But why should I? I'd fucked Ray last night. And I knew for a fact Jeremy had been with other girls.

I'd already done it then. I was an infidel. It was too late to go back. And honestly, it felt good. Not the whole, having sex with someone who wasn't my husband part, that sucked. But fucking someone again. It'd been far too long. And I wasn't prepared to go another half a year without that euphoria.

And I always had wanted to fuck a Werewolf.

I plopped to the couch and took in deep breath of the eucalyptus scented wax melts. Tinkerbell erupted in barks, running from my bedroom toward me. I reached to the side table and flicked on the light.

"Hey, baby." I ran my fingers down the back of her neck. "Do you need to go pee?" She excitedly wagged her tail. "Okay, just one minute."

I reached for my phone in my purse and dialed the number Liam had given me. After three rings, he groggily answered the phone. "Hello?"

"Hey, this is Laila. I'm sorry, did I wake you up?" I asked.

"No." He yawned. "No, I'm up. What's going on? Do you have any information?"

"No. No, I'm sorry. I know it's late. I just wanted to call you before I lost my nerve," I said. "Do you still want to get that drink?"

"Uh, yeah," he said, still disoriented but sounding happy. "Sure. When are you free?"

"Pretty much any day after eight thirty," I said. "Would tomorrow work for you?"

"Yeah. Tomorrow sounds good." His voice began to sound more awake. "Is nine-ish alright with you?"

"Yeah, that'll work. Should I text you the details?" I asked.

"Sure," he said. "Thanks for asking."

"Alright, I'll see you tomorrow then."

"Tomorrow," he said.

CHAPTER ELEVEN

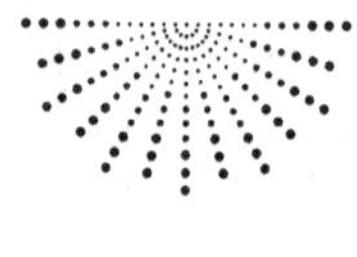

LAILA

Loud, almost deafening pop music vibrated to my ears from the speakers in the corners. The smell of greasy bar food drifted to my nose. The taste of iron touched my tongue from all the nervous nibbling on my lip. Warm air wafted around me from the open patio that overlooked the bright city.

A bar. A nice bar, better than the one I'd been in last night with Ray, but a bar. In the city, because I didn't want to run into anyone I knew and have to awkwardly explain that I was on a date. It was closer for him, and I'd teleported so I didn't have to worry about traffic on my way home. Plus, I wanted to keep things casual. A restaurant with quiet music and soft flickering candles would've sent the wrong message. I wasn't looking for love. I was looking for temporary bliss.

My gaze shifted over Liam on the other end of the table. He really was cute. In a very clean-cut, dorky way. He had a touch of facial hair but kept it neatly trimmed. His pouty lips looked like they'd be nice to kiss. He pushed up his glasses, giving the waitress a sweet, friendly smile.

She smiled down at us. "What are we having tonight guys?"

I sat my purse in the booth beside me. "Whiskey on the rocks, please."

"Just sweet red wine, if you have any." Liam pulled off his jacket and laid it on the bench beside him.

"Alrighty." The waitress scribbled on her tablet. "One check or two?"

"Two," I said as Liam simultaneously said, "One."

He met my gaze, giving an awkward smile. "I'm sorry, that was kind of misogynistic to assume I was paying for you."

It kinda was. But this was a date. That's how it was stereotypically done. Still, I appreciated the fact that he called himself out for playing into that misogynistic bullshit.

I smiled. "No, it's alright. I'm not going to turn down a free drink. You can pay for me if you want."

He looked back to the waitress. "One then."

As she turned away, he met my gaze. I grinned. "You do seem like a red wine kind of guy."

"And you're clearly a whiskey kind of girl."

"Yeah, well" —I shrugged— "Wine doesn't really do it for me these days."

"I bet." He smiled.

I gave an awkward smile, unsure of what to say. Did he just call me an alcoholic? I mean, justifiably. I had been on quite a bender. Still though, not exactly the sweetest thing he could have said.

"I'm sorry, this is a little weird for me. I don't usually do this sort of thing."

"Thank god," I said. "Yeah, me neither. I haven't been out like this in… Fuck, I don't even know. A year and a half or so? I'm not sure, but it's been a good minute. I mean, I did go out with someone a few weeks ago, but he was a prick and… Yeah, we didn't even make it past drinks."

He cocked his head to the side. "But didn't you get married after you came home?" Then he pressed his smiling lips together, eyes widening a bit. "Geez, that probably made me sound like a stalker. I'm not, I swear. There was just a lot of chatter around the whole thing."

Nah, I knew how word spread. Jeremy and I were talked about. It wasn't exactly a shocker. Liam didn't give me creeper vibes. It's not like I trusted him with my life or anything, but that wasn't all that weird of a question to ask.

I laughed. "No, that's okay. But yeah, you're right. I got out in June, we got married in September. But during that time, I wasn't really myself. I barely left my apartment until Jeremy and I broke up."

"Yeah, it was hard on my sister when she came home. She was doing alright at first. Excited to be home and everything. Then that bomb went off and… I don't know. She didn't feel safe anymore."

That bomb had been what did it for me too, so I knew exactly what he meant.

"Yeah. Almost like he was picking us off." I pushed hair behind my ear as the waitress set our drinks in front of us. I muttered a thanks as she turned away. "How old is she?"

"Thirteen," he answered with proud. "As of last month, anyway."

I gave a smile back. "First birthday home in a while?"

Liam nodded, lifting his wine to his lips. "She was ten the last time we saw her."

"That's great," I said. Bad wording. Bad, *bad* wording. "I mean, it's great that she was home for this one. Not that it was great that she missed the last two."

He smiled. "Yeah, I knew what you meant."

It was great that he was just as awkward as I was. In the past, I'd never been this uncomfortable with people. But aside from Jeremy, he was the only other person I dated in the supernatural world. Which, granted, was incredibly refreshing. Comforting, even, but it was still pretty weird.

"What's her name?" I placed my hand above my glass and sipped through my straw.

"Emma," he said.

"I'd like to meet her at some point. If she wants to meet me, anyway. I know it's weird but seeing the people that made it out makes me feel better about the people who didn't."

"It's not weird. And she'd love that. She's a little bit obsessed with you."

I raised a brow. "Really? Why?"

He chuckled. "Our family doesn't really fit in anywhere. We're hybrids, you know, but not like you. Our powers aren't innately good like yours. Even in our pack, we're still kind of... I don't know. I don't want to say discriminated, but... Put it this way." He leaned forward in his seat a bit. "If it weren't for the fact that our family had been in the pack for generations, we wouldn't have been allowed to join."

"See, I'll never understand that. The whole purebred lines that the history books go on about. We know for a fact that mixing races creates a stronger offspring. It doesn't cause birth defects or anything like the incestuous 'pure' races do from fucking their siblings and cousins. There's no reason for there to be a stigma around it."

Aside from humans, anyway. Certain races couldn't mix with humans. Like Angels and Demons. If they did, that's how second-generation Demons—beasts, as we called them—were born.

"Yeah, well." He took another sip from his wine. "All hate comes from a place of fear."

"Yeah, I guess so."

"It's kind of funny though, isn't it? Even our kinds are racist. We blame each other for everything. Vamps hate wolves, wolves hate Guardians, Guardians hate Angels, Angels hate Demons. My mom, she had three kids to a Demon and even she was racist. My whole family is. It seems like hybrids are the only ones who aren't."

"She passed away?" I sipped my whiskey.

"Yeah, a month and a half ago. She was sick for a while, so it wasn't really a shock. Just not really how I pictured things."

"Oh, I'm sorry," I said. "It's really hard to lose a parent."

"Yeah, thanks. I just try to keep busy, ya know? Emma keeps me on my toes. I don't have much time to be sad."

I pushed a smile. "So you take care of her then?"

"Yeah. I mean, Dad's not really an option." He laughed. "And I'm more stable than most of the family. It made sense. After everything Emma's been through, I couldn't just uproot her life. She was just getting used to being home, ya know? My cousin and my aunt help a lot though. They check on her while I work and stuff. It's not like I don't have help. It's just... Family sticks together, ya know?"

"Yeah, I feel the same way. So you're a nurse, you said."

"Yeah," he said. "I'm a trauma nurse. Which comes in handy in our line of work."

"I would think so. Common work for people like us. I know a lot of nurses actually."

He gave an awkward laugh. "I feel bad. I want to ask you questions about yourself, but I've already heard a lot."

"Oh yeah?" I laughed.

"You're practically famous." He paused. "God, that sounded like I was fan girling, didn't it?"

"Not really. I get it. The par animos were a myth before we proved that they weren't. And I've got a lot of abilities. Last year... That really put my name on the map. It's kind of weird. Being so important to a group of people that doesn't exist to the rest of the world."

"You were human before, right?" he asked.

"I thought I was."

"What's that like?" Liam sipped his wine. "Being normal and everything."

I shrugged with a smile. "I don't know. Boring, I guess? Nothing exciting ever happened. I watched a lot of TV. I spent a lot of time at the park near my house. I did a good bit of drugs in my teenage years."

He chuckled. "Didn't we all."

I raised a brow, giving his neat button up and khakis a once over. "*You* did drugs?"

"What—I don't seem like the kind of person who likes to have a good time?"

"You came to a bar with a girl and got red wine." I grinned, gesturing to his drink. "Most retired partiers at least go for a beer."

"Hey, wine is great. Jesus drank wine."

"Jesus was never a partier."

"Fair enough," he said. "But there's no reason to hate on wine. It does the trick."

"True. If you drink a few bottles. Especially for a wolf." He laughed. "I can't believe you ever partied though." I narrowed my gaze a bit. "You were one of those band geeks who occasionally hung out with the stoners, huh?"

"Actually," he said confidently, "I was a drama geek; band was lame. I dropped that in middle school."

I laughed. "Yeah, I could see that."

He smiled. "What clique did you belong to in high school?"

"Burnouts and skaters," I said. "Never really fit the mold, I guess. I didn't know why then, I just thought I was weird. Then in my senior year, I got my powers. I almost failed because of how many days I missed in the last term."

"So, it was traumatic when you learned what you were?" he asked.

"You could say that," I said. "Honestly, I didn't really care about my powers at first. It was the whole soulmate thing that freaked me out."

"Yeah, that must have been weird. You were seventeen, you said?"

"Barely eighteen. But yeah. It was surreal. Still is sometimes."

He glanced at my hand as I raised my glass to my lips. "So you said that Jeremy's not really in the picture anymore."

"I did."

"But you still wear your wedding ring."

"I do."

The dreaded question. But one that needed addressed. I had no intention of taking off that ring. I had no intention of wearing a new one. I loved my husband, and I knew that one day, eventually, we'd work through things. Not any time in the foreseeable future, but one day. And he had the right to know that before anything went down between us.

He gave an awkward smile. "Do you mind if I ask why?"

"How much time do you have?"

He smiled, giving a shrug and leaning back in his seat.

"Jeremy and I are... I don't know. We aren't together. But he's..." I paused, searching for the words. "The bond makes things complicated."

"What do you mean?" he asked.

"Essentially, we're one soul split in half." I lifted my drink and took a long gulp. That wasn't one hundred percent true, but it was close to it. I believed it was true, at least. "Even if we don't want to be, we're still instinctively drawn to each other. It's primal. The way I feel about him, it's not like I feel for anyone else. And I don't necessarily mean that in a romantic way. It's just... It's hard to explain. I don't care for him just as a partner. I love him that way too, but I also love him the same way that I love everyone else. It's like he's my best friend, and my cheerleader, and my hero, and my damsel, and my family all wrapped up in one giant, tangled spider web."

"I have an idea of what you're saying," he said. "But if that's how you feel, why aren't you together?"

I found my glass, raised it to my lips, and chugged until it was gone. "We're going to need more drinks."

He tilted his head back to swallow what was left of his wine.

"How much do you know about the Skouldas?" I asked.

"Not much, I guess. They're powerful. Pure blood Guardians going back as far as history dates. They've got a reputation for being ruthless. And dicks." I chuckled, and he smiled. "But they've helped a lot of people, I know that. Besides that though, I'm not all that familiar with them."

"Alright, where to begin then." I rubbed my hand against my mouth. "Jeremy's an addict. He was clean for as long as I knew him but then I was taken. And he relapsed."

"Can't say I blame him," he muttered.

"Yeah, me neither. But he was clean by the time I got back. A momentary lapse in judgment under the circumstances, he said." I lowered my hand to my lap and spun my wedding ring. "Jeremy and I got married in September. And in January, he overdosed. Which would have been one thing, but I didn't know he was using. I just found him on the bathroom floor. I get him to the hospital, and he's in really bad shape. They have me stay in the waiting room. And Jeremy's ex, she volunteers at the hospital sometimes, and we run into each other."

"Olivia Ainsworth, right?" he asked.

"Yeah, you know her?"

"Vaguely," he said. "We've worked together a few times. Volunteering at the hospitals. Not friends, but yeah, I vaguely know her. Her family's kind of a big deal too."

"Yeah, that's how they met, I think. Both of their families are high up in the Chambers."

He sipped his drink. "But go ahead, go on."

I probably shouldn't have. But I explained what had happened when we broke up. The messages I'd found in his phone, how I interpreted them, the fact that Olivia was at my home the night I gave birth to Micah in that tiny cell.

Probably should've kept those skeletons in my closet. But in fairness, it seemed like he should know what he was walking into. However, I didn't consider the nasty picture that painted in his head of Jeremy.

The truth was, yeah, what he'd done was fucked up. But that didn't make him a bad person. It just meant that he was flawed. I was too. The problem was, he was good at hiding it.

"Was that the last time you guys talked?" he asked.

"No. We talk on a semi regular basis. We've only seen each other once since things ended but we talk on the phone sometimes. Usually just when one of us gets hurt."

"Because you feel each other's pain, right?" he asked.

"Yeah. But it's never very long. Usually a quick hi-goodbye sort of thing."

He pushed up his glasses. "If this is overstepping, you don't have to answer. But can I ask you something?"

"Sure."

"Your son. He didn't make it, did he?" he asked softly.

I turned my gaze downward. "No. He's gone."

Liam was quiet for a moment. "I'm sorry for your loss."

"Thanks," I muttered.

"Given all that though," he said. "I take it you aren't really looking for a relationship."

I turned up to meet his gaze. With a laugh and a shake of my head, I said, "I don't really know what I'm looking for. I don't know that I really want to be with someone. But I know that I'm tired of being alone."

"Yeah, I can relate."

"Dating seems fun," I said. "Never really got around to that."

"Well." He smiled. "I don't know about you, but I'm having fun."

I smiled back. "Yeah. Me too."

As the night went on, things got less awkward with Liam. He was kind of weird but not in a bad way. Just a different kind of weird than I was.

He was smarter than me, at least if we're talking book smarts. Aside from the fact that he had a degree, he was just generally well informed. He didn't have a know-it-all type of attitude. He was simply a smart person who liked to have intelligent conversations. We discussed important things like politics and religion and science. It was refreshing to talk about the world instead of our disastrous lives.

There was a bit of flirting, but Liam wasn't very good at it. He was interested; I could see that. It was clear that he didn't want to come on too strong. Overall, he seemed as generally unsure of how the whole dating thing worked as I was.

I didn't really know what I was doing either. But as the drinks kept coming, the flirting got a little less awkward and a lot more fun.

I liked him. Not even close to as much as I liked Jeremy in the beginning. But still, he was nice all the same.

He was a good guy. And I was lonely. So I took the dive.

Around eleven thirty, I stood and insisted that Liam dance with me. We were both horrible, but it was oddly reassuring.

The rest is a blur in my mind now. Not that I was drugged or anything along those lines. It just feels so insignificant in the grand scheme of things when I look back on it.

I kissed him while we danced. Once things got a little heavy, I pulled him into the bathroom.

I could have teleported us back to my house but sleeping with someone else in the apartment I shared with Jeremy seemed dirty. In addition to that, there was this strange sense of security to hooking up in a public place.

I knew that I could get out of any sexual encounter I didn't want to be involved in. Hell, I could turn anyone who touched me, in a way I didn't like, to ash without so much as batting an eyelash. But there was something about there being a group of people behind the locked bathroom door that brought me comfort. It even turned me on a little bit.

It was hot and passionate but not overly dominating. Things weren't the same as they had been with Ray or Jeremy. It was the first time I was with someone who didn't know I was raped. In a way, I liked that he didn't fuck me differently than he would anyone else. It was nice to have sex and not be seen as a rape victim that had to be handled with care.

CHAPTER TWELVE

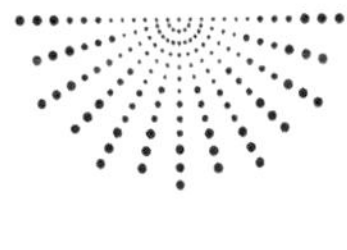

JEREMY

arm, comforting air slid in from the cracked window to my left. I listened to the soft sound of the acoustic in my lap, strumming along to a tune I was working on. It was coming along, but something about it wasn't quite right.

"Hey, you." Leah leaned in the doorway. "Long time no see."

I smiled. "I've been here all week, so you have yourself to blame for that."

She smiled back, pushing purple hair from her green eyes. "Sorry, I would have come back sooner. But honestly, I've enjoyed Hannah going to college and not being my responsibility anymore. It's refreshing."

I grinned. "Nah, you've just been enjoying fucking Haley."

Her smile widened. "Yeah, that too."

"I'm happy for you." Can't say that I wasn't jealous, I absolutely was. I missed having a relationship like the one she'd created with Haley. But I *was* happy for her. "You deserve it. You gave up the best years of your life to take care of us."

"Hey, the best years of my life are not over. I'm only twenty-nine; I'm not dead yet." She joined me on the bed. "I've got a lot left to do here."

"I didn't mean it like that. I just meant thank you. You deserve to be happy."

She frowned. "So do you."

I forced a smile. "I am."

Leah chuckled. "You might be able to fool everyone else, but I know better."

"I'm okay, Leah. Really, I am."

I wasn't. Life sucked. But it was better than it'd been. I may not have been happy, but at least my wife wasn't being held hostage and tortured every minute of every day.

Things were shitty. But they'd been worse.

"Have you seen her?" she asked.

I gave an awkward laugh and looked back to the guitar in my lap. "I haven't seen her since I helped Celena and Wyatt in West Virginia. Well, then there was that day here."

It flashed behind my eyes, sending an ache to the pit of my stomach. I'd come home between gigs in June. I didn't bring my car though, and I'd only been there for a few minutes. When she came in, I was in the bathroom shooting up. Then I heard her talking to Leah, so I shoved my needle in my pocket, staggered to my feet, and went out into the kitchen.

I smiled at her and started to say hi. Then her jaw pressed to a line and she disappeared.

"I don't know why she left like that."

"She hates me."

"She doesn't hate you—"

"She does. I kind of hate her too."

She definitely hated me. We both knew it. And it hurt. I hated her for not hearing me out. I hated that I lost my best friend. But most of all, I hated her because...I couldn't really hate her. I hated what I'd done, and I hated that I couldn't get over her. I hated how bad I wanted her back when she wouldn't even let me see her. But I made her hate me. It was *my* fault. And that's what I hated the most.

"But I don't want to talk about that right now," I said.

"Then let's talk about something else," Leah said. "How's your music? A few of your performances went viral, ya know."

"Yeah, I know. It's good. I didn't like performing that much before. I still don't, really. But playing and singing... I don't know. It makes me feel alive."

She grinned. "You don't puke before a show anymore, do you?"

"No." I laughed. "I don't even get nervous anymore. I've kind of let go of the low self-esteem. I never believed people when they said I was good before. Now I know that I'm good. Sounds kind of cocky, I guess—"

"Not at all," Leah said. "Being confident doesn't make you vain. You're good, Jeremy. You've always been good. I'm glad you finally see that."

With my music, at least. I knew I sucked at just about everything else. But I was a good musician. I had a voice, and I had mad skills on a guitar. It was about all I really did have, but it was something.

"Thank you." I smiled.

"For what?" she asked.

"For always supporting me. For supporting all of us. In every way, I mean. Financially, physically... Emotionally." A small, genuine smile pulled at her lips. "You didn't ask to be a mom, but you did a damn good job at it."

"I didn't ask for it." She held her smile. "But I wouldn't have had it any other way."

I smiled back.

She raised her arms around my shoulders in a hug. "I'm glad you aren't pushing us away."

I hugged her back, placing my chin on her shoulder. "I'm just happy I have you guys. I don't know where I'd be without you."

"Me neither," she said quietly, tightening her arms around me a bit.

Being at home for the past few days hadn't been easy. Adam was dating Laila's sister which made being around him kind of hard because it was a constant reminder of her. Brody spent a lot of time at his internship when he wasn't at school. Not that I would have wanted to hang out with him that much anyway, but he didn't have the time regardless. Hannah was at school or work a lot as well. When she was at home, she was overwhelmed with schoolwork or Kai, so I hadn't seen much of her either. I'd seen Kai more than anyone. And that fucking sucked.

I liked Kai. He was a good dude. He worshipped the ground my sister walked on, he always had a smile, but he was my wife's twin. They had the same emerald-colored eyes and nearly jet black hair, their expressions were similar, they even wore similar, vibrant hippy-like clothes.

I thought about Laila all the time. But being here without her and being surrounded by the memories haunted me.

The whole time I'd been here, I'd hoped Leah would come home. The two of us were closer than I was with any of my other siblings. Matter of fact, I was probably closer to Leah than anyone alive.

I kind of needed her. I didn't need her to do anything. I just needed her time. I needed her friendship. I needed to sit down and smoke a blunt and just bullshit. I needed companionship because I felt like I was on a deserted island in the middle of the Atlantic.

But I couldn't tell her that. She was focusing on herself. She was happy. I couldn't guilt her into being there for me when I could see how badly she needed to live her life. I couldn't drag her down.

As Leah pulled away, a shooting pain rang up my elbow toward my bicep. I grimaced. My hand ran along it and squeezed the muscle.

"Are you okay?" Leah asked.

"Yeah, just Lai. She hit her arm on something. A corner, maybe?"

"Damn," Leah said. "That's got to be annoying."

A splitting, stinging pain sliced across my palm. I gripped it. "Fuck," I muttered. "I should call her."

Leah brought herself to her feet. "Let me know if you need me."

"Sure." I found my phone on the side table. She started from the room as I scrolled to my favorited contacts. I clicked on her picture and held the phone to my ear.

After two rings, her chuckling voice answered. "I'm fine, just stupid."

I smiled at the sound of her laugh. "What happened?"

She audibly sighed. "I'm a little drunk."

I chuckled, setting my guitar on the ground beside the bed. "I can tell."

She laughed again. Fuck, I missed that laugh. "I tripped and fell on the end table by the couch. A vase fell off and shattered. I was trying to pick up the pieces, and I started to fall backward so I kind of closed my hand around the glass."

"Jesus, babe."

"Yeah, I'm a dumb ass."

"No," I murmured. "You're clumsy."

She laughed again. "I'm sorry, I hope I didn't wake you."

"No, I was just talking to Leah."

"Oh, alright." There was a touch of disappointment at the edge of her voice. "I'll let you go then."

"It's okay, she just left. I'm happy to hear from you," I said. "Do you have a minute? Can we talk?"

There was a long pause. Just as I was about to ask if she was still there, she cleared her throat. "Yeah, sure. What's up?"

A quiet laugh left my lips before I rubbed my hand along them. "I don't know. Nothing really. I just miss you."

"I miss you too," she murmured.

My stomach flipped. The only sound coming through the speakers was her breath. She hadn't said that once since the breakup. I prayed that she would a thousand times. I already knew that she did, but I thought it'd be nice to hear her say it. It wasn't though. Because unless that was accompanied by a 'come over and let's talk,' why did it even matter?

"I've been in town for the past week or so." I broke the silence.

"Yeah, Jenna told me you were working on her car," Laila said.

"I figured she would."

"Has it been nice? Being home, I mean?" she asked.

"I guess. Quiet though. Everyone's doing their own things these days, ya know? I don't know." I shifted my body to lie back on the pillows. "Doesn't really feel like home anymore."

It got quiet for a moment. Then she blew out a heavy breath. "Yeah. I know the feeling."

I knew she'd probably tell me no again, but I had to ask. "I'm leaving tomorrow. I have some shows lined up in South Carolina for the next few weeks, so I don't know when I'll be back unless someone needs me."

"That's exciting," she said softly. "I'm sure you'll have a lot of fun. You should check out Charlotte on your way down. There's a really cool scene there. I stayed there overnight a few months ago with Jenna right before the whole pandemic thing hit, it's a fun place to see. There's a cool night life. Oh, and there's this restaurant. I'll have to check to see what it was called but they had this amazing mushroom risotto. You have to try it."

I smiled. "Yeah, text me the information when you get a chance and I'll check it out."

"Sure, I will in the morning."

"Thanks," I muttered. Then I rubbed my anxious shaking hand against my mouth again. "I, uh... I was hoping that maybe on my way out of town, maybe I could stop by the diner? Maybe we could have a cup of coffee together or go for a walk or something?"

She grew silent. A moment or two later, she quietly said, "I don't know, Jeremy."

"I don't have to stay long or anything. I just... I really want to see you."

"I know," she murmured.

"It's... Um..." A knot stiffened in my throat. "Everywhere I look, there's something here that reminds me of you. And I know it sounds crazy, it's been years since we slept in this bed together, but somehow, it still smells like you. Maybe it's in my head, I don't know. I just miss you. I always miss you, but I miss you a lot right now."

"Jeremy..." she whispered. "I don't know."

"Baby, you said we'd stay friends, and I've only seen you twice in six months and the second time, you teleported away before I could even say hi. We're basically just Facebook friends."

"I know."

"You said you missed me too," I murmured.

"I do," she said. "I just don't know what I want right now."

"You don't have to, baby. It doesn't have to mean anything; it's just a cup of coffee," I whispered. "Please. Please let me see you."

Silence for a moment. "You should probably quit calling me that."

"What?" I asked.

"You called me baby."

She was right. It was silly. But whether she'd admit it or not, I knew she liked hearing me say it. And I liked saying it. It made things feel normal.

"Are you going to divorce me?"

"No," she said. "I'm not planning on it anyway."

"Then you're still my baby," I said. A quiet chuckle left her, and it brought a smile to my lips.

"I should tell you something," she murmured. I waited for her to continue. Then she cleared her throat. "I... I went on a date tonight."

It shouldn't have hurt. I'd fucked at least twenty other girls since the breakup. But for some reason, those words felt like a dagger to the heart. Or like a hole had been punched through it. My stomach ached, my hands shook, water even welled in my eyes.

She wouldn't even look at me. She wouldn't let me get within a hundred feet of her. But she went out with someone else. She had every right, we weren't together, but it didn't make it hurt any less.

"Oh." I kept my voice level. "Did you have a good time?"

"It was a little awkward," she said. "But it was okay."

"Really?" I asked. "Anyone I know?"

"You might know his name," she said. "Liam Moore?"

At least it wasn't Brody. Or Max. That would've been a real gut-punch to my pride.

"Sounds familiar," I muttered. "What is he?"

"He's a hybrid. Mom's a wolf, Dad's a Demon," she said. "His sister's one of the survivors. That's how we met. His brother's still inside, he wants to help us look for them."

"Oh," I said. "Yeah, that makes sense I guess."

After a moment, she said, "I do miss you."

"Then let me come see you," I murmured, pushing the thought of her with someone else from my mind. "I can clean up that glass so you don't cut yourself again."

She chuckled. "It's alright, I picked it up already."

It got quiet again. She wasn't going to let me come over, even if we both knew some part of her wanted me to. "So no coffee?"

Another moment of silence. "I should get to bed. I have to open in the morning."

Yet again, I wasn't getting an answer. She knew I was too polite to show up unannounced, even if she did live above a public place. A restaurant that, by technicality, I could enter any time that I wanted because it was just as much my property as it was hers.

I wouldn't. I knew that would do nothing but piss her off. *Then* she might file for divorce. We weren't together, but that window was still open. She hadn't divorced me yet for a reason. I wasn't going to force her hand.

"I love you, Jeremy," she said quietly.

"I love you too, Laila," I said.

"Sleep tight," she murmured.

"Sweet dreams, baby," I said softly.

I took in a deep breath and threw the phone to the bed and rubbed my eyes with the tips of my fingers. My hand fumbled to my pants pocket where I had a small plastic bag with a few pills. I pulled it out, set one on the side table, crushed it up, leaned my head down, and inhaled. Then I found the joint I'd rolled earlier from the top drawer and sparked it at my lips.

This was my life now. I'd reached a content state of depression tied up in drug abuse. I knew what I wanted but I couldn't have it. I couldn't be where I wanted to be or do what I wanted to do.

I hated what my life had become. I was twenty-five years old with no career, no real job, and no degree. I'd already lost a child, a brother, and every parental figure that I ever had. My siblings, the only friends I really had, were all happily living their lives without me. And my wife wanted nothing to do with me.

All I had was a couple guitars, a bag of clothes, my dad's old car, some pills, and a cell phone.

CHAPTER THIRTEEN

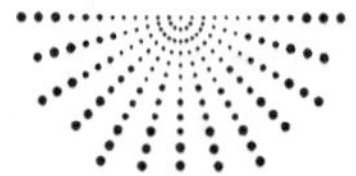

LATE JULY, 2020 - LAILA

"Here are your drinks." I set two Cokes and a Sprite at the table of four. "Your meals should be up in a few minutes, but is there anything I can get you guys for now?"

"I forgot when I ordered," the young woman at the end said. "But can I get extra ranch for my salad?"

"Oh, yeah. Sure thing."

"Thank you," the girl said.

"No problem." I gave a friendly smile before I started behind the bar.

The bell above the door rang, and Liam walked in. He wore pink scrubs and carried a small bouquet of roses. I smiled as our gazes met. "Aww, are those for me?"

He grinned, sat at the bar, and laid them on the counter. "They sure are."

"You're sweet." I picked them up, sniffed, and smiled. "Thank you."

I wasn't really sure why he did stuff like that. We both had a clear understanding that we weren't a couple. We were fucking, we weren't boyfriend and girlfriend. But I did love flowers.

He smiled, shrugging. "Somebody was selling them at the corner down the street. I thought you'd like them."

"Yeah, I do. Thank you. Didn't you just get off work though? Don't you need to get some sleep?"

"Yeah, I'm beat. But I wanted to see you."

"Well, I don't think I have time to sneak off," I said. "But I'm glad you came by. Are you hungry? I can have Max whip you something up."

"Yeah, I could go for some bacon and eggs," he said.

"Coming right up." I smiled, pulled my tablet from my apron, and scribbled on it. I clipped it to the wheel and turned back to Liam with a gesture to his scrubs. "You were on maternity ward duty today?"

"Yeah, I keep getting pulled. They're really understaffed up there. I don't mind it though, the babies are cool."

"That's good." My phone began to buzz in my pocket. I clicked the ignore button through the apron. "Was it a quiet night?"

"Mostly," he said. "It was pretty peaceful."

My phone buzzed again, and I creased my brows.

If someone called more than once, that was something of a code in our family. That meant something was wrong. My heart skipped a beat.

I pulled it out. Ray. "I'm sorry, I have to take this. Just one minute."

He smiled. "No problem, I'll be here."

I slid the green button and started into the kitchen. "Hey, Ray. Is everything alright?"

"Yeah, everything's fine. Sorry, I know it scares you when anyone calls back-to-back but." He stuttered, speaking fast. "Can you come here? I—I, uh, I need to talk to you."

"Well, I have a minute now, what's up?" I asked.

"I don't want to talk about this on the phone," he said quickly. "It's important, Laila. Just come here, please."

I made my way to the steps toward my apartment. "I thought you said everything was okay. Is someone hurt?"

"No. It's not like that. I just need to talk to you about this in person," he said.

"I'm a little backed up here at the moment, but I could come by this afternoon—"

"Laila, you're going to want to know about this sooner rather than later. I'd come to you but that'd take hours. Have someone watch your tables or shut the place down for the day. Just get over here. This is important. Trust me, you want to hear this," Ray said. "And you're going to need some time so make sure you aren't in a rush."

"You're freaking me out, man." My heart picked up in my chest. "Is Lydia okay?"

"Yes, Laila. We're fine. Just come to the living room ASAP. I'll explain when you get here."

"Alright," I said. "I'll see if Sophie can wait the tables while I'm gone. Give me ten minutes."

My gaze shifted around the mostly still boxed up living room. The smell of fresh paint wisped into my lungs. I heard rustling in the powder room off the main room.

"What's the problem, Ray?" I spun around in search of him, heart hammering in my chest.

"One second." He yelled from the bathroom. The toilet flushed before the door shut and he rushed out.

I heard the toilet, but I hadn't heard the spigot.

"Aren't you going to wash your hands?" I wrinkled my nose. "That's gross, your hand was just on your dick, dude. We're recovering from a pandemic, aren't you in the habit of washing your hands yet?"

He rolled his eyes, walked back into the bathroom, and quickly rinsed his hands. "Happy?"

"I don't think you used soap, but good enough, I guess," I muttered.

He walked to the couch and sat. "Have a seat."

"You said everything was okay—"

"It is. But you're going to want to sit for this. Just have a seat, alright?"

Still puzzled, I sat beside him. He began rummaging through a box of papers that sat on the floor. "What's this about, Ray?"

"Okay." He took in a deep, recollecting breath. He put his hand to his face and rubbed his eyes. "I've been unpacking and this morning I found this box."

"Alright." I raised a brow. "What's in the box?"

He pulled out a sketch book. "You know Lydia's an artist."

I vaguely remembered her saying that she liked to draw, but only vaguely. I hadn't seen anything she'd made.

"Sure."

"Alright. She doesn't show me a lot of her stuff, just things she's submitting for projects at school and everything, ya know?" I nodded, and he went on. "But these were here so I figured I'd take a look."

He handed me the journal and gestured for me to look inside. I flipped open the frayed book to find some detailed sketches of flowers. Gorgeous, incredibly intricate, all in gray pencil. "These are beautiful, but I don't see the relevance. She controls earth; makes sense that she likes flowers."

"Keep looking," he murmured.

I flipped through the notebook. A few pages in, I noticed a picture of a baby. They looked young, maybe a month or two. As the pages went on, the baby got older.

"Well, she's a twelve-year-old girl. Doesn't really surprise me that she likes babies."

"Right. That's what I thought at first too. But there's a lot, Laila. Hundreds of pictures of this baby. The one that was the weirdest to me was this." He fumbled in the box for another picture. This one was drawn on a small white canvas with charcoal.

My breath caught, instant spin going to my stomach.

Peterson.

He was smiling next to Amy.

She held the baby in her arms with her lips pressed gingerly to his forehead.

Two of the worst people in the world. Two of the only people alive that made my hands shake. But they were essentially Lydia's parents most of her life. So, I rationalized it away.

I cleared my throat. "What are you trying to tell me, Ray?"

"When I saw this, I was wondering if that's what Amy told her. That he was her dad. So, I asked her. And when I did, she gave me this really weird look."

"What do you mean?"

"I asked if that baby was her," Ray said slowly. He squeezed the bridge of his nose. "I can't confirm this because I don't have powers. But you can go in her memories to make sure she's right."

"Make sure she's right about what, Ray?"

He was quiet for a moment. "I asked who that baby was. And she said it was yours."

My stomach sunk. A weight fell to my chest. "What?"

His throat bobbed with a swallow. "I told her your baby died when he was born, and she shook her head. She said that Amy and Peterson *took* him the day he was born."

"No, she and I talked about Micah. She knew he was dead."

"Did she ever say the word dead? Or did she say taken?"

My heart picked up speed in my chest. I blinked hard, trying to rerun our conversations through my mind.

The day that I escaped, the day that I destroyed the compound, when I collapsed beside her on the kitchen floor of that apartment, she said, "Why aren't you with your baby?"

Come to think of it, I didn't think there was a time that I referred to him as dead around her. She was eleven years old at the time. I tried to keep our discussions as kid friendly as possible.

"Laila," Lydia's quiet voice said from the doorway to her bedroom. I turned to see her watery eyes and red blotchy cheeks. "Can we talk?"

I couldn't manage a verbal response, so I nodded.

She started toward us and looked at Ray. "Can you give us some privacy, Dad?"

He nodded, stood, and started to the kitchen.

On one hand, the world felt like it had stopped spinning. On the other, it felt like the ground had been ripped from below me. I couldn't process what I had just been told. It couldn't be true.

Then I thought back to the day I awoke in his office. He told me Micah was dead, but he offered no proof. Why hadn't I questioned it? Why the fuck did I believe that man?

But most importantly, it'd been more than a year. If my baby was still out there, what had happened to him in that time? Why had I *wasted* so much time? I'd spent the last thirteen months mourning him, and he wasn't even dead.

The night we found Daniel, just before in fact, Jeremy said something in reference to Chris. That he shouldn't have stopped looking. "*We shouldn't have stopped looking until we found a body.*"

Why wasn't that the first thing I'd done when I broke out of my cell? Why wasn't looking for my baby the first thing I did? Why?

Lydia sat beside me and placed her small hand over mine. "I thought you knew, Laila. I—I... No one told me he was dead, or I would have told them he wasn't. But you said he was taken from you. I thought you knew."

My hand began to quiver. She tightened her palm around it.

"Do you want to see my memories of him?" she asked.

Still unable to form words, I gave a nod. She released my hand and outstretched her palms to mine. I laid them on top of hers and closed my eyes.

Behind my eyelids flashed images of Amy's apartment. A small, clear incubator was being wheeled into the room. Inside of it lay a silent child in nothing but a diaper. Wires connected to little gold patches all over his tiny body.

Lydia got closer and put her hand against the glass. He looked up at her with big, vibrant blue eyes. Eyes I knew all too well. Jeremy's. Big, round, and the most vibrant shade of blue. He had thick lips shaped just like mine, but they were a little wider. His nose, though much smaller, was the shape of Jeremy's. He had his daddy's black hair and my doughy cheeks.

The first image of my son I'd ever seen.

The image shifted to one of Amy holding him in her arms on the last cushion of the couch. She smiled down at him in awe. Her fingertip grazed his rosy cheek. She leaned down and kissed his forehead. Her eyes closed, and she breathed in his smell.

Then an image of flashing red lights. The explosion shaking the walls. Still, he didn't cry.

"Stay here, baby," Amy said quickly. She wrapped the tiny baby in a soft blue blanket. She lifted him to her arms. "I'm going to get him to the plane. I will be right back for you, okay?"

Lydia's hands pulled from mine. We opened our eyes and met each other's gaze. Both of our faces were damp with tears.

"I'm so sorry, Laila," she whispered. "I thought you knew."

I couldn't make words form or leave my lips. I was dumbfounded. I could barely even think. It was as if my mind had gone blank. The only thing I thought of was that image.

That sweet baby boy in an incubator. Those round cheeks. Those tiny little lips. Those shocking, electric blue eyes. That strong, angled nose.

His daddy had to know.

"I—I have to call Jeremy." I wiped my cheeks.

"Are you mad at me?" she said with a desperate gaze.

"No. Not at all, sweetie. This is just... It's a lot," I said quickly. "We'll talk more soon, okay?"

CHAPTER FOURTEEN

JEREMY

I gestured to the bill on the granite counter before me. "But I didn't order room service."

"Are you sure?" the desk clerk asked.

I didn't even know hotels this low of quality offered room service. I definitely didn't order any. "Yeah, a hundred and ten percent," I said.

My phone vibrated in my pocket. I pulled it out and glanced down. Laila's picture lit up the screen. I was usually the one to call her. I hadn't gotten hurt. If she needed something, she usually texted.

"I have to take this. Please just make sure the room service is taken off my bill." I turned from the counter and slid the green bar. I headed toward the large glass doors, pushed one open, and started outside. "Hey, baby."

She sniffled. "Hey."

"It's been a while," I said. "How have you been?"

"Um..." She cleared her throat. "Pretty good, I guess. What about you?"

"I've been alright." I smiled, lowering myself to the bench and breathing in the fresh air. Warm sunlight shined against my black hoodie, making me wish I'd worn a zip-up rather than a pullover. "Hey, I did go to that place in Charlotte. You're right; the risotto was amazing."

She chuckled, but somehow, it sounded sad. "I'm glad you liked it."

"But what's up, Lai?" I asked.

She scoffed a bit. Then it got quiet. Her voice lowered. "A lot actually."

"That doesn't sound good." I tilted my head to the side. "Is everything alright?"

"No one's hurt or anything, if that's what you mean. But I need to talk to you."

"Isn't that what we're doing?" I gave a quiet laugh.

"No. No, I mean, I need to talk to you in person."

My heart practically shot out of my ribs. Butterflies flapped in my stomach. My eyes widened. A large smile pulled at my lips. "Really?"

"Yeah." She sniffled again. She didn't sound happy the way that I did. It was like she was on the verge of crying, which wasn't promising, but she said everyone was okay. "Yeah, it's important. Are you busy?"

"I'm heading to lunch right now, but I can come by. Are you home?" I asked.

"No. Not yet, I will be soon. But I have a lot of work to do at the diner," she said quickly. "I—I don't know. Are you busy this evening?"

"I have a show at nine. I could come before but you'd probably be working," I said. "Are you okay, baby? You don't sound good."

"Yeah. Yeah, I'm okay. I'm stressed but..." It sounded like she was fighting the urge to erupt in violent tears. I felt an anxious swirl spin through her stomach. "I just have to see you in person."

She was crying, and she wanted to see me in person. That wasn't promising. If I didn't know better, I'd think she found something shady I'd done. But everything shitty I'd ever done to her had been out on the table for a long while.

There was only one thing I could think of that'd cause that mixed reaction. And it hurt, and I'd do it if she really wanted it, but I had to ask. Of course, I'd beg her not to first. But I wanted to prepare what I'd say if it was what I thought it was.

My heart thudded. "Are you serving me?"

"Huh?" she asked.

"With divorce papers. Are you serving me?" I asked. "I just want to be prepared if that's what this is. I'll still come over but—"

"What? No. No, that's not what this is. It's not about us. Well, I guess it kind of is. I don't know. But no, I'm not divorcing you."

"Oh, good. Thank god," I said. "Is it... Is it good news then?"

She cleared her throat. Then she sniffled again. I felt her eyes sting with tears and a stiff tightness in her throat.

"Baby, don't cry," I murmured.

"I'm alright." She cleared her throat again. "I'm okay. It is. It's good news."

"Oh, good," I said. "Good, I'm glad."

"I'll be closing up the diner around nine. Do you think you could come by after your show? I have some paperwork to get done anyway."

"Yeah. Yeah, I'll be there. My set's an hour and a half. I should be able to get there by eleven. Is that okay?"

"Yeah, eleven's perfect. That'll give me enough time to get everything cleaned up and finish up my paperwork," she said. "Unless you want me to come to you. I can, if that's easier."

Hell no. If she was inviting me back into our home, I was gonna jump on that opportunity. I missed Moe's. I missed that couch. I missed the rug in the living room beneath my bare feet, and the soft sheets, and the smell of her perfume in the bathroom. No way I was going to have her come see me at some dirty hotel if she'd let me come home. Even if she wasn't *really* letting me come home.

"No, I'll come by. I don't really have a place out here. It makes more sense for me to come to you," I said. "Should I just meet you at the diner?"

"At the apartment's fine."

I smiled. "Alright, baby. I'll see you tonight then."

"Okay, sounds good."

"I love you," I said gently.

"I love you too," she murmured.

"Bye, Lai," I said.

"Bye, baby," she said. Then the call abruptly ended.

My stomach flipped. She hadn't referred to me as a pet name of any kind since the breakup. It made me giddy, like a teenage boy who just got a 'Yes' to the big dance coming up. I knew it didn't mean anything. She was stressed, spoke too fast, and slipped up. That's why the phone cut out so quick. But I was holding onto hope.

<hr>

As the day went on, I grew more and more excited. I was nervous, but excited. I trimmed my beard, I stopped by Leah's to get a nice shirt, I even stepped out of my falling apart shoes into my "fancy" Converse. I didn't think Laila really cared about all of that, but it made me feel better.

The last time I saw her in person for any length of time was in March. It was late July now. I hadn't gone that long without seeing her since we met.

But the harder I thought, or overthought, the more anxious I became. Something must have happened for her to call me out of the blue and want to see me like that. I couldn't figure out what would be important enough for her to want to see me unless something was wrong. But she said it was good news.

I pushed the curiosity from my mind and tried to focus on how happy I'd be to see her. I wondered if she'd be happy to see me too.

As the day dragged on, I only took enough pills to keep from getting sick. There was a little bit of an airy hue to the world around me, but I wasn't really high. I didn't want to be. I wanted to be focused when I saw her. I couldn't be nodding off.

I picked up lunch at some food truck, I got dinner, I grabbed my guitar from the hotel, and I went to the venue. My body was on autopilot because I couldn't think about anything but tonight.

All day, I rehearsed what I would say when I saw her. Pathetic, I know. But if I could see her, if she could see me, maybe we could make it work. Maybe we'd see each other and fall back into where we were before. I was going to tell her what really happened with Olivia, and I prayed she'd hear me out.

I'd quit using. I'd quit drinking. I'd quit smoking weed if she asked me to. I'd do anything. I didn't mean that in just the metaphorical sense. I genuinely would have done *anything* if she were willing to let me come home.

Then I sang on the small stage, performing songs she'd helped me write, most of which were about her. My head wasn't on the music, it was on her. She was all I could think about. I think it made my sound better. Hopeful.

I finished my set around ten thirty-five and hurried back to my hotel room. I dropped my guitar and other miscellaneous shit off. I made sure to leave my drugs behind because that was the last thing I wanted to talk about that night. However, I did bring a few pills because if I was there a while, I didn't want to get sick. The only other things I brought with me were my bag of weed and my phone.

At ten fifty-five, I teleported to the bottom of the steps of her apartment.

The familiar scent of grease and old wood filled my nostrils. I watched shadows move beneath the door shining on the wall at the landing at the top of the steps. When I heard her voice, my stomach filled with butterflies. Flexing my shaking hands, I started up the stairs.

Holding my breath, I raised my fist and knocked on the old door.

CHAPTER FIFTEEN

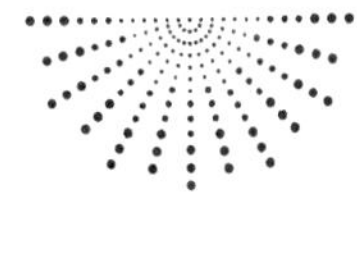

LAILA

I landed in the kitchen. My heart raced a mile a minute. My breaths were short, hands shaking. It felt like my chest was squeezing shut. Like my lungs had collapsed in on themselves. I couldn't breathe, I couldn't see straight. I knew I needed to breathe, but it felt like I couldn't.

"Leah." I started toward the living room. "Leah, are you home?"

"Yeah, I'm coming," Leah hollered from the powder room.

I brought my hand to my mouth and chewed on my nail, pacing back and forth against the hardwoods.

Don't get me wrong, I was ecstatic that my son was alive. But I was infuriated with myself for not realizing it sooner.

He just turned one. He was thirteen months old.

I missed the first thirteen months of his life.

He was with them. They were holding my baby. They were breathing in his smell, they were touching his sweet little cheeks, they had him.

They had taken *everything* from me.

And I didn't even know how to find them. I didn't know how to get my baby back. They had him, and I had no clue how to get him back.

"What are you yelling about?" I heard Leah say from the steps. I continued to pace. When she saw me, she said, "What's wrong?"

But I just kept pacing and chewing my nails.

How could I have believed that he was dead? What fucking reasoning did I have to believe Peterson? *Why* did I believe that vile, disgusting human being in the first place?

"Laila." Leah grasped my shoulders and searched for my gaze. "Laila, what's wrong?"

Tears trickled from my eyes. "Micah's alive."

Her face screwed up. "What?"

"He's alive," I repeated. She was practically a blur in my anxious, disoriented gaze.

"What? How do you know?" Leah gripped my shoulders, practically keeping me upright.

"Lydia. Lydia, she—She always—I always said things like, 'He's gone' and 'taken from me.' I never said dead. I never—She's a kid. She'd been through so much, I—I—I tried to use kid friendly words, you know? I didn't—I should have asked her. I should have been more specific. She thought I knew. She—She—"

Leah gestured to the couch a few feet away. "Okay, sweetie, I need you to sit down."

"I didn't know. She thought I knew, but I didn't. I didn't know, Leah. I wouldn't have let them take him." I spoke quickly as she helped me to the couch. I could feel my breathing picking up and my heart racing faster. "I didn't know. I didn't know."

"Laila, slow down." Leah ran her hand along my back. "Breathe, alright? You have to breathe."

My eyes were practically sprinklers. "That bitch, she has my baby. *He* has my baby. My baby isn't dead, he's with them. How am I supposed to... I ..." My throat felt tight and I fought the urge to erupt in violent, ugly cries. "He's thirteen months old..." Everything started to blur. Realizing I was having a panic attack made me more anxious, and I began to hyper-ventilate. "My baby... He's... Oh my god, what am I going to do? They-they have my baby. They—"

Leah grabbed my hand and held my gaze. "You have to calm down, Laila."

I blinked a few times. "I have to calm down."

Almost instantly, my breathing was level and the blackness on the edges of my vision faded. Leah released my hands, and I looked away blinking quickly.

As the muscles of my body eased, I muttered, "Thanks."

She pulled her knee onto the couch. "Have you talked to Jeremy?"

I wiped my cheeks. "Yeah, I called him before I came here. I didn't want to tell him on the phone. He's coming over tonight after I close the diner."

"So I shouldn't tell anyone until tomorrow then," Leah said.

"Yeah. I should have told him before I told you, but I had to talk to someone."

"I'm sure he'll be okay with that," she murmured.

I slid my shaking hands up and down my thighs. "I thought he was dead."

"We all did."

"But I'm his mom." I looked down at my hands. "I should have known."

"You couldn't have," she said. "I was in your head. I've been in Haley's a thousand times. Nothing happened that would have led either of you to believe he was alive. The doctors even rambled about it when they were in your cell that day."

"But I should have known, Leah. I should have known. I've wasted the first year of his life not looking for him because I thought he was dead. I've just been wasting time. What if they're hurting him? What if they torture him like they did to me? Oh my god, they probably put the trackers in him too." I shook my head as I raised my hand to my eyes. "Fuck, I..."

"Just breathe, Laila," Leah said softly. "Just breathe."

CHAPTER SIXTEEN

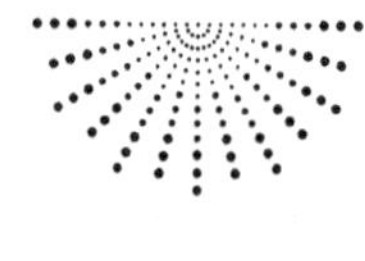

LAILA

I sat at the dining room table gazing at the clock on the wall. Ten fifty-four.

My fingers clenched the glass in my hand, trying to keep it steady.

Fuck. What was I even going to say when he arrived?

Hey, so our son isn't dead. Sorry for the misinformation.

Jesus fucking Christ.

I had just gotten past the worst of the mourning. And suddenly he wasn't dead. I never had a god damned thing to mourn in the first place.

A quiet knock sounded at the door. Tinkerbell erupted in obnoxious barks, darting from the couch to the entrance.

My stomach flipped. God, I hoped he didn't hate me after this. I'd hate me. If I were in his shoes, had he told me our baby was dead when he wasn't, I'd hate him.

I stood and walked to the door. I grabbed ahold of Tink's collar and held her back with one hand. Then I opened the door handle with the other.

Jeremy stood on the other end in his usual glory.

My heart skipped a beat. Jesus, why did just looking at him make me feel like a little girl going out on her first date?

His long black waves were combed neatly around his strong jaw. The thick scruff along his cheeks and upper neck was recently cropped but not

96

so close to the skin that it was a shadow. His thick lips turned up in a smile. He quickly lowered himself to the ground. He reached out to pet Tinkerbell, and I pulled her back.

"You got a dog?!" He reached further out and petted her head.

"She's kind of a bitch, I wouldn't get too close at first," I said.

"That's okay." Jeremy continued to pet her throat. "You can bite me, buddy. I won't be mad." Her tail wagged as he ran his fingers from her head down to her shoulders. His big blue eyes looked up to mine. He smiled that sweet, boyish grin I loved so much. "What's her name?"

"Tinkerbell." I smiled back.

"Of course it's a fairy." He grinned, looking back to Tink. "You can let her go, she's not going to hurt me."

"We're still working on the jumping," I said.

He laughed, standing back to his feet. He kept rubbing her face between his hands. "I think I can handle it."

"If you say so." I released her collar. She took a few steps forward, happily wagged her tail, jumped up, and pressed her paws to Jeremy's chest. He placed his arms around her shoulders and quickly pet them before sliding toward her neck. He kneaded her thick fur as she began licking the air.

Damn, I loved him. Even Tink loved him. She hated most people, but she knew instantly that she could trust him.

She hated Liam. I invited him upstairs once before we were heading out to get drinks. The moment he walked in the door, she latched ahold of his wrist and wouldn't let go. Had he not had wolf healing, he would've needed stitches.

I laughed, gesturing to her. "She wants to lick your face."

He made a face. "Really?"

"Yeah, she's a weirdo."

He awkwardly leaned down a bit. Tink happily licked his chin and upper neck. Then she dropped back to all fours. Her tail continued to wag as she looked up at him.

"That's weird," I muttered. "She likes you."

He raised a brow with a grin. "Thanks?"

"No, I didn't mean it like that. She just hates almost everyone. Brody's not even allowed up here anymore. She does okay with him at the house, but she only lets a handful of people in here."

"She's just a good judge of character." He scratched her head once more and shut the door behind him.

"Clearly." I smiled. He smiled back. "Do you want to come sit down?"

"Yeah, sure," he said as I started toward the dining area.

I made my way to the table and lowered myself to a chair. He trailed close behind. Then he sat in the seat he'd claimed as his once upon a time.

It was so strange. He sat down, and for a second, it felt like nothing had changed.

His gaze met mine. He smiled, pointing to my head. "I like your hair."

"It was either a new hair color or a face tattoo. I went with the more temporary option."

"Probably a good move." He grinned. He squinted a bit, looking at my neck. "That turned out beautiful. Is it healed yet?"

"Oh." I laughed, giving a nod. I pulled my hair behind my shoulder and turned to better face him. "Yeah, it just healed. I haven't gotten around to posting it yet. Thanks for hanging in there through the pain though."

"Yeah, any time." His fingertip gently traced the outline of the butterfly. As our skin met, my stomach spun, and goosebumps rose over my body. Butterflies of my own danced from my stomach further down. But that's not what the meeting was about. This was not a hookup. This was a serious conversation. "It's gorgeous."

I turned back to face him. "It's better than the bite mark."

He smiled. "You're beautiful either way."

My cheeks warmed. "You'd say that no matter what."

"I would. Because you are."

Damn it, he needed to stop being cute. I needed to tell him. But the small talk was so comforting. So I kept it going. I had a feeling he was in no hurry to rush out.

"I saw that video of you performing. The one that went viral, I mean. You were amazing."

"Which one?" he asked.

"Your cover of *Circles* by Post Malone." I gave a bare yet playful smile. "I would've thought you'd go with *Fall Apart*."

He laughed, awkward smile coming to his lips. "Well, I didn't want to refer to you as a whore, so..." I chuckled, and he smiled. "I hate that one honestly."

"Why?" I asked. "It was amazing."

"I was getting over a cold, my voice sounded weird."

"I liked it."

"Well, thanks."

We smiled at one another for a few heartbeats. Then I gazed over him and felt my heart skip a beat. Fuck.

This was why I didn't want to see him. Because when I did, I was that same seventeen-year-old girl I was when we met. No matter how much I hated him when he wasn't there, those big blue eyes and that sweet boyish grin made it all fade away.

"So what's all of this about, Lai?" he asked gently.

Ah, yes. Reality.

I lifted my whiskey to my lips and tilted my head back to chug what remained in the glass. When it was empty, I stood and rubbed my forehead, then past my brows down my cheeks.

"Are you using?" I asked.

His smile fell, but his tone was playful. "Is this an intervention or something? Because I'm pretty sure you're supposed to have more people—"

"No," I said quickly. "No. I, um. I was going to get another drink. If you're not sober, I was going to ask if you wanted one."

"Oh," Jeremy murmured. "Yeah, I could go for a drink."

Well, that answered that question. Not that I was happy about it, but I couldn't sit there getting shit faced while he watched sober. And at least he wasn't lying.

"Any preference?"

"Whatever you're having's fine."

I stood and started toward the kitchen. He stood behind me. Then he walked to a picture that hung on the wall.

"Is that from the wedding?" He pointed to a photo of me with all of my sisters.

"The bachelorette party." I grabbed another glass from the cabinet. "I love that picture."

He smiled over his shoulder as I poured our drinks. "Yeah, it's a good one."

I gave another smile, walking toward him. I handed him his glass and looked it over. The memory of his arms around me on the couch that night flickered through my mind. The sound of his laugh as I told him I'd made out with Max once. The shocked, humored gaze. "That was a good night."

"It was," he said quietly.

I felt his gaze on me and turned up to meet his with a smile. "What?"

"I'm just glad you invited me over."

"Thanks for coming on such short notice."

"You could ask me to come at three in the morning, and I'd be here before you could end the call."

Giving a nod, I said, "Yeah, I know."

Jeremy took a sip of his whiskey, holding my gaze. He pulled it from his lips and laughed. "Almost five years since we met, and this is the first time we've had a drink together."

"I guess it is, huh?"

"It is." He smiled.

I looked between his big blue eyes. This innate, almost primal urge told me to lift myself to the tips of my toes and touch my lips to his. But I couldn't do that. We needed to talk.

I turned away and made my way back to the table. I set my drink down, pulled up my jeans, hoisted myself onto the end, and let my legs dangle off of the edge.

"I brought a joint if you want to smoke." Jeremy turned to face me. "It's not as pretty as yours but it'll get the job done."

I smiled. "Yeah, I'm down."

He reached into his pocket and lifted out a thick white joint. As he held it to his lips, he patted his pockets for a lighter. His gaze met mine. I laughed and brought a flame to the tip of my finger. He smiled, took a few steps forward, leaned down a bit, and ignited the end. Once it was sparked, he took a few hits and passed it to me.

As I breathed in a drag, he awkwardly looked for a place to sit. Was sitting beside me on the table weird? Maybe. Not sure what the weight capacity was on it either. But sitting in a chair would make the eye level differential pretty weird too.

This was so strange. He was Jeremy. He was my husband, my soul-mate, the love of my life, and we were both so uncomfortable. Why did this have to be so awkward?

"Do you want to sit on the couch?" I asked.

He agreed, and I teleported onto the cushion on the far left. The sound of his laugh echoed from the dining area. He made his way toward the couch.

I pulled my knees up to my chest and smiled. As he drew closer, I extended the joint to him. Our fingers grazed. He lowered himself to the last cushion. He took a hit, angling himself to face me a bit. He looked around the room, smile across his lips.

"You haven't changed anything," he murmured.

"Well, you didn't want any furniture and it's all new. There wasn't a reason to."

He still looked around. "It's nice being here. Thank you for letting me come by. It feels like home."

His gaze met mine as he passed it my way. I didn't want to go there. I didn't want to fight with him. But when he said that, as if I booted him to the curb for no reason, a fire crept up inside of me. He caused all of this. It was his fault he wasn't at home anymore, not mine.

"It still would be if you hadn't cheated on me."

Jeremy's gaze narrowed a bit, watching me take a drag. "I didn't cheat on you, Laila."

"Really, Jeremy? You're going to keep lying?" I raised a brow. "I read the messages."

"You read what you wanted to read in those messages," he said.

I huffed. What I *wanted* to read in those messages? I didn't want there to *be* any messages. But there they were. Him talking to his ex about 'what happened' the night I gave birth to my son in captivity.

"Sure, I'm the one who was in the wrong. What—I didn't have the right to go through your phone either?"

"That's not what I meant."

"How can you even say that? There's only a handful of ways to interpret, 'Laila's asleep, can I come over?' And, 'She thinks I'm with Adam, can I stop by?'" I snapped.

"Because context matters," Jeremy said. "It was never what you thought it was."

"Then what was it, Jeremy? A quick lay while I was giving birth to our son in that fucking cell with a bullet hole in my leg?"

"No." His brows fell deep above his eyes. "I didn't sleep with her while we were together—"

"Oh, but you did when we broke up?" I questioned.

"What? No. God, no," Jeremy said. He closed his eyes, looked away, and shook his head. "I'm sorry. I don't want to fight with you."

I huffed. "Yeah, of course."

"What's that supposed to mean?"

"You're sorry now because it's too late. You weren't sorry then—"

"That's not true. I apologized immediately—"

"Yeah, because an apology is an admission of fault—"

"In a car accident, not a marriage," he said quickly. "Apologies are the backbone of marriage."

"Apologies don't erase infidelity—"

"I never cheated on you!" It came out as nearly a yell. His eyes were wide. And when he took that tone, my brows raised, head tilting to the side. He closed his eyes again and drew in a deep breath. He took a hit off the joint before turning his gaze back to mine. "I'm sorry because I hurt you." His expression softened a bit. "I'm sorry because I lied. I'm sorry because I ruined our marriage before it had a chance. But I'm not sorry for something that I didn't do."

I sucked my teeth. He took another hit off the joint and passed it back to me. His gaze was steady with mine as I took another hit.

Steady, and honest. Hurt as I was, maybe I should hear him out.

"You never even let me explain my side of the story," Jeremy murmured.

I breathed in another long drag.

He was right. I hadn't. And I did want to know.

"What's your side of the story then?" I asked.

He shifted in his seat until he was facing me. "Where should I start?"

"Maybe with why you had the bitch at my house the night that I gave birth to our son," I said.

He lifted his drink from the table into his hand. "I didn't *have* her here." I raised a brow and huffed. "Do you want to hear what actually happened or are you happy going on with your life thinking that I fucked her when I didn't?"

I lifted my drink from the table and raised it to my lips. "Go ahead."

"The night that you had Micah, I was working downstairs. I was getting ready to close like I always did. I was clean at the time, by the way. I stopped everything when we figured out a way to communicate."

I chewed the inside of my pursed lips.

He continued, "I was literally about to put the closed sign on the door when she walked in. And she was fucked up. Like, drunk out of her mind. Her car was parked crooked in the lot and I couldn't let her drive home. I got her some coffee and told her she needed to sober up."

His gaze was steady with mine, just as honest as it'd been. "So she starts talking. Rambling, really. And she said some shit that was really fucked up, so I tried to teleport her home—"

"What'd she say?" I asked.

"I don't know. It started with some story from high school when we were still together. Then she basically said she was sorry for the shit she did when we were kids. I told her it was cool, ancient history or whatever. But she kept on. Started saying that neither of us would feel like this if things hadn't ended the way they did. That you wouldn't be missing, or pregnant, because we would still be together."

I scoffed, and he said, "Exactly, that's what I said. I told her she was wrong. And that her and I were so far in the past, I could never think of her that way again. I still would have met you at some point and when I did, even if she and I were still together, I would have left her for you."

It shouldn't have given me an ego boost, but it did. I knew that he wasn't lying. The truth was, I would have left any guy I was with when I met Jeremy too.

"What'd she say?" I asked.

He gritted his teeth together. "Her exact words were, 'But she's gone now.'"

"Cunt," I muttered.

He took in another breath. "So I said it was time for her to go home. And literally, all that I did was put my hand on her shoulder. That's it. I didn't touch her waist or grab her hip, I just barely touched her shoulder so I could teleport her home," he said. "And she grabbed my shirt and kissed me. I pulled back right away, Laila. That was it, that was the only thing that happened between us that wasn't platonic."

That face did look genuine. He stuttered when he lied. He'd give this awkward, sad smile. But his eyes were wide open, shifting between mine.

"What happened after that?"

"I took her home. I laid her in her bed. I turned out the light. And I came back here," Jeremy said, earnestly staring into my eyes. "That's it. That's as close to infidelity as it ever got."

I waited for a stammer. I waited for him to swallow. I waited for him to bite his lip. But he didn't. He just looked at me and waited to hear what I had to say in response.

"I need another drink."

CHAPTER SEVENTEEN

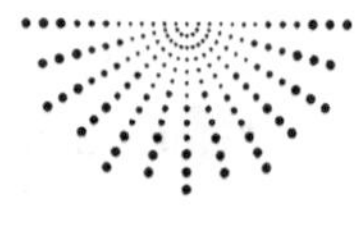

LAILA

Jeremy slurped up the rest of his whiskey before setting his glass on the counter beside mine. I met his gaze. "Do you want to take a shot with me?"

He smiled. "Yeah, I'll take a shot."

I grabbed a few glasses from the cabinet, set them on the counter, and poured the Crown into them. Once they were filled to the brim, I handed Jeremy his and took mine. "To our first shot together."

He smiled and clanged his off of mine. We both raised our glasses, tilted our heads back and swallowed. I shuddered as I set it back to the counter.

I probably shouldn't have been drinking with him. It definitely wasn't the mature thing to do. But the news I was working into wasn't going to come out easily. And the liquor helped.

Staring down at the empty shot glass as the burn settled in my stomach, I turned my gaze back to Jeremy.

"To our second shot together?" I asked.

He grinned. "Maybe a third too?"

"Wise man." I pulled two more glasses from the cabinet. We stood there in silence as I poured four more shots. I slid two in front of Jeremy and set the other two in front of myself. I lifted one in each hand and met his gaze. "To our second and third shots together."

He smiled. The two of us raised our glasses, tilted our heads back, swallowed the first shot, then the second.

By that point, the taste wasn't too bad. I gripped the counter for stability. It wasn't like I was completely shitfaced, but I was drunk. I kind of needed to be. We hadn't even gotten to the conversation that brought him here.

I hoisted myself to the counter and pulled my legs up into a lotus position. "So care to explain those other texts? The ones where you met up while I was asleep? Or when I thought you were with your brother and you were out with her?"

Jeremy leaned against the counter about a foot from me. He stood so close that I could smell his cologne.

"I know they look bad. I reread them after everything went down, and they look way different than they were," he began. "It was never anything remotely close to sexual. It wasn't even really friendship. It was just a place to go where I... I don't know. Where I felt like I didn't have to pretend like everything was okay."

To some extent, I understood that. I was far from okay during that time too. But why'd it have to be her who he confided in? Why couldn't it have been me? Or Leah, or Adam, or Wyatt, or Celena? Why couldn't it have been literally any other person alive?

I rolled my eyes. "Should've gotten a therapist."

"Yeah." He gave an honest nod. "I probably should have."

"If it wasn't about sex, then why did you lie?" I searched his gaze. "Why did you hide it?"

He paused. "Well, she's my ex. I knew you weren't fond of her and I doubted you'd want me to be around her at all. Let alone one-on-one."

"Well, yeah. But because she had feelings for you."

"Brody had feelings for you, and you guys still hung out all the time."

"Yeah, but I didn't lie about it," I said. "And Brody doesn't have a prescription pad with his name on it. And I'm not a recovering addict with a recent relapse."

Frowning, he turned his gaze to the ground. "That's fair."

The room fell silent.

"Look." I poured some whiskey into my glass. "I get not telling me at the end. I was pissed and I didn't give you the chance. But why didn't you tell me sooner? Like before we got married?"

"I don't know. I know that I should have. I thought about telling you all the time. I could have avoided all of this if I had and I hate myself for that. I used to lie and say it was because you were already going through so much but that wasn't it." He rubbed the back of his neck and closed his eyes for a moment. "Olivia was my way to get high. I knew she was in love with me, and I didn't have feelings for her or anything, but I kind of... I guess I used her. She let me come over and get high because she was scared that I'd die if I were alone. And it's wrong that I took advantage of her like that. Maybe it seemed justified because of the shit she did to me when we were kids? I don't know. I know that it was wrong, and I just... I don't know. It just made things easier. I didn't have to worry about you or Adam or Leah or someone catching me nodding off."

"She gave you drugs?"

"Couple times. Mostly, I stole them. She didn't exactly try to stop me."

"Were you clean when she gave them to you?" I asked.

"The first time I relapsed, she gave me the pills. So yeah, I guess."

I huffed. "The bitch was that desperate for your affection that she was willing to help you lose your sobriety."

"In all fairness, I manipulated the shit out of her." His eyes were full of guilt. "I used her feelings to get what I wanted. And I know that was shitty. I don't want to excuse it. It was wrong, I know that."

"But I don't understand *why*," I said. "The drugs, I get. You're an addict. But why her? You could get drugs anywhere."

"I didn't always get them off of her." He looked at the ground. "I just went to her place to do them. Otherwise, I was going to do it alone. I was on oxies then. I didn't want to die but I knew that snorting those could be dangerous. She was the only one who knew I was using. Anyone else would have told you, but I knew she wouldn't because that would mean she wouldn't see me anymore. But after I ODed at her house, I stopped going over there. That was the last time I talked to her before we got married."

My chest tightened. It was because he was that desperate to keep it from me. He was always so open with me. We talked about everything. Unless... unless it was something he was ashamed of.

I raised my glass to my lips. I took a slow sip and set it in the gap between my thighs. "You promised me you'd tell me if you wanted to relapse."

He ran his tongue along his lips, eyes averting mine. "Yeah, I know."

"But you didn't."

He murmured, "No. I didn't."

I gazed at him. "Why? Why didn't you want me to know? Was it just because you were ashamed?"

"Honestly?"

"I'm over lies, so yeah. Honesty's probably your best bet."

Jeremy took a sip from his glass and met my gaze. "You'd give me an ultimatum. Get clean or lose you."

That wasn't true. I wouldn't have left him just because he was using. I would've thrown his drugs out, I would've swept the alcohol and paraphernalia from the house, I would've made him go to meetings and a therapist. But I wouldn't have left him.

Still, I ran my tongue along my teeth. "And you'd choose drugs."

"No. I'd choose you. I'd always choose you."

Hearing those words leave his lips made me fall for him all over again. My stomach flipped, a warm feeling moved from my chest through my body, and I wanted to erase the past year. I wanted to go back to where we were before any of it, or even after my capture but before the bomb. But it wasn't that simple.

Especially now that I knew Micah was alive. The track marks ascending his forearms were plenty of reason to suppress that feeling. Not because I couldn't love him while he was using, but because I wouldn't have drugs around my child. I wouldn't let my son find his dad dead on the bathroom floor with blue lips the way that I'd found his dad.

"Then why, Jeremy?" I asked.

"I'd choose you. But I knew I'd relapse and end up hiding it from you anyway. The only way an addict gets clean is if they want to. Not because they have to."

"And you didn't want to."

He rubbed his eyes down to his beard. "I was really depressed. What happened to you, and Micah..." A shiver went up my spine when he said his name. "I know I should have talked to you about it. I shouldn't have tried to hide how fucked up my head was. That part, I did keep from you because I didn't want to hurt you. When you started doing better, I didn't want to ruin that with how shitty I was doing. I didn't want you to think that I felt that way because of you. Even though I was depressed, I still loved you. And you still made me happy and I didn't want you to think that I wasn't. I didn't want to sulk for pity. I just wanted to feel better. And the drugs... I know they ultimately made it worse, but for a while, they let me forget how shitty life was. Not my life with you, just..."

"Overall." I lifted my glass. "Yeah. I get it."

He held my gaze. "I didn't want to hurt you. That was never my goal."

"You just weren't ready to be sober."

Another frown. "No, I wasn't."

My eyes moved over his arms again. Those beautiful, slender yet strong arms, covered in splotches of blue and purple. "Are you ready to get sober now?"

"I'd get clean if I had a reason to."

I took another gulp from my glass. "If what I'm about to tell you isn't a good enough reason, I don't know what is."

He squinted a bit. "What do you mean?"

"I asked you to come because I have something big to tell you."

"You said it was good news, right?"

I blinked the sting in my eyes away. I looked down. "Yeah, it is."

His hand found my chin. He lifted it to meet his gaze. He looked between my eyes with slightly furrowed brows. "Then why do you look like you're about to tell me something awful?"

Because it was my fault.

None of this would've happened if I knew Micah was alive. I'd have gotten him out of there before I even attempted to get any other survivors. He wouldn't have relapsed because we'd have our son. He wouldn't have been depressed.

This all fell on my shoulders.

He moved his thumb to my cheek and wiped away a tear that escaped my eye. "What is it, Lai?"

After a calming breath, I said, "You remember Lydia."

"Kind of hard to forget her."

"Well... A month or so ago, Ray got a job offer in upstate New York. His hometown." He nodded slowly, paying close attention. "It was a really good opportunity for them, and he has family there. It made sense, ya know?"

"Sure," Jeremy murmured.

"They've been gone for a couple weeks, but today, Ray called. And I was busy, I didn't answer, and he called again. I was worried something happened, but he said everything was okay, just that we needed to talk. Specifically, he said I had to come there now. That he'd come to me, but it would take too long to get here when I could just teleport. He told me to close the diner down if I had to, just get up there because I would want to know this as soon as possible. So I went and he told me to sit."

"That's never a good sign," he murmured.

"You know how Lydia's an artist, right?"

"I vaguely remember that," Jeremy said.

I hopped from the counter and started toward my purse on the other side of the kitchen. I reached inside and pulled out one of the sketches that Lydia told me I could keep. My fingers gripped the folded white paper in my hand. I held it tight between my fingertips as I walked back to Jeremy at the counter.

With trembling fingers, I extended the paper to him. He took the sketch. I watched his face as he unfolded the paper. When he opened it, he gritted his teeth.

"That's Amy and Peterson, isn't it?" he asked. I nodded as he gestured to the baby. "That's Lydia?"

"That's what Ray thought too. But no."

"Who is it then?"

Tears began to puddle in the corners of my eyes as I looked down at the image. One fell from my cheek and landed on the page. Jeremy gently raised his thumb to my face to brush the wetness away.

"You're going to have to give me a little bit more than that, Lai," he said quietly.

I turned my gaze up to meet his. "I... Ray asked her who it was." The lump in my throat got bigger and my teeth began to anxiously chatter. "She—She didn't..." I wiped my cheek and searched for a way to go on. "She gave him a really weird face and said..."

Jeremy gently ran his thumb along my cheek. "You don't have to talk about it if you don't want to, Laila."

I held his gaze. "You have to know."

"Take your time then."

My voice was barely above a whisper. "She... She said that it was Laila's baby."

His brows fell, pulling together.

"He—He told her. He said that Micah died and... And she looked at him like he was crazy." The tears fell down harder.

"I don't understand."

"I—I... When she and I talked about Micah, I—I always said things like 'gone' or 'taken from me.' I... I never..." My cries got heavier; my body began to quiver. "I never said dead because she's a kid. I used kid language... I—I never..." I began to gasp between my words. "I didn't know, Jeremy. I didn't know."

He carefully placed his hands on either side of my face and wiped the tears with his thumbs. "Baby, I still don't understand."

I pressed my trembling lips together. "They took him. He didn't... Micah didn't die."

He cocked his head to the side. "What?"

I bit my chattering teeth together. "Micah's alive."

His eyes widened a bit. It was as if he was waiting for me to say April Fools.

"I didn't know, Jeremy. I didn't know." My tears began to turn to obnoxious, ugly crying. "I didn't know."

His eyes were still discs. "Our son's alive?"

"I didn't know," I said between chattering teeth. "I didn't know."

A joyful smile came to his lips. Then he moved his hands from my cheeks around my waist. He pulled my body close to his and squeezed me as tight as he could.

His arms were the safest place in the world. I felt his lips press to my hair as his hands gently coasted along my back. He held me even tighter.

I rested my head against his chest and tightened my arms around his ribs. I stayed there for a moment, closing my eyes and trying to refrain from crying.

CHAPTER EIGHTEEN

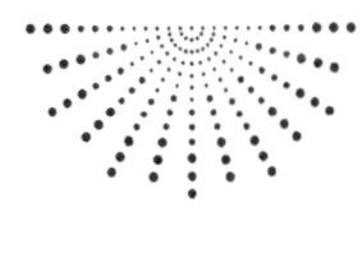

LAILA

His arms were still around me. They practically held me upright. I struggled to keep my tears from turning to sobs. My arms tightened around his back, breathing in the scent of citrusy cologne. At least he didn't hate me.

"I can't believe it." Jeremy murmured. He pulled back a bit to meet my gaze. "You're sure?"

"I saw him in her memories."

He smiled, and another tear fell from his eye. "Can you show me?"

I moved my hands from his back out in front of me. He laid his palms on mine and closed his eyes.

I watched his expression as he saw Micah's little face for the first time. Tears began to drizzle. He smiled. And then he frowned. After a moment, he opened his eyes and met my gaze.

His smile widened. He wiped his eyes. "He's beautiful."

I nodded as my teeth continued to clamber.

"Baby, this is good news." He gently held my face in his hands. "Why are you crying?"

"I should have known," I said quietly. "I'm his mom. I should have known."

"You couldn't have."

"But I *should* have." The tears began to pour, still holding his gaze. "He's thirteen months old, and I missed it. I missed the first year of his life, Jeremy. They've had him for all this time and I've never even got to hold him. It's not fair."

He gently ran his hand along my back. "It's not."

"I wasted all of this time mourning him and he isn't dead. And I missed it all. I missed his first laugh, probably his first words, his first steps. I'm missing everything and I don't know where he is. I don't know how to find him." My voice shook. "What if they're hurting him like they hurt me? What if they put the trackers in him already? What if he's in pain? I'm not there to keep him safe. I—I failed him. I failed all of us. I just want him to be safe, but he isn't. They have him and..."

"Hey." Jeremy gripped my face in his hands and turned it up to meet his gaze. "We're going to find him."

"How?" I cried. "It's impossible. It... He... Peterson is so smart, Jeremy. You know that—"

"I don't care how smart he is." Jeremy wiped my cheeks with his thumbs. "I don't care, Laila. We're getting our son back. I don't care what we have to do, I don't care who we have to kill. We're bringing him home."

My teeth continued to chatter. "I don't know how."

"Neither do I. But we're bringing our baby home."

My tears got heavy again. "He's not a baby anymore. He doesn't even know us."

"It doesn't matter," Jeremy said. "That's our son. We're bringing him home, Laila. It doesn't matter what we have to do or who we have to kill. We're getting our son back."

I bit my trembling lip.

"Come here." He placed his arms around my waist and tugged me into him. I buried my head into his chest. He squeezed me tight, lips pressing to my hair. I held him as tight as my arms would allow.

"We're going to find him," he said. "We're going to bring him home."

I hugged even tighter and closed my eyes. I pushed my head further into him, listening to his heartbeat beneath my ear. He stiffened his arms around me. Then he sweetly lifted me in the air, spinning me in a little circle. He chuckled at my ear. He held me tight and set me back to my feet.

I turned my gaze up to him, still holding his waist tight against my body. He smiled down at me, pushing hair from my face.

"He has your eyes." I brought a small smile to my lips.

"He has your chin." His thumb and forefinger gently pinched mine with a smile. His thumb moved upward, grazing my lower lip. His gaze went from my mouth back up to mine. "And your lips."

I swallowed hard as I looked between his eyes.

Holy shit, I'd forgotten how much I loved those eyes. Most blue eyes are cold and stiff. But Jeremy's were warm and inviting. They were a deep, vibrant shade that were as welcoming as the ocean on a ninety-degree day. They looked livelier than I'd seen them in a long time, glimmering with radiant beams of hope.

It was one of those moments where the world around me ceased to exist. Something about him would always be able to consume me in a way nothing and no one else could.

I'd been seeing Liam for a month or so, but it wasn't serious. He wasn't my boyfriend, although I knew he wanted to be. But I couldn't do it because I didn't want him. Not the way that he wanted me.

I wanted this. I wanted my husband, and our son, and a happy, sweet little life.

"Kiss me," I whispered.

His eyes smiled before his lips. His hand at my chin moved to my neck. He leaned down and firmly touched his lips to mine.

My stomach flipped as the hardness of his mouth molded into the softness of mine. The taste of whiskey and weed danced on my tongue as my lips parted against his. His bottom lip brushed mine, pushing hair behind my shoulder.

Our tongues barely grazed each other's. I tilted my head the other way, leaning onto the tips of my toes to reach his face better. I moved my fingers from his face around his shoulder.

Warmth flooded through my body, tingles stretching from my mouth over every pore.

Fuck, he was the best kisser. I'd enjoyed that night with Ray, and all the dates I'd shared with Liam, but nothing compared to this. Somehow, when Jeremy and I kissed, it felt like the perfect fit. There was no better way to describe it. Like I was a lock, and he was a key. With enough jiggling, any piece of metal could open me up. But it was seamless with Jeremy. He hardly had to touch me, and I fell wide open.

He knew exactly how to run his hands over my skin. Soft, but not too soft. Firm, but not hard. Gentle but dominant. Liam was good in bed, Ray was better, but neither of them knew what I liked. Neither of them knew that perfect amount of pressure to squeeze my ass with. They didn't know how to use that feather like touch on my cheek. Neither of them knew how to be emphatic and gentle at the same time.

As he lifted me up and sat me on the counter, I clenched my hands around his neck and locked my legs around his lower back. Those strong, calloused fingers drifted from my hips to my chest all the way to my face. He held it close, firm, almost protective. As though he never wanted to let go.

I found the bulge in his jeans, stomach flipping when he let out a deep breath against my lips. As I fumbled with the zipper, he laughed. "Laila—"

"Just take off your pants."

He raised a brow, smile wide. "Are you sure?"

"Do you want to fuck me or not?"

Another half laugh. He held my cheek tighter, thumb brushing my lower lip. "That's a stupid question."

"Then take off your pants and fuck me until I forget all the bullshit that's brought us to where we are."

He made a noise in his throat that almost resembled a laugh.

Then he gently grabbed a fistful of hair at the back of my neck and pulled my head to the side. I closed my eyes when his lips touched the skin just below my ear. He squeezed my hip with his other hand, pulling me as close to him as he could. I yanked his pants down and snuck my hand into the waistband of his boxers.

Jesus fuck, he was so hard. I wasn't sure if I'd ever wanted him as badly as I did in this moment.

Kissing my neck still, his hands coasted over my body, and mine did the same, yanking and pulling, until all of our clothes laid in a pile on the hardwoods, and we were nude against the countertop, hands exploring every inch of each other.

The moment we were naked, he yanked my body close to his, and an overwhelming sense of comfort tied up with arousal coursed through me. Skin to skin contact was always intimate, but it felt like more than that. This wasn't just about sex. It wasn't about intimacy. It was vulnerability.

We opened ourselves to one another in a way that we hadn't in half a year.

When kissing wasn't enough, when the tease of his cock against my inner thigh was too much to bear, I turned around and rubbed my ass against him. He let out a breathy moan, grabbing my hips and bringing them tight against him. Pulling my hair to my back, Jeremy's lips lowered to my neck, grazing the butterfly gently as his free hand glided to my clit.

The passion was there, but my eyes closed, head rolling against his chest, sensation of comfort taking hold.

Liam kissed my scar once, and it'd yanked me from the moment so quickly. I wasn't sure why. I knew he wouldn't hurt me, but I supposed it was a trigger. Each time Jeremy kissed that spot though, I thought about the first time he touched me after I escaped. I thought about how gentle he'd been with me, how aroused pleasuring me made him, and bliss overtook me.

The trust I had in Jeremy was greater than it could ever be for another person. No one felt as safe as he did. No one was as familiar, as comforting.

And that was exactly why I wanted more. Kissing him was sweet. The gentle, teasing strokes along my clit forced little pulses through my core. But I wanted him to fucking *rail* me.

"You're so wet." His hot breath tickled my ear.

I moaned again, feeling his dick getting harder against my ass. "Just fuck me."

He laughed, squeezed my hips, and tugged them back to him. "Yes, ma'am."

I wanted to smile, but he pushed himself inside, and I gasped at the sudden stretch throughout me. Gasping, I felt my eyes heat in their sockets, head rolling against his chest. Our eyes locked, and he smiled. He kept rubbing my clit, but thrusted in deeper.

And it was glorious. His touch, those gentle rocks into me, that loving look in his eyes. It felt like I was safe, like I was whole for the first time in months.

But I wanted to get fucked. I wanted to lose touch with reality. I wanted to feel pure, inexplicable bliss. I wanted to forget everything else existed and drown myself in pleasure.

"Jeremy," I moaned, tilting my head into his chest.

"Yeah, baby?" he murmured.

"You don't have to be so gentle," I whispered. "Fuck me 'til it hurts."

"Oh?" He smirked, thrusting a bit harder. "That's what you want?"

I gasped when he went in as deep as he could, only managing a nod in response.

His smile widened. "Grab the counter."

My stomach flipped, pressure building deep inside me. I did as he said and started to bend over, but he grabbed ahold of my hair and pulled my head back as far as it could go, tilting me slightly sideways so my gaze locked with his. Fuck, I would've done anything to capture that moment in a picture.

"I said to grab the counter," he murmured, hand on my clit sliding up my torso to my throat. He didn't squeeze, but he held it, forcing my eyes to stay on his. "I didn't say to bend over."

And he slammed inside. I squealed with pleasure, thankful for my stability against the counter. He pounded deep into my cunt, hitting that perfect place against my G-spot. My ass arched closer toward him, neck aching at the contortion, but that place the head of his cock massaged had my knees trembling with bliss.

"This what you wanted, baby?" he murmured, voice gravelly.

This was exactly what I had meant. I wanted him to fucking pound me, and he did.

Holy *fuck*, he did.

"Mhmm." I closed my eyes.

He chuckled.

If anyone else would have grabbed me like this, or squeezed my throat like that, I would have killed them on the spot. Liam knew better than to grab my neck, he'd learned the hard way when I left a hand shaped burn on his shoulder. But this wasn't Liam.

It was Jeremy.

Once upon a time, I practically had to beg his shy little ass to smack mine.

Jeremy was the only person alive that I was comfortable enough with to literally put my life into his hands. He could slap me across the face, and I'd love that pain.

We loved each other more than just about anything on earth. But at that point in our lives, we hated each other almost just as much. He hurt me. I hurt him. There was a lot of damage done.

We were angry. That frustration and pain bred this passion that I could never experience with someone else.

I hated being controlled after what happened to me in captivity. But for some reason, I *wanted* Jeremy to control me. I wanted him to be angry and aggressive like he used to be before it all happened.

Maybe it was because I felt guilty over the way I ended things. Maybe because I knew how much he wanted our baby, and I just learned I let that bastard get away with Micah. Maybe I wanted someone to hurt me because I couldn't do it to myself.

Maybe it was just because Jeremy was the only person alive I trusted enough to completely let myself go with.

I didn't know, and I didn't care. All that mattered was that I was lost.

Everything else was gone, and Jeremy and I were the only things that existed.

He pulled out of me, grabbed my hips, and spun my body to face his.

Gasping, trying to level my vision, I held his biceps for stability. "Why'd you stop?"

"I want to see your face." He grabbed my hips and hoisted me around his waist.

I laughed as he kissed my neck and began carrying me to the living room. His hands at my hips moved to my ass. They squeezed for a moment. Then—still walking—two fingers slipped inside of me. I moaned at his ear, and he laughed.

He set me down on the couch, fingers still inside of me as he brought himself to his knees. His lips trailed down my chest, carefully tracing his tongue along my nipple. His thumb moved on my clit and his lips continued to coast down my body. He kissed my stomach, then my hip, and then my inner thigh. He opened his lips and gently sucked my skin into his mouth. His gaze stayed on mine as he dropped the tip of his tongue to my clit.

He spun it in a slow, teasing circle. I moaned, tilting my head back. His other hand moved up my chest. He squeezed my boob, thumb brushing against my hard nipple, fingers rolling against my G-spot.

I squirmed with pleasure, whole body tingling, stomach rolling with bliss and temptation. It was amazing—*he* was amazing. Those skilled, guitarist fingers were great for more than plucking strings, and the man's tongue was practically a vibrator. But I wanted more.

I struggled to keep my eyes from rolling to the back of my head. "Baby."

"Yeah?" He moved his lips back to my clitoris.

"Fuck me."

Aren't you enjoying this? he spoke into my mind. He flicked his tongue until my leg shook. Then he grinned.

Jesus Christ, enjoyment didn't come close to how much I loved what he was doing down there. He was so fucking good at it. His fingers inside of me hitting just the right spot, his tongue against my clit doing no different. But I craved the intimacy of his eyes on me, watching the euphoria shine in his gaze as he fucked me. I didn't want it to end yet, and I knew I would in this position. It was overwhelming, overstimulating, and I didn't want it to end.

"But I don't want to come yet."

He smiled and he moved his tongue in a circle. *I'll just make you come again.*

I laughed. "But I can't even reach you."

He shrugged, grinning. *That's okay.*

His tongue spun in a fast circle before flicking up and down. The scratchy texture of his beard against my lips was that little hint of pain that magnified the pleasure, and god damn, I couldn't help the squeal that billowed from my lips.

Holy fuck, it felt so good. *He* felt so good. He'd done that so many times, he knew exactly what it took to make me scream.

And those bright blue eyes locked on mine just made it better. He smiled each time I moaned, but he didn't change anything. Liam always went harder when I moaned louder, and then he ruined what felt so fucking good to make me scream in the first place. But Jeremy knew that the moan meant "don't stop," not "go harder."

His fingers moved in perfect sync with his tongue against my clit. Every so often, he'd spin it in a circle and then flick fast and hard from the hood of my clit to the bottom where it met my skin. When I pushed my hips closer to his face, he did it even faster until I was screaming his name.

Then a wave of euphoria rushed over me as my muscles contracted around his fingertips. It was a deep, rumbling sense of bliss that left me momentarily blinded and trembling with pleasure.

But he didn't stop then either, he kept doing exactly as he had been with the biggest grin, forcing it to last longer, making my thighs tremble around his face. I squirmed and screamed with pleasure, rolling closer into him. My heart slammed so hard and so fast that I could hardly bring in an even breath, but I wouldn't have had it any other way.

When it finally stopped, he laughed. Wiping his lips and straightening up, he gripped my hips and pulled me to the edge of the couch.

Before I'd even caught my breath, he leaned closer and slammed his cock inside of me. I sighed against his lips, and he laughed again. His hand slid up my chest, caressing my skin. It sent warmth throughout my entire body, leaving me in an orgasm induced haze that was somehow a crossroads of pleasure, familiarity, and home.

When his thumb found my clit, I gasped, and he smiled.

"You're trying to kill me, huh?" I laughed.

"Do you want me to stop?" He smiled, still moving his thumb against my clit. The other found my face. It grazed my lips, pulling down the bottom one and looking between my eyes.

"Please don't," I whispered.

He bit his smiling lip. Then he moved his hips out and back in harder than the last. I tightened my arms around his chest. He placed his hand at my neck onto my spine and pulled my body up to his. He kissed me harder and thrusted deep, so deep that I groaned his name in bliss. I had no idea how he could multitask like that, but *fuck*, he knew what he was doing.

He rested his forehead against mine and looked deep into my eyes. "I love you," he murmured.

"I love you too," I whispered against his lips, twisting my arms around his neck.

He grabbed the side of my face and held it close to his, eyes stuck to me. "Fuck, you feel so good."

"Yeah?" I murmured.

His forehead was still against mine. "I missed this so much," he whispered. "I missed *you* so much."

"I missed you too," I whispered. I touched his face, rubbing the tips of my fingers through his thick scruff. My eyes shifted between his. The warmth of his breath against my lips, the feel of his hands against my skin...

He was perfect.

For a second, I thought about forgetting the past year. I thought about ignoring what had torn us apart. But then I remembered how much it hurt to pull that perfect face from the bathroom floor and my heart ached.

I pushed that thought from my mind.

This moment. That's what I needed to focus on.

How euphoric I felt with his dick inside of me. How safe those hands felt. How beautiful those blue eyes were. How careful his kisses were when his lips pressed to mine.

He pulled my face closer to his. His tongue traced along my lower lip, then gently grazed mine.

I just had to stay in this moment.

CHAPTER NINETEEN

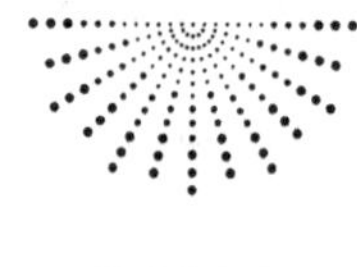

LAILA

At some point or another, we made it to the bedroom. Then we did it again, and again, and again. It wasn't exactly as I'd planned the night going. But it was a hell of a lot better than I'd prepared myself for.

I struggled to catch my breath, resting my head on Jeremy's fast rising and falling chest. I breathed in the smell of his cologne mixing with sex and sweat, feeling liked I was floating. "Jesus."

He laughed and kissed my forehead. His arms tightened around my waist. "What was that—Like six for you?"

I shook my head. "I have no idea, I stopped counting after three." He chuckled and kissed my hair again. His hands squeezed my waist a bit tighter. "That was the best sex I've had in years."

"Hey, we had great sex in January," he said.

"Yeah, but not like that." I raised my head and placed my chin on his chest. "That was amazing."

He grinned. "It was pretty great, huh?"

I smiled. I didn't have to say it, but I wanted to see his response. "Better than any of the sex you've had since we broke up?"

"Possibly the best sex I've ever had in my life. What about you?"

That was a good answer.

I smiled. "It's always better with you."

He smiled for a moment. Then it pulled down slightly at the edges. "I don't know if I should say this."

"What?" I traced my fingertips along the short hair on his chest.

Some form of sadness flashed in his vibrant eyes. "Leah said you were seeing someone. Is that... Is that true?"

Oh, yeah. Liam. I'd just about forgotten he existed.

"There's no title between us."

He was quiet, lips lowered in a frown. He looked so sad. And my chest tightened with guilt.

"We weren't together, and you've been with other people too," I murmured.

"Yeah, I know."

It's not like either of us could be upset with the other. When I ended things, I'd made it clear that I was okay with that. Still though...

I wasn't sure if I wanted the answer to the question I was about to ask either. "Are you seeing anyone?"

"No. Nothing like that."

"Like what then?" I asked.

He scratched his head. "I've had some hookups since the breakup."

I leaned up onto my elbow. "How many is some?"

"I don't know the exact number."

"Like five?" I asked. His gaze averted mine. "Ten?" My eyes widened a bit when he didn't respond. "Fifteen?" He looked away, unable to meet my gaze. "Christ. More than fifteen?"

A moment of awkward silence. "I really don't know how many."

"Jesus, Jeremy," I muttered. "Should we have worn a condom?"

"I don't have anything," he said. "I used a condom every time and I just got checked. It's not like I'd knowingly give you the clap or something."

It was a little shocking at first, but in fairness, it shouldn't have been. He got around quite a bit before we got together. That's how he learned to be so great at it. He was a good-looking guy, he had the bad boy persona, and he played guitar. Obviously, it wasn't very difficult for him to get laid.

"How many people did you sleep with since we broke up?" he asked.

Oof. Ray.

"Two."

He studied my expression. "Was it someone I know?" I scratched my head. "It was. Oh, fuck, was it Brody?"

I crinkled my nose. "God, no. That's gross. He's my brother."

"Yeah, in law."

"Still gross. Wasn't trying to keep it in the family."

He thought for a moment. "Max?"

My lips curled, head shaking. "Also gross."

"Who else is there?" he asked.

He was going to find out one way or another. It was inevitable, I'd told his sisters. It was better he hear it from me than someone else.

I scratched my head again. "I slept with Ray before he moved."

He creased his brows, jaw tightening.

"I hadn't been with anyone since you and I ran into him at the bar. We were really drunk. It was a shit day... We were friends. It wasn't intimidating. It was just, like, a steppingstone to get back out there."

He ran his tongue along his teeth. "I was friends with him too."

"It's not like I did it to hurt you."

His hand still resting at the small of my back squeezed slightly, pulling me into him, eyes growing distant.

"It was just a really shitty day," I murmured. "I'd killed someone before I went to the bar, I just wanted to disappear for a while."

"Who'd you kill?"

"Some preacher," I said. He raised a brow. "Yeah, I guess that didn't sound too good, huh?"

He laughed.

"It wasn't unprovoked. I mean, I guess he didn't hurt me personally. But he... He raped a sixteen-year-old girl in my support group. She was fifteen at the time. And he gave her HIV."

He crinkled his nose, jaw tightening again. "Was it painful?"

"Not really. It was pretty quick. But he's gone and that's all that matters."

"Good riddance," Jeremy said.

I rested my head against his chest again. I may not have been down to cuddle with Ray or Liam after we fucked, but this was my husband. This was my best friend. And talking with him, even if he didn't like what I had to say, felt so comforting.

"So am I bigger than Ray?" he asked abruptly.

I made a face, turning up to meet his gaze. "What?"

"My dick," he said. "Is it bigger?"

I laughed and shook my head. "Yeah, Jeremy. Your dick's bigger than Ray's."

He grinned. "What about your boyfriend?"

"Liam's not my boyfriend," I said.

"Alright, is my dick bigger than Liam's?" he asked.

I rolled my eyes, half laugh escaping my nostrils. "Yeah. You have the biggest dick in the world. Is that what you want to hear?"

"Well, now I feel like you're lying." Jeremy smiled, rolling onto his side to face me better. One hand rested around my waist as the other twirled my hair that laid against the sheets.

I was definitely lying. Liam's dick was huge. Almost painfully huge. We had to stop multiple times because it was starting to hurt and I didn't want Jeremy to pop into my head and see me getting railed by some other guy. But of course, I wasn't going to tell him that.

Jeremy's was just above average in size. Ray's was significantly smaller but still satisfying enough to get the job done. Really, it didn't matter. They all did what needed done in their own way.

At the end of the day, sex with Jeremy was always better than sex with anyone else, regardless of size. I loved him. Even when I hated him, I was still in love with him.

"Do we really have to talk about this?" I laughed.

He sighed. "At least my dick's bigger than Ray's."

"That's the spirit."

After a quiet moment, Jeremy pushed hair from my face. "We should probably have a conversation about what just happened."

I didn't want to go through the whole 'what did that really mean?' conversation. Because I didn't know. I knew that I loved him, I knew that the sex we'd just had was amazing, I knew that I wished things were like they used to be.

But they weren't. Things couldn't magically go back to what they were before our lives blew up on us.

Whether I loved him or not, I wasn't ready to jump right back into things. I wasn't ready to pick his body up off the bathroom floor again.

However, it was nice to talk to my best friend. It was nice to spend time with him. I may not have been ready to get back together. But I didn't want to go another four months without seeing him.

"So it was a onetime thing?" he asked.

Biting my lip, I shook my head. "I wouldn't say that."

He raised a brow. "Oh?"

"Whatever this was doesn't mean we're back together," I said. "But the situation with Micah changes things."

He gave a gentle smile, eyes shifting between mine for a moment. "Does that mean you're not going to teleport away the next time we run into each other?"

"I won't do that again."

He smiled. His hand cupped my cheek. "Am I allowed to see you?"

"Call first," I said. "But yeah, as long as you don't just show up."

"Fair enough," Jeremy murmured. "Are we keeping this quiet? The fucking, I mean."

"I would like to," I said. "Just until I figure things out."

"Are you going to tell your boyfriend?"

"Not my boyfriend. But yeah. I'll let him decide how he feels about it. He's well aware that I'm married, and I've made it pretty clear that I'm not interested in a relationship. So... I don't know how he's gonna feel about it, but yeah, I'm gonna tell him."

Jeremy was quiet for a moment. "You haven't kicked me out yet so that's a good sign."

I pulled a smile to my lips. "Do you want to go again?"

He raised a brow, smile tugging up his lips. "Jesus, woman."

I sat up and started to my feet. "Well, if you don't want to—"

"Get over here." He grabbed my hips and pulled me on top of him.

CHAPTER TWENTY

JEREMY

The sweet smell of Laila's perfume lingered in my nose, then became overshadowed by musty dog. A scratchy, slobbery tongue licked my face. I opened my eyes. A big white fluff ball with pale blue eyes stared back at me.

She wagged her tail. I smiled, reached out, and pet her scruff. Her head rubbed into my palm.

Last night felt like a dream until I turned and saw her sleeping with a pillow curled under her head. Her cherry red hair laid on her ivory skin like blood on the snow. The apples of her cheeks were a light shade of morning blushed pink. The slight part of her heart shaped lips was easily the most beautiful thing I'd ever seen. I wanted to push mine into them as I had most of the night, but she looked so sweet.

It wasn't a dream come true, but it was close. We might not have been "together," but I was lying naked beside her in the bed we'd picked out together. It was a hell of a lot closer than I had been the morning before.

And our son was alive.

Micah was alive and my bare legs were entangled with his mother's as the sun peeked in through the open window.

It was the closest to a dream come true as I had lived in a very long time.

Except for my runny nose, watery eyes, stiff muscles, and clammy skin.

I had to get high soon or the less attractive withdrawals were going to kick in.

But there was no way in hell I was leaving yet. For the first time in more than half of a year, she wanted me here. I wasn't leaving until I was told to.

I thought about taking Tinkerbell outside to piss but I knew I'd have to walk through the kitchen where I was sure Max would be cooking. She said she wanted to keep things quiet, which was not Max's strong suit. If he saw me walking down those steps at seven in the morning, there's no way he wouldn't know what happened the night before. I wasn't going to do anything that would jeopardize this opportunity.

Instead, I carefully crawled from the bed and tiptoed to the kitchen. I put a pot of coffee on and grabbed my boxers and jeans from the floor. I didn't bring my whole supply, but I kept three hydrocodone in my wallet for situations like this.

It wasn't much. Barely enough to feel anything. Hell, it probably wouldn't do a damn thing since I'd been shooting but it was better than nothing.

I pulled on my boxers, walked to the bathroom, and crushed the pills on the sink as I'd done hundreds of times at that point. I rolled up a dollar bill from my wallet and quickly sniffed the powder into my nostril.

There I was, thinking about how I wouldn't do anything to fuck it up, then doing exactly as I had the day she told me to pack my shit. But if I didn't, I'd get sicker. I didn't want to get sick; I just wanted to enjoy any time with her she was willing to give me.

Once the coffee was brewed, I poured two cups and carefully walked them into the bedroom just as Laila's alarm sounded. She grumbled, mumbling something along the lines of, "I know, shut the fuck up," as she sat up in the bed.

I laughed. "Hey."

A smile tugged at her lips. She rubbed her tired eyes. "You made coffee."

"Used to be our routine back in the day." I set her cup on the end table.

"Once upon a time." She lifted the mug to her lips and took a sip. "Damn it. Why does it always come out better when you make it?"

I lowered myself to the bed beside her. She tugged the light blue sheet to her chest. "I don't know, I just throw some coffee in the pot and press start."

"Yeah, but the cream to coffee ratio is what makes it so perfect." She sat the cup in her lap. Her gaze met mine and she squinted a bit. "You're high, huh?"

I looked down at the steaming coffee in my hands.

Please don't tell me to leave.

"I know you aren't clean," she said. My eyes met hers. "I'm not exactly the poster boy for sobriety either. Just don't lie to me about it, okay?"

It wasn't an easy thing to be honest about, but it was only fair. "I was getting sick. I just wanted to keep the withdrawals at bay."

Laila gaze searched mine for a minute. Then she took another sip of her coffee. "I don't know how I didn't know before. The blue in your eyes look so much bigger."

"I didn't let you see me until it was wearing off," I muttered.

She gave another nod, showing not an ounce of emotion on her face. I used to be able to read her like a book, but now, she'd gotten so good at hiding what she was thinking. She looked at the side table. "Jesus, I'm dehydrated."

"I'll get you—"

She set her coffee down on the table. "It's okay, I have to pee anyway."

The blanket fell as she put her feet to the ground. When she stood, I got my first good look at her body in more than half of a year. I'd seen plenty of it last night, but it was in the heat of the moment, and I didn't get to take it in.

She looked a hell of a lot different than I remembered. It wasn't a bad thing. She was still fucking beautiful. But she looked like a woman now.

She didn't look like she was nineteen anymore. But her curves moved just as smoothly from her ribs into her waist out toward her hips. Her ass was just as tight as it'd always been, but it looked a bit wider than it once had.

She didn't have a flat, smooth belly anymore. The skin was littered with stretch marks and scars. She'd gained back most of the weight she'd lost in captivity.

It was funny though because I'd been with a lot of women in the past six months. Society might say that their bodies were more appealing than someone like Laila. Someone... normal. Someone who didn't have perky tits and a flat, smooth stomach. Someone who didn't have cellulite on the back of their thighs. Someone whose hips flowed from their waist into their thighs without love handles.

But still, there wasn't anyone alive who I thought was sexier than she was. She was imperfectly perfect. Every detail that might not be seen as perfect was perfect to me because I adored her.

The dark red hair and mural over her back almost made her look like a different person entirely. All of those scars had been elegantly camouflaged into what looked like the garden of Eden. Bright flowers of a thousand different shades covered the marks she'd resented with every fiber of her being. They were intertwined with vines and branches like a magnificent orchard of foliage.

"What?" Laila met my gaze in the mirror. She grinned, yanking a pair of jeans up over her legs.

"You're just beautiful." I smiled.

Pulling a T-shirt from the drawer, she turned and met my gaze. "You should take a picture. It lasts longer."

Over the last seven months, I'd looked at plenty of pictures of her. I didn't need another. I needed to capture that moment.

"The real version's better."

She bit her grinning lip. Then she put her arms through the sleeves and tugged her black T-shirt past her stomach to her hips. "If you need clothes, your dresser's still full. Might be a little musty but they're clean."

"That's alright, I'll just wear the clothes I came in," I said. "But have you told anyone else?"

"Just Leah. I wanted to tell you first, but I was kind of a mess after we got off the phone and I just needed to talk to someone."

"It's okay. Leah knows everything anyway." I smiled. A tiny grin pulled at her lips. "We should probably fill everyone in then, right?"

"Yeah, definitely," she said. "What is today?"

"Sunday, I think."

"Good. Hannah's off school, Brody doesn't have his internship, Mom and Jenna are off work. I'll tell everyone to meet up at the house later."

"What time are you thinking?" I asked.

"I don't know. Maybe threeish?"

"Are you working today?"

"Just some administrative stuff." She crossed her arms to her chest and leaned against the dresser. "Shouldn't take more than a couple of hours."

"Alright. I'm going to go back to North Carolina and check out of my hotel then. I'll have to drive my car back up tomorrow, but I'll be there at three."

"You don't have to come back right now. We don't have anything to go on yet, it's not—"

"I'm coming back." My voice was firm. Not mean, but firm. I stood. "Look, I heard what you said, Lai. We aren't together. I get that. But this isn't about us, this is about Micah. I need to be available if something comes up. This is about my kid."

A half smile came to her lips. "I'm happy you feel that way."

I gave one back. "I'll stay at the house. But I'm going to be involved in this. I don't just want miscellaneous updates; I'm going to dig too. I don't want anyone to be able to tell my kid I didn't look for him when he's old enough to understand all of this."

Her smile lifted higher. "I'm glad you're coming home."

"It isn't really home. But it's as close as I can get for now."

She laughed. "For now, huh?"

I smiled. "For now."

She smirked. "Go put your clothes on."

"Take your clothes off, put your clothes on." I grinned. "I can't win with you, woman."

She waved me off, smirking. "Shut up."

I smiled, making my way to the kitchen. Just as I stepped into my jeans and began to pull them up to my hips, a knock erupted at the door.

I shouldn't have answered it. But it was almost instinctive. It was my home once.

As I pulled it open, a guy about my age holding a cup of coffee in each hand stared back at me. He wore a white thermal beneath pink scrubs and white tennis shoes. Thick black glasses framed his dark brown eyes on his melanin-rich skin.

When our gazes met, he furrowed his brows.

I tilted my head a bit, gaze finding the hospital badge clasped to the breast pocket of his scrubs. *Liam Moore.*

"Well, this is awkward," I said.

"Oh shit." Laila joined us at the door. "We had plans."

Liam glanced at her and then back to me. The shirtless guy standing with his pants unbuttoned in the doorway to the apartment of the girl he'd been seeing.

"We did." He turned to me. "You must be..."

"Jeremy," I said. "And you're Liam?"

"You're..." He glanced from me to Laila, then back to me and then Laila.

"The husband?" I asked. "And you're the boyfriend. Pretty weird on both ends. So I'm going to grab my shirt and head on out."

"That's probably a good idea," Liam said with a darting gaze.

I made a face and let out a bare laugh. Laila and I might have been on a really rough part of our road, but she was still wearing her wedding ring. So was I. Pictures from our wedding and her maternity shoot still laid around the house like nothing had ever happened. We may have been separated, but she was *my* wife. The irony of the dude's threatening attitude was genuinely amusing.

Shaking my head a bit, I turned back to Laila. "I'll see you at three. Let me know if you need anything." I turned back to Liam and gave a fake, almost sarcastic smile. "Nice meeting you, Liam."

He said nothing as I teleported to the kitchen and grabbed my shirt. Laila gave me an odd look, somewhere between annoyed and amused. But I just grinned at her and teleported back to my hotel room.

CHAPTER TWENTY-ONE

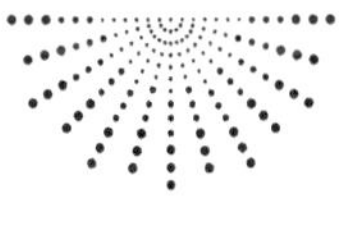

LAILA

Warm summer air coasted around me. I looked at the cars driving past on the road beyond the parking lot. The sharp taste of menthol combined with tobacco settled into my lungs. This wasn't exactly an easy conversation to hold. But Liam deserved to know. I would have held off, but after he showed up to my half-dressed husband answering the door, I didn't have much choice.

"Your son is alive," Liam murmured.

I nodded, flicked my cigarette to the grass, and clicked the button to extend Tink's leash. She romped out into the higher grass.

"And that's why your husband was here. Because you had to tell him," Liam murmured, as if he was trying to excuse what obviously happened.

I nodded again, exhaling a large cloud of smoke.

"You slept with him," he said even quieter.

I turned to meet his gaze. Yeah, I'd made it clear that I wasn't looking for a relationship with him, but I knew it still hurt. With a sigh, I gave a slow nod.

"But you aren't with him," Liam continued.

"No. But I understand if you want to end this. What I did was pretty shady."

I almost hoped he'd say that he did. That this had been fun, but he didn't want to deal with the drama. That we should just be friends from here on out. Because that's kind of how I felt. I liked Liam, and I enjoyed the dating. But—even if I wasn't ready for it yet—I knew this story ended with Jeremy and I back together. I didn't want Liam's feelings caught up in the middle of that.

His tense fingers pulled a fist full of grass from the soil. "Not like we ever concluded that the two of us were exclusive."

"It was still pretty fucked up."

Liam looked up and met my gaze. "I knew what I was getting into when this started. You and him are legends in our world. I can't act like I'm ever going to be to you what he is. I knew that from the get-go."

"I know. But I'm sorry, Liam," I murmured. "I didn't want you to find out like that. I don't blame you if this is too messy."

He was quiet. "Do you want to end this?"

Did I? Yes and no. Yes, because I didn't want to hurt him. No, because I did really like Liam. He was sweet, and kind, and funny.

"This is a lot, and I don't want you to get hurt."

As his fingers wrapped around mine, the other grasped my chin and turned it up to meet his gaze. "I don't want to end this."

"Liam," I murmured. I put my cigarette out on the grass and blew out a heavy breath. "I don't know how I feel or what I want. But I don't have the energy to care about a love triangle right now. Getting my son home is all that matters to me. I'm not concerned with trying to sort out my emotions because nothing I feel for him or you is anywhere close to as important as bringing my son home is."

"I completely understand, Laila."

"I'm sorry, but I should get back to work. I have a lot of calls to make."

"I should probably get home and get some sleep anyway."

As I began to stand, he took my hand and pulled me toward him. He pushed his lips to mine.

I pulled away and forced a smile. "Text me."

"I will definitely do that." He grinned.

Honestly, I felt pretty gross. I liked Liam, but I loved Jeremy. I knew who it was going to be. But it was almost like I was keeping Liam on the hook for when Jeremy fucked up again. I gave him the out, I told him I understood if he didn't want to deal with this. And he didn't take it.

I poured a cup of coffee at the kitchen counter, breathing in the scent of warm apple candles. Bright light shined in from the French doors. Warm air brushed against my bare arms.

Adam bobbed down the steps stifling a yawn. "What's all of this about?"

"When everyone gets here, you'll know." I placed the pot back on the burner.

"Whatever you say."

Jeremy landed by the steps. His eyes met mine, lips curving to a smile. "Hey."

"Hey." I gave a smile back. He brushed past me to the coffee pot and poured himself a cup.

Adam's face screwed up, looking between us. "Okay, I really have to know what the hell is going on here."

"Nice to see you too," Jeremy said.

Adam cocked his head to the side. "Is this to tell us that you guys are getting back together or something? Because you could have just texted—"

"No."

"Unfortunately," Jeremy muttered. His hand grazed my arm, reaching past me to the bottle of creamer.

Adam huffed. "I have no idea what this could be about then."

"Everyone's going to be here in like ten minutes, just chill, man." I put a hand on my hip.

"Sorry, there was an accident on the highway, and it backed up traffic for like twenty minutes." Brody came through the doorway and placed his jacket on the table. His gaze turned to me and Jeremy on the other side of the island. "Hey, man. Long time no see."

"Yeah, sorry, I've been busy lately," Jeremy said.

"Yeah, we've noticed," Adam muttered.

"I'm not going to be such a stranger though," he said.

I made my way around the counter and joined Adam at the bar with my cup of coffee. "Where's Jenna?" I asked Adam.

"She's in the bathroom," he muttered.

"Geez, she's been in there for a while." I sipped my coffee.

"Yeah, I think she's coming down with something," he said.

"Jeremy!" Hannah barreled down the steps toward her brother. Kai chuckled behind her. She darted across the kitchen. Jeremy laughed. She jumped in the air, placed her arms around his neck, and he lifted her in a little twirl.

"What are you doing here?" she asked as he set her down.

He looked at me and gave a smile. "We'll talk about it when everyone's here."

Her gaze turned to me, smile coming to her lips. "Are you guys—"

"We're not together." I sipped my coffee.

"Damn," she muttered. "What's up then? I had plans tonight, you know."

"You're going to want to hear this." Jeremy hoisted himself to the counter.

The front door shut, and I heard Mom call, "Is anybody home?"

"Back here!" I yelled.

"Oh good." Leah came down the steps. "Everybody's already here. I just ordered pizza, it should be here in an hour or so."

"Hey, baby." Mom set her purse on the counter. She gave me a quick hug and kissed my head.

"Nice to see you, Rachel." Jeremy smiled.

Mom looked up, eyes widening for a second. Then she looked between us and a smile came to her lips. "Wow, how have you been, kiddo? It's been so long."

"December, I think." Jeremy smiled. "But I've been alright. How about you?"

"Oh, you know. Living the dream." Mom chuckled.

"Sorry, guys." Jenna burped, bobbing into the kitchen. "I don't think that Long John Silver's is sitting well with me."

"Long John Silver's doesn't sit right with anyone," Brody muttered.

I glanced around. "Everybody's here now, right?"

"Looks like it," Leah said.

Jesus. I'd spent all day rehearsing how I was going to let the family know. But now, I had no idea what to say. They'd have a million questions. But I knew the number one would be, 'How didn't you realize?' And I didn't have an answer for that. Truly, I had no idea why I believed it.

I brought myself to my feet. Quietly, I murmured, "I don't even know where to start."

"Do you want me to?" Jeremy hopped from the counter as I made my way around the island.

I gave a nod. He could be the one to say it. I liked that better. It was too hard for me to put into words. At least no one would blame him for it.

As he began, I walked to the wet bar, grabbed the bottle of whiskey from the lowest shelf, and poured myself a three-finger glass.

"So yesterday, Ray called Laila and told her he needed to talk to her in person as soon as she could get to him," Jeremy began. I lifted myself onto the edge of the counter. I kicked my feet, gazing down at the liquor in my hand. Then I took a long gulp. "She goes and talks to him and he gives her this picture Lydia drew. Did you bring it with you, Lai?"

I gestured to the folded-up sketch next to my purse that laid on the counter.

Adam grabbed it, unfolded it, and squinted for a second. Then he handed it to Jenna. "That's Ray's wife, right?" I nodded. "So who's the dude?"

"That's Peterson," Jenna murmured, creasing her eyes at the picture.

"So who's the kid?" Adam asked.

Jenna passed the photo to Mom. "That's Laila." Mom's finger grazed the image. "Or damn near close."

"Yeah. Close," I said.

"Because it's Micah," Jeremy said.

"What?" Hannah asked.

"Micah's alive," Leah said. "Lydia showed Laila her memories of him."

"What?" Kai asked.

"What do you mean?" Brody asked with a similar expression.

"Lydia met him." I took another drink. "Amy and Peterson took him. He didn't die the day that he was born."

"How is that possible?" Adam asked.

"Yeah, I don't understand," Jenna said. "I thought you saw him die."

"Not exactly," I said. "He was glowing like our hands do when we heal so I didn't really get to see him. I just knew that he wouldn't cry."

"Then how did you know that he was dead?" Adam asked.

Because I was a fucking idiot. "That's what Haley and Chris thought. Then Peterson said the same."

"And you believed him?" Brody asked.

My heart sunk.

He was right, I had no reason to trust a word that left the man's lips. I didn't understand why I had. But it hurt so bad to hear someone else say it.

"Yeah, I did. I knew something was wrong when my water broke, it was a weird color. I don't know, it made sense at the time."

"This is amazing." Hannah gave a wide smile. "I'm an aunt. You guys are parents."

I scoffed. My head shook a bit as I took another long gulp of my whiskey.

I wished that were true. Truly, from the bottom of my heart, I wished that it were. There was nothing I wanted more than to be a mom. But I wasn't. I may have given birth to him, but Mary had given birth to me, and she wasn't my mom.

The people that raise a child are who their parents are. And the person raising mine was a sadistic, raping, serial killer.

"Micah's alive," Mom murmured, smile coming to her lips.

"We don't know that," Brody muttered. "I mean, Lydia was brought home, what—A week after Micah was born? Just because he was alive then doesn't mean he still is. A pandemic's come and gone since then, there's no way to know he survived."

My heart sunk to my stomach. A flood of fear made its way from my brain to my already tense extremities.

I hadn't even thought about that.

He was right, it was possible that Micah was dead. I didn't want to believe that, but that didn't mean it wasn't possible.

"He's alive," Jeremy said. "Peterson would have kept him quarantined during the virus so that's not an issue. And even if he didn't, kids were less likely to die from it than anyone."

"But you don't know that," Brody said blatantly, as he often did. "There's no way you can be sure. You shouldn't get your hopes up too high. He could be long gone at this point. And even if he is alive, he's more than a year old now. Taking him from them would be ripping him away from the only family he knows."

The heart that had sunk to my stomach suddenly felt like someone was squeezing it until blood squirted outward in every direction. At the same time, it felt as heavy as it would have if I ripped it open and filled it with bricks.

He always said that. That Micah was *his* son. Maybe he was right. Maybe Micah wouldn't even want anything to do with me.

"*We're* his family," Jeremy said. "They're his captors."

"Yeah, but he doesn't know that," Brody said. "All he knows is them. A one-year-old can't understand the difference."

I chugged the rest of my glass and jumped from the counter. A knot the size of a basketball was forming in my throat and I didn't want to be there when it erupted. I walked to the island, brushed past Adam to reach in my purse, and pulled out my pack of cigarettes.

"What the fuck is wrong with you, Brody?" Jeremy snapped.

"I'm just saying," Brody said. "You guys have been through enough already; I don't want you to have to mourn your kid again."

"He isn't fucking dead," Jeremy said.

"Are you alright, Lai?" Jenna asked as I made my way to the back door.

I nodded, unable to bring words from my lips.

"Why would you fucking say that?" I heard Leah blurt as I opened the door and stepped outside. "You don't think they know that they haven't gotten to be around their kid for the first year of his life?"

"I was just saying the truth—"

"No, you had to rain on everyone's parade just like you always do," Leah said as the door floated shut behind me.

I started down the steps, fumbling with the pack of cigarettes. Tears formed in my eyes. That weight in my chest got heavier. My shaky hands struggled to keep the box steady before I dropped it to the ground.

"Are you okay?" Jeremy asked from the porch. The door clicked shut behind him. His footsteps thudded against the wood, drawing closer.

I nodded, clenching my teeth together to keep them from chattering. I bent over, lifted the box to my hand, pulled a cigarette from the pack, and held it to my lips. He gingerly placed a hand on my back. My shaking finger ignited to light the cigarette.

"Brody's an asshole," Jeremy murmured. "He doesn't know what he's talking about."

He wasn't being an asshole; he was being rational. He was right. We didn't know what would happen. We shouldn't have gotten our hopes up.

"I shouldn't have believed him. I should have known. If I—If I would have—I shouldn't have listened. I didn't even believe him at first, I don't know why I..."

Tears began to roll down my cheeks. I closed my eyes, wiped my face, and held the cigarette back to my lips.

"That doesn't matter—" Jeremy began.

"Yes, it does. It does matter." I pulled the cigarette from my mouth and met his gaze. "Because if I would have known, he would be here. I would have gotten him back that night. I wouldn't have let them take him. What if we never find him? We don't know anything, Jeremy. We haven't gotten a single lead since this all started. Neither has the FBI. We have *nothing* to go on." The tears got heavier. "They have my son, and I don't know how to get him back. He's right, Jeremy. We shouldn't get our hopes up."

A tear welled in his eye. He held my gaze. "You don't believe that."

I shook my head, and my lip began to quiver.

He was right. I did believe that we would find him. The moment I saw those images Lydia drew, what I felt was guilt. Guilt for not realizing, guilt for losing him, guilt for believing Peterson. But then Brody said it, and I couldn't get it out of my head.

"I don't believe that either," he murmured.

My teeth chattered. My tears grew heavier. "They have our baby. And I don't know how to get him back."

His hand at my back moved around my waist. I leaned forward, and he tugged me close against his chest.

"I don't know how to get him back," I repeated.

"We'll figure it out," he murmured. "I don't know when and I don't know how, but we will. We're going to bring our baby home."

CHAPTER TWENTY-TWO

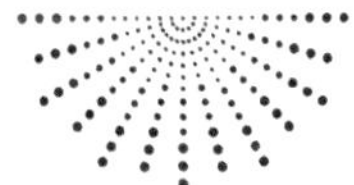

LATE AUGUST, 2020 - LAILA

My heart raced as I breathed in the humid August air. I looked up at the sky, in search of dust and clouds of smoke like there usually were. But it was different this time. The lights weren't flashing like strobes at a rave. The alarms weren't blaring in my skull the way they always did. The only sound was the whistling of the wind through the partially demolished walls.

I knew this place all too well. Or at least, this part of it. I'd had this dream a thousand times. But it wasn't the same as it'd been all those times before.

Instead of a force field at the edge of the cliff where I'd blown the building apart, there was a yellow line of police caution tape. The dust had well settled around the high grass outside of the building.

It was this place now, not the night that we unlocked as many doors as we could and told everyone to jump off of the precipice I'd created.

Another difference was my awareness of the fact that I was dreaming.

It felt the same as the others. I was just as terrified as I'd been the thousand other times I'd lived this dream. Once you've had freedom, being trapped is a different form of petrification.

But something else was different too.

This time, his voice was clearer than any time before.

"Mommy," he said in the doorway.

Instead of shrouded in a sun like glow of white, his little body was as typical as any other child.

He wore what I'd worn.

That itchy, lint ball littered navy blue scrub like uniform.

His eyes shined the brightest blue, the same electricity pulsing through them that pulsed through his dad's.

His pale, sandy lips turned down, quivering.

His little nose struggled to take in deep breaths, eyes locked with mine.

"Mommy, I need you." Tears streamed down his ivory skin. His cheeks were quickly turning to a blotchy rose.

But as I jumped from the metal table and darted across the room toward him, I noticed that he wore something else that neither of us would ever be able to take off.

The scars.

I reached through the doorway to grasp him. But again, it was different. Because this time, there was no forcefield that separated us. I took his hands and felt his flesh beneath my palms. It was a dream, and even as it was happening, I knew it was a dream. But I felt his skin.

It almost sent a shock through my body, the way that Jeremy's did from time to time. But it was hot to the touch, just as mine often was.

"Mommy," he cried again.

"I'm here." Tears clouded my vision. "I'm here, baby. I'm here."

"No, I need you here.*"*

"I'm right here," I repeated.

"You have to find me." He put his hands on top of mine. "You have to find me, Mommy."

"I'm trying, baby." Tears drizzled from my eyes. "I'm trying so hard."

Suddenly, my hands held nothing.

"You have to find me, Mommy," he said at the end of the hall.

I shot my head toward him as quick as I could. I staggered to my feet, clutching the cool cement wall. His body was beginning to radiate a white light in every direction.

"I'm coming, baby." I rushed down the hall. But as I drew closer, he disappeared. The bright light of his body shined from the doorway that led to the foyer between the wings. Gripping walls as I ran, I felt a violent, sudden, radiating pain in my abdomen. I grasped my stomach but kept running.

"You have to find me, Mommy," he said from the next hall.

"Stay right there, Micah!" I screamed, holding the cold metal frame as I struggled through the next doorway.

He was just ahead, maybe ten feet from my reach.

Then Amy appeared.

"There you are, buddy." She leaned down to Micah with a smile. "What are you doing in this silly old place?"

As she grazed his glowing white face, I screamed, "Don't you fucking touch him!"

She acted as if she didn't hear me. Then she caressed his cheek.

"I wanted to see Mommy," Micah whispered.

Amy frowned. I staggered toward them and collapsed to the ground a few feet before I was close enough to make contact.

"Mommy's right here, kiddo," she said.

"But Daddy says—"

"I know what he says."

I struggled, practically swimming across the floor, screaming profanities.

"Laila isn't ready for you, Micah," Amy murmured. "She doesn't understand sacrifice. She can't be the mommy that you need."

"Don't listen to her, baby," I said between gasping cries. "I love you, Micah. I love you more than anything."

"I take good care of you, don't I, buddy?"

Micah gazed at me through his white glow and gave a slow nod. "I just want to see her though. Can't we visit her? Just once?"

Amy shook her head. "I don't think so."

"Please, Amy." Hot, salty water burned down my cheeks. I tried to stand but it was as though my body were full of cement. "Please, just let me see my baby. Please."

He stared at me as Amy placed her arms around his shoulders in a tight embrace.

Slowly, his sweet little lips mouthed, You have to find me, Mommy.

I wept a long, desperate sob at the top of my lungs.

Then they disappeared.

I gripped my chest and slammed forward in my desk chair, heaving in air, wide eyes flickering around my quaint little office.

Forcing in slow deep breaths, I began to bring myself back to reality. My gaze shifted to the clock. Five twenty-four.

Damn it. The last time I looked, it was nine fifty-two. At some point, I must have dozed off and gotten a full night's sleep.

I rubbed my tired eyes and wiped sweat from my brow. My heart gradually began to slow down in my tight ribcage.

Just as I seemed to regain my composure, a quiet knock thudded at the front door.

I jumped.

"Jesus Christ." My hand flew to my chest again. Then I stumbled up, still half-drunk from the night before.

I took slow breaths, trying to steady myself against the desk. Another knock sounded, a bit louder that time. Still more disoriented than I typically was after a nightmare, I took another glance at the clock.

We had some morning bird customers but not *so* early on a Sunday.

I started out of the office, through the kitchen, and into the front of the house. I squinted a bit as I approached the front door.

A young woman, no more than thirty, stood behind the glass. She had long, billowing copper curls against her peaches and cream skin. Her face was small and dainty with soft features. She had a small, button nose over thick, modest red lips. Thin black wings lined just above her thick mascara. She wore a pale pink trench coat and held a black designer handbag on her wrist.

Not the type of person I usually saw at Moe's Diner.

I reached for the handle and pulled the door open. "Can I help you?"

"Perhaps." A thick English accent edged her voice. "Are you the hybrid?"

I jerked back. "I'm sorry?"

"Laila Callidy? The wife of the Skoulda boy? You know, the one the Chambers don't like." She took a step back to look at the sign above the diner. "I could be mistaken but I thought the website said this was the place. I know it's early. My apologies, I'm a bit jet lagged myself."

I mean, yeah, that was me, but one hell of a way to ask.

"Who are you?"

"You don't know me." She looked me over. "But I do know a thing or two about you. Although, you may know my surname. Surely, your husband does." She extended her thin, jewelry covered hand to mine. "Moriah La Fay."

My eyes widened a bit. I extended my hand to hers and gave it a slow shake. "Wow, okay. Nice to meet you. I feel like I'm in the presence of royalty."

She gave a soft, genuine laugh. "Oh, no. The pleasure is all mine, truly. I've only got a name, you're the one with the reputation."

"Sure. I'm sorry, would you like to come inside?"

"Yes, thank you. We have a lot to discuss." She pranced past me.

CHAPTER TWENTY-THREE

LAILA

"Darling little shack you've got here." Moriah smiled. Then she wiped the table with a wet wipe before she set her purse down.

I tried not to be offended. In fairness though, that bag was probably worth as much as the whole building.

"Thanks," I said. "Do you want a cup of coffee? Or tea, maybe?"

"Coffee is fine, thank you," she murmured.

I walked around the bar, poured some grounds into the filter, plopped it into the pot, and pressed start. I made my way back to the table and sat across from her.

I didn't know much about Witches, but I knew of the La Fays. Jeremy had mentioned them a time or two. Particularly, he'd mentioned Thomas, who was on the Chambers with his grandparents.

They were a legendary coven that dated back to the days of King Arthur. Morgan La Fay was one of the most powerful Witches to ever live. As the centuries went on, the coven tapped into her power through ancestral magic. At one point, they were known as the most powerful coven in the world. They didn't do much, mostly just hoarded their wealth. But practicing ancestral magic was an art form. With Morgan as their however many greats grandmother, their abilities were almost boundless.

"So what brings you here?" I met her icy eyes. "I'm sure you didn't come across the pond for a cup of coffee."

"I was in New York on some business. But no, I didn't stop by for refreshments," she said. "This isn't exactly something I find pleasure in, but I've heard the chatter. You're looking for a Witch, no?"

"A specific Witch. One able to cast a lot of very powerful barrier spells."

She pressed her thick, injection filled lips together and widened her eyes a bit. "Well, I believe you're in luck then."

I knitted my brows.

"I'm not like you and your clan, Laila." She rolled her eyes. "I don't *save* people. I have no interest in being a hero or ending the treachery around the globe. Best of luck to your kind on that one, but it's not really my cup of tea."

"Then why are you here?"

"Well." Her finely manicured, red stiletto nails clicked against the Formica tabletop. "I have a very large family. Much larger than yours, in fact. Many sisters, loads of drama. You know how that goes."

"Sure."

"That being said, you know my coven, but you don't know us." I gave a bare nod and waited for her to go on. "One of my eldest sisters, Anastasia, she's been gone for a long time."

My head tilted. "Was she taken?"

Moriah laughed. "Hardly. She was asked to leave about ten years ago for practicing dark magic. I'm sure your husband knows the story. Anastasia always had a few screws loose, if you know what I mean." I waited for her to go on. "She'd done some awful things. Neighborhood pets found at pagan altars, dancing naked in the woods under a full moon coated in their blood. Our family was constantly paying off a reporter here or there, always scrambling to clean up her messes. Then she killed a young girl. She needed a virgin sacrifice for a spell she was working on, blah, blah, *blah*. It wasn't pretty. A lot more difficult to disguise than a neighbor's dog."

Spoken so casually. As if murdering young girls and people's pets was just normal for her.

Anastasia La Fay didn't ring any bells. Although, I wasn't one to keep up with the drama in the supernatural world. But Jeremy grew up in it. I'd ask him.

"I can imagine," I muttered.

"Yes, well," Moriah muttered, "We aren't close. We were once, I suppose. But after that murder... That all changed. We don't chat on the phone or follow one another on social media. I don't believe she has any of that, in fact."

"Right," I said slowly, still waiting for the part where this tied into me and my life.

"But she does write me letters from time to time. They never have a return address or a post card. And they're almost always nonsense, as anything with Anastasia always tends to be." An eye roll. "I received a letter about a month ago. It doesn't make much sense, but I think it might be more valuable to you than it is to me."

Ah, the good part.

I cocked my head to the side. "What does it have to do with me?"

She scratched her head a bit. "She talks about you. Well, in a manner of speaking. More specifically, she cites the mother of 'He who shines brighter than the sun.'"

My eyes widened.

Micah was literally born in an ambiance of white light. It definitely sounded like she was describing my son. If this Nastya bitch was the one working with Peterson, it made sense for her to know that. But how could Moriah know with certainty that that was about my son?

"How do you know that's referring to me?" I asked.

"She refers to the par animarum. Only a couple of those that I'm aware of and you're the only one who's had a kid." She squinted a bit. "But it looks like that phrase meant something to you."

"You could say that."

"She references the Bible a lot in this letter. We're" —she huffed, letting out a half laugh— "obviously not Christians, so it's a little bizarre to me."

The zombie in the basement flickered through my memory.

"The book of Revelation?" I asked.

"Yes. She mentions that she's protecting him. He who shines brighter than the sun. She implies that he's the Lamb, or something?" She crinkled her nose. "I don't know, it's all very bizarre. Perhaps it will mean more to you than me, I don't know." She reached into her bag and set an envelope to the table. Then I caught a glimpse of a small plastic bag she held in her palm before I got a look at it. "I didn't want to risk sending it in the mail. I could have called but you never know who's listening."

"Sure."

"There was one other thing before I leave," she murmured. "Anastasia asked me to cast a spell on your son. I haven't, of course, for obvious reasons. I stick to myself; I don't want your clan nor the other supernatural followers you've accrued to have me on their hit list."

"What kind of spell?"

"My guess would be that she's already bound herself to him. *Our* bloodline can be bound to him with the minuscule amount of DNA she has pushed into him. But I have no desire to do that. Like I said, I'd like to stay in your good graces."

Why in the fuck would she want someone else to be bound to my son? What purpose would that serve?

"Anyway, she gave me these." She extended a small Ziploc bag. Inside was a small lock of wavy black hair and a tiny blue sock.

My eyes began to water before I even took it. Then I did and that tight feeling in my chest softened. That same sense of purity I felt when he was born vibrated in my palm.

It was a piece of my baby.

"That's really all I was here for. My Uber is outside, so I'm going to get on my way. But I hope this helps somehow. I'm sure you're eager to be reunited with your child."

I opened the bag and took the lock of hair into my hand.

Velvet. It was like velvet between my fingers. Just as it felt when I touched it for the first time.

"Is this enough to cast a locator spell?" I asked as she stood.

"Yes. But I wouldn't if I were you. You'd need all of that and if I know my sister, it wouldn't work anyway. I'm sure she's cast something very powerful to conceal their location."

"Thank you."

"I hope it helps."

I looked up and met her gaze. "But why would you tell me this? She's your sister. You don't even know me."

"Read the letter. Whatever is going on here, it's big. End of life as we know it, big. Disastrous."

She paused and looked me over. "Like I said before, I'm not out to save the world. But I don't want to burn with it either. I don't know the details, but I've read the prophecies. The par animarum are said to rise up and take their power back from the god who tore them apart. You seem to be on the right side of history, Laila Callidy. I don't know what the end of the story looks like, but I do know one thing." Her blue-eyed gaze grew a bit more serious. "You're bigger than us. And at the end of the day, I'd like to have someone like you owe me a favor."

CHAPTER TWENTY-FOUR

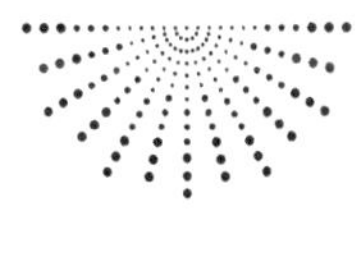

JEREMY

My phone vibrating on the nightstand pulled me from my dreamless sleep. I rubbed my eyes as I grabbed the phone and held it out in front of me. 6:02.

A text from Laila appeared beneath the time, reading, *Hey, I know it's early. I'm sorry. Just call me when you get up.*

I yawned and flicked on the lamp next to the bed. I clicked the call button and held the phone to my ear. After a single ring, she answered.

"I'm sorry, I didn't think a text would wake you. You can go back to bed and call me when you're ready to get up," she said.

"It's alright, baby. I went to bed early, I'm good. What's up?" I asked.

A heavy breath hummed through the speaker. "Can you just come over? It's not much, I guess. But I got some more information that might help us find Micah. Maybe, I don't know. It's something."

And suddenly, I was wide awake. I shot up in the bed. My eyes parted wide open. I pulled the blanket off my legs. "Yeah, definitely. Let me get some clothes on and I'll be right over."

"Alright, cool. I'm making breakfast, do you want anything?" she asked.

"Yeah, sure." I started to my feet.

"The usual?" Laila asked.

"Whatever you're making's fine. No need to go all out or anything."

"Alright. I'll see you soon then."

"Yeah, just, like, five minutes."

"Sounds good. Love you."

"Love you too," I murmured with a smile.

Once the call ended, I went to the bathroom and took a quick piss. Then I went through my usual routine. I crushed some pills from the medicine cabinet and reached for the bent spoon I kept beside them. My fingers stopped on it though, knowing that I'd be too high to stay focused. Instead, I sniffed it up, dabbed my finger in the powder, and rubbed what was left along my gums.

I threw on a pair of jeans, a baggie T-shirt, and a black hoodie.

The past few weeks had been pretty weird. Exciting, in a way, but still pretty fucking weird.

Laila and I hadn't slept together again since the night I came back. I would have loved to, but it wasn't the right time. She was kind of a wreck, and I knew she regretted that night together a few weeks ago. She didn't say it, but I could see it in the way she'd tighten her hoodie closer around her body when I walked in the room. She struggled to meet my gaze, she wrung her palms against each other when I was around, she tilted her knees the opposite direction when I sat near her.

Then again, maybe she was just trying to keep anyone else from realizing what had happened that night. Because when we were alone, she'd hold my hand and rest her head against my chest. We'd kissed a handful of times, but it hadn't gone past that. I'd become something of a band aid for her shit days.

I hated being only that, but it was a shred of something. Even though she was still fucking that Liam guy, I was the one who got to comfort her. I was the one who got to see the side of her she locked away from the world. The soft and gentle, fragile version she was too proud to show anyone else.

I hadn't slept with anyone else since her. It just didn't seem worth it if it wasn't my wife. I'd grown pretty friendly with her Instagram account though.

It was kind of fun. Not beating off to her pictures, that was disappointing. But in general. The whole courting ritual felt like it did when we first met. The quiet hushed kisses as we skirted off into the hallway to murmur little anecdotes.

Knowing that she was still seeing Liam wasn't great. But knowing that she couldn't confide in him the way she did with me stroked my ego. Also, seeing how generally uncomfortable he was around me gave me a primal sense of security. We were both fighting for her. He was winning on the physical aspect, but I was a shoe in for the rest.

We hadn't gotten any leads on Micah until then. Laila wasn't wrong; Peterson was a genius. But no day went by when we weren't looking into something. It was mostly dead ends, but we weren't giving up.

I tried not to think about Micah and Chris too much when we weren't working on the case.

Knowing that my son was out there somewhere was reassuring. Yet, thinking about that piece of shit holding him when he cried left me nauseous. Not to mention infuriated. I hadn't even gotten to see him, besides the images in Lydia's memories. And that bastard got to know him.

The man who raped my wife and covered her in scars. The man who managed to hold more than three hundred of our people captive for more than a decade. The man who ripped open their flesh and jammed little pieces of crystal to disguise GPS trackers before sewing them back together like voodoo dolls.

He got to be a father to my son. He got to wipe his little tears and feed him a bottle. He got to see him smile. He got to feel his little hand wrapped around his finger. He got every experience with my son that I should have had. And it fucking hurt. A time will never come that it doesn't fucking hurt.

———

I trudged up the sloped walkway to the diner. As I took each step, I watched Laila through the glass window behind the counter. She was doing that thing where she ignored the world and focused only on the task at hand. In that case, refilling the salt and pepper shakers.

Painting on a smile, I walked into the diner. "Hey, you."

Laila smiled back and set our plates down on the counter. "Just in time. I just got this off the stove."

"Good timing then." I pulled off my jacket and set it on the counter. "It smells great."

"Eh, I burned the bacon a little." She walked around the counter and sat beside me.

"Bacon's bacon," I said. She took a piece from the plate and chewed at the edge. "There's coffee, right?"

She nodded, starting to her feet. I grazed her hand. "I got it."

Laila smiled. "Thank you."

"Mhmm." I started around the counter and grabbed a few mugs from under the sink.

Laila wasn't looking her best. Her long, unwashed red hair was tied up in a messy, knotted bun at the back of her head. She had deep, dark purple circles beneath her brilliant, bloodshot green eyes. Her pale pink lips were crusting around the edges against her greasy, paper colored skin.

She was drowning. Not only could I feel it, but it was written all over her. But she smiled anyway. She was still taking care of her shit. I'd begun to see what Jenna meant when I was working on her car that day. Laila had moved past wallowing on the unpleasantness of her life onto the same depressed contentment most people in our world reached.

"You said you got a lead, right?" I asked.

"Yeah, kind of. Not really much to go on. More information than anything."

I met her gaze as I poured coffee into our mugs. "What happened?"

A long pause. "So you know the La Fay's."

"The Witches? As in Morgan La Fay's descendants?" She nodded. "Yeah, I'm familiar with them. Not like we're friends, but I've heard stories. Why?"

Laila took in a slow, heavy breath. "Moriah La Fay paid me a visit this morning."

Moriah. I'd met her once. She was okay. Snooty, pretentious—all around, kind of a bitch. But compared to her father, she wasn't too bad.

"Why?"

"She thinks her sister is the one working for Peterson. Anastasia, to be exact." She paused. "So do I."

Nastya La Fay. She was a good bit older than me, at least going on thirty-five now, but I had definitely heard the stories. She was a lunatic. She was the personification of 'evil witch' folklore. There were stories of her eating human flesh and others of her killing birds and sewing their feathers to her skin as a part of a ritual. I wasn't sure how much of the rumors were true, but I knew the part about her being exiled was. Some ten years ago, rumors surfaced that she died. I assumed that they were true because no new information had surfaced about her since about then. If it weren't for that, I'd have already questioned if she were the one working with Peterson.

"Of course it's the sociopath that kills virgins," I murmured. "Guess I shouldn't have expected it to be the Good Witch of the North."

Laila laughed, shaking her head. I slid her the cup of coffee. "Wouldn't be our usual luck, huh?"

I smiled, licking my lips before they fell to a frown. "Why do you agree?"

"Anastasia keeps in contact with Moriah. Not reciprocal communication, but she writes her letters. She gave me this." Laila pulled an envelope from her back pocket and laid it on the counter. "And these. She wanted Moriah to cast a binding spell with them." She reached into her hoodie pocket and delicately set a baggie on the counter. Inside was a tiny lock of bluish black hair and a small blue sock.

I reached for the bag and opened it. "Is this Micah's?"

"I think so. It feels like him, if that makes any sense."

She harnessed spirit. It made sense for her to be able to feel some type of connection to an object like the one in my hands.

"I haven't read the letter yet. I wanted you to be here," Laila said quietly.

I lifted the lock to my hand. My finger traced along it with a smile. It was soft, and silky. Somehow, it almost felt familiar. I raised it next to a piece of my hair that didn't make it into my ponytail. "It's the same color as mine."

Laila smiled. "It's long too. Especially for a fourteen-month-old."

I looked down at it with a smile. It was the first thing I ever held in my hand that belonged to him. It was the closest I got to holding him since he was born. And it really wasn't much, but it definitely made me smile.

"Must have your hair because mine was like an inch short until I was four." Laila smiled, blinking a tear away.

I nodded, grinning. "My dad had long hair too. They say balding's on the mother's side. Was your dad bald?"

"Full head of hair 'til the day he died."

"But who knows, maybe he'll want it short."

Tears glistened her eyes a second later. "Another first that we missed."

"It'll be the first haircut we're there for. So in a way, it kind of is a first. But maybe he'll want it long like mine and we'll never see him get a haircut."

"Yeah, maybe."

"Do you want to eat before we read the letter?" I asked.

"Yeah. I'm not sure if I'm ready to read what's in there just yet. Moriah said it was pretty bad."

I frowned. "We'll smoke a blunt while we read it then."

Laila looked down at the coffee in her cup. "That sounds like a plan to me."

CHAPTER TWENTY-FIVE

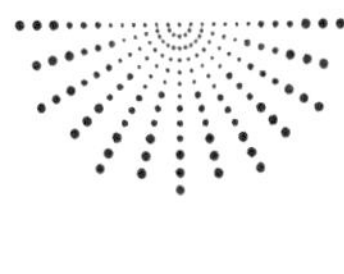

JEREMY

We sat on the shortest of the three steps to the back of the diner. It was a cool morning for August but refreshing when compared to the ninety-degree days we'd had recently. The smell of humid dew settled in my lungs. Crickets chirped in the bushes, almost in sync with the morning birds singing their songs. A beautiful sunrise shined above the woods behind the diner.

It looked so pretty. But it felt so... sad. Though I was happy to have a lead, Laila was just off. Her eyes looked heavy above the dark circles that lined them. She kept her narrow shoulders tucked inward.

I held the white envelope between my fingertips. Laila passed me the blunt and extended her hand for it. I set it in her quivering palm.

She sat close, shoulder brushing mine. Then she handed me Tink's leash. Her fingers grazed the letter meticulously, as if the outside of the sealed envelope would somehow give us some clue if we stared at it long enough.

"Laila," I said softly.

"Hmm?" she asked, still gazing down at the envelope in her palm.

My fingers gently touched hers when I passed her the blunt. "Do you want me to read it first?"

"No. No, that's okay."

I gave a nod. She hit the blunt and continued to look down at the envelope. "What's on your mind?"

"I don't know."

I placed my hand on hers and laced our fingers together. She looked up at me. Her hand squeezed mine. She pulled her brows together, water welling in the corners. That face, it was so hard to describe. But it was like the definition of pain and terror tied together. Like she didn't know how to keep on moving. She'd been going through the motions, she was on two feet, but it was like that day in the hospital bed when she made it out. Like she had no will to live.

"I just don't want this to be another dead end." Laila bit her lip. "I'm so tired of dead ends."

I frowned. "Me too."

Her eyes stung with tears. "I don't know what else I can do, Jeremy. I've been looking at the same bits of information for months. Years, really. And nothing. I just keep coming back with nothing."

I bit my bottom lip. "Yeah, I know. But this is something. At the very least, we know the name of the Witch working for him. That's going to come in handy at some point or another." A sad smile pulled up my lips. "And we have a sock. And a little piece of hair."

Tears bubbled against her irises. "How can you be so optimistic about this? How are you just okay, Jeremy?"

I wasn't. Honestly, I was a disaster. But she needed me. I promised to be her strength when she was weak, and I was doing everything I could to hold up that vow.

"I'm not really okay. But I don't know. It's easier not to think about it too hard for too long."

She scoffed. "Lucky you." Shaking her head, tears began to dribble from her eyes. "It's all that I can think about. I'm crying all the time. I can't fucking sleep. I—I don't know what I'm supposed to do. I'm just walking around on autopilot."

Laila paused, pressing her quivering lips together.

"I know that I'm okay in most regards. I'm functioning and everything. I'm doing what I have to do, I'm living my life. I'm not in that stupid fucking cell. But... But I'm not okay." Her teeth began to chatter as she met my gaze. I'd seen some really awful expressions on that beautiful face, but that look brought chills to my skin. She looked more devastated than I knew was possible. "I'm not okay, Jeremy."

I twisted my other arm around her shoulder. I pulled her into me and kissed her hair. She touched my chest. Her fingers grasped my shirt. She rested her head against my shoulder and took another hit off the blunt.

"You will be," I murmured. "We both will."

I wasn't sure if that were true. But I'd said that before, and I was right. This wasn't the type of wound that time could heal, but I had to believe that things would get better. I had to believe we'd find our son and get the life we wanted. Because if I didn't believe that, there was no point in going on.

We stayed like that for a while. Being sad together was easier than being sad alone. Holding her as we passed the blunt back and forth wasn't going to make things better. It sure as hell wasn't going to bring Micah back. But for a minute, we weren't alone.

As the blunt burned out, I set it on the concrete step. Laila turned up to meet my gaze. I kept my arm around her shoulders. "Should I read it out loud?"

"Sure. Unless you want me to read it when you're done."

She flipped the envelope over in her hand. "It's okay, I can do it."

I extended Tink's leash as she chased a bug in the gravel ahead of us.

Laila cleared her throat and pulled her hand away from mine to wipe her face.

"*Dear Moriah,*" she began. "*I'm sorry it's been so long since my last letter. I'm not sure that you even read them but I'm going to keep writing them regardless.*

"*I know how the family feels about me. Although it hurts in more ways than words can begin to describe, I know that you all have every right. Things I've done have been unforgivable. But I'm going to right my wrongs. I can't change the past, but I <u>can</u> change the future.*

"*It's just as they say, Moriah. A time will come when I too eat from the Tree of Life. I am they who have come out of tribulation. I too will wash my robes in the blood of the Lamb.*"

Laila swallowed hard.

"*My robes will be made white once more by He who shines brighter than the sun. He will make me clean. The blood on my hands will wash into the blood of him, and he shall make me clean once more. He will take away all of that pain. He will make me clean.*

"*Until that time comes, I will remain in my filth. But as I do, I will give him shelter. I will keep the Lamb safe. He needs our protection.*

"*You have to bind yourself to him. If something should come of me before I am made clean, he will need someone to keep him safe. The time for his resurrection is yet to come, it must be aligned with the fall of Wormwood.*

"*The Lamb is all things good and right in the world. He's the living mani-*

festation of true love. Only the par animarum could bring forth a child like He. He must be kept safe, even from them.

"They will not allow him to be what he is. They will prevent the sacrifice and thus prevent the resurrection that will whiten our robes. He will not shine when the sun turns black and the sky rolls like scroll and we all will perish.

"Please, Moriah. Do as I have asked. And, one day, you too shall eat from the Tree of Life.

"With love,

Anastasia"

My hands tightened to fists, jaw clenching tight.

They're insane.

They believed my son was the prophesied child from the book of Revelation. That he was a sacrifice which would cleanse the earth. The reborn messiah.

Then they said that he needed to be protected.

To be kept safe, from *us*. The people who loved him more than anything, the people who wanted to bring him home.

All we *ever* wanted was to keep our son safe. *That* was what started the war. Not because we wanted vengeance on the god that tore us apart.

I drew in slow breaths, struggling to remain calm. Laila folded the paper back up and set it inside the envelope. She sat it down on the pavement. Then she closed her eyes and shook her head.

"They're going to kill him." Water drizzled from her eyes. "They're going to kill our baby."

"We don't know that—" I began.

"She said it right there," Laila barked. Her breaths became short. Then she stood and began pacing. She could barely get an even breath into her lungs as she walked back and forth the beside the dumpster. "'They'll try to prevent the sacrifice.'" Her eyes filled with tears and her lips quivered. "They're going to kill my baby."

Tinkerbell ran across the parking lot to Laila. She jumped against her torso and licked her face. Laila lowered herself to the dog and let her lap away the tears that ran down her cheeks.

I stood and walked toward them. My fingers coasted along Tinkerbell's scruff as she obediently sat. Laila looked down at the ground, wringing her shaking hands. I reached beneath her face and pulled her gaze up to meet mine. "We'll get to him first. You read the letter, she said the time has yet to come. We're not going to let that happen."

"You don't know that. There's no way you can know that."

"I do, Laila. I *know*. No one thought you'd come home either, but I knew you would. I didn't have any reason to believe it, but I knew you'd come back." I carefully cupped her cheek. "We're going to bring our son home. He isn't the savior or the reborn Jesus. He is *our baby*. And he is, Laila. He's ours. He isn't Peterson's, or Amy's, or Anastasia's. He is *our* child. And we're not going to stop looking until we find him."

"We don't have a way *to* find him." Laila's bloodshot, watering eyes darted between mine. "They're going to kill him and there's not a damn thing I can do to stop it and if he's gone, I don't..." Her teeth chattered. "I've lived the past year thinking he was dead, and I—I can't lose him again. I know I don't have him now, but I—I can't. I don't—There isn't a point. If he's dead, I don't want to be alive."

My eyes filled with tears. "Don't talk like that."

Snot dripped from her nose. Her tears got heavier. Her breaths became shorter. Within a moment or two, her sobs were so violent that she couldn't manage a breath through her hyperventilating lips.

"Come here." I placed my arms around her shoulders and pulled her against me. She put her shaking hand around my back and laid her head against my chest. "I know you're scared, baby." I ran my hand against her back. "I'm scared too."

And I was. But I was more angry than anything. That they took him. About what they said in that letter. That they idolized him, yet planned to kill him.

My shirt grew wet with her tears. "I just want my baby."

"I know." I nodded against her hair. "So do I. But we have to stay strong for him. We have to be strong because when we do find him, it's going to be harder on him than it is on us. We just..." My arms tightened around her. "We just have to stay strong."

CHAPTER TWENTY-SIX

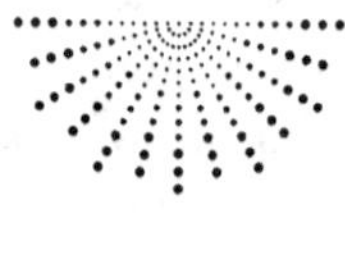

JEREMY

It took a while before Laila regained even part of her composure. She cried for at least half an hour. She nuzzled her head against my chest, struggling to bring air into her lungs while I held her trembling body against mine. She stayed on the verge of the panic attack her body desperately craved, but wouldn't allow it to consume her.

Around seven thirty, Max pulled into the parking lot. It wasn't until then that Laila pulled away and forced herself to stop crying. As he got out of his car, she met my gaze. Wiping her cheeks, she said, "I need to get to work."

"Do you need some help?" I asked.

She struggled to dry her cheeks with her wet hands. "No, I'm alright."

"No. You aren't." I pushed hair from her face behind her ear. She looked down. Whether she'd say it or not, she needed me. She needed to breathe. She needed to relax for a moment.

I cupped her cheek and brushed a tear beneath her eye. "Why don't you go get a shower? I can handle things down here for a little bit."

"That's okay—" she began.

"When was the last time you bathed, Laila?" I asked.

She turned her gaze to the ground. "I don't know."

"Go take care of yourself. Get a shower, drink a cup of coffee, and breathe for a couple minutes. I can handle this."

"Jeremy..."

"Please let me help you," I whispered. "I know that I can't do much, but I can do this. I ran the place for a while, you know."

A sweet, sad smile came to her lips. She rubbed her puffy eyes.

"Just let me handle this. You handle you." I gave a smile back.

She stared down for a moment. Then she looked up to meet my gaze. "Liam's coming by soon."

Ugh.

I didn't like it. But if going out with him, or... doing other things with him, helped her cope, then okay. Whatever helped her get through the day. Whatever gave her a will to live was okay.

It wasn't really. It made my stomach hurt, it made my chest tight, but I loved her. And I wanted her to be happy. Regardless of who or what brought her that.

"That's okay. I can be nice. He knows we talk, right?"

"Yeah but—"

"I'm just going to wait some tables and hold down the fort for you. And then I'll leave. But you need help, whether you're willing to admit it or not. And I'm here. I might as well pitch in." I raised my hand to her cheek and brushed hair behind her ear. "Please, just go relax for a few minutes. Let me handle this."

A smile, a real smile, pulled at her lips. "Thank you."

"I'm always here for you, baby."

Laila took Tinkerbell's leash from my hand. "I need to feed her too. But I shouldn't be long."

"Take all the time you need," I said. "I miss being here anyway."

"Alright. Thanks again. I owe you one."

I smiled. "No, you don't. Just go shower."

She smiled back through swollen lips. Then she called for Tinkerbell and started upstairs. Just as the door shut, I breathed out a sigh. My thumb and forefinger rubbed into my eyes as Max started from his car.

As he drew close, I felt his hand pat my back. "Rough morning, man?"

"Something like that."

He gestured toward the diner. Then he sparked a cigarette at his lips. "She isn't doing too good, huh?"

That was the understatement of the century. "I don't think so."

"I'm worried about her, man." Max took a hit off his cigarette. "She's just..."

"Yeah, I know. I'm worried too."

"You helping out down here? I could use a hand getting the fall decorations up from the basement. Laila said she was going to do it tonight, but they're pretty heavy and I don't trust her not to kill herself bringing them up."

"Yeah, I can grab 'em real quick."

"Awesome," Max said. "I miss when you were together and I wasn't the only set of muscles around here."

A quiet chuckle left my lips. "Yeah, you and me both, man."

***

I heard the bell ring at the front door as I trudged up the basement steps. My arms ached from the weight, but it was a good feeling. I was there. And I was doing something to help her. I couldn't find our son, but I could carry some shit up the steps. At least that took one thing off of her plate. When I was downstairs though, a thought had come to me.

That picture Lydia had drawn. Micah was older in it. Definitely not the infant she'd met. And it made me wonder. Was that how she pictured him? Or had she seen him somehow since then? I made a mental note to ask Laila what she thought.

A man cleared his throat at the front of the house, as if asking a server to hurry up and seat him.

"Just a second." I set the giant box of autumn décor down in the office.

"Don't rush for that tool," Max mumbled outside the door.

Lovely. The dude who was fucking my wife had arrived.

I dusted my hands off on my thighs. Then I made my way out of the office, through the kitchen, to the front of the house. Liam stood on the other side of the counter holding a small bouquet of sunflowers.

I gritted my teeth and forced a smile. "Aww, man. You shouldn't have. I'm more of a roses kind of guy anyway."

Actually, I preferred Lilies. But they were Laila's favorite flowers. And I wasn't going to give him any ideas to score brownie points with my wife.

Liam licked his teeth, squinting a bit. "Where's Laila?"

"Upstairs." I leaned against the counter behind me and took a sip from my coffee. "She had a rough morning, I told her I'd handle things down here so she could get a shower."

"Oh." Liam gave a short nod. Then he pressed his teeth to a hard line.

He was a Werewolf. I knew what was going through his head. That I'd just pissed all over his favorite tree. But nothing he said or did was going to make me stop being there for her. And whether he liked it or not, this wasn't his territory. He may have been fucking her, but that didn't make her his. Laila was no one's but her own, she always would be.

I smiled and raised a brow. "That's not a problem, is it?"

"Why would it be a problem?" he said.

I laughed. "The look on your face. Makes me think you have a problem."

"I'm fine. Thanks."

"Mhmm," I said. "Well, she might be a little bit. I told her to take her time. Do you want something to eat?"

"We're going out," he answered. "But thanks."

"Yup."

He still glared at me like I was the scum of the earth.

Really, I didn't want problems with the guy. I was trying to be decent. I didn't like him, but Laila did, and I knew fighting with him would make her bad day worse, and I didn't want that. But he was fucking my wife. Most guys would've been treating him far differently than I was. There wasn't a reason for him to be a dick to me.

I set my forearms on the counter in front of me. "Look, man, I haven't done anything to you. You can quit looking at me like you want to bite my head off."

"I didn't realize I was." He narrowed his gaze.

I squinted a bit, then laughed again. "You do realize that I'm the one who's married to her, right? If I can be this civil, so can you."

"You're married but you're not together," Liam said.

Dick thing to say. True, but still. It stung, so I got smart back.

"Not at the moment. But she hasn't divorced me so."

He gritted his teeth. "Yeah, well. She hasn't let you come back either so."

"Maybe not. But at least I have a title."

He set the flowers on the counter and leaned over it. He was only a foot or two from my face. His dark brown eyes darted between mine. "Has it occurred to you that maybe I'm not looking for a title?" He leaned in a bit closer, obviously trying to intimidate me. "Maybe I just want what I have? What you want and can't have?"

I clenched my jaw. Then I gave a smile and straightened myself back up. "If you just wanted sex, you wouldn't be bringing her flowers and going out on a brunch date, dude."

"Ah, well." He brought himself upright. "At least I get a brunch date. What do you get, man? A single fuck in a year? Her drunk calls at four in the morning?" He laughed. "You guys have history, I get that. I know what you are, I've heard the stories. But even with that bond, I'm the one that she wants."

Maybe to some extent. And yeah, it hurt that they were screwing. But I knew what he didn't. That even sexually, no matter how great he was in bed, it didn't touch how good it was with me. Because I felt the same way. No girl I fucked compared to Laila, even if they had a better body, or a prettier face, or knew how to do something amazing with their tongue.

None of that mattered. At the end of the day, I'd rather fuck her than anyone else. I knew she felt the same way. And the only reason she wasn't fucking me was because she wasn't ready for us to get back together. She wanted to sleep with someone for the relief without the complications of emotions. Which I understood.

But it was me that she really wanted. I knew that.

Another chuckle. "Keep telling yourself that."

"I'm sure it hurts." Liam's gaze shifted between mine. "Seeing the girl you love with someone else. But at some point, you're going to have to get over her. She doesn't want you anymore."

Get over her. As if I wasn't the one holding her and wiping her tears an hour before. As if we weren't searching for our missing child together. As if we weren't both still wearing our wedding rings.

I sucked my teeth. "Watch yourself, dude."

He gave a half-smile. "C'mon, we both know I could take you. And it's not like you'd do anything here anyway. She'd hate you for starting shit at her diner. She'd probably hate you for hitting me at all."

I ran my tongue against my teeth and leaned against the counter behind me. Lifting my coffee to my smiling lips, I said, "She probably would, huh?"

He smiled back as if he'd won. In a way, I guess he did. In a hand-to-hand fight, he'd lay me on my ass. He was a wolf, obviously he was stronger than me. But I could kill him in a second if I wanted to. I wouldn't because he was an ally. He fought alongside me to bring her home.

But that wasn't the only reason I wouldn't attempt to hurt the guy. He wasn't wrong; Laila would be pissed. Beyond pissed. She'd probably punch me in the face and ignore my calls for another six months.

Things were still shitty between us, but she was talking to me. I had my best friend back. I was the one she called when she needed someone again. Things were going to get better. I wasn't going to ruin that by trying to assert dominance.

"Oh, hey." Laila came through the swinging stainless steel door. "I didn't realize you'd be here so soon. I have to wait for my waitress to come in at eleven before we can go."

She looked more like herself then. There was no denying she was miserable; the contour and eyeliner didn't erase the depression. But she had her happy face on. She was back to pretending life was beautiful and grand.

I met her gaze. "That's alright, I can stay until she gets here. Is it still Sophie?"

Laila gestured around the diner. "That's okay. Really, you don't have to do all this."

"No, I'm happy to." I smiled back. "Go. Have fun. I didn't have anything to do this morning anyway. I was just going to sleep 'til noon so I'm glad I came by."

Liam scoffed, rolling his eyes.

Admittedly, I was kind of a loser. All I did was get high, play music, and sleep. But what else was I gonna do? I'd been making money playing shows, but I didn't want to be halfway across the country if something with Micah came up.

Still made my jaw clench that he had to show off how little he thought of me.

Laila turned to him and arched a brow. "You good there?"

He forced a smile and avoided my gaze. "Yeah, I'm great. Are you ready to go?"

"Sure. Just got to grab my purse. We're taking your car, right?"

"Yeah, that works for me."

Laila turned back to me. "Well, if you're going to work my shift, I'm going to have to pay you. So fill out a time sheet before you go."

"You're going to pay me out of the account I already use?" I laughed. "That's stupid, Lai. Don't worry about it."

Laila held open the swinging door. "Fair enough. But can I talk to you for a second before I head out?"

I brushed past her and walked into the kitchen. As the door shut behind her, she put her hands on her hips. "Were you a dick?"

It's not like I was gonna sugarcoat it. "Not as big of a dick as he was. But yeah. A little, I guess."

She crossed her arms. Her voice lowered, leaning in slightly. "You didn't say anything about the letter, did you? Because I don't think I want to talk about that with him. Maybe the Witch part but not the details."

"No, that wasn't exactly the topic of conversation."

"Good. You have the letter though, right?"

"Yeah, I've got it. And you have the bag, right?"

"I'm going to hold onto it if that's okay."

"Yeah, that's fine," I said. "But hey, I was thinking about something. Do you think we could talk to Lydia?"

"Probably," she said. "Why?"

"Well, you know those pictures she drew. She only knew him for the first few days of his life," Laila said. "But in the drawings, that isn't a newborn. He's what—Six or seven months old? Maybe even older?"

"I hadn't thought about that."

"I mean, maybe it's just how she pictures him now, I don't know. But it's worth asking."

Laila paused, squinting. "Remember the zombie in the basement?"

"Jesus Christ, if one of the waitresses walked in right now, you guys would be fucked," Max muttered at the fryer.

I ignored him and turned back to Laila. "Kind of hard to forget the zombie in the basement."

"When it went back to Peterson..." Laila paused, head tilting slightly. "He said something. I don't remember exactly, but something about me on our wedding day. And we didn't know how because we only had like twenty people at our wedding. But Lydia was there. Moriah mentioned that she probably bound herself to Micah. But what if she bound to Amy to Lydia too?"

Me and the family had wondered about that too, how he knew what she looked like on her wedding day. Binding Amy to Lydia would have made sense, it'd give them an inside look at our lives. Considering ancestral magic was the La Fay expertise, it'd line up.

I ran my hand along my jaw, giving a nod. "Maybe. But that would mean that the two have been in contact and I hope like hell that isn't the case."

Laila bit her bottom lip. "Ray mentioned something about me bringing them here soon. Lydia wants to see her friend and he has a box to pick up from the police department. It's a Sunday, I might be able to bring them down for a few hours later. It's early though so I'll call him in an hour or two."

"Yeah, just let me know. I want to be there. Even if Lydia doesn't know anything, I was going to ask if I could keep a few of her drawings."

"Hopefully today. If not, we'll go from there. But I should probably head out. Show Leah that letter. We'll see if she can make any sense of it and ask her if she knows anything about Wormwood. I'm going to call Mary later and ask if she knows anything too. Google said that it's either a star or an angel but there's no fact to back it up."

"I'll go to the sanctuary library at the hospital. I might be able to find something on it there too." I forced a smile. My stomach spun as I said it, but I did mean it. "But you go. Have fun."

She huffed. "I'll try."

I really did want her to be happy, but seeing her lack of enthusiasm to go out with that asshole brought me a bit of comfort. Then she turned away. And as she did, my eyes slid from her pink blouse down her body.

Those jeans stuck out in my mind. They were tight as hell with little bronze buttons on each pocket. Her ass was like the definition of a peach in them. They'd been her favorite pair before she went into captivity, and mine too. I'd ripped them down her legs and fucked her against the counter I was leaning against a few years prior.

"And Laila?"

She glanced over her shoulder. "Yeah?"

"Walk away a little slower." I gave a childish grin. "Your ass looks amazing."

She laughed, cheeks turning pink. "Fuck you."

"Is that an invitation?" I smiled wider.

She rolled her eyes, still smiling. Then she flipped me off and headed through the swinging door. I placed my hands on the counter and looked out into the dining area through the serving hatch.

"So is that a no?" I called. She glanced over her shoulder with a bashful grin. Her head shook, struggling to pull her smile down. Then Liam took her hand. I smiled still. "A double negative becomes a positive, you know."

She laughed. "Get back to work."

Liam glared at me. Then turned his gaze back to Laila, forcing a smile. "Ya all set, baby girl?"

"Yeah, I'm good to go."

He looked at me. Then he leaned down and pushed his mouth to hers.

She kissed him back, but fast.

My smile dropped. A pit fell through my stomach.

That split second when she touched her lips to his felt like a millennium. It wasn't a passionate or loving kiss, but it was still enough to make my heart feel like it was ripped from my chest.

Knowing it and seeing it were two vastly different things.

As she pulled back, his gaze found mine. A smile tugged at the corners of his mouth. Laila looked at me and swallowed hard, brows raising at the center. She felt awful. It was all over her face. We might not have been together, but she didn't want to hurt me any more than I wanted to hurt her.

"That was a dick move." Max set a plate on the serving hatch.

I turned away. Watching her walk away didn't seem like much fun after I thought about the fact that she was walking away with him.

As the bell rang above the door, I said, "I don't like that guy."

"Me neither. Something about him rubs me the wrong way. He's just so cocky, you know? I know she likes him and everything, but" —he gave a shrug— "I'm team Jeremy."

I managed a smile. "Try putting in a good word for me?"

He took a sip from his coke. "She'll come around eventually."

"Hopefully," I muttered.

CHAPTER TWENTY-SEVEN

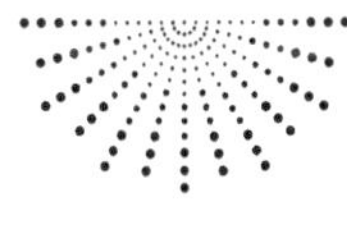

LAILA

The smell of the car air freshener wafted to my nose. Music played quietly through the speakers. My body bumped up and down over the potholes along the winding backroad. I watched the green foliage whoosh by out the window.

But my chest felt tight and my stomach hurt.

Jeremy's expression on the other end of the serving hatch kept flashing behind my eyes. His mouth open, the way his brows pulled together, his lips curved down.

By that point, I was mostly spending time with Liam because I enjoyed his company. We'd only had sex once since Jeremy had been back, and it wasn't close to the same as it'd been before. We'd kissed a couple times, and he'd tried to take it a step further, but I kept turning him down. After being with Jeremy again, I couldn't climax with Liam. Honestly, I was so deep in thought about Micah, I wasn't sure I could orgasm at all.

And I'd been on the other side of that stick. I knew how much it hurt to see the person I loved with another person like that. I wouldn't wish it on anyone, let alone Jeremy.

I glanced at Liam behind the wheel. "That was kind of a shitty thing to do."

Liam turned down the music. "What's that?

"Kissing me like that." I veered to look at him.

"I'm not allowed to kiss you?"

"That wasn't a kiss. That was marking your territory."

"And him talking about how great your ass looked wasn't?" Liam pivoted his gaze from the road to meet mine.

"We were in the next room," I said. "So no, it wasn't."

"He knows I'm a wolf, doesn't he?" Liam asked. I didn't respond, but I must've made a face. "Alright then."

"But I'm not your territory," I said. "Just because we're dating doesn't mean I'm yours."

"Obviously," he muttered, almost too quiet for me to hear.

"I'm sorry?"

He was silent for a moment. "Nothing."

Granted, I did like Liam. And in another lifetime, maybe I'd have given him a bigger chance. But the fact was, my life was a mess. I'd made it loud and clear that I didn't want to get caught up in a love triangle. Going out to the movies and getting something to eat together was a nice distraction when I couldn't get my mind to shut off. But not once had I told him there was a chance for anything more than what we had.

"I thought you understood that I wasn't looking for anything serious. I wasn't looking for anything actually. You just showed up at my doorstep," I said.

"Yeah. I know," Liam said. "I see your point. I'm sorry. It won't happen again."

I looked over him for a moment. That's when I realized that whatever we were doing meant something a lot different to him than it did to me. I was a relationship girl, Liam was a relationship guy. But I didn't want to be in a relationship with him. I didn't want to be in a relationship with anyone. What I wanted was a *distraction* from love. But he wanted to *find* love.

I tilted my head, looking him over. "Do you want something more than this?"

Liam turned to meet my gaze. "You're right, Laila. I'm sorry. That was shitty. I shouldn't have done that. I won't do it again."

I wasn't sure if he avoided the question because he didn't want to argue or if it was because I was right, and he had a broad misunderstanding of my intentions here. But either way, it'd been one hell of a morning. I didn't particularly want to argue or hurt him either. I just wanted to go out with a friend and try to breathe.

"So where are we going?" I asked.

"Just a movie, if that's cool with you," Liam said. "I have to work at five, so I figured we'd make it short today."

"That's probably a good idea. I have a lot of shit to do later." I rubbed my eyes.

"Work stuff?" he asked.

"Micah stuff."

"Is that why he was there? You found something?"

"No, not really. I mean, yeah. That's why he was there, but I didn't really find anything. I know who the Witch working for Peterson is. I'm not sure how it's going to help though."

"Who is it?" he asked.

"Anastasia La Fay, we think."

"You're sure it's her?" he asked. "How do you know?"

It wasn't that I didn't trust Liam. I did, I didn't think he'd run his mouth and tell someone he shouldn't have. But he wasn't a telepath. If he had that information in his head, the psycho telepath working against my family could get it out of him. Keeping vital information like that on the down low was best.

"It's kind of a long story. But she sent her sister a letter and..." I paused. "I don't want to get into the details, but she, um... She's been with my son."

"That must be why the barrier spells are so strong. The La Fay's are..."

"Insanely powerful?" I asked. "Yeah, I know."

***

Rain drizzled down around me, slapping my cheeks. The taste of menthol and tobacco touched my tongue. I looked out over the crowded parking lot, listening to the dial tone against my ear.

"Hey, Laila. Long time no talk," Ray answered.

"Hey, man. How are ya?" I flicked some ash to the ground before breathing in another drag.

"I'm alright. Just getting ready to go over to my sister's for lunch. What about you? How's everything been?" he asked.

"Okay, I guess. A lot going on," I said. "But I'm not calling to bitch and moan. I was actually hoping we could get together. I have a couple things I want to talk to Lydia about. I got some information on Micah, and I don't know, some thoughts came to mind that Lydia might be able to help us with. I wanted to check with you first and make sure that's okay though."

"Yeah, that's alright with me. She's been talking about you recently, I think she misses you. She looks up to you or something."

I laughed. My head shook. If I was the type of person kids looked up to, I felt really bad for the next generation. I was a damn shit show.

"So when were you thinking?" Ray asked.

"I know it's short notice, but I was hoping tonight," I said. "We can come to you, or I could bring you back here for the day and take you home in the evening. If you're too busy, maybe something one day this week."

"No, that's okay. Today is probably best. I'm picking up overtime this week so I'll be pretty busy in the evenings and Lydia's about to start school so the daytime wouldn't work either. And Lydia wants to meet your dog, so we should probably come to you," Ray said. "As long as we're back by nine, we'll have enough time to get ready for bed and be up for work in the morning. What time do you want to pick us up?"

"I could come grab you as soon as I get back to the diner. We could have dinner here so you don't have to worry about rushing to eat before you come over. But what time works for you?"

"How about I just call you after we get back from my sister's?" Ray asked. "That way, no one has to rush or anything."

"Works for me. That'll give me enough time to get in touch with Jeremy."

"Sounds like a plan."

"Alright, I should get back in there. Just give me a call and let me know when I'm good to come grab you guys."

"Will do."

I wish I could say I had fun that morning. But I didn't really know what fun was anymore. The closest I got to fun was the peace that came from the bottom of a glass of whiskey. Emptiness and numbness may not have been happiness, but it was closer than misery.

Suddenly, sitting beside Liam felt wrong. Even if he hadn't said it, I knew that this meant so much more to him than it did to me. And I felt bad.

It also felt like a giant waste of time. Sitting there feeling like shit wasn't helping my mental health. I should have been working on something that would help me find my son, but I wasn't even sure where to look. I did text Mary and ask her to meet up, but she didn't respond.

My therapist, who I'd blown off my last four sessions with, would tell me that I was overthinking. That things weren't as bad as I thought or that they would get better. But it's easy to say things like that to someone else when your life isn't in shambles.

My son was gone. Being held captive by the same people that held and tortured me for more than three months. A mere drop in time compared to what Chris or Haley endured. Still, the time I spent inside those walls and behind that locked door changed me.

But I knew what life was before that place. Micah knew nothing but that. He wouldn't even fucking know me when I got him back.

If I got him back soon, he could still be a normal child. Maybe not normal per se, given the massive array of abilities he must possess, but normal enough. But the older he got, the less I'd be able to give him a sense of normalcy. His normal would be vastly different than mine. If they didn't kill him first.

Having sex had been a nice get away before. A rush of endorphins and serotonin, some oxytocin. It made me feel good. But I couldn't even bring myself to want it now. Especially not with Liam. All I could think about was that line.

The blood on my hands will wash into the blood of Him, and He shall make me clean once more.

Even as Liam drove us home, no other thoughts touched my mind. Micah.

Micah's alive, and they're going to kill him. They're going to kill my son because they're delusional and believe that he is the Jesus of our time.

That insanity was the reason I hated religion. No matter which religion it is, there's always a shroud of madness over the decency. Religion destroys lives.

In hindsight, it made sense. The way that Peterson treated me wasn't because I was Elite. He treated me like royalty because of the prophecy. He believed I was the mother of the child that would bring heaven to earth.

Little did he realize that heaven is essentially hell. The good isn't any better than the bad. It sounds like it doesn't make sense. But when I considered the fact that Demons are simply Angels who went against the will of God, the more I realized that God wasn't innately good.

God wasn't good. God was the reason someone was planning to murder my child.

God sickened me.

CHAPTER TWENTY-EIGHT

JEREMY

I spent the morning at the diner doing what I'd done before the separation. Serving customers, filling ketchup bottles, scrubbing a few tables. It was kind of refreshing, really. Then Sophie came in and took my place. I headed home.

After spending most of the afternoon googling some shred of information containing the word Wormwood and finding absolutely nothing, I went downstairs and gave Leah the letter. Practically in silence, she nodded, opened her laptop, and began to dig.

She was scared. That's why she didn't say a word. Prophecy meant more to her than it did to me. All that I was concerned with was the fact that the murder of my child was a part of whatever nonsense those idiots were following.

I was scared. But not about the end that Anastasia talked about in her letter. I should have been, but that wasn't it. I was terrified that Laila was right. They could kill Micah well before we were able to find him.

I thought about it as I tied the tourniquet around my bicep and tapped my forearm for a vein. What it would feel like to lose him again. What it'd do to me, how it'd destroy Laila. How much it'd hurt to hear for the second time that my son was dead before I even got to meet him. Before he got to lie in the crib I'd put together for him. Before he got to see that Winnie the Pooh cubby I'd spent hours making. Before I got to put him to sleep in the rocking chair that my mom used to rock me and my siblings in.

But once the blood filled the needle and I pushed it back into my vein, the euphoria began to set in. The misery lifted and I floated off into something lighter.

Somehow, I made my way back to my bed. Lying my head against the pillows, despite the sense of relief from the drugs, Laila texted, and I was full of guilt. She said that she was bringing Ray and Lydia back to the diner later and I could come over whenever I was ready.

If I hadn't just shot up, I'd have been there in the blink of an eye. But I didn't want her to see how fucked up I was, so I didn't open the text. I wanted to be there, I wanted any minute she'd give me, but she'd be disgusted to see the way I looked then.

But she got her little fix to make it through the day. She had her sweet little brunch date and those stupid fucking sunflowers. I didn't get my thrill from a quick fuck in the back of some random asshole's car. I got mine from a needle and some little green pills. And I knew mine was more destructive than hers, but we both had to get through the day somehow.

After an hour and a half of nodding and strumming at my guitar strings, I felt close enough to sober that I could see her. I placed my guitar back on the wall, put my hoodie back on, and teleported to the basement of the old diner.

"Back so soon?" Max asked as I made it to the top of the steps.

"Looks like it," I said. "Is Laila upstairs?"

He wiped his hands on his apron, then started toward the office. He made a waving motion over his shoulder, gesturing for me to follow him. "Yeah, she's been up there for a while now. She said to tell you to come up when you got here. But let me talk to you for a minute."

"Sure, what's up?" I trailed behind him.

He shut the office door and reached into his pocket. "You aren't sober, are you? Because I don't want to be the reason you relapse."

I rolled my eyes. "No, Max. I'm not sober."

"Alright, cool. I mean, not cool but cool." He pulled a small tied off end of a plastic bag from his pocket. "My dude gave me this. Trying to get me into the party drug scene, I guess. I tried some, it's really good but I'm not trying to sell anything that isn't weed, ya know?"

I opened my hand for it. "What is it?"

"Molly. Might have some coke in it, I dunno. But I saw how upset Lai was this morning so I was going to give it to her. But then I figured if I gave it to her, she might go do it with what's-his-face. And I don't want to give him my drugs. So I thought I could give it to you, and you could do it with her."

She did love molly. When she was in that funk last year, it really helped her feel more like herself. She'd been on quite the bender, maybe she'd want it. But I wasn't sure if she'd want to get fucked up with me. And I wasn't sure if she'd feel gross about it now that Micah was back in the picture.

"I mean, I can offer it to her, but I don't know if she's going to want it. This shit with Micah... I don't know. It might make her feel irresponsible or something."

"Don't let it be like that, man. Make it about you guys. You have the opportunity right now, ya know? She's mad at Liam, you're the one going out of your way to help her and shit. This is your chance. A couple key bumps and she'll talk to you. Trust me, I know Laila. She loves molly." Max smiled. "That's all you need. She wants to be with you, I know she does. And you want her, right?"

"Well, yeah. Obviously I want her, but I don't want to take advantage of her. She's fragile right now," I said. "I can't just give her drugs and expect things to get better."

"Laila isn't fragile like a flower, Jeremy. She's fragile like a bomb."

I raised a brow. "Isn't that a meme?"

"She loves memes. Just try it, alright? If she doesn't want it, give it to Leah. I know she'll take it."

I guessed it was worth a shot. I'd offer.

"Alright, man. I'll try. But later, there's too much shit going on right now."

"Well, let me know how it goes. But I really think it could help things. Even if you guys just get fucked up and talk."

"We'll see, I guess. Do you want anything for it?"

"Nah, I got it for free. It isn't much anyway. But if it helps, we're getting drinks and you can pay. At this point, man..." He paused. "Look, I just want to see her happy again. Even if it's just for a few minutes."

Couldn't disagree with him there.

After talking with Max, I headed upstairs. The steps creaked beneath me, the smell of French fries filling my nose. It was nice being back, but it felt so weird to knock on the door. Felt even weirder after this morning.

"Hey." Laila pulled the door open with a smile.

I smiled back, leaning down to pet Tink. "Hey."

"I'm going to get Ray and Lydia in a few minutes, but do you want a drink or anything?" She walked to the kitchen and grabbed a bottle of water from the fridge.

"No, I'm good. But thank you." I smiled.

She smiled back. Then she walked to the couch and sat down. I sat at the other end and met her gaze.

I really didn't know what to say. Sure, I could've asked, 'how was your date?' But I didn't want the answer. I didn't want to hear about how much fun she'd had getting fucked by that asshole.

I'd pushed it from my mind earlier that day, but when I sat down, I couldn't help but wonder. Was he right? Was he what she wanted? I mean, I couldn't blame her if that were the case. But... that thought just made this whole thing so much more uncomfortable. I wasn't gonna leave, I wanted to spend time with her, and I wanted to get a glimpse into Lydia's mind, but still. I was a little queasy.

She let a trill escape her lips. Then she smiled. She pulled her feet onto the couch and wrapped her arms around her knees. "Thanks for this morning. Helping with the diner and everything."

Thank god she knew how to start a conversation.

"Yeah, I was happy to. It was nice. I love this little shit hole."

"Hey, don't call my diner a shit hole." Her tone was playful. "This place is my baby."

I laughed. "I didn't mean it like that."

"It is kind of a shit hole though. I just had to cancel tonight's show because of the rain," she said. "The stage area in the basement decided it was going to flood again."

I hadn't noticed when I landed, but the stage was on the other end of the basement from the staff steps. It did have a habit of flooding, usually at this time of year.

"Damn, really? I told you forever ago we needed a French drain."

I almost corrected myself, I should have said 'you,' not 'we.' But she didn't seem to notice.

"Yeah, I have someone coming out tomorrow to start digging. It's gonna be two or three grand so I kept putting it off. But I easily lost a good eight hundred bucks by having to shut down tonight. So I figured now's the time, I might as well just get it done."

"Probably a good idea," I said. "But I could do that, you know. French drains are easy, you just dig a whole, throw down some gravel, then a pipe, more gravel, and fill it back in."

"I seriously could not ask you to do that," Laila said. "That's a big ass job. Plus, there's codes we have to follow and shit. It's just easier to have someone come do it. But really, thank you." Her voice softened a bit, gaze shifting between mine. "You don't have to be as nice to me as you are. I don't want to take you for granted. I really am grateful. For everything. You kind of talked me off the ledge this morning and... And thank you."

"You weren't on the ledge." I smiled and gave a slight shake of my head. "That note was emotional. It's okay to break down sometimes. We all fall down, we just have to get back up."

"Maybe I wasn't on the ledge yet, but I was getting close. But you're right, I can't let myself get to that point. I have to keep it together. And I want to apologize. That whole thing with Liam... I didn't plan that or anything and I'm really sorry you saw it."

My smile dropped. "We've both been with other people. I mean, yeah, it hurt. It hurt a lot. But it's not like it's a secret that you're seeing him."

"Yeah, but that wasn't cool. I... I wouldn't want to see that. I remember seeing that memory of you with Ally and it broke my heart. Hearing it isn't the same as seeing it. That won't happen again."

"No, it's not," I said. "Laila, can I ask you something?"

"Sure."

I was pretty sure I knew the answer. But I wanted to hear her say it.

"Do you love him?" I asked quietly.

She frowned. "It isn't like that. I mean, yeah, I love him. But just in the way that I love any of my friends. Not um..." She laughed quietly and looked down at the couch. "Not like I love you."

My lips lifted in a smile. I'd hoped that'd be her answer, but the tightness in my chest softened to hear her say it. It gave me a shred of hope that we'd get back to where we always should have been. Me, her, our son, in that little apartment, taking turns with him and the diner downstairs.

"What is it like then?" I asked quietly.

"It was just sex." She bit her lower lip. "It's more friendship than anything."

I understood that. I'd had 'just sex' plenty of times. But I never went out with those girls. I never bought them flowers. And I did understand that it was probably easier for her to be with one person than a bunch of them after she'd been raped, but it still felt like it was more than that.

"Breakfast dates aren't usually just sex," I murmured.

"He works overnights," she said. "And he takes care of his little sister. I work a lot. It's just a matter of availability."

"Maybe for you," I said. "But it isn't just sex to him."

She was quiet for a moment. "Yeah, I know."

I looked away. If she knew that, if she didn't want the same thing, why was she still seeing him? That wasn't exactly a fair thing to do to him. Not that I cared much about his feelings but making him think he had a chance wasn't good for anyone.

"I'm sorry that I'm hurting you," she murmured. Her gaze met mine over her knees, hugging her shins. "I'm just under a lot of pressure right now. I don't... It's just a lot to handle all at once."

"Well, it's not like I don't deserve it." I managed something of a smile. "I hurt you too."

"We're a mess."

"Masters of our own destruction."

"I wish we were as good at building as we are at demolishing."

"We were."

"Once upon a time." Her smile grew sad.

"Maybe we could again," I said quietly. "Build, I mean."

She smiled. "Maybe."

I smiled back, feeling my heart swell. For the first time in a long time, she verbalized it. I wasn't reading something that wasn't there. It wasn't a yes but maybe was better than no. There was a chance.

We had a chance.

CHAPTER TWENTY-NINE

JEREMY

When Laila said she was going to pick up Lydia and Ray, I went to take a piss. As I made my way back into the living room, I found Ray standing by the door. He casually hung his jacket on the coat rack. Like he'd done it a thousand times.

I wondered if they did it here. If he hung his jacket on that hook before he fucked my wife in our bed.

I tried to stay levelheaded, I really did. And maybe I was projecting a bit after this morning. But I couldn't even look at him without visualizing him screwing my wife.

"Hey, man," I said.

"Oh, hey." Ray gave a friendly smile. "How are you doing?"

"Seen better days. What about you? How have you been?"

"I'm good. Great, actually. I love my new job. Laila told you I moved, didn't she?"

"Yeah, she did. Upstate New York, right? Near Buffalo?"

"Yup, that's the place. A little town, a lot like this one. But it's home, you know?"

The longer I looked at him, the more pissed I got. I was sure Laila was the one to initiate it, because I knew Ray didn't have the balls. That should have shown me that he wasn't the one at fault really. But it just pissed me off more.

Thinking about her giving him the flirty smile that she used to give me.

Thinking about his hands traveling her naked body. Thinking about her moaning for him.

Fuck, I was pissed. We'd been friends. Maybe not *best* friends, but we *were* friends. He watched me cry over her. He saw how much losing her destroyed me.

Then he fucked her.

"Sure," I said. "Where'd Laila and Lydia go?"

"Laila took her dog out to pee and Lydia wanted to tag along. I think she just wanted to talk about girl shit, I don't know."

"Oh, good," I muttered. I began cutting away at the distance between us until we were only a foot or two apart. "We're friends, right? We never had any beef?"

"Yeah, man. We're friends."

I nodded. Something of a chuckle left my lips. I ran my thumb and fore finger down my cheeks toward my mouth. But then I saw it again. Him, her...

Almost involuntarily, I raised my fist through the air and dropped it hard into the side of his face.

Ray stumbled backward, catching himself on the edge of the counter. He gripped his jaw and looked up at me. "What the fuck was that?"

"Friends don't fuck each other's wives, Ray." I grasped my aching wrist. "What—You didn't think I'd care?"

"Jesus," Ray mumbled, regaining his balance. "Damn, Jeremy. I didn't know you could punch like that."

"Well, fuck you too."

"No, I'm sorry, man," Ray began. He straightened up, wiping his bleeding lip. "I didn't mean it like that."

I clenched my jaw. "You fucked my wife."

Ray held his throbbing jaw, gaze sympathetic. "Yeah. Yeah, I know. And I'm sorry for that. It shouldn't have happened. We were both drunk, and lonely, and she came on to me. I mean, kind of. I guess I started it, but—"

"Shut the fuck up." I tightened my hand to a fist. "Why would I want a play by play?"

"You're right. I'm sorry. You guys were broken up, she said you were seeing other people—"

"Yeah, but we were friends. You were at our wedding. You don't fuck your friend's wife, dude."

Ray gave another nod. "You're right. I shouldn't have let that happen."

"No shit."

"If it helps, she said your name a couple times—"

"No, Ray." I gritted my teeth together. "That doesn't help."

"I should probably quit talking now," Ray muttered.

"Yeah, you probably should." I tightened my jaw.

"Hey, are you okay? I felt…" Laila began in the doorway, gaze traveling between my hand and Ray's bleeding lip. She sucked her teeth. Then she turned behind her, carefully holding the door so Lydia couldn't see inside. "We'll be downstairs in one minute, kiddo. Go save us a table, alright?"

Tinkerbell barreled through the door.

Lydia said something I couldn't make out. Then Laila closed the door and stepped inside. She gestured to my hand. "Did you hit him?"

"I did."

"Are you kidding me?" She put her hand to her hip. "What are you—Fifteen?"

I shrugged. "He fucked you."

Liam was different. I didn't know the guy. But Ray shouldn't have done me like that. I wouldn't fuck his wife—even if she weren't a psychopath—because you just don't fuck your friend's wives.

She traced her tongue along the inside of her teeth. "A week before, I felt another girl's nails digging into your back. Don't act like you're innocent here."

"I'm not," I said. "I get why you did it, but we were friends and he—"

"I don't care, Jeremy," she snapped. "I'm no one's god damned property."

"I didn't say you were. I just said that—"

"It's alright, Laila," Ray interjected. "I deserved it."

"No. You didn't," Laila said. "And I'm the one that made the first move."

My stomach spun. "Yeah, that's been established."

"You can't just go around punching people because I've slept with them, Jeremy." Her piercing gaze moved between mine. "You don't get to make decisions for me and—"

"I'm not," I said. "This wasn't about you, this was about loyalty to friendship. If I fucked one of your friends, tell me you wouldn't punch them in the face, Laila."

"He's right, Lai." Ray nodded. "This is what guys do. Girls cry, guys fight and call it square. We're good now, right, Jeremy?"

I mean, not really. I'd never completely get over that. I damn sure couldn't trust him anymore. But I wasn't gonna punch him again.

"Yeah. We're cool."

She rolled her eyes. "Well, sit down, Ray. Let me heal your face."

I began to roll up my sleeve as he sat. Laila turned to me and huffed. "Uh-uh. Your ass can get an ice pack."

A surprised chuckle left my lips. "You aren't gonna heal me?"

"You knew it was gonna hurt. You made your bed, now you got to lie in it."

I laughed. "Alright. Fair enough."

CHAPTER THIRTY

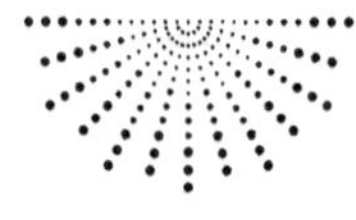

LAILA

I set our plates to the table and slid into the booth next to Jeremy. "So your dad said you liked your new school?"

Lydia sipped her strawberry milkshake. "Yeah, it's nice. Kinda weird though, we start way earlier than we did here. But there's this big library with thousands of books. And I signed up for the track team. I'm not really good at sports and stuff but running's easy."

"I ran track in middle school." Jeremy smiled. "Cross country actually, not track. But I started with track."

"Yeah, what's the difference?" Lydia asked. "Some of the girls were saying that track's for pussies."

"Lydia." Ray's tone was firm.

I chuckled. Jeremy laughed. Lydia had developed quite the personality after the initial culture shock of escaping captivity. Aside from the scars, I'd have thought she'd lived a perfectly normal life.

That gave me hope. Maybe Micah would be the same way. Maybe when we got him back, after a little bit of time with us, maybe he'd be normal too.

"It's just a word, Dad."

"A word you're too young to use," Ray said. "We've had this conversation before."

"I'm not talking to a teacher or something." Lydia turned her gaze back to Jeremy and me. "You guys don't care if I say pussies, do you?"

"We aren't your parents." Jeremy glanced at Ray. "Listen to your dad, kid."

"I second that notion," I said.

"Thank you," Ray murmured.

"But they're right, track's for pussies," Jeremy said. I chuckled, and he smiled. "Track is literally just running around a track. It's harder on your joints too. In cross country, you run in all terrain. Mud, grass, rock. It's basically fast hiking. You'd probably like it, a lot of it's running in the woods and stuff. It's more about agility than speed."

"That's way cooler," Lydia said.

"Considering what we are, it's never a bad thing to be a good runner." Jeremy gave a friendly smile.

"And most of the time, you won't be running on an all-weather track," I said.

"Guys," Ray said.

I looked around the empty restaurant. "What?"

"They're right, Dad," Lydia said. "I know you don't like to think about the fact that I'm different but I am."

Ah, I saw now. He had an issue with her talking about her abilities. But around here, that made up a big portion of our conversations. The kid had a right to embrace who she was, at least around people like us.

"I have to go to the bathroom. Could you guys try and keep the curse words to a minimum for the time being?"

"We'll keep it classy." I smiled. "Or we'll try, at least."

Ray exhaled deeply. "Just stick to damns and shits. Try to hold back on the F bomb."

Lydia rolled her eyes. She took another sip from her milkshake while Ray made his way to the bathroom. "He acts like I'm five. I'm almost thirteen, you know. I'm not a little kid."

I laughed. As if being almost thirteen made her an adult. I was twenty-two, and I didn't feel close to grown yet.

Jeremy gave a smile. "I saw a lot of bad things by the time I was thirteen too. It made me think I was so mature for my age. But trust me, you're going to wish you could be that innocent again one day. Hold onto it, kid. One day you'll be twenty-five and realize that all of the answers you have to the world just become more and more questions."

"He just doesn't get it."

"No dad does at thirteen," I said.

"It's not even that. It's the whole Fae thing. He acts like I'm human and I'm not. I know that he is, but everything's different for me. What Mom and the doctor did was horrible, and I hate them for it, but I got to be what I was there. And with Dad…" She sipped her shake. "I don't know. I think my powers remind him of her. I feel like I have to hide them."

I knew that wasn't the case. He didn't want her to use her powers because he wanted her to have a happy, normal, human life. Which was sweet, it really was. But it wasn't realistic.

"You can call me any time, kid," I said. "I can pick you up and we can spend the day growing shit and playing mind games."

"Yeah, I think I might do that sometime. It's lonely. Being the only special one in the family."

"A blessing and a burden," I said.

She slurped from her milkshake. "But Dad said you guys wanted to talk to me about something. Questions you had about Micah?"

"Yeah, we did," I said.

Jeremy reached into his hoodie pocket and laid her drawing on the table. "So we were thinking about something. How long ago did you draw this?"

"I don't know. A few months ago. Around Christmas time, I think. Why?"

"Well, I was just wondering. You only met Micah when he was a baby. Like fresh out of the womb, premature little guy. But this baby's a lot older than that," Jeremy said. "Is that how you picture him?"

"I don't know. I just… I don't know, it's hard to explain. I just get these images in my head sometimes, so I draw them. I see Micah a lot."

"What do you mean? Like you're looking through someone else's eyes?" I asked.

"No, not exactly. I've done that before and this is different. It's just, like, a flash. From a different perspective though. Kind of like how in a dream, sometimes you're looking down on a conversation? You're not really in it, but you see it. That sort of thing."

"It isn't when you're asleep, is it?" Jeremy asked.

"No, just randomly. Sometimes when I'm walking down the street, sometimes when I'm doing my homework," Lydia said. "It's never bad stuff. Just like, little images. I don't think it's a power thing, I think it's just a human thing."

"No, I don't think it's a power thing either," Jeremy said after a moment. "At least, not your power. If I didn't know better, I'd say it's astral projection. But that usually feels more real. Like you're actually there. I think this is a Witch thing."

Lydia turned her head to the side a bit. "What do you mean?"

Jeremy pulled his phone from his pocket. He typed for a minute and turned the screen to her. "Okay, she might look a little different now, this is a really old picture. But did you ever meet this lady when you were living with your mom and Peterson?"

Lydia studied the image on the phone. I saw Moriah standing beside her, although she was clearly much younger. At least a good decade ago. Her style was similar though. She looked frilly and soft, wearing the same thick mascara and red lipstick as I'd seen her in this morning.

But the woman beside her looked different. She bore the same small, gentle features. But her icy blue eyes were even colder than Moriah's. Her dark brown hair hung loosely around her long oval shaped face. She gazed into the camera with this expression that wasn't easy to explain. It was more of an intuitive thing than anything because an outside perspective may say she didn't look much different than her sister. But her gaze held this emptiness. When I just looked at her eyes, it was as though I were looking into nothingness.

"Yeah, that's Nastya," Lydia said. "She lived a floor beneath us. I didn't like her very much."

"I don't think I like her either," Jeremy muttered. "But did she ever cut off a piece of your hair? After Micah was born, I mean."

"Yeah, why?" Lydia asked.

"I think that she cast a spell that bound you to one of them. Maybe her, maybe Micah. That's why you see him sometimes."

I didn't really know what that meant. Was it good news? Was it bad? I wasn't sure, and Jeremy was maintaining a puzzled, yet serious poker face.

Why would they do that? To keep tabs on her, maybe?

"But what does that mean?" Lydia asked.

"It means that you're linked to him," Jeremy said. "You don't see much of the details because he's so small and his thoughts are so simple. That, and she has other spells cast to seal his location."

"But why would they bind her to Micah?" I asked. "Wouldn't it make more sense to bind her to Peterson or Amy?"

"No." Jeremy shook his head. "In theory, yes. But if she were bound to Amy, there wouldn't be a way to conceal their location. They're blood, the binding would be stronger than any spell Anastasia could cast. And if she already bound herself to Micah, she couldn't bind herself to anyone else or it would weaken the bond between the two of them. Peterson's human, the bond wouldn't hold over time without mutual power feeding it." He put his hand over mine.

They bound Lydia to Micah as a Trojan horse. That's why they let her go. Amy gets into Micah's thoughts to channel Lydia. If she went into Lydia's head, Lydia would feel it and she would tell us. But Micah's young. His thoughts aren't complex and overwhelming. It's just a link. Flashes, meandering thoughts. Enough to go unnoticed for Lydia. That's why all she sees of Micah are simple moments. Because he's too young to organize complex thoughts and connections.

But why would they try to kill her then? I projected into his mind. *Amy deliberately shot her before we left.*

Maybe she didn't want to use her, but knew that was the only way to break the bond. Or maybe it was just to prove a point, that she was loyal to Peterson. Or maybe to guide us away from this conclusion.

"I don't understand," Lydia said. "Can we break it?"

"Anastasia could," Jeremy said. "But we'd need Micah to break it without her. Binding spells are triads. To break them, you need two ends of the triangle."

"Is that why I get random pains sometimes?" Lydia asked. "My therapist says they're phantom pains, but they feel so real."

I fought back a gasp. My stomach sunk, then spun. Oh god, were they hurting my baby?

Images of Daniel's scarred back flashed behind my eyes. What if they were torturing him like they tortured me? What if he was in agony every moment of every day just as I had been?

"What kind of pain?" I asked.

"Just needle pricks and then some aches sometimes after one. It's gets dull after a little while though."

A steady breath left me. Needle pricks weren't so bad. It still wasn't ideal. But at least his back wasn't torn to shreds.

A relieved smile came to Jeremy's lips. "You feel his pain."

Her breaths picked up. "Does that mean he feels mine too?"

"Yes. That's exactly what it means," I said.

That's why. Micah felt her pain when she shot Lydia. I didn't know why she got better so fast and you didn't, but it makes sense now. Jeremy squeezed my hand that rested on my lap. *He healed her. Through their bond, he healed her. That's why Amy did it. She knew Lydia wouldn't die but we would think she didn't care. Micah won't let anything happen to her.*

That's why Anastasia bound herself to him and why she told Moriah to. To protect them. A personal self-healing device.

Is that possible? Healing without coming into contact with each other.

I've heard of it. Only with magic though. It wouldn't work with a bond like ours unless we were bound with a specific spell and I harnessed spirit like you. Our bond is tied to our souls, this is tethered specifically to the consciousness between two Fae who have telepathic abilities.

"Is there a way to find him through me?" Lydia asked quietly. "Could I help you get him back?"

"I don't know. I can ask some Witches though. It might be possible."

"If she can channel Lydia through the bond's telepathic binding to Micah," I said quietly, "does that mean I could too?"

"Maybe," Jeremy said. "But his thoughts, their bond, he doesn't know how to use it yet. Healing was an instinctive power he had at birth, probably due to the trauma you experienced during your pregnancy and the birth itself. But any thoughts he'd have wouldn't be logical enough to make sense of."

"How can I know when she's in my head?" Lydia's tone was laced with fear and confusion. "Or when he is, I mean. But I... That's..."

"It's probably when you see him. Those little flashes. She has a Witch magnifying the connection on top of Amy's. That's why you only see an image or two. But she probably has a full episode. At least a couple minutes. It's how she's checking up on you," Jeremy said. "The day of our wedding, were you getting any flashes of Micah?"

Lydia swallowed hard and gave a nod. "A lot of them."

"That's how Peterson knew what you looked like on our wedding day." Jeremy met my gaze.

"Does this mean..." Lydia began blinking hard. "They used me. They're using me to keep tabs on you."

Truthfully, I didn't believe what I was about to say. What Jeremy said made more sense. But I wanted her to have just an ounce of solace.

"No. It's a mother making sure her baby is okay."

"But—"

"Lydia, she knew you weren't going to die." I began. "She knew Micah would heal you. He probably started healing you before Kai did, and she knew that. She wasn't trying to kill you that day. She was trying to let you go. But she wanted him to think that all that mattered was his cause. She was setting you free, Lydia. She knew you wouldn't go unless you thought she hated you. She had to give you a reason to want to be with your dad.

Maybe she used you too, but she did it to set you free. To give you a normal life. It still had to fit in with his plans, but this was her way to get you out. It's brutal and it's painful and wrong, but it wasn't just to use you. It was to free you. That's why she left you in the room that day. She knew I was coming for you."

She fell silent as she tried to take it all in. After a moment, she met my gaze. "Then why did she take Micah?"

I thought about telling her the truth. Because they think they can use him as some tool to bring on the end of the world.

But she was the Trojan horse. I couldn't tell her what we knew. Not the details.

"Because Peterson wanted him," I said. "Not because she was replacing you."

I didn't believe that either. But again, maybe it'd give that little girl some peace.

CHAPTER THIRTY-ONE

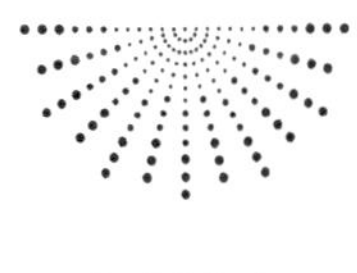

LAILA

After giving Ray a brief description of what we'd gathered, or at least suspected, we ate our dinners while making a list of questions to ask a Witch who might know more about it than we did. We all had several, but Jeremy and I meandered on the same one we wouldn't say aloud.

If they killed Micah, would it kill Lydia?

I almost didn't want to tell Ray. I also didn't want to break whatever bond they had because it was a connection to my son. In a way, he knew me because of it. He saw his dad lift me into the air and kiss me at the altar because of it. He probably knew my voice because of it.

But most importantly, I knew they hadn't hurt him because of it. And I would know if they did.

It was horrible to want to use Lydia in the same way they were using her, but when it came to the safety of my child, morals floated away.

Around eight thirty, I took Ray and Lydia home. When I was sure Lydia was out of hearing distance, I told him about the letter. He came off more sympathetic than anything, probably because he didn't think about the physical connection between them. I told him he couldn't tell Lydia any of it. He assured me it would be the last thing the two of them discussed. With a nod and goodbye yell to Lydia, I teleported back home.

Jeremy was sitting on the couch with Tinkerbell, pulling on her chew toy with the hand that wasn't resting on an ice pack.

"Oh, hey." He smiled. "Sorry, she was barking, and she sounded lonely so I thought I'd keep her company until you got back."

He looked so sweet like that. There were few things that made me look at a man and melt inside. Playing an instrument, holding a baby, and being kind to an animal. Three things Jeremy was great at.

He was a little shit though. I felt it when he punched Ray, and he knew I'd feel it. But I did get it. Had one of my friends fucked my husband, I might've killed them.

I placed my hands on my hips. "Want me to heal that?"

"It's alright. I'll just have Leah or Kai do it when I get home."

I frowned, sat beside him, and lifted his wrist from the ice pack. He winced, and I met his gaze with a half grin. "Oh, I'm sorry. Did that hurt?"

He narrowed his gaze but smiled back. "I'll live."

I raised my other hand over it and let the bright light radiate from my palm into his. I felt the pain as the swelling gradually receded but ignored it. In a few seconds, he was able to tighten and loosen his wrist freely. When I finished, I ran my fingers along the section of skin that was red and puffy before. "Is the pain gone?"

He kept his hand on mine. "Yeah, it's good. Thank you."

"You're welcome." I lifted his hand and set it on his lap. I pulled my feet up onto the couch until I sat lotus style. My knees rested against his outer thigh. "Did you get in contact with any Witches?"

"Yeah. Yeah, we're going to meet up with Helena tomorrow to talk about it. I didn't go into detail over the phone."

I gave a slow nod. "Good. That's good."

"I didn't find anything on Wormwood though. But I did leave a message for Mary. She's going to meet me at the house tomorrow evening. She said she had a lot going on today, and to tell you she was sorry she didn't answer your call."

"So now we wait."

"And now we wait." He was quiet for a moment. He reached into his pocket, pulled something out, but held his hand around it. "Look, so...If the answer is no, I completely understand. No pressure or anything. But Max gave me this earlier and honestly, I think we could both really benefit from it. But still, if you don't want to, you don't have to. And it wasn't my idea, it was Max's, so don't get mad at me for suggesting it."

"What is it?" I asked. He opened his palm and extended his hand. Inside sat a ripped off corner of a Ziploc bag. A small amount of white powder looked back up at me. I picked it up, arching a brow. "Molly?"

"Yeah. Max said he got it for free and he thought you could use it. But he didn't want you to do it alone, so he gave it to me. But if you want to do it alone, you can. I can leave. Or I could give it to Leah. It doesn't really matter."

Shit, I could use a little bit of ecstasy after the day I'd had. Then again though...

"Wouldn't it make me a hypocrite to do drugs with you?"

He laughed. "You did it last year, and I was here. It's not like you're forcing me. And we aren't shooting up together. It's a party drug. But if you want me to leave, I can."

A time would come when I wouldn't *dream* of having anything more than a few glasses of wine. But that was in the distance.

I was more depressed than I'd ever been, and I wanted to feel good. Then I thought back to the night with Leah the year before. I thought about how good it felt to open up to him. I thought about how good it felt to talk about my feelings with him. I thought about how I was able to let the pain fall away that night.

And I wanted to feel that way again. I wanted to feel that way with *him* again. And a big part of me was curious what he'd be like on MDMA too.

"No, I don't want you to leave."

He pressed his smiling lips together.

I looked down at the powder in my hand. "Doesn't look like we're getting Micah back tonight. I could use a pick me up."

***

Jeremy strummed his guitar beside me as I angrily chomped away on a piece of gum to keep from grinding my teeth. I closed my eyes, tilting my head from side to side with the beat as he played.

It did feel hypocritical. That was the first time I had been happy in a long time too. Most of the time, I just drowned the pain out until I was numb. But that night, I genuinely felt happiness. I was still anxious and depressed, but for a little while, I was able to breathe. The world looked colorful again. It was probably how Jeremy felt when he was banging dope.

But I pushed that thought to the back of my head. I pushed Micah to the back of my mind for the night too. I pushed Liam and Wormwood and Anastasia as far away as I could because I needed to fucking breathe for a minute. It was kind of selfish, and incredibly childish, but what the fuck else was I going to do that night? Cry on the kitchen floor with a creased drawing of my missing son and his little blue sock and finish off a bottle of Crown? What good was that going to do?

I was still going to get up the next morning and open the diner. I was going to be there when the Witch got to Leah's. I was going to be there when Mary came by. But in the meantime, I needed to stop fucking thinking.

"You alright over there?" Jeremy smiled, bumping the neck of his guitar against my bicep.

I opened my eyes. "Yeah, I'm good. Why'd you stop playing?"

"Just had to make sure you were still breathing." He grinned, lifted his bottle of water from the table, and took a long chug. "You should drink, you look a little dehydrated."

I took the bottle from his hand. After a quick sip, I noticed the sweat beading at his forehead. "You look hot. Take your jacket off, psycho."

"I'm alright."

I wondered if he'd seen me staring at his forearms the night we slept together. Then I felt a little guilty. "I know you have track marks, Jeremy. But I don't want you to have a heat stroke. Take off your jacket. I promise I won't make you feel bad about them."

Setting his guitar on the ground, he pulled his arms through either sleeve and laid it along the arm of the couch. "Honestly, I don't think it's the jacket making me hot. You're a damn heater."

"Oh, shit. I'm sorry. I should move." I started to shift my feet off the couch.

"Don't you dare move." He gave a playful smile, and put his cool hand over mine. It probably wasn't actually cool, it just felt cool to me because my already high body temperature was way higher than usual.

I smiled back and laid my head against the couch cushion. "I don't want you to get too hot. I can't have a heat stroke, you can."

"I'm fine, Laila. Really." He laced his fingers through mine. "You're okay though?"

"Yeah, I'm okay. I'm great actually. I feel really good right now."

His smile widened, turning to face me. "I see that."

I smiled back. Then I nuzzled my face against the cushion. "Was this couch always this soft?"

"I think so." He chuckled.

"This was a good pick." I closed my eyes. "I wanted that other one, the one that reclined, remember?"

He smiled and laid his head against the couch cushion beside me. "Yeah, I remember."

"But you said no because the suede was easier to clean," I said.

"And the warranty on the other one was shit." His smile stayed against his lips.

"It was a good choice. Even with Tinkerbell, the hair doesn't even stick to it. Ugh, I love this couch." I fell backward onto the arm.

He laughed and ran his thumb along mine. "A lot of memories on this couch."

"Mostly good ones." I smiled as I sat back up.

"Mostly."

I cuddled into the soft suede and closed my eyes. My fingers tightened around his as I enjoyed the buzz for a minute. It was nice. Him being there. Smiling. Happy. For a moment, only a short moment, it felt like the good old days.

Silence crept in. Then he said, "Okay, can we talk about this?"

I opened my eyes. "About what?"

He looked down at our hands before he found my gaze. "What are we doing?"

That was a great question... that I did not have the answer to. Though I hadn't officially told Liam that I couldn't keep going out for brunch dates and I was over the kissing and fucking, I knew that I was. I also knew that I loved my husband. That I wanted moments like this every day for the rest of my life. That I wanted to find my son and have the little family we'd planned almost two years prior.

But we were fucking train wrecks.

"I don't know."

He cupped his hand around mine. He gazed down at them for a moment. Then he cleared his throat.

"I... I don't really know how to say this. I know that you're not sure what you want right now, and I know that you don't have the energy to figure it out right now. But... I just—I need to know something."

"What is it?" I raised my other hand to push hair from his face.

"Am I holding on for good reason?" His eyes shifted between mine. "Because I feel like I am. I know you love me, I can feel it. I can see it, but I just feel... I don't know. Is there some part of you that still wants me?"

"Jeremy..."

It made sense for him to ask. I would too if I were in his position. He and I talked daily, we kissed when no one was around, we held each other's hands.

I did want to be with him. I wanted our little family together. But we didn't have our son, I was drinking like a fish, and he was still doing pills. Were we even close to emotionally ready to be what we wanted to be? Neither of us were in any place close to stable.

"If not, I get it. It's not going to change how I feel, and I'm still going to keep trying, but I just... I need to know." His big, sad blue eyes grew even more dopey. "I need to hear you say it."

"I want what we used to have," I said quietly. "I want to hit reset on the past two years because the first three were the best of my life. But these past couple have been so painful. I wish I could go back and keep all of the bad stuff from happening. I wish I could go back to before Mary killed Moe and keep it all from going down the way that it did. I don't need this place, I'd be more than happy to just be the manager again and live in that little bedroom with your big, crazy family. And I wish I could keep me from getting taken. I wish you could have been with me when Micah was born. I wish we could be what we were before all of this."

"I know that." He cradled my cheek. He gently tucked hair behind my ear. "But do you still want *me*?"

"You wouldn't be here right now if I didn't," I murmured. "Part of me is always going to want you, Jeremy."

A smile came to his mouth. His thumb gently slid down my cheek. "So I'm not crazy for holding onto you."

"No. You aren't crazy."

"So you think we could make it work between us again?"

"I don't know."

He frowned, holding his gaze steady with mine. After a moment, he leaned forward and gently touched his lips to mine. I leaned into it, relaxing into the comfort and safety they brought me. His hands lifted to gently hold my face.

They felt like they always had. Hard and strong, but slow and careful. He gently opened them against mine and slid along my bottom lip before moving to my top. Then he pressed his forehead to mine and pulled his lips back an inch or two.

He felt so good. *Everything* felt so good, but especially him. The firmness of his lips, the strength of his calloused fingertips against my cheeks. It sent a tingle from my mouth through my entire body.

The way he felt almost made me forget about everything else. The past year, the ache of guilt, the mess we'd dug ourselves into.

He could always do that. No matter how bad things were, he could always make me feel like I was floating through space.

"Was that okay?" he asked quietly.

My lip grazed his. "That was perfect."

"*We* were perfect." He continued to hold my face between his palms. "We can be perfect, Laila. You know we can. We can make this work."

I licked my lips and tasted his mouth against my tongue. "There's so much damage done here." I moved my hands to his cheeks. "I love you. I love you so much, but—"

"No buts," he whispered. His sad eyes looked as if they were about to overflow with tears. "That's all we need. We just have to love each other, and the rest will fall into place. It will, it'll work. We just have to love each other. It worked before, baby, we were great. We still have that, we love each other. We can make this work."

I frowned. "I wish it was that easy."

"It is, Lai. It is, we just have to fight for each other. We know what we want." He moved his hands to my arms. His eyes were nearly watering. "We just have to—"

I pushed my lips to his to cut him off.

Love got us through some horrible shit. Love was the reason we were here. But love hurts. We couldn't have love without pain, and I didn't want pain.

When things were good, they were great. But when things were hard, it was hard to remember the love. It was hard to be patient and kind and caring when I was dying inside. We both failed in that regard.

I couldn't pick his dead body up off the floor again. I couldn't feel that pain again. And I couldn't save him. I couldn't make him want to get clean. I couldn't make him want to be healthy.

He had to do that on his own. It couldn't be for me. He had to do it for him, or it wouldn't stick.

And he couldn't take the treachery I felt away either. He wasn't an anti-depressant; he couldn't make me ready to love again. He couldn't bring back my will to live.

But we could do this. We could get lost in each other for a moment.

I lifted my legs around his, kneeling over him. Then I sat on his lap. The bulge in his pants pressed against my groin. His hands slid to my hips, gently coasting upward beneath my shirt until his hands caressed my bare back.

All I wanted in that moment was to feel him. I didn't want to think. I just wanted to forget it all and feel something that wasn't shit for a while. But he wouldn't let it be that simple.

"Laila," Jeremy murmured as I undid the button of his jeans.

"Yeah?" I asked. He touched my chin and tilted it up to meet his gaze.

"You were with him this morning," Jeremy whispered. "I don't, um... It isn't you or anything, I'm not trying to slut shame you. I just don't think I can..." He cleared his throat. "I don't think that I can have sex with you knowing he did a few hours ago."

"We didn't sleep together."

"Oh." A smile pulled at his lips. "And you aren't just doing this because you're rolling balls?"

I laughed. "Does it matter?"

His smile fell. He cupped my cheek in his hand. His eyes searched mine. "Yeah, baby. It does."

"Why?" I moved my hands from his jeans up his chest and around his neck. Then I leaned forward and pressed my lips to the skin just below his ear. His hands at my hips tightened, breathing getting short against my neck. "Don't you want this?"

"I always want this." He gave a soft laugh. "But I don't want it to be just sex, Laila. I want you. I want us."

"It's never just sex with you," I murmured at his ear. "You're my husband. I love you."

His hands slid from my hips to my back. He held me tighter as my lips curved into the skin of his neck. "Then tell me you want me. Tell me you want more than this."

"I love you, Jeremy." I touched my lips to his neck again. "But I won't make you a promise I can't keep."

"I love you too." He found my chin. He carefully pulled it from his neck and shook his head with a frown. "But this isn't enough for me."

I was quiet for a moment, thinking of the right thing to say. "I can't promise you that we can go back to what we were. I wish I could, but I can't."

"You don't have to," he said softly as his hand found my neck. "I don't expect you to figure it all out right this second. I just need to know that you want me. That you want us again. That, maybe not today, but one day, we'll get back to where we were."

His thumb moved from my jaw to my bottom lip. It ever so slightly grazed my mouth and sent a warm chill to my skin. His eyes moved from my lips back to mine, softly, gently. "I need to hear you say that I matter to you. That I'm not just a quick way to numb the pain. You're so much more to me than that. I want to matter to you the way that you matter to me."

"Of course you matter to me." I moved my hand from his neck to push hair behind his ear. "You mean more to me than anyone besides Micah."

He smiled. Then he pulled my face back to his and pushed our lips together. His hands moved from my back to the front of my high waisted jeans. He rushed to unclasp the buttons and snuck his hand inside.

CHAPTER THIRTY-TWO

JEREMY

That was the first night since the day that I overdosed that I felt like there was a fighting chance again. She said it, she wanted me. I mattered. I wasn't chasing an empty dream. She loved me. and she wanted what I wanted.

The subconscious part of my mind knew exactly why she wouldn't let me come back. If I would have detoxed months ago, she probably would have taken me back that night. Hell, she may have taken me back weeks ago when we found out Micah was alive.

But I wasn't stable. She couldn't depend on me. I spent at least a couple hours of every day nodding off on the toilet. Thinking back on it, I had to have known that.

She fell asleep with her head on my chest around one thirty. I lay there for a while listening to her breathe and admiring the way she looked in the glow of the moonlight.

But at some point, my nose started running and my legs got restless. I had a few pills in my pocket. That's why I hadn't managed to fall asleep yet, I needed to get high. So I grabbed my pants and carried them to the bathroom. I didn't shut the door the whole way because I knew the sound of the knob would wake her.

Then I did what I'd done a thousand times. Dusted off the counter, used the decorative candle to crush them up, and slid my credit card through the powder to split up even lines. I rolled up the dollar bill, lowered myself to the counter, and took a long sniff.

In all fairness, it could have been worse. I could've been using a needle. That probably would have been more disturbing given her hatred for them.

The door creaked open, and I heard her voice. "So this is what it looked like that day, huh?"

My stomach dropped. Sure, we'd just done a couple lines of molly. But what did I do when she wasn't watching? Got up to go get high.

I turned quickly and wiped my nose. "I just—"

"You couldn't sleep. You're so far in that you probably can't sleep without it anymore, right?" Laila tightened the white sheet around her chest. "I've done a lot of research. There's a lot of information out there for people that love addicts, did you know that?"

I didn't know what to say. I felt like a kid who got their hand stuck in the cookie jar.

"You know what they tell us?" she asked. "They say that you have to love them through their addiction. And I do, I do love you. They say that we can't make you get clean; you have to want to do that for yourself. And I know that you're using, and I try to act like it doesn't bother me because that's what I'm supposed to do. I'm supposed to love you from a distance and wait for you to be ready to get sober, but seeing it play out in front of..." She huffed. Her eyes filled with tears. She let out an ironic laugh.

"You were right here." She gestured to the ground. "And I'm not supposed to make you feel guilty, so I'm sorry if I do but you were right fucking *here*. Your lips were blue." Her eyes flooded with tears. She gazed at the ground with her hand still extended toward it. "You wouldn't open your eyes and you weren't breathing. And I didn't feel it because overdosing on opioids doesn't cause pain." She looked back up, salty water glistening her cheeks. "Your leg was bent all weird, and you must have hit your head on the way down, but you were so fucked up that neither of us even felt it, so I couldn't even keep you safe. I wouldn't have even known you were dead if I wasn't here and didn't hear you fall off the toilet."

"Laila, I'm so sorry—" I reached out to wipe her tears.

She pushed my hands away and continued, "But before I found you, I had this indescribable feeling of emptiness. It's hard to explain. Almost like there was a black hole inside of my chest that was sucking my life into it. You probably know that feeling, you felt me die. But I didn't ask Adrian to stab me, I didn't want to leave you. And I'm so mad at you because now I understand why that had to happen. I'm *glad* that she's dead, Jeremy, because I'd rather it be her than you. Because if Adrian hadn't stabbed me all those years ago, then I would have never known what Hannah was and she wouldn't have been able to save you. You would have been dead. You would be gone, and I would be a widow and... And I'm happy it's her who's dead and not you, and I hate that I feel that way." Her curling lip started to swell. "You would be gone forever. And my last memory of you would be you lying dead on our bathroom floor. For what, Jeremy? For a couple pills? For a short high?" Her teary eyes overflowed. She pressed her teeth together to keep them from chattering. "You'd leave all of this for that? You'd leave me for that?"

I was so fucking close. She looked at me that night the way she used to. I could see it, she was almost ready to ask me to come home.

And I fucked it up again. She found me doing exactly what I'd done that caused the breakup in the first place. She didn't just have PTSD from the months she spent in captivity, she had PTSD from what I'd done to her. And now, she was reliving that moment again.

"No. Laila, I—"

"I didn't even know what was happening. I had no idea, Jeremy. Not until Adam put the naloxone up your nose. Then it all clicked, and I kept thinking, 'How didn't I know? Why wouldn't he tell me? He promised he would tell me, why didn't he tell me?'" She raised her hand to wipe her cheeks. "You go on and on about how sex isn't enough for you. That you want more than this. But how am I supposed to want more from you when you're like this?"

"Baby, I'm so sorry." I reached out to take her hands. "I'll get clean. I swear, I'll stop. I will, I just need a little time to wean myself down. Please, just give me a little time."

She pulled her hands away. "I'm going to go to bed. You can sleep on the couch if you want. Or you can go home. But I want to be alone. I'll see you tomorrow when we talk to Helena."

"Laila." I grabbed her hand.

She yanked it away and turned back to me with furrowed brows. "No, Jeremy. I'm sorry, I understand that you didn't choose to be an addict. But we do choose what kind of parents we're going to be. This isn't just occasional abuse or relapse; this is full blown addiction. And I'm getting my son back. When I do, I won't have this shit around him. He can't grow up like this. I want him to be normal. I don't want him to have a traumatic childhood that he has to spend his entire life healing from. So get clean if you want to be his parent. Because you won't have that opportunity if you're using."

For the first time since we'd broken up, anger flooded through me. She tossed the biggest double standard at me. We'd just gotten high together and then she was going to keep my son for me as if she were any better?

"And are you going to stop drinking? Because I don't know how many times I've picked your drunken, puke covered body up off this bathroom floor either. I had to *bathe* you after you gashed your head open because you were too drunk to use your fucking feet."

It was like vomit. The words tasted awful as they left my lips. As soon as I spoke them, I wished I could swallow them back down. It was the truth, but it wasn't a fair argument.

She'd been tortured for months. She felt safe for the first time since she was taken, and she wanted to lose touch with reality for a minute. She wanted to spend some time with her friend and feel the way she used to. I should have never held that against her, but she was holding my son over me.

Laila's vibrant eyes glowed a bright green. She clenched her jaw and tightened her fist. "I know when not to drink. I know when to not get high. And I lost my fucking son. I thought he was dead because of me. I was the reason over a hundred people were still being tortured. I just killed dozens of people I had sworn my life to protect. I hated myself. I didn't want to fucking be alive." Her voice was coated in pain and fury. "I was hurting, and I thought you wanted to help me. I didn't know you'd use my moments of weakness as ammunition in an argument. So fuck you for throwing that up in my face." Her teeth gritted and her voice raised. "Fuck you for vowing to respect me and honor me for the rest of our lives while you were standing in front of all of our friends and lying to me. Fuck you for ruining this marriage. Fuck you for hurting me. Fuck you for telling me through sickness and health." She turned away and started to the bedroom.

"You vowed to be my strength when I was weak." I walked after her into the hallway. "You vowed to be there through sickness and health too and you didn't even notice that I was dying."

"Because you lied to me!" she yelled, turning around. She walked closer, tears pouring down her cheeks. "You told Olivia, but you didn't tell me. You told Adam, but you didn't tell me. You fucking lied, Jeremy. I would have been there for you if you didn't keep it from me, but you did. I couldn't be your strength because you had me convinced you were the strong one. And it's *my* fault? How is it my fault that *you* lied?" She raised her hand from the sheet and pushed my chest. "How is this my fault? What did I do wrong? Why, Jeremy? Why do I fucking deserve this?"

The questions didn't sound rhetoric as they left her lips. They were angry, but she wasn't just saying it for the hell of it. She blamed herself for everything. She wanted to know what she did to karmically justify the life we had in front of us.

And it broke my heart. Because maybe losing Micah was partly her fault. But our failed marriage was one hundred percent on me.

She'd been doing better. Then she found me like that. She found those messages with Olivia. And then she wanted to die again.

If we had Micah, she wouldn't be the mess she'd become. She'd have her shit together. She wouldn't be snorting lines of ecstasy and drinking bottle after bottle of whiskey.

Me though? If we got Micah back at that very moment, I'd still put a needle in my vein the next morning. I'd say that it was because I needed to come off them slow. But then I'd crush it up and say, 'oh, I can't let all of that go to waste,' and bang the whole thing.

Because I was an addict. She wasn't. An abuser, definitely, but not an addict. She could maintain a life and still use drugs and alcohol recreationally. But I couldn't. I always had to go hard, because if I wasn't fucked up out of my mind, what was the point?

I hurt her. I hurt her so much, and I hated myself for that.

And she was right.

I couldn't hurt my son the way that I'd hurt her.

"It isn't," I whispered. She stared up at me with angry, glowing green eyes. Her expression was hard to explain. She was furious, but her gaze was laced with pain. "It isn't your fault. And you don't deserve this. Any of it. You don't deserve to hurt."

The glow of her eyes gradually began to recede, but the tears continued to trail down her cheeks.

"I'm sorry I said that, about you drinking. I know you're responsible. You can drink and do drugs and still hold your life together. But you're right. You can't trust me around our baby if I'm on drugs. I could OD, or nod off, and anything could happen and..."

My lip began to quiver, and I bit it to keep it steady. Tears burned my eyes. "I know you're going to be a great mom. You already love him so much. I won't say something like that again. Just please don't hold my son over my head either. I love him too. I know I'm shitty at a lot of things, but

I'm not going to be a shitty dad. I haven't even met him, and I already love him so much. Please don't use him against me."

Laila wiped her cheeks. The glow in her eyes softened. She gazed at me in silence for a long moment. "I shouldn't have said that. I'm sorry. I wouldn't keep my kid from his dad. All that would do is hurt him. I just saw you standing there, and then I remembered you..." She pressed her lips together, eyes watering again.

"Yeah. Yeah, I know."

"I'm sorry. I... I shouldn't have talked to you like that."

"I shouldn't have gotten high in the room that I died in a few months ago." I shook my head. "I'm sorry."

Her gaze turned toward the floor. "I'll see you tomorrow. At Leah's, right? To talk to that Witch?"

"Yeah, twelve thirty."

She gave a fast nod back, still looking down. "Twelve thirty."

My gaze shifted over her. That long, red hair. Those pretty green eyes. The tattoos, the scars, everything that made her into the woman she was now.

And I realized that I was a fucking idiot.

I knew what I wanted. I knew what I had to do to get it. It was gonna be a bitch, but I had to make the choice and put in the effort.

I had to get clean. Not even for her. Not even for Micah, not really. For me. To be the dad I swore I'd be. To do better for my family than my dad had done for me. To have something to be proud of again.

"I know you don't want to hear this, Laila, but I'm going to make it right. I'm going to give you a reason to believe in me again," I whispered.

She tightened the sheet around her chest. Finally, she looked back up. "I never stopped believing in you, Jeremy. I just can't be the only one here who does. You're the one who gave up on being the best version of yourself. I know that I'm not either. I shouldn't cast stones in a glass house. But I'm trying. I'm going to do better. You told me that once, remember? That you'd do better."

She smiled slightly. "Yeah. Yeah, I remember. And I did. It took some time but." She paused. "I did."

"I will too."

"I hope so, Jeremy," she murmured.

I placed my hand at the back of her head, leaned forward, and touched my lips to her crown. "I'm going to. I swear, I am."

She tucked her arms around my back and brought her chest to mine. I felt her body quake, fighting back a sob. "I don't want you to die. I want my son to have a father. I know how good of a dad you'll be, and I want you to be around long enough for him to see that."

Tears welled in my eyes. I leaned my head against hers. I felt her warm, fiery skin beneath my hands and squeezed tighter. Those eight words hit harder than any addiction lecture I'd ever had to sit through.

I want my son to have a father.

I wanted that too. I wanted that more than I wanted anything.

"I don't want to die either," was all that I could make out without my glistening tears turning to weeps.

She tightened her arms so hard around me that I almost struggled to breathe. I meant it that time. I wanted to do better.

I didn't want to be sober. But I wanted to be a good dad more than I wanted to get high.

I knew that after a couple months, I'd be okay without it. I just had to make it through the first week and the rest would get easier. If I could get past the worst of the withdrawals, I could do it. I'd done it before, and I could do it again.

CHAPTER THIRTY-THREE

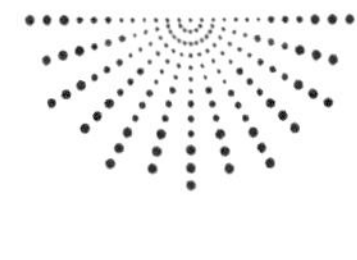

LAILA

I stood at the bathroom mirror dusting a thin layer of bronzer just below my cheekbone. Once I did either side, I moved my blender to my concealer coated under eyes. I dabbed hard in a desperate attempt to cover the deep circles. After my fight with Jeremy last night, I had a hard time falling back to sleep. The comedown from MDMA was never a fun time but that argument certainly didn't make it any easier.

Liam texted three times so far. They were the same sweet texts he sent every morning.

Good morning, gorgeous
I might be asleep by the time you get this, but I just want you to know that I
hope you have a good day.
Let me know if you need anything<3 And let me know if you need to cancel
our plans for this weekend. I know you have a lot going on so no worries if so

What the fuck should I say to that when I was up half the night rolling my nuts off and fucking someone else? Especially when I wasn't ashamed that it happened.

I *enjoyed* last night. I was happy with Jeremy. Until that fight, I felt like I was floating. I guess it could have been the drugs. But Jeremy always had a way of making me forget the rest of the world. I hated that he made the rest of my thoughts foggy, but I loved it in the same breath.

I slid my phone back into my pocket, began blending my makeup, and drifted away to the music that played off my speakers. I couldn't think about all of that.

This was about my son. It wasn't about Jeremy or Liam or any of our stupid fucking feelings. This was about Micah.

***

The smell of warm apples and coffee drifted to my nose. I looked out the French doors at the bright afternoon sun. Chatter from the TV in the front room vibrated to my ears. I lifted my purse and set it to the counter.

"Hey, lady," Leah said. "Looks like you had a long night."

I sat beside her and laid my head against the granite countertop. "Is it that bad? I thought my makeup covered up the bags."

"No, you just have a giant hickey on the back of your neck." She gestured to where my hair rested against my back. "I thought you didn't let Liam do that."

I sat up quickly and pulled my hair over my shoulder to cover it. Her eyes widened, and she smiled. "It wasn't Liam, was it? You little hoe. Who was it?"

Jeremy turned down the steps. He looked just as exhausted as me with deep purple circles beneath his bloodshot blue eyes. He may have even looked worse than me. He was a little clammy, wiping his nose and rubbing his eyes. As he pushed hair from his face, he revealed a big purplish bruise near his ear.

Leah gasped. Then she excitedly grasped my bicep. "You guys slept together."

Ugh. Well, it was Leah. She was bound to find out eventually. The bitch knew everything.

Jeremy smiled. "What?"

"Don't even try to lie to me." Leah grinned. "But oof, you slept here. Ouch."

"Fuck off." Jeremy made his way to the fridge and pulled out a bottle of water.

"Well, there was no celebratory group text so I take it I shouldn't mention this to anyone," Leah muttered.

"It doesn't mean we're back together," I said quietly. "There's a lot going on right now. We can worry about us later."

"Micah's the top priority." Jeremy poured a cup of coffee. "Not us."

He set the coffee in front of me. I gave a smile. He smiled back.

"He's what this is all about."

"Right. Speaking of which. I have some thoughts on that letter you gave me." Leah closed her laptop. She laid it on the counter and opened the paper.

"Okay, see these little specks up here?" Leah pointed to some orange dots at the bottom of the page near the signature that appeared slightly smeared into the closing.

"Yeah, it looks like coffee or something," Jeremy said.

She lifted it to her nose and sniffed. Her head shook. "Tea, actually. Wyatt sniffed it, he said it was definitely tea, but not like any he's smelled before. So I had an idea. They might be able to identify the brand. There aren't all that many orange teas out there. If it's a specialty blend, and expensive, which it probably is if this is Nastya La Fay, maybe I can track down the people who've ordered it. So I ordered a bunch of variety packs online with high end brands. Maybe it's stupid, but I might be able to get something. I might be able to cross reference it with wholesalers and get us a list of places which might just give us a general vicinity of where they are."

"Talk about a hail Mary," Jeremy muttered. "But it's something. I like it, let's go for it."

These were the types of pathetic leads we were chasing. Little tiny snippets that couldn't possibly lead us to my son. But we had to chase something.

Leah looked at me. "It's not ideal, I know. But we have a few leads with Lydia and Anastasia. Maybe she'll be able to help. If not, Mary might have something for us. Oh, she stopped over, by the way. She said she'd heard the name Wormwood at some point a few hundred years ago, but doesn't know much about it. I guess she's dealing with some shit going down in her new clan. But she's going to ask around and get back to us in a couple days."

"Damn," I muttered. I stowed the letter away in my purse. "Alright. Well, hopefully the Witch has some information that we can go on in the meantime. What's her name again?"

"Helena," Jeremy said.

CHAPTER THIRTY-FOUR

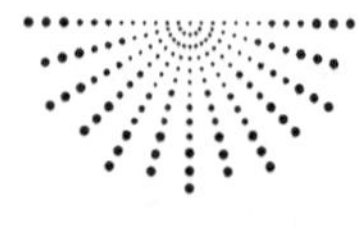

LAILA

"This must be the famous hybrid," a raspy voice said from the doorway to the kitchen. I turned and got the first glimpse at the Witch whose name I'd heard a hundred times over the years.

She was an older woman with long locs ending on strands of beads. Jeremy was a few inches over six foot tall and Helena was still a good bit taller than him. She had sharply padded shoulders but svelte and elegant arms. Her facial features were soft. She wore sparkly golden eye shadow sprinkled over her thick, false eyelashes above light brown eyes. She wore a nude ombré that faded from a dark, almost purplish color to a light, soft shade of pink where her lips met.

"That's me." I smiled, stepping down from the bar stool.

She smiled and extended her hand to mine. "Quite a name you've made for yourself."

"I haven't done that much."

"You will." She smiled. Then she pulled away and placed her bag on the table of the breakfast nook. She glanced at me and then back to Jeremy. "So why wasn't I invited to the wedding?"

Jeremy laughed and looked at me.

"I'm to blame for that." I raised my hand. "Our last big gathering didn't go very well. I wanted it small."

"Mhmm," she said. She sat at the breakfast nook. "Let's get down to business then, shall we?"

"Sure." Jeremy sat at the bench across from her. I slid in beside him as Helena began to unpack her bag.

"You said that you recently discovered that your son was alive." Helena laid a small purple cloth over the table. In the middle, she set a small metal bowl. She lined an array of crystals in a perfect circle around it.

"Yes. Yesterday we learned that he was bound to another young girl that was being held by them."

"And she's Fae too?" Helena asked.

"Yeah. But Micah's Elite. Lydia only has earth and spirit."

"So they're bound through consciousness," Helena said. "That's good."

"What do you mean?" I asked.

"The bond connects their minds. Their physical bodies are tethered too, similar to the way the two of you are connected." She gestured between us. "You feel each other's pain but only in an empathic sense. Your bodies are connected but they don't fuel each other."

"So if something happens to Micah. Lydia will know, she'll feel it. But it can't kill her."

"Not unless she has some predisposition. Heart condition that may cause cardiac arrest due to the stress of his pain. An aneurysm at risk of rupturing," Helena said. "Healthy kid won't die from empathy. Might fuck up her head but she'll live."

Well, I supposed that was a relief. I was more concerned about Micah dying than Lydia, but it was nice to know that she wouldn't die if he did.

"Is there a way to break it?" Jeremy asked.

Helena cocked her head to the side. "Would you want me to if I could?"

Neither me nor Jeremy could meet her gaze because no, we wouldn't want to lose the only tether we had to our son.

"If you had two pieces of the puzzle, I could be the third to break it. But no. Not just with the kid. I'd need them both. Or the Witch who cast it. Binding spells are triads. There's always a third link."

"So that's why she wanted Moriah to bind herself to him."

"That's what I would do. If another Witch as powerful as her bound her to him, she'd have *way* more power than any La Fay should."

Thank the stars that Moriah brought that to me then. At least I really knew where her allegiance was now.

"What about binding one of us to him? Would that be possible?" Jeremy asked.

"Is it possible?" She arched a brow. "Absolutely." My heart skipped with excitement. Then she said, "If we had him here. But not with a lock of hair. Honestly, I'm not even sure it'd work for Moriah. It might strengthen her powers on some existential level? But it wouldn't help you find him. The barriers she has in place block everything out. The only way binding him to one of you would help is if we had blood or soul—and we'd need a good bit of either. A tiny lock of hair wouldn't do shit but let you tap into his abilities. Which I don't think will help you either."

My stomach dropped, and I fought the swell in my throat.

That was why she'd given Moriah his hair. Nastya clearly believed heavily in her cause. She was willing to help her sister by strengthening her power through my son, but she wasn't willing to risk losing their savior.

"Is there a way to track his location through their link?" Jeremy asked. "The way that I can find Laila and she can find me through ours."

"Not if there's a Witch who knows how to conceal their location. How did she block it from you for so long?" She looked between Jeremy and me.

"She was in my head," I said. "Not the Witch, another Fae."

"Hmm," Helena murmured. "You're sure this is Nastya La Fay?"

"We think so," Jeremy said.

"That type of ancestral magic is strong. Way stronger than mine. I can do some research. Maybe work up a spell of my own. But it's going to take a good bit of time. And I'm going to have to use my own resources."

Jeremy made a face. "How much are we talking?"

It began to piece together then. Any time someone mentioned Helena over the years, he'd roll his eyes and scoff. There were plenty of people in our world that Jeremy didn't like so I never questioned it. But now, I saw why.

We helped people for free. Helena helped people for a hefty price. But I got it. I wouldn't ask for money in exchange for saving a life, but I inherited a business. We all had to make a living and this was how Helena made hers.

She gave a quiet chuckle. "Jeremy, what you're asking me to do is suicide. We know who Anastasia La Fay is. You're asking me to risk my life for your kid."

"What if you come up with nothing, Helena?" Jeremy leaned across the table.

"Five thousand if I find nothing that helps in six months."

Jeremy snorted and crossed his arms against his chest. "And if you do find something? What then?"

"Well, reimbursement for materials of course," she said.

"Oh, of course." Jeremy nodded with furrowed brows.

"Ten thousand if I get you a lead," she continued.

"Jesus Christ," Jeremy grumbled.

"And fifty if I get you a successful location. Paid after you have your son in your arms."

"Fifty thousand dollars," I said.

Sounded more than reasonable to me. I'd give her every penny in my account if it brought my baby home.

"Two thousand five hundred down as a deposit to start looking for the first six months."

"And if you give us multiple leads, is that ten thousand each until we reach the fifty thousand?" I asked. "At which point, you'll continue to work for us free of charge."

Helena gave a smile. Then she chuckled. "Up to seventy-five. Then I'll work for free. For one year, then we'll have to work out another contract."

"Look, I'll pay seventy-five thousand dollars to get my son back," I said. "More than that even. But if I find out you're withholding information at any point to prolong your paycheck and cutting into the time I could be spending with my child, things won't end well for you."

Helena smiled wider. Then she turned to Jeremy. "I like her."

He smiled at me and looked back to her. "Yeah, me too."

Helena reached her arm across the table. "You got yourself a deal, girl. I wanna get your kid back. I keep my word. Find me on Yelp, I have a four-point five-star rating. Would be five, but some people give me three and say, 'I love her work.' If you love my work, where are my other two stars?"

I laughed.

She gave a smile. "There's something I'd like to do for you two. If you'd like, anyway. On the house."

"You're already robbing us, it isn't really on the house," Jeremy muttered.

"What is it?" I asked.

"Well, a complimentary reading, of course." She pulled her tarot from her bag. "But a magnification spell for your bond too."

"What do you mean?" I asked.

"It wouldn't change much. The only difference would be your ability to tap into one another from a distance. It wouldn't be as much of a strain." She looked between us. "And you'll be able to feed off of each other's energy. Basically, it'd make your powers more potent. I've always wanted to cast it, but no one is willing to use their power to fuel someone else's. But you guys already do that. It'd keep you safe."

"I don't understand. Would it weaken our powers?" I asked.

"In most people," Helena said. "At least, when the other person is borrowing your energy."

"But not us," Jeremy said. "Our energy is already connected. It's why we're stronger when we're together."

"It would make morion and hematite impervious to Jeremy. He'd use energy from your Fae abilities that would feed his Guardian abilities."

"She's basically talking about an amplifier. It would just make what's already there stronger," he said.

Jeremy being unaffected by morion and hematite? Hell yeah. Then he'd have no weakness, just as I had. If by some short chance they ever tried to kidnap him like they had me, he'd have the same fighting chance that I did.

"We should do it then. We need to be as strong as we can be. If you're okay with that, Jeremy."

"Yeah, it's a good idea."

Helena pulled a small athame from her bag. "Not afraid of a little blood, are you, Laila?"

"No. Blood and I are old pals."

"Alright then. You'll have to let this heal on its own. Don't use any of that Fae magic or it'll cancel out."

"Looks good." Helena rubbed some of the blood herb mixture into the slit at my wrist. "It's probably going to get infected, so you should get on antibiotics ASAP. But leave this solvent in the skin for at least twelve hours before you clean it out."

"I have to work later, am I alright to wrap it in gauze?" I asked.

"Covering is fine, just don't remove it." She stood, walked to the sink, and began washing her bloody fingers.

"Can I get through, babe?" Jeremy placed his hand over his pale lips. His skin was a light, almost greenish color.

I stood. "Are you alright?"

"Yeah." He started to the bathroom. "Just not feeling great."

"Weak ass stomach." Helena gave a playful grin, drying her hands on a dish towel. "If he isn't back by the time I'm done with your reading, then I'm heading out. I can catch him later."

"I'll be leaving when we're done here too."

It didn't seem like Jeremy was all that interested in having his tarot read anyway.

But I was. I wasn't sure why; tarot and witchcraft had never really been my thing. I suppose I was just looking for some sign. Anything that would give me reassurance. Anything to give me hope.

That's all I wanted. Just a little bit of hope.

She sat in front of me. "So I'm going to give you a large reading here. Past, present, and future. Three cards for each."

I watched her carefully shuffle them around in her hands. She closed her eyes and she laid them in neat little stacks. Then she gingerly flipped the first card over.

A man in a dress holding a rose in his hand looked up at me. He carried a sack attached to a stick that hung behind his shoulder.

"The fool." I laughed as I bit my lower lip. "This is my past, right?"

"Yes. But this isn't an inherently bad card. The fool represents the beginning of the cycle. The inner child, innocence. This was your origin."

Seemed logical to me. Prior to last year, I'd been quite the fool.

She moved to the next card. A man and woman stood on green grass. They were both naked. A snake wrapped around a tree's trunk behind the woman, and a burning tree was erected behind the man. In the clouds above them floated a man with big black wings and flaming red hair.

The lovers.

Another laugh. "Well, that's a given."

She smiled as a quiet chuckle left her lips. "Not much need be said for that one, huh?"

"I suppose not."

Then she flipped over the next card. A woman in a long white gown, pouring water from one glass to the other.

"The temperance," Helena murmured. "It represents balance. Diluting wine with water, one foot in the creek, another on the grass. Balance."

Also accurate. I'd been pretty balanced in my past. Not so much these days, but I had been for a time. "Sounds about right."

Helena moved to the next row. "This is your present. This is where you are now, where you've been in the recent past and where you'll be in the near future."

This one didn't look so pretty. It was a pillar on fire. People jumped from windows, the backdrop was black, lightning struck its top. Couldn't help but feel like this particular card should've been in the past because I wasn't currently blowing up any buildings.

"The tower," I murmured.

"It's also a card of rebirth. Burning the bridge to build anew." She gave a smile. "The death of an imaginary ego. A sudden awareness of your need to be reborn."

Well, when she put it that way... Yeah, I could definitely go for some rebirth.

She moved onto the next card.

I looked down at the man hanging from a rope. "That's lovely."

"Also not an inherently bad card. It represents everything you know being turned upside down. Letting go of your ego. A dramatic shift in your world," Helena said. "Does that sound familiar?"

An internal huff echoed within me. There was a lot of ego death going on here. Which was entirely accurate. In the last year, I may have gained a lot of confidence. But I also realized my lack of control in the grand scheme of things.

"It all sounds pretty familiar," I muttered.

She moved onto the next card. As she flipped it over, my heart skipped a beat.

A woman on a thrown in the middle of a field of grain. Her stomach protruded wide from her abdomen, at least eight months pregnant. She wore a crown of stars atop her head.

All that I saw there was a mother.

The empress.

"The great mother. The Goddess of fertility and beauty." Helena gave a soft smile.

I smiled back.

"And now the future."

The moment I'd been waiting for. Perhaps my bit of hope.

She flipped over the first card to reveal the world. "The completed journey. Grounding. Seeing reality for what it truly is instead of shrouded by emotion."

"Sounds refreshing." I smiled.

She smiled back and lifted the next card. It was the same as the second one she'd placed. "The lovers."

"Of course," I said. "Wait, why's it there twice?"

"I'm using two decks."

"Why's that?" I asked.

"Because sometimes the future lies in the past and vice versa."

Huh. Well, aside from the last year, my past hadn't been so bad. I hoped that she was right.

She flipped over the last card, and my heart melted.

"The sun," I whispered.

He who shines brighter than the sun.

A smile edged up my cheeks. There was my bit of hope.

"This is the best card in the deck you could get for the future," Helena said softly. "It represents joy. Ecstasy. Celebration and positive energy. Warmth, love, happiness. It is your regained sense of innocence."

That reading gave me hope. One day, we *would* get our happily ever after. One day, it *would* all make sense. A time would come when we understood the world and the lives we lived. We'd understand it in a way that no one else ever could.

CHAPTER THIRTY-FIVE

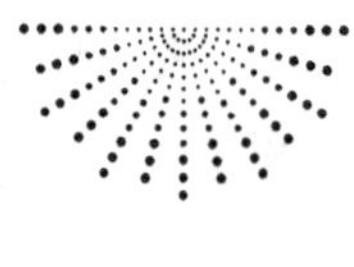

JEREMY

Gripping the bathroom sink for support with one hand, I splashed cold water against my face with the other. I cupped some water in my hand and slurped it up. Gurgling for a moment, I spit it back to the sink. I panted hard to stay steady.

I laid my head against the wall behind me and gazed at myself in the mirror. I looked almost as shitty as I felt.

My face was almost green. Snot dribbled from my nose, and water ran from my eyes. My muscles felt like tight, hard pieces of metal grinding between my nerves. It felt like my throat was on fire from the acid stinging its way up my esophagus. My ribs throbbed from the contractions of my abdomen. Even my asshole stung from the diarrhea.

Not a pretty sight. So much of me wanted to go upstairs and jam that needle into my forearm. Or crush a pill and put it up my nose. Or swallow it whole. It didn't really matter, as long as I could stop feeling like shit.

I was irritable. I was hungry. I was dehydrated. And it only just started. It was going to get a lot worse. And last for a week at least.

But then, there was a quiet knock at the door.

"Hey, are you alright?" Laila's soft voice said from the hallway.

And then, I was reminded of why it was all worth it. Miserable or not, if it meant I got her back, if it meant I got the family I craved so badly, it was worth it.

Micah and Laila were all that I wanted. I loved the way I felt when I was high, but I hated the guilt it brought on. And being with her never brought me guilt. Being a good father would never make me guilty either.

They mattered more.

I wiped my face with the hand towel and opened the door. I forced a smile. "Yeah. Yeah, I'm alright. Just think I'm coming down with something."

She ran her hand along her stomach. "Yeah, feels like you got something going on. Do you need me to get you any aspirin? Or Pepto Bismol?"

"No, I'm okay. Thank you though. I have some ginger ale, I have weed. I'll be alright in a couple days."

"Well, Helena left. She said she'll do your reading another time."

"It doesn't matter. I'd rather she spend her time looking for something that'll help find our son."

She smiled. "It was kinda nice actually. Restored my faith in the future a bit."

I gave a smile back.

But honestly, tarot was bullshit. It was originally created as an interactive card game in the 1400's with Christian roots. I had no idea why it became a part of witchcraft in the first place. Still, if it brought her a little bit of peace, I wasn't going to interfere with that.

"Hey, I'm sorry about last night. It shouldn't have gotten to that point. It probably shouldn't have happened at all."

I frowned. "Don't say that."

"I just... I wasn't trying to hurt you. I was coming down and I wasn't exactly feeling my best, but I could have handled it better. I said things I shouldn't have." She frowned too. "I'm sorry."

"We probably needed it," I said. "We fight, Laila. We argue. We challenge each other, we always have. It's been a while since we had one of those blow outs. Things needed to be said."

"They could have been conveyed in a less dramatic manner." She gave a sad smile. Then it slowly fell. "But I don't think we should do that again. Not any time soon, anyway."

I knew what she meant. And she was probably right. We weren't the friends with benefits kind of couple. No one can be friends with benefits with someone they're in love with and not be a couple. After all, what separates friendship from a relationship is sex.

Either we needed to be friends, or we needed to get back together. She wasn't ready for the romance. I needed to get my shit together before I was.

It was best if we kept sex out of the equation until we were both ready to get back together.

"What, molly?" I smiled.

She narrowed her gaze a bit but still smiled. "You know what, Jeremy."

"Yeah, I do."

She rubbed the bridge of my nose. "It's not that I... I don't regret it, and I don't want you to think I didn't enjoy it. It was fun, and sweet, and..." A smile pulled at her lips. Then it quickly dropped. "I know that you know what you want. And I wish that I did, but I don't. There's just so much going on right now. And if I keep fucking you, I'm... I'm leading you to think that we're at a point that we aren't."

"I know you aren't ready to get back together, Lai. We talked about it last night, remember?" I gave a gentle nod. "I get it. I hurt you and I haven't done much to prove that I won't again. I don't blame you."

She slid her phone from her pocket. Then she sighed down at the picture of Liam lighting up her screen. She shuttered it and slid it back into her pocket.

He wasn't making things any easier either.

But the fact that she ignored his call gave me a short-lived ego-boost.

"And now someone else's feelings are in the mix."

She met my gaze. "I'm just really confused right now. And I... It's not that I don't want you around or that I want to go back to how things were before you came back. I'm happy that we're spending time together again. But right now, I just... I need you to be my friend. I don't want distractions, I just want to find my son."

Exactly as I'd thought a moment prior.

A soft smile tugged at my lips. "I have a lot of work to do on myself too, Lai. I kind of need a friend more than a wife right now too."

She smiled back. Only slightly, but it was there. At least we were on the same page.

Laila cleared her throat. "That new server just quit. Said she got a better job offer somewhere else. So I'm going to be pretty busy this week until I find a replacement."

"Well, if you need a hand—" I began.

"You're sick as hell and we just got past a pandemic. You can't handle food right now." She laughed. "No, but thank you. You just feel better. And let me know if you hear anything from Mary or Helena. I will too."

Yeah, that was good thinking. I felt like total ass. If she needed me to, I would be there without a second thought. But I really needed to lie down.

"Sounds good."

"I'm pretty sure chicken noodle is the soup of the day today." Laila gave a sweet smile. "Do you want me to bring you some by later?"

My smile widened. "That'd be really nice of you. If you have the time, I don't want to be a burden."

She smiled too. "I'll drop some off tonight. I'll call first to make sure you aren't asleep. I probably won't stay long, I have those plumbers coming early tomorrow to work on the French drain. I'm gonna go home though. I hope you feel better."

Fuck, me too. But I was glad she wasn't gonna stick around for long. Not because I didn't want to see her, I just didn't want her to see me in the shape that I was in.

"That's okay. Drive safe."

She turned and started down the hall. As she pulled on her jacket, she smiled. "You can text me if you want. I know you aren't feeling good, so if you're just bored and..." She let out an awkward, shy laugh. "I don't know. Just text me if you have time."

That sweet smile, that maladroit little giggle, it made it all worth it.

I was gonna make it through this hellacious week. I was gonna be her friend. And I was gonna get my wife back.

"Yeah, I will."

Once she pulled on her boots, she turned back to me over her shoulder. "And Jeremy?"

"Yeah?" I asked.

She still wore that gentle smile. "I love you."

My smile lifted. "I love you too."

We were going to move past the last year. I knew we would. I'd get clean. She'd let me come home. We'd find our son. And we'd get our happily ever after, damn it.

I just had to stay clean.

She turned, headed out the door, and gently shut it behind her.

Leah grinned, leaning in the doorway that led to the front sitting room. "I told your ass to come home. I knew it'd help things between you two."

"We aren't in a great place or anything. But I guess it's better than where we were."

"I know she says she doesn't want to have sex again but we both know Laila. She'll get horny and she'll call," Leah said.

The sex last night had been great, don't get me wrong. But I didn't want that. The sex didn't matter if I didn't get to hold her while she slept and make her coffee in the morning. Honestly, last night had only happened because *she* wanted it.

"No. No, she's right. We shouldn't keep playing games. It's painful and messy and... She says she doesn't regret it, but she does. And I don't want that, you know? I don't want to sleep with anyone else, but I don't just want to be her booty call either."

"So that's what last night was? A booty call?" Leah asked.

"No, not exactly. It just kind of happened."

"Then why'd she give you the boot?" Leah asked.

Once we sat on the couch, I went into the story. I explained it all. How it started, how amazing it was, and then how it ended.

Biting my lip, I twirled my wedding ring. "I can't be the one thing I want to be more than anything if I don't get my shit together. It's not even about her. I love her, and I want her, but it's about my kid. I want to be a good dad."

Leah studied me for a moment. Then she smiled. "You're detoxing."

I gave a nod. "I'm going to get clean."

"But you aren't telling her?" Leah asked.

"No, I'm not. Not yet, anyway. I don't want her to think this is about her. That's what she'll say. That she guilted me into this. That it's not what I really want. But it is. I want to be proud of myself again. I might not have a career, or a marriage, or an education, but if I can get clean, I can be proud of something again."

Leah's smile softened.

"And I can be a good dad." I licked my dry lips. "Because that's all I really want, you know? I just want my kid to know that I love him. Last night, Laila said something, about wanting to raise a kid that doesn't have to heal from their childhood. I'm still healing from mine and Micah's going to have his own trauma already by the time we get him. I don't want to make that worse. I..." I blinked to keep my eyes from watering. "I found my dad when he died. And I don't want Micah to have to live that. I've already overdosed what—Four times?

"I can't. I've put all of you through watching me die, but I can't let Micah go through that too. If I die, it's going to be when I'm old and gray or because I went down fighting for something I love or because of some freak accident. It's not going to be because I wanted a quick fix."

Leah's green eyes twinkled with tears. "That's great, Jeremy. You're about, what—Twelve hours in?"

"Maybe I should go to a meeting and get one of those stupid little white key chains."

"They aren't stupid."

Eh, she was wrong about that. The twelve steps were entirely centered around religion. And that wasn't it for me. I needed a reason to stay clean that wasn't God. And I had that. I had a damn good reason to get clean. But the keychain thing was intended as a joke.

However, it would be nice to collect one of those ten or twenty years clean ones. I'd never made it that far. But I liked to think that I would.

"The first one is. I don't want it to be just for today. This is it. I'm never touching the shit again."

"Just take it a day at a time, Jeremy," she said.

She was right. Come to think of it, going a decade without getting fucked up was kind of a hard thought to grasp. Taking it one day at a time did feel a hell of a lot easier.

"The detox is the hardest. Once the sickness stops, the worst of it's over. Or at least, that's what I'm going to tell myself to get through the next week or so."

Leah smiled. "Got to keep putting one foot in front of the other, right?"

"One foot in front of the other," I said. "Hey, do you think you and Adam could help me go through my stuff and find all the shit I have? I just don't want the temptation right there. I know I could still go get more, but I'm not going to. I just don't want it in arm's reach."

"Yeah, of course." She smiled still. Then she sat forward. "Well, I had plans with Haley but I'm going to cancel, and we are going to binge watch Netflix all week."

"You don't have to do that. It's okay, really. I'm going to be fine."

"No, you need a friend." She stood. "I'm gonna run to the store and get all the junk food I can find that doesn't taste too bad coming back up. I have a pretty good list for that. And a bunch of water, and ginger ale, and we're going veg out on the couch for a while. You don't need to be alone when the cravings kick in."

They'd already kicked in. But I wasn't gonna turn it down. I'd missed my sister a lot lately.

"Alright. Sounds like a pretty decent way to spend my misery."

"Got to look for the good in everything, right?"

CHAPTER THIRTY-SIX

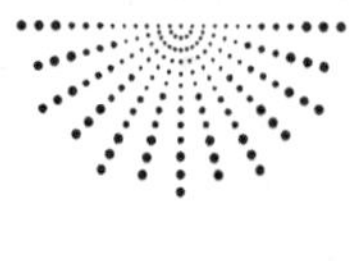

LAILA

After last night, I knew what I had to do. I didn't know exactly *what* I wanted. But I did know who. And I had to stop playing games with their heads.

My fist raised to the old wooden door on the small, covered porch. I was nearly holding my breath. Then I heard quiet footsteps pedaling toward me on the other side.

As it swung open, the preteen girl holding the handle physically gasped. Her big brown eyes widened. "Oh my God. You're Laila Callidy."

Shit.

I had promised I'd meet his little sister. And now, here I was. Meeting her. Just as I was about to tell her brother we had to stop seeing each other.

I smiled and extended my hand to her. "You must be Emma."

"Oh my god. I can't believe it's you." She practically bounced with excitement. "I—I never thought I'd get to see you again. You look amazing, I love your hair."

I smiled. "Well, I'm happy to meet you too."

"We met before. That day, when you let us all out. Oh god, I can't believe you're here." She raised her hands to cup her face. "This is so crazy."

"What are you doing, Em?" Liam called from inside. His footsteps drew closer.

222

"Can I hug you?" she asked with a big smile.

I smiled back. "Yeah, of course."

She opened her arms and practically collapsed into me. Her tight curls pressed against my chest, arms locking around my back. I gasped a bit, struggling to catch my breath through her strong grasp. But I chuckled anyway, hugging her small shoulders.

Liam made his way to the front door with a spatula in his hand.

I admired his beauty for a moment. His strong shoulders and perfectly toned chest. His green and blue plaid boxers resting at the edge of his V-shaped hips just above his dark washed jeans.

He had a touch of a five o'clock shadow along his prominent jaw line and around his mouth. He looked a bit tired, but still happy. His eyes always looked happy, gleaming like magnificent shining rays of honey through pools of melted chocolate. But when his lips smiled too, it was enough to fill any gloomy space with a beautiful, positive energy.

Jeremy was just as gorgeous but in a vastly different way. Liam had this soft yet sexy beauty that made me want to settle down. He looked like the kind of guy one would want to go to farmer's markets and PTA meetings with.

But when those long black waves fell in front of Jeremy's sad, electric blue eyes, it was almost impossible to fight the urge to collapse into his sleek, strong arms and beg him to ruin my life. He looked like a gorgeous celebrity I dreamed of fucking once and never seeing again. And I knew he had some PTA vibes in there.

Despite that sadness he carried, there was an angelic vibrancy to those blue eyes. There was tranquility and a sense of freedom. And one day, he would find that same sense of liberty and calm without that shadow of sorrow.

He was the one. The dark, tortured man I would spend the rest of my life with. Once things settled down, anyway.

He'd always be dark, that would never change. But dark is not innately bad, nor is light innately good. To all things, there must be balance. Jeremy just needed to find his.

Liam smiled when he met my gaze. "Oh, hey, baby girl."

"Hey." I made out as well as I could.

"You're gonna break her back, Em," Liam said. "She isn't a wolf, you can't hug her like that."

"Oh, right." Emma pulled away with a grin. She kept her arms around my waist but loosened her grip and rested her head against my cleavage. I laughed slightly, patting her back.

"What're you doing here?" He smiled.

"I was just wondering if we could talk."

He bit his inner cheek, reading my fake grin. "Yeah, of course. I just made lunch though, we were just sitting down to eat."

"Do you want to have lunch with us?" Emma said as she pulled away.

Ah, fuck. For whatever reason, this little girl idolized me. I'd feel like the biggest piece of shit if I didn't give her a moment of my time. On the other hand though, after this conversation with Liam, maybe she'd feel differently about me anyway.

I looked at Liam over her shoulder. He mouthed, "It's up to you."

"I'm a little busy today—" I began.

"Oh, come on, you see my brother all the time." A frown tugged at her lips.

"Emma—" Liam said.

"Just have lunch with us," she urged over him. "I eat quick."

Damn it. What was I supposed to do? Tell her no? I didn't actually have anything to do aside from a bit of paperwork. The girl's mom had just died, she felt like she was in the presence of a legend, how could I say no?

Liam mouthed that he was sorry.

I gave a smile. "What'd you make?"

"Yay!" Emma said. She took my hand and pulled me down the hallway past her brother into the kitchen. She scooted out my chair, gestured for me to sit, and lowered herself beside me at the small square table that sat a few feet from the sink.

It wasn't the first time I'd been in Liam's house, but it was the first time I saw it in the light of day. It looked a lot different when we drunkenly fumbled around ripping off each other's clothes. Honestly, it was a bit of a mess. Not as bad as Ray's was before Lydia came into the picture, just neglected.

There was a layer of dust pasted to the oven hood with a film of grease. Piles of mail stacked up on the old Formica counter by the rickety back door. The dingy yellow paint was stained a grayish color around the tops of the room from years of cigarette smoke, leaving me contemplating whether or not I should quit smoking. My shoes squeaked as I lifted them from the sticky floor. The counters had big ugly splotches of spaghetti sauce and sugary sodas.

Desperately, I resisted the urge to grab the dirty rag that hung over the spigot and scour every surface of the place. I almost was sickened with myself for having sex on that counter two weeks ago. Then I pondered if some of my DNA was still lingering on it.

"So what grade are you in, Emma?" I asked with a bare smile.

"I should be in eighth, but I got dumb in there, so I'm in sixth."

"Emma tested a little lower than most kids her age." Liam grabbed another plate from the cabinet. "But she isn't dumb."

She rolled her eyes. He turned to the table and set a grilled cheese and a bowl of tomato soup in front of her. "I don't even know how to do pre-algebra."

"Hey, neither do I." I gave a smile. "Math doesn't really matter these days anyway, we have Google for that." Behind her, Liam made a face at me. "But you'll get the hang of it. You just have to study really hard."

"I guess. I don't know, I just don't like school."

"I didn't like school either," I said. "Kids are mean, especially at your age."

"The problem doesn't seem to be the other kids." Liam set a plate in front of me and another where he sat. Then he turned back to the counter to grab two more bowls. He laid them in front of us and lowered himself to the old wooden chair. "Isn't that right, Emma?"

"He started it, I just responded."

"What happened?" I asked.

"She punched some little boy in the face and broke his nose." Liam lifted the grilled cheese to his hand. "He had to have reconstructive surgery. They're talking about suing."

"It would have healed fine on its own, he just wanted a free fix for his beak face." Emma dipped her grilled cheese in the soup and took a bite.

I couldn't help the chuckle that left my lips. Granted, I probably shouldn't have laughed. But it was funny.

Liam furrowed his brows at me. Emma smiled. I cleared my throat and put on a serious face. "Why did you hit him?"

"Because he's a jagoff."

Liam rubbed his eyes beneath his glasses. "Emma."

"What? Jagoff isn't a curse word," she said.

"Jesus Christ."

"Now that *is* a curse word," she said. "I bet Mama's rolling over in her grave."

"Can you just be quiet for, like, five minutes?" Liam raised his pointer finger. "Or just one. I'd be happy with one."

"Nope. You're stuck with me for another five years."

I smiled. Their bickering was endearing. Liam's commitment to caring for her despite how much of a pain in the ass she was melted my heart. He really was a great guy.

Just not the guy for me.

"What did he do?" I asked.

"He called me the corpse bride." She gestured to the scar on her neck. "So, I punched him."

Good for her. I'd have punched him too. Fuck that kid.

I began to shrug when Liam shot me a 'this is a teaching moment' kind of expression. I cleared my throat. "Kids can be assholes." I grimaced, realizing I swore. "But you have to rise above it. And I'm not telling you not to speak up for yourself. But you can absolutely do that without violence. Just make him feel bad about himself too." Liam widened his eyes and shook his head vigorously. "Or kill 'em with kindness. Tell him you're sorry he feels that way, but if he doesn't like you, he can look away because your body is not his business."

"Nah. I like punching. No one's said a word to me since and I like it that way."

Liam rubbed the bridge of his nose.

I wasn't very good at the whole being civil thing. I was, and still am, a bitch. Getting through high school, I definitely didn't 'kill them with kindness.' I fought, I yelled, and I cursed. Still do. But I did see why that wasn't the ideal way to raise children.

Still, in that moment, I wasn't sure what to say or do. I didn't have kids yet. I didn't know what the fuck I was doing. Hell, I didn't know how to talk to kids.

For a moment, I wondered if I'd even be a good mom. Surely, I'd do better at it than the lunatics that had my son. But I'd already failed as a parent when I got into that van. I failed every day since he was born. I hadn't realized he was alive, I drowned myself in drugs and alcohol, I failed. After all of that, how could I be a good mom?

"So are all the legends about you true?" Emma lifted the bowl of soup in her hands toward her mouth.

"I don't know, what are the legends?" I asked.

A grin came to her lips. "That Jeremy Skoulda's your soulmate."

I was caught off guard by her nonchalance. "Yeah. Yeah, that's true."

"Then why are you dating my brother?" she asked. "I've seen Jeremy, he's way cuter than Liam."

"Alright, that's enough. Go to your room," Liam said.

"What? It's a legit question," she said. "You're boring, all you do is work and run through the woods. Jeremy's cool, he plays guitar. I saw one of the videos on YouTube, he's amazing. And really cute. Are his eyes really that blue? Or does he wear contacts?"

"Emma, finish your lunch in your room," Liam repeated, sterner that time. "This conversation is over."

"But it was just getting good."

"How about you and I go talk outside for a minute?" I said to Liam. "Emma can finish her lunch while we figure some stuff out."

"Good idea."

I stood with a smile. "It was really nice meeting you, Emma."

"Yeah, you too. Too bad my brother's a di—"

"I swear to God, if you finish that sentence, Emma," Liam said with a darting gaze.

"You'll what?" she asked. "Beat my ass?"

"I'll change the Wi-Fi password." He narrowed his gaze. "You know I will, little shit."

She rolled her eyes.

I laughed and pushed my chair in. Then I gestured to my plate. "Do you want me to wash this?"

"Naw, that's Emma's job. If she wants her twenty dollars to go bowling on Friday anyway." He shot her a parental gaze. She rolled her eyes again.

Liam pulled the door shut behind him. "I'm sorry. She's had a lot of behavioral issues since she came home. We have therapy three times a week, but I don't think it's doing a damn thing. She's just gradually becoming a bigger and bigger pain in the ass."

"No, that's okay. Don't apologize, I like her. She's spunky." I smiled as he sat on the porch swing. I thought about sitting beside him, but I didn't want to be directly beside him and give him the opportunity to get a kiss in. "Every kid her age is a little shit. But she's been through a lot more than most. You got to give her some credit. I would have punched that little fucker in the face too."

"You're a bad influence, ya know that?"

I leaned against the column that held up the roof. "Probably shouldn't smoke a cigarette then, huh?"

Grinning, he said, "No, probably not. She's probably peeping through the blinds as we speak."

A cigarette would've made this a lot easier. Especially when he pulled on that sweet, happy smile. "So you just showed up without calling me back. That could mean a lot of things."

I bit my lip and gave a slow nod.

He squinted, eyes shifting over me. "Not a good thing judging by that face."

"No, not a good thing."

"What's wrong?"

"I, uh..." I paused. "Well, I'm not really sure where to begin."

"What is it?"

"After yesterday, with finding out about that Witch and everything, I had some things I wanted to talk to Lydia about. Well, I guess Jeremy did. Not really my idea. But you've heard me talk about Lydia, right? You know who she is?"

"Yeah, the little Fae girl that got shot by her mom, right?"

"That's the one," I said. He waited for me to go on. "We had some questions to ask her. So I picked them up and took them back to my place for dinner."

"Did you get any leads?" he asked.

"No. Not really. Just some information. Nothing particularly worth mentioning." Part of me wanted to tell him everything, but I knew that I shouldn't. Amy was a powerful telepath. The less people who knew what we knew, the better. "Anyway, so I took them home. And I got back, and Jeremy and I hung out for a while. He, um... Well, Max gave him some molly. And he offered it to me. I don't do it all the time or anything, but I..."

"You're an adult, you can get fucked up sometimes if you want." His brows creased in a bit of question, as if he were hoping that was the end of the story.

I gave a steady nod. "Right. But it's not really the drugs that I need to tell you about."

He looked down. Then he cleared his throat. He leaned forward, propping his elbows against his knees. His sad gaze turned from the ground to mine. "You hooked up with him again, huh?"

Pressing my lips together, I nodded.

He turned down. "You, uh... Has this been, like, an ongoing thing?"

"No. Just last night and a few weeks ago when he first got back."

"Are you guys back together or something?"

"No. No, definitely not. The night ended with a big fight so…" I trailed off. "No, that isn't in the plans."

"I knew I shouldn't have talked to him yesterday. Probably just made him want to chase you more."

I fell silent.

Truth was, I knew there was never going to come a time when he stopped chasing me. Not unless I specifically told him I never wanted to see him again. Not unless I filed for divorce and cut every tie to him. And even then, the moment I fell and broke a bone or cut my hand, he'd be there. He'd leave when I told him to. But he'd be there.

Still, I could never do that. Even with how hurt and mad I'd been since the separation, it wasn't that I never wanted to be around him again. I just needed time. Because we were one within two.

In every life, no matter what he did or what I did. We were connected on a deep, cellular level. Jeremy had explained it like quantum entanglement once—not that I completely understood it. But he'd said that the two of us were constantly linked. And nothing, absolutely nothing, could change that. No distance, no span of time. The two of us would always be entangled.

"I just… I know I made it clear that I still loved him and everything, and you said you weren't looking for anything serious, but um… I think that you've developed some feelings for me, and I don't want to hurt you, but I feel like I already have."

He was quiet for a moment. "Yeah, I mean… I wasn't planning on catching feelings for you. It just kind of happened. I know what the par animos are, I knew some part of you would still want him. But after everything I'd heard, everything you said…" He released something of a laugh and sucked his teeth. "After everything he put you through… I don't understand why you'd put yourself through that shit again."

"He was going through a lot too. He was just better at hiding it than I was."

"Yeah, and that's just it. He kept so much from you. He had it made in the shade and he fucked it up in two of the worst ways possible. He cheated on you and he was lying to you about a drug addiction," Liam said. "I don't think he's good enough for you. I don't think he's good enough *to* you. You deserve better. You shouldn't just let him back into your life, Laila."

"He isn't always bad. He's been good to me."

"He's a low life," he said. "He uses you."

I bit my tongue for a second. He wasn't saying those things to hurt me. He was saying them because he knew what was coming and wanted to sway my opinion. But the fact of the matter was that I'd always defend Jeremy. Even if I agreed and saw his faults as well. I couldn't continue to let him talk shit without upholding my husband.

"You don't know him. You have this alpha male mentality that makes you want to tear him down. And he's a lot of things, but a low life is not one of them. Yes, he's a drug addict. It's a problem. But he took care of my diner when I was held captive for over three months. He took care of *me*. He went through something awful too. If you're suggesting that him using my money for day to day living costs is taking advantage of me, then you're entirely unjustified in thinking so. And we share a bank account but I'm not the only one making deposits. Yes, I make more money than he does, but he works on cars and he plays shows. He has income too." My voice hardened, gaze narrowing. "Look, I understand what you see in the situation. I especially know how a good chunk of people in the health care field feel about addicts. But you only know a chapter of the story. You don't know enough about him to be a judge. So please, don't talk about him like that again."

He was silent for a moment. "I'm sorry."

Once his attitude dropped, I lessened mine too. "I never expected things to be like this between us, Liam. I got into a serious relationship when I was really young. I don't know how friends with benefits relationships work, it just seemed like an easy option. And you're sweet, and you're hot, and I thought it was a good idea. And I still... I like you a lot, Liam. I really do. But this isn't fair to you."

He looked up from his hands to meet my gaze. "What you had with him, the way you guys love each other... Do you at least want that with me?"

"That's not really fair. We're bonded souls, I didn't choose to love him—"

"That's not what I asked," he said. "Do you *want* to love me like you love him?"

Did I?

A swirl spun in my stomach.

Maybe that was what I wanted. I did want to be with someone like Liam. Someone put together. Someone who handled their business. Someone who didn't spend day after day with a needle in their arm.

But that was just it. Jeremy had been a guy not so different from Liam once. He'd been responsible. He'd been the kind of man I could envision growing old with.

Last year had fucked him up. It'd fucked me up too though; I wasn't close to the girl I was before I was taken. Destiny had come and beaten us to the ground. I couldn't condemn him for that. We were both healing, and we were both hurting.

It was too complex. I couldn't tell this guy that yes, I wish he was the one I was bound to on a molecular and spiritual level. Because he wasn't. The togetherness of his persona drew me to him. But that didn't make me wish that he were my soulmate. I just wished that my soulmate had that same grasp on responsibility and security that Liam did. But no, I didn't wish it were Liam instead of Jeremy.

"I can't really answer that, Liam," I said. "It's a lot more complicated than that."

He turned his gaze downward. "I know I can never compare to what you guys have. I'm not stupid." Liam looked up and took my hand. "But I like you a lot, Laila."

"I like you too," I murmured.

"Are you... You aren't going to sleep with him again, are you?" he asked softly.

"No. No, it shouldn't have happened in the first place. We were fucked up, and I was emotional. So was he... It just... It just happened."

"But it won't happen again?" he asked quietly.

"No, it's not going to happen again. Not any time in the foreseeable future, anyway. But it's confusing—"

He stood and pushed his lips to mine. His hand cradled my face as the other went behind my back and pulled my body close to his.

It wasn't the same comfort I felt when I kissed Jeremy. It was something different altogether. It was passionate and fiery.

He was a great kisser. He was great in bed too. He really was a great guy. And that's why I had to do the right thing.

I had to let him go. He wanted something I would never be capable of giving him because I already had it with someone else.

None of this even mattered. What mattered was getting my son home. I could work out the details with my love life when I had some inkling that'd keep my son from becoming some crazy Christian apocalyptic sacrifice.

His hand stayed on my cheek as I pulled back. Those pools of chocolate swirled with honey looked between my eyes for a moment. I knew I was about to break his heart. It made me wish I could stop time for a moment.

"It doesn't matter to me, Laila. I'm not him. I know I'm not him, and I'm okay with that. As long as you want this, I want this. Even if it's just this."

"I can't keep hurting you, Liam."

"Anything that makes you feel good hurts a little." He smiled. "But I think the good's worth the pain. Don't you?"

I kept trying to say it nicely. I didn't want to scream in his face that he'd never be the one. It seemed like I'd already said that, but he just didn't want to grasp it.

Jeremy always knew what I meant. I could be blunt, I could beat around the bush, and he'd still understand me. Liam, I supposed, was more of a typical man. I had to say exactly what I meant word for word for him to understand.

"Liam." Taking a step back, I frowned. "I do like you. I really do. But I just want to be your friend. I don't want anything else. When I said I wasn't going to sleep with Jeremy, I meant that I wasn't going to sleep with anyone. This isn't me saying that I need time to figure out what I want. I know what I want. I want my family. I want my son, and my husband, and the life we were planning before I was kidnapped. Whatever's been going on here has to end. Not because you're a bad guy, not because I don't like you as a person. Just because... You want something from me that I can never give you."

"Oh," he muttered. He took a step back too. His gaze averted mine. He brought himself down to the porch swing.

"I'm not saying that I want to stop seeing you. I like spending time with you. We're friends, and I really like this friendship. I just need to focus on finding my son right now. And this love triangle is just... It's distracting."

"Right. Yeah. Yeah, I get it."

He got quiet for a moment. "I didn't really expect it to last forever."

"I'm sorry, Liam," I murmured. "I don't want this to be one of those we never see each other again sorts of things. I meant that, about being friends with benefits. We are friends if you still want to be. I just think we could do without the benefits."

"You're fun to drink with, and you make good commentary at movies." He gave a soft, yet almost sad smile. "Plus, I'd hate to end things with you on a bad note. There's a really good chance you're going to be the one who saves my brother. I'm just happy we built this friendship at all. If we could still hang out, and work on the case together and everything, I'd really like that."

I smiled. "Yeah. Yeah, I think I'd like that too."

PART II

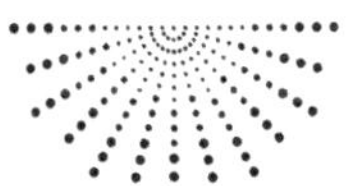

GETTING BACK TO THE BEGINNING

CHAPTER THIRTY-SEVEN

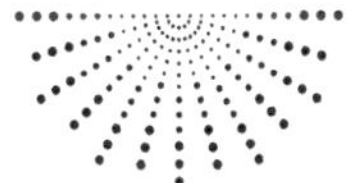

MID-SEPTEMBER, 2020 - LAILA

Music buzzed from Leah's Google Home on the entertainment stand. I lifted my feet from the hardwoods onto the couch, tucking them underneath me. I popped a chip into my mouth, grabbed my grinder full of herbs, dumped it into the white paper, and began rolling it together.

Leah held up a glass bottle in either hand. "Red or white?"

"I'm feeling red." I licked the paper shut and held it to my lips.

"I second that." Hannah raised her hand.

"Red it is then." Leah began twisting the corkscrew into the bottle. Suddenly Tinkerbell came charging across the room. Barks echoed through the ceilings so loud, it could shatter glass. She jumped against Leah's legs, gnawing at the bottom of the bottle.

Leah leaned down to pet her. Tink continued to jump at the bottle. "Laila, why does your dog hate wine?"

I laughed. Handing the joint to Hannah, I stood and started across the room to pull her down. "She thinks it's champagne. She wants to catch the cork when it flies out."

"You're a psycho, dog." Leah continued to twist the screw into the bottle. Tink pulled me, pushing her back paws into my feet as she barked and whined.

Honestly, I had no clue why my dog did the weird shit she did either, but I loved her quirky personality.

I laughed, leaned down to Tink, and wrapped my arms around her chest. "But you're my psycho, huh, baby?"

She licked my face and wagged her fluffy tail.

Leah popped the cork off, and Tink sprinted to her hind legs. She bounced toward her like a kangaroo. I stumbled onto my butt. "She's not going to stop until you give it to her."

She twisted it from the screw and handed it to Tink.

Tink grasped it between her teeth, tossed it in the air, and caught it as it fell. I laughed, watching her chase it around the room like a ball.

Life may have been shitty lately. But that dog always made me smile. She'd comfort me when I cried, she forced me to take her out on days when I'd have rather lay in bed, she made life worth living.

She was the only thing that made sense. Tinkerbell was the only thing that brought me any sense of joy without some taste of shame or disgust. She needed me, and I needed her. She was always happy to see me. Never turned down cuddles. She loved everything I fed her, even if I burned it.

That's how love is supposed to be. Simple. It's not supposed to be complicated and painful.

Smiling, I stood and walked back to the couch. "So Leah." I plopped down beside her. She handed me a glass of wine, arching a brow at my overly chipper tone. "Are you as pumped as I am for this road trip?"

Back when the virus hit in March and concerts stopped happening, my heart about broke. Then come May as things settled down, I got an email for a discounted ticket to a band I barely knew in Virginia. I didn't really have that much interest until I saw that it fell on me and Jeremy's anniversary. Then I bought two. I figured being out of town that night would be a better idea than lying in the bed Jeremy and I stayed in all week the year before.

Her eyes widened. "When is that again?"

I creased my brows. "No. You can't cancel on me, that's not fair. We've had this planned since May."

"Shit, girl, why didn't you remind me sooner?" She sipped her wine. "Haley has shit going on next week, I told her I'd help. She might need someone to heal and they don't know any other Fae."

"Oh, great excuse." I narrowed my gaze. "You think I won't be mad if it's because you're saving people. But fuck you, I'm mad."

She laughed. "Someone could die, Lai."

"Yeah, yeah. Fuck you." I turned to Hannah. "Do you want to come with me on a road trip to Virginia next week? All expenses paid. I'll even buy you food. I'll try and sneak you some booze from the bar too."

"Is it on the weekend?" she asked. "'Cause I can't afford to miss any school right now. We just went back, and I have to start out on the right foot."

I frowned. "It's on Tuesday."

"Sorry, babe," Hannah said. "Why don't you ask Liam? You guys are still hanging out, aren't you?"

We were. Only as friends, and not as frequently as we had before Jeremy got back. But still. I didn't want to share a hotel room with my ex-fuck buddy on my wedding anniversary.

I raised my glass to my lips. "That doesn't really seem appropriate."

"What do you mean?" Hannah asked.

"You don't know what Wednesday is?" I asked. "That big deal you all made about how we couldn't elope. We had to have a big wedding. I spent almost a thousand dollars on that cake alone, and you don't even remember."

Hannah's eyes widened a bit. "It's been a year already?"

I took in a heavy breath. "A year on Wednesday. Which is when I will be driving back from my day trip to Virginia."

"What about Jenna? Or Adam?" Leah asked.

"School started back, so Jenna's back to work. And Adam's the worst person to bunk with. He talks in his sleep, he snores, and he has to piss every ten minutes. I'm not driving with him for eight hours."

"What about Jeremy?" Leah asked.

I gave a huff of a laugh and took a sip from my drink.

It added up then. She knew good and damn well that the trip was coming up; we'd been planning for months. But she always had to put her nose where it didn't belong.

"What's so funny?" She laughed.

"You did this on purpose."

She bit her smiling lip. "You guys need to talk."

I rolled my eyes. "You're a meddling little bitch, you know that?" Leah smiled wider. "And we talk all the time."

"Yeah, but it's fake," she said. "You both know what you want. You're just playing games now."

It wasn't *fake*. It just wasn't what it used to be. We were friends. Really, just friends. Every now and then, we'd have a moment where I thought about leaning in and kissing him. But then one of us would pull away.

Neither of us were ready to get back to where we'd been a year before. For the moment, it was best for things to be as they'd been.

"I don't—" I began.

"No, don't tell me you don't know what you want." Leah laughed. "You do, you know you want Jeremy."

I glanced at the steps, lowering my voice. "Is he upstairs?"

"Nah, he's at your house," Hannah said. "Something about a leaky sink in the basement? I don't know. Max called earlier."

"C'mon, Lai. You're just being stubborn." Leah looked at me, brows pulling together.

"I can't deal with it all right now, Leah," I said. "It's drama, and it's messy, and there's so much baggage on both ends, and all that matters is my son. I don't want to worry about Jeremy. I'm worried enough about someone else that I can't help."

While that may have been true, we had nothing.

Absolutely nothing. We hadn't heard back from Mary. That tea thing hadn't amounted to anything.

I could keep saying it was about my son all I wanted, but the truth was, I was terrified of getting hurt again. I was scared that one day I'd be doing paperwork and I'd hear a bang upstairs. I was petrified that I'd fall back into a routine with him, then he'd die on me. It'd hurt so badly in any circumstance, but it'd hurt so much more if I'd just gotten used to having my husband back only for him to leave like that again.

"The two of you are better together than you are apart. No matter how much you want to pretend that isn't true, it is. But if you don't want it to be like that, then don't let it be like that. At the end of the day, don't you think you should spend your first anniversary with your husband?" Leah's lips curved downward. "Look, if you really would have ended things, I would support you. You haven't though, neither of you have filed for divorce. You flirt constantly. And if you guys are anything, you're friends. You should spend that day together. It doesn't have to be romantic or sexual, but it should happen. And I think you know that. Things between you guys were in a drastically different place when you bought those tickets and planned to get out of town for the day."

She wasn't wrong. But still. Jeremy and I in a hotel room after a concert would end one way. It'd take a lot of willpower on both sides not to. He and I needed to stay that coronavirus, six-foot distance to keep from ripping each other's clothes off when we were alone and booze was involved.

I took a sip from my wine. "Did he put you up to this?"

"I don't think he even knows you're going out of town. Unless you told him."

I hadn't.

Maybe she was right though. Maybe it'd be nice to get away with him. I'd have to constantly remind myself not to get caught up in the moment, but it'd been too long since we went to a concert together. And it was our anniversary. It did feel right to spend it with him.

"Laila," Hannah said quietly.

"Yeah?"

She cleared her throat and tilted her head slightly. "I don't know if you've given this any thought, we don't know how far in the distance it is, but um..." Hannah shook her head a bit. "If you and Jeremy aren't going to be together, what kind of arrangements will there be for him to see his son?"

I looked down and gave a shrug.

"I know that your primary concern is bringing him home. And I get that, I do." Hannah said softly. "But have you thought about how you'll raise him separately? The logistics of it?"

"We all spend so much time together already," I said. "And I work a lot, so maybe... I don't know, Hannah. I haven't worked out the kinks."

No, I had not thought about custody arrangements for our missing child. Thinking about Micah coming home was all I thought of, but every time I pictured that, Jeremy was there. It wasn't just me and Micah, it was me, Micah, and Jeremy. We were a family.

But Jeremy and I weren't even a couple. And then it hurt. So I just closed us out of the picture and only thought of my son. His sweet little smile, those big blue eyes, that long black hair. That's what I focused on. Because that's all that really mattered.

"I get that you think it's selfish to focus on something that could bring you a shred of joy instead of just numbing the pain," Hannah murmured. "But having a good relationship with his father is going to be an important part of your son's life. Even if you aren't together, like Leah said. How could it hurt?"

I said nothing.

"You know that you'll have fun." Hannah grinned. "Even if it's platonic. You love being around each other."

"I'll think about it."

Even if I went alone, I was going on that trip. My therapist convinced me I had to at my last appointment. I'd told her that I was going to sell the tickets because I couldn't be in Virginia if something with Micah came up.

To which she said, "Why? What difference will it make? You can teleport. You're just trying to punish yourself."

And she was right. I knew that I couldn't keep up with the guilt. It was a never-ending loop. I'd thought I'd found an escape from it months ago but after learning Micah was alive, I got locked back inside.

I was doing everything in my power which only made me feel like more of a failure when I came up with nothing. Micah was still young, and I had a way of keeping tabs on his safety, but it almost made it harder. Lydia gave me updates but there hadn't been anything significant yet.

Recently though, she'd started to feel aches around her knees and sudden impact pains on her butt. He was walking. Clumsily toddling and falling, but walking. Another milestone I didn't get to see. Growing from a baby into a toddler, and I wasn't there to witness it.

When I saw kids around his age at the diner or grocery store, I couldn't stop smiling at them. Then they'd walk away, and I'd go out to my car and cry. Part of me was beginning to understand those maniacs that stole other people's children. I couldn't do that. I never would because I knew how badly it hurt to live without my child.

But I wanted my baby. I wanted back what was taken from me. I was missing so much of his life. I hated it and I had to stop thinking. I needed a distraction. I needed a cleansing breath before I did something crazy.

CHAPTER THIRTY-EIGHT

JEREMY

My alarm buzzed on the nightstand just as the sun peeked in through the faded blue curtains. I snoozed it on the first ring and rubbed my eyes for a minute. I lay there stifling yawns, watching the warm light coming in from the window gradually brighten the room.

Once that second alarm sounded, I sat up in the bed, ended the alarm, and started to my feet. I carefully pulled the sheet and comforter back over the bed and placed my pillows on top. I opened the curtain, then the window. Everyone else was still asleep, but the world was just starting to wake up.

The birds chirped outside. The smell of the early autumn air drifted up my nostrils. I lowered myself to a lotus position on the ground and took some calming breaths.

I'd gotten used to starting out my day much differently before the last twenty-nine days. Meditating with the window open was what I used to do before I met Laila. It was in some recovery book Annie gave me before she died. They said that routine was important for addicts.

I was doing it on my own, so it was kind of hard to feel like there was some purpose in sobriety if I didn't reform some type of structure to my life. Even if the rest of my day was shit, I was being proactive. I was giving myself something to be proud of.

My morning ritual, if nothing else, was a reason to get out of bed. But most days, it was more than that. It genuinely made me feel better. I opened my window, I sat on the floor, I breathed for a while, I showered, I brushed my teeth, and I got dressed.

I couldn't say that I was happy. Happiness was the finish line, but I had barely run my first lap. I had a long way to go until I reached it, but I could see it.

Running was like a state of contentment. Every time I made it through a day without getting high, it was like finishing another lap. And each time I passed it, I got a glimpse at what it would feel like when I finished the race, but I just had to keep running.

That contentment was better than sitting the race out entirely. Sitting on the side lines was painful. And I didn't want any more pain. I had to keep chasing the goal. First it was a day, and then a week, and now a month. Every day was a victory in its own way.

I wasn't quite sure what the final lap looked like. Going home? Being able to truly call myself a husband again? Finding Micah? Becoming a dad? Bringing my brother home?

I had no idea what the final victory was. But I had to chase it. I had to do something that wasn't escaping.

Around 7:30, I finished up my morning ritual by starting downstairs to have my cup of coffee. Besides weed, it was the only drug I wasn't giving up.

I started a pot. Then I heard a soft whine from the living room. I walked past the counter to the hallway into the front sitting room.

Tink lay at Laila's feet on the couch. She wagged her tail and whimpered at the orange fire flicking from her fingertips.

Laila's brows were crunched down. Words too quiet for me to hear left her frowning lips. Another bad dream.

It was odd. This time, I was doing better—not just pretending to be okay—and she was the train wreck. I wished I could help her. But I couldn't. I was there for her as much as she'd let me, but for the most part, all I could do was watch her self-destruct.

Then she grasped the throw blanket and caught it aflame.

"Shit." I grabbed another throw blanket and threw it over her. She gasped and slammed upward. "Shit, I'm sorry. Tink was whining, you caught the blanket on fire."

"Fuck." Her glowing green eyes began to slowly recede. She looked down at the hole in the blanket, smacking away the singing edges. "Shit, I'm sorry."

I made my way around the couch and lowered myself to the coffee table. She raised her hand to her tired eyes. Makeup from last night clumped up in the corners. Sweaty, sticky red hair stuck to her cheeks.

"Are you okay?" I asked.

Her head shook back and forth a bit. She closed her eyes, breathing in and out slow. "Another night, another nightmare."

I wanted to reach out and give her a hug. I wanted to tell her it was all okay. But she didn't want that.

"Is it the same one you used to have?"

"Yeah. Yeah, that one was. I fell asleep around midnight and woke up from a different one around three though. I'm sorry, Tink usually wakes me before I catch anything on fire. That hasn't happened in a long time."

"I think that was like, eight bucks at Target." I smiled. "Do you want to talk about it?"

"It's just the trauma. The first one was about Chris." Her head shook again. "The other one was about Micah. But it isn't identical to the one I used to have. Some things have changed." She rubbed her eyes. "I'm sorry, you don't want to hear about this."

"I do." I smiled. "It helps to talk about it. If you want to talk about it."

Laila gave a soft smile with a nod. "The ones with Chris are hard. Harder than the one about Micah, in a lot of ways. I hear him. Screaming and crying. I don't see him though. I think it's poetic or something, ya know? Because I only saw him the one time. The rest of the time we just talked through our cells."

I gave a compassionate expression as she looked up to meet my gaze. Some part of me was glad I hadn't seen my brother that night. Imagining him so vulnerable in that place made my stomach ache. It was easier just to not think about.

"The one about Micah is... It's different. A lot's changed. It used to be the night that we escaped, but it's that place now." She paused, squinting in thought. "And Micah's there, and he's still older but he's not glowing. I see him now, he's a kid. He looks a lot like you actually." A soft smile pulled at her lips.

I smiled back.

"And he's telling me that he needs me, and I tell him that I'm here. And there used to be this force field around the room but it's gone now so

I reach out and I touch him. And I know it's a dream, but it feels so real. It's like I'm there, like I can really feel him. His skin is so soft." She trailed off. "Then he teleports to the end of the hall, and he tells me I have to find him. And I try to use my powers, but I can't." Tears welled in her eyes. "And I chase him down the hall, and then I'm bleeding, and Amy's there. And Micah asks if he can see me and she…"

Her nostrils flared a bit. She paused to regain her composure. "She's nice to him, and he's nice to her. But then she picks him up and over her shoulder, he mouths, 'You have to find me, Mommy.'"

The way she described it… It didn't sound like a dream. It sounded the way Wyatt described his visions. Fae aren't usually prophetic, but we didn't know what Laila's Guardian abilities were. So I had to wonder…

I tilted my head to the side slightly. "What do you think it means?

"It's PTSD and survivor's guilt. The dream's changed because I found out Micah's alive. It's just my subconscious mind harassing my consciousness."

"Maybe," I said. "But maybe there's more to it than that."

She stifled a yawn. "What do you mean?"

"I don't know. Maybe there's something there that we missed on our first walk through, ya know?" I asked. "We didn't get much time to look over everything before the cops got there. But it's been long enough, we could probably get in there unnoticed now."

Laila was quiet, eyes growing fearful. "I'm not ready for that."

I forced a reassuring smile. "Yeah. Yeah, I get it. Just a thought."

The thought still lingered in my mind. But I'd give her some time and bring it up again. If she still didn't want to go, I'd get a team together and go without her.

She managed a smile back. "Is there coffee?"

"It's brewing." I stood and started to the kitchen. "Are you hungry? I was gonna cook something."

"No, I'm good. Thanks though." She loosely folded the blanket, tossed it over the couch, and followed behind me.

"So I've been meaning to ask you something." I pulled a few mugs from the cabinet. "You've been going to that therapist for a while, right?"

"Yeah, about six months." I pulled the creamer from the fridge as she continued. "Why do you ask?"

"I don't know. I mean, your therapist isn't like us, right?" I asked.

"Her wife is but yeah, she's human," Laila said.

I poured the coffee into our cups and set hers on the counter. "So she accepts our insurance then?" I sipped my coffee and met her gaze.

She tilted her head to the side slightly. "Yeah, she does."

"Does it help?" I asked. "Therapy, I mean."

She studied me carefully. Then she smiled, giving a nod. "It does. She gives good advice. Whenever I don't skip my appointments anyway. Why do you ask?"

An awkward smile came to my lips. "I don't know. I have some issues, you know? Seems like I should grow up and work through them."

She smiled a little wider. "Yeah, it can't hurt."

"I think it probably will. But growth does, ya know?"

"I guess it does. But I think hurting's a part of healing. She specializes in addiction too. That's one of the reasons I picked her. I can text you her number."

"That'd be cool. Thank you." I smiled wider. "Maybe she can give me some pointers with you."

She narrowed her gaze but held her grin. "She's not going to tell you what I say about you, ya know."

My smile lifted higher. I raised my hand to my chest. "Wow, you talk to your therapist about me? I'm honored."

"Fuck off." She laughed, rolling her eyes. "Have you heard anything from Helena? Or Mary?"

"Yeah, Helena called. She's in Europe right now. Looking for some rare ingredient that might magnify a locator spell. Asked for another two grand for 'travel expenses.'" I held up air quotes. "Nothing on Mary though."

"Did you give it to her?" Laila asked. "The two grand?"

"I gave her five-hundred. I told her that should cover a decent hotel, and if she wanted a lift, I could take her. She wasn't pleased, but I don't care. We're not paying for her to fly first class when either of us could just teleport her. And she has connections over there, she doesn't even need to stay in a hotel. She's just money hungry. All those Witches are."

That was why I didn't like them. They didn't want to help; they wanted a paycheck. I understood that everyone needed to make money, but if we tapped out that seventy-five grand, we'd be paying her more than twice what we paid Max. And I'm sorry, but the guy worked harder than she did.

Laila's eyes softened. "I'd give her every penny if it brought him home, Jeremy."

"I know. But you can't go broke for nothing. She knows you have money, she knows my grandparents have money. She's going to milk it,

Lai. I'm not saying she isn't doing her job. She's good at what she does and she's going to help. But she *would* take you for every penny if she thought you'd let her. That's why she's not my biggest fan."

"As long as she isn't backing out, you negotiate however you have to. But don't be afraid to give her what she needs."

"I got it. I've known Helena a long time, I know how to work her. Don't worry."

Laila chewed her lip and gave another nod. "I did talk to Mary. Last week, I think. She said she's trying to get ahold of someone. She didn't say who, just that they aren't easy to reach. She thinks they have some information on Wormwood that'll be helpful."

"Sucks that tea thing was a bust," I muttered.

"It was a hail Mary, like you said. I didn't really expect to get anything out of it."

"Yeah, me neither," I said. "I was just hoping."

As I leaned down to sip my coffee, I felt her gaze on me. I smiled, setting my cup down. "What?"

"Huh?" Laila asked.

"Do I have something in my teeth?" I held a friendly smile. She made a face, and I laughed. "I don't want to call it staring but you don't usually look at me for that long."

"Oh, I'm sorry." She laughed and turned away. Shaking her head, she bashfully pushed hair behind her ear, gazing down at her coffee. "I... I think I want to ask you something. But it could come off in a way that I don't want it to, and I don't know how to phrase this."

A slow breath left my nostrils, but I kept my smile in place. "Unless you flat out tell me otherwise, I know where we stand, Lai. If that's your concern."

Slowly, she looked up and met my gaze. "Okay, well, I'm going out of town next week."

"Oh." I made a mental note to call the florist and cancel the order I made for our anniversary. Kinda sucked, but it was what it was. We weren't together. "Do you need me to take care of the diner?"

"No." She laughed. "No, Max wanted the overtime anyway."

I cocked my head to the side. "Do you need me to watch Tink?"

"No, Hannah said I could leave her here."

"Got to throw a dog a bone here, baby." I smiled.

Her gaze met mine. She smiled, cheeks a little red. "Okay, so when I made these arrangements, you and I were barely talking. And it seemed like a good idea at the time because I wouldn't have to be here on Wednesday." As I gave a nod, she bit her lip. "You know what Wednesday is, right?"

I laughed. "Yeah. I know what Wednesday is."

She gave a gentle smile. Then she cleared her throat. "Right, so it seemed like a good idea at the time. But then everything changed, and I... Well, I bought a ticket for Leah. And I've had the hotel room booked for months. I wasn't going to go, but I saw my therapist last week and she thinks I should go. I'm not in the greatest place mentally and I... I really have to get away for a day or two. Like a little reset."

She had a habit of blurting things without giving me all the details, so I didn't really know what she was talking about.

"So I brought it up to Leah last night and she bailed. And Jenna's back to school, and Adam's not fun on road trips, and Brody's in his own little world, and Hannah's busy with school and..."

It sounded like an invitation if I was hearing her correctly, but I had no idea where to or what for. Still, I was gonna say yes. There were very few things she could ask for that I'd turn down, especially then.

"Baby, I have no idea what you're asking." I laughed. "Tickets to what?"

"Oh, right. A concert. It's in Virginia," Laila said. "I'm not even sure who I'm seeing. I went into a little concert frenzy and I bought a bunch of tickets to every band I've ever even remotely liked after she shutdowns ended. Supporting artists and whatnot." She paused. "I don't know how to say this without it sounding weird."

"You aren't..." I laughed and raised a brow. "You aren't asking me to go with you, are you?"

Her cheeks got bright red, a smile resting between them. "Well, not if you say it like that."

Still holding my smile, I tilted my head. "So Liam couldn't make it?"

She narrowed her gaze. "I didn't ask Liam."

"No?" I asked.

"No. Liam and I aren't like that."

"Like what?" I smiled. I propped my arms against the counter and leaned toward her a couple inches. "You said that the whole thing doesn't imply anything, right?"

She bit her smiling lip. "I can go by myself if you don't want to come."

"No, I want to come." I grinned. "Just wanted to make sure I'm not getting the wrong impression."

Laila forced her smile down. "I want you to come. But I don't want you to think this is something that it isn't."

"I get it, Lai," I said. "You aren't ready for what I want. And that's okay. Maybe one day we'll be on the same page. We aren't, and it's not perfect, but it's okay. We're friends again. At least we're in the same chapter."

The truth is, I was content with where we were then. I wanted her back. Obviously, I wanted her back. But I had my best friend. Even if I didn't get to say we were together, I had her in my life again.

And the flirting was kind of fun. I liked watching her blush.

CHAPTER THIRTY-NINE

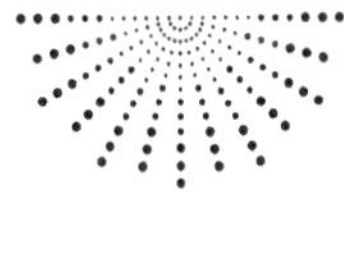

LAILA

The scent of French fries mixed with mildew, reminding me that I desperately needed to call a cleaning service. I struggled my way up the steps, glancing at my feet over the side of the overflowing box in my arms. There hadn't been enough room in the basement sink to wash them. So my lazy ass decided to stack them into the box the shipment of liquor had come in instead of taking multiple trips. Now, it was starting to crumble in my hands.

"Max," I called. "Little help down her please."

He mumbled some curse words. Then his feet pattered to the doorway, just as I started to lose my grip. I braced it with my knee against the wall. "Jesus Christ, Laila." He started down the steps. He grabbed a few off the top that were about to fall, and I readjusted it against my hip. "We have bussing trays for a reason, dumbass."

"Well, there's none down here and this seemed easier than coming up to grab one." I shifted my hands to get a better grip.

He collected more in the front of his shirt. Rolling his eyes, he turned and started up the steps. I trailed behind him.

"Make two trips, dude." Max carefully set glasses in the sink.

"Meh meh meh, make two trips." I set the box on the counter. "Fuck off."

Smiling, he went back to a burger on the griddle. "Damn it. Now I burned it. You can go out and apologize to the customer 'cause this isn't my fault."

"Just make another. Does that one have seasoning on it?" I asked.

"Nah," he muttered. "Want me to save it for Tink?"

"Yeah, that'd be great. Thank you." I wiped my hands on my apron. "Who was it for?"

"I don't know, one of Sophie's. There's only two tables so shouldn't be too hard to figure out." He walked to the fridge and got a fresh hamburger patty from inside.

"Alright. I'll take care of these in a minute." I started toward the front of the restaurant. Sophie was bussing a table in the corner. That only left one taken. Brushing past the counter, I started to the table by the door where a woman sat facing away from me.

"I'm so sorry, ma'am, but it's going to be a few minutes on your burger." I approached the table. "I had to borrow my cook for a moment, and he burned it so—" I stopped abruptly.

She looked up from her cup of coffee.

Two big brown eyes, a gorgeous crown of tight black curls pulled into a bun, and a gentle smile.

Tina Davis.

The too curious FBI agent assigned to my case when I was kidnapped.

"No worries, Laila." She smiled. "I've been in the car for a while, I'm in not in any rush."

"Tina." I forced a smile. "Wow, it's nice to see you. How are you?"

She shrugged but kept the smile. "I'm alright. And you?"

"I'm hanging in there."

"I like the tattoos." She gestured to my neck.

"Better than the scars, right?"

"The hair's pretty too. But do you have a moment? This isn't just a social call."

Ah, fuck.

If it were news on Chris and Micah, she'd have called. And her smile was just a little bit... suspicious. This was bigger. It had to be.

"Sure." I lowered myself to the booth across from her. "Have you gotten any new information?"

"We think so." Her gaze was steady on mine, unblinking. Almost all-knowing. "I'm sure you've been in contact with Ray Ramirez."

Okay, so definitely something to do with Micah. But what did she think? That I played some part in it? Surely she knew better.

"I have."

"You're friends. I'm sure he's told you what his daughter told us," she said, testing the waters to see what I knew and what I didn't.

"About my son?" I asked. She nodded. "Yeah. Yeah, I know."

"From what we've gathered, we know for a fact that there are at least another fifty to seventy-five people still being held. And we are still utilizing our best resources in an attempt to find them, but there's a lot of red tape in terms of international security."

Okay, maybe I was wrong. Maybe this was just a formal way of her relaying what I already knew. But there was something off in her eyes. She knew something.

"Micah's just another on the list. I get it."

"I wish I could say that wasn't the case."

"So what's this about then?"

She held my gaze for a moment. Then she lifted her coffee to her lips and took a sip. "I'm not the only one working your case, Laila. But it did hit home for me. I'm the closest to it, at least in terms of experience and not simply peddling papers. I think that's why it was given to me."

"I'm sorry, I don't follow."

Tina's gaze shifted upward, washing over my diner. She gestured around. "Last year, after our interview here, I remember feeling relieved somehow. I knew that something didn't quite fit, but I ignored it."

My heart sunk to my ass. Jesus Christ. She knew we fucked with her head.

Damn it. I really don't want to have to kill her.

She reached into her bag, then laid a small manilla envelope on the table in front of us. The word *Tina* was written across it in meticulous, cursive black letters. "Until this showed up at my door."

She gestured to it. I lifted it open and pulled out a small scrap of paper.

They aren't what you think they are.

A small flash drive sat at the bottom of the envelope.

Shit.

Shit, shit, shit.

Not only did she know, but this flash drive, it must have had proof. That bastard had just exposed us to an FBI agent.

This is bad, this is really bad.

"It hasn't left my possession, Laila," Tina said. "To my knowledge, it was only sent to me. That isn't to say that it won't or hasn't been sent to someone else, but I just want you to know that nothing on here has been or will be repeated by me. Now, I'm gonna head out. Don't worry about that burger. I want you to watch this. Then, we'll have lunch. And we're going to talk."

CHAPTER FORTY

JEREMY

The smell of gas and oil filled my nose. Cool autumn air brushed against my cheeks. I struggled against a bolt of the tire of the Jeep. I was wrenching with everything I had, but the little bastard wouldn't give.

"It's a tire." My arms ached, pulling back as hard as I could. "Not a fucking submarine hatch, Adam."

We'd been over this a thousand times. One time, *one* time, he didn't fasten the bolts tight enough. It loosened the rest of the lug nuts. Then he was driving down the road and the car started to shake. He pulled over and the wheel was only an inch or two from falling off the frame. I told him to tighten the bolts better next time he rotated his tires. And from that moment on, he acted like they were the locks to the grandest treasure in the universe.

My phoned buzzed in my jeans pocket. I dropped the tire iron to the ground. It was best I take a break anyway.

I plopped to the cement and pulled it out. Laila's face lit up my screen. I smiled.

"Hey, beautiful," I answered. "What's up?"

"Ugh, ya know. Tired of this fucking life." Her tone was bubbly, but there was a touch of seriousness at the edge. "Do you think if I learn to shapeshift, I could just become someone else? Fake my death type of thing?"

I laughed. "I don't know. From my experience, no matter how far you run, your problems seem to be pretty close behind."

"Maybe I'll try that someday. It's worth a shot."

"What's wrong?" I picked up my water and took a sip. "Did something happen?"

"Well, Tina Davis just paid me a visit."

"The FBI agent?" I asked. "Why?"

"She gave me a flash drive. She says it was dropped at her doorstep," Laila muttered. "There was a little note with it. It said they aren't what you think they are."

My heart began to race in my chest. "Oh, shit."

"I don't really want to watch this alone," she said quietly.

"I'll be right over." I stood.

A million thoughts were running through my mind as I sat down on the couch beside Laila. What if he put a video of them using their powers online? What if he sent it to a news station? What if there was a video of my son on here?

Exposure could be the worst thing to ever happen to us. Then again, the government had released clear documentation of alien spacecrafts in our skies only a few months prior and no one seemed to bat an eyelash.

Then my mind travelled to the Chambers and the Council. When I'd asked for help finding Laila, they told me that it was a 'human problem.' Bet they wouldn't be saying that if tomorrow morning's episode of CNN was someone turning into a Werewolf.

Laila started up her laptop.

"What do you think it is?" I asked.

She stared at the loading screen. Shaking her head, she reached for her glass of whiskey on the table. "One of us using our powers, judging by Tina's face. Or maybe a compilation of all of us. I can't see her giving me a tape of them doing something bad to my son."

Fuck. That screen needed to load faster.

I reached into my hoodie pocket and pulled out a joint. The lock screen flashed. I rummaged my pockets for a lighter. Laila extended her finger with a flame and typed in her passcode with the other.

"Thanks," I muttered. Taking a few slow drags, I watched her open the attachments. They were labeled by date.

L.C. 3/29/19
L.C. 4/1/19
L.C. 4/4/19
L.C. 4/8/19

Laila. Callidy. Every Monday and Friday for all of April and most of May.

That bastard sent the FBI agent on Laila's case the videos of him torturing her. Why? What kind of sick fuck would do that?

Laila sipped her whiskey. "Well, that answers that question."

"We know what this is, Lai. We don't have to watch it," I murmured.

She gazed at it for another moment.

I took another drag off the joint and offered it to her. She breathed in a long hit. Then she clicked the first video and immediately pressed pause on the black screen. After exhaling the smoke away, she turned and met my gaze. "I don't know why I called you. You don't have to watch this."

"Neither do you," I murmured.

"There could be something in here. Maybe something he says or something in the image itself. I have to watch it, Jeremy."

"Then I'll watch it with you," I said quietly.

I had no desire to watch those videos. But there were a few reasons I had to. She was already a glass of whiskey in. Not a shot, but a glass—and that was just since I'd gotten here. If there was something there that we needed to see, she'd be too inebriated to notice unless it was pointed out to her.

But more importantly, I knew what reliving those moments was about to do to her. I knew how badly she was about to hurt. And I had to be here.

I hadn't been there for her while it was happening. I couldn't comfort her then. But through this, I could.

She held my gaze. "I don't want you to see me like that."

"Baby, I felt it," I said quietly. "I was there. Not physically, but I was *there*, Laila. I can handle it. You're not watching this by yourself."

"Jeremy—"

I took her hand from the keyboard and twined my fingers in with hers. I brought her knuckles to my lips. "I'll be okay, Lai."

Her eyes shifted between mine for a moment. I felt them burning. It was taking everything in her not to cry. But she gave a slow nod. "Just don't look at me any differently, alright?"

I ran my thumb along the swell of her tense knuckle. "Nothing can change how I see you, Laila."

An unwilling smile came to her lips before quickly falling. Our fingers remained laced together. Then she set them on her lap and pressed play with her other hand.

The camera rustled around, facing a drywall ceiling with the light of a computer illuminating its view.

"Today is March 12th, 2019. We are on day two since the capture of subject seven-seven-six, Laila Rose Callidy, age twenty-one," he said.

It was the first time I'd heard his voice aloud. I'm not sure what I expected, but it wasn't that. Soft. Nearly dainty for a man. It wasn't a high pitch, but it didn't sound intimidating. It hardly even sounded masculine.

I felt the goosebumps rise on the back of Laila's hand. As he went on, her skin got warmer. Her breathing grew short. Her shaking hand lifted to her whiskey, and she took a long gulp.

She was visibly shaken from merely the sound of his voice.

And that… it made my chest tight and my blood boil at the same time.

Such a wee little man. Someone so incredibly powerless compared to her and yet he held all the power in the world over the both of us.

"What's so fascinating about this subject is who she becomes, not who she is now." The camera adjusted to face out a window into a large, well-lit room. The walls were white, nearly thirty feet tall at least coated in a shiny, nearly sparkling large tile; like that of a school gymnasium.

It was a torture room. Similar to the one in our basement, but on a much larger scale. Contrary to popular belief, white's your best décor option when it comes to blood and gore. It's impossible to miss on such a bright surface which makes for easy cleanup.

There was almost nothing in the room besides my unconscious, naked wife lying stomach down on a metal table turned roughly eighty degrees so that she was nearly standing. I'd know that body anywhere. The two little dimples just above her small, perky butt. The long black hair resting against her shoulders.

Some type of metal bracket connected to the table held her down at either ankle, another across the back of her thighs, one held either bicep, and both wrists.

I couldn't help but make the inverted association to the way she was laid out like Christ on a crucifix. I hadn't thought of it before that moment, but Jesus was also slashed across his back for hours before his murder.

"That's what we're here to do today. We're going to unlock every bit of potential Laila holds. No matter how long it takes, or how much it hurts, regardless of how much she hates me for it. This has to be done, whether she realizes it or not."

As he spoke, two men, wearing black military-like suits came in from the stainless-steel door in the corner. They talked amongst themselves, laughing as they looked over Laila's naked body.

I gritted my teeth and fought the urge to shudder. Not that looking emotionless was the best move either, but I didn't want her to pause and say 'this is too much for you, leave.'

"Laila is incapable of unlocking her full potential in her current environment. She's sheltered in her relationship, her family life. She's rarely exposed to danger that will trigger the resurgence of her abilities.

"Considering who she will become, her capture was not ideal to me in terms of longevity and allegiance. But we're running out of time, and she has to be prepared. It took me a long time, but it finally occurred to me that I'm a part of the story. Ironically enough." He chuckled. His laugh faded, turning into a sad sigh as we heard the click of a button. "Please begin."

The man on the right pulled something from his back pocket. He raised it through the air. And out came a long, leather whip. It slammed against her spine in a quick, snapping motion.

I tried not to wince, watching her back arch in anguish and lines of crimson appear across her pearly white skin. Her head curved back as far as it could against the restraints.

Her hand tightened around mine as she turned and met my gaze. "Are you okay?"

"Yeah, I'm alright."

She turned her gaze back to the computer screen. Then she took a sip from her glass.

Again, he slashed the whip against her back, that time reaching so far down that it slid against the top of her ass cheek. I struggled not to flinch again, watching her hands shake against the cuffs. Her ankles were attempting to kick her way out only to stiffen again as the leather sliced again and again.

Orange sparks began to light her fingertips. The men laughed and slammed the whip through the air again. That last slash set her body ablaze. The flames licked her skin as if she were a campfire on a cool, fall night.

The men jumped backward, nearly stumbling.

There was another click of the button. Peterson said over the intercom, "Again."

They looked back through the window. Their heads shook, eyes wide in fear.

"*Again*," Peterson repeated. "That's an order."

They breathed heavily, hands shaking. They turned back to Laila. Just as the whip cracked against her flaming skin, vibrant licks of blue and violet traveled up the whip, drastically shifting into a tunnel of fire. It was almost cone-shaped. It touched the men's skin and they erupted in a violent purple blaze.

Then they were just pillars of dust.

Laila closed her eyes. Her head shifted from the screen. She put her hand to her mouth and shook her head a bit.

Peterson laughed, clapping his hands together in glee. "I knew she had it in there. Beautiful. The first occurrence of full incineration on impact and I captured it on film. Stunning."

Then the camera shifted before the video ended.

I traced my thumb along the back of Laila's. She kept her eyes closed with her head turned the other direction.

"Lai," I whispered.

She continued to look away.

I gently raised my hand to her chin, ever so slightly tugging it toward me. If she would have resisted my touch in the slightest, I would have pulled it back. But she turned her head with my hand to meet my gaze.

Her eyes weren't watering, but they were as red as the blood we'd just watched spill from her flesh. Her teeth were pressed together behind her pouting lips that struggled to stay steady. She wasn't going to let herself cry, but she wanted to.

"You did what you had to." I held her chin above my thumb. "It's okay, baby."

"Yeah, I know. I just... I didn't see it then, you know? I heard it. But seeing it's just different."

"At least they went quick," I murmured. "The way they died was nothing compared to what they were doing to you."

Her tone was somewhere between hurt and ashamed. "They didn't all go quick. That was just my first round."

"Good. Those fuckers deserved it."

Her gaze turned down.

I moved my hand from her chin to the side of her face. She leaned into it slightly, closing her eyes and lifting her fingers over mine.

"I remember thinking about you in there." Her voice was nearly a whisper, fingertip stroking the back of my hand. "Just praying I'd get to touch you one more time. Sometimes I'd sit there, and I'd think about this. Holding your hand. Such a little thing, I guess, but something about our hands together makes me feel safe, and I missed it so much. Chris told me I needed to remember one good thing when I was in that room. I had to think about something good that I wanted to feel or eat or smell one more time if I didn't want to lose my will to live, and that's what I wanted. I just wanted to hold your hand again. At least one more time, I wanted to hold your hand."

I managed a sad smile, heart swelling as I squeezed her palm tighter.

Her eyes settled on them for a moment before they met mine. "I'm so glad I got to hold your hand again."

"Thank you for letting me," I whispered.

She had no idea how happy I was that I got to hold her hand again.

CHAPTER FORTY-ONE

JEREMY

As we flicked through each video, Laila poured a new glass of whiskey. By the time we made it to the sixth, she was too obliterated to so much as notice—let alone care—about the man she killed by thrusting a giant tree root from beneath the building through his chest. That one was pretty wild.

By the time I clicked play on the eighth, Laila drunkenly collapsed to my bicep and drifted away. Looking between the slow breathing, sweet and vulnerable girl then to the mass murderer on the screen, I almost had to chuckle. Out of context, that would be hard to explain. But that's what I loved about Laila. She was a living, breathing oxymoron.

Once I made it to the last dated video, I scrolled a bit further to find one more. It was labeled *THE END*.

I pressed play.

Then I saw him for the first time.

Still, not as bad as I pictured him. But there was a look to his eyes that sent shivers down my spine. It wasn't in a terrified, run for my life kind of way. Just off. Like I could see the crazy wheels spinning frantically behind his pools of muddy brown.

He wore a freshly ironed, white button-up with a perfectly creased collar cresting the black tie at the base of his neck. Over it sat a long white doctor's coat. An array of pens protruded from his breast pocket on both his coat and his shirt.

He wore thick, black framed glasses above an inviting smile. The kind one would see on a priest or a guidance counselor. He looked nice. Presentable. I'd be more likely to walk on the other side of a road if I saw someone that looked like me than if I saw someone that looked like him.

"Agent Tina Davis," he said. "I'm sure you know who this is by now given the fact that this is probably the last video that you're watching. I would like to formally introduce myself. My name is Doctor Robert Peterson. I'm the man responsible for the capture and or death of nearly eight hundred supernatural creatures since two-thousand and four.

"You're probably wondering why I'm confessing my crimes to you. You may turn this over to your supervisor. You may throw them all under the bus to your government, including Laila and the rest of the two-hundred and something men, women, and children. You may let them endure the same torture and treachery they endured from me for however long they did. But I doubt that you will. However, there's a few reasons I don't care if you do.

"As you can see, your government doesn't stand a chance if they all band together. They make up a good portion of Earth's population, and they have a lot more fire power than you do. Laila is only one of thousands. Millions, maybe, if you include the ones who don't know what they are. Admittedly, Laila is an incredibly unique specimen. But her powers are primarily related to the world around her. What others can do are even more unimaginable. Teleportation, invisibility, nuclear capabilities, the power to manipulate energy in such a way that could shut down every telephone and internet tower around the globe.

"Aside from that, I know who I am in this story. I know my fate. I'm the villain. I don't get a happy ending. But see, you're someone in this story too, Ms. Davis. You'll keep her safe in a way that I can't. But you have to know who she is. Who they all are.

"I wish I could give you all the information now. But there isn't more I could say without giving it all away too soon. What I do want you to know is that this story is far from over. But when it does eventually take its final bow, just know that is hardly the end either. This is all only the beginning. The prologue, if you will."

This odd, gleeful, almost joyous smile came to his lips.

"Until we meet again, Tina."

He hadn't done this to expose us, not to the world. Just to Tina. He wanted her to know what we are. But I didn't know why.

Was it like he said? So that she could cover shit up for us? Who was she in all of this?

I raised my thumb and forefinger to my tired eyes. After a silent moment, I closed the laptop and moved it to the couch cushion beside me. Then I turned my gaze to Laila. Her cheek rested on my arm as hers twisted around mine, clutching it like a teddy bear.

What she did in those videos—though, admittedly, kind of terrifying—was amazing. I wouldn't verbalize that; she'd equate it to him. But her ability to fight without even looking... She was a badass.

She was also the sweetest, kindest person I'd ever met.

For a moment, I just looked at her. My heart wrenchingly beautiful little oxymoron.

I wanted to hold her a while longer. I wanted to keep her safe. In that moment, she was weak. She needed someone to take care of her aside from herself.

But no matter how much I loved her, I couldn't stay the night. Not unless she asked me to.

I moved my arm around her shoulders and teleported us to her bed. Her eyes fluttered a bit as we landed but stayed shut. I carefully helped her down onto the pillows.

As I pulled the comforter over her, she began murmuring to herself. Sweat beaded her forehead. I couldn't make out much. Just a "no" and "stop" here and there.

I pushed hair from her face behind her ear. I kept my hand against her cheek for a moment. Then I watched her stiff expression gradually soften.

I pulled my hand away and stood. Just as I turned to head toward the door, her quiet voice broke through the silence.

"Jeremy," she murmured.

I turned and met her gaze in the pale moonlight. "Yeah, Lai?"

She groggily tightened the comforter beneath her chin. Her green eyes peeked over it. "Thank you for taking care of me."

I smiled. "Thank you for letting me."

She tried to smile but couldn't bring herself to. "Baby."

Hearing that word leave her lips gave me chills. A flock of butterflies flapped in my stomach.

Tears filled her eyes. "Did you watch them all?"

Licking my lips, I nodded.

"So you saw the one where I was shot?" she whispered.

"Yeah." I walked back to bed and lowered myself beside her. "Yeah, I did."

The tears in her eyes began to escape. They slid down her cheeks and landed on the white pillow. Her hand slid to mine, still gazing at me. "I didn't want to kill anyone else. I just wanted it to stop."

I pulled our hand to my lips and kissed the back of her knuckles. "You did what you had to do, Lai."

She clenched her trembling jaw together. Then the tears began to fall faster and harder from her eyes. I moved my other hand to her cheek. My thumbs brushed away the water. "I killed them all for nothing. I didn't protect Micah, or myself, or any of the others. They're dead for nothing, Jeremy, and I killed them."

"It wasn't for nothing," I said softly. "You're home, baby. You're safe. You made it out."

Her teeth began to chatter. Shaking her head a bit, she murmured, "It doesn't feel like it."

I frowned, squeezing her hand a little bit tighter. "It's going to be okay."

Silence set in for a moment. "I'm really drunk."

"You are, huh?"

"I-I'm too fucked up to defend myself if something happened and usually, I wouldn't care, but that brought back a lot of memories I usually try to bury and I..." Her lip quivered, struggling not to sob. "I'm scared, Jeremy."

"It's okay, Lai," I murmured. "You have a good security system, and I'm just a thought away. Nothing's going to happen to you, I promise. You're safe."

"I don't feel safe," she whispered. "Is there any way you could... Could you maybe... Could you stay with me tonight?"

My heart skipped.

I smiled and kissed her hand again. "Yeah, I can stay with you."

She smiled. Silent, heavy tears continued to bead her cheeks. "Jeremy?"

"Yeah?" I asked.

"Can you hold me?" she whispered so quietly that I almost didn't hear her.

I blinked away tears of my own. "Sure, baby. I'll hold you."

I released her hand and teleported behind her. I reached my hands around her waist and interlocked them just below her ribs. She took my hand in hers and pulled it up to her chest like a teddy bear to a homesick child. Her voice was quiet as a mouse. "This is the only place in the world where I feel safe anymore."

My stomach flipped. I kissed her hair. I closed my eyes and held her body to mine a little tighter. "We're stronger together than we are apart."

"I wish we were strong enough to bring them home," she whispered.

"We will, baby," I said quietly. "We're going to bring them all home."

"I don't want to be too late," she murmured.

"We won't be," I said. "We're going to bring them home. Micah, and Chris, and all the others."

"But—"

"Don't think about the buts," I whispered in her ear, closing my eyes. "Don't think about what can go wrong. Think about what'll go right. Think about how happy we'll be when we see him for the first time. And the smile on Leah's face when she gets to see Chris again.

"Think about how when we get Micah back, we can take him to the park together. We'll get to see his little smiles, and bandage up scraped knees, and wipe his tears when he cries. And how he'll learn to play catch with Tink. And his first day of school, and his first trip to Disneyland, and his first picture with Santa, and his first Halloween costume. Think about the first time he tries to play my guitar, or the first time he helps you bake cookies.

"You have to think about the good, baby," I murmured in her ear. I gently kissed her hair and took in a long whiff of her perfume. "You have to, because we're going to bring him home. We can miss him, and we can be sad that he isn't here, but we have to remember that this is temporary. This isn't the end, Laila. Our story with him has barely even started."

CHAPTER FORTY-TWO

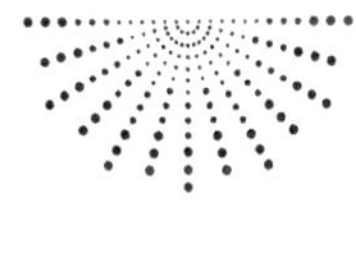

LAILA

I watched Jeremy lift a piece of sausage off Micah's plate. "Since when do you like sausage?" I asked.

Chewing behind a smile, he said, "I've always liked sausage."

"Nuh-uh, Daddy," Micah said from the booth beside me. "Mommy made it last week and you said it tasted like shit."

My mouth dropped, trying hard not to smile. "Oh, is that what Daddy said?"

Jeremy's cheeks got pink. An embarrassed smile came to his lips. "You're not supposed to say shit, Micah."

"He didn't say it, he quoted it," I said. "Totally different thing."

"Totally different." Micah nodded.

"So that's why you always ask for bacon. You think my sausage tastes like shit." I grinned.

"It doesn't taste like shit, Mommy." Micah bit into it. Turning up to me with a mouth full and a smile, he said, "It's good."

I dabbed syrup from his cheek. "Don't say shit, baby, but thank you."

"You boil them first." Jeremy's nose curled. "They get all rubbery."

"Well, screw you." I laughed.

"Laila," a voice said from the bar.

My head turned.

He wore the same navy blue scrubs. He had the same buzzed cut hair.

He was still skinny. He looked almost identical to how he did the day that we escaped.

But he had eyes. The same electric blue eyes his three brothers, sister, and the little boy beside me had.

"Chris?" I started from the booth. "What are you... Is it really you?"

"I don't have a lot of time," he said quickly. He walked toward me and grabbed a hold of my upper arms the way Adam did when he had something important to say.

"That was a dream." He gestured to Jeremy and Micah. "But this isn't. This is real, Laila. It's me. Don't forget this, okay?"

I knew this was a dream. I had plenty of these. These were the ones I craved, the ones that I woke from and cried, but not the ones that I woke from screaming.

They didn't feel real. I couldn't smell Jeremy's cologne, or feel Micah's skin, or taste Jeremy's lips. These were dreams, I knew that.

But Chris's hands on my biceps felt real. So real I wondered if they'd bruise.

"Chris." I wrapped my arms around his chest.

He put his around me. I closed my eyes, breathing in the smell of sanitizer on his clothes just as I had on my own during those three months of captivity. His heart thudded beneath my ear. His palms around my shoulders were firm, real. It felt so real.

But I felt something else too. The way I felt the warmth of a fire before I drew close enough to get burned. A massive, pulsing orb of energy.

And it felt just like that little lock of black hair Moriah had given me.

"I'm so sorry I didn't get you out." I began to cry. "I promised you that I would and I—"

"You did get me out. I'm just stupid." He pulled away. His gaze slid over me. "Jesus, I did not expect you to look like this."

"And what is that supposed to mean?"

He smiled. The crinkle at the edge of his eyes reminded me so much of Adam. "I don't know, just thought you'd be less girly. Maybe taller. Jeremy has a thing for blondes. I didn't think you'd be a red head."

"I'm actually a brunette," I said. "But how are you here? What is this?"

"They're using me, Laila. Micah's age is my only frame of reference in time, I don't even know what month it is." He spoke fast.

My heart skipped a beat.

Chris was with him. Not just that bitch, not just that sociopath, but his uncle.

"You've seen him?" I asked. He nodded. A smile a mile wide came to my lips. "What's he like? Is he okay?"

Chris smiled. "He's the sweetest baby I've ever met. Way better than Hannah was. But yeah, he's okay. For now, anyway."

"What do you mean?"

"I've heard bits and pieces. I don't know all the details. But they think he's some miracle child—"

"The Lamb they plan to sacrifice in order to bring on the apocalypse," I said. "Yeah, I know."

"They're trying to contact someone. Wormwood, they called them."

"We've been trying to figure that out," I said. "But no one knows who that is."

"Neither do I. But you need to do something for all of us, okay?"

"Anything."

"You have to go back there." His blue eyes locked with mine. "I know you don't want to, but you have to."

"Go back where?" I asked.

"Shit." He looked over his shoulder and dropped my upper arms. He turned back to me with wide eyes. "I don't have any more time. Just go back. You'll find it, I know you will."

"Where?" I asked again.

"Wherever they were holding us," Chris said. "You'll find it, and then you'll find us."

Then he was gone.

"Wait," I yelled, heart hammering in my chest. "Wait, Chris! Chris, find what? What do I need to find?"

"Laila," Jeremy's voice said.

I opened my eyes and shot forward in the bed. My hand flew to my chest. A cold sweat pearled from my forehead down my cheek.

I looked around the room. My heart thudded against my chest, echoing into my ears. I ran my hands along my upper arms.

My hands felt just as real against my skin as Chris's had.

"Another nightmare?" Jeremy asked softly as he sat up against the pillows beside me.

I nodded, wiping sweat from my brow.

Go back there. That's what he told me. To go back to the place where it all happened, the place that seeded all of my worst nightmares.

But it was a dream. Right? It'd been a dream, it had to be. He had eyes.

Wishful thinking. That's what it had to be. A fantasy. That's what my therapist would say. But why did it feel so real?

"Laila." Jeremy placed his hand over mine. "Are you alright?"

"Yeah. Yeah, I'm okay." Taking in a slow, heavy breath, I pulled my hand from his and rubbed my eyes. "Chris can't astral project, right?"

"No, just teleportation and energy manipulation."

"And he can't dream walk either?" I asked.

"No, that's not an ability in our bloodline. That's more common in Native people than French Americans."

I nodded.

"What happened?" he asked.

No matter how real it felt, Chris didn't have an ability capable of entering my dream. It had to be a dream. Nothing more.

Plus, I didn't particularly want to tell him about my fantasy of the three of us as a family. It would've sent the wrong impression. Especially after I cried and asked him to stay the night.

"It doesn't matter. What time is it?" I asked.

"Seven-thirty," he said. "Your alarm didn't go off yet. I didn't want to wake you up too early. But you started mumbling and sweating so I figured I probably should before you burned the place down."

"Thanks," I muttered. "How long have you been up?"

"I don't know. An hour or so."

I turned his way and arched a brow. "And you just laid here for an hour?"

He smiled. "You asked me to stay. I didn't want you to wake up and wonder where I went."

That was why I loved this man. He didn't make me feel pathetic for being a mess last night. He was just... Here for me.

"Well, thank you." I smiled. "And thanks for last night."

"Any time." He smiled back. Then he yawned and stood from the bed. "But I should probably get back to the house. I didn't even bring my phone last night. I need a shower and I should probably give Leah the flash drive. She might be able to find something tech related on it that we don't know to look for."

Lovely. My sister in-law watching me being tortured wasn't exactly a pleasant thought. But he was right. She might find something that we missed.

I brought myself to my feet and pulled my fuzzy robe on. "I guess that makes sense. She, uh... Have her watch the videos too. Both of us are pretty biased and I was pretty drunk last night."

"Yeah, might not be a bad idea. I don't think there's anything on there, though. I think he just wanted Tina to know what we are."

I tightened my robe around my waist. "What are we going to do about Tina?"

He frowned. "She seems like a nice lady, I don't really want to kill her."

"Me neither," I muttered. "But if it comes to that."

He turned his gaze to the floor. "Let's hope it doesn't. We'll talk to her, test the waters, and see if she'll keep this quiet. Homeland security isn't knocking on the door, so I think she's planning to keep this to herself. But I'll talk to Leah and see what she thinks."

"I'll tell her we can meet up to discuss it after our trip. I'll lie and say we're leaving town today. I might park the Forester at your place to cover my ass. It'll give us a couple of days to figure out what we want to do."

"Sure," Jeremy said. "Yeah, that's our best bet. I'd like to be there when you talk to her if that's okay."

"That's a good idea." I took in a slow breath. "So you didn't see anything that might help in the videos?"

"No, it was what I expected it'd be. But there was one more video at the end you might want to watch. Or maybe you wouldn't want to, I don't know."

"What do you mean?"

"It was weird. Almost like a vlog," Jeremy said, biting his lip. "It was a message to Tina."

"It was Peterson?" I asked.

"Yeah. I don't know why I expected him to be bigger. He's scrawnier than me."

"You aren't scrawny."

A boyish grin lifted his lips. "I'm a little scrawny."

"You're slender." I smiled. "I don't do scrawny."

"Well, you don't do me, so." He gave a half-smile.

I rolled my eyes and smiled back. "I've got to get dressed. Get out of here."

He smiled back. "I have a couple of errands to run but I should be at the house if you need anything. Otherwise, I'll see you on Tuesday morning?"

"Tuesday."

CHAPTER FORTY-THREE

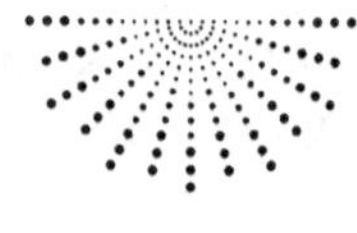

LAILA

After Jeremy left, I took a long, hot shower. I laid my head against the meticulously tiled wall and basked in the warm water coasting down my body. But I couldn't stop thinking about that damn dream.

I knew it was a dream. It couldn't have been him; he couldn't just teleport into someone's mind. But it felt so fucking real. The first half felt like a dream, but once Chris got there, it felt like I was just as awake as if I'd drunk ten cups of coffee.

The more I thought about it, the more I thought about the dreams that haunted me almost nightly since I learned Micah was alive. They felt just as real.

"You have to find me, Mommy."

"No, I need you here."

"You have to find me, Mommy."

His little voice echoed between my ears like a basketball bouncing on the hard floor of an empty school auditorium.

Then Chris's voice did the same.

"This is real, Laila. It's me. Don't forget this."

"You have to go back there."

"You'll find it, and then you'll find us."

I couldn't go back there. I was terrified of that place. There was no reason to be; I'd destroyed a good chunk of it. Still, the thought sent a chill down my spine.

But it was a dream. I had to stop thinking about it. I had to stay focused on the rest of my shitshow of a life.

As the water grew cold, I shut the spigot off and started out of the shower. Just as I finished drying off and tying my hair in a towel on top of my head, the music playing from my phone's speakers turned to a ring. I dried my hand a little better. Then I grabbed my phone. Liam's name flashed across the screen.

I slid the green bar and held it to my cheek. "Hey, you."

"Hey, baby girl. What're you up to?" Liam said in his usual sweet and joyous tone.

"Just getting ready to start the day. What about you?" I held the phone between my shoulder and face. Then I pulled my jeans up over my ankles and hopped them up my hips.

"I am enjoying my first day off in six months," he said. "Well, not enjoying it as much as I'd like to. I'm cleaning the house, and this toilet is disgusting."

I chuckled as I put the phone on speaker to pull my shirt on. "You had a day off, like, two weeks ago."

"Ah, yes. I did. But I still had Emma."

"Oh, I see." I opened the door to let in enough air to un-fog the mirror. "And you don't today?"

"I do not." I could practically hear his smile. "She's spending the night at my aunt's. Are you doing anything tonight?"

"Not really, I just have to finish packing for my trip on Tuesday. Why do you ask?"

"Oh, you're going on a trip?" he asked. "Where to?"

"Nothing crazy, just a little daycation to Virginia," I said. "I just really need to get out of my head for a day or two, ya know?"

"Yeah, I can relate." He laughed. "That's actually why I'm calling you."

"What do you mean?"

"How would you like to go on a little trip with me?" he asked.

There was no way in hell I was going on a road trip with Liam. "What kind of trip?"

"The psychedelic kind." He laughed. "I don't have a lot of friends, and the ones I do are nurses and hate drugs. But you like drugs, and I like drugs. Tripping alone is kind of a bummer, ya know?"

Huh.

"Oh, damn," I said. "I mean, what is it?"

"Acid," he said. "One of my coworkers confiscated a ten strip off her nephew. She was too paranoid to throw it in the garbage. Didn't know what else to do with them and just gave them to me. We went to school together; she knows I used to really like tripping. It's been a good minute. I just don't want to do it alone."

"Well, there's no way in hell I'm taking half a ten strip." I laughed.

"But you'll take a couple hits?" he asked.

"God, I don't know. I haven't done acid since I was sixteen."

Not the type of trip I'd envisioned. But I loved hallucinogens as a teen. Molly and acid were my two favorite drugs aside from weed. The joy it gave me... That was something I desperately wanted right about then.

Maybe it'd be fun.

"Yeah, same," he said. "It was the best shit when I was a kid though. I went on a little acid binge the summer before my junior year in high school and it was the best summer of my life."

"Yeah, me too," I muttered. "Not about the binge, just the loving it part."

"So is that a yes?" he asked excitedly.

Another laugh. "I don't know, Liam."

"Oh, come on. It'll be fun. I'll bring Emma's laser show projector and a little strobe light thing, and we'll have the time of our lives," he said.

Acid was a blast. I loved what it did to my mind. I loved that I lost touch with reality. I loved that I couldn't pull my cheeks down until I came off of it. I had some of the best sex of my life on acid, everything tasted better, and the world looked beautiful.

I wanted to feel that way again. I wanted to smile so big that my face hurt for two days. I wanted to lose touch with reality. It seemed like a good idea at the time.

The thing about tripping though? It's all about your mindset. You control where the trip takes you. And I had absolutely no control of my shit storm reality as it was.

I genuinely thought it'd be a great time.

Spoiler: it wasn't.

"Alright, fine. But no strobe lights."

"Deal," Liam said. "Alright, awesome. I'm gonna try to get some sleep so I'm not a zombie when we come down tomorrow. You probably should too. I'm thinking around eight or so?"

"Eight sounds good. That gives me enough time to get everything handled around the diner, run some errands for stuff I need for my road trip, and then finish packing."

"Cool shit," he said. "Awesome, I'll see you tonight then. Your place or mine?"

"Mine would be good, that way I don't have to leave Tink at Leah's or anything."

"Sounds good. I'll see you tonight then," he said.

Tripping used to feel like this beautiful, connective, spiritual experience. I still remember my first trip. I was fifteen. Adrian ordered pizza and we stayed up all night talking about our lives as we played Crash Bandicoot on Max's old PlayStation 3 in her gloriously furnished bedroom. I hung out with my two best friends, feeling for the first time what it meant to be alive. I swore that it changed my entire perspective on life. It didn't, but it did make me see the beauty of the world around me for those twelve or so hours.

I'd never had a bad trip. It didn't even cross my mind that things could go wrong. It should have been my first thought. I'd seen Demons, Werewolves, Vampires, and the horrors of the supernatural world in the flesh now—things I never even imagined existed the last time I tripped.

As if I wasn't manic enough, somehow willfully hallucinating seemed like a good idea.

CHAPTER FORTY-FOUR

JEREMY

She'd called me into her office a moment prior. It was nice. It smelled like lavender. The walls were a comforting, neutral gray. A bundle of carnations perched from a glass vase on the mahogany table beside her floral printed armchair.

I hadn't rushed out of Laila's because I had to get home. I rushed out to make it here.

Truthfully, I'd wished that we'd have scheduled for a few weeks later. But she said she had an opening for the next day, so here I was.

This wasn't exactly something I was looking forward to. I guessed it was necessary though. I needed to talk to someone who couldn't repeat my thoughts or relay it to Laila.

Yeah, I'd been doing alright. But I knew I was fucked up. I needed this.

"Well, I feel like I'm meeting a celebrity." Doctor Williams smiled, extending her hand for mine. "I've seen your videos on YouTube, you're an excellent musician."

"They aren't really my videos. People just recorded and put them up on their personal accounts. Some little shit's getting a paycheck from YouTube on my music."

She chuckled. "Well, at least they spelled your name right."

I laughed. "I guess that's a plus."

She smiled. Then she sat and gestured to the couch. "Please, have a seat."

Ugh. I hoped she wasn't going to tell me to lie down now.

I lowered myself to the white couch. I place my elbows on my knees and folded my hands in front of me. My lips vibrated in a trill. "So how does all this work?"

"Therapy?" She raised a brow. I nodded, and she chuckled. "You talk."

"Well, yeah. I know that, but, like, where do we start?" I asked.

"That depends on why you're here," she said. "Are you here to talk about your son? Or your addiction? Or your marriage?"

What was there to talk about? Laila had already told her my life story.

"I don't know. All of it, I guess? I'm a little broken, I just need to be fixed."

She chuckled. Then she lifted her coffee from the table and took a sip. "Recovering from anything, whether it be addiction, or trauma, or a bad break-up, is healing, Jeremy. I can't just snap my fingers and fix you."

"Be pretty cool if you could," I muttered.

She smiled. "Believe me, I wish it were that easy. My work would be a lot less frustrating if it were. But most of the time, just talking helps a lot."

"I'm not very good at that."

"Talking?" she asked.

"Yeah. At least, about myself. I can talk about other people for hours. That's probably why I'm married to Laila." I looked down at my wedding ring. "I don't know, I just like other people's lives more than mine."

"Become a therapist, you'd love it."

I laughed. That wouldn't work for me. I had this drive to fix other people's problems. Rather than giving advice, I'd end up diving headfirst into other people's lives and trying to repair them on my own.

"So tell me about yourself, Jeremy."

"You already know a lot about me." I laughed. "I don't know. Maybe this would work better if you asked me questions."

"Alright. Then, as cheesy as this sounds, let's start with your child-hood. You lost your parents when you were young, right?" she asked.

So damn cliché. But maybe a lot of my problems did start there. What the hell did I know? I wasn't the psychologist.

"Yeah. Yeah, I did."

"Would you like to talk about that?" she asked. "Their deaths and how they affected you?"

"I don't know. If it's going to help, then yeah. I guess."

"Tell me about your mom then," she said. "What was she like?"

A sad smile pulled at my lips. "I don't remember her very much. I was six when she died. I just have fleeting memories from time to time. I remember her smile though, and the smell of her perfume."

She smiled. "And your dad?"

There went my smile. "Mostly, I just remember his death. I remember the good times too, there were a lot of them. He wasn't a bad parent or anything. It's just kind of hard to forget finding your dad's corpse hanging from a ceiling fan, ya know?"

Her tone was gentle. "That must have been really hard."

I bit my cheek. "Yeah. It still is, I guess."

"How old were you then?"

"Eight." I remembered that clearly. It wasn't long after my birthday. We'd had a big party, Dad seemed so happy at it. I didn't remember the party itself that clearly, but I remembered how happy he looked.

I guessed that's where I got it from. He pretended to be okay when he was really dying inside too.

"And your aunt took you in after his death?" she asked.

"Yeah. She moved in with us. Into Dad's old room, actually."

Still, I had a hard time walking into that room. It was Leah's now. It'd been more than a decade, but any time I opened that door, I could still see him hanging there. Face purple, bloated and deformed, long black hair dangling in front of it.

I fought a shudder.

"She passed too, didn't she?" Doctor Williams asked.

"Yeah. Not long after we lost Chris."

"How did she die?" she asked.

"A Demon killed her. My other brother, Adam, he killed him though." I paused. "I don't know, it was pretty shitty."

"Death always is," she said gently. "How old were you then?"

"Seventeen," I muttered. "Almost eighteen."

"How did you feel after her death?" she asked.

I gave a soft laugh followed by a shake of my head. Obviously, I'd been devastated. We all were. But I wasn't just sad. "Ashamed."

"Ashamed?" she asked. "Why?"

"I'd been on drugs for a while," I muttered. "A couple days before she died, I overdosed. For the second time actually. She was scared I wasn't going to stop until I turned up dead. So, while I was unconscious, her and Adam teleported me to my room. They lined it with hematite and morion so I couldn't use my powers to get out. I was sick, and I was furious. She said that she couldn't get me into rehab because I could teleport right out."

My eyes stung with tears. "I told her it was bullshit. That I wasn't a little kid, and I could make my own choices. I don't know, a bunch of shit. I called her a cunt. The last thing I said to her was 'I hate you.'" A lump formed in my throat before I swallowed it back down. I'd been such a little shit. "And she said, 'You can hate me all you want, but I'm never going to stop loving you. One day, you'll have kids, and you'll understand. They might hate you for making the best decision for them, but you'll love them no matter what they call you.'"

Doctor Williams passed me a box of tissues. I set them on the couch beside me. Guess I wasn't as good at hiding how I felt as I thought.

"How long were you clean after that?"

I cleared my throat. "Almost six years."

"And when did you relapse?" she asked.

"March of last year," I murmured. "When Laila was taken."

She watched me carefully. "That sent a shock through the entire supernatural community. My wife even got me a gun because she was so scared. I know what it did to every supernatural creature I've met. I can only imagine what it did to you."

I released something that resembled a laugh. "It was bad."

"Because of your bond, you could feel what was happening to her, right?" Doctor Williams asked. I nodded, gazing at the floor. "That must have made things even worse for you."

"Not really," I muttered. "In some ways, yeah. The pain was awful but if it hurt, that meant she was still alive. It made me feel like a failure. But she was alive."

Doctor Williams said, "What were you using at the time?"

"Just alcohol at first," I said. "Not like that was a good thing either. I'm an addict, I can't drink any more than I can take pills or dope."

"At what point did you move back to pills?" She propped her elbow on the arm of her chair and placed her chin in her palm.

"The night Laila was raped." She waited for me to go on. "I... I, um... I felt it. As it was happening, I mean. And then afterward when everything was sore and bruised and..." I cleared my throat and shook my head a bit. "It was brutal. I just... I just felt completely defeated. She was hurt. Like, a different kind of hurt than any time before. And I wasn't there. I didn't keep her safe, and I couldn't talk to her or hold her, and I couldn't take her to Leah to be healed and she needed me, and I wasn't there, and... I just wanted to make the pain go away for a little bit."

"How long were you using after that?"

"It was a onetime thing at that point. Her sister said something about how if I could feel her pain then she could feel mine. And I was high, and I thought about it, and it made sense. So I... I cut I love you into my arm." An awkward laugh. "It sounds really creepy to say out loud."

"Once you could communicate with her, you stopped using?" she asked quietly.

"Yeah, for a while."

"When did you start again?" she asked.

"I think July of last year. Laila and I got into a big fight. We both said hurtful things. Me more so than her, but... It was stupid. I don't even know why I did it."

"Your triggers are clearly linked to emotional pain, Jeremy," Doctor Williams said. "Some people are triggered by places, others by needles, or seeing others use. But yours seem to be directly tied to emotional trauma."

Well, duh.

"Yeah. Yeah, I guess."

She pushed up her glasses. "So when was the last time you used?"

"Thirty days ago today actually." I gave a bare smile.

"Wow, congratulations. That's a milestone."

"Yeah. That's why I'm here, I think. I don't want to relapse again. I want to stay clean and I know I can. I had a lot of clean time under my belt before I relapsed this last time. I just don't like NA. But I know I have issues, and I want to work through them."

"That's the first step." She smiled. "Recognizing you have a problem and wanting to do better."

I gave a bare smile back. "Yeah, Laila doesn't know about this. Me getting clean, I mean. So please don't tell her. I just, uh... I don't want her to know until I've got my shit together a little more, you know?"

"Everything you say here is confidential, don't worry," Doctor Williams said. "So what made you take the leap and want to get sober?"

"I got into a fight with Laila."

She laughed. "Why does that not surprise me."

"It wasn't really about her though," I said. "I mean, yeah, I want her back and I know she won't be with me if I'm using. But that wasn't it."

"What was it then?" she asked.

"It's a long story." Doctor Williams crossed her legs and waited for me to go on. "Um, alright. Well, we were hanging out a few weeks ago. We had a pretty good night." I cleared my throat and scratched my head. "She was going to let me spend the night, but I couldn't sleep. I was getting some mild withdrawals. And, uh... Well to make a long story short, she walked in on me snorting some pills.

"She was reasonably upset. And then she started talking about how she found me on the floor and... I don't know. It resonated with me. She's been through a lot, but the way she looks when she talks about that... It's how she looks when she talks about losing Micah. And I know that feeling. I had that feeling when she died, and I wouldn't wish it on my worst enemy. It's like half of me was gone," I said. "And my siblings, putting them through that again terrifies me. We're close, you know? We're not just brothers and sisters, we're friends. It fucked them up pretty bad too and that's not fair either." I paused, licking my lips. "But she said something else. It really pissed me off at the time, but then I thought about its and... I don't know."

"What did she say?" Doctor Williams asked.

"About Micah. That I won't get to be his parent or something if I don't get my shit together." I twirled my wedding ring. "But she's right. If I were still using, how could I be a parent to my kid? I could nod off and anything could happen. He could fall and bust his head open, or turn on the stove and cause a fire, or fall down the steps, or drown in the toilet, or who knows. Kids get hurt. Or I could overdose, and he could find me. And I can't put him through that."

"What I'm getting here is that your worst fear is your son living what you lived. Is that the case?"

"Yeah. Yeah, I guess. Almost twenty years later, and I still have nightmares about finding him. It used to hurt when I thought about it, but now it just makes me angry. I know I haven't really gotten to be a dad yet, but I already love my son more than I love anything. Even more than I love Laila, which is saying a lot. But still, if I had him, I'd never let him go. I could never willingly leave him like my dad did to us. He *chose* to end his life. It just makes me so angry because I would never do that to my kid. Part of me hates him for it and I don't want Micah to feel that way about me. I don't want to fuck him up like my dad fucked me up. I want to be a good dad. I'm *going* to be a good dad, but I can't be if I'm using."

"That makes a lot of sense."

"I just don't want him to be like me, you know? Like the me I've been recently. I want him to have someone he can look up to. I want to *know* that I'm doing everything in my power to be a good dad and a good person. What they're doing to him, what he's seen or is going to see by the time we find him if we don't soon... I just want to show him what it means to be good."

She gave a soft smile. "You've got a good head on your shoulders, Jeremy. You just have to remember to use it."

CHAPTER FORTY-FIVE

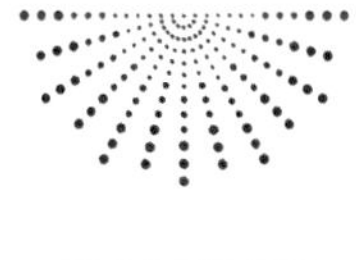

JEREMY

I pulled off my jacket and dropped it onto the granite island. Then I dug in my jeans pocket and laid the flash drive down in front of Leah. She met my gaze and picked it up. "What's this?"

"Essentially? A snuff film of my wife's torture."

Her face screwed up. "What?"

"Peterson." I sat beside her. "He sent this to Tina Davis."

Her eyes widened. "The FBI agent?"

"She's watched it. She knows about Laila's powers. He told her a lot. Things we can do, how many of us there are."

"Shit." Leah's eyes widened. "Shit. She hasn't told anyone, has she?"

"No, I don't think so. But we have to figure something out. Even if she hasn't told anyone, Peterson is becoming a bigger problem. If he's willing to expose us to the FBI, he's willing to expose us to the world. Maybe that was his goal all along. Gather enough data to know how to kill and control us and then tell the world we exist and give them the resources to destroy us."

"I'm going to talk to some Angels. If I can contact Sariel, we can arrange a meeting with the Council. We're talking about mass exposure here; this isn't a joke." Leah's voice was firm. "I'll contact Mary and tell her it's urgent. But in the meantime, don't say a word to Tina. We'll see what the Angels think first."

"Laila said she's going to arrange something for after we get back from Virginia. Thanks for that, by the way. I know it wasn't her idea."

"She needs to quit being stupid. She's making herself miserable for no reason. And you need to tell her you're clean. Hiding shit is how you got into this mess in the first place."

"Yeah, I will," I said. "I just want more clean time under my belt first. I don't want her to think I just got clean to get her back. And that's what she'll say, I know it is."

Her green eyes shifted over me. "She wants you to be clean, Jeremy. She won't condemn you for that."

"She might. I'm just not ready for that yet."

Narrowing her gaze, she said, "You're ready, and we both know it. If you tell her you're clean, it's going to change everything."

"Maybe. But do you know how many times she's told me no, Leah?" I raised a brow. "Do you know how much it hurts when I beg her to take me back and she tells me no? It's pathetic. I'm tired of begging. I'm not going to show off every small accomplishment like that's enough of a reason for her to take me back. She needs a friend right now and that's what I'm going to be unless she asks me to be more than that."

A soft smile came across her lips. "Getting clean isn't a small accomplishment, Jeremy. But that's a very mature perspective."

"That's what I was going for. I also went to therapy this morning."

"Oh?" She sipped her coffee.

I nodded again, lifting my to-go cup from the counter. "It was kind of nice," I muttered. "I'm pretty fucked up. I need to work on that."

"Well, you're doing a good job." Leah smiled. "I'm proud of you, man. You're trying really hard to be the best version of yourself that you can be, and I applaud you for that."

It felt so good to hear her say that. Yeah, I called Leah my sister. But in all actuality, she was more of a parent. And it always feels good when a parent says they're proud.

I smiled. "I just can't stop trying."

She smiled back. "No. No, you can't. But I'm going to start digging on this flash drive. There might be something on here. I'm assuming you haven't watched it?"

"I wish I hadn't," I muttered. "Laila said she was going to, and she didn't want to do it alone."

"Damn." Her eyes widened. "How did that go?"

"She thought it wouldn't bother her, but it's... It's hard to watch. She got black out drunk and fell asleep."

"So that's why you weren't here?" She raised a brow.

"She woke up when I took her to bed. She was scared. She didn't want to be alone."

"Sappy fuckers." Leah started to her feet. "Is there anything on here I should know beforehand?"

"It's brutal," I said. "So ya know, prepare yourself. And don't look at her like she's a victim afterward; that'll piss her off. And don't tell her I told you she was scared. That'd probably piss her off too."

"Will do."

"You might want to watch the last video first. See his face. Get you warmed up." My stomach turned. "It's really hard to watch, Leah."

"Laila's cool with me watching it though?" she asked. I gave a nod, and she sighed. "Then time for me to put on my big girl pants. You guys lived it. I'll be alright. If it helps us find my brother and nephew, it's worth it."

"Don't let anyone else see it though. I don't know how she'd feel about that."

"Probably not good." Leah stood, collected her laptop, and started upstairs. "Tell no one to bother me until further notice. I'm behind on work stuff, and I have phone calls to make and now I have this. I need peace."

"Will do. Let me know if you find anything." I stood. "I'm running to the store to get stuff for my trip. Text me if you need anything."

"Cool, I have a list on the fridge. It's the big grocery trip of the month but I'm trying to find your child and keep a roof over our heads, so have fun," Leah called as she ascended the stairs.

"My lucky day," I muttered.

CHAPTER FORTY-SIX

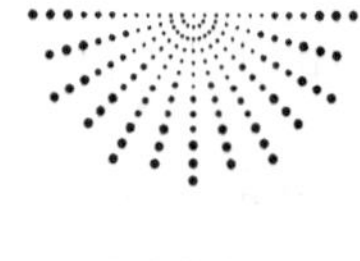

LAILA

The first couple hours or so of my trip were pretty fun. It wasn't some beautiful, uplifting experience or anything along those lines, but it wasn't unpleasant. Liam and I sat on the floor of my apartment listening to Moe's old record collection as we talked about how cool the walls looked as they breathed.

Honestly, it was kind of hard to explain. My thoughts were always foggy when I tripped. They ran in circles, mostly incoherent, stumbling around dumb shit. I focused on things that didn't matter like the spinning of the ceiling fan above the coffee table in the living room.

I remember thinking that I was having fun but having this impending sense of doom in the back of my mind that I couldn't seem to break past. It was like the barriers of some wall I'd assembled in my brain were beginning to crumble.

When I went to the kitchen to grab a couple of drinks, my gaze caught on the sketch of Micah on the fridge. My heart sunk as I raised my finger and slid it along the page.

In my hallucinating mind, I swear I saw his head turn to me. His little hand even waved. I smiled.

Then, suddenly, I had this sixth sense feeling that someone was watching me. Of course, I was hallucinating, but my mind was allowing me to see what my conscious thoughts didn't want to fathom.

I turned.

Chris stood by the bar into the living room.

I grasped my chest and dropped one of the bottled waters to the ground.

He didn't look the way he had in my dream. He looked how I imagined he genuinely did. His empty eye sockets stared back at me. Blood dripped from them. He looked skinnier than he had. His skin was pasty, chafing on his cheeks and neck.

Bright red blood left the corner of his lips. "You'll find it and then you'll find us. But you have to look for it, Laila. You can't just keep sitting around and waiting for it to fall in your lap."

"Chris." I began quietly approaching him.

He drew closer. His hands gripped my shoulders. His empty eye sockets turned down to me, as if he could see me. "It wasn't a dream, Laila. You have to find us before they kill him."

"But how?" I reached out to touch him. My hands drifted right through him, and he glitched like a video game.

"You have to go back." His voice shook. "Find it, and then find us. Find us before it's too late."

And then he was gone.

Of course, he was never there. I was tripping my balls off and I was already in a bad state. It was my own mind telling me what I had known I had to do for months.

I had to go back.

"Laila." Liam started to his feet. "Who you talking to, baby girl?"

"I think Chris has been trying to send me a message." I tilted my head, focusing on the dream. "He was here. I know he was."

"You're tripping, Laila." He reached out to gingerly place a hand on my shoulder.

"No, I know," I said. "But I've been having these dreams. I had one last night. He—He told me it wasn't a dream. I don't think I'm crazy, Liam. He's been trying to tell me something, I know he has."

"What did he say?"

"That I have to go back," I said. "There's something there. He said, 'You'll find it, then you'll find us.'"

"What do you mean?" he asked. "Where?"

"Where they were holding us." I squinted, trying to look at the counter without seeing it breathe in and out. "I have to go back, Liam. There's something there, I know there is."

"Let's get a team together. We'll go over every inch of the place."

I should have listened. But—tripping my balls off or not—I believed I had a lead. And I couldn't ignore that. I couldn't ignore a chance at finding my baby.

"No, I've wasted enough time already. No, I'm going tonight. There's something there. I have to find it and then I can find them. I have to find them, Liam. I have to."

"We should wait," he said. "We aren't in a state of mind to deal with that."

"I'm going, Liam." I started to the door. I pulled my jacket over my arms and stepped into my boots. "With or without you, I'm going. There's a fifty percent chance I'm wrong, and in which case, no harm done. The place has been abandoned for over a year, no one's there. I'll be fine."

"I don't think this is a good idea, Laila," Liam insisted. "We're tripping and—"

"You can stay here then." I adjusted the zipper on my boot. "But I'm going."

He frowned. "Let me get my shoes on."

<hr>

I stood in the cool dewy grass staring up at the partially demolished building. I'd never seen it from this perspective. I'd only seen it from inside. It looked a lot like I'd imagined it would.

The moon cast a bluish, white glow on the chipped cement. Waves roared against the shore to my left and right. Vines and ivy had begun to climb their way up the walls. The grass was nearly knee length high and infested with bugs.

It was vacant. Abandoned. And nature was taking back what belonged to it.

A large capital H shaped of stone and cement. The stress test room, Peterson's office, and the significant captors five-star suites were in the longest section. Either end was where the wings for the common captors sat.

On the far right, the top two floors were blown off. I don't know why anyone would believe an explosion caused it. Maybe a tornado, but certainly not an explosion. There were no burn marks. The ground of the second floor was in almost perfect condition. It looked like it had been designed that way because it had been. I tried to destroy it piece by piece.

It was almost disappointing when I looked at it from the ground up. I'd barely made a dent in the big picture.

I wished those waves that crashed against the hillside beside us would grow large and strong enough to tear the building to the ground. I supposed I could make that happen if I tried hard enough.

But I wasn't here to destroy this time. I was here to rummage the wreckage. I supposed that's what I'd been doing for the past year anyway.

It was a good thing I didn't burn it to the ground that day after all.

"Are you sure you want to do this?" Liam asked quietly. He looked the place over. "We don't have to right now. We can come back another time."

"I'm sure." I started toward the main entrance. "I have to do this."

He tailed close behind. "I just don't think this is a good idea."

"Then I can take you home." I started inside. "But I'm doing this, Liam."

"Laila—"

I turned and quickly locked my gaze with his. "I'm doing this. Decide now if you want me to take you home."

"I just think we should wait—"

"So you want me to take you home?" I raised a brow.

He held my gaze. "I don't want you to do this on your own. So fuck me, I guess."

CHAPTER FORTY-SEVEN

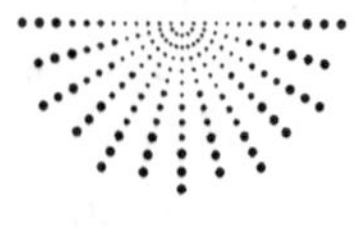

JEREMY

My fingers spun the turning keys of my old acoustic guitar. I strummed it and listened closely over Hannah and Kai's conversation at the table.

"Does this sound flat to you?" I interrupted them with a strum.

"Do it again." Hannah creased her brows a bit. I strummed again, and she shook her head. "No, it sounds good."

"Are you sure?" I slid the pick against the strings once more and fidgeted with the key. "It sounds off to me."

"Nah, it's good," Hannah said. "Do you want some pizza? I don't want to wrap up two slices."

"Yeah, I'm hungry." I set my guitar on the ground, started to my feet, and walked around the bar. I reached into the box. "So how's school, Han?"

"So far so good. Mostly just syllabuses and professor introductions. It's pretty stupid."

"Well, it's not so bad. You only have six more years." I smiled.

"*Only* six more years." She took a bite from her pizza. "No big deal or anything."

"Not at all," I said.

"So have you found anything about Micah?" She sat at a bar stool. "Leah put a 'Do Not Disturb' sign on her door. She usually does that when she finds something."

"Probably not but maybe. Peterson sent that FBI agent videos of Laila killing the people who were torturing her with her powers."

"And she didn't arrest her?"

"Nope. I don't think anyone with a heart could. The videos make you feel for her. She's... She's begging them to stop. She doesn't want to do it, you can see that she isn't trying to hurt anyone. Her body is defending itself. He sent it to her in particular, not the FBI. He said something in the last clip, something about how she's a part of this story?"

"And that's what Leah's watching? Those videos?"

I gave a nod.

"Jesus," she said in a low murmur. "I don't think I could stomach that."

"It wasn't easy." I reached into my jacket and pulled out a joint. Rummaging through my jeans pocket, I found my lighter. Then I lifted it up and held it to the end.

"*You* watched it?"

I lit the joint. Breathing in a long hit, I said, "I did."

"Why?" she asked. "Why would you want to see that?"

"Laila was going to watch them either way. I didn't want to. But she asked me to stay with her and I have a really hard time telling her no."

"You should work on that," she muttered. "Jesus, I can't even imagine watching something like that at all. Let alone to someone I love. Are you okay?"

I hit the joint again and passed it to her. "It was hard to see her in pain. When I felt it happening, I didn't understand the context. She didn't really talk about it when she got home, at least not with me. But in every video except for the last one, she won. She ended it. And I know how awful it sounds but it made me proud of her. She was so... I always had to protect her. And in some ways, I still do but to see what she's capable of... I could never tell her I feel that way. She'd immediately correlate it to his responses, so please don't tell her I said this but, it kind of helped me. It made me realize how strong she is, and in its own way, it was kind of beautiful. Not what happened to her but how she reacted to it."

"Murder is beautiful?"

"Justice is beautiful," I said. "I know how that sounds, I do. I know it's cryptic and brutal, but she... She had to rely on me for so much before. And I think that's part of what made me so crazy about her, ya know? The whole damsel in distress type of thing? But she isn't. She hasn't been for a long time, and I... I don't know. I'm just starting to see that. And I still love her. I still want her. But it feels like growth. Accepting that she doesn't have to need me for me to care for her, if that makes any sense."

"Yeah. Yeah, it does." Hannah smiled. "If it helps, I think you're growing too. But not into someone new. Into you."

An hour or so later, Hannah, Kai, Adam, Jenna, Brody, and I sat around the living room. We laughed, playing an intense game of Cards Against Humanity. It was kind of boring from time to time, but I enjoyed it. It would get quiet then suddenly loud and chaotic.

They all sipped wine, or some dark colored liquor, and I was sober as a surgeon, but I was just as happy as they were. In a way, that encouraged me. That I could enjoy being around some of my favorite people in the world while being sober.

I'm not sure that any of us were really happy. But I think we were close for a little while.

My earlier conversation with Hannah couldn't have been more ironic though, because as I stood from the couch to get a drink, my heart nearly stopped beating.

A splitting, stabbing pain shot through my abdomen.

I doubled over and grasped the couch for stability.

"Are ye all right?" Kai started to his feet.

It wasn't my pain, it was hers. I knew it was, and I knew exactly what that sensation was. She'd just been stabbed in the gut.

I pulled myself up and tapped my front and back pockets. "Where's my phone?" I slid it out. The intense, stabbing throb in my lower left side remained steady.

My fingers trembled, scrolling to Laila's contact. The call went straight to voicemail.

A sudden jerk pulled against her skin, pain intensifying.

I focused on her, trying to see through her eyes. But instead, I could only enter her thoughts. They were a jumbled ball of yarn, twisting and catching on themselves, struggling to break free.

It was noisy, like the bustle of a concert as the crowd applauds for the opening act. Everything was sloppy and incoherent. Almost like many voices were yelling and chasing the words they just breathed. It wasn't the drunken confused thoughts Laila often had.

They were running in cycles; loops, tracing around each other and overlapping like a car spinning in obnoxious, tire peeling donuts. I couldn't understand any of it. The only thing I could make out was this primal, aggressive, almost animalistic fear.

After only a second, I realized where I knew that feeling from. I'd only done acid once; hallucinogens weren't really my thing. But the loops in one's head are impossible to associate with almost any other drug.

When I realized I wouldn't be able to get into her head, I started looking for her energy. The closest way I can think to explain it is like looking over a crowded room for someone in a neon-colored shirt where everyone else is wearing black.

Then I recognized the place.

My heart sunk.

Adam was gripping my shoulder with wide eyes. Everyone else stared at me. "What's happening, Jeremy?"

Jenna stood close behind him, gazing up at me with wide, fearful eyes. Hannah perched on the arm of the couch toward me. Her shaking hand clenched a glass of wine. Brody was already walking toward me with a look just like Adam's. Kai said something that didn't register.

"She's back there. She's hurt, something's wrong. I'm going to get her, be ready to heal, Kai."

Brody and Hannah yelled something, but I was gone. Adam was still gripping my shoulder as we spun through space.

The wind twisted around us like a turbine to a plane. Lightning flashed in the night sky above. Water poured from the black clouds to the earth. The waves crashed against the shorelines hundreds of feet away.

I started running through the door.

Adam jogged close behind me. I bolted through the entrance propped open with a rock. I hadn't seen this part of it before, but I didn't have time to take it in. I just followed her power.

I could feel her energy just as strong as the wind that rushed against my clothes. It was so powerful that it fluttered my hoodie in something of a tornado against my skin. Seeing the series of small cyclones in the room around me, I knew it was her. I'd never seen her manipulate air in such a large range before. Yet, I didn't know that I'd ever felt her that scared before.

We jogged up a few flights of stairs, chasing her energy. It felt like the longest two minutes of my life. Running through those dark hallways brought me back to that night. The broken, hanging light fixtures. The dust spinning through the air. The crisp, cold touch to the atmosphere.

As I felt closer to her, I heard a man yelling incoherently. Or begging, maybe.

Then her screaming in reply.

A bright violet glow coming from a room down the hall lit the stairwell of the fourth floor. I could feel the heat as soon as I pushed open the heavy metal door.

Nearly out of breath, I darted down the hallway to the vibrant light. Her yelling was almost entirely incoherent, nearly a sob. Another voice yelled against her, loudly demanding she calm down before she killed them both.

"Laila," I called as I got closer to the doorway.

Then I turned my gaze into the room.

And I can't pretend like I didn't almost piss myself.

She stood with her back against the wall in front of me, hand clutched to her stomach as the other outstretched from her shoulder. But she was invisible, engulfed in violent purple. Merely an outline of fire in the shape of a human.

I'd seen her body glow. I'd seen her hands and arms ignite. I'd seen her lose control but never anything like that. Never had I seen her entire body engulfed in a ball of fire so large that I couldn't find her beneath them. Especially flames that weren't red or orange.

As I got closer, she began crying. I felt the pain surge through her body with every sob. She doubled over and yelled, "Stay back."

I took a few steps closer. "Baby, it's me."

"I can't stop," she said between gasping tears. "*Get back!*"

"I'm not going anywhere." I raised my hands in surrender with a smile. "It's okay, Lai."

"I hurt him." She made out between cries. Hyperventilating, she gestured toward the corner of the room to my right. I followed the direction of her gaze to Liam on the floor. His face was black with smog. He grasped his ankle in agony. A look of outright terror shined in his eyes, nearly rocking in a fetal position.

Big strong Werewolf my ass.

"And I killed him," Laila said, voice shaking as the flames grew. Her head shifted to a pile of ash a few feet in front of her. She raised her fiery fists to either side of her head. "I—I didn't mean to. I should have kept him alive. He—He knew something, that's why he tried to kill me. He tried to kill me and I just—I just—"

"Get him out," I muttered to Adam behind me and took a few steps closer. "Laila, it's—"

"Don't tell me it's okay!" she screamed, still clutching either side of her head. "It's not okay. Nothing is fucking okay."

Adam brushed past me and helped Liam to his feet.

I took a few steps closer. "Look at me, baby. Look at me."

"Get back, Jeremy." Her voice shook as she pushed her body tighter into the steel corner. "I can't—You'll—I'll hurt you, you have to get back."

"You won't," I said softly. I let my smile widen as I got a bit closer. "You won't hurt me, Lai. I know you won't."

"No." Her shaking head moved like a flaming ball on top of a glowing mannequin. "No, please." Her tears got louder. The air spun faster, fire licking toward me. "I can't hurt you too. Please, please stop."

"You're scared." I drew another foot inward. There were only a few feet between us as the purple color began to fade to red. Sweat trickled from my forehead down my cheek but I retained my composure. I carefully pulled my jacket off of my arms and dropped it to the ground. "But you're okay, Laila. Everything else doesn't have to be, but you are. You're okay."

She was holding either flaming hand to her face, stifling her heavy sobs. I gently stared her down, arms open. Her eyes were in there somewhere, they had to be because I felt her gaze on me. But they were hidden behind the bright blaze that burned from every inch of her petite body. It gradually turned to orange as she cried. "I can't make it stop."

"Yes, you can. You're already cooling off a little." I smiled and moved in another foot. I gently reached my arm out. She retreated further into the corner. She collapsed to the ground and carefully pulled her knees to her chest. Red surged from her skin for a second before turning back to yellow with orange and only a few licks of red. She became a glowing ball of fire on the ground.

I lowered myself in front of her. "You control it, Laila, it doesn't control you. You're scared, and you're hurt, and you're hallucinating, but you're in control of it. You can make it stop, but you have to breathe, okay?" I said softly. "Just breathe, baby."

"I'm—I just, I can't," she said between heaving cries. "I can't—I don't know how to make it stop. I don't—" I reached my hand out. "Stop, Jeremy." She frantically shook her head again. "I don't want to hurt you. Please. Please stop."

I ignored her and gently pushed my fingers through the edges of the flames.

It fucking hurt. I literally just put my hand in a fire, obviously it hurt. But I had to pretend that it didn't.

She grimaced as my fingers singed and burned hers through the bond. The smell of burning flesh filled my nostrils.

Then the flames on her body collapsed into her skin.

She kept her face tucked low into her knees, panting out labored breaths. Her body was shaking, curled in a ball, struggling to bring air into her lungs. It was only then that I saw her blood spilling out onto the cement at our feet. She was naked, shivering as the wind brushed long red hair into her blood smeared face.

I reached for the jacket behind me. After lifting it from the ground, I draped it around her shoulders. Just as it touched her skin, she opened her eyes. They widened in shock. Her teeth chattered as she turned her gaze to mine.

"There she is." I touched her cheek and gave a smile. "See? I told you, you wouldn't hurt me."

CHAPTER FORTY-EIGHT

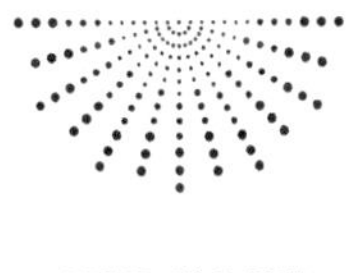

JEREMY

er shaking hands grasped my wrist to heal the superficial burns. She struggled to steady her breaths. As it mended, her eyes grew a bit less frantic and a little more disoriented. I pulled it away and reached out to touch her face. "Can you walk?"

Her head shook and she gripped her bleeding stomach. "I don't know."

"Here." I took the sleeve of my hoodie and pressed it to the oozing wound. Then I wrapped the top portion around her shoulders. "I can't teleport out of here because of the barrier spells. We'll have to get outside first."

She brought herself to her knees, trying to stand. But she stumbled. Her white lips trembled.

"You're losing a lot of blood. We'll move faster if I carry you."

Her wide, puppy dog eyes turned to mine. "Don't let Adam see my butt."

I smiled, chuckling. I reached an arm below her knees and the other behind her shoulders. The adrenaline still pumped through my veins, making it feel like I was lifting a feather to my arms.

"I don't know what I was thinking." She closed her eyes, pressing her palm into the bleeding wound. "This was so fucking stupid."

I positioned her body better against my chest and started out of the room. "Who stabbed you?"

"It was a guard, I think. Everything looks weird and trippy though. I—I'm not sure but it—It looked like a guard."

That didn't make sense. Why would a guard be here?

"It's been a year and a half." I started down the nearly black stair way and slowed a bit to make sure we didn't fall. "There's no reason in hell that a guard should have been here still."

She turned her confused gaze up to me. "But what—What does that mean?"

I thought back to yesterday morning. When she'd woken from that dream. Jesus Christ, was I the one who planted this idea in her head? Yeah, I thought there might be something worth looking into here, but I hadn't wanted her to check it out while she was tripping face.

"Why did you come here, Laila?" I carefully moved my foot down the next step, looking over her to the ground.

Blinking hard, her voice cracked, "I had a dream, and then a hallucination, and Chris was there." She grimaced as we took another step. She moved her hand and outstretched it toward the ground. A flame appeared.

"Thanks." I picked up speed down the stairs, now able to see where I was going. She closed her eyes and breathed heavily. I tried to step gently because I felt the pain with each bump, but she was losing a lot of blood. I had to hurry. "I'm sorry, I know this hurts."

"It's okay," she murmured. "He said it wasn't a dream and he touched my arm and I felt it. I really *felt* it."

"That's why you asked if he could dream walk this morning," I murmured as we made it to the next floor.

She groggily nodded against my chest. "He said there was something here. And if I found it, I'd find them."

"And you didn't find anything?" I asked.

Her breaths got further apart. The flame in her hand got smaller.

"Stay with me, Lai." I wistfully picked up the pace and took two steps at a time.

Her eyes fluttered open. The light in her hand grew a bit brighter. "It hurts so bad." Her skin began to feel cool under my palms.

"You've been through a lot worse." I turned down the next flight of stairs. "You're gonna be okay, this is nothing. It only hurts so bad because you're having a really bad trip."

She huffed. "I'm an idiot."

I mean, yeah. This was fucking stupid. Not coming here, but coming to the place where the worst horrors of her life occurred tripping nuts?

Yeah. Fucking stupid. But I wasn't gonna say it. Clearly, she knew that much.

"You were right," I said. "Someone was here for a reason. Somehow, Chris contacted you and they knew. They came here to get whatever he was talking about before you realized it wasn't just a dream. We'll come back with a team; we'll find it."

She nuzzled her head against my chest.

"Lai, you've got to stay up."

"I'm not sleeping," she muttered with closed eyes. "You just smell good. Like home. And I'm cold, and you're warm."

I laughed. It was sweet, it made my stomach flip, but she still needed to stay awake. I rushed out the door of the first floor into the foyer. "We're almost there, just hang on for a few more seconds."

I hurried through the grand entrance. Just clearing its large floor felt almost as long as an entire flight of stairs.

"Do you think we'll ever get to be parents?" she whispered.

My heart throbbed. Fuck, I really hoped so.

"We will," I murmured, speed walking down the sidewalk to where Adam and Liam leaned against a tree.

"I don't think the universe wants us to." Her voice was barely above a whisper. "I don't know if I'd be very good at it anyway. I like to think that I would, but I don't know if I really would. You would, but I don't think I would."

She was wrong. I knew that then, and I know that now. Yeah, she fucked up when she got in that van. But once we had our babies, she was the best mother in the universe.

Adam stood, pulled his jacket off of his arms, and started toward us.

"You already are, Lai," I said. "You've already done so much for Micah."

"Yeah, and look how that turned out," she muttered.

"You alright, Lai?" Adam asked as he laid his jacket over her legs. She gave a slow nod but kept her eyes closed, clenching my shirt.

"Is this the border?" I asked.

As Liam limped toward us, Adam said, "Yeah, about ten feet behind you. We're good."

"I got her, you get him." I glanced at Liam.

We swirled through the air. We landed in the living room about a foot from Brody.

"Jesus Christ." He clutched his chest.

I brushed past him to set Laila on the couch.

"Holy hell." Kai walked from the recliner beside me. "Laila," he said softly, touching her hand that rested on the bleeding wound. "Ye alright, love?"

As she opened her eyes, I grabbed a blanket from the back of the couch and draped it over her cold legs. She met Kai's gaze. "Not really, but I'm alive."

"At the moment." I gestured to her stomach. "She lost a lot of blood."

Kai lowered himself to his knees beside her. I kissed her forehead and straightened back up. Her bloody hand reached out for mine. Her gaze turned up to me as Kai pulled the cloth from the hole in her abdomen.

"Can you stay?" she asked quietly.

I gave a smile, lowered myself to the ground beside her, gave her hand a tight squeeze, and pressed my lips to her forehead once more.

CHAPTER FORTY-NINE

JEREMY

"Stop," Laila said, pushing Kai's hand away with her hot, flickering fingertips.

He looked to me and furrowed his brows in frustration. Then he glanced back at her oozing wound. She breathed in and out slowly, raising her bloody hand to her pale, clammy cheek.

She was anxious and out of control. Each time Kai would start healing, she'd set herself on fire and start flailing. Kai was impervious to the flames, but I wasn't. I'd try to hold her down, but then she'd burn me, push me away, and cry apologies about how she didn't want to accidentally kill me.

She lit up in flames the first time she'd been stabbed too. Leah tried to heal her, but she did the same that she was doing now. I had no choice but to take her to the hospital. They did what they had to in order to calm her down there. I knew she wasn't going to like it, but if she didn't chill out, that was our only choice now too.

I raised my hand and wiped sweat from her brow. "Lai, if he keeps stopping, he's not going to be able to heal it."

"I know." Her breaths were as uneven and shaky as her hand. "I just need a minute. Just give me a minute."

"We don't have a minute." Kai looked over her paper white skin. Her lips were just as pale. They faded into her cheeks without any color to tell them apart.

I glanced at Hannah over my shoulder. "Go see if Leah has any Xanax, Han."

She started away and gestured for Brody to follow her.

Laila forced open her heavy eyes. "I don't need that."

"If you don't calm down, Kai can't heal you." I moved my thumb along another bead of sweat on her cheek. "I'll have to take you to the hospital, and—"

She frantically shook her head. Tears welled in her eyes. Her words were soft, shaking as they left her lips. "No, I don't want to go to the hospital. I'm okay, I'm going to be okay, I just—Just please don't take me to the hospital. I can't go to a hospital right now, I—I don't want stitches and gauze and—"

"I won't, baby." I wiped a tear that came from her eye as I looked between them. "But I won't let you die either. You're scared and that's okay. But you have to calm down."

Tears streamed down her cheeks. "I'm trying."

"I know," I said. "I know you're trying, but you're tripping balls, Lai. Coming out of a bad trip isn't easy. If we took you to the hospital, this is the same thing they'd do. Whether it was against your will or not. I won't make you take it, but you need to, baby. Leah and I both tried already, and we can't make you calm down. The Xanax will help."

"I don't like benzos," she said with sad, wide green eyes. Her teeth clambered together.

Of course I understood why she was scared and didn't want to take them. But she'd die if we didn't get her healed soon. I was amazed she wasn't in shock already.

"You're safe here." I moved my hand to hers. I twined my fingers through them and lifted her knuckles to my lips. "Nothing's going to happen to you, Lai. It won't be enough to knock you out. It's just to help you calm down. And I'll be right here. I'm not going to let anything happen to you."

She clenched her shivering jaw. "It's going to take too long to work anyway. I'll be dead by then."

"Not if you snort it." Leah came into the living room. She sat on the coffee table behind where I kneeled in front of the couch. "You have to take it, Laila. Either you take it and let Kai heal you, or Jeremy takes you to the hospital. Those are your options."

Her erratic breaths jumped faster from her lips.

"Or we can melt it down and you can shoot it," Leah said. "I'm sure Jeremy can find a vein for you."

I narrowed my gaze at her, and she smiled.

Not gonna lie though, I always wished I had her veins. I'd fantasized about putting a needle in them countless times. It's a thing we do. Look at other people's arms and fantasize about jamming a needle in them. Most of mine in my arms were blown out and difficult to shoot in. Not that I ever actually wanted to put a needle in her arm, that thought freaked me out actually. But damn, did I wish I had those veins.

"No," Laila said, vigorously shaking her head. "No, I—"

"She's just being a bitch." I rolled my eyes. "Shooting benzos isn't exactly safe. But snorting it isn't a bad idea. It isn't extended release, is it?"

"Don't keep those on hand. I like instant gratification."

I turned back to Laila. She looked at me with a trembling lip. "It's up to you, Lai. But they'll have to give it to you either way if we take you to the hospital."

She looked at it in Leah's hand. "I guess I'll snort it."

Leah looked at me. "Got a dollar bill?"

I reached into my back pocket, grabbed my wallet, and turned back to Laila.

Her lip quivered as her eyes met mine. Her eyes filled with tears, and her lip trembled. *Please don't let anything happen to me.*

Of course she thought it. She had too much pride to admit aloud how scared she was.

I smiled and ran my hand over her cheek. *I got you, baby. You're gonna be fine.*

Her eyes filled with tears. She gave a nod.

After about fifteen minutes, Laila was struggling to open her eyes. When they shut, I told Kai to do it. As he began, her eyes shot open in agony. But I took her face in my hands and murmured something soft enough that her hands stopped sparking. Her body still trembled, but I told her to squeeze my hand and she channeled the pain a bit better. Her other hand wrapped around my wrist that held her cheek as she held my gaze.

Felt like she was breaking my fingers for a second there, but I digress.

Once Kai could work without her pushing him away, it only took a few minutes to close the bleeding wound. Her color began to come back a minute or two later. Then she groggily laid her head against the couch cushion behind her, eyes closed.

"How much did you give her?" I turned to Leah, still holding Laila's hand.

"Ten milligrams, I think."

"Half of that would have been sufficient."

"I just got this couch not even two months ago. Blood is one thing, that's why I got leather. But fire is another," she said. "She needs the nap. She'll thank me for it tomorrow."

I thought about arguing. But after the bad trip she'd just had, yeah. She could use the nap.

"Probably not." I carefully pulled my fingers from hers, lifted the throw blanket from the ground, and placed it over her half-naked, blood-covered body. Now that she was healed and taken care of, I could deal with the person I was furious at. "Where's Liam?"

"In the kitchen," Leah said. "But dude's pretty fucked up too. Go easy on him."

"I just want to know what the fuck happened," I muttered. "Can you stay with her in case she wakes up?"

Leah nodded and plopped into the recliner. "Throw me the remote."

I lifted it from the table, tossed it toward her, and started to the kitchen. Adam sat across from Liam. He took a casual gulp from a water bottle. As if he hadn't just let my wife run into that place and get stabbed.

"Is she alright?" Adam asked with a look over my blood covered shirt and forearms. Liam turned and glanced over me.

"She'll be fine in a couple hours," I said. "Kai healed her."

"He self-healed once we got the piece of metal out." Adam said. "Slower than most wolves. Probably the Demon blood or something, I don't know."

I walked to the sink. Then I met Liam's stare as I washed my hands. "So you're tripping right now too I'm assuming?"

He gave an awkward nod.

"Do you not know the number one rule to doing acid, dude?" I rubbed soap up and down my wrists.

"I don't know," he muttered.

"You don't do acid with someone when they're in a bad state of mind," I snapped. "And you gave acid to the most depressed, angry, super-powered hybrid the world has ever seen."

"I didn't force it down her throat."

"But you gave it to her." I glared. "And you let her go back there? With *you* as back up? You can't even teleport and you thought it was a good idea to go thousands of miles away without letting anyone know?"

"It was her idea, not mine." Liam stood. "And everyone knows there's no way to keep Laila from something she's hell-bent on."

"You have a phone, don't you?" I turned off the spigot and dried my hands with the dish towel. "I'm pretty sure you have my sister's number. You could have called us. We would have come. If we had, I wouldn't be wearing my wife's blood right now."

"It's not like the idea was heavily considered when she said she was going. I told her I wouldn't let her go without me and—"

"Yeah, a lot of help that was." I dropped the dish cloth to the counter. "You're a wolf, how did someone even get past you to stab her?"

"I was a few rooms down," he said.

I narrowed my stare further. "You weren't even with her? You wouldn't let her go by herself, but then you left her alone in the place where she was tortured for months while she was tripping on acid?"

"It wasn't like that—"

"Are you seriously that fucking stupid?" I took a step closer, and Adam stood. "You really don't give a shit about her at all, do you?"

"It's not like this was in my plan for the night, dude."

"Oh, yeah?" I felt my jaw tighten. "Then what were your plans?"

"Jeremy." Adam took a step forward.

"No, I just want to know. Get her fucked up and fuck her? Take advantage of her?" My eyes narrowed further. He opened his mouth to speak, but I kept going. "And what was your plan when you went inside that place? Just leave her by herself in her worst nightmare?"

"She said we'd cover more ground if we split up." Liam's hand clenched at his side.

Right, but didn't dispute that he planned on trying to fuck her.

"Why don't you just leave her alone?" I blurted almost unwillingly. "Clearly, you aren't that concerned with being there for her. You almost got her killed tonight—"

"Why don't you?" Liam took a step toward me. "How many times have you almost got her killed?"

Actually, not that many. We operated as a team in a fight. She had my back and I had hers. She got hurt sometimes, so did I, but never like she had tonight.

"She's my wife, I'd never abandon her. Especially not in that fucking place. And not that I owe you a damn thing, but any time she's gotten hurt, my top priority has always been getting her healed. Before anything else. Whether I'm bleeding or not, if she's in bad shape, I fucking get her help. But more importantly, I wouldn't let her go there at all when she was like that. And I damn sure wouldn't have given her acid right now." I moved forward, eyes darting between his. "She's the mother of my child—"

"You say that like you're a real husband. You aren't even a parent." He snapped. "You've never even met your kid. It's not like you're co-parenting or something, you're just the pathetic ex chasing an empty dream."

I clenched my hand to a fist and practically lunged forward. Adam stepped between us, facing me. "She'll be pissed. You know she will. All fighting him is going to do is make her bad trip even worse. He's fucked up, it wouldn't even be a fair fight. You guys have made a lot of progress lately, don't let this little shit fuck that up."

I gritted my teeth together and clenched both of my hands to fists. "Get him the fuck out of my house."

CHAPTER FIFTY

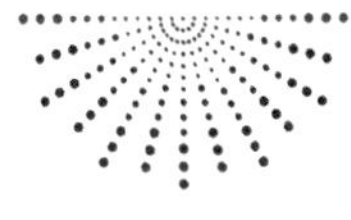

JEREMY

After I stopped angrily shaking, I grabbed a bottle of water and made my way back to the living room. Laila was vertical then. She slouched over her knees and groggily wiped a rag against her cheek. Leah sat beside her pointing to splotches of blood on her face.

I gave a smile as I made my way around the couch. "Feeling better?"

She turned to meet my gaze with a delirious, stoned grin. Her voice was barely above a whisper. "Jeremy."

Not sure why, I loved strong women. But I loved the damsel moments too. And that 'help me, thank you for coming to my rescue' look in her eyes made my heart skip with pride.

I smiled and sat on the coffee table across from her. "You okay?"

She gave a slight smile. "Yeah, I'm okay."

Leah stood. "You got it from here?"

"Yeah, we're good," I said. "I'll take care of the couch after she gets cleaned up."

She started to the stairs. "Bleach is under the sink."

Laila continued wiping blood from her cheeks.

"Taking a shower probably isn't a good idea, huh?" I asked. "Small spaces and everything?"

"I'm a little too woozy to stand." She looked down. "I'm really sorry, I didn't think anyone would be there. I just felt like I had to and..."

"You're trying to find our son," I muttered. "Don't apologize for that."

"I'm tripping face, Jeremy." She met my gaze. "How stupid was that? Dropping acid with all this shit going on right now."

I may have been pissed at Liam for giving it to her. But I understood why she took it. She wanted an escape from reality. It was stupid, but no more stupid than me banging pills. And it was always close to impossible to be mad at her. Didn't make the decision any less idiotic, but I understood it.

"I'm not really one to talk." I gave a sad smile.

Tears puddled in her eyes. "You were never too fucked up to control your powers."

"It's different for you than it is for me. You have different powers than me. You've been through different things than me. I've had my powers my whole life, you've only had yours for a few years."

She looked down. Her head shook slightly. "I feel like I'm losing control of everything. I don't know what to do anymore. I'm not good at any of this. The only thing I'm good at is work, but I don't even care about that." Her lips trembled before she quickly pressed them together. "I just want to be a mom, but I don't think I'll be good at that either. I already failed him; I don't even deserve him."

"That's not true, Lai." I took her hand and gently twisted our fingers together. "You didn't choose this. None of this is your fault."

"I got in the van." Her eyes began to water. "They didn't drag me in kicking and screaming. *I got inside.* I did that, Jeremy. No one else. This is *my fault.*"

I frowned. "We can't turn back the clock, baby. If we could, I would have the day you were taken. I would have never told you to leave. Hell, I wouldn't even have taken Daniel in."

She looked down. I reached forward and lifted her chin to face me. "But we can't hate ourselves over what could have been. All we can do is build a better future."

A silent moment.

"Do you want to borrow some clothes and get a shower in the morning?" I asked.

She gave another nod. "Can you take me upstairs? I don't want to go home."

"Here's some clothes." I walked toward the bathroom attached to my room. Laila stood facing the mirror running a wet washcloth along her bare stomach. My eyes caught on her chest where the hoodie laid open, falling just below her ass like a short dress.

As she turned to meet my gaze, I cleared my throat and looked away. Bracing herself against the sink, she stepped into the old, bleach-stained pants and laughed. "You've seen them before, I'm sure you'll see them again."

I set the T-shirt on the counter and turned around. "Hopefully under better circumstances."

A hushed laugh escaped her.

I walked back to the bedroom and lowered myself to my bed. "Are you okay to stand and everything?"

"Yeah, I'm alright," she said. "Kind of trippy and drunk feeling but I'm okay." I nodded, trying really hard to not think about her boobs as she glanced at me from the doorway. "Thank you, by the way. For coming to get me and everything."

"Well, I couldn't let you die," I said. "But you're welcome. I'm just glad you're okay."

The spigot turned off. She walked into the room and met my gaze. She'd washed off most of the blood that was visible along with her makeup. Her hair was partially wet in places as she pushed it from her face. "I'm sorry if I ruined your night. I didn't realize all that would happen."

"Stop apologizing," I said.

Her knee grazed mine as she sat beside me. She pulled her feet under her thighs in a lotus position. "I've put you through so much shit, Jeremy. I've gotten drunk and busted my head open, I've pushed you away when you needed me as much as I needed you, and now this and I... I'm a hypocrite. And I'm so sorry."

"Lai—" I began.

"Just, let me say this." She took my hand and met my gaze. "That day, I should have been there for you. You were hurting too, and I should have been there. I shouldn't have denounced you; I should have helped you. You've helped me every time I've fucked up and I treated you like shit the one time that you did. I didn't even give you the opportunity to explain, I just immediately... You've always been good to me. Even when you hated being alive, you still did everything you could to make me want to live. You helped me. You saved me in more than just a metaphoric sense and

I'll never be able to make up for that." Her beautiful eyes grew sad. A frown pulled her lips down. "I don't deserve you, Jeremy."

It was sweet to hear her say that. But it wasn't close to true.

I did her dirty. Yeah, I loved her through everything. But that didn't absolve me of the fact that I'd fucked her over,

A smile tugged at my lips. "You haven't always been easy to love, but I can't love anyone like I love you. But you're wrong. You did the right thing when you told me to leave. It would have been one thing if it was a temporary relapse, but it was going on for a long time. I should have told you as soon as I fell off the wagon. Or at least before we got married. I deliberately lied to you for months. The lies, that's what hurt you. And that's not okay. You had every right to do what you did. You didn't deserve what I put you through."

Her big, dilated green eyes looked between mine. She chewed her bottom lip. Then she leaned forward and gently touched her lips to mine, hand finding my jaw.

I leaned into her and slid my lips against hers. My other hand found her waist. Still kissing, she got onto her knees, lifted her body around me, and sat on my lap. My heart slammed against my ribcage as I felt her ass against my dick.

No matter how much I wanted to shove it inside of her, I couldn't. Not when she was this fucked up and I was stone-cold sober.

"Lai." I pulled away.

She leaned back and looked between my eyes. "Yeah?"

"You've been through a lot tonight," I said. She played with hair at the back of my neck. "I won't take advantage of that."

"Kiss me then," she murmured. "Just kiss me."

And jizz in my damn pants?

"Baby." I gave a quiet laugh.

"You make me feel warm," she murmured softly. Her arms tightened around my neck. "And safe, and alive, and I love you. I love you so much. I love the way I feel when I'm with you."

I looked from her eyes down to her full, dewy lips. "So do I." I looked back up to meet her gaze. "That's why I want you back. But this isn't the same, Lai."

"If I told you I wanted you to come home, you'd tell me I was too fucked up to make that decision." She leaned forward and kissed my cheek. "But you know that I want this." Her breath at my ear sent a shiver up my neck. Her lips touched my jaw. My dick hardened against her. I tightened my arms around her in a hug. I'd hold her, but that was the extent of it. "And I think you want this, right?"

I laughed. "I'm not fucking you tonight, Laila."

"Then kiss me," she whispered at my neck. Her lips curved into my skin again before she pulled her head back to meet my gaze. "Or push me away."

I couldn't justify sleeping with her after everything that happened that night. She was always horny when she was fucked up, and when we were a couple, I loved it. Fucking her when she was under the influence of just about anything made it incredibly hot. But I was sober then, we weren't a couple, and the past day had been absolute hell on her. I wouldn't use that and have her regret it in the morning.

I could justify making out and feeling her ass grind against me though.

"Get over here." I thumbed her chin and touched my lips to hers.

She laughed and kissed me back. I lifted her into the air and lay her on the bed. Our lips stayed locked together as I pushed her up the comforters. I placed my knee firmly between her thighs as I kneeled above her, holding her face in one hand and pulling her chest up to mine from behind with the other.

I knew she would have let me rip her pants off and fuck her as angrily as I wanted to, but I wouldn't. Not until we were together.

But fuck, I just wanted to touch her. I wouldn't let it go past this, but the little sigh that left her lips as I moved my knee a bit gave me a bigger ego boost than fucking any random girl ever could. The way her hands tightened on my back as I slid my hand up her ribs and gently pinched her nipple brought a giant grin to my lips. Her legs wrapping around my hips as she pulled me against her made me feel like I was floating.

She wanted more, and it was killing her that I wouldn't give it to her. It was a little sadistic to enjoy teasing her as much as I did but she seemed to like it.

In most terms of our relationship over the past few weeks, things were better than they'd been in a long time. She was close to letting me back in. I wouldn't fuck her, but I wanted her to want me. Kissing her neck, holding her waist just right, and nibbling her ear left her practically begging to go the rest of the way. But if she wanted me to fuck her, she'd have to sober up too. And start treating me like her husband again.

CHAPTER FIFTY-ONE

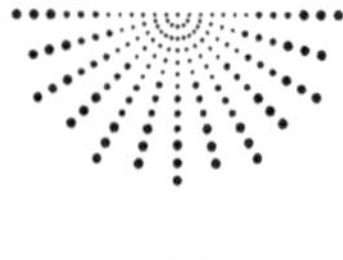

LAILA

The smell of Jeremy's cologne filled my nose from the pillow beneath my head. Warm cotton sheets caressed my cheeks, still feeling a bit tingly from last night. Bright morning light shined into my eyes. A quiet cling rattled behind me.

I turned. Jeremy struggled with the curtain rod, trying to pull it into place.

A smile edged up my cheeks. He'd been bitching about that curtain for as long as I'd known him. I'd told him a thousand times to get a new one and he always said no. Because it wasn't broken, it was just a bitch.

I wondered if that's why he hung onto me too.

"You can leave it open." I sat up and stretched my arms above my head.

He turned over his shoulder. "Are you sure? It's early, you could sleep for a little while."

I stifled a yawn. "Then I won't be able to sleep tonight. I'm alright. What time is it?"

"Eleven thirty." He sat beside me on the bed. "I think you passed out around seven."

"Four hours." I gave a slight smile. "Sounds about right. Did you get any sleep?"

"Maybe an hour or two, I don't know."

I felt like the biggest piece of shit. What I'd done last night was beyond idiotic. And doing it with Liam hadn't exactly been a wise move either. I was sure it left the wrong impression in Jeremy's mind.

A knot stiffened in my throat. "I'm sorry, I really didn't think I was going to ruin your night like that."

"It's okay." He smiled. "I'm just glad you're alright."

"Well, thank you."

"Always."

Still, Liam had been there and clearly in a better state than I'd been. I had to ask. "Do you know if Liam's okay? I saw him when you got there but I didn't see him when we got back here. He made it home, right?"

Jeremy pursed his lips a bit. "Yeah, he's fine. Adam took him home. Said his phone got broken last night so don't try to call him."

"I melted mine too," I muttered. "Did you guys talk at all? Do you know if he saw anything?"

Jeremy made a face of annoyance. "Yeah, we talked. I don't think he saw anything though."

A slow breath left my nose. "Did you guys argue or something?"

"I don't know. A little, I guess. He's a dick, man. I just don't like him."

"Jeremy."

"It's not even because of you two or anything," Jeremy muttered. "He's just so arrogant and holier than thou. Yeah, I wasn't exactly being nice but he's an amateur and he had no place being there. He was your only backup and he let you get stabbed. You're the healer, he was supposed to have your back and he didn't. If it weren't for our bond, you would have died last night. So yeah, I was a little pissed. But he threw some low blows. So fuck that guy. I'm sorry, I know he's your... Whatever he is, but he's a fucker. Don't ask him to come with you on a lead again."

He had every right to feel that way. In his shoes, I'd have been livid. But last night was on me. It wasn't on Liam.

"It really wasn't his fault. I mean, yeah, I definitely don't want to take him on something like that again. But he didn't know what he was doing. He's the brains, not the brawn, ya know? The place was empty, it made sense to split up to cover more ground. I would have been fine if I weren't tripping, I just didn't even hear the guy coming. I was focused on this little mouse. I ended up incinerating the poor little guy anyway." I paused. "Tripping and superpowers don't make a good combination."

"Not when you go back to the place where you were tortured and held captive." Jeremy pulled a smile to his lips. "You're supposed to sit in the woods and play around with your abilities. It makes you feel like a god."

A quiet laugh. "Either way. After that, I'm never tripping again. I will never take acid again. Ever. Not in a million years."

"Yeah, that's probably best. It wasn't easy to calm you down. Leah and I were trying to at the same time and you just wouldn't let us."

"I'm sorry," I said. "I think I just had my guard up. Being there kind of..."

"It's alright." He smiled. "At least one good thing came out of it."

"Our make-out session all night?" I grinned.

He gave a bashful smile. "Two things then, I guess."

"What's the other thing?" I asked.

"There's something there that could help us," Jeremy said. "There wouldn't have been a guard there if there wasn't."

"Has anyone else searched it yet?" I asked.

"Yeah. Adam, Brody, and Kai went last night. We're trying to get ahold of Wyatt to see if he can help us sniff anything. It's been a while, but most of the building has been protected from the elements. We're hoping that Micah's hair will be enough for him to catch a scent. He knew Chris's so maybe if we can follow the path he walked that night..."

"It'll lead us to whatever Chris was trying to show us," I said. "A long shot. But we can try. I can call Celena, I'm sure she could help."

"We called, she said she had too much shit going on. Something with her dad, I guess he broke a hip and she's helping him out? I don't know. But I'm gonna call Wyatt in a little bit here. I mentioned asking Haley, and Leah said there was no way she'd go back there. But we have a few people keeping surveillance to make sure no one can get inside to destroy whatever evidence they were looking for last night."

"If they haven't already," I said.

"There may have been two last night. One left the other to take care of you and Liam while the other took whatever you guys were looking for. We won't know until we can do a thorough search. Do you want to be there?"

Did I? Hell no. I hadn't wanted to go in the first place. But Chris had come to me in particular. Maybe I'd understand it in a way the others wouldn't. Whatever *it* was, anyway.

"You don't have to." Jeremy took my hand and gently twined our fingers together.

"No, I will. I didn't want to face that place. And last night was bad, but I think it kinda helped in a way? To see how empty it is now?" I forced a smile. "Maybe I just needed to get fucked up to face my fears."

"I wish that was my problem when I get high."

CHAPTER FIFTY-TWO

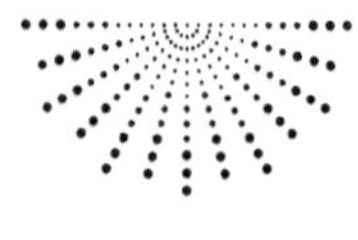

LAILA

"Did you see what he looked like?" Adam asked against the kitchen counter.

"Not really. All I saw was the outfit they all wore. I didn't recognize him, but Peterson had so many working for him, I couldn't have told them apart if I tried unless they had some notable feature. For all I know, it wasn't even a guard. I was tripping my balls off."

"Liam said it was definitely one of the guards," Brody said.

Jeremy passed me a cup of coffee over the island. I gave him a smile. He returned it. Then I looked between the boys. "You guys didn't find anything when you went this morning?"

"We din't know much'a what we're looking for," Kai said.

"You know the place better than we do, Lai," Adam murmured.

Unfortunately, I sure did. "Has anyone heard from Wyatt?"

"Just did." Jeremy sipped his coffee. "I'm going to pick him up in an hour."

Being back inside of those walls was so painful. So incredibly painful. I didn't want to go back. But there was something there and I had to be the one to find it.

"Well, let me get a shower and some clean clothes on. Then we'll go."

"Can we all talk for a moment before you do?" a soft voice said from the doorway to the hall.

My gaze met hers, and I smiled. She looked as she always did. Neat blouse, clean slacks, well maintained hair, and soft, barely-there makeup. She looked at me and smiled back. Barely, but she did.

"Nice to see you, Mary."

She smiled softly, giving a short nod. "You too, Laila."

"Did you find anything?" Jeremy asked.

"I have some information. I'm not sure what help it will be," she said. "But it's something."

"There's coffee." Leah gestured toward the counter. "Help yourself."

Mary made her way to the island. "That's okay, I can't stay long. But thank you."

"So what is it?"

"I finally heard back from my contact. They were pretty vague, but I think you'll want to hear this." She looked almost sad, although it was always close to impossible to place Mary's emotions. She leaned against the counter to face the room. "Did you guys read up on Wormwood in the Bible?"

"We did."

"But there's no explanation as to what it really means," Leah said.

"'The third angel sounded his trumpet and a great star, blazing like a torch, fell from the sky on a third of the rivers and on the springs of water. The name of the star is Wormwood. A third of the waters turned bitter, and many people died from the waters that had become bitter,'" Jeremy recited. "Not very descriptive though."

"But did you do any other research?"

"Wormwood's derived from the Hebrew word la'anah meaning curse," I said.

"Right." Mary nodded. Her thumb and forefinger rubbed against her eyelids for a moment. "Look, I don't know all of the details. I wasn't given much information. All I do know is that this is big."

"What do you mean?" Brody asked.

Mary ran her tongue along her teeth. "I started asking questions in Heaven. Most of the Angels who haven't been around very long only knew what you all knew. What I knew. But when I was finally able to contact Zaphkiel, I wasn't just turned away for bringing it up. I was physically removed from his chamber and instructed to stop asking questions."

"Zaphkiel?" Kai murmured.

"The Angel of God's knowledge," I said.

Mary was quiet for a moment. "It was bizarre, and a little frightening if I'm being honest. That's when I reached out to some other contacts."

"Your mystery source?" I asked.

Whoever this mystery source was also knew that I'd be taken captive. They knew that I'd lose Micah. They knew a *lot*. But there was no probing it from Mary.

I just cracked it up to a really powerful psychic.

"They're very ambiguous. It isn't easy to get a clear understanding of what they're trying to tell me."

"Who is it?" Jeremy puzzled. "Maybe we can try talking to them. They might be more susceptible to talk with us given the circumstance."

"That isn't an option."

"Why not?" I knitted my brows.

"I've mentioned it myself, but they won't. They refuse," she muttered. It was like she wanted to say something, but physically couldn't. "They're familiar with the two of you. But they won't. They say that this is something you have to figure out on your own."

"What does that mean?" I asked.

"You could say they're prophets in their own way." She paused. "Look, I can't get into those details. That's not my place. But I can tell you what they told me."

"Which is?" Leah asked.

"Wormwood isn't a person. Not exactly, anyway. More like a group of people." She paused, searching for the words. "I don't understand all of the details. I don't think that my source does either. All that I know is that Wormwood is not from this planet. Not even from this galaxy."

My brows fell further.

The old books I'd read in the underground library spoke of God coming to earth. That he lived another life before he was god of this land. The Archangels, they weren't born here either. Essentially implying they were aliens. Which, rationally, did make sense. They didn't just appear one day, they came from somewhere and cultivated life here. So it didn't come as much of a shock to hear that there were more people from another world as well.

But what was odd was her expression as she said it. Like she was scared.

"It isn't an Angel?" Jeremy asked.

"They don't work for us, but our races have an allegiance with them, according to my source. There's more back story here but they won't tell me everything. But they told me to tell you that this is dangerous. And that my getting involved with it is the same. Just collecting the information is risky." She paused. "If you don't hear from me for more than six months, assume that I was executed. I don't expect your sympathy, but please know that I do care deeply for every one of you. You all have good reason to hate me, I've done some awful things. But I know that when it's all said and done, you will ultimately understand why I've done what I have. You don't have to forgive me. I love you regardless of how much you hate me. But I just want you all to be aware in case this is the last time we see each other."

My stomach spun.

Well, that explained the terrified expression. But why would she get involved in this if it were as dangerous as she said it was? The only people I knew who could execute Angels were other Angels. Did that mean she was going to fight her brothers and sisters?

"Mary." Adam's tone was somewhere between scared and firm. "What're you going to do?"

"I'm going to do everything in my power to prevent my grandson from being sacrificed."

"And that's going to get ye killed?" Kai asked with watery, reddening green eyes.

"It may. And if it does, I want you all to realize that I was trying to protect you from what's coming."

"But Mary—" I began.

"It's alright, Laila," she said with a gentle smile. "Doing what's right isn't always doing what's expected of you. I know who I am. I know what my duties are. But I'm not just an Angel, I'm a mother. I'm a mother to every person in this room and all I want to do is keep you safe. That's what I'm going to do until it gets me killed. Don't act like you don't understand; you would die for your child too."

She was right, and she always would be. I'd do anything for my children. Absolutely *anything*. I'd burn the world if it meant they got to live.

"A thousand times over," I murmured.

Mary managed something that resembled a smile. Then she cleared her throat and let it fall. "Biblically speaking, God gave his only child as a sacrifice to save the world. I wish I had that kind of courage, but I never will. Keeping you safe, protecting my children, that's more important than any other person or concept alive."

She met Jeremy's eyes with a sad gaze. "I can't ever expect or ask for forgiveness for what I did to you, Jeremy. But please believe me when I say that I didn't want to hurt you. I was doing what I thought needed to be done. I see the error in my ways now that I realize I couldn't have prevented what's come to pass and what has yet to occur. Nevertheless, please believe me when I say that I love you. I can't keep everyone safe, but I will do everything in my power to help you find your son."

Jeremy clenched his jaw. His eyes were gentle though, pained. "I wish I could say I understand, but I don't, Mary."

She bit back tears of her own. "I know you're tired of hearing this but one day you will."

He gazed at her for a moment, practically holding his breath. "For what it's worth, I love you too. I can't say that I forgive you, but I do love you. And I appreciate that. About Micah, I mean."

She gave another bare smile. Then she looked around the room. "I'll try to check in at least every other month. I will let you know immediately if I find a shred of information that can help you find Chris and Micah. In the meantime, be safe, kids. Try to enjoy the lives you're living. You never know when it can all come crashing down around you."

CHAPTER FIFTY-THREE

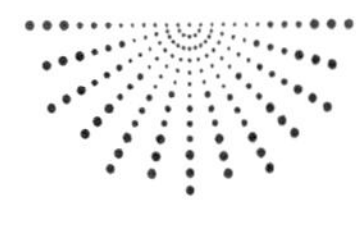

LAILA

Yet again, here we were. Standing outside of that half-demolished building. It felt different than it had last night. I'd been on this adrenaline rampage, desperate to find something. And I supposed I was doing that now too. But I was looking at it now through a lens of realism.

This was the place that destroyed me. This was the place where I'd been bolted to a table, tortured, beaten, raped, and experimented on. This was the place where I lost my baby.

I'd do just about anything to distract from the weight that fell to my shoulders when that reality set in.

"Are you okay?" I placed my hand on Jeremy's forearm.

He looked up from the ground to meet my gaze. "Yeah, why?"

"You haven't said much since we talked to Mary," I murmured.

"Yeah, I'm alright. Just sucks, ya know?"

"I can't even imagine."

His lips made a loud trill. He rubbed the back of his neck. "I never really liked Mary. She was like the strict stepparent. She was bitchy, never particularly kind or affectionate... But after Annie died, she was the closest thing I had to a parent besides Leah.

"I just don't get it. I would never, *never*, do to my kid what she did to me. I think that's why I want to be a good dad so bad. Because I didn't have a good relationship with any of my parents. My mom was good, but I was so little when she died... and Annie did what she could, but she had six of us, and I was the most fucked up of all.

"And Mary was always there. She wasn't exactly compassionate, but she was good too. She was strict and annoying, but she cared. I know that she loves me but that's what doesn't make any sense. I don't care what she thinks she was trying to prevent by doing what she did. Now that I have a kid, even though I'm not really... Ya know, getting to be a parent and everything, I just can't wrap my head around it. I'd never hurt Micah like she hurt me. Never. I don't care what's at stake, I don't want anything more than I want to keep my son safe."

It was another kind of betrayal. Even her killing Moe, as awful as that'd been, somehow, what she'd done to Jeremy was far worse. Maybe that sounds arbitrary, but to me? Rape was far worse than murder.

"I don't get it either. I... What Ally did to you, it's an awful thing to experience."

"The crazy thing is, I don't really hate Ally for what she did. I know I should. Maybe because she died, and we were kind of friends before it happened. I know that she had a choice in the matter too, but at the end of the day... I don't know. She kind of had a gun to her head too, ya know? It's not like she was some sick sadist. She didn't have any more pleasure from it than I did, it was a means of survival. Not like that makes it better. It's still awful. But I can understand why she did it. But Mary..."

"It doesn't bother you?" I asked quietly. "What Ally did?"

"It did for a while. But I don't even remember it. It still makes me feel kind of... I don't know, dirty—I guess—if I think about it hard enough."

That, I could not relate to.

I wish I could. I wish I could be as accepting as Jeremy was. But those moments on that table, looking down at him below my bloated, pregnant belly, his maniacal smile as I screamed for him to stop, how bad my back ached with each thrust...

It destroyed me. Even if my situation were similar to Jeremy's, I still wouldn't have any sympathy for that man. But then again, he'd always been far more understanding than I was.

"It's okay for it to still... I mean, there's nothing wrong with you still having a hard time with what happened to you." Jeremy gazed up at the building as we drew a few feet closer. "Especially being here and everything. I'm sure it's hard."

"I try not to think about it a lot. I'm okay most of the time. Most of my nightmares are about Micah or Chris these days. But hearing his voice on those videos... I don't know. I wish it didn't bother me."

"What happened to you was a lot different than what happened to me." The wind blew a long black lock in front of his gentle, compassionate eyes. "You were at the most vulnerable time of your life. You were pregnant, and tied down, and already in so much pain... He hurt you in every way he could, Lai. It's not the same as what happened to me. You don't have to have the same reaction."

"Yeah, I know. Just makes me feel weak," I murmured. "It's hard to face, but I have to face it every day when I walk past Micah's empty bedroom."

He frowned. "One day it won't be."

"I hope."

CHAPTER FIFTY-FOUR

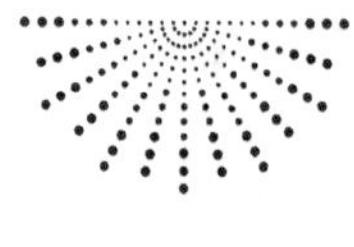

LAILA

We stood just outside the door. And my heart raced harder than it ever had.

Jeremy was beside me this time. So close that I could feel his warmth. And yet, somehow, no matter how safe he usually made me feel, I still had to clench my shaking hand to a fist. I had to remind myself to breathe. Everything was blurry around the edges of my vision. My stomach hurt. I wanted to run away.

But I wanted to find my son more.

Wyatt lifted the piece of hair to his nose. "You're sure this is Micah's?"

"Pretty sure."

He sniffed again. "Kinda smells like you guys. That's not usually how it works. Might be the Fae in him. I've never smelled this before though. Do you have any idea where they would have been keeping him, Laila?"

"Yeah, in Amy's apartment according to Lydia's memories," I said. "I can take you to it."

"After you." He pulled open the large glass door.

My legs felt like lead as I lifted them onto the marble floors. But heavy as they may have been, I had to do this.

Jeremy tailed close behind as we started inside. Adam and Brody stayed watch.

Then, I got my first good look at the place that would haunt my memories for the rest of my days. It wasn't cold and dreary like the cells or the stress test room. Though dusty and cluttered with pieces of the plaster and broken light fixtures, it was pleasantly inviting. Even a bit extravagant.

It reminded me of the Elder's hall. Just a tad more modern.

On either side of the ballroom like area was a long counter with hookups to a computer behind each. They must have been seized by whatever government agency was investigating. A comfortable, modern black office chair sat behind each as well, one knocked over and the other hurriedly slammed into the wall behind it.

The walls were painted a smooth, delicate shade of gray. A modern, ball shaped chandelier laid on the ground in the center of the room. The floors were an elegant white marble placed so closely together that it was impossible to tell where one ended and another began.

It looked so normal. Extravagant, even. Like the ground floor of a beautifully designed skyscraper or even the foyer to a massive palace. Simple with clean modern lines and no cluttering décor.

And yet, it was my worst nightmare.

It reminded me of Peterson. The place was warm and inviting at first glance. But the doors adjacent to either reception desk were practically the gateways to hell.

Jeremy touched my arm. "Lai."

"Huh?" I turned to meet his gaze.

"Which way?" Wyatt gestured between the two doors.

"I think either will work." I cleared my throat. "The building's shaped like a capital H. We're in the center of it now. Those doors go to hallways. One door leads to cells, the other leads to the center of the building where the first-class captors were kept as well as the medical center, offices and the stress test room."

"Then to the left cause the right is wrong." Wyatt started toward the door.

I wanted to laugh at his stoner pun, but I just couldn't.

I continued to gaze around. It felt so strange. Haunted, yet still so beautiful. I'd destroyed so much of this place, and that brought me a great sense of pride. But it was so bizarre to stand in that part of the building. I could almost hear the phantom screams in the distance as I and the other captors begged them to stop torturing us. I could almost feel the snaps against my back. I could nearly smell the blood running down my legs.

But then it would suddenly go quiet again. And the pain would disappear. And my legs felt dry once more.

Textbook PTSD flashback, I supposed.

As Wyatt walked through the doorway, Jeremy turned back to me. "Are you coming, Lai?"

I took in a slow breath. "Yeah, right behind you."

"Are you sure?" he asked with a concerned gaze.

I forced a smile, nodded, and started toward him. "Yeah, I'm good."

He gave a sad smile back. "How 'bout you stay beside me?"

I gave another nod. He placed his hand on the small of my back as I made it through the doorway into the dark hallway lit only by Wyatt's flashlight. As Jeremy took a step inside, the door shut behind him.

The click of the knob as it clasped shut sent a shiver up my spine and down my extremities. Jeremy's hand traveled from my lower back up to my shoulder. It gently coasted down my chilled arm.

"It's unlocked, baby," he murmured.

I cleared my throat.

"Which door are we going through?" Wyatt called, a few yards ahead.

"The one on the end," I said.

He gripped the door handle and pulled it open.

I started toward him. Jeremy was right beside me as we made our way into the next dark hallway. I looked into the corridor I should have known like the back of my hand but I only recognized from a few drugged, fleeting glimpses.

My trembling fingers tightened to fists as the memories I didn't realize I had begun flooding back. They weren't much, just images through fuzzy, blinking eyes. I remembered being wheeled down the long hall on a hospital style bed with every extremity tightly bound to it with thick, cool leather straps.

Jeremy's fingertip touched my pointer finger and gently hooked around mine for a second. I looked up at him and swallowed hard. He gave a soft, sad smile I could hardly see in the lack of light. I moved my hand to his and carefully intertwined our fingers together. It took the edge off the loneliness.

"Which door from here?" Wyatt asked.

"I'm not sure. We're looking for a stairwell. We need to get to the third floor. The room we're looking for has a set of glass French doors. The glass is shattered though."

He began to open each door and take a peek inside. Then he reached for the doorknob attached to the extremely thick metal door to my right. Seeing it from that side made my stomach ache. Not only did it have a handle, but a large submarine hatch type wheel as a lock.

"Not that one. That's not it."

"What is it then?" Wyatt asked as he stepped away.

I cleared my throat. "That's where they tortured us."

"Oh," he said. "Sorry."

"Don't worry about it." I started toward a door on the left. I kept Jeremy's hand in mine and squeezed tighter, spinning the knob with my free hand.

The first thing I noticed was the large window overlooking the ocean. The memory of Peterson's lips on mine and the taste of his blood after I bit him flashed through me. I pulled it shut faster than I opened it.

I walked fifteen or twenty feet ahead to the next door. I turned the knob and pushed it forward. As I did, the first and only thing I saw in the barely lit room was the cushioned maternity table in the center. Thick metal clamps hung open from the head of it down the sides with more on either stirrup.

My breath caught, chest growing tight.

It hurt. Just seeing it hurt. The memory spun behind my eyelids, and phantom pains stabbed through my lower abdomen. I could practically feel that tearing sensation inside of my womb once more. My throat tightened, just as it did when his hand clasped around it. The sounds of my screams echoed through my ears.

"Down here, guys," Wyatt said, midway through the long hall.

Jeremy squeezed my hand a bit tighter. But I continued to stand like a statue. My legs wanted to tremble, but I tightened the muscles to keep them steady. With his other hand, he reached forward and pulled the door shut in front of us.

My stare stopped on the white wooden door inches from my face.

"We're looking for the stairs, right?" Jeremy asked.

Our source of light bobbed with Wyatt up the steps.

"C'mon, baby." He held my hand a little tighter.

"This is where..." I trailed off.

"I know." He moved his hand from mine around my shoulder. His fingertips gently trailed up and down my upper arm. "Let's just keep that door shut."

CHAPTER FIFTY-FIVE

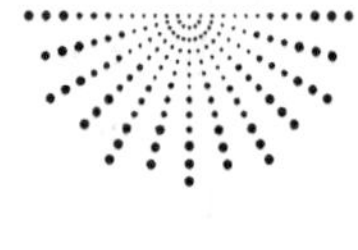

LAILA

"Is this it?" Wyatt called as Jeremy and I made it up the steps.

I gazed out the wall of windows overlooking the ocean. "This is it."

Wyatt sniffed the hair in his hand and turned back to Jeremy and me. "Good news, I can smell him here." He scrunched his nose up a bit. "I think I smell his shit actually."

"Probably an old diaper," Jeremy said as we drew closer.

Our feet crunched on the broken glass in the doorway. Wyatt gestured ahead, pointing with the flashlight. "After you guys."

My body swiveled that direction. I walked through the threshold. The once thriving foliage was now piles of broken branches and dead petals beside pots of dried-up soil. The room was warm but sent a cool shiver down my spine.

I started inside silently, hearing only the sound of dehydrated leaves crunching beneath my shoes. The cracks under the soles of my feet brought with them a sense of pride when I remembered Lydia was no longer here to feed this place with beauty it didn't deserve.

As we made our way to the living room, Jeremy's gaze narrowed. He started toward the window and gazed out into the dark room. His eyes scanned around, little visible in the lack of light.

But he'd seen the videos. That upward leaning metal table was impossible to mistake.

He turned to look at me. "This... This is where Lydia lived?"

I swallowed hard, nodding.

"And that's where..." he murmured.

I looked down, unsure of what to say.

"Micah was right here," Jeremy muttered. His eyes slid around the modern living room, then out the window into the dark room with ceilings three stories high. "And they were torturing our people right there."

I fought the tears that wanted to make their way from my eyes. Tears welled in his as an awestruck, pained look washed over him.

"The smell's coming from back here, guys," Wyatt said.

I followed him past the kitchen down a hall.

That door looked just like the ones we'd hung in our apartment during the remodel. It was simple and homely, the typical six paneled doors you'd see everywhere those days.

He pushed it open and as he did, I felt sick.

The walls were painted a soft, cloudless sky blue lined in vibrant white trim and baseboards.

A large stuffed monkey sat in a modern gray rocker. Its big brown legs rested on the footrest in front of it.

A white crib laid neatly made with white sheets and a baby blue comforter.

Above the crib were letters carved from wood, hand painted in a rainbow of colors spelling out, MICAH in a perfectly situated arch.

My hand moved to my mouth as my eyes filled with tears.

Peterson said he wasn't going to take my son from me if I joined him. Obviously, that wasn't true.

Not that I trusted a word he said either way. But why the hell had he said it like I had a choice if I hadn't? Was this his agenda all along? Did he have the intent of torturing me against that table while forcing my son to watch from the window above between Paw Patrol and Peppa Pig?

I gritted my teeth, nostrils flared. "That fucking liar."

"What do you mean?" Jeremy asked behind me.

"Setting up a nursery like this doesn't happen overnight," I said. "They were planning on taking him all along."

"Uh... guys." Wyatt's voice shook beside the dresser next to the rocking chair. "Do you think this is what Chris was talking about?"

I turned toward him. "What is it?"

He raised an aged, five by eight standard chapter book toward us. His gaze was somewhere between confused and terrified as he handed it my way.

"*The Last Beginning,*" I read the white print aloud. Violet smoke encased and curled out of a green tree of life emblem on a black backdrop speckled with twinkling stars. "So what?"

"Look at the author," he murmured.

My heart nearly stopped at the byline.

Laila Callidy
and
Jeremy Skoulda

CHAPTER FIFTY-SIX

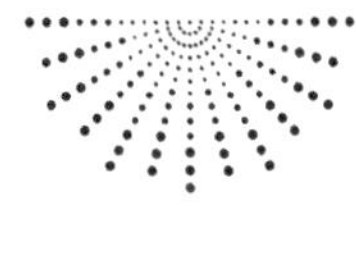

LAILA

L eah looked between Jeremy and me. "You didn't write this?"

"I'm pretty sure we'd remember writing a book, Leah," Jeremy said.

"This is insane," she murmured. Her gaze shifted from a picture of the two of us on our wedding day on the back to the blurb beside it. Her thumb slid against the frayed pages, flipping them. The cream-colored paper emitted a small cloud of dust as she thumbed. "There's highlighter on almost every page, notes in the margins." She opened the first page. "Did you guys see the date of publication?"

I shook my head.

She turned the open book to us. "All rights reserved, 2062."

"What?" I snatched the book from her hands.

"It says it right there," Leah said.

Jeremy furrowed his brows as far as I did. "That's forty-two years from now."

"I know what year it is, Jeremy," she said.

My thumbs flipped past the title page, reading the words of the preface inside my mind and immediately recognizing them. Not the words themselves so much as the style. Style is like a writer's footprint. It can't be synthesized; it can't be copied.

It was mine. I knew my style. Blunt, to the point, not incredibly poetic. I knew how I wrote, and I wrote those words.

But I *hadn't* written those words. Not all of them. Not yet, anyway.

"This is me," I murmured as I read. "This is how I write."

"Let me see," Jeremy said beside me. I angled it toward him. He began reading, murmuring the words under his breath. "Here." He pulled the book in front of him. He began flipping through the pages until he reached chapter one. He skimmed for a moment. "This is definitely your style."

"Then you had to have written it," Leah said.

"But I didn't, Leah," I insisted.

"Yes, you did." Jeremy pointed to a section on the sixth page. "This, this was in one of the files on your computer. This whole paragraph. I read it when you were captured."

I creased my brows, gazing down at it.

"It's our story," he murmured. "This is the day that we met."

I quickly read over the page about the day that Adam, Adrian and I went to the Mumford and Sons concert in Burgettstown in 2015. I described the bounce of the car.

Then the shriek of peeling tires when we slammed into that deer. The blood pouring from its nose as I crouched to the ground beside it. The coarse feel of its fur.

I did. I wrote it. "But..."

"It's better," Jeremy muttered. "It's been edited, it's a little more detailed. But you wrote this, Laila."

What in the actual fuck? Why did he have this? What did it mean?

Even if it were real, even if it weren't some trick he was playing on our minds, what was so important about Jeremy and I that he'd read a book about us? Why would he write notes in the margins of a love story? Because that's what this was. A dark one, but a love story nonetheless. One that was only an origin and very little actually happened in.

Adam read over our shoulders at the bar stool. "We need to read it the whole way through."

"There might be something in here," Brody said. "Chris wouldn't have sent us to find it if there weren't."

Jeremy murmured to himself for a moment, flipping through the pages. Then he looked up with a boyish grin. "You think I have a tightly toned torso with strong shoulders and a finely honed chest?"

I felt my cheeks get hot. "I was seventeen, shut up."

His smile widened.

"Well, let's hunker down in the living room," Leah said. "If this book did come from the future, there's bound to be something in here that'd be useful. We should all read it together. We'll take turns."

"Oh, look," Jeremy said. He chuckled, pointing to a paragraph a few chapters further in. "Laila thinks you're the least attractive brother, Brody. 'Not because he was ugly, he wasn't a bad looking kid. He looked a lot like Adam—who could have been a model if he took better care of himself.'"

"Well, fuck you too." Adam grinned.

My cheeks grew flushed.

Yeah, I'd written that. I remembered writing it clearly.

"'But the harshness of his personality made him less appealing than either of his sweet and kind older brothers. Even less so than the images of Chris that hung scattered around their home." He laughed, and Brody furrowed his brows at me. "'At that time, he was just an overall bitter person. He grew less bitchy as he aged, but at that point he was happy being unhappy. He rarely looked slightly pleased with the world around him. He almost always made this face that was hard to describe. It was an odd expression with a scrunched-up nose, furrowed brows, and sour, pursed lips all at once. Almost like he was taking a shit while sucking on a lemon.'" Jeremy looked up, nearly cackling. "That's it, that's the face. I've been trying to think of a way to describe that expression since you were born. But that's it. Sucking on a lemon while taking a shit."

Yup. I wrote that too.

I tried to hide my blushing cheeks as I met Brody's gaze. "In all fairness, I never intended for anyone to read it. And you were really mean to me when we first met. You held a knife to my throat once if memory serves."

"Because you were annoyingly positive all the time," he said. "And a reckless, naïve little shit."

"This is going to be fun." Adam laughed.

CHAPTER FIFTY-SEVEN

JEREMY

Laila, Adam, Jenna, Brody, Leah, Hannah, Kai, and I all sat comfortably around the living room for the following six hours. We took turns reading a chapter aloud and passing the book to the person beside us. Tinkerbell sat at my feet resting her head peacefully on my shoe.

Laila chewed her nails as she sat in the chair slightly in front of me to my right. She didn't let people read what she'd written often, if at all. I had from time to time but never something so big.

It was surreal to hear our story of young love told as an adult. Most of what was written were things she'd written at seventeen or eighteen, hardly more than a child, yet told with poise and confidence.

Some scenes were hard to read. Some we skipped entirely because they were far too explicit for my siblings' ears. Some sent a warm feeling to the pit of my stomach, hearing her utter words about how much she loved me and how much I meant to her.

And others made me sick. Hearing how hurt she was when she found out I'd been lying to her about what I was. It really resonated because that pain wasn't much different than what had happened last year. I lied to keep her safe. Yet, the lies hurt her more than telling her the truth would have. It was a paradox, really, one that I was trying really hard to escape.

As we read, I'd begun to realize how I had failed her. I was so worried about protecting her from all of the inevitable aspects of our world. But if I would have been less protective, if I would have made her learn instead of always swooping in to save her, they would have never been able to take her.

Some chapters were written from my perspective. And it was fucking bizarre. They were my thoughts. They were moments I'd experienced that no one knew about but were written in neat, perfectly formed sentences. I had never journaled or written anything aside from a few lines of poetry for a song in my life. Yet, sentences that I had only ever thought were printed on the pages in front of me. I wrote it. But I didn't write it.

The story started the night that we met. It went into the details of what Laila experienced as a human while I was lying to her about what I was. It talked about our first date and the first time she heard me sing. It told the story of our first kiss. She talked about our first New Years together, and the kiss we shared at Moe's that night. It even told the story of how she and Leah became best friends.

She talked about the way her body felt tingly the night after we'd made love for the first time. The night her powers were activated. She spoke about how terrified she was the first time she saw her irises glow in the mirror. She explained the way that it felt when she held fire for the first time without being burned. She talked about the way that I made her feel safe when the world felt like a battlefield.

The final chapter was the night that Adrian killed Laila and Adam killed Adrian. As her recollection of that night left her lips, it sent tears rolling down her cheeks as well as everyone else in the room. It was written from a newer, adult perspective. But the agony behind the words were just as fresh as they'd been that night.

Adam's gaze as the words rolled off her tongue was almost too pain filled to meet.

"*'The worst of it all was that I was alive, and Adrian never would be again. I had been given a second chance thanks to the fifteen-year-old girl I would one day call a sister, but Hannah couldn't save everyone. She barely knew what she was then, she certainly wasn't capable of bringing two people back into dying bodies in the same night.'*" Laila wiped her cheek.

"*'It's been decades, but if I think about that night hard enough, it's almost as if I'm reliving it. I can still remember Jeremy's expression as he rolled my dead body over and gripped my face in his bloody hands. I can still hear him crying out for Leah as I struggled to hold on to the life that was slowly slipping away from me. I can still hear him telling me to stay with him, begging me not to die. I can still taste his tears as they fell from above into my blood-filled lips and mixed salt into the flavor of iron. I can still smell the crisp and moist February air. I can still feel the stinging sensation of snow on my skin where my hoodie rode up in the fall to the ground.'"*

She cleared her throat. Jenna blew her nose into a tissue. Even Leah wiped the corners of her eyes.

"'But that night was only the beginning of an incredibly long, exceedingly trivial parable. It took years before I finally understood why Adrian killed me that night. I will always carry the weight of her death on my shoulders, but this story has very little to do with Adrian. Her death was an untimely but necessary event in my life's history.

"'I wish there were a way for her to have lived. But knowing what I know now, I'm not sure that I would have been the person I needed to be without her death. Now that it is all said and done, I realize that some people who enter our lives are meant to be in it forever while others are only meant to leave a scar to remind you of a person you once were.

"Adrian was the first deep scar I ever attained, and somehow, the one that aches the least."

My eyes caught on the butterfly that covered that bite mark on her neck, the vine that coated the cicatrix along her throat, the ones ascending her wrists now coated in flowers...

Fuck, that line hit harder than almost any other in the book had.

Adam brought himself to his feet. "I—Uh, I need a minute."

Laila nodded, wiping her cheek. As he started up the stairs, Laila turned her gaze to me and passed me the worn book. "The epilogue is written from your perspective."

I cleared my throat and took the book from her hands.

"That night changed everything. The night that I saw my best friend die would forever be etched into my memories like a tattoo that never stopped healing. When I saw Laila die, a part of me died with her. But when she came back, I realized that I never wanted to live without her again. I remember thinking that I had to die first because the thought of living without her was unbearable to fathom.

"'The way she stared up at me as blood splattered from her heaving lips would forever haunt my dreams. I had failed that beautiful girl who gave me the privilege of loving her. For the moments before I realized she was alive, I thought about how the world had been stripped of the best person to ever walk its green grass because she loved me.

"'I could never forget that feeling of shame and guilt, remembering Adam begging me to leave Laila alone when he learned that we were dating. He told

me that I would ruin her life if I kept seeing her. He insisted that she deserved normalcy. That I would steal that from her if I let things progress. Some part of me wished I'd listened to him because he wasn't wrong. I did. I ruined her life.

"'Laila deserved so much more than I was capable of giving her. But she loved me anyway. Despite every awful part of who I was, she loved me in a way no one else ever had.

"'When she came back, after she'd stopped hyperventilating and we disposed of Adrian's body, we lay in my bedroom silently holding each other for hours. She held my shirt between her fingertips like a life raft keeping her afloat in a shipwreck. I was a rock giving her stability in a life where she had forgotten what that word meant.

"'Still, I don't think Laila holds onto anyone like she holds onto me. She isn't capable of being as vulnerable with anyone as she is with me. Despite her façade of strength and independence, she needed me as much as I needed her and always would. She didn't see it then, but she was my rock as much as I was hers. Being with her was the only thing that made sense. It still is.'" I met her teary, passion filled gaze as I flipped the page.

"'I'll never forget lying in that bed with her warm body curled in my arms. For the first time in my life, I prayed to whatever god gave me the chance to hold her again. I prayed that I would never have to lose her because that was the worst thing I ever faced.

"'I thought that I couldn't live without her then. I was wrong. There were times that I would have no choice but to live without her by my side. When she left me, I realized that I kept breathing even when I didn't get to say that she was mine. Every breath felt like a thousand stabs to my chest when she hated me but no matter how much hate she had in there, she would always have more love for me than anything.

"'We would never have the old and gray together happy ending, but we had our own version of a happy ending one day. It took a long time before we got there, but when we finally did, after all the mountains we'd climbed and hurdles we'd jumped, we realized that we couldn't keep looking to a past that couldn't be changed. All that we could do was try to be happy despite it all. It wasn't too hard when we allowed ourselves to get lost in each other.'"

CHAPTER FIFTY-EIGHT

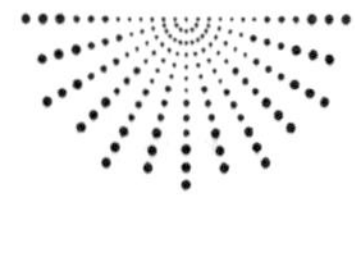

JEREMY

"It's clearly written by an older version of both of you," Leah murmured, still thumbing through the pages. "But it just doesn't make any sense."

Laila pulled the book away. She gazed at the back cover. "How could Amy have a book we haven't even written yet?"

"Look at the pages," I murmured beside her. "It's old. It doesn't even exist yet, and it's old. The cover's faded, the pages have been turned a thousand times."

"What if..." Laila began quietly as she raised her hand to rub her mouth. "We couldn't find Peterson on any facial recognition algorithm, right? All his guards, none of them were reported missing and I killed a lot of them."

I knew what she was thinking. Because I was thinking it too. I didn't know how. To my knowledge, no one was capable of it. But a few years prior, no one believed in the par animarum either. Yet here we stood.

"The one we caught in that airport when you were captured," Adam murmured. "The one who killed himself, we couldn't identify who he was either."

"Peterson... When he talked to me, it was like he was... Like he already knew me," Laila murmured. "I know it doesn't make any sense, but he did. And when I asked him why he was doing what he did to me, he said it was because I had to learn. I had to live up to my reputation or something."

"You think that he's..." Leah began.

"Not from this time." Laila rubbed her hand across her lips.

"I don't know how that's possible," Brody said. "Time travel doesn't exist."

"Not yet," I murmured. "But if this book was written in 2062, and it's already this old..."

"Mary knew that I was going to be captured. That's why she killed Moe, that's why she hired Ally..." Laila said. "Then earlier, she said something about how she sees the error in her ways now that she realizes that what happened and what is going to happen couldn't be avoided." She rubbed the bridge of her nose. "Her contact, she called them a prophet."

"But they aren't prophets." My eyes widened. "They're time travelers. That's why they're only giving her shreds of information."

"But that doesn't make any sense," Hannah chimed in. "Why tell her certain things but not details?"

"Because timelines are intricate," Laila said. "Too much information from a time that has yet to occur could alter the timeline too far from what it's meant to become. It's called the chaos theory, more commonly known as the butterfly effect."

"What Mary did..." I murmured, thinking back to my philosophy class in high school. "She created a casual time loop. By trying to prevent an event, she created it."

"What do you mean?" Leah asked.

"When she killed Moe." Laila's eyes shot open. "That's how I met Ray. That's how we discovered Chris was alive. Had Moe never been killed—"

"You would have never met Ray, we would have never found out Chris was alive, we would have never dug into Peterson and none of this would have ever happened," Brody said with wide, awestruck eyes.

"But if that were true..." Kai searched for the words. "If she knew it would happen, wouldn't she've known how to stop it?"

"Not necessarily," I said.

Time travel. A giant chunk of our story that confused the fucking shit out of me in the beginning. It fascinated me when I was young, so I knew a good bit about the different paradox theories. But how it fit into our story was so complex that it couldn't be explained in less than a few dozen epic sized novels.

"Mary once said that you can't elude destiny," Laila murmured. "The timeline her source is from might be slightly different than ours. The way things happened that led them to the same outcome would have been different but ultimately brought things to the same place."

"My head hurts." Jenna rubbed her temples in the recliner.

"Think of the timeline like a river system. Each stream is similar," I said. "They're all a little different, but they're similar too. But despite their differences—"

"They all end at the same place." Adam ran his hand along his mouth.

"You realize what this means if you're right," Leah said. "Mary was trying to prevent Micah from being taken. And if she failed... That means you were destined to lose him."

Laila looked down.

No, I couldn't believe that. She was trying to protect Laila in the beginning. That's what it'd been about. And shit, I'd have killed a man for my kid too. But today, she said she was going to do everything in her power to help us bring our son home. Yet, she knew now that this destiny couldn't be prevented.

If we were destined to lose Micah, she'd have said that we wouldn't find him. Instead, she said she'd help us.

I met Leah's gaze. "Maybe. But maybe we were destined to find him. Maybe that's what this has all been. A tragic learning experience in the game of life."

CHAPTER FIFTY-NINE

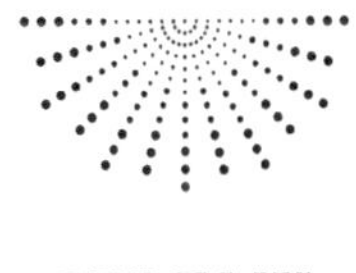

JEREMY

"Hey." Laila leaned against the doorway into the kitchen with her arms crossed against her chest.

I looked up from the mac and cheese on the stove and gave a soft smile. "Hey."

"That was a lot." She made out just above a whisper.

"Yeah," I said. "Yeah, I've been through a lot of weird shit but that was definitely the weirdest. Even for us."

"Definitely the weirdest." She started through the kitchen.

"The weirdest part is the accuracy," I murmured. "No one could have written those things but us. No one knows about that stuff. How we hid Adrian's body, that thing you described me doing when we fucked the night of your birthday." She laughed, and I smiled. "I don't know. I don't get it. But that was us."

"It was definitely us."

"But are you okay?" I asked.

"Kind of in shock. A little trippy from last night still so that doesn't help." She sat at the island "What about you? Are you alright?"

I set the ladle onto the spoon rest. "Yeah. Yeah, I'm okay. Really confused. But I'm alright."

"Some of the things I said in there, after I found out what I was... I never intended for you to hear that. I was scared, and confused, and I was angry at you for lying to me all the time to cover your ass and I... I'm sorry."

"Your entire life was just ripped out from under you, Laila. You don't need to apologize."

"That comment I made..." she murmured. "What I said about wishing I didn't love you..."

I'd heard it. But it went in one ear and out the other. Some fraction of me felt the same way. No matter how much I loved her, we fucked each other's lives up more than a handful of times. We were people. And people were allowed to have thoughts like that from time to time.

"It's okay, Lai."

"It isn't because of who you are or anything you did wrong. You were the best thing that ever happened to me, Jeremy. You're the kindest, sweetest, most perfect person I've ever met." Her gaze shifted to the ground. "But loving anyone as much as I love you is terrifying."

A gave a smile. "I can relate, Lai."

Her green eyes met mine behind a piece of dark red hair. "It didn't scare me until you died. I guess I didn't realize how much you meant to me until then. I think that's why I ended things the way that I did. I think I thought that I could love you less if we weren't together anymore. I thought that I needed to learn to live without you because one day I might have to."

"Did it work?"

"What do you mean?"

I looked between her emerald gaze. "Do you love me less?"

A sad smile pulled her lips upward. "I love you as much as I did the day that I said it for the first time. Maybe even more."

I smiled back. "Yeah. Me too."

She was quiet for a moment. "We probably shouldn't go to that concert tomorrow. There's so much going on here. I should use my time away from the diner focusing on this, not having a good time."

"Your attempt at having a good time is what led us to this. You said it yourself, you wouldn't have had the courage to go back there if you weren't tripping and convinced that you had to. If that isn't the universe telling you that you need to allow yourself to be happy for a minute, I don't know what is. But if you don't want to, it's okay. We don't have to."

She thought for a moment, nibbling her lower lip. "If we don't drive, it'll only be a few hours."

I smiled still. "We could leave twenty minutes before the show started and still have enough time to get a decent spot. And we'll check our phones every five minutes to make sure we're available if anything happens."

Her smile lifted a bit. "I think I'd like that."

"Me too." I gestured to the stove. "Are you hungry? Want some mac and cheese?"

"Sure," she said. "Can I ask you a huge favor?"

"Depends on what it is but probably." I smiled. "What do you need?"

"I parked my car here yesterday to cover my ass with that FBI agent. And I teleported Tink here earlier, but she gets so scared and sick, so I'd rather just drive home, but I still don't feel quite right and I'm not sure I should get behind the wheel."

"You want me to drive you home?" I asked.

"If you don't mind."

"Yeah, baby," I said. "I'll ride you home."

"Do you know what's so weird about the whole thing?" Laila said. I looked either way, checking to see that no cars were headed down the highway. Then I stepped on the gas and cut the wheel to the left, turning onto the main road Moe's was situated on a few miles down.

I pet Tink's scruff as she licked my face from her perch on the center console. "It's all pretty bizarre."

"The overall poise and serenity it's written with. I mean, yeah, a lot of it were things I wrote when I was young and frantic, but other parts... It's me writing it, I know it is. But it's so much more peaceful than I've ever been. This version of me, this older me, she understands and accepts all of the tragedies we've been through. And I don't understand how." She gazed out the window. "She's at peace. And I don't know how to get to that place."

"She's sixty-four." I laughed. "If you hadn't grown in forty-two years, that's what would be weird."

"I guess. But how? How am I supposed to just accept everything that's happened?"

"I don't think it's that simple," I said. "Our lives have been problem after problem after problem with no resolution." I met her gaze as we stopped at a red light. "Maybe the peace comes with the resolution."

"I hope we get there soon," she murmured.

"Yeah. Yeah, me too."

If only.

She turned to look at me as I pulled into Moe's parking lot. "What do you think you meant?"

"What part?" I asked.

"At the end. You were talking about how you learned to live without me, but then you said we didn't get the old and gray together happy ending." Her nostrils flared, fighting tears. "Do you think that means that I'm going to die by the time you write that?"

My stomach sunk as that thought crossed my mind for the first time. Jesus fuck, I hoped not.

But I held my composure, shaking my head as I smiled.

"That's not how this works. I'm going to go first, and I don't want to hear you say otherwise. You're part Angel, your life expectancy is at least a good century longer than mine. You can't die before me."

Tears welled in the corner of her eyes. "I don't want either of us to die."

I held her gaze for a moment. "We're all gonna die someday, baby."

She stared down at her hands. I put the car in park. Her hands fumbled with the keys in them for a moment. "I should probably head inside. I'm exhausted. I need to get some sleep. I'll call you in the morning."

"Sure." I gave a bare smile. "Sleep tight."

As she unbuckled her seat belt, I glanced at the clock reading 12:12. "And Lai?"

She turned up to meet my gaze. "Yeah?"

I leaned forward and gently touched my lips to hers. I grazed her cheek. She pushed her lips closer into mine. Mine delicately grazed the softness of hers for a slow, gentle moment.

I pulled away and rested my forehead against hers. With a quiet laugh, I murmured, "Happy anniversary."

CHAPTER SIXTY

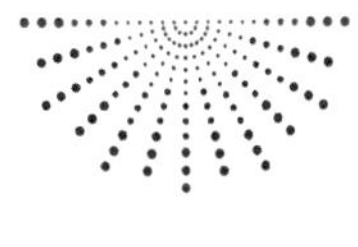

LAILA

I lay there in my bed for a good three hours struggling to swallow the thick swell in my throat. The past thirty or so hours were so much to take in given that short span of time. My heart felt like a hundred-pound weight in my chest, pulling me farther into the fluffy comforter than I knew was possible.

Going back to that place didn't give me a prideful sense of facing fear. It brought me back to the same weak little bitch I was when they closed those van doors and snapped Daniel's neck.

If I were as strong then as I was now, I could have split the vertebrae inside their necks without batting an eyelash. I could have forced the blood from their bodies in a messy, crimson bomb before they even had time to aim that gun at me. I could have split the earth and plummeted their bodies inside of it by barely swirling my fingertips.

And I would.

The girl I was then wasn't capable of murder. Not mass murder in front of a small child. But this battered, trauma filled, childless mother would kill anyone or anything to protect her child.

Knowing what I know now, I would kill every last one of them if it meant that I got to birth my baby with his father by my side and raise him in that little hole in the wall diner.

There was a time when I wanted the excitement of this life, yet seven-teen-year-old me would probably be disgusted with the cold-hearted bitch

I'd become. However, I didn't let that bother me too much. Seventeen-year-old me was a stupid, insignificant, little twat. She was barely less experienced than the girl who willingly climbed into her captor's hands while carrying one of the most powerful children to ever exist inside of her womb.

She thought she was so powerful merely because of what she was one day capable of becoming. She was a child, but she thought she was already a warrior.

What my captivity taught me more than anything was how weak I truly was. Granted, it also beat a lot of that weakness out of me. It made me strong. But it forced me into humility.

Power without humility is useless. When I was composed of pure confidence, I was incapable of seeing my limits. Even with my nearly boundless capabilities, I had weaknesses that I blinded out by an idea of who I could become. I had barely touched the surface of what I was capable of, but because my childish mind had been told how powerful I was, my head was as big as the Kool-Aid Man's.

Then was that book. It didn't give us much insight, and I failed to see how it connected to finding Micah and Chris. It may have come from the future, but it gave me hardly any information into it. The only thing it really did give me was a sense of understanding in who I would become. It showed me that eventually, I would get past my desolate mindset.

It showed me how much Jeremy loved me. It reminded me of how much I loved him. But it also reminded me of that little girl I was once and reminded me to be proud of how far I had come. It showed me that I could get past it all. That my husband and I could get past it all.

It told me that eventually, I would learn who instructed Adrian to kill me. And truly, there was no way in hell that I could figure that one out then. But I was glad to know that one day I would.

But most importantly of all, it told me one thing about Peterson.

He was not from my time. He may have appeared twenty years older than me, but I was at least fifty years older than him.

And hearing my elder self's confidence gave me a mere glimpse into what he meant.

One day, I would be more than powerful enough to destroy my enemy.

One day.

"Hey," I said to Leah as I walked into the kitchen with Tink at my side.

"Hey." She closed her laptop and pulled off her headphones.

I placed my purse on the counter and sat beside her. "Working hard or hardly working?"

"A little bit of both I guess."

"What are you watching?" I asked.

"The videos of that dude we caught after the bomb. I don't know, Laila. I'm just so confused. If they're from the future, why are they still convinced the world is going to end? Micah will be forty-three years old when this book is published. Clearly, the apocalypse doesn't happen if you and Jeremy are alive to publish it."

Guessed it taught us one other thing.

"I don't understand either."

She rubbed her mouth, pulled off her glasses, and set them on top of her laptop. "Hannah's going to keep reading through the book while I go over these videos. There has to be something in there."

"Should I help you look over them?"

She laughed and turned to meet my gaze. "Are you just trying to get out of that concert tonight?"

"No, not really. I'm actually looking forward to it. But if I'm needed here, then that's where I should be."

"You aren't needed here." She smiled. "Go out and enjoy your anniversary. We'll let you know if we find anything."

I nodded, chewing my lip.

Leah pulled a smile to her lips, arched a brow, and looked over me. "Is there something else on your mind, Laila?"

"Nothing important."

I thought about asking what she thought of the book we'd read the night before. I was wondering what her opinion was, because mine had started to shift. I always wanted to get back together. And I wasn't certain I was going to ask him to come home at that concert. But I was getting tired of loving him from a distance . And that book reminded me of a faith in our love I had let fall away in the last year.

But I wasn't sure yet. He was still using, and after that bad trip, I was done with drugs and partying. I wanted to move onto that calm, serene woman I'd read of the night before. He and I needed to have a serious heart to heart before I made any final decisions. And I knew that if I mentioned it to Leah, she'd get excited. But since I wasn't sure, I didn't want her to know what was running through my mind.

She raised a brow. "Jeremy's not unimportant."

"Get out of my head." I rolled my eyes. Then I started to my feet and made my way to the coffee pot.

"I didn't get that from your head, I got it from your face." She stood from the island and followed me. Her voice lowered as I poured my coffee. "That whole knight in shining armor persona did something for ya, huh?"

"Shut up." I poured coffee into a mug.

"You're going to take him back, aren't you?" she said excitedly in a hushed tone.

I raised the cup to my lips and took a gulp. "You need to chill."

"I won't tell him." She smiled wide.

"Why do you care so much?" I laughed. "You've never been much of a romantic."

"Honestly?" Leah asked. "You make my brother a better person. When he's with you, he feels important. He's in an okay place without you and everything but he wants you more than he wants anything. And I'm pretty sure you do too. The way that you love each other, that isn't something that should be pushed away. You're forcing yourself into misery for no reason."

"It isn't for no reason."

"Then what is it, Lai?" she asked with a genuinely confused expression. "You know he didn't cheat and that's the reason you broke up with him."

"Look." I glanced toward the steps to make sure he wasn't trotting down them. "We're on our way to figuring things out. But that'll be something between the two of us. Once things are said and done, you'll know. But in the meantime, just don't try to meddle, alright?"

She puzzled at me for a moment. Then a smile pulled at her lips and she raised a brow. "Alright. I'll mind my business. But just for the record, if you weren't my friend, I would hate you for what you're doing to my little brother. I know he did you dirty, but this punishment game isn't fair either."

I fought an eyeroll. "Just mind your business, Leah. Please."

CHAPTER SIXTY-ONE

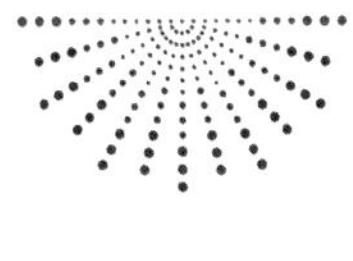

JEREMY

I knocked on Laila's apartment door. Then I heard her argue with Tinkerbell when she barked. "It's open!" she called.

I made my way inside and lowered myself to greet Tink. She excitedly jumped at my face, wagging her tail. The smell of her slobber slithered up my nose. I set the flowers down on the end table as I pet her scruff and chuckled.

"I'm sorry, Max needed some last-minute help so I'm running a little late," she called from the bathroom. "Just give me, like, two minutes."

"Don't rush." I ran my hands along Tinkerbell's fur. She licked my cheek for a moment before scurrying her way back to the couch. "What did Max need?"

"Remember a couple years ago when the cops got called because of a fight at one of the concerts downstairs?" she said.

"Yeah, that was right after you took over, right?" I asked.

"I think so. One of the guys that got hurt is suing the other guy and they needed to know some details from the report I had to file with the insurance company. I don't know, a bunch of dumb legal jargon." Her voice drew closer. "It was stupid. But I just have to feed Tink and let her out really quick and we'll go." Laila rushed into the living room. A weird styling clip held up half of her hair as she pulled a loose, purple flowing shawl over her white spaghetti strapped shirt. I laughed. She met my gaze with a smile. "What?"

"We're teleporting, Laila, we don't have to worry about traffic." I smiled. "Going out's supposed to be a fun thing. Breathe a little."

"There's just a lot going on right now. But I'm going to have fun as soon as I get there."

"How about I take Tink out while you finish getting ready?"

"I am ready."

Well, if she planned on wearing her hair like that, I wasn't gonna judge. She was gorgeous no matter what. But just to check…

"Did you turn off your straightener?"

Her eyes widened a bit. Then her hand raised to her head. "I didn't do my hair, did I?"

"It looks like you started it." I smirked. "But it's kinda cute. Kind of like an older, more metal version of Pebbles."

She placed her hands on her hips. "As in Flintstone?"

I laughed. "Just take your time. I'll feed Tink and take her out. Is there anything else you need to do before we go?"

"I just need to put the dog channel on for Tink." She unfastened the hair clip from her head, leaned forward, and tucked hair her hair into a ponytail.

"Your dog watches TV?" I asked.

"She has some issues, alright?" Laila leaned down to pet her. "If we don't put the doggy channel on, she likes to eat my shoes. And I mean that literally, she doesn't just chew them. She eats them. Even if I put them away. She's learned how to open my closet."

I laughed as Laila leaned up. Her eyes caught on the lilies at the entry table. She smiled and met my gaze. "You didn't have to get me flowers, Jeremy."

But I did. It was our anniversary. That asshole Liam had been buying her flowers—the wrong ones, might I add—and whether she'd admit it or not, it was a date. I had to get her flowers.

Plus, the ones in the windowsills were wilting. She needed more.

"Your vase was empty the other day. You love flowers. You should always have some in here."

Her smile widened a bit. "Well, thank you."

The smell of vapes, weed, and patchouli filled my nose. I could hardly see through the low, blue lighting. Wiggling to the bar through the dense crowd felt just about impossible. But it was nice too. I loved the vibe of a concert.

"Can I get a Coke and a Crown and Coke?" I called over the loud music.

"We're out of Crown," the bartender said almost inaudibly over the blaring speakers. "We have Jack though."

"That'll work."

"That'll be sixteen even," she said quickly, turning to the soda fountain.

I set the twenty on the counter and looked out over the crowd. Laila's bright red hair was easier to distinguish than it'd been when it was black.

She didn't seem to fit in at a group like that. Again, it came back to the dramatized personification of an oxymoron that Laila was. It was some near reggae, hippy band playing.

Laila was a little too heavy to be at a place like this. She was covered in gruesome scars but adorned them with dainty flowers and butterflies. The songs she sang along to were about world peace and compassionate love, but she had just killed a man the day before.

"The spiked one's on the left." The bartender sat the drinks down in front of me. She reached into her apron to give me change but I shook my head.

"That's yours, thanks." I turned away. I sipped my Coke as I made my way through the crowd. I kept my gaze on Laila in the strobing lights, somewhat worried that they'd be a trigger for her. But she seemed happier than I'd seen her in some time.

Some guy approached her and placed his hand on the small of her back. He was a typical hippy fuck boy—skin as white as mine, but wearing locs that came to the middle of his back. As a man with long hair, I didn't typically judge other guys for theirs. White guys with locs though? Yeah, I immediately labeled him a hippy fuck boy.

He leaned down to her ear. She physically laughed, shook her head, yelled something, and took a few steps away. He drew a bit closer and touched her shoulder. Again, she stepped back. Her gaze met his, yelling something I couldn't make out.

When I got close enough, I passively stepped between them. I handed her the drink with a smile. Then I put my hand around her waist, gently tugged her into me, and pressed my lips to her forehead.

"They were out of Crown, so I had to get Jack," I yelled over the music.

The guy beside me turned around and started away. As he did, I moved my hand from her waist. She laughed and turned up to me. "Thank you."

"He didn't want to take a hint," I said. "Figured that'd do the trick."

She grinned. After finishing off what was left in her first cup, she tucked it under the next and took a gulp. Then she held her hand out to mine. "Do you want to get closer?"

I smiled, nodding back. She started into the cluster of people with friendly apologies. She pulled me along like a kid with a toy cart. People glared, getting closer together, but she continued to politely poke past them.

To this day, I still have no idea what band we listened to that night. It wasn't really my taste. I liked a soft, milder rock. Or at least, a more alternative rock. My personal style fell somewhere between art and folk rock, so I was a little out of my element.

It wasn't that I *hated* reggae folk music. But it definitely wasn't my thing. I was a little rougher around the edges than Laila was. At least, I was in the beginning. Over time, her skin got thicker than mine. But even as thick as it was then, I knew how badly she wished she could thin it back out. That's probably why she enjoyed that show so much. It was almost like a reminder of the soft, sweet person she'd once prided herself in being.

Either way, I had one of the best nights of my life that night. It was the first time in nearly a year that Laila and I did something together that wasn't fucking or crying. We just had fun.

We didn't start out as friends—not in this life—but above everything else, that's what we were best at. That's why we were so great once. Because we had fun together. Seeing her happy made me happy and I like to think that seeing me happy made her happy too.

It was only for a few hours, but during that time, we weren't broken, miserable disasters. We weren't super powered creatures burdened with the pressures of being a hero.

We were just two souls in a crowd full of people desperately attempting to forget the bullshit of their lives for a little while.

CHAPTER SIXTY-TWO

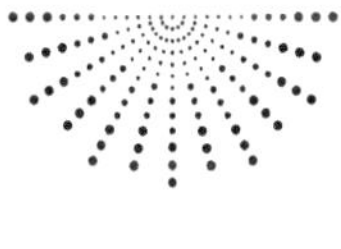

LAILA

Cool autumn air brushed hair into my face. The smell of cigarettes and gasoline touched my nose. My gaze shifted over the small, quiet city ahead. Norfolk, if memory serves. It was about the size of Pittsburgh. Otherwise meaning, though it was labeled a city, it really wasn't.

"Thank you for coming." I looked up at Jeremy and smiled. "I know the whole burning sage stuff isn't really your thing."

Jeremy gave a smile. "It was cool, I'm glad you invited me."

"I'm glad you were here." I smiled still. "Are you hungry?"

"I could eat," he said. "What're you in the mood for?" I turned my gaze to the yellow sign a few blocks down, then back to him with a grin. "Waffle House? Really?"

"What do you have against Waffle House?"

He laughed. "You own and live above a diner."

"I didn't choose the diner life, Jeremy. The diner life chose me," I said.

He laughed, grinning. "Waffle House it is."

We walked quietly for a moment, enjoying that after concert high, trying to hear normally again. The rest of the world slipped away as that vibrating sensation from the bass began to ease from my chest. I wasn't thinking about the chaos of our life, I wasn't thinking about the remorse, I wasn't thinking about the things that tore my marriage apart.

I was just enjoying the peace the music had given me. It's funny because I wasn't the musician. But I love music. I love the way it makes my body feel when it's loud enough. I loved the way the blood within me felt like it was bubbling with the bass as we walked.

For the first time in a long time, I felt good. I hadn't smoked, I'd only had two small drinks, so I wasn't tipsy. I just felt good. And I wanted to wrap myself within that feeling because I knew it wouldn't last long.

After a minute or two, I turned up to meet his gaze. "Jeremy."

He looked up from the ground. "Laila."

"Do you remember when we went to Venice?" I asked.

"I do."

I felt my hands tremble a bit. "Do you remember what you asked me that night?"

"I asked you a lot of things that night," he said.

I cleared my throat. Then I stepped in front of him. I reached onto my tip toes and touched my lips to his. His hands found my hips as he craned down to kiss me back.

My hands rested on his chest, and I met his deep blue eyes. "You asked if we could pretend all of the shit that happened didn't happen for the night."

He smiled, holding my gaze. "Is that what you want?"

"I just want to forget everything for a little while."

He moved his hand to the side of my neck. Then kissed me slow and hard. Just the way I'd answered him two years ago when he asked the same question.

<hr>

"You cannot put Panic! At the Disco into the same category as Justin Bieber." I stabbed a piece of waffle with my fork. "That's unacceptable."

"I'm just saying, they're pretty mainstream now," Jeremy said. "They're great, don't get me wrong. But I'm sorry, they're just not the kind of band I'd like to see live any more. They're at stadiums and shit. It doesn't give you that same general admission, we all paid the same amount of money to see them so suck it up if you get hit in the face as I'm making my way to the front thrill."

"That's fair." I laughed. "Do you ever want to be that big?"

He sipped his Sprite. "What—Performing at stadiums?"

"Yeah." I took a bite of my waffle. My smile stretched up my cheeks. "Like being a *star*."

He laughed. "No. No, not at all. Honestly, you wanna know what my biggest fantasy is?"

"Sounds kinky," I muttered. He laughed, and I smiled. "What's your biggest fantasy?"

"Just being normal." His eyes lightened with hope. "A normal, simple life. No more powers or nightmares or kidnappings or murders. I dream of my biggest problem being a flooded basement or a car that keeps breaking down. Just something that isn't time travel or the FBI breathing down our necks."

I lowered my voice, leaning across the table. "Yeah, I know what you mean. I love what I am. I have pride in my heritage, especially the Fae. I love that I've used my abilities to make a difference. But I wish I could pass the baton to someone who wants the burden."

"If only it were that easy," he said. "But we're supposed to forget about that tonight."

"We are," I said. "So, what was the biggest crowd you performed for while you were gone?"

He took a bite of his pancake. "I think I opened for this one band in Florida for just over a thousand, so nothing too big."

"A thousand people isn't very big?" My eyes widened. "Jeremy, that's amazing. Two years ago, you couldn't perform in front of ten."

He chuckled. "I don't know. It was fun sometimes, I guess. It made me feel good and alive but... But I like being close to my family."

I smiled. "I can understand that."

There was a pause for a moment as I sipped my coffee. Then Jeremy laughed.

"What?" I asked.

Biting his lip, he looked up and met my gaze. "I was going to ask if you ever wanted to publish your work but that seems a little redundant now."

Huh. Yeah, definitely redundant. But a fair question.

"Part of me always did. But fictionized. Not you, not me, not your family. I couldn't publicize the truth—it's exposure. Maybe it's still published as fiction in its time as some weird, artistic author that writes themselves into their story. But it hasn't crossed my mind in years. I haven't even written in years."

He raised a brow. "Years?"

"Yeah. I don't know, I used to write at least once a week. Then at some point it was once every other week, then once a month and before I knew it... Years."

"You should write," he said. "Music's one of the only things that gets me through things that nothing else can. I'm sure writing's the same for you."

"It was," I said. "But I wouldn't even know where to start. I'm busy enough as it is."

"Even if it's just a sentence." He smiled. "Or help me work on a song. You're a writer, you have to write. Passions give us purpose and if you're forgetting what that is, put the pen to paper and you'll remember. Even if you think you don't want to, once you start, you know you won't want to stop."

"Maybe."

"No maybe." He grinned. "Take five minutes every day and write something. You sit on the toilet after you pee scrolling social media for five minutes when you wake up, you can spend that time doing something that you really love."

"More like half an hour." I laughed. "I should really get one of those cushioned toilet seats."

He smiled. "You know I'm right."

"Yeah, yeah." I leaned back in the seat. A long yawn left my lips as I stretched my back.

Jeremy set his fork down on his plate and wiped his hands on his napkin. "I think I'm full. Are you ready to head back?"

"Yeah, Tink probably has to pee. Let me go wash the syrup off my hands real quick." I scooted out of the booth.

CHAPTER SIXTY-THREE

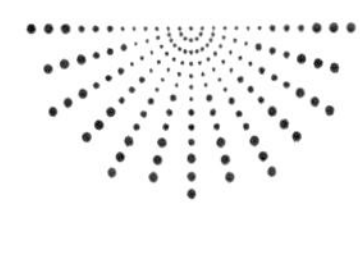

JEREMY

After getting back to the apartment and taking Tinkerbell outside, Laila and I sat down on the couch to smoke. She looked happy that night. I hadn't seen her look happy in so long, but it seemed like she genuinely was for a little while. I wasn't sure if it was that book or if she was still a little disoriented from that acid trip, but it was like seeing rain for the first time after a drought.

I didn't want to leave and risk waking up to see that forced, depressed smile on her lips again. I wished that I could stay in that night for the rest of my life. I wanted to capture that night in a jar and take a hit of it the next time I was lying there in bed fantasizing about her beside me.

That night reminded me that even when things are at the worst, we could still find something to be happy about. If there was a moment of joy that passed through, we had to hold onto it because they're farther apart than the painful parts.

I felt like I used to.

I felt happy.

I felt happy, and I wasn't fucked up.

"I miss this," Laila said quietly. Her gaze met mine as she repositioned herself until her knee touched my thigh.

I looked up from the joint in my hand, smile tugging at my lips. "I thought you wanted to pretend that didn't happen tonight." After taking another hit off the joint, I passed it to her. "But for what it's worth, I miss this too."

Her eyes stayed on mine as she breathed in a slow hit. They stayed on me through the cloud of smoke as she exhaled. Then she set it in the ash tray.

"Jeremy," she said.

"Laila." I smiled.

She grew quiet again. Then she leaned forward and pushed her lips into mine. They barely met, just enough for me to feel their touch. Her hand moved to my chest. I lifted my hand to her neck and tugged her face closer toward mine. Then she gripped my shirt and came in closer.

She moved her hands to my shoulders, brought herself to her knees, and swiveled her body around mine. I held her waist, basking in the warmth of her skin. She lowered herself to my lap and slowly moved her hands against my torso. Mine slid along her curves. Her kiss was slow and gentle in a loving, careful sense. I could feel her pulse racing against my thumb as I touched her neck but she was slow and steady.

After a moment or so, she pulled back a little. Her lips were still touching mine as I opened my eyes. I pushed hair from her face and leaned back to meet her gaze. "Are you alright?"

She gave a smile, but somehow, it looked sad. "Yeah, I'm good."

I touched her cheek. "What is it, Lai?"

Clearing her throat a bit, she said, "I don't know how to say this."

I creased my brow a bit and moved my hand away. "What's wrong?"

"I was a bitch." She still held my gaze. "I... I was hurt and I know that I had the right to be hurt, but I was a bitch. I wasn't fair to you. I never gave you a second chance and that isn't fair."

I pushed hair behind her ear. "What do you mean?"

"When I asked you to leave... I didn't even give you the chance to explain."

The sentiment may have been sweet, but that didn't change that she'd done nothing wrong. I'd fucked up. And I had to deal with the consequences of my actions.

"You weren't a bitch. You were right. What I did was fucked up. I would've left me too. But it is what it is now. We can't change what's in the past."

"But it's still affecting the present," she said. "And I don't want it to. Everything that's happened didn't have to."

"Laila, you didn't choose the circumstance we've been dealt any more than I did," I said softly.

"I chose *this*." Her eyes filled with tears and her head shook. "I chose to throw this away and I shouldn't have." My stomach began to swirl as her green eyes danced between mine. "I'm done playing these games. I want this."

She said it. She finally said it.

I smiled and took her face in my hands. I leaned forward and pressed our lips together. As mine opened against hers, I tasted the liquor on her breath, and my dancing stomach sunk. It wasn't the taste that bothered me but the reminder that she wasn't in a place to make the decisions I wanted her to.

The past few days had been pure emotional turmoil on her. I was there when she needed someone. I was her hero for a little while. As much as I loved the appreciation, I couldn't take advantage of it. She was intoxicated and emotionally exerted. If anything was going to happen between us, it had to be when we were both at a level state of mind.

As her hands traveled down the buttons of my shirt and gently pulled one open, I took them from my chest and twined our fingers together.

"What's wrong?" she asked.

I took her hand from my shirt and laced our fingers together. "We should talk about this in the morning."

Her lips fell to a frown. She leaned back. "It's too late, isn't it?"

"What?" I asked.

Laila climbed off of my lap and moved to the couch cushion beside me. "I didn't expect you to wait around forever, it's okay."

I furrowed my brows. "What are you talking about?"

"I've put both of us through hell for the last nine months." She looked down. "I get it, I do. I just didn't realize—I thought that this was what you wanted too—"

As I realized what she was rambling about, I took her face in my hands and pressed my lips to hers. After I felt her heart pick up against my thumb, I pulled back and met her gaze. "Of course I want this, Laila."

She smiled. "Then why'd you stop?"

"Because you're drunk," I said.

"I had two drinks. I'm not drunk." She tilted her head to the side. "Are you?"

"No, I'm not."

"Then what does it matter?" She laughed.

Either way. Two drinks may not have affected her in the most profound way, but it still could have done something. And I wouldn't be that guy. I wouldn't use this moment to my advantage. She needed to be sure this was what she wanted.

"You might not be drunk, but you're at least tipsy. It's been a shitty couple days, Lai."

"If I'm 'at least tipsy,' then so are you so why does it matter?"

Now seemed as good a time as any. I'd been clean just over a month now—which, granted, wasn't much. But it was something. It was more than I'd had in more than a year. Maybe she'd realize I was serious about my sobriety.

I cleared my throat. "I haven't been drinking, Laila."

She studied my eyes. "You aren't high either?"

"I'm a little buzzed off that joint, but no. I wanted to wait to tell you until I had more clean time under my belt. But I haven't done anything in a while."

She tilted her head to the side. "You're sober?"

"I still smoke obviously," I said. "But yeah, I'm clean. Thirty-three days tomorrow."

Her eyes stung with tears. "That's amazing. Congratulations."

"Thanks."

"Why didn't you tell me?" She smiled back, searching my gaze.

"I didn't want you to think I was getting clean to impress you because I wasn't. But what you said about Micah, about me not being able to be his parent if I kept using—"

"I didn't mean it like that—" she began.

"No, you did. But you weren't wrong. I can't put my kid through what I've put the rest of my family through." She began to say something, but I cut her off again. "You found my dead body and you're my wife. But if it would have been Micah who found me, he would hate me for the rest of his life. I know because I've lived it. I hate my dad for what that did to me. I don't want my kid to ever think that I would abandon him because I won't. I didn't want to die that day and I did. One day I will, and it will stick, but it won't be because I wanted to get high. It won't be because I'm running away from my problems."

A true smile crept up the corners of her lips. "I'm really proud of you."

I smiled back. "Yeah, me too."

"You should be."

I let my smile come down a bit, lifting red hair behind her ear. "But it just doesn't feel right to have sex when I'm sober and you aren't, ya know? At least with the way things have been."

"Always have to be a gentleman, huh?"

"Isn't that what you like about me?"

"That's what I love about you." She grinned.

Biting my smiling lip, I said, "So we can talk about everything in the morning?"

"Sure." She gave a gentle nod. "But I'm still going to feel the way I feel right now."

"I'd just feel better if we waited." I smiled. "I've fucked up a lot of things. If we're going to do this, I want to do it right."

"I can wait until the morning." She gave a playful grin. "But until then, is kissing okay? Because I really want to ki—"

I pushed my lips to hers, grabbed her waist with one hand, her neck with the other, and pulled her into me.

CHAPTER SIXTY-FOUR

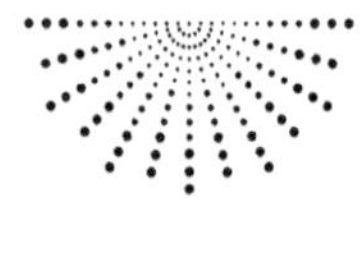

LAILA

Jeremy and I made out on the couch for half an hour or so before I teleported us to the bed. I tried to put my hand in his pants again. Then he laughed and lifted it back up to his chest. He could say that it was because he wanted to "do it right" all he wanted, but I think he just enjoyed watching me beg.

His hand crept along the seam of my jeans as I kneeled above him, then up my shirt and beneath my bra, pulling me closer against him with the other.

We were basically dry humping like freshmen at a high school dance with no moment of finish that brought it to a close. Eventually, I got tired, laid my head against his chest and gave up. He wasn't going to budge, and it was just making me more sexually frustrated.

His arms twisted around my waist and he kissed my forehead one more time before we fell asleep.

It was the first night in months that I didn't dream. I actually got to rest. It was probably just exhaustion from the concert, but it was wonderful. I was beyond grateful because I needed to be well rested for the conversation we were having in the morning.

I'd known for a while what I wanted. That's why I stopped having sex with Liam. That's why I never filed for divorce.

I knew that this was ultimately where I wanted to end up. But reading the words I'd written about Jeremy reminded me how stupid I was being once again. My pride had a way of hurting me differently than anything else could.

He made me happy. He was the father of my child. He was my husband. He was my best friend. We were both finally to the point where things weren't complicated between us. No drugs clouding our minds, no other people's feelings involved, just the two of us and the hope in finding our baby together.

Life had punished us enough. I had to quit punishing us too.

When I woke up the next morning, Jeremy was in the shower. I hurried on some clothes, tried to brush up my makeup from last night, took Tink outside, grabbed a couple pieces of coffee cake and two cups of coffee from the diner, then sat at the table.

As I waited for him to get out, I rehearsed what I planned to say. But the second the faucet turned off, I forgot everything I'd rehearsed.

My heart began to slam against my ribcage like a drum and I forgot every line of the speech I'd prepared.

He came out of the bathroom a few minutes later with damp hair. He glanced into the bedroom before realizing I was in the kitchen. He met my gaze. "Hey, beautiful."

"Hey." I smiled. "Ready to have that talk?"

He raised a brow, grinning. "Are you?"

I laughed as he started toward me. "I sure am."

Jeremy smiled, pulled the chair out, and sat in front of me. He leaned forward and kissed me. I relaxed into that sweet feel for a moment, letting it soothe my tense muscles. I touched his jaw, holding his face close to mine.

As he pulled away, I smiled and met his gaze. "What was that for?"

He grinned. "I just wanted to make sure we were on the same page."

I laughed, feeling my cheeks warm.

He smiled, fingers finding mine. "So are we on the same page?"

I squeezed his hand. "I think we are."

"You want to get back together?"

"I do."

He pressed his smiling lips together. "Maybe we should talk about what that looks like now?"

"Can't we just skip to the part where we're together and this is in the past?"

"We were broken up for a long time, Lai." He gave a sad smile. "Getting back together could mean a lot of things. Like, do you want me to move in? Do you want to date for a while first? Or are we just jumping right back into where we were?"

"I wouldn't say it's really jumping," I muttered. "We see each other almost every day. We talk all the time. We've slept together twice since you've been back. I don't even know how many times we've kissed. And I talk to you on a deeper level than I talk to anyone else."

"Well, yeah," he said. "But you're sure this is what you want?"

I held his gaze. "Isn't this what you want?"

"I've begged you to take me back a thousand times. You know it's what I want." He smiled. "But I don't want to break up again. I want to be able to call you my wife and it have meaning. I want to be with you for the rest of my life. I want to know that you're sure."

I looked between his serious, almost piercing gaze. It was soft and meaningful, but firm at the same time. He wanted the same reassurance he always gave me.

"I want you to come home, Jeremy," I said softly. "We've been through a lot of shit, and we're still going through a lot of shit, and I'm sure we're going to go through a lot more shit. But I want to go through it with you. We can't have that life we wrote about in that book again. That's over. It isn't all rainbows and hearts on my notebook and it never will be again. Things are never going to be soft and sweet the way that they used to be. They're messy. They're always going to be messy because of what we've been through and what we are. But I love you and I'm tired of wasting time. I want this, Jeremy."

As I spoke, his eyes gleamed and a smile crept up his lips. "I love you too."

"You said that's all we needed if we wanted to make this work." I gave a soft smile, holding his gaze. "We'll figure out all the details along the way. But we love each other. That's all we need."

He leaned forward and kissed me. I pulled away and laughed. "I haven't brushed my teeth yet."

"I don't care." He reached in and pulled my face back to his smiling lips.

CHAPTER SIXTY-FIVE

LAILA

Being with Jeremy as more than just a hookup for the first time after almost a year of being apart was mesmerizing. The last two times we had sex, it was angry and gritty fucking. But this time was slow and sensual love making. The makeup sex was definitely better than breakup sex.

His hands moved along my skin like he was holding the most precious object he'd ever touched. They were somehow firm while still soft and gentle.

His lips slid familiarly along mine before they moved along my jaw and down my neck. He had this way of being ginger while maintaining a steady stream of passion.

We changed positions, rolling back and forth for hours, holding each other close. Our faces stayed near each other's as I rolled on top of him. Moving my hips up and down, I pulled away to let a heavy sigh escape my lips.

"Laila," he murmured at my ear.

"Yeah?" I made out between moans.

His other hand slid along my waist, leaving a layer of warm tingles in its path. "Promise me that you want this forever," he whispered.

I smiled, kissing his neck. My eyes closed, breathing in the scent of his citrusy cologne. "I promise."

I ground my hips against his pelvis. Pressure built in my stomach, traveling down to my clit against his mess of dark curls. Fuck, he felt better than anyone else ever had or could. His hands on my skin, his dick inside of me; it wasn't just good, it was euphoric. I felt like I was floating.

"I love you," he murmured at my neck.

"I love you too."

His hand at my waist moved to the side of my neck, pulling my lips back to his. He teleported us to the edge of the bed, sat forward, placed his arms around my naked chest, and pulled me as close against him as he could get.

In that moment, so close against each other, practically hugging while inside and around one another, it truly felt as though we were one within two.

Joy, and passion, and friendship, and love all combined into this beautiful, almost cosmic sensation. The sex alone was amazing, but it felt like so much more than that. It felt... it felt like I was high. Not on drugs, not on life, but him. He was captivating, consuming, and yet—somehow—so freeing.

All in the same instant.

"Baby, are you okay?" Jeremy suddenly pulled away.

I opened my eyes. And I gasped.

Bright light radiated from every inch of my body. It was a goldish purple, almost shimmering color. It reminded me of the blinding white light I healed with, but it was so much prettier. The way it slid from my bare skin almost resembled smoke, but it glowed like the light of a star.

I jerked backwards, nearly falling off him. Jeremy held my hips—probably in fear that I'd break his dick if I did. "Jesus Christ, does this hurt?"

"No." He gave an odd, joy filled smile. "Not at all. It feels amazing." He gazed between my eyes; pupils so dilated they nearly overtook his irises. But he smiled still, blinking slightly. "Fuck, you're beautiful."

"What is this?"

He shook his head. "I have no idea. But it's..." He laughed. His hand shifted from my waist up to my head, gently caressing my hair. "It's euphoric."

"You're high?"

"Not really." His strong, calloused fingers slid into the curve of my waist. "Go in my head. Feel it."

He teleported me onto the bed. He gently kissed down my neck. My eyes closed, legs tightening around his waist.

I engulfed myself in his mind, still feeling his slow, gentle thrusts inside of me. I saw myself through his eyes as he stared down at my glowing face. It almost looked as though a Snapchat filter had been tossed over me. Hues of gold and purple emitted from my cheeks and chest. Sparks of purple and white flickered through it, almost like glitter, but a light source on its own.

His body felt warm and fuzzy, yet tingly and exhilarated at the same time. Happy. Somehow, it felt safe and sweet yet almost fearfully powerful all in the same thought. It was kind of like being high, but no high I had ever felt. It was as intense as being drunk yet filled with the same sense of clarity and happiness I felt after my morning cup of coffee.

"Do you feel it?" he murmured at my ear, still gently pulsing in and out of me.

"It's amazing," I whispered. "What is it?"

He kissed my neck. Warm chills erupted over me at the feel of his tongue against my skin. "I have no idea, but don't stop."

Well, I didn't know how to if I wanted to.

But I didn't want to.

The feel of his dick slowly sliding in and out of me with that warm, enticing sensation in his mind merging together was the best thing I'd ever experienced. It wasn't a rush of pleasure, but a steady, pulsing stream of it. Nothing had ever felt so good in my entire life. Not in a gritty, 'fuck me harder, baby' sort of way. But in a 'I never want this sensation to leave me' kind of way.

It was love, it was strength, it was joy, it was ecstasy, it was passion.

It was everything.

Jeremy's fingers moved through my hair, holding it between his fingers. He murmured, "Your hair was red five minutes ago, wasn't it?"

I opened my eyes. "What?"

He leaned back a bit. His fingers held the end of my hair up between us. I blinked hard, making sure the light coming from my skin wasn't playing a trick on me.

Brown. A warm, almost mahogany color.

"Isn't this your natural color?" he asked, smiling.

I nodded as he gently moved his hand to the side of my face. "How is that possible?"

He shook his head, almost in a daze. He laughed, still holding my gaze, and gently moved in and out of me. "I don't know but it's beautiful." He lowered his lips to mine. "You're beautiful."

As he did, the rest of the world began to drift away. It shouldn't have, whatever was happening was fucking bizarre. But I just couldn't help myself.

It felt like I was molding into him, into this experience.

My eyes closed, fingers sliding through the thick scruff along his jaw. It felt like we were in perfect sync for the first time in... I didn't even know how long.

It was the strangest sensation and more difficult to describe than anything else. It was the same comfort I got when lying naked with him or holding my newborn to my bare skin. That same rush of endorphins and oxytocin but magnified by a thousand. Just an overwhelming sense of love. Not passion, not excitement, but love, joy and peace.

Yet, it was simultaneously arousing. The fluid continuously gushing around his dick pulsing in and out of me was proof of that. But that normally tense pressure gathering in my pussy was softer. It was the best sex I'd ever had, but not because it was rough and passionate. It was... loving. Gentle, slow, and bringing me closer to finish with each thrust.

I lifted my eyelids for a moment, and then they flung open.

The skin on his neck in front of me glowed the same way mine did. What I had just felt in Jeremy's mind hit similarly, yet so different too. Mine was amazing, but his was shocking and more intense. That same sense of love and joy, but rather than peace, it was a sense of intense euphoria.

I was almost dizzy, but not quite. It was more like that spinning sensation of a first kiss. It sent a cool chill over my bare skin, but in the best way imaginable.

It gave everything my eyes could see this beautiful, warm grayish glow. But the color radiating from him was different. Swirling undertones of blue throbbed throughout, not much different than the color of his eyes.

But light wasn't even the right word for it. While it was, in fact, light, it didn't permeate. It surely would have lit a dark room, but it looked more like smoke than the rays of light.

Everything looked brighter. It even felt brighter, if that makes any sense. It was the way the world looked when I fell in love for the first time. Yet, much more intoxicating. The aura he was releasing made me feel lighter and happier than I'd ever felt in my life.

"Jeremy," I whispered.

He pulled back and met my gaze. His eyes peeled open at his glowing hands on the bed beside my head.

"What the fuck?"

I leaned forward, molding our mouths together. "Don't stop." I pulled him back down.

Slowly, he kissed me back. He leaned further inside of me, but instead of thrusting, he ground up and down. His pelvis hit just the right place against my clit, euphoria overtaking me.

My nails dug into his back, heavy moan falling from my mouth to his. He breathed heavily, resting his forehead on mine. His eyes opened, shifting between mine.

"What is this?" he whispered.

"I don't know, but it's amazing."

His dark hair hung against my cheeks, hot breath warming my skin. "I've never felt so good in my life."

"Neither have I," I whispered. My leg tightened around his waist, pulling him further inside of me.

He breathed out something between a sigh and a groan. "Fuck, I'm gonna come."

I'm not sure why, but I tightened my legs around him. It was almost involuntary. And he didn't attempt to pull back.

His hips ground up and down at the same pace, pressure growing heavier at my clit.

So good, it felt *so* good. I didn't want to climax yet, I didn't want him to either, but I didn't want to stop. I wanted to make this moment last a millennium.

I wanted him. *All* of him.

"Are you close?" he whispered.

I nodded, long moan dropping from my mouth. Our eyes stayed on each other's, intensifying euphoria spreading through my body and pleasure rocking through where our bodies joined as one. The bliss was hurriedly climbing, I was almost at my peak, breaths so close together I was surprised I didn't faint.

Warmth filled inside of me, heavy breath falling from Jeremy's mouth. And just as it did, I reached the top. My muscles contracted around him, yanking him in further. His mouth dropped open, his eyes shifted between mine, and his thumb brushed my lower lip.

The light permeating from us grew so bright that had it been night, we would've lit up the parking lot outside the window.

Pleasure overtook me, still caught up in that glorious stream of love and beauty.

It may not have been the most powerful, leg trembling, screaming orgasm I'd ever had. But it was definitely one of the best.

Just as it ended, the light radiating from our skin began to slowly drift back into our bodies. Jeremy laughed, and I smiled. Then he dropped to the bed beside me and tugged my waist into his chest.

CHAPTER SIXTY-SIX

JEREMY

"Okay, walk me through this again." Leah pulled off her glasses and rubbed the bridge of her nose. "You were fucking and then you just started glowing?"

"Pretty much," Laila said.

"It wasn't really *fucking*," I muttered.

It may have been the sweetest, most gentle sex we ever had. As cheesy as it sounds, it felt as though we were making love. Then that thing happened. And don't get me wrong, whatever it was had been amazing. But really fucking strange too. I had a pretty broad understanding of the supernatural creatures and abilities in our world, but never had I seen anything like we'd just done.

Leah raised a brow. "And you did too?"

I raised my hand and let the light leave my skin. She put her glasses back on and looked over it. "You can touch it, it doesn't hurt."

"I'm not touching your weird sex power." She crinkled her nose. "For all I know, that shit makes you guys feel like your rolling balls and sets me on fire."

"I doubt it," Laila said.

"It isn't like rolling either," I said. "I guess in a way it is—in the sense that it makes you happy but it's not the same."

"No, not at all," Laila said. "I've never felt anything like it before."

"It's beautiful," I murmured. "That's the only way I can think to describe it. Distracting, in a way. Like, it engulfs your mind. You can still think, you can still make decisions, but it makes you... I don't know what word I'm looking for here."

"Happy?" Laila asked. "Tranquil, and happy at the same time."

Leah gazed down at my hand. "I swear to god if you kill me, you better be prepared for me to punch you in the face when Hannah brings me back."

"Fair enough."

As her fingers touched mine, a soft, dewy expression of joy washed into her green eyes. Her mouth tugged upward in a wide grin. She giggled.

"Dude." She laughed, looking between Laila and I. "What the fuck is this?"

Laila laughed. Leah continued to snicker with a giant, childish grin. Then I pulled my hand away. She continued to chuckle. Then it slowly faded, and her head shook. She looked at me. "No, that's fucking weird. I can't even think of a way to use it defensively."

"I can," Laila said. "Give yourself a second to come down and you can think of a thousand. If I could have touched a guard in there and over-whelmed them with joy, I could have made it out without over fifty murders under my belt. And when someone's going to die anyway, we can take that pain away."

I smiled softly as I met her gaze. She was aggressive and angry, but she'd always be soft and fluffy inside.

"Have you ever discovered a new ability during sex before, Laila?" Leah asked.

"I've never discovered a new one. I've used them accidentally at times, but no. Never unlocked one like that before."

"Yeah, I have the scars to prove it," I mumbled.

"When was the last time you guys slept together before this?" Leah asked.

"Is that relevant?" Laila asked.

I met her gaze. "The night before I got clean."

"So before Helena cast that spell," Leah said.

"You think that has something to do with it?" I asked.

"The par animos fables are gibberish. Parts of it are entirely accurate, like the physical bond, but others we have no clue about. We know that you're powerful. Your souls are massive compared to the rest of us. But we don't know much else. Your powers are associated with sex, we know that because intimacy is what the bond is about. That's how your powers manifested, that's how yours grew so rapidly." She looked between us. "When Helena magnified your bond, maybe she woke something up that you would have discovered in two decades. It sped up your body's evolution."

"Okay, but what the fuck did it do to my hair?" Laila pointed at her head. "This shit is long; do you have any idea how much money it cost me to have it colored?"

I laughed. I liked her hair red. It was pretty. It brought out the green in her eyes. But like this, she looked like her. Different, actually, she'd colored it a nearly black shade for as long as I'd known her.

But I liked this better. The soft brown with her vibrant green eyes reminded me of a forest. Earthy, like she was. The red looked fiery, which she was, but that was only a fraction of her.

"Maybe you aren't meant to be a red head," Leah said. "I told you you'd end up going back to dark."

She made a face. "I liked my red hair."

Leah laughed, pulled a piece of purple hair in front of her eyes, and then held it in front of Laila. "Hey, I'm just saying."

That was a good point. It hadn't been a chemical reaction, Leah's hair would've returned to its natural color too. It had to have been something else. What that was, I had no idea.

Laila's spare phone—the one she used for all things paranormal related—dinged in her pocket. She pulled it out and frowned as she read the message. She rubbed her eyes.

"Who is it?" I asked.

"Tina. She wants to know if we're still on to meet up later." She typed.

"Are you?" Leah asked. "Because I haven't heard back from the Angels."

"I'm going to tread lightly," Laila said. "But yeah, I have to meet with her. She has video evidence of not only me using my powers, but also me murdering almost twenty people. Regardless of the Angel's opinions, I have to address it. Any reporter in the world would kill for those videos. I have to protect myself and every other supernatural creature he could release footage of. To do that, I have to have a conversation with her. I'm going to fuck with her head. Not make her forget, just make it impossible for her to tell anyone. She'll be on our side afterward, regardless of where she stands now."

"Where are you meeting?"

"I'm not sure yet," Laila said. "I told her I'd give her the location twenty minutes before. Just as a precaution."

"Good call."

"Are you going to be there?" Leah asked me.

"Yeah, that's the plan."

"Good," Leah muttered. "Make sure she doesn't have any copies and make her turn them over to you if she did. She can't have that type of dirt on us."

"Top of my list."

Tina was a nice lady. But I'd be damned before I let her destroy everything I just got back. I'd do whatever needed done to keep our secrets—and my wife—safe.

Leah looked between us and smiled. "So is this what I think it is?"

I smiled, turning to meet Laila's gaze. Her cheeks got a little pink, smile spread across her lips. I put my arms around her waist and kissed her head. "We're together."

"Finally." Leah stood. "Now we can get onto things that actually matter."

CHAPTER SIXTY-SEVEN

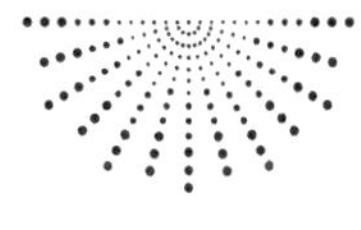

LAILA

The smell of warm espresso filled my nose. My gaze shifted over the crowded coffee shop. Quiet jazz played over the radio speakers above. I leaned over the high-top table and took a long sip of my iced macchiato. Damn, that thing was delicious. I wondered if I could find anything nearing the same quality back home.

Jeremy leaned in a bit closer and lowered his voice. "Are you sure she's coming alone?"

"Of course I'm not." I turned to meet his gaze. "But it's not like I could talk about this on the phone. We'll see when she gets here. If anyone's with her, we disappear into the crowd and teleport home."

He looked toward the door with a tight jaw. "If she's smart, she told someone. Maybe not the FBI, but a friend or a relative. She's a cop, there's no way in hell she isn't wearing a wire in case we kill her."

"Ray didn't," I said.

"His wife and kid are like us. That was different," Jeremy muttered.

"This can't be avoided, Jeremy." I took his hand in mine. "We have to deal with this at one point or another. It isn't going to go away. Peterson sent it to her for a reason."

"What if she did tell the FBI?"

I'd already thought of that. Peterson was able to hide from them, even from us and we had a shit ton of superpowers. If he could do it, so could we.

"I have some cash stashed at the diner." I sipped my iced coffee. "We'll pack a bag and go."

He turned from the door and met my gaze. Then he smiled, squeezing my hand. "Where to?"

"Mexico sounds fun. I've heard you can get weed really cheap down there. Or maybe China. Or Antarctica. Or a deserted island in the tropics." I smiled. "We can build our own civilization. And then if the feds find us, we can start over somewhere new. Maybe Scotland. It's pretty there. I really want to scratch it off my bucket list. We could buy an old castle by the ocean and walk Tink on the beach every morning."

"A castle?" He grinned. I nodded, holding my smile. "Never pegged you as a castle kind of girl."

I laughed. "I think I could be pretty happy in a castle."

My tastes were diverse. I loved cabins, tents, castles, and just about everything in between.

He chuckled, gently sliding his thumb along the back of mine. "So that's what this was about, huh? You didn't want to be alone if you had to run from the government?"

My lips raised in a half smile. "I thought when you married me you agreed to be my partner in crime."

His hand squeezed mine. He lifted it to his lips and kissed my knuckles. "Always, baby."

Behind his head, I saw Tina making her way through the door with her phone in her hand. A moment later, my phone buzzed. Her name lit up my screen. When I saw no one was behind her, I waved and she looked around. As her gaze met mine, she smiled.

She carefully made her way through the crowd. Jeremy tightened his hand around mine and lowered it to my lap. "Laila." She sat at the high top table across from us. "Jeremy."

"Hi, Tina." I smiled. "How are you?"

Her smile faded. "I'm a little terrified to be honest."

I held my smile. "You shouldn't be."

She met my gaze. "I take it you watched the tapes?"

"We did." Jeremy gritted his teeth together. "Still think I have something to do with it after seeing it for yourself?"

"No, Jeremy. I don't."

"Good." He tightened his jaw.

"But it made a lot of things that didn't add up come together. How you got all of those people off the island. Why they called you their savior. Why none of them, not even one, was willing to give a story to the media." She looked between us. "How you were so sure Laila was alive when I was sure she was long gone."

"What do you know about that?" Jeremy's tone was accusative.

She smirked a bit. "Just a hunch 'til you said that."

He gritted his teeth together.

Truthfully, I wasn't worried about Tina. She was a no one. I knew that even then. But Jeremy never did well with cops. I wasn't sure which direction I was going to head but I knew taking care of her wouldn't be too difficult. I was more worried about the fact that Peterson sent the tape to her at all. Because if he sent it to her, I had no clue who else he'd be willing to send it to.

"What do you want, Tina?" I asked.

"He said he was responsible for the capture or death of almost a thousand people, Laila," Tina said. "What you did in those videos" —she leaned forward and lowered her voice— "I didn't see a murderer. I saw someone who was terrified doing what they had to do to survive. You were looking for those people. You were trying to free them, and you became a prisoner of war. What you endured, all those people you helped escape, that's the work of someone who I want to help. I can help you find them, Laila. We both have resources that the other doesn't."

Her expression looked genuine. Although I didn't know her all that well just yet, I had liked her when we met. She worried me when we met again, but only because she implied Jeremy had something to do with my capture. Not because I thought she was a vile individual.

"Why do you care?" Jeremy asked. "You know that the people he's holding aren't like you."

She narrowed her gaze at him. "I became a cop because I wanted to help people. They might be different than me, but so far, not one of the people found has been a previous violent offender. No felons or bank robbers. They're good people."

"Some of them probably aren't, you just wouldn't know because we're smart enough not to get caught," I said.

"Regardless." Tina turned back to me. "No one deserves to endure what that man did to you. The people he took might be different, but they are good people and they deserve to live.

"Christopher Skoulda was eighteen years old with a full ride to Columbia before he disappeared. Haley Mitchell was the best EMT in her county. A man named Kurt Eaton fought in Afghanistan from nineteen ninety-six to nineteen ninety-nine when he lost his leg, only to be captured and tortured there for three years. One of the survivors even fought in Vietnam." She steadily looked between Jeremy and me. "I don't know you, not this side of you. But I know that you're good people. You didn't want to be a part of this any more than you wanted it to exist.

"These people, they are *people.* I don't care what you all can do. I heard you begging them to stop, Laila. You didn't want to kill them, but you did what you had to. I don't know how, but *you're* the reason all of those people are back with their families.

"He reached out to me but I'm with you. Whatever I can do within my power to help bring the rest of those people back, I want to do. No one, especially no child, deserves to grow up the way Lydia Ramirez did."

I looked over her for a moment, studying her expression. She meant what she said. And she wore a loose shirt with no bra. I'd have seen a wire if there was one.

"Did you make any copies?" Jeremy asked.

"Of the videos?" Tina said. He nodded, and she shook her head. "No."

"Would you be willing to prove that?" he asked.

"You can go through my computer if you want but I'll tell you what, kid, I wouldn't know how to do that if I tried."

I laughed. "We don't need to do that." I reached across the table and met her gaze. "Just touch my hand for a second."

She looked down at it. "And you can tell if I'm lying?"

"Something like that."

She cleared her throat. Then she put her hand on mine. Inside her mind, I did something of a metaphoric keyword search of myself. I focused on 'Laila' and a million files appeared.

My case was a puzzle she couldn't figure out. Even reports she had written now laid in a file nearly entirely redacted. She had argued with her husband time and time again about the importance of my case when he complained about the way she buried herself in her work. She spent so much time on it that it drove a wedge between them. They weren't even sleeping in the same room anymore. She was obsessed with finding those people almost as much as I was.

I sifted past the emotional stuff onto the more recent memories. At just the image of my back by the third, she couldn't control the urge to vomit. Her eyes stung with tears as she watched each one. She stayed up all night after watching them, tossing and turning as a million thoughts traveled through her mind.

How could someone pull something this big off for this long and go unnoticed?

We failed almost a thousand people. Serve and protect my ass.

A twenty-something year old waitress did more for those people than we have done in almost a decade.

Tina ripped her hands back. "I was frustrated, Laila. I didn't mean that in a—"

"Please stop looking at me like I'm about to kill you." I smiled. "Trust me, I wish you could have been the one to save us and take the glory. And as long as you aren't a threat, you have nothing to worry about. I haven't done what I've done because I enjoy it."

"You understand what this means." Jeremy's piercing gaze locked with hers. "You can't tell anyone about those videos."

"I already gave it to you. Telling someone would be pointless, I have no evidence to back it up," Tina said. "I have to do psych evals to keep my job. This wouldn't look good. I don't want to bring this to the public eye any more than you do."

Tina leaned a little closer. "You saw those files, Laila. Almost all of them were redacted after homeland security got involved. After you were found, there was almost nothing in the news about it because any police files related to it are almost entirely blacked out. Even under the freedom of information act, you can't find anything on what happened to you guys. I've been heavily encouraged by my superiors to keep it as quiet as possible. Your people are quiet, so that helps. But someone up high is helping to cover this up. Maybe one of you works at the FBI or CIA. Or maybe it's someone working for him. I don't know, but I do know that someone very important is pulling strings to keep this quiet."

I did see the files. And the same thoughts ran through my mind. Part of me did wonder if it was Peterson. But he wanted Tina to know about us, and he asked her not to take it to her superiors or the media. So that wouldn't pan out.

But I did know that the Chambers had their claws in several governments around the world. And that's what I cracked it up to. It made perfect sense. They didn't want our people exposed any more than I did.

So I didn't think much more into that aspect. They were keeping it quiet high up and Tina was keeping it quiet down low. As far as I was concerned, I just formed an alliance with an FBI agent.

PART III

AT LEAST WE AREN'T TOTAL SHIT SHOWS ANYMORE

CHAPTER SIXTY-EIGHT

NOVEMBER 5, 2020 - JEREMY

After the day that Laila and I got back together, everything in our lives changed. It wasn't easy to figure out how we fit in each other's worlds now. I'd already been at the diner almost daily since I'd been back, but falling back into our routine could have been a little easier than it was.

We argued a lot. It was never intense screaming matches but there was plenty of annoyed bickering. She bitched about my wet towel on the floor, I bitched about her inability to dump out the coffee grounds when she finished brewing a pot. That was actually the fun part.

Adjusting to her erratic sleep schedule around her nightmares wasn't easy. Remembering how hot she was at night was going to take some acclimation. Max banging around in the kitchen at five a.m. wasn't exactly pleasant. All of Tinkerbell's weird little doggy triggers were a lot to get used to.

But I was home. And I fucking loved it.

I missed a full night's sleep without waking up to getting burned or Max yelling in the diner downstairs, but I wouldn't trade it for anything.

I just fucking loved *her*. And I was so grateful she wanted me there. It wasn't peaceful. It was busy and exciting. In a lot of ways, I was more stressed than I'd been when we were broken up. But I loved every minute of it.

We hadn't gotten much information on any leads, but we were noticing some weird details. Not anything that would immediately help us find our son, just some odd connections

There were things the zombie in the basement said that were beginning to stick out and point to some odd conclusions. Laila said that Peterson told her she'd bring light to the world. The Bible states that Lucifer is the bringer of light, but Lucifer was a real person. I'd never met him, and I had no desire to, but he was the leader of Hell. So I didn't see the correlation, but there had to be one.

The book hadn't given us anything which left us wondering why Chris led us to it in the first place. It helped remind the two of us why we loved each other so much, but it hadn't given us even an inkling as to where they could be or how we could find them. The timeline it was set in had long passed, it had nothing to do with Chris, let alone Micah.

Tina hadn't been any help, but she hadn't given us any problems either. We'd been in contact with Helena. She was still working on a tracking spell strong enough to find Micah but hadn't had any luck yet.

We hadn't heard from Mary either. We all feared the worst. She made it clear how things might end for her. Despite how much I hated what she'd done, I didn't want her dead. I never did, not even in the beginning after I realized what she caused. I didn't want Ally to die either. But people died doing what we did. Maybe Mary was just another one on the list.

Laila was still having a really hard time. I wasn't doing great either but I was a lot better at blocking it out than her. She cried a lot. Most of the time, she didn't realize I heard her from outside the bathroom door. Or she thought I was asleep when they quietly erupted from her eyes when we lay in the dark bedroom trying to fall asleep. I tried not to comfort her because if she wanted it, she'd ask for it. I just held her a little closer until the two of us drifted off to sleep.

I couldn't do much about what happened to Micah and Chris. I wished I could, but I couldn't. But I could be here. Even if she didn't want me to wipe the tears away, she wanted me beside her. Aside from bringing them home, that's all I really wanted too.

Sitting at the kitchen table with closed eyes, I focused on the sound coming from the strings and hollow piece of wood on my lap. I wasn't sure what this song was going to be about, but it sounded hopeful. Sweet, and gentle.

The front door opened. I looked up and gave a smile.

"Hey." Laila smiled back. She kissed my cheek, pulled off her sneakers, and sat down at the table beside me.

"Hey." I smiled and put my guitar down. "How was work?"

"Another day in the life," she said. "I really hope this waitress sticks. I haven't had a full staff since Celena and Wyatt left."

"I'd really be happy to help." I took a sip from my bottle of water. "I'm bored anyway. I miss it."

"You're basically the handyman around here." She smiled. "I can't have you fixing toilets then serving food."

"We need a new one by the way. That third stall in the men's room is leaking at the bolts on the tank. They're too corroded to get off. We could try and go the cheaper route and replace the tank, but the toilet itself is pretty old. Something's probably going to break on it soon anyway." I laughed. "But you like the work. Part of you is hoping that waitress quits, isn't it?"

"It keeps my mind off things, ya know?"

I smiled. "Yeah, I do. Actually, I've been wanting to ask you what you thought about something I've been considering."

She took a piece of candy from the table and began unwrapping it. "Which is?"

"I think I want to go back to school," I said. "Probably just online classes at the community college or something because of the way our lives get. But I think I want a career in something."

She smiled wide. "I think that's a great idea."

"Really?" I asked. "'Cause I feel like I might be a little too old."

"You're twenty-five. Even if you do a six-year program, you'll be done by the time you're thirty-one." Laila gave a sweet smile. "I think it'd be a good thing for you."

"Thirty-one." I chuckled. "Jesus, I'm getting old."

She smiled and took my hand. "What do you want to go for?"

"Just pre-requisites for now but I'm thinking something with music. Maybe like a music teacher or something," I said. "I'm not sure. I just think it'd be good to start working toward something, you know?"

"Yeah, I completely agree." She smiled. "Have you talked to anyone about enrollment?"

"I have," I said. "The fall semester already started so the soonest I can start is January."

"Well, that's okay. That'll give you some time to prepare yourself." She held her smile. "I think that'll be good for you."

"But I really want to help around here more, Lai." I smiled. "There's only so much I can do with trying to find Micah. I need a distraction too. I've thought about looking for a job in town somewhere but considering how erratic our life gets, I need something with flexible hours."

She stood and moved in front of me. Her hands moved to my shoulders as she leaned down and pressed her lips to mine. "I could use a program manager for the shows downstairs. That'd take a whole work load off me and it's right up your alley."

I smiled and moved my hands to her hips. "That would be right up my alley, huh?"

She smiled back. "I know that I try to do everything on my own all the time and I'm trying really hard to stop doing that. I don't push you away because you don't do a good job or anything, I'm just having a hard time adjusting to a second set of hands. But I'm going to try to ask for help."

I smiled and tugged her down onto my lap. "Well, I'm here when you're ready for help."

She kissed me. Then she leaned back. Arms still around my shoulders, her eyes came to mine. "How are you doing? Adjusting to things, I mean."

"I'm good." I smiled as I pushed hair from her face. "I'm really good."

"You aren't... You know, thinking about getting high?" Her hand moved to my jaw.

"I'm always going to think about getting high," I said. "But I'm not seriously considering it or anything. Life isn't perfect right now and I wish things were a little better than they are, but I don't want to ruin what I do have, Lai."

"Just please tell me if that changes, okay?"

"I will, baby."

And that was the truth. I was happy. Not as happy as I could've been, but I had a routine again. I woke up each morning, took Tink for a walk, grabbed a shower, had coffee downstairs, then helped out with miscellaneous things. If it was a light day, and Laila swore she didn't need me, I'd take Tink for another walk. Then I'd come upstairs, clean a little, make dinner, and play some music. I'd found some peace in sobriety.

Still, I wanted to work. Every now and then, I'd be sitting there playing guitar and think about how much better it would sound if I were fucked up. But then I'd think over the last year. I'd prop open the window, I'd drop to the floor, and I'd meditate until the sensation passed.

If I were working as much as she was, I wouldn't have the chance for that moment to set in. But I was doing okay. I just needed something to focus on. I needed something to keep myself busy.

And soon enough, I'd have the perfect project.

A gentle smile pulled at her lips. She turned her eyes to her hands. Her teeth chomped on her lower lip as she thought. I lifted her chin to meet my gaze with a soft smile. "How are you doing with everything?"

She forced a smile. "I'm okay."

"You can talk to me." I brushed hair behind her ear,

She looked down. "It isn't you. I don't want you to think that you're doing anything wrong," she said. "I'm just having a hard time."

"Do you want to talk about it?" I asked softly.

"It's all been said before."

"Have you still been going to therapy?"

"Yeah." She moved her arms around my back in a hug.

I kissed her hair. "Has it helped?"

"Sometimes."

I tightened my arms at her waist.

I'd gone to therapy a time or two too. And it helped.

But neither of us would be truly happy until we had our baby in our arms.

CHAPTER SIXTY-NINE

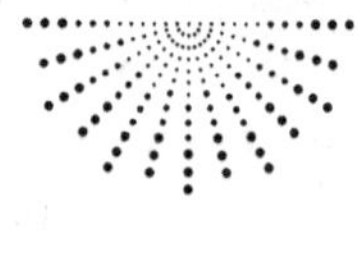

LAILA

The past month had been the first glimpse into happiness that I had since I found out that I was pregnant with Micah. Nothing was easy, but it wasn't quite as hard with Jeremy by my side.

I was still filled with guilt, but I tried my hardest to allow myself to enjoy being happy before the remorse crept in. Chris once said that I had to hold onto the happiness when it came through. I had no problem giving others that advice, but it wasn't easy to take when he came to me in a dream insisting I had to find him before it was too late.

And we'd looked, but that message didn't bring them home. It brought Jeremy and I back together though. Maybe that's what we needed. Maybe we needed to be together to find them.

Regardless, it still wasn't easy.

My business was running well, our profits were near the highest they'd ever been. My husband was home and things between us were going great. My mom and I had a good relationship, I was pleased with where I was in relation to my siblings and friends.

But I didn't have my baby.

My son was still being held by some insane, megalomaniac and his super powered, motherly side kick.

It was hard to think about anything that wasn't him. Yet, I had to because it was too hard to fathom the horrible mother I'd already been by allowing it to happen. Just thinking about it sent me into this pit full of shame and self-loathing.

Every day was a battle inside of my mind, constantly struggling to maintain my composure. I had to not think about it. If I didn't push it from my mind, it would consume me.

The morning after Jeremy told me he was going to go back to school was like any other. We drank our coffee, we read the newspaper, we kissed before I started my shift. He took Tinkerbell outside for her morning walk while I shuffled papers around on my desk.

It was a normal, calm day. But his plans to start school were about to fall apart in the best way possible.

Warm coffee slid down my esophagus, sweet flavor settling on my tongue. Quiet rock music muffled behind the sound of Max clanking together pots and pans in the kitchen outside the door. I pulled my sweater tighter around my shoulders, that autumn chill having snuck in. My fingers thumbed through my notes for next week's schedule.

Then my phone sounded. It was a notification sound I didn't get often, I wasn't sure what it was from. I lifted it from the desk.

Did you forget to log your latest start date?

I clicked into my menstrual tracking application.

You period was projected to start on October 30th.

It was November 6th.

My stomach sunk before it filled with butterflies. A fluttering sensation pounded in my chest.

I had to assume I was just a few days late. It was rare for me, but it happened.

I couldn't get myself excited. If I wasn't, the disappointment of being wrong would be too devastating to handle.

But I couldn't wait. I had to know.

I dropped my phone into my purse and turned out into the kitchen. "Hey, Max," I called, looking around for him.

"Down here, hang on!" he yelled from the basement steps. I started toward them. He came upstairs, dusting his hands on his dirty jeans. "Sorry, I had to put that blow up jack-o-lantern away. Jeremy put it in the wrong place so I couldn't fit the damn skeleton in that cabinet. What's up?"

"Could you hold down the fort for a little bit?" I pulled my jacket from the coat rack over my arms. "Jeremy'll be back soon. Just tell him I have a quick errand to run. I shouldn't be more than an hour or two."

Max wiped sweat from his brow. "Sure. Where's Jeremy? He said he'd look at my car. The check engine light's back on."

"He's taking Tink for a walk. He'll be back soon." I lifted my purse back over my shoulder.

"Alright, cool." Max nodded.

"Thanks, I owe you one." I hurried out the back door to my car.

As I drove to Walmart, I had to force myself to stop fantasizing about being pregnant. After losing Micah, all that I wanted was a baby. I hadn't, not at first, but now I knew he was out there, and I craved holding a newborn in my arms. I didn't want anything in the world more than I wanted to be a mother.

There was this steadfast tremor in my fingers as the possibility of losing another child washed over me, even if it was just the thought of another child. I had no evidence that I was pregnant, but if I wasn't, a negative result was going to be devastating. Not because I lost anyone but because I lost the idea of being who I wanted to be yet again.

I wondered if that concept would hurt as much as losing Micah had. Surely not. But a negative symbol would tear my heart in two.

If I wasn't, I wasn't going to tell Jeremy I was ready to try to get pregnant—even if that was what I wanted. Because if something came up with Micah, I couldn't risk losing another child in the battle to find him.

But if it'd happened on accident...

After I purchased the tests, I did the same thing I did the day I found out I was pregnant with Micah. I grabbed a paper cup from a cleaning cart and scurried off into the Walmart bathroom. Come to think of it, I believe I sat in the same stall.

My heart thudded in my chest as I stared at the tests in front of me. I cupped my hands together in something of a praying motion in front of my lips. My toes anxiously tapped. I nearly held my breath, watching the little timer flipping up and down on the plastic, digital white stick.

I waited for it to read *Not Pregnant*.

But almost simultaneously, the timers disappeared.

And the same word appeared on every test. Tears formed in my eyes.

My lips couldn't help but pull into a smile. It turned to a joyous laugh. My feet stopped tapping, my heart stopped racing. For a moment, I was truly, genuinely happy.

Pregnant.

I was pregnant.

CHAPTER SEVENTY

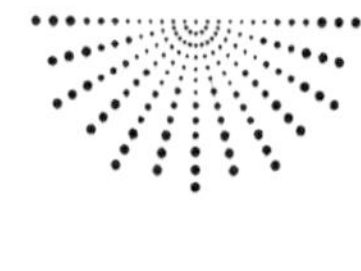

LAILA

I hated these places. The smell—whatever the fuck that smell was. Cleaners, or medications, or whatever the hell it was made me nauseous. The sticky linoleum beneath my feet squeaked with each step. Beeps on monitors from the rooms in the distance brought me back to my time in one similar after I escaped.

But this time? This time, I had a feeling I was going to walk out of here with some good news.

I approached the desk, waiting patiently for the nurse who spoke into a large black phone. She held up her pointer finger and gave a smile.

Then she dropped the phone back to the receiver. "Can I help you with something, ma'am?"

"Uh, yeah. Yeah, I think so." My voice lowered. "I probably could have gone to a regular doctor, but I was just hoping to be seen today. Do you have any openings with an OB/GYN?"

"We take everyone on an as needed basis." She smiled. "What do you need to be seen for?"

"Um." I cleared my throat. "I, uh, I need to confirm a pregnancy."

Her smile widened. "Yeah, we can definitely get you in for that. Our OB floor is pretty slow today. We should be able to get you in right away." She spun and opened a desk drawer. She reached in, retrieved a small clear container with an orange lid, and an alcohol swab. "Collect a urine sample in here, bring it back to me, then we'll get you set up in a room. If the result is positive, we'll do an internal ultrasound to confirm how far along you are. Then we'll need to collect some blood samples."

Good thing I'd drunk four cups of coffee, because I did, in fact, have to pee again.

"Alright, great. Thank you."

I sat on the chair beside the maternity table in the small yellow room wearing a pale pink hospital gown. The table would have been comfortable for most people, but I hadn't even been to the gynecologist since I was cleared immediately after returning home last year.

Something about being on any hospital bed made my stomach churn but the thought of putting my feet into those stirrups made me ill. I would do it when I had to, but not a moment longer than I had to.

Still, as I sat, my stomach spun with butterflies and my mind danced with fantasies.

Another baby. I'd get to be a mom. They wouldn't be Micah, but they'd be *my* baby. I'd hold them the moment they were born, and I wouldn't let go. I'd wrap them in a blanket and touch their little fingers. I'd smell that sweet, new life aroma against my chest.

And Jeremy would be there. We'd have a family. It'd be missing a piece, one that we craved as much as air, but we'd have at least part of what we wanted.

Then I opened Google, went to Amazon, and clicked onto the registry I'd formed for Micah's baby shower. I started clicking all of the suggested items and smiled wide. Green, everything green until I knew the sex. Boy or girl, green was fitting.

As the door began to open, I laid my phone on the chair beside me. When I realized who my practitioner was, my hands tightened to fists.

Her blue eyes stayed on the page in front of her as she pushed up her glasses. "Hello, my name is..." She looked up and met my gaze.

"Hi, Olivia."

And she just stared at me like a deer in headlights for a moment.

"Laila." She cleared her throat. "I'm sorry, there wasn't a name on this chart."

"That's alright. I didn't give them one for a reason."

"Sure. Right, well, um..." Licking her lips, she cleared her throat again. "Your hair looks nice, is that a new color?"

"The color it came with." I forced a smile.

She gave a smile back. "It looks good. You look great."

"A lot better than the last time you saw me," I said.

She turned her eyes downward. "Yeah, you could say that."

Awkward. No, not just awkward. Infuriating.

She knew what she was doing that day. She had to have. When she said, 'he told me that he told you everything.' She could've phrased it differently. She could have said it without leading me to believe they'd been fucking.

Okay, she wasn't the only one to blame. That came down on Jeremy. But she'd wanted us apart since day one.

And either way, I didn't want her judging my pussy. I knew what that shit looked like, and it wasn't porn star perfect. Hers may have been, and I didn't want her to get a chip on her shoulder about how she had a prettier vag than me. She already had the advantage in the ass and tits department, she didn't need the gratification of knowing that my lady bits weren't all that pretty.

Petty, maybe. But still. Nah, that bitch wasn't gonna stick her fingers inside of me.

My lips pressed to a line. "No offense or anything, but I really don't feel comfortable with you putting a probe up my twat. Could I get a different provider?"

"Yeah. Yeah, of course." She turned to the door. She gripped the door handle for a second before releasing it and swiveled back to me. "Before I go, I, uh... I'd like to talk with you for a minute if that's okay."

I sucked my teeth. "What would you like to talk about, Olivia?"

Her cold blue eyes met mine. "I'm very sorry for all of the pain I caused you."

"We aren't friends," I stated. "You don't owe me an apology."

"No, I do." Her eyes shined with honesty as they looked between mine. "I should have told you he was using."

"No, you shouldn't have," I said. "You were his friend. You didn't owe me that betrayal of his trust."

"Yeah, but if I had—"

"You should have gotten him help. You shouldn't have given him drugs. You shouldn't have let him come to your house to get high. You really shouldn't have fucking kissed him." I stood. "You shouldn't have given him the resources to lose his sobriety. You shouldn't have let him manipulate you so that you could get a few moments of his time. You shouldn't have made it sound like you guys had been fucking when you hadn't. But no. You shouldn't have told me."

She looked down. "Either way. I'm sorry for the pain that my mistakes caused."

Ah-ha. I knew I was right. She didn't deny it, so clearly I was. She'd made it sound the way she had that day so that I would believe something had happened that hadn't.

"Well, thank you." I crossed my arms against my chest. "He's doing good now though so that's all that matters."

"That's what I've heard. You guys are back together now, aren't you?"

I tightened my jaw. "We are, yeah."

She gave a smile. "Good for you guys. I'm happy for you both."

She wasn't. I knew that and so did she. But she'd accepted her fate. She was done trying to get between me and my husband. Now, I can feel bad for her. It must not have been easy to love someone who had a soulmate. Then though, I kind of hated her.

"Sure," I muttered. "Thanks."

She made a gesture to my stomach. "And congratulations, by the way. I'm sure you're both really excited."

"Yeah. Yeah, um... He doesn't know yet. I literally just found out. That's why I'm here, I just wanted to confirm it."

"Oh. Oh, okay." She held my gaze. "Are you... You know. Going to keep it?"

I narrowed my gaze. "Why? 'Cause if I terminate, you think that'll make Jeremy leave me and come back to you?"

"No. No, of course not—"

"It's really not any of your business, Olivia, but yes. I'm going to keep my child." I gritted my teeth together. "I was just telling you that he didn't know so that you wouldn't go run your mouth and tell someone before I got the chance to talk to him. I was planning on waiting until the second trimester to make any announcements anyway in case something does happen, and I lose it. That's what's medically recommended, right?"

She stood there silently, opening her mouth as if she was going to say something before closing it back. She stammered like that for a moment. "Right. Of course. I don't betray patient confidentiality."

"Great," I said. "Thanks."

"I'll send another provider in as soon as they're available."

"Sure."

As she reached for the doorknob, she steadily held my gaze. "Laila, I want you to know that Jeremy and I stopped talking entirely a few weeks before you got married. We've only talked once since then, shortly after you broke up with him. He showed up at my doorstep completely shit-faced. I doubt he even remembers it. He was drunk, belligerently yelling at me, calling me a bitch and a liar. I guess he had it in his head that I told you the two of us slept together, which never happened. Not since we were kids anyway. He ended up falling over and passing out. I called Adam and he came to get him.

"But after that, I realized there was never a chance for the two of us. I wished there were, but I'm past that now. It's been almost a year since that night. My viewpoint has completely changed since then. I have a boyfriend that I'm crazy about. We're talking about marriage and kids and the whole nine," she said. "Jeremy's never going to want anyone more than he wants you, Laila. I don't know why I didn't see that then, but I see it now. I just want you to know that I see the big picture and I realize you two are in an entirely different portrait than I am. And that's okay."

I knew that already. Not about him showing up at her door, but that there was nothing between them and never would be again. But hearing her say it aloud gave me a sense of peace. I can't say that we became friends afterward. But I did have a newfound respect for her.

And I felt a little guilty for snapping.

<hr>

The doctor repositioned the probe inside of me. "So this isn't your first pregnancy?"

I winced. "No, this is my second. But you can tell just from looking at my hoo-hah?"

She chuckled, shaking her head. "No. No, I can tell from your uterus. It's slightly tilted, did you know that?"

"No, what does that mean?" I sat up abruptly. "Is something wrong?"

"No." She gazed at the screen. "Tilted uteruses are very common. It just makes it a little harder to see the baby at this stage."

"Oh, good." I leaned back against the bed. "Good."

"You seem very anxious, are you okay?" She raised a brow. "Am I hurting you?"

"No. No, you're fine. I just don't do well with doctors. Gynes in particular." She gave a slow nod and waited for me to continue. "I'm Laila Callidy. You probably know my name."

"Sure. Of course. Thank you for your service."

"Yeah, you're welcome."

She turned back to the monitor. "I take it you don't like the fame?"

"I just wanted to bring those people home. I didn't do it for recognition."

"Sure," she murmured, gazing at the monitor. Then a smile pulled at her lips. "Alright, stay exactly where you are but look at the screen here." She tapped away on the keyboard, clicked the mouse a few times, and turned the monitor toward me. "See this little circle right here? Almost looks like there's a tadpole inside it?"

My eyes filled with tears as I looked at the little black blob on the machine.

The first time I saw Micah on an ultrasound, I was petrified. I didn't even know if I wanted to be a mom yet. I had no idea how Jeremy would feel. I'd been heavily drinking and smoking weed. I just lost a dear friend and was a little broken inside.

But when I saw that baby, despite the little twinge of fear, I was overwhelmed with joy. I couldn't even make out a humanoid form yet, but I loved that baby from the moment I saw them.

"See this little pulse right there?" she asked softly. Nodding, I kept my hand over my mouth as I stared at the ultrasound. "That's your baby's heartbeat."

"Are they healthy?" I asked.

"We can't see very much at this stage. Your little guy's measuring just under a quarter inch. Given your last menstrual cycle, I'm going to say you're right around six or seven weeks pregnant," she murmured. "But from what I can see here, everything looks good. We'll see more in the coming weeks but for the time being, I'm going to request some standard blood work. We'll have some done today and then once weekly for a while to make sure baby's on track."

"Can I get some pictures to show my husband?"

She smiled back. "You sure can."

CHAPTER SEVENTY-ONE

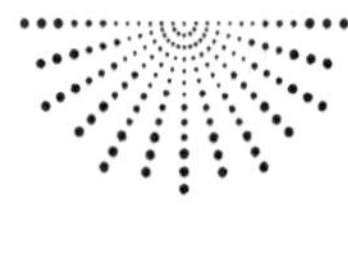

JEREMY

The smell of garlic drifted to my nose from the skillet on the stove before me. Grease popped, landing on my arm. I jolted back at the momentary burn. Then I took a step away, reached to the plate of roasted mini-potatoes, and tossed one to my mouth. Parsley, oregano, and basil popped on my tongue.

Damn good meal. The roasted vegetables were almost done, the salad on the counter looked perfect, it was gonna be a nice night.

"Baby," Laila called from the door.

"Hey, gorgeous." I glanced at her over my shoulder. "Are you in the mood for chicken? Cause that's what I'm cooking."

"Chicken sounds good." She smiled, placed her arms around my waist from behind, and rested her head on my back. "But can the chicken chill for a minute?"

I turned to face her. "What do you mean?"

She smiled. "There's something I need to talk to you about."

"Uh-oh."

Starting a conversation with one's partner with that line is usually bad news. But she was smiling. Sometimes she did that when she was about to yell though. But I'd been good, she didn't have anything to yell about.

I started rerunning through the last week in my mind. Wait, had I forgotten anything? Her birthday wasn't for four more months. Our anniversary was more than a month ago.

"What's wrong?" I asked.

She raised a brow, still holding her smile. "Why does something have to be wrong?"

"Usually, you just tell me what's going on," I murmured. "If we have to talk, it's usually bad news."

She was practically bouncing with glee. "It isn't bad news."

"What is it then?" I asked.

"I'm not doing anything sweet and cute this time. I'm just going to say it."

"Alright." I arched a brow. She was silent, just smiling. "Ready when you are, Lai."

She took in another deep breath before slowly releasing it with a grin. "I'm pregnant."

My eyes widened. "What?"

"I'm pregnant," she repeated with a quiet laugh.

"You're pregnant?" I asked, eyes still wide as a smile came to my lips.

Her head moved in a slow nod. Tears welled in her eyes and her hand went to her stomach. "I'm pregnant, baby."

My hand holding the spatula released it and I threw my arms around her. I laughed as her arms closed around my waist.

The moment those words left her lips, my perspective completely shifted.

I was going to be a dad. I was *actually* going to be a dad. Not to a child that wouldn't know me, but a kid that I could call mine. Someone that I'd do anything for to protect. Someone that I'd be damned before anyone took from me the way they had my son.

Boy or girl, I didn't give a damn. All that I cared about was keeping Laila safe until that baby came and I could keep them safe myself. Someone would have to kill me to keep me from being there the day that baby entered the world.

I craned my head back a bit. "Are you sure?"

"I took a few tests at Walmart. They were all positive, so I went to the hospital and they confirmed it. We're going to have a baby."

I laughed, grabbed her waist, and hoisted her into the air. She giggled as I spun her in a circle. Her arms tightened at my neck, legs lifting outward. My lips turned up in a smile, and nothing could bring them down. I set her onto the counter. "Enjoy doing that now because I'll be fat as hell soon."

I moved hair behind her ear with a smile. "How far along are you?"

"Around seven weeks." She smiled. "My due date's June 26th."

"Another Cancer?"

"Gemini, actually."

"Damn." I slid my hand on her hip to her stomach. "You're going to be a handful, huh?"

She laughed and lifted her fingers over mine. "I'm sure she will."

"She?" I asked. "Didn't you get mad at me for assuming our baby's gender last time around?"

"Yeah, yeah." She made a shooing motion. "I just have a feeling she's a girl. I don't care either way, and I don't care what they choose to identify as later in life, but I just have a feeling. I feel... I don't know, it's like a softness I didn't have last time. Or maybe soft isn't the word, maybe it's feminine. I don't know. I just have a feeling."

I smiled, holding her cheek in my hand. "I don't care either. As long as they're healthy."

"The doctor said everything looks good. You can't see much yet but from what she could see, everything looked good."

"You had an ultrasound already?" I asked. "Baby, why didn't you call me?"

"I wanted to make sure first." She grinned. "It could have been a false positive or something, you know?"

A sigh. "As long as I get to go to the next one."

"You'll be at every single one of them." She smiled, lifting her arms around my neck. "You'll be beside me when she's born. You'll be there when she cries for the first time and takes her first steps. You're going to be there for everything, baby."

I smiled too. Tears bubbled in my eyes. "Every single thing."

She smiled so big.

A thought occurred to me then. Of course, as much as I'd read on pregnancy, I was still kinda dumb in the conception regard. But we'd only been back together for four weeks. And I didn't understand then that the first two weeks of pregnancy aren't from conception, they're the two weeks after the last period prior to ovulation. But I was a dude, and I didn't really know how all that worked.

"Seven weeks you said, right?" I asked.

She nodded, still grinning. "Seven weeks."

I paused. "But six weeks ago... Okay, I don't care either way. You're my wife and I love you. Your baby is my baby, but... Is it mine?"

Her face said she didn't appreciate me asking that. "Yes, Jeremy. It's yours."

"Okay, good. Good." I thought a moment longer. "But you and Liam were together the day before you and I got back together, so... Are you sure?"

"Liam and I stopped fucking well before the night that you and I slept together and you snorted pills in my bathroom. Since that was months ago, yes, Jeremy. I'm sure. But if you don't believe me, you'll know when she comes out and isn't black."

"Of course I believe you, Lai." I smiled. "I just wanted to make sure."

"Just shut up and kiss me," she said.

I grinned, thumbed her chin, and lifted her face to mine. I kissed her long and hard as her hands moved to my neck. "I love you." I touched her belly. "I love you both."

Her lips pulled in a smile against mine as she quietly said, "We love you too."

CHAPTER SEVENTY-TWO

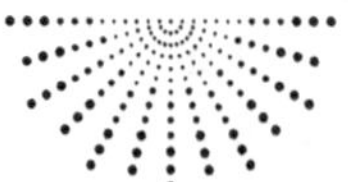

DECEMBER 9, 2020 - LAILA

"Hey, baby, did you get to the store yet?" I kicked my shoes off at the front door. My fingers ran through Tink's fur before I stood back up and hung my jacket on the hook by the door. I set my purse on the counter. "I need a couple things I forgot to put on the list. I always forget about the vacuum bags."

"No, I haven't gone yet," he called from down the hall. "We could go together if you want. Leah wanted us to stop by anyway, she needs help coming up with the list for Christmas dinner."

I started toward the sound of his voice. Light casted into the hall from the guest bedroom.

I hadn't touched Micah's room in years. The last time I passed through that threshold, I was still pregnant with him. When I got back, I could barely bring myself to turn that doorknob. It brought a different kind of emptiness to the pit of my stomach that nothing else was capable of.

Going into that room was harder than having my back torn to shreds with the end of a leather strip. It was harder than being tied to that table as Peterson forced himself inside me. It was harder than giving birth to my son in that painfully cold, tiny cell. It was harder than anything else I had ever faced because it was a manifestation of the worst downfall I ever caused.

Jeremy stood shirtless in front of the window reaching onto his tip toes, hanging fairy lights around its frame. There were small swatches of different shades of pink and purple painted on the sage green wall. A recently assembled white bassinet sat confidently beside the old rocking chair with its empty box on the floor beside it. In the white crib laid a new, flowery comforter.

I gazed around. "What are you doing?"

"I know that we aren't one hundred percent certain on the sex yet." Jeremy gave a sweet smile over his shoulder. "But flowers are cool, right? And even if it is a boy, there's nothing wrong with pink. Oh, and look," he said, grabbing a bag on the chair. He pulled out a small white box and turned it to face me. "It's a wipe warmer. How cool is that? You put the wipies inside and it heats them up so it's nice and toasty on the baby's butt. And that's important because I know how much you hate being cold and she'll probably be the same if she has your powers and everything."

I saw the look of excitement over his face as he smiled proudly at the work he was doing. He got Micah's nursery put together just weeks after I told him I was pregnant, and it meant a lot to him then too. It made me smile like a little girl last time around. I still appreciated his thought this time, but it also infuriated me.

"Why would you do this?"

He tilted his head to the side. "What do you mean?"

"This." I gestured around. "All of this."

"I thought it would make you happy," he murmured.

"Well, it didn't. You can't just come in here and destroy his bedroom."

His confused gaze softened. "I wasn't trying to destroy anything, Lai."

"Well, you did," I said. "He never even got to see it. How could you just take that away?"

"Baby," Jeremy began softly. "It's just a couple paint swatches—"

"On his wall," I blurted. "In *his* room. He's going to have a hard enough time adjusting as it is, and we're not even going to have a bedroom to put him in? What are we supposed to do, build him a doghouse outside?"

"Of course he's going to have a bedroom. But this baby needs a place to sleep too and we only have a two-bedroom apartment." His tone was still soft, but I was fuming. "He's not here and we're going to need this space—"

"We're bringing him home, Jeremy," I snapped. "He's not here right now, but he will be."

His gaze was soft and gentle. His lips lowered to a frown. "I know he will, Lai."

"Then why would you do this?" I gestured around. "You don't think we're going to find him by the time the baby's born, do you?"

"Baby," he murmured, stepping forward. He reached out to push hair from my face, but I flung his hand away.

"I can't believe you would do this without talking to me." I blinked the sting in my eyes away. "We're getting close, I can feel it. We're going to find something soon and when we do, and we finally get to bring him home, he has to feel like it's home. And doing this ruined that. This is his bedroom, Jeremy. You can't just act like he doesn't exist anymore because we're having another baby."

"I'm not, Lai. I wouldn't do that." He reached out to touch my cheek.

I swatted it away and turned down the hall. I opened my bedroom door and telekinetically slammed it shut. Jeremy caught it with his hand and tailed close behind me.

"Leave me alone." I sat on the bed, fighting the thickness in my throat.

"I'm sorry," he said gently. He lowered himself beside me and took my hand in his. I tried to pull it away, but he interlocked our fingers together and raised my knuckles to his lips. "I should have talked to you first."

And he should have. But I shouldn't have lashed out because he did something sweet. We were both excited about the baby. I got my kick buying clothes and blankets and breast pumps and boppies. He got his working with his hands.

My teeth began to chatter as I struggled to keep from crying.

He frowned, touched my chin, and turned my face to meet his. "What's this really about, baby?"

Shaking my head, the hormones got the best of me and I couldn't contain myself. A sob escaped. "It isn't fair to do that. It isn't fair to change his room for this baby when he never even got to see it."

He ran his thumb along the back of mine. "None of this is fair to anyone."

My eyes flooded with tears until I couldn't see without wiping them. My soft cries turned to violent sobs. He gently took my face in his hands. He thumbed my cheeks as a few tears of his own formed in his brilliant blue eyes.

"Come here." He tucked a hand around my shoulders and pulled me into him.

I laid my head against his chest, shaking it as I wiped my eyes and failed to regain my composure. "I don't want to replace him. I love him just as much as I love this baby and it isn't fair. I can't ever replace him. He's my baby too."

"We're not replacing anyone." He coasted his fingertips along my spine.

I closed my eyes, hands shaking at the small of his back.

"I'm really sorry, I should have checked with you first," he murmured. "I think there's half a can of paint left in the closet. After the pink dries, I'll throw a coat of green on top, okay? I'll put everything back to how it was. Winnie the Pooh isn't gender related, we can keep the set up that we have. I just... I wanted to do something for my kid, you know? I don't know what else to do to help Micah, and I can't carry this baby for you, and I just wanted to do something. I wasn't trying to replace him, I just wanted to do something that I could."

"I shouldn't have yelled at you," I murmured. "I know you weren't trying to be malicious, I just..."

"It's okay." He kissed my hair and tightened his arms around me. "It's not an easy situation for anyone. I should have been more considerate. I'm sorry, baby."

"It's okay." I nuzzled my head further into his chest. He pushed hair behind my ear and kissed my head.

He slid his hand to my belly. "We're going to do everything right with this one."

We didn't. There's no way to do *everything* right as a parent. But we tried.

CHAPTER SEVENTY-THREE

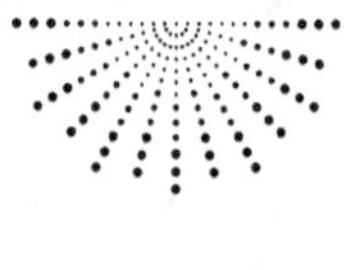

JEREMY

After we went to the store to grab some groceries, we returned to the apartment and had dinner. Laila was out cold by eight thirty. When she fell asleep, I found that old can of green paint, cracked it open, and painted over the samples on the wall.

I completely understood how that could be painful for her, especially after seeing the nursery Amy had for our son at that prison. In her head, it could have seemed like I was filling the void Micah's disappearance caused with the excitement of the new baby. She was extremely emotional from the hormones in addition to battling depression, survivor's guilt and some serious PTSD. In hindsight, I should have considered that there was a reason why she always kept that door shut.

But the fact of the matter remained. We had a baby on the way. They would need a bed, and a rocking chair, and a wipe warmer. They needed a room too.

Yet, Micah would need a bed and dressers and a toy box. The second bedroom wasn't small, but it wasn't large so the concept of the two of them sharing it wasn't ideal. Plus, putting a toddler and an infant in the same bedroom could be problematic with crying fits and sleeping schedules.

After straightening the room back up to its former glory, I took a shower and sat on the couch. As I smoked a joint while playing my guitar, it became abundantly clear that we had to find something bigger. We needed more space.

As much as we loved the apartment, it just wouldn't work for two adults, two kids under five, and a dog.

I set the joint in the ashtray, laid my guitar on the couch, and logged into our banking app to check our savings account. Obviously, I wasn't going to make any major decisions without a serious conversation with my wife, but I wanted to see what we were working with.

When I saw how much money was in there, I almost shit myself.

After deposits made from the diner and accrued interest on the money Laila inherited when Moe died, in addition to all the money she'd made selling his stocks and selling off his other properties and assets, our savings account came to a total of $876,643.59. Not to mention the two thousand or so in our spend account for daily necessities and bills.

We didn't need much. We certainly didn't need a nearly nine-hundred-thousand-dollar house. We just needed something private with enough room to grow.

A decent sized yard for Tink and the kids would be ideal. Something on the outskirts of town would be nice given our way of life. It'd be great to have a garage to work on cars and have a little work area. Laila would need an extra bedroom or just enough room for a home office. She hated doing laundry in the basement, so we'd need one on the main floor. She always said she wanted to live by the water so maybe something near the lake would be good.

But as I scrolled on Zillow, there was almost nothing like that. We lived in a small suburban town surrounded by state forests. A lot of the houses were smack dab in the middle of town with no yard. The one's that weren't were extravagantly priced with tons of pointless amenities that we didn't need like marble floors and smart home systems. Finding something private wasn't easy unless we were willing to pay a couple hundred thousand just for the land.

And just as that thought crossed my mind, I had an epiphany.

I grabbed a piece of paper, wrote a quick note to Laila to call me if she woke up and needed me, and teleported to the old cabin on what was now Leah's property.

The little old shack rested about halfway up the driveway to the main house. It sat about a hundred yards off the road. An old, overgrown flag-stone path went from the road to the small cabin.

It wasn't looking great those days. Not that it was ever a five-star resort, but there was a time when it looked like a pleasant little hunting cabin. Now, it looked like something out of a horror movie.

But it didn't have to.

I had a good understanding of carpentry. I was young when I helped my dad work on the house, but Annie taught me a lot. She never depended on anyone—especially a man, despite the fact that she was raising four boys—to do a job that she could do herself. When I was fourteen, Adam, Chris, and I helped her remodel the kitchen. We tore out walls, bolted down cabinets, refinished floors. We weren't experts, but we learned.

When I was a bit younger than that, she and I poured a vat of cement and built the garage ourselves. It wasn't a massive project, but it taught me to frame out walls. I learned to lay shingles and hang drywall.

After Laila first inherited Moe's estate, she hired contractors to do the mild remodeling downstairs for insurance purposes. But in the apartment, she basically left me to my own devices. She told me what walls she wanted knocked down, she picked out cabinets, flooring, paint colors, light fixtures, and told me to have at it. I did every bit of the remodeling aside from electrical and major plumbing. Not to toot my own horn, but the place came out beautifully.

Still, I knew that I wasn't an expert. But I could learn.

The project I was planning in my mind was dramatically more challenging than a small garage or a cosmetic remodel, but I knew I could do it. I'd need some manpower behind me, but it could be done.

I could see it as I started toward the overgrown, decrepit cabin.

As I opened the door, it all began to manifest in front of my eyes.

We'd keep the fireplace in the middle of the room that could be seen from anywhere I stood. We'd clear out some trees around the property to give the kids a nice yard. Laila could grow a garden around the old creek I used to play in with my brothers and sisters as a kid. We could build a swing set and a jungle gym with slides and a rock-climbing wall. Maybe we'd even dig out a pool down the line.

I could see it. It was already home, but it could be our kid's home too. I could see the house. I could see us spoon feeding our babies in their highchairs at the counter. I could see Micah running around in the back yard with his brother or sister and Tinkerbell. I could see our children growing into adults and coming back for Christmas dinner with their kids.

This was it. This was the room we needed to grow.

CHAPTER SEVENTY-FOUR

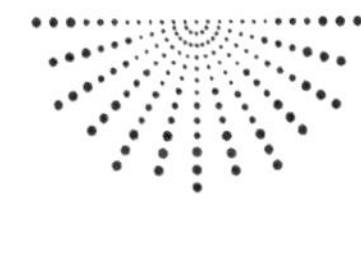

LAILA

"Baby." Jeremy shook my shoulder. "Baby, wake up."

I rolled over. "Shhh."

He laughed and moved to the other side of the bed. Pushing hair from my face, he spoke again, which I did not appreciate while I was sleeping. "I'm sorry, I know it's early. But I've been up all night and it's seven, so you got a good eleven hours of sleep." He continued shaking my shoulder a bit. "C'mon, baby. Get up, I wanna talk to you about something."

He knew better by now. We'd been sharing a bed for five years. No one wakes me up but my alarm, damn it.

I rubbed my tired eyes. "Are you on crack?"

"No, I don't like speeds." He smiled with dark circles beneath his bright blue eyes.

"Then why were you up all night?" I stifled a yawn.

"Okay, so I was thinking about what you said last night. About the kids and bedroom situations and everything, right?" he said with a shit eating grin.

I yawned. "What about it?"

"This place is beautiful. I know you love this apartment, and so do I, but it's small." He took my hand in his. "We have a baby on the way and... Well, I guess we kind of have two babies on the way, right?"

An endearing way of putting it.

I rubbed my eyes. "Yeah."

"That being said, we're probably going to have more kids too, right?" he asked.

"I don't know, Jeremy. Probably. Why?" I wiped crusts from the corner of my eye.

"Well, this is only a two-bedroom apartment," he continued. "And we're going to have two kids soon, and even if we didn't have any more, we still wouldn't have enough room for the four of us and Tink."

"You want to move?"

"Not particularly, but it's not like we want to live above the diner forever," he said. "Max is loud, he's sure to wake up the baby when he comes in at five in the morning. Not to mention the concerts on the weekend. Plus, we're overflowing with shit already. You're kind of a pack rat."

I narrowed my gaze. "Did you seriously wake me up to bitch about how much shit I have?"

"No." He smiled. "I woke you up because I have an idea. I haven't worked out every detail yet, but I think I solved the problem at hand. I mean, not yet. It'll take a few months at least, but I think I could get at least most of it finished before the baby's born. If not, definitely by the time they're a few months old. No more than six months, and that's the absolute max. Unless something crazy happens, which is always possible I guess."

"Jeremy, you need to chill." I yawned again. "I literally just woke up."

Still grinning, he said, "I'm sorry, I've had a lot of coffee. Can you overdose on caffeine? Cause I feel a little weird right now."

"Probably the sleep deprivation," I muttered. "What's all this about, babe?"

"Here." He stood and extended his hand for mine. "Come with me."

"Where?" I pouted.

"You'll see, just put your slippers on." He wiggled his fingers out to me.

"It's too early for your shit, dude."

"C'mon, Lai. This is important."

I tossed the blankets to his side of the bed and stood. "You're killing me, man. Killing me."

He laughed. I stepped into my slippers and he handed me my jacket. "You love me."

"You're lucky I love you." I pulled my arms through the sleeves. "Alright, mister. You wanted to wake me up so bad, show me what's so important."

He stepped behind me. "Okay, close your eyes."

"Jesus Christ."

He placed his hands over my face, blocking my vision.

I felt the familiar swirl as we landed in the old cabin. I knew that weird, old person smell anywhere. It was a cross between moth balls and rotting wood. It mixed with the dewy air outside and the smoke from the embers in the large, stone fireplace that sat in the center of the studio styled cabin.

"What are we doing here?" I asked.

"Hey, it was supposed to be a surprise." He pulled his hands away.

"You should have covered my nose then. God, it's making me nauseous." I placed a hand over my mouth and the other over my belly.

He moved in front of me. His smile stretched up his cheeks as his arms opened on either side. "Okay, just be patient with me for a minute here. I went on Zillow and I started looking at houses. But privacy is important if we're going to buy, and you're talking at least a hundred thousand just for a couple dozen acres. Not to mention having the house built, tapping into sewer lines or installing a septic tank, or tapping into the water line, or getting electric hook ups. Plus, we need something close to Moe's and most of the stuff I saw was pretty far away. But we're only fifteen minutes from Moe's here."

"Let me get this straight. You want to move from our small, two-bedroom apartment into an itty bitty hunting cabin with my dog and our two children?"

"Not exactly." He grinned. "Okay, so it'd be a lot of work if you agree to this. Like, a shit ton of work. It'd take up most of my free time for the next six months at least. But picture this, okay?" He moved toward the fire place. "This would be the only thing that we keep. We'd literally build the house around it. Everything else gets gutted. We reinforce the foundation then we build new exterior walls a good ten or twenty feet in every direction, depending on how much space you want. The square footage would more than triple."

A house? Was that what he was telling me? That he wanted to build us a house?

He moved toward the door at the back left of the cabin and gestured behind him. "Back here, we have our bedroom. Same size as our room now, but with a big bathroom and a walk-in closet for all your shit." Then he gestured from the ground upward. "And right here, we have a big, grand staircase. Or maybe something more modern with rails or glass or something if that's what you want."

Glass? Not glass. Glass on windows, but a house was not a mall. I did not want a glass railing.

"Then here." He moved to the galley kitchen. "We keep this the kitchen, but we completely rework it. New cabinets, new lights, drywall instead of these hundred-year-old logs. And new floors everywhere. Oh, and new countertops too. I know you love granite, but we can do a cheap Formica if you want to cut back on cost. And we put a big window in over the sink so we can look out at the kids and Tink playing in the backyard while we're washing dishes. And a big sliding glass door. Or maybe French doors with a doggy door into the backyard. We keep the island and get new pretty light fixtures. And where the pull-out bed is, we put in a big sectional. Or we use our couch, I know you love that couch."

A doggy door, that sounded amazing. Taking Tink down a flight of stairs, on a leash, at four o'clock in the morning was a real pain in the ass. But her letting herself in and out? Yeah, I liked that idea.

"But that part can come later, you're the decorator. And then upstairs, we put in at least four bedrooms. Not too big, but not too small. Maybe a jack and jill bath or something? And we're up on the hill here, so I could put a little balcony up there somewhere to give us an awesome view of the sunset. Maybe even over the whole back porch. I don't know, I haven't given upstairs that much thought yet. But kids want to decorate differently all the time, so we'll figure that part out later. But we need at least four bedrooms. Even if we just have two kids, we always have friends and family over and you never know when someone's going to need a place to crash. And we can stay at the apartment while I work. We'll keep the baby in our room for the first few months anyway so if we get Micah back soon—"

"Jeremy." I watched him frantically move around the cabin.

He let out a slow breath, maybe the first since he started going on. "Is it a bad idea? Because it was just an idea. We could buy something if you want, it'd probably be quicker to get moved in and set up. But it'd be a lot more money for something big enough. And if we had someone else build it, we'd be spending way more money and we'd be on their schedule. Depending on who I can get to help me build, I could get this place up quick. But I guess we aren't really poor; we could afford either option. But it'd cut our savings in half at least, which would really suck because you've done amazing at managing the money. It's at almost a million dollars now.

How did you get that interest rate on the savings account anyway? They're almost never over one percent—"

"Breathe, Jeremy." I laughed, reached out, and placed my hands on his shoulders. "Breathe."

He laughed and put his hands on my hips. "I'm sorry, I got a little excited."

"I see that." I smiled.

"So what do you think?"

I loved it. But just to bust his balls, I said, "I don't know." My eyes scanned the room. "That's a lot to take in right after you wake up."

He laughed. "I'm sorry, I just couldn't keep it all in there."

I smiled and pushed long black waves from his face.

That was truly one of the best moments of my life. It was even better than our wedding day. Watching his excitement as he talked about building us a big old family home. It still makes my stomach spin and sends that warm, homey feeling through my body.

I could say that we fell in love as teenagers. But this was when we started to fall into the love we were always meant to. Lovers, partners, best friends. Family.

Two sober adults that had busted their asses to get where they were. We were both in a really shitty situation with Micah. But this...

This was the most felicitous thing anyone had ever said or done.

"You're sweet." I smiled. "Who are you, Noah Calhoun?"

"Noah who?" he asked.

"Ya know, Nicholas Sparks?" I said with a raised brow. "Ryan Gosling? The Notebook?"

"Not ringing any bells, baby."

"You never watched *The Notebook*?" I asked. He looked at me like I was crazy. My jaw hit the floor. "You know, these two kids fall in love, and they fuck for the first time in this big, old, abandoned house, and he says that one day he's going to buy it and fix it up. Then they break up and he ends up buying the house and making it beautiful again and they get back together and then they live happily ever after. Then they die in each other's arms."

"That doesn't sound very happily ever after," he murmured.

"We're watching it tonight. It's iconic. You're gonna cry, you'll hate how much you love it." I pulled away. I started toward the back door. Then I pushed it open and gazed at the snow falling out over the trees. "It *is* a pretty view."

"This has been an important place for us," he said behind me. "We completed our bond here; you used your powers for the first time here. And my family is a ten-minute walk away, a few seconds by car on a good day, so built in babysitters. Plus, when everybody else starts having kids, we'll all be really close so all of the cousins will grow up like siblings. And these woods were so much fun as a kid. We'd find salamanders and frogs and we'd have fires in the woods. And we're not far from the school, it's five minutes closer than Moe's. We're over here all the time already. And we're only fifteen minutes from your mom too."

I turned to meet his gaze. "Did you talk to Leah about this?"

"Yeah, she doesn't care. She likes the idea of us being close. The house was originally supposed to go to Chris anyway, she was just second in line for it after he disappeared. And there's not a safer place in the world for our kids than living right down the road from a house of supernaturals who would kill anyone who tried to hurt their nieces or nephews."

I gave a dramatic sigh, looking around the old cabin. "There's almost no natural lighting in here."

"I can add windows." He smiled. "A whole wall of windows, if you want."

I smiled and met his gaze. "I *have* always loved this fireplace."

"We can roast marshmallows on Christmas Eve." He smiled. "Dad used to do that with us. They lived here, you know. He proposed on Christmas Eve right in front of it before they had Chris. This was the only structure on the property when he bought it. While he was building the main house, this was their home."

"I didn't know that." I gave a gentle smile. That look on his face was everything I needed to say yes. "We'd have to clear a lot of trees to have a decent sized yard though."

"Yeah, but that's easy. You can just burn them. And you've always said you wanted to live by the water, and I know it isn't much, but there's a good size creek a few hundred yards out back. You can hear the water rushing if you sit back there for a while."

I smiled still. "Yeah, I know the stream."

"And you've flown here, you know how gorgeous the view is if we put in a balcony," he continued.

"This is true."

"And we can put a washroom right over there off the kitchen so we don't have to go to the basement to do laundry. Oh, and the basement. It's small, but it's big enough to put in a little game room. Maybe a pool table or something. We don't need a torture chamber, there's one right up the road."

"Things only we say." I laughed as I turned around.

He smiled and cupped my cheek in his hand. "This can be our home, Lai. We don't have everything we want right now, but we will. We're going to find Micah and when we do, I want him to have a good life too. I want him to have a normal childhood with silly little holiday traditions and memories in his family home. And this baby too. And whatever other kids we have. I want to be able to tell them how I built their bedrooms and pass this place down to them when we die like my parents did for us. This place, this property; this is home. It's kept us safe time and time again. I know there's some bad memories too—"

"Yeah, like when I got stabbed right about"—I began side stepping until I was just in front of the TV— "here."

"But there's so many good memories too." He placed his hands around my waist. "I saw you naked for the first time right about"—he teleported in front of the couch— "here."

I laughed as I met his gaze. "How much do you think this would cost?"

"A lot," he muttered. "But most of the work I can do myself. I might need some help from Brody and Adam, Wyatt would be a huge help too. Your telekinesis could help with a lot of the heavy lifting too. I'd have to have someone come in to do the electrical and parts of the plumbing, but we already have the hookups so it wouldn't be too high. No more than ten grand each. Oh, and HV/AC. That's gonna be a pretty penny. I have an idea of what I'm doing, but we'd probably be better off having someone do it for us. Still, though. Most of it I can do. I know how to frame out walls. I know how to put on siding and build roofs. Drywall and insulation is easy. It's a bigger project but I did an alright job at the apartment remodel, right?"

"You did an amazing job." I smiled.

He exhaled deeply. "A lot of the cost is going to depend on what you want. Granite or marble countertops are going to be twice as expensive as a cheaper alternative. We could go with a basic tub shower combination for all the bathrooms or we could do a shower and a tub for the master. We could get some real expensive hardwoods or do a floating vinyl. We can cut back on some other places too. But for everything to be simple and still nice and new looking? I'm thinking about a hundred grand, give or take fifty thousand."

"That's not too bad." I looked around.

"So you want to do this?" he asked with a smile.

I laughed, turning back to meet his gaze. "We have some kinks to work out. But I think it's a great idea, baby. You're right, this place is home. I'd love to live here."

The only other times I'd seen Jeremy smile as big as he did when I said that was when I said I would marry him and when I told him I was pregnant. It meant the world to him. I hadn't thought much about the future in terms of living arrangements, but this was brilliant. It was cost effective, it was sentimental, and it would be beautiful. Everything about it made perfect sense.

He leaned down and kissed me, lifting me in the air and spinning for a moment before he carried me to the couch.

"I love you," he whispered.

"I love you too," I murmured, grabbing his shirt and pulling him closer to me.

CHAPTER SEVENTY-FIVE

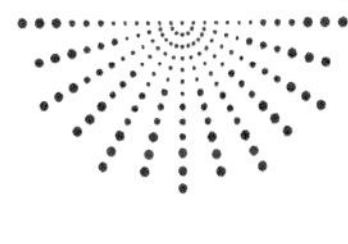

LAILA

The smell of coffee and bacon drifted up my nose. Heat from the stove behind me warmed my skin. Quiet talking and laughter floated from the front of the diner through the kitchen. The taste of this morning's coffee still lingered on my tongue. I reached onto the tips of my toes, shoving a bag of buns onto the top shelf of the pantry.

Then the bell rang above the front door. "Just a sec!" I called.

"No rush," Liam's voice said.

I furrowed my brows, but smiled. Then I started past the griddle to the swinging stainless steel door. He stood on the other side of the counter in a pair of jeans, blue button up, and black sweater vest.

"Hey, you." I gave a friendly smile.

He smiled back. It was a different smile than the ones he used to give me. It was just as sweet, but without any intent behind it. "How ya' doing, baby girl?"

I leaned against the counter. "Oh, ya know. Living the dream. How about you? I'm sorry, I know it's been a little while."

"Don't apologize. It's not like I called either."

My lips vibrated in a trill. "Guess not, huh?"

He smiled. "No hard feelings or anything. It was a really wild night."

"Yeah, to put it mildly." I glanced around at the diner before meeting his gaze. "What's going on, Liam?"

"Could we talk somewhere more private?" he asked. "This is... Well, it's important."

––––––––––

Snow fell from the dark gray clouds above. Cool winter air nearly burned my cheeks. Early morning traffic raced past on the highway on the other end of the parking lot. I lowered myself to the second step to the back door, practically hugging my knees to keep from shivering.

"So what's going on?" I tightened my coat around my arms.

Liam stood a few feet ahead. He shoved his hands in his pockets. "Okay, so that night, when we went back there, my phone got destroyed."

"Oh, right. Shit, I'm sorry, man. I can pay you back—"

"No. No, that's not why I'm here." He turned around and lowered himself to the step beside me.

"What is it then?"

"I had to get a new phone. I didn't have the old phone or anything, but they said they could transfer everything over from the cloud, right?"

"Sure," I muttered.

Liam ran his hand over his mouth. "Okay, so I had an older phone before. But this one, it has Google send me notifications a million times a day with dumb shit. Yesterday, I got this pop-up that said to 'clear the clutter' and there was this group of pictures under it that I vaguely remember taking. From that night."

"Did you find something?"

"I don't know. Maybe." He pulled his phone from his pocket and held his fingerprint over the sensor. "Did you guys find anything on your second search?"

"Something, yeah. But it hasn't been any help. All it's given us is more questions."

"Well, maybe that's not what Chris was telling you to look for," he murmured, opening his gallery.

He scrolled for a moment. I looked over his shoulder, seeing the images of the compound. My stomach spun, a knot forming in my throat.

"Okay, look at this." Liam clicked on the first one. He had taken it as he walked a few yards behind me. He began flipping through them, about ten taken from that perspective. "Do you see it?"

I saw my cherry red hair, I saw the brick building, but I didn't see much else.

"See what?"

"Look. Right here." He zoomed in on the image.

Then I saw it. A small, barely noticeable blue orb levitating several feet in front of me. My body blocked part of its aura.

He began flipping through the photos, pointing out a similar glow in every one he took that I was in. "It moves in every picture so it isn't a camera flare or a spot on the lens. And it's only in the pictures you're in."

My heart skipped, stomach flipping.

A lead.

For the first time, we had a fucking lead. A real one. Not a splotch of tea on a letter, not a pop up of a face similar to Peterson's on a facial recognition algorithm. A real, solid fucking lead.

"Can you send me these?" I asked.

He nodded as I continued to stare at them. "I think he had something important to show you. And I don't think it was what you found, or we'd have a location by now."

I still looked over that blue glow. "Chris can't astral project though. I don't know what we could be seeing."

A thought occurred to me then. Chris couldn't. But I could. And Micah was half of me.

My heart skipped a beat.

Was a piece of my son's soul guiding me through the building that night?

"I don't know much about Guardians, but I do know about Witches." I looked up to meet his gaze. "We know they have the La Fay Witch. She uses ancestral magic, that's what makes her so strong."

"Right."

"The Skouldas are a powerful bloodline. So is yours. There's no way that bitch wouldn't use it. Peterson didn't want to lose you, but when he did, they made sure to come back and grab Chris." Liam looked between my eyes. "Maybe they wanted you for the same reason they wanted Chris. Ancestral magic. Binding the powers of generations together to feed something. Or maybe just to use Micah until he'd be old enough to use his powers himself. Maybe they needed a closely related living relative to combine with his powers so that they could use it how they wanted."

My eyes widened.

That's what he meant. When he said we could stay together, he didn't mean that I could have with Micah what Amy had with Lydia. He meant that he'd have Nastya bind us together.

"That's how he came to me in the dream. He's using Micah's power," I murmured. My gaze shifted around the snowy gravel before a quiet, pride filled chuckle left my lips. "Micah will be able to astral project one day."

Those dreams. They weren't PTSD. I was chasing Micah down those halls for a reason. He was going to lead me somewhere.

The door behind me nudged my back.

"Lai," Jeremy said, "what're you doing out here? It's freezing. You aren't smoking, are—" He stopped abruptly when he saw Liam beside me.

Liam gave an awkward wave as he stood. "Hey, man."

"Hey." Jeremy's jaw tightened for a moment. "What's up, babe?"

I thought about telling him everything Liam had just told me. But then I decided I should wait until Liam left to fill him in.

I smiled, stood, and faced the door. "I'll be in, just give me one minute."

He glanced at Liam. "Nice to see you, man. Happy Holidays."

"Yeah. Yeah, you too." Liam nodded.

Jeremy pulled the door shut.

"Thank you for this." I met Liam's gaze. "This looks like a solid lead. If you're right, if he was there that night, his spirit would've left a trail. I have a good Witch; she can help us follow it if it exists. If there's something there, he probably spent special attention to whatever he wanted us to find. He probably lingered there the longest."

"That's what I thought too." He pulled a pack of cigarettes from his back pocket. He placed one between his lips and sparked it with his flaming fingertip. "I hope it leads somewhere. Emma... She needs her brother back, ya know? I'm there but he's her twin. They've been through the same things. They can support each other."

"I know the feeling." I gestured to the cigarette at his lips, giving a smirk. "Those'll kill ya, ya know."

"That's kind of the idea." He quoted with a grin.

I smiled. "Just make sure you send me those pictures please."

"Why'd you quit?" He smirked, taking a hit off his cigarette.

I willed my smile higher. We weren't quite at the announcement stage yet. I glanced at him over my shoulder. "I kind of like living sometimes."

He smiled. "Congratulations."

I furrowed my brows, turning back to him. "What?"

"The baby," he said. "Congratulations."

My heart raced. "How'd you know? I'm not showing yet, am I?"

"I smell her." He gestured toward my stomach. "Her heartbeat's real fast too."

My lips curved up in a smile. "You can't actually smell a fetus's gender."

"Not a bit of testosterone." He smiled. "Daintier than you always smelled. Softer. She's got a lot of Fae in her. How far along are you?"

"About fourteen weeks," I said. "We're announcing on Christmas Eve."

"Yeah, there'd be testosterone by now. She's a girl."

"You're sure?" I smiled, running my hand along my belly.

"Yes, ma'am. I work on the maternity floor all the time, I see plenty of pregnant patients. I can smell DNA. Trust me, I can smell sex," he said. "Congratulations, Laila. Really, I'm happy for you. I know how much you wanted this. All of this, I mean."

I knew what he meant. He wasn't talking about the lead. Not even the baby. He was referring to the little family Jeremy and I were creating.

I smiled. "Thanks, Liam. For everything. I'll let you know what we find."

CHAPTER SEVENTY-SIX

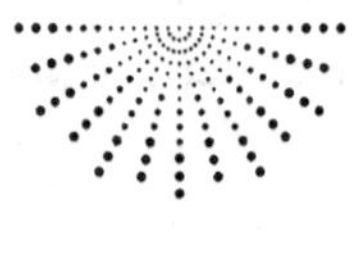

JEREMY

Lifting the coffee pot with one hand, I held the mug with the other. I lifted it to my lips and took a sip. The warm, bitter flavor touched my tongue.

I had to wonder, why was Liam here? I knew he and Laila had been friends, and it wasn't like I was jealous or anything. Laila wasn't one to keep secrets, not from me anyway. Still, there had to be a reason. They hadn't seen one another since September.

"I knew it." Laila flung her arms around my waist from behind and squeezed hard.

I laughed, spilling some coffee on the counter. Spinning around to meet her gaze, I tucked my arms below her waist. "You knew what?"

"It's a girl." She grinned. "We have to start looking into names. How do you feel about Millicent?"

I wrinkled my nose. "We are not naming our daughter Millicent."

"I like Milly. What other names are there that we could use as a full name and keep Milly as a nickname?"

"My mom's name was Melissa and Annie called her Milly sometimes," I said.

She crinkled her nose a bit. "I made out with a girl named Melissa once. I don't think I could do that."

"What about Malina?" I asked. "I bookmarked it on one of those baby name apps the other day."

"What's it mean?" she asked

"Something about a tower. From the tower, I think?"

Her eyes widened. A smile spread across her lips. "Malina. I like it. Malina Skoulda."

Well, that was easy. But I liked it. Milly.

I slid my hands from the back of her hips toward her stomach. "How do you know she's a girl?"

"Liam could smell it." She placed her hands over mine. "I'm glad he came because he said he could hear her heart beating. I know that Micah didn't move this early either but I'm just so excited and I've been a little worried. I want to get one of those doppler things to listen to her heartbeat."

I smiled, watching her grin down at her little belly. She'd been covering it with big flowing shirts and heavy jackets. But I couldn't wait until she'd start showing it off. "What did Liam need?"

"Oh, right. We have to call Helena once she's awake. I'll need to find my checkbook. I think I have a box in the safe."

"Baby." I raised my fingers to lift her chin. "What's going on?"

"Right," she said. "Liam was going through pictures from that night on his phone and he noticed something weird. He just them to me. I don't have my phone on me, but I'll show you when we go upstairs."

"Sure," I murmured, waiting for her to continue.

"There's this little blue orb in every picture of me. It looks like you guys' energy balls." Laila met my gaze. "Like Chris."

"That's how a soul manifests on film when it astral projects. But Chris can't do that."

"But I can." A smile came to her lips. "That means Micah could."

I turned my head to the side. "But what does that have to do with anything?"

"Liam said this, and it makes a lot of sense. Nastya La Fay uses ancestral magic, right? That's why she's so strong."

"Right."

"And Peterson was adamant about keeping me. About giving me what Amy had. Raising Micah there with him." I nodded and she continued, "But when I escaped, they made sure to keep Chris. Why would they do that?"

I thought for a long moment. As it clicked, I wondered why I hadn't thought of it before. In fairness though, there were so many variables it made sense to overlook a few details.

"Unless she was trying to bind them together," I murmured. "So that they can use Micah's powers before they've even manifested. Chris is bound to Micah and they're both bound to Nastya. Chris is older, he can handle the kind of power Micah doesn't know how to use yet."

"Exactly," she said. "But if Chris was there that night, if he astral projected—"

"Helena can use a spell to show us where he was inside the building," I said. "Whatever he was trying to show you."

"The book had nothing to do with it," Laila said. "Maybe it was put there that night to lead us to believe we found something when we hadn't."

"A false clue," I murmured with a nod. "To throw us off."

"Still fucking weird," she said. "But yeah. We found it and stopped looking. We just assumed that was what Chris was there for."

CHAPTER SEVENTY-SEVEN

LAILA

The partially demolished building was coated in snow, making it even more eerie than the last time I stared up at the monstrosity. It looked like a post-apocalyptic abandoned prison or insane asylum.

The wind blew against my running nose. Jeremy tucked his arm around my shoulders. Then he gently coasted his hand up and down my arms. I leaned in a bit for warmth. I pulled my coat closer around my waist and struggled not to look at the towering, gloomy building a few hundred feet away.

Instead, I looked to Helena. "Thank you for coming on such short notice."

"There's an extra fifty dollar an hour charge if I have to leave the country, just so you're aware," Helena said.

"We've given you over ten grand since we worked out this arrangement, Helena," Jeremy said. "Can't you waive the travel fee?"

"No." She raised a brow. "I sure as hell can't. Y'all ain't broke, you can afford it. And there's an additional fifty-dollar hourly fee for forcing me to work in the elements too."

"Are you kidding me? After all these years, all the business we've given you."

"Yeah, I know." She reached into her bag. "Your family makes up a good percent of my income."

"Jesus Christ," he said.

"Just get me something to go on here." I gestured toward the building. "I don't care about the price. I just want to find my kid."

Helena gave a nod and pulled out a small vial. "You said he astral projected into your mind, right?"

I nodded.

She handed it over. "There should be some residue left in there. Not enough to bind you to him, but enough to follow the trail it walked here. This'll pull it out and lead us along the path he walked and gather where he spent the most time."

I looked down at the bottle. The flavor, which I imagined was about to be horrendous, wasn't the reason my stomach spun. There were hundreds of herbs a pregnant person can consume that could cause them to miscarry. Even chamomile is bad during pregnancy.

Jeremy placed his hand over the vial. "What's in this, Helena?"

"What—You think I want to kill your wife?"

"I didn't say that," he said.

She gestured toward my stomach. "It won't kill your kid either."

"How did you—"

"I'm a Witch. A pretty good one." She rolled her eyes. "Take the damn potion, Laila."

I looked down at the murky brown liquid in the bottle. "Alright, alright. Hold your horses."

I pulled off the cork. I glanced up at Jeremy, held it to my lips, and took it down like a shot. My balance grew disoriented as the dirty, alcohol like tea danced on my tongue. It sent a swirl to my stomach.

"Oh my god, that's awful," I said.

Helena began chanting in another language.

"Don't puke, Lai." Jeremy held me steady "I know it's disgusting but if she doesn't extract what energy is left in you while you keep that down, you'll just have to drink it again."

"I'm alright." I swallowed the saliva in my mouth in attempt to flush the flavor.

Suddenly, a stabbing pain vibrated through my skull. I groaned out. My hands went to my head. Jeremy held me up as I doubled over in pain. It was a nails-on-a-chalkboard, cringing sensation inside of my mind that sent chills all over my body.

"What's happening?" Jeremy's eyes shot to Helena.

She shook her head as she continued chanting in front of me.

"I'm okay." I grasped my head.

The pain still radiated inside of my skull, but I closed my eyes and pushed it away. If it weren't gonna kill Milly and it would help us fine Micah, I could handle it. Once the shock was over, I could withstand almost any pain imaginable. An intense, sudden migraine was bearable.

"This wasn't a part of the deal, Helena." Jeremy grasped my hips and held me upright. "You didn't tell us it was going to hurt her."

"It's not that bad."

"I feel it. It *is* that bad," he insisted.

Helena wrapped up her chant, and the throbbing stopped. My body straightened back up. Glowing blue light slid from my eyes, nose, and mouth and formed a small ball just in front of my gaze.

"You're overprotective. You wouldn't let me do it," Helena said to Jeremy. "See? She's fine."

"Yeah, I'm good."

Helena side stepped and gestured to the path. "After you."

I looked between her and the glowing, swirling blue light. "Isn't it supposed to lead the way?"

"You control it. Tell it when to go and it will," Helena said. "Tell it when to stop and it will."

CHAPTER SEVENTY-EIGHT

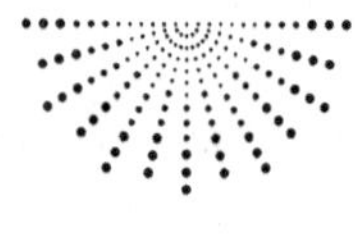

LAILA

Jeremy tightly closed his hand on my hip. I turned away from one of the empty cells whose door laid on the floor beneath the threshold.

It was cold, like last time, but the snow outside made my hands tremble. Although, a chill would've slithered down my spine regardless of the temperature. Come to think of it, my hands would've shaken either way too.

I leaned closer to Jeremy, squeezing my hand around his.

"You really hate this place, don't you?' Helena murmured.

"It's hard," I muttered.

"Why?" she said. "You ought to be filled with pride. All these rooms are empty because of you."

"Some," I said. "But at least a couple hundred are at full capacity somewhere else."

She shook her head as we approached the blue orb. "You don't give yourself enough credit, kid. What you did here, what you pulled off, that was a massive accomplishment."

"That's what I tell her," Jeremy said.

"Sure," I said. "But also my biggest failure. I got my brother in-law out and got him taken back just as quickly. They took my son right out from beneath my nose in this place."

"What—Do you think you're a bad parent because your newborn was kidnapped while you were unconscious and bleeding out?" she asked. "'Cause there's some serious fault to that logic."

We approached the orb. "Go," I told it. It continued down the hallway and stopped at the end.

"Shit, you haven't done anything and you're already better parents than mine." She laughed. "You're willing to spend as much money as you have to find a kid you've never met. Mine told me to never contact them again and moved away. Never gave me their new address either. Not even a phone number."

I creased my brows, glancing up at her warm brown eyes. "Jeez, I'm so sorry."

"Don't be," she said. "People like them don't deserve to be graced by a queen like me."

"I can't even imagine." It was intended to be a thought, but typical for me, it fell from my lips. "Who could do that to their baby?"

"The same kinda people who put their kids in conversion therapy."

My heart swelled. "Oh, wow. I'm so sorry. I didn't know you were gay."

"I'm not. I'm a woman who likes men. I always was. But it was another time then." Helena laughed. "Mom used to make comments about how strange it was that I was so powerful for a boy."

I turned my head to the side.

She looked down at me then at Jeremy and laughed. "What—You didn't tell her I was trans?"

"Why would I?" Jeremy asked.

She turned back to me as we continued to stroll. "You couldn't tell?"

"No, not at all. I just thought you were tall."

Helena chuckled, shrugging. "People usually know."

Honestly, it's not like I was the most observant person. But she was definitely passing, at least in my eyes. Still, now I was happier that she was the Witch the Skoulda clan depended on. I liked supporting people in the LGBTQ+ community. I also liked supporting small businesses. And women.

She looked down at my stomach. "Say this little one is like me. Or gay, maybe. You wouldn't care, would you?"

"No." I ran my fingers along my little bump. "Of course not."

She looked at Jeremy, and he rolled his eyes. "You know I don't give a shit about anyone's sexuality or gender unless I'm fucking them."

"Then you're already better parents than mine," she said. "Having a kid is about loving them. Y'all are pretty good with the love. You were just put in a situation out of your control."

I looked down and slid my hand over my stomach. Jeremy squeezed the other. "You haven't had any luck with a tracking spell?"

I commanded the ball to move forward once more.

"I've used every single one I've found. And I mean, ever. We're talking hundreds of locator spells. They don't suggest that he's dead or anything. But they've never led to a location. I've spent a few of that ten grand you've given me on ingredients alone. And nothing. Same outcome on the spell I gave your sister. Not to mention the fifteen I've crafted on my own. The last one made a dent and she had to fight back. It almost had her, I'm telling you. I almost had 'em. Then everything on my table simultaneously caught fire."

"Maybe this is what we need. Whatever we're gonna find tonight."

The blue light stopped at a door on my left. It moved into it and bounced back. It moved to me and then back to the door. Almost as if it were alive with its own consciousness.

I wondered whose it was.

Chris's or Micah's.

"Move." I instructed it. It swiveled out of the way. I raised a purple flame to the hinge. I watched the violet light melt the metal and send it dripping to the ground as I had the night I set us free.

Helena and I stepped out of the way. Jeremy pulled the door down. Cool, brisk winter wind brushed in through the hole in the wall. It was like a small, enclosed patio but the door to it was propped open with a heavy rock. The wind whirled inside.

I stared out at the long runway ahead of me. This was where they'd been. My baby, Chris, all the others. Carted down a covered walkway that led to a plane that'd taken them somewhere far, far away.

Jeremy squeezed my hand tighter. He raised my knuckles to his lips. I struggled a smile.

Then I looked at the orb. "Go."

It slammed out into the winter air flying so fast it nearly teleported. It lowered itself to the ground by the edge of the wooden frame just below the glass window. And it stopped.

I approached and kneeled beside it.

A flame came to my hand for light. My eyes narrowed. I squinted, looking into the plywood. Small messy symbols were scratched into the wood. I raised my hand and ran my fingers along the different shapes and lines.

Jeremy crouched beside me.

"Where have I seen this?" I murmured.

If only I knew why symbols Chris and Leah 'made up' as children looked so familiar to me. But that isn't all that relevant to this part of the story. I'll get there one day.

The blue orb slammed into the carvings like it had against the door. Then it dispersed, like smoke in a bottle wafting through the air when the cap's removed.

"Chris," Jeremy murmured, a big smile stretching across his lips. He ran his fingers along the carvings. "Fucking genius. No idea how he did this blind, but fucking genius."

"You know what this is?" I asked.

"It's a code." He reached into his pocket and pulled out his phone. Laughing, the camera flashed. "Him and Leah had this little language when we were kids. They created it. They'd talk about us and we didn't know what they were saying. They made their own alphabet and number system for it, they went all out. They were the smart ones, ya know?" He laughed again, dusting snow off the symbols before snapping a few more pictures. "I guess being a conniving little shit as a kid can pay off."

"He sent us a message." I smiled.

"I'm not sure, but I think this one was a number." Jeremy's finger slid over the next carving. Under his breath, he counted. A second later, his eyes widened. A giant smile pulled at his lips.

He threw his arms around me. He pulled me to the ground on top of him, yelling out in excitement and joyously kicking his feet. "He's a fucking genius!"

I was a little confused, but I knew my husband. He wouldn't have shown such enthusiasm if it were nothing. The carving in itself was exciting, but he knew we had it.

I laughed, rolled over, and met his gaze. "What is it?"

He smiled the most hopeful grin I'd ever seen. Then he sat up and held my face in his hands. "Fifteen decimal points, and a bunch of numbers between them."

Jeremy was the smart one. I was in my own way, but he clearly saw something here that I didn't.

I raised a brow.

He laughed, brought himself to his knees, and took my face in his hands. "They're coordinates. They're latitude and longitude coordinates, baby. He must have heard the pilot say them while they were getting ready to load him onto the plane. That's why he didn't just tell you in the dream. He wrote them down as he heard them. He didn't remember them all now because he wrote them as he heard them."

My heart pounded and a giant grin came to my lips. "They're coordinates."

"They're coordinates." Jeremy smiled.

That was it. We had it. I was more excited than I'd ever been in my entire life. For the first time since he was born, I knew where my baby was. And I was gonna bring him home.

"Finally. I can quit busting my ass trying to challenge a Witch ten thousand times as powerful as me," Helena muttered. "That'll be seventeen hundred dollars. Are you going to be paying with check or card? I also accept Paypal."

CHAPTER SEVENTY-NINE

JEREMY

"What do you mean you don't remember it?" Laila yelled at Leah from where she stood at the end of the island.

Leah held her hand over her open mouth, eyes wide. "I was six. It was a game to play pranks on you guys. How the fuck does Chris even remember it?"

"He's had plenty of time to think. It's not like he's had many new memories to take in over the last decade, Leah," I barked. "He was counting on you to know this. You can't just not remember. My son's life is in your hands right now—"

"I know!" Leah screamed, clutching the sides of her head. She breathed heavily with wide, unblinking eyes, staring down at the photo in front of her. "I know."

I fell silent as my anxious breaths turned to pants.

"Everybody needs to calm down for a minute." Brody stood from the breakfast nook. He pushed his short hair back as he looked between us. "She's not going to think straight if everyone's yelling at her. Just give her a minute. We all want to find them. Just give her a minute, guys."

Laila clenched her shaking hand to a fist.

"There's a key." Hannah's eyes widened. "There's a key. Me and Wyatt, we found a key once. In middle school, I think."

Leah gasped. "Second grade. He brought it to show and tell."

A joyous smile came to my lips. "There's a key."

Leah started to her feet and darted to the maid stairs. "I'm going to search the attic. There's a lot of shit up there so it might take me some time. But I got this. I saw it last year, I think. No one follow me, you'll get in my way."

As she made it halfway up the steps, she turned to Laila and I. "Get some sleep. I'll figure out the code, get the coordinates, and then research the area on satellite and Google the general vicinity. You guys need to be prepared for what you're walking into. Get a full night's sleep 'cause it may be a few before you get another."

"You're up to date on all your continental vaccines, aren't you?" Adam looked between us. "I know I am."

Laila's hand subconsciously slid to her stomach. I looked down at her little bump beneath her black hoodie.

My stomach sunk. The baby in her belly had been about the only thing I'd thought of for the past month. But it'd completely slipped my mind once we had a lead on Micah.

Fuck. We needed Laila to do this. But I couldn't risk losing our second child to find our first.

"Let's go get some rest, baby," I murmured, starting around the island.

Her eyes stayed on the counter. "I'll see you guys in the morning. We'll be here as soon as we get up."

My heart hadn't stopped racing since I saw those carvings. Finding Micah meant the absolute world to me. It meant just as much to Laila. But Milly.

She was innocent in all of this. We needed to protect her too.

Laila couldn't do this. She couldn't.

We couldn't lose another baby to those bastards. We couldn't.

I knew she didn't agree. That's why she hadn't spoken since we got back to the apartment. She hopped in the shower, used up all the hot water, then collapsed to the bed.

And I sat there with Tink, running through the possibilities in my mind.

They could take her again. He'd said that he would. In the basement the night of the bachelor party, he said he'd have her again. That it wasn't a threat, it was a promise. And I'd still taken it as a threat, but now, knowing that he came from the future, my stomach ached.

We had to keep her out of this. She had to stay home. We couldn't lose

Milly like we'd lost Micah. We couldn't. It'd kill us. Losing Micah practically already had. Our baby girl was our only hope left, and if we lost her too, if we lost two babies to that monster, we wouldn't have the will in us to keep going.

I sat beside Laila on the bed. She was in her white camisole and baggy sweatpants. Damp, dark brown hair hung around her torso as her hand rested carefully on her belly. I looked over the little bump too, heart swelling. "Are you okay?"

Her gaze rested on her belly. Her hand trembled against it. "Yeah. Yeah, I'm okay."

"I don't want you to come," I blurted.

Laila looked up with big, watering green eyes. "I don't want to come either. But I have to, Jeremy."

"No." I placed my hand on her stomach. My head shook. "No."

"Baby." She reached out to touch my face.

"No." I vigorously shook my head. Tears formed in my eyes. I held her gaze and kept my palm against her belly. "He said that. When he was in that guard's head in the basement. He said that he'd have you again one day. I can't live through that again." The tears dribbled over and I cupped her face in my hand. "No."

"Jeremy." Her voice was a soft, barely audible whisper. Water streamed down her cheeks. Her anxious, quivering hands held my jaw. "I have to."

"You can't." I moved my hand along her stomach. "We can't. We can't lose her too, Laila. You won't be able to live with yourself if you do."

"I know." Tears flooded her bloodshot eyes. "But I can't abandon Micah for Milly." Her eyes overflowed with water, but she kept her quiet voice steady. "I already left him there." Her lip trembled. "I have to get him back. They're both my children. I have to protect them both. Finding Peterson and killing him isn't just to protect Micah, it's to protect her too. This isn't going to stop until we kill him."

"I'll do it."

"Baby." She moved over top of me and wrapped her arms around my shoulders. I slid mine around her waist and rested my head against her chest. I squeezed her so tight. I heard her heart beating beneath my ear. I closed my eyes as they overflowed with tears.

I knew what she was thinking. That I couldn't. That he would kill me first. And I knew that she was right. She had amenity with him that I didn't.

He might kidnap her. He might torture her. He might rape her, but he wouldn't kill her.

But he would kill me.

"Please don't do this to me again." I tightened my arms around her warm body, salty water dampening her chest. "Please, Laila, please don't do this to me."

Her head shook against my shoulder as her arms locked around me. "We're doing this together. It's not going to be like last time."

"No." I tightened my arms at her waist and listened to her heart thumping away at my ear. "You can't. Please, baby. Please. Just stay home."

"I'm stronger than you, Jeremy," she murmured. "If you go in there without me, there's no way you're walking out with Micah. You'll die."

"You have to believe in me," I whispered, hugging her tighter. "I can do this, Laila. I can get our son back."

"I know you can." She kissed my hair. "I know you can, baby. But we have to do this as a team."

She was lying. We both knew it. I couldn't do this without her. But she couldn't come. She couldn't. We couldn't lose Milly like we'd lost Micah.

"Don't do this, Laila," I begged, holding her as tight as I could.

"History isn't going to repeat itself," she murmured. "I'm stronger than I've ever been, Jeremy. No one's taking me anywhere I don't want to go."

"Who are you trying to convince?" I looked up to meet her gaze. "You can't do this, Laila. You can't. Please."

Her lips trembled. She touched my neck and lowered her lips to mine. "I love you so much."

"That's why you can't do this." I pulled back, eyes shifting between hers. "You're walking right into a trap, Laila. He said he was going to take you again. I know you remember that. Don't let him be right. If you love me, if you love our baby, you have to stay here."

Her eyes filled with water. Brows pulled together, lip quivering, her head shook. Her face screwed up in an ugly cry. "I love this baby so much. Please don't say that."

My chest tightened, stomach spinning, as I watched guilt flood over her. A quiet breath left my lips. I reached up to take her face in my hand. "I'm sorry, I didn't mean it like that."

The tears continued to leave her eyes. "I don't want to lose her any more than I wanted to lose him. But I have to bring my son home too."

"Let me be the hero this time." I held her face in my palms. Her hands traveled to my cheeks. "Let me keep you safe this time. Please, Laila. Please don't do this to me again."

"This is my war, Jeremy," she whispered. Her teary eyes sparkled in the light of the lamps. "I can't stand on the sidelines and watch my people get slaughtered. I have to fight it. We can win if I fight it. I waited last time and that's why I lost him. We'll lose if I don't. And—"

"No," I said over her as she continued.

"Our son will die, and everything will have been for nothing." Her hands went to my hair. "I love you so much."

"You can't." She'd blinked her tears away, but mine continued to fall. "You can't risk yours and this baby's life."

Laila wiped my cheeks and looked between my eyes. "Just tell me you love me."

"No." I shook my head. "No, not until you promise that you'll stay home."

"Jeremy," she whispered.

"Please." I moved my hand to her soft hair. "Please. Don't do this."

"Tell me you love me," she whispered, kissing my cheek.

"No." I twisted my arm around her back, the other to the back of her head, and held her tight against me.

"Please," she whispered, moving her lips toward my jaw.

My eyes burned with tears. She leaned back to meet my gaze. Her fingers began undoing the buttons of my shirt as we looked at each other with the saddest, most heartbroken expressions.

"Just tell me you love me," Laila murmured again.

I loved her more than anything besides those babies. That's why I wouldn't say it. I needed her to listen to me. I needed her to see what decision she was making.

But she knew. She knew what she was doing, and she hated it. She wasn't going to let us go after Micah alone. She was putting herself and our daughter at risk, but only for the sake of saving our son. She had to right the wrong she made two years ago. She had to fix this.

She wouldn't back down. She was going to go after them no matter what.

I couldn't stop her. All I could do was stand by her side and guard that belly the best I could.

I scrunched up my face and struggled not to cry. Holding my trembling bottom lip down with my teeth, I gently nodded. "I love you."

She smiled, water leaving her eyes. "I love you too."

Then she pushed her lips to mine.

We had a lot of sex over the years, but that was the first time we cried while we fucked.

Neither of us knew what tomorrow had in store for us.

We had no idea what we were walking into.

We could lose everything.

They could kill Micah.

We could lose the little girl growing in her belly.

Both of us and everyone we loved that came along could die.

It could be the last night we spent together.

CHAPTER EIGHTY

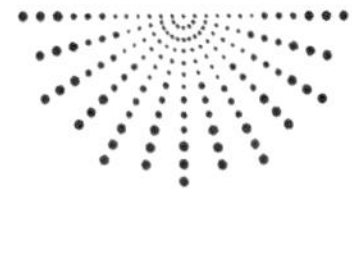

LAILA

"It's a small town in Brazil off the Amazon River." Leah clicked around on the screen to a satellite image. "The coordinates led to a private airport here on the outskirts of Alter do Chão. And I do mean outskirts, that's just the biggest city nearby. It's practically in the rainforest. But while I was digging, I figured if we wanted to be sure they were, I should hack into local cameras, right? Run the facial recognition algorithm I synthesized from the local police department and over lay—"

"Just show us what you found," Jeremy said, huddling closer to the laptop.

"Amy wasn't treated like the other prisoners." Leah clicked away. "I thought she might be allowed outside. I got her last driver's license photo and age progressed it. Then I ran some programs. Low and behold." She clicked on a window.

Amy appeared. She was wearing a pale, lilac sweater, and a pair of dark washed blue jeans. Her long, copper hair was pulled into a neat bun behind her head. She stood on the other end of a cash register, handing a cashier money.

"That's her, right?" Leah asked.

"That's her."

"This was taken four days ago. They're still there, I know it. They have no idea we're onto them," Leah said.

Jeremy licked his lips, like he often did when he was nervous. He didn't believe that. I wasn't sure I did either.

"Are there any structures?" I moved the mouse to the window for the satellite images. I looked down at the runway surrounded by vegetation. "A building like the one in Canada? He said in that video he'd held or killed at least eight hundred of us or something. This could be the second location."

"No," Leah murmured, worry in her gaze. "No, no structures. I didn't understand what part of the message meant at first but now I think I do." She looked between us. "There was a word and a down facing arrow after the coordinates."

"What was it?" Jeremy asked.

Leah was quiet for a moment. "Ground. Down facing arrow, and ground."

"Shit," Jeremy murmured.

I ran my hand along my mouth. "Underground."

"Underground," Leah said.

"That's going to make finding it a hell of a lot harder," I muttered.

"Might make getting in easier though." Adam came down the steps holding my sister's hand. "Probably only a few entrances. Find them all and we can kill off every single guard that tries to escape."

"You guys have guns, right?" Jeremy asked.

Brody gestured to a bulge at his hip and then pulled up his pant leg. "Two pistols each."

"It's going to be different this time." I looked between Brody and Adam. "I killed off a good chunk of them last time. I think I got a good fifty just while you guys were getting people out. And we don't have a small army behind us."

"Let's hope we're better shots," Adam murmured.

"Even if there's a group of three, one pistol isn't going to be enough to get them before they get you. Your powers aren't going to work, you need something a little more heavy duty."

"We have a couple AKs," Brody said. "Once we get down there and figure out a place to set up camp, we'll bring the trunk."

"Good call," Jeremy said. "Helena said my powers are still going to work, but I'd rather be safe than sorry."

"Battle weapons aside," —Leah pulled my attention from the two pistols on Brody's body— "We know that Peterson's smart. He'd stay near an airport. That's why he liked the location in Canada, he had a personal landing strip."

"Yeah," I said. "He'll have a back-up plan."

"That's why we went this morning and installed deer cams on the outside of every airport we could find in a twenty-mile radius of this place." Adam sat at the counter.

"I'll be watching those while you're inside," Leah said. "A plane starts loading up with a bunch of prisoners, I'll know where they are. Laila and Kai can teleport to it, even if it's in the air."

"And do what?" Kai asked. "Getting in and out of a tiny space like that where we'll be swarmed with as many guards as there are prisoners idn't gonna be easy."

"I'll take it out of the sky," I said.

Adam's face screwed up. "I thought we were trying to save them."

"Gently," I said. "Jesus, my kid could be on it, obviously I'm not going to kill anyone. I'll knock off the turbines and lower it back to the ground. I'm good enough with air to pull it off."

"Laila," Jeremy said quietly.

"I'm doing this, Jeremy."

"I know this can't be easy for you to face after what happened." Leah looked his way with a soft gaze. "But we need Laila. She's stronger than all of us."

"She's pregnant," he blurted.

Her mouth dropped open. "What?"

"Jeremy." I furrowed my brows at him.

"I'm sorry, baby, but you might not be here to announce it next week if you do this." Jeremy met my gaze before looking around the room. "There's a good chance that this is a trap. Peterson said he'd get her back. He said he'd take her again. You remember that, right? He had some book that described our lives in the most grotesque detail imaginable. He knows what's going to happen. He knows more than we do. We can't walk right into this. We can't hand our second child over to him on a silver platter."

"They didn't know what message Chris left me," I said. "That's why they gave us the book. To throw us off."

"You're pregnant?" Jenna smiled, walking toward me from the steps. She placed her hand over my belly. She smiled up at me and met my gaze with quick forming tears in her eyes.

"How far along are you?" Leah asked.

"Fourteen weeks." I touched my stomach.

"Do you know what it is yet?" Hannah made her way across the room with a smile.

"She." I smiled. "Her name's Milly."

"Milly." Adam grinned. "That's what Annie called Mom."

Jeremy smiled, nodding.

"Jeremy's right," Jenna said with tears in her eyes. She touched my stomach. "You can't do this."

"But we can't do *this* without her." Brody looked at me with an expression I'd never seen on his face before. It was a shrouded look; terror blanketed with confidence. "We're not going to get an opportunity like this again."

"Did you even talk to Mom?" Jenna asked.

"I won't be gone long. And when I come back, I'll have my son."

"Laila," Hannah said. "You're pregnant. You can't possibly think this is a good idea."

"I agree," Adam said. "You got shot twice on the way out last time. This is too risky."

"What losing Micah did to you—" Jenna began before I cut her off.

They were right. They were all one hundred percent right. I didn't want to do this. I didn't want to risk my daughter's life, but that was the decision he forced me into yet again. Risk one child to save the other.

A time would come when I had no fear of any battle, pregnant or otherwise. But I wasn't invincible yet. We didn't have a concrete plan, we didn't have proof Micah was even alive, but Chris reached out to *me*. He reached out to me because he knew I was the only one strong enough to pull off what had to be done.

And I hated it. But I had to right the wrong I made almost two years before. I had to get my son back before he was any older.

"Losing Micah is the reason that I have to do this." I looked around. "I lost my son—"

"And you could lose our daughter." Jeremy's jaw tightened. "What will it do to you if you do?"

"This is *my* fault," I blurted looking around with darting eyes. "My son is being held captive by this maniac because of what *I* did. I chose to get in that van. *I* am the reason I was held captive and tortured for three months. I am the reason Micah came too early. I am the reason that they took him out of my cell and I never saw him again. This is because of me and I—"

"You're going to do exactly what you did last time and dive headfirst into their trap?" Hannah asked. "How? How could you do that again after what it did to every single one of us?"

I gritted my teeth to a line as I fought the urge to scream profanities.

She was the person I protected over Micah in the first place. But she was my sister, and I wasn't going to cast stones. It could very well be the last time we saw each other.

"I'm not the girl who walked into that van." I held Hannah's bright gaze. "I was young and overconfident. I wasn't scared of dying yet. I should have been, but I wasn't. Now, I am. I'm more terrified than I've ever been in my life. I'm more scared now than I was when I woke up in that cell."

"Then you have to stay." Jeremy took my hand and squeezed it. "Please, baby. Please. Just stay."

"Then we got nothin'." Kai stood from his silent seat at the breakfast nook. "Laila's the best weapon we got. She's stronger than the lot of us."

"We know what we're up against," Jeremy insisted. "We can handle this."

"Talkin' out yer fanny flaps." Kai scoffed at Jeremy. "All 'a us here know we ain't walking outta there in one piece if she don't come."

"Stay out of it, Kai," Hannah said.

"I stay outta everything." Kai gave a similar expression. "But ye can't all berate my sister like she idn't doin' everything she can. It's her babe locked up in that place, ye expect her to just forget that? Yer bloody mad."

I'd never seen Kai angry before, but he was then. His accent was so thick, I honestly had a hard time understanding him. But the situation hit home. He wanted parents that gave a damn. He wanted parents willing to climb leaps and bounds to find him if he was lost. And he was smart enough to know what I knew.

They would fail without me. Jeremy and Kai would be the only people they had with abilities. I was the arsenal.

"My powers are still going to work," Jeremy insisted.

"No, Laila's right." Leah rubbed her mouth. "She's the fire power. We need her."

"Leah." Jeremy narrowed his gaze.

"I'm sorry, Jeremy, but she is." Her eyes met mine. Blowing out a breath, she went on. "I know it hurts your pride a little, but at the end of the day, her and Kai are the only ones who stand a chance here. Your energy might help, you can take down a few guards at once with it, but Laila can take down squads in a second and leave no evidence behind. She has to be there."

"Anything could happen—" he began.

"You're my cover, Jeremy." I took his other hand in mine. "You have my back in there. I'm not doing this alone; we're going to be together every step of the way." Tears formed in his creased blue eyes. "We're a team. This is the biggest challenge we've ever faced; we can't do it ten thousand miles apart. We're stronger together, remember?"

He frowned. "I remember."

I smiled and gave a nod. "We stick close. Always in each other's eyesight. That's where we went wrong last time. We stay together. We have two healers, so we split into two groups."

"No, you have three," Leah said. "I've sat out every battle we've fought and it's time I join in. I'll stay outside to monitor the cameras, but I'll be there if you need me. Anyone gets hurt and you don't have time to heal them, you bring them to me. Haley wants to come. She'll stay with me unless you need the hands."

"We protect the healers." Brody came to the counter and leaned over it. "We keep them safe, and no one dies."

"I'm coming," Hannah said, voice shaky.

"No—" Kai said.

"Oh, so your pregnant sister can go but I can't?" She arched a brow, looking at Kai. "If anyone dies, I need to pull them back to their body before rigor mortis sets in. I'm coming."

"Hannah," I began quietly.

"No, I don't want to hear it. This is just as much because of me as it is because of you. We're doing this and I'm going to be there. I'm not losing another person I love, not even that baby inside you. No one else that I love is dying. And what if they try to fulfill the prophecy when they realize you're coming? I have to be there to bring my nephew back. I'm an adult now, I've made my decision. I'm coming."

"You're old enough," Adam said. "You're ready."

"We might need you," Brody said. "Don't let me stay dead if I go down in there, alright?"

Hannah nodded.

"So we're all in on this one," Leah murmured. "I'm going to order pizza for lunch and then we'll go find a place to set up camp. In the meantime, we should all spend a few minutes together. Even with a necromancer, we don't know how this is going to end. We should all try to take a deep breath for a minute because it might be a while before we get another."

CHAPTER EIGHTY-ONE

JEREMY

Laila didn't say a word to me the whole time we sat around eating pizza. She was silent on the ride to her mom's.

Okay, maybe I shouldn't have blurted that she was pregnant to the whole family. But I didn't want her to get involved with this. And I was sure Leah would agree with me and tell her to stay home—she had a better chance of swaying her opinion than anyone.

It wasn't safe for any of us. But it especially wasn't safe for her. And more than anything, it wasn't safe for my daughter.

She held my hand as we walked up the drive to Rachel's door though.

Maybe she wasn't mad at me. Maybe she was just scared. But I wasn't accustomed to silence from Laila, she usually never shut up. Not that it bothered me, she kept life interesting. Her aura was engulfing. She had this way of making the rest of the world disappear when she smiled and laughed.

Fuck, I couldn't go months without seeing that smile again. I couldn't.

"Hey, Mom." Laila opened the door to her mom's living room from the small patio. "Are you home?"

"Whatcha doing here, babe?" Rachel called from the bedroom. I carefully shut the door behind us. "I didn't realize you were stopping by."

Rachel stepped from the hallway into the living room. Her brows fell over her eyes, looking between us. "Oh god, what happened?"

"Nothing." Laila gave a sad smile and made her way across the room. "Everything's good."

She looked at me. My face must have said it all because she turned back to Laila with wide eyes. "What's going on?"

Laila said nothing.

"We have a lead on Micah," I said. She turned back to me. "We think they're in Brazil somewhere around the rainforest. We don't know much, but we're going. We're just about certain that they're there."

"Well, that's great news." Rachel looked from me to Laila. "That's great news, isn't it?"

"It is," Laila said. "It's great news."

"Tell her the other good news," I murmured.

She glared over her shoulder. "We do have some other news. We were going to wait until next week to tell everyone, but with this, I'm not sure we'll be back next week."

"What is it?"

Laila cleared her throat, forcing a smile. Her hand went to her stomach.

Rachel's eyes widened. "Are you...?"

Laila smiled. "I'm pregnant."

Her eyes filled with joy as a smile flung to her lips. "Oh, congratulations, baby!"

I swallowed as I watched them hug.

Her problem before was her overconfidence. Whether she realized it or not, she was still being just as big headed as she once was.

I didn't want to say that it was her fault because it wasn't. Neither of us would have ever asked for any of it. We always wanted the same thing. Simplicity.

But god damn it, it was like watching a rerun with better farewells. She looked like she knew something bad would happen. She had the same bad feeling I did, and she was coming anyway.

"Thank you." Laila ran her fingertips along her barely bloated belly.

Rachel looked at her and then at me. "Why do you look like that then?"

"Because this is dangerous," I said. "We're going up against the people that took our son. The same people that ruthlessly beat her and drugged her and ran god only knows what kind of experiments on her. Because she ended up with three bullets inside of her the last time she was around these people. She coded twice in three days last time. Then he swore that he would take her again. That was barely more than a year ago. And now she's pregnant again and I'm terrified that history is going to repeat itself."

Laila lowered her lips in a frown as she met my gaze. Rachel looked between us, clearly debating what to say next. But Laila took her hands and smiled.

"I'm going to be fine, Mom. Really. I am. I'm ready for this. The things I can do, as far as I've come, I'm ready. This is my war. I have to fight it. Pregnant or not, I have to fight it. That's my baby in there. If you were in my shoes, if you were pregnant with me and someone took Jenna." Tears began to slide from her eyes. She gritted her teeth together. It reminded me of the face she made the day that she died. The anger and pain mixed together into a beautiful portrait of love and fear. But she just squeezed Rachel's shaking hands tighter. "You would do whatever it took. You would risk my life for hers if you knew that you were the only chance she had."

Rachel's eyes began to water. "If there was a chance you could both live, I would take it."

Laila's eyes flooded. She nodded quick. Then she moved her hands around her mom's shoulders and squeezed as tight as she could. It was like she needed that reassurance from a mother. She needed to hear from the best mother she knew that she was doing the right thing. Although, she may have just needed to hear it from anyone.

But fuck, I was pissed Rachel didn't tell her to stay home.

Losing her was the worst thing I ever experienced. Feeling them torture her and not being able to do anything was worse than living through hell. When he raped her and I heard her in my ears begging him to stop as she sprained her limbs against the restraints trying to break free, I was broken.

I failed her in every way. I felt every minute of her pain and was unable to stop it.

And I would feel it again if she ended up back there. I would feel their whips and needles and scalpels and I wouldn't be able to stop it. I would fail her again.

What I still struggled to accept was the fact that she was the powerful one. She had to do the things that I couldn't. And if I couldn't save her, and I couldn't save Chris, I wouldn't be able to save Micah.

She saved herself and she almost saved Chris. She could save Micah. I couldn't, but she could.

"When are you leaving?" Rachel asked with her eyes closed against Laila's shoulder.

"About an hour," I murmured.

"Well." Rachel pulled back. She wiped her cheeks and forced a smile as she looked between us. "I made some chili. Do you guys want to eat before you go?"

"We—"

"We would love to." Laila gave a quiet laugh. "I love your chili. Just let me pee real quick."

"Sure." She smiled. Then Laila started down the hall.

When I heard the bathroom door close, I turned to Rachel with watering eyes. "Don't let her do this."

She frowned. "You're not used to being on the other end of this stick, are you, Jeremy?"

I creased my brows.

"Seventeen years." Rachel tucked her sweater tighter around her torso. "I was married to Luka for seventeen years and every single time that he walked out that door, I didn't know if he would walk back in. And sure enough, one day, he didn't. And I'm sorry, sweetie, I wouldn't wish that pain on anyone but that is what we signed up for. That is who they are. Laila is never going to stop helping people. That's who she is. And not even just helping, but *saving* her child? Nothing and no one is going to stop her. I know she's not invincible, but she sure has a hard time staying dead."

I turned my gaze to the ground.

That was some of the best advice I'd ever been given. Rachel was right. I had to accept that Laila would always do what Laila had to do. She would do whatever it took to meet her goal. She fucked up when she got in that van and she had to make it right. And I had to accept that.

I wouldn't.

But she was right.

"Does she need you for this, Jeremy?" Rachel asked. "Does she need your help for this?"

I gave a nod and chewed my inner lip.

"Then be there. If she needs you, be there because she doesn't ask for help unless she really needs it anymore. Do what she needs and keep her safe. Don't let them hurt her—"

"Don't make him promise that," Laila murmured, coming back down the hall. "I'm going to do my best to keep everyone safe. But if I don't—"

"Don't say that—"

"*If I don't.*" Laila cut me off, wide eyes against mine. "If I fail, then no one is to blame but me. I want to make that very clear. This is my war. No one is forcing me to fight it and it is no one's job to protect me. If I don't make it home, no one needs to feel how I have felt since this all started."

I blinked tears away, gaze shifting between those beautiful, nearly glowing emeralds.

It didn't matter. If something happened to her, if she got hurt out there, I was still going to feel like it was my fault. If something happened to Milly, I'd say it was my fault for failing to protect her.

But she needed to hear me say it.

"Okay?" She pressed her trembling lips together.

Licking my lips, I gave a slow nod. "Okay, baby."

CHAPTER EIGHTY-TWO

LAILA

As we stepped out onto Mom's porch, I leaned up onto the tips of my toes and pressed my lips to Jeremy's. I felt his scruff against my cheeks, basking in the warmth of his skin. He placed his hand at my waist. He closed his eyes for a moment, and I ran my hand along his chest. I dropped flat to my feet and looked up to meet his gaze.

"You go back to the house. I want to talk to Max just in case anything happens. I—I don't want to say hi to Tink because she'll get too excited and I only have a couple of minutes. But Mom has the key so she's going to come grab Tink when she gets off work. She won't be home by herself for very long."

He raised his hand to my face and gently slid the back of his fingers along my cheek. "I'll see you at the house."

I brought myself back to my tiptoes and touched my lips to his. He placed his hand on the small of my back and held me close for a moment. Then he leaned down and wrapped his arms around me in a tight hug.

"Everything's going to be fine." I hugged him tight. I stared at the snowflake wreath that hung on the door behind his head. Jen, Mom, Dad, and I made that together when I was in grade school. And it'd weathered so many icy winters since then. I had to hold onto hope that by next Christmas, I'd be making a wreath like that with my babies too. "Everything's going to be okay."

He kissed my hair and squeezed me a little tighter.

I didn't believe that. Something didn't sit right about any of it. Chris led me there, I knew that. But something wasn't right. Still, I had to do it. I couldn't sit on the sidelines. I had to be there.

———

"Max," I said. A timer on the back of the oven buzzed. He anxiously flipped a burger before rushing toward the fryer and pulling the basket from the boiling grease.

"Yeah, one sec." He turned to Sophie. "Did you just take my chicken tenders? Those were Mandy's, yours had a baked potato."

"Max," I repeated.

"Jesus Christ, what, Laila?" Max turned to meet my gaze.

I smiled, looking at his muddy brown eyes. "I need to talk to you for a minute."

"Well fuck your burger, I guess, Sophie." He dropped his spatula to the griddle. He started toward the office, raising his hands in question. "What's up, dude? We're in the middle of Christmas season lunch rush. Those old ladies who never leave the house are out and they are brutal. Do you know how many plates have come back to the kitchen today? A shit ton, put it that way."

I smiled as he closed the office door.

My best friend. The thought of never seeing him again terrified me. But if Jeremy and I didn't make it, I knew he'd do right by Moe's Diner. He'd be good in my place.

He looked me over. "Did you finally break? Is this it? Full manic episode?"

I rolled my eyes and laughed. "No, Max. I'm not out of my mind."

He crossed his bulky arms against his chest. "What's up then?"

"I'm going to be gone for a little while," I answered. "I don't know how long. Might only be a few hours. But more likely a couple days. Possibly weeks. I doubt we'd get to months."

He creased his brows and turned his head to the side. "Okay, where are you going?"

"If I'm gone for more than two weeks, you can file a missing person's report. On all of us. Me, Jeremy, his brothers, and sisters. But I don't think it will come to that. If it does though, you should know that my lawyer has a draft of my will. Almost everything goes to my kids if they make it. But you get a sizable inheritance."

Max was the only person I could be blunt with about this. If I told Jeremy how terrified I was, he just might be able to convince me to stay. But Max would just take it in. He'd listen. He wouldn't tell me what was right or wrong, he'd just listen.

"Laila." Max took a step forward. "What are you talking about?"

"I really think that everything's going to be fine. But if it isn't, if something happens to me, don't let this place go to shit. Jeremy will get the place if he makes it, but if I don't, he probably won't either so." I gave an ironic laugh. "No pressure or anything, right?"

He studied me for a moment. "Is this about Micah?"

"We think we found him, but we have no idea what we're walking into. I don't know what's going to happen, but..." I brought on a smile. "I love you, Max. Thank you for being my best friend through it all. You've been a part of my life for as long as I can remember, and I couldn't have imagined what my life would look like without you in it. You work so hard here, and you do such a great job, and I... I love you, man."

He just stared at me. I wasn't sure if in disbelief or terror.

I just smiled wider. "You don't have to say anything. I know you feel the same way. Just don't forget how much you mean to me when some shitty customer throws your food back at you, alright?"

He stood stiller than stone as I wrapped my arms around him in a tight embrace. He stunk like rotten onions and weed, but I smiled anyway.

CHAPTER EIGHTY-THREE

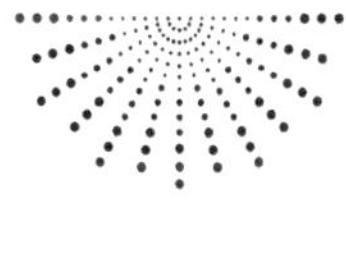

LAILA

Sweat beaded at my forehead as I looked out over the empty parking lot of the dingy motel. The hot, humid air drifted into my lungs. It was so thick that breathing felt a little difficult. But maybe that was the anxiety.

I looked up at the bright, sun coated hillside. What felt like a thousand homes of stucco and brick teemed with life. Some were bright and vibrant shades of blue and pink. People yelled and laughed in the distance, mixing with the sound of donkeys smacking their hooves against the ground.

If I was gonna die, this seemed like an okay place to go. I'd rather die with the sun on my cheeks than in the snow.

Jeremy placed a large hat over my head from behind and said, "Você retomou o she portugês?"

I smiled. "I have no idea what you just said."

A quiet chuckle left his lips. "So you don't know any Portuguese then."

"Not all of us got to travel the globe from the time they took their first steps." I grinned. "And Portuguese wasn't an option at our high school."

"Yeah, that's true," he said. "Isn't it weird that we were in high school at the same time and didn't meet until you were almost finished?"

I'd thought about that over the years too. It was odd. Our town was small, one would have thought we'd crossed paths at one point or another. And perhaps we had. But the timing hadn't been right until that dark night in 2015.

"Yeah, it is." I gave a laugh. "Technically, I think Brody was the first one of you I met. Not directly or anything, but I think we had a class together in freshman year. He was quiet. I was loud and annoying. We kind of clashed."

He squinted a bit. "Really? You met Brody first?"

"We didn't really meet," I said. "It was home ec, I think. I just remember his name during roll call."

"No shit," he muttered.

"It's probably for the best that we didn't meet then," I said. "I was really weird in high school. But I think I heard your name on the morning announcements a few times during freshman year telling you to report to the office."

He laughed. His elbows propped onto the hand rail, he leaned over it, and he shook his head. "I probably wasn't there to hear it."

"That's probably why we never met." I smiled and leaned against the railing beside him. "You were always cutting class."

"That's probably true." He smiled and met my gaze. "I'm glad I didn't meet you then. I was a little shit."

Grinning, I narrowed my gaze a bit. "That's when you were dating Olivia, huh?"

He grimaced. A slow breath left his nose. "I was."

"Wasn't she a cheerleader?" I asked.

"She was."

"So that's your type, huh?" I smirked and bumped my shoulder against his. "Peppy bitches who do robot dances in short skirts for a bunch of guys in tights?"

He laughed and met my gaze. "Did someone get turned down for the squad?"

I laughed, pushing his shoulder. In a mocking tone, I said, "My routine was just as good as everyone else's."

"Did you really?"

"Hell no."

He smiled. "She wasn't really my type. But she's a Witch. Not a very good one, but she knows about this world. Her parents knew mine. It was more about availability than anything."

"Hmm." I placed my chin on my palm. "So what is your type?"

Jeremy grinned as he looked me over. "If I had to choose?"

I nodded, smile stretching and eyes widening slightly.

"Probably dark hair." His thumb and forefinger took a piece of my hair between them. "About five five. Green eyes." He smiled, moving his thumb and forefinger to my chin. "Covered in tattoos."

"Ya don't say." I smiled and moved my hand to the side of his neck. "Sounds like someone I know."

"Oh yeah?" He touched his lips to mine.

I kissed him back for a moment. Then I pulled away. "Ya know, Chris said you liked blonds. Am I *really* your type?"

Another laugh. "Your hair could be blue, and you'd still be my type."

"What's wrong with blue hair?" I raised a brow.

"Nothing." He smiled. "Do it. Blue hair'd be cute on you."

"Good answer." I grinned and kissed him again. A moment later, I pulled back to meet his gaze. I rested my forehead against his. "I think we met at just the right time."

"Me too," he murmured, pushing hair from my face.

I threaded my fingers through his. "Everything comes down to timing."

Silence set in for a long moment. Our eyes stayed on our fingers twined together.

Truth was, I was doing everything in my power to think about something that wasn't this mission failing. I don't know why I did, but I had a feeling it would. It just felt too easy.

We were past two years since we started this now. Two years, and the only evidence we ever had was handed to us on a silver platter. I supposed the message Chris had left was a bit more elusive, but it'd still been too easy.

And there was a pit in my stomach. The last time I had a pit in my stomach like this was when we visited Cage Stevenson and Janis and Elijah Wilson's.

That feeling had been right last time. I just prayed it was wrong now.

Jeremy gently moved his hand along my jaw. "Are you sure you're ready for this?"

I looked away. A trill made its way between my lips. "Do you want me to give you the answer that's going to make you feel better or the truth?"

"The only thing that's going to make me feel better is if I know that you and our daughter are safe." His thumb traced along the back of mine. "So the truth."

I turned back to meet his gaze. "I'm as ready as I can be. Physically, I'm not worried. I don't think Peterson wants me dead. For whatever sick reason, he loves me. I know I'm not going to die at his hand."

Jeremy looked between my eyes.

"I want to keep this baby safe. But I have to get my other baby to safety too. They're going to kill him, Jeremy." I looked between his deep blue eyes. "And I know how strong you are. I know that you'd give it everything you got with or without me to bring Micah home. But you're one person with the power of ten. I'm one person with the power of a hundred. And you don't have the amnesty that I do. You, he would kill. The guards are going to shoot for my legs, but they'll go for your head first. Every one of you. I'm the only one that they won't. We have to use that, baby. I know you want to keep me safe from everything, but this is my war. I'm the way we win with the least number of casualties possible."

Jeremy was quiet for a moment. His eyes slid between mine. He squeezed my hand. "You said eyes on each other at all times but that isn't gonna cut it. You keep your hand on mine until we see our son. Then we hold his. But until then, you hold my hand, and you don't let go. Okay?"

I smiled.

He gave a sad smile and squeezed a little harder. "Deal?"

I nodded, tightening my hand around his. "Deal."

CHAPTER EIGHTY-FOUR

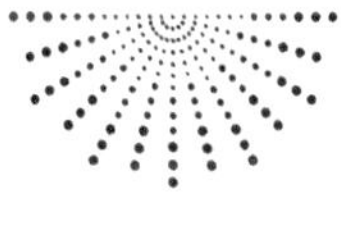

LAILA

We sat in the parking lot of some run-down gas station I couldn't attempt to pronounce the name of if I tried. Brody and I were ducked down in our seats as Jeremy meandered through the aisles grabbing miscellaneous items.

Brody had backed me up at the house. He, Leah, and Kai were the only ones that did. And that meant a great deal to me. Everyone else was concerned more about Milly than Micah. But he saw what I did. The outside perspective that we couldn't do this if I weren't there.

I turned down the music. "Thanks."

"For what?' Brody took a sip from his drink in the back seat.

"Backing me up on coming here." I stifled a yawn.

"It'd be stupid for you to stay," he said. "I see Jeremy's point and every-thing. All of their points, I guess. But the fact of the matter is that you're stronger than all of us. Leah might be able to hack those microchips if we find the place, but it took her months before. After they realized what she did, I'm sure they amped up their software. We're going in there powerless besides you and Kai."

I said, "Yeah, I'm sure I barely put a dent in his army. If this is a second location, I'm sure it's armed just as heavily. Even with machine guns—"

"We don't stand a chance without your power," Brody murmured. "That's not the only reason I backed you up though."

"No?" I shifted sideways to meet his gaze.

"This is your fight, Lai. That's your kid in there. You hated yourself for his death just to realize he wasn't dead but kidnapped." He perched forward between the seats of the rental. "You won't forgive yourself for what happened to him until you have him back. Of course you had to be here. That's your kid."

At least someone was on the same page as me. "Thanks for being here too. You're a good shot."

He smiled. "This is my fight too ya know." His tongue ran along his lips before he bit the bottom one. "That's my big brother in there. And my nephew. It didn't feel real until I saw him that night but then it all came back. He smiled when he heard my voice. It was different than it used to be without his eyes and everything. But he smiled. My voice has drastically changed since he disappeared, but he remembered it. He needed me that night and I fucked up. He was right there when that fucking tranquilizer hit me. He's powerless in there, and he's down a sense. He needs us. All of us."

"Yeah. Yeah, he does."

The car fell quiet for a moment as I watched Jeremy approach the counter and begin to speak to the cashier.

Brody laid his face against the back of the driver's seat with a soft smile. "Can I tell you something?"

"Sure."

His smile lifted higher. "I think I have a girlfriend."

A smile came to my lips. "Really?"

He nodded, still smiling.

That was the best news I'd heard since I found out I was pregnant. Brody deserved love. He'd wanted it for a long time, and I was glad that now, he had it. Or at least, a chance at it.

"Who is she? How'd you guys meet?" I asked.

A quiet laugh left his lips. He closed his eyes. "The same way Leah met Haley."

"She's a survivor?"

"Yeah. Yeah, she is," he said. "Her name's Gwen. Gwendolyn Acker."

"That's a pretty name." I smiled. "What is she?"

An awkward laugh. His eyes closed, and he rubbed his mouth. "See, that's why I haven't told anyone about her yet."

I grinned. "Well, I was fucking a Demon a few months ago so no judgment here."

He turned his head and pulled the neck of his hoodie to the side. Two thin fang marks stared back at me. My eyes widened. "She's a Vampire?"

We didn't innately hate vamps. Some of them were decent enough. But we'd also killed plenty of them. I'd never heard the name Acker, so I had no reason to hold a grudge against her. Hell, I didn't have a reason to hold a grudge against any of the races. A human hurt me more than any Demon or Vampire ever could.

But Brody looked happy when he talked about her. I didn't know Gwen yet, but she'd help him grow so much as a person. She'd help him realize that life is what we make of it. She'd help him see that life can be a beautiful thing.

"Hybrid." He pulled his hoodie back to its place. "Born wolf, turned vamp."

"What's that like?" I turned to face him better. "Liam tried but I never let him. He said it felt good but it's kind of a PTSD trigger for me."

He laughed. "It's kind of amazing. You get sort of high for an hour or two during and after. It's really hot to be honest."

"And she just knows when to stop?" I propped my chin in my palm.

"Yeah, she's pretty experienced. I wouldn't trust a new vamp to do it."

"How experienced we talking here?" I asked with a grin.

"She's pretty old."

"Ooh, so you're into the cougar vibes," I teased. "How old is she?"

"She was turned at nineteen. But she was born in 1891."

My eyes widened. *Major* cougar vibes. "Holy shit."

"It's a little weird when I think about it hard enough," he said. "Actually it's just pretty weird in general. But she doesn't look like she's a hundred and twenty-nine so I forget a lot."

I tilted my head slightly. "Does she know you're here?"

A deep exhale. "Yeah."

"I take it she doesn't approve?"

He was silent for a moment. "She wants to forget about all of this, ya know? She was one of the first that he got. He had her for fifteen years. A good chunk of her life is wasted because of that fucker. She doesn't want to waste any more. She doesn't want me to die for this. Neither do I, but I can't sit it out either. That's my brother in there. My nephew too."

Couldn't say I blamed her. If we weren't smack dab in the center of that disaster, I wouldn't have wanted my loved one to go off and fight in this battle either.

"So that's why you backed me up."

He smiled. "Projecting a little, I guess."

I pulled a smile to my lips and met his gaze. "Do you love her?"

His smile lifted a little higher. "Yeah. Yeah, I think I do."

My smile widened. "Then I'm happy for you."

"Yeah, me too. Thanks."

I smiled back at him. Then I turned my gaze back to Jeremy who was still chatting with the cashier.

"Thanks for not being a bitch when you found out how I felt about you," he muttered. I turned back to meet his gaze. "I never should have acted on it, but still. Your reaction made things easier."

"You're my friend, Brody. It's not like you wanted to feel the way you did."

"Still though. Thanks."

"You don't feel that way anymore, do you?"

He neatly combed black waves falling in his eyes. "No. Not really. I still love you. I'll always love you, you're family. But not the way that I used to." He looked between my eyes. "I'm not even sure why I did. Maybe because I knew I could never be with you? Or maybe because I always kind of resented Jeremy and I thought he wasn't good enough for you? I don't know," he muttered. "But it doesn't really matter anymore. I had to come to terms with reality. It'd never happen, and it'd never work if it did. I'm a dick and you're a bitch, we'd never work as a couple."

He wasn't wrong. He was way too firm to be with someone like me. I wasn't the calmly manipulate my man into what I wanted type. I was the, 'I'm gonna say and do whatever I want and you're gonna deal with it or we won't be a couple' type.

I laughed. Then I gestured toward Jeremy walking out of the store. "I like passive guys."

"Yeah, 'cause he puts up with your shit." Brody smiled.

A laugh left my lips. Also true. Most men, or people in general, would have a hard time dealing with my attitude. But Jeremy was the exception. He hated that he loved my attitude.

Jeremy opened the passenger side door and climbed inside.

"Okay, so I got some information." He closed the door.

"What is it?" I asked.

He handed me a bottle of water and a bottle of pop to Brody. "Amy comes through every morning. Always pays in cash. Always grabs a cup of coffee and a pack of cigarettes."

"Does she ever have Micah with her?" I asked.

He pulled snacks from the bag. "No, no kids. But she always has someone in the car. He never comes in, but he's always there."

"Probably a guard," Brody murmured with a nod.

"So I guess it's time for a good old fashioned stake out." I twisted off the lid to my bottle of water. "But we should move to that parking lot across the street behind those shrubs. We'll have a clear view between them, but they won't see us."

"Yeah, that's what I was thinking." Jeremy opened a bag of beef jerky.

Brody reached into his pocket and held his hand out toward us. "Here. Leah said to take these when we get close. When we get eyes on her, we swallow them."

I opened my hand. "What is it?"

He dropped it to my palm. "It's a tracker. Small enough to pass through our intestinal tract in a couple days, about as long as the battery in it'll last. But that gives her a few days to locate us if we get captured. Wait to take it until we see her so it's inside of us for as long as possible."

I looked down at the small piece of plastic in my hand. It was about the size of an 800 milligram ibuprofen. It looked like a slightly larger version of a chocolate chip.

Another tracker in my body.

With a bite on my lip, I slid it into the lining of my bra.

"We should take shifts sleeping." Jeremy took my hand. "But we should call back and let everyone know to be prepared. We call them as soon as we get eyes on her. Then we follow her at a safe distance until she leads us to them."

CHAPTER EIGHTY-FIVE

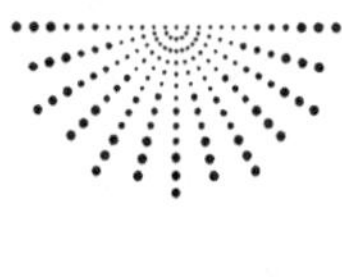

JEREMY

My gaze shifted around the deserted gas station parking lot. The only other car was the cashier's that had been here since we arrived. I decided to take the first shift. I was wide awake. I wasn't sure I'd sleep at all, hence the third Red Bull in the cup holder.

The thought of bringing my son home kept sliding through my thoughts. He was still young enough that he wouldn't remember those monsters. He was still young enough that he'd know me as his dad.

I wondered what it would feel like to hold him in my arms. I wondered what it would be like the first time he said 'dad' or 'daddy' or 'da-da.' I wondered if he still looked like me as he did as an infant.

Then... I wondered if we'd ever bring him home.

What if this was all a set-up? It did feel like one. It was just so... simple. Tracking this place down had hardly taken us more than a day. How could one lead have brought us this close?

But I had to stay positive. I had to. As much as I could, anyway. I turned the dial up on the music a bit as Laila rolled from one side to the other to face me. She hadn't slept yet either. And she really needed to. If she was gonna be our fire power tomorrow, she needed all the strength she could muster up.

I ran the back of my fingers along her cheek. "You should really try to get some rest."

"Yeah, I know. I just can't." She snuggled my hoodie closer to her face in a makeshift pillow. "My back hurts and I have to pee."

"Didn't you just pee like fifteen minutes ago?" I smiled.

"I have a literal person sitting on my bladder." Her hand moved to her belly.

I twisted our fingers together. "You could go back to the hotel for the night. He said she usually comes around seven. I can call you when she gets here, and you could teleport back."

"You wouldn't call me," Laila murmured with a smile. "You'd try and handle it yourself."

"Brody would." I gestured toward his drooling face in the back seat.

She rolled her eyes. "I'm okay. I'll just keep teleporting back to the hotel every five minutes."

"You're going to need your rest," I whispered, moving my thumb against the back of her hand. "You used a lot of energy last time. It drained you."

"I didn't have much of a will to live after last time." Her fingers twisted between mine. She pulled our hands to her lips. She kissed the back of my knuckles before resting our hands beside her face. "But I'm not going anywhere this time, baby."

I smiled and squeezed her hand tighter in mine. "You better not."

She lowered her voice to a near whisper. "I am scared. But do you know what I'm scared of?"

"Being locked up in a cell by that lunatic again?" I turned to better face her.

"No. Not really. I hated that cell, but it wasn't the worst part about it. In a lot of ways, it was my safety net. My powers worked in there."

I traced my thumb along her jaw. "What is it then?"

"I'm scared of this being another dead end."

I frowned. "I don't think it is. Might be a trap. But I don't think it's a dead end."

Her eyes grew dewy. "I just want him back before he's old enough to remember it. I don't want him to know Amy or Peterson." The tears in her eyes spilled to the makeshift pillow beneath her head. "He probably calls her mama and it just..." She wiped her cheeks. "It's just so fucked up. All I want is to be a parent to my kid and... It—It's not fair."

I used my thumb to wipe her cheek. "That could all change in a few hours."

"Yeah. Yeah, it could."

"We're getting our son back, Lai." I pushed hair from her face. "I can't say that it'll be tomorrow for sure. But we're getting close. We got Amy on film. That has to mean something. They're here, I know they are. We're going to find them."

"Do you want me to take the first shift? I don't think I'm falling asleep any time soon."

"Nah, I'm alright," I murmured. "I just chugged a Red Bull. I'm ready to fight a bear right now."

She laughed. A smile pulled at her lips. "Ugh, I'd kill for a Red Bull. Or just one hit off a joint. Just one."

I'd been pretty pushy about her health with both pregnancies. I bitched about her third cup of coffee, I rolled my eyes when she insisted on drinking unpasteurized milk from the local farm, I told her to sit down and relax all the time. She hated it. Primarily, I think, because she knew I was right, and she shouldn't be doing those things. But we could die in a few hours.

"I have some weed if you really want to smoke."

"And you won't frown at me disappointedly for weeks?"

I laughed. "A hit isn't going to hurt the baby."

She smiled. "Well, I'm glad that I have your blessing but I'm okay. I don't have a tolerance; I'd be too high. And I'd rather not risk it anyway. I was still drinking and smoking until I was eight weeks pregnant with Micah. I was terrified something was going to be wrong until I had a few ultrasounds and the doctor said everything was normal. That's probably why I waited so long to tell you."

I smiled. "And he was fine."

"Apparently," she murmured. "All this fuss over him, he must be perfect."

I squeezed her hand. "I'm sure he is."

As I looked over her, my chest tightened. Something had been weighing heavy on my mind for the last few hours. I knew Micah would come home eventually. And I wasn't proud of the person I'd been for most of his life so far. But I was trying to do better. And if I weren't around to prove to him that I could be a good man, I wanted him to at least think that I was.

"Baby," I whispered, moving my hand to her cheek.

"Yeah?" She met my gaze.

"I know you're going to be okay. But if something happens to me, I—"

"Don't talk like that." She squeezed my hand tighter. "Nothing's going to happen to you."

"But if it does." I forced a smile. "Just in case."

She frowned.

"Can you lie to the kids about me?" I asked quietly.

Laila sat forward, face screwed up. "What do you mean?"

"I'm not what I want my kids to be. I barely graduated high school. I'm not successful. I'm an addict. I'm a murderer." I slid my thumb against her cheek. "I'm a lot of things I wish I weren't. But if I don't make it, please don't let them know that. All I want them to know is how much I love them. And how much I love you."

She smiled, leaned forward, and pushed her mouth to mine. Her hand held my neck as her lips parted and brushed carefully for a second. Then she pulled back and touched my forehead to hers.

"That's all that matters, Jeremy." Her warm hands touched the skin just below my ears. "Nothing's going to happen to you. But one way or another, our kids are only going to know what we teach them. It doesn't matter if we're perfect. We're doing everything within our power to keep them safe because we love them. That's all that our kids are going to see. Just love. Okay?"

"But if I don't—"

"Don't say that," she repeated, tears welling in her eyes. Her head shook and her hands tightened against my face. "Nobody's dying, okay?"

I frowned as I pushed hair behind her ear. "Alright, baby."

She got the message. Even if she didn't want to admit that there was a chance I'd die in the morning, there was. I didn't want to. But killing that piece of shit and getting my son home was worth the risk.

As long as my kids knew I loved them. As long as they knew I'd fight for them, I'd kill for them, and I'd die for them. I wanted to live for them. I wanted to, but if I didn't, all I wanted them to know was that I'd have been the best father that I could be if I had the chance.

CHAPTER EIGHTY-SIX

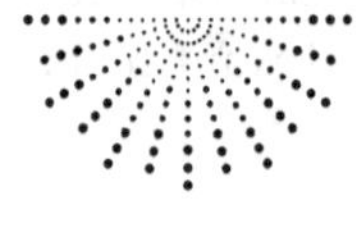

LAILA

"Babe." Jeremy shook my shoulder to wake me. "Laila, that's her."

"What?" I shot forward.

"That's Amy, right?" he asked. "Right there, getting out of the Beemer at the pump."

I squinted as my eyes adjusted. My racing heart sunk.

Her long, glistening copper hair flew in the wind. She wore a pair of dark washed denim pants over short heels with a pale blue blouse beneath a classy black blazer. Both of the times I'd seen Amy, she looked like she was going in for a job interview. Business casual.

It sickened me. Not only was she free of scars but she got to see color. She got to *wear* color. She got to curl her hair after washing it with some high-end shampoo and conditioner. She got soap, and coffee, and salads, and whatever the hell else she wanted. She got normalcy while everyone else got slashes on the back, scars on every extremity, and drug dependencies.

I swallowed hard, watching her long legs strut toward the small store. "That's her."

"Think we should take care of the guard and driver first?" Brody rubbed his eyes. "I could teleport in and take care of both of them real quick."

"No," Jeremy said. "She's not going to tell us where they are and it's not like we can get in her head. She'll immediately send Nastya a message."

"No, we follow them." I pulled the small chip from my bra and set it on my tongue. I quickly swallowed it down with a gulp of water. "Even if it's into a trap."

Jeremy pulled his phone from his pocket. "I'm letting Leah know we're about to be on the move. Watch her."

I nodded.

I carefully examined Amy's casual pour of coffee into the paper cup. My skin got warmer before I clenched my shaking hand to a fist. She walked to the counter and raised her sparkling sunglasses to the top of her head.

Jeremy started the car and shifted it into drive. He held his foot on the break and took my hand. He slid his fingers through mine.

Then she walked through the double glass doors and made her way through the parking lot.

I pulled my seat belt around my body and clicked it into place. She stepped into the passenger side. My fingers tightened around his as we watched her door shut.

The brake lights came on, and parking lights went off. They shifted into drive and started out of the parking lot from the same direction they pulled in from.

"What're you doing? Go." I gestured toward them pulling out of the lot.

"We need to keep a distance," Brody said from the back seat.

"If we're right behind them, they'll see us. We pull out after them." Jeremy slowly backed out of the space. "We don't put the pedal to the metal unless we have to. We stay back and we watch. We aren't going to lose a white BMW on these roads in the early morning. They stick out like a sore thumb."

"Just don't let your mental guards down for a second. That's all she needs. One second in your head and you're powerless."

"Yeah, well." Brody loaded his gun in the back seat. "I'm counting on being powerless."

Jeremy's fingers gripped mine a little tighter before he moved his thumb against the back of my hand. He kept his eyes on the car a few hundred yards in the distance as he said, "Don't let go, alright?"

I swallowed the lump in my throat.

"I'm putting the car in cruise." Jeremy glanced at Brody in the rearview mirror. "If we have to teleport out, you take the wheel. Even if they ditch the car, we might be able to get something from its GPS system so try to keep it from going up in flames. But if you can't avoid it, teleport out. Go back to camp and we'll send you signal as soon as we can."

"You think we're going to have to teleport out?" I asked.

He licked his lips. "If she even suspects she's being followed, she's going to try to get in our heads. When she realizes she can't, she's going to realize who we are and what we're doing. When she does, I don't know if she'll tuck and roll or if we'll be surrounded by armed vehicles in seconds. Either way. If possible, we want that car. It's new. It's sending a signal somewhere. If we can get a map of where it's been, even if we can't get anything out of Amy—"

"We have a map of where she's been."

My husband always was the brains.

***

"No way this bitch goes this far to get coffee and a pack of smokes every morning," Brody murmured in the back seat. We stayed a reasonable distance behind the white BMW with a few cars between us on the small highway.

Jeremy pushed up his aviators. "Yeah, this is sketchy."

I glanced out the window toward the left. But a glowing green sign there looked familiar. I wasn't sure where from, but it was definitely familiar. "Haven't we seen this store before?"

A slow gasp collapsed into Brody's lips as he looked out the window on the right. "That's our hotel."

"Shit." Jeremy smacked the steering wheel, pain vibrating up my wrist. "We just made a giant circle. Motherfucker. She knows."

"They went past our hotel for a reason," Brody said. "They know we're here. They know where everyone is. They're warning us."

"Call Leah." I sat up in my seat. "Tell her to get everyone out. Find somewhere else to go under a new alias and send us the rendezvous."

"Got it." He pulled his phone out.

"Where are they going?" Jeremy murmured as we made a right hand turn behind them.

Brody muttered into the phone in the back seat as we got directly behind them with only a few empty car lengths between us. Just as we turned onto a tree canopied, dirt road, Amy swiveled her head toward us. A smile pulled at her lips.

The other head in the backseat swiveled our way.

Chris.

His empty eye sockets stared back at us. A devilish smile I didn't realize he was capable of edged up his lips.

"Jesus Christ." Jeremy jumped, color draining from his face.

Suddenly the white BMW began to shake back and forth. Amy's head rolled back in a laugh. "Get ready to take the wheel," Jeremy called to Brody.

He shoved his phone into his pocket.

"What's happening?" I watched the car tremble.

"That's what happens when someone who doesn't know what they're doing tries to teleport out of a moving vehicle."

It wasn't Chris behind that vacant stare.

That devilish, maniacal grin was the same I'd seen on the zombie's in the basement.

Peterson.

Jeremy squeezed my hand. "As soon as they're out, we're jumping on their trail. Be ready, baby. We're moving fast, there's gonna be an impact when we land."

The car ahead shifted from one side to the other. Then Amy and Chris disappeared.

Then we spun through the quantum levels of our existence.

CHAPTER EIGHTY-SEVEN

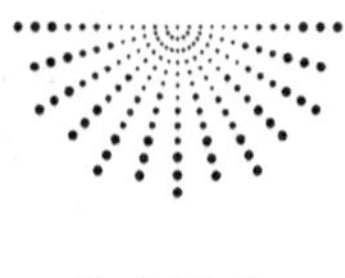

LAILA

Icy water ripped around my skin. I struggled not to gasp. Water still went up my nose, but hopefully not enough to drown.

I guess Peterson knew that much. If you're going to come from a sudden stop after moving fifty miles an hour on the highway, land in something that will absorb the impact.

I nearly lost Jeremy's hand when the water smacked my skin like a belly flop on every inch of my physique. He pulled me into him, paddling toward the sunlight. I joined in kicking my feet against the cool liquid until we met the warm air with deep gasps.

"Are you okay?" Jeremy asked, moving his arms through the water to keep us afloat.

I coughed up salty water that ran down my throat, surveying the cool blue ocean around us. "Where'd they go?"

He wiped his eyes, looked around, took my hand, and teleported again. We landed on hot sand. Jeremy grabbed my wrist to keep me from falling. I blinked around in the bright sun. A sudden sweat appeared over my body.

No beach in sight—a hot, empty desert.

As my gaze adjusted, I saw Amy trying to pull Chris from the ground. He coughed on all fours.

I dropped Jeremy's hand and teleported above her. My hands wanted to ignite. I had to fight the urge to burn her alive. Instead, I grabbed a fist full of her hair and ripped her off of Chris. Whether it was him in there or not, he was struggling air into his lungs.

As I pulled her back, her hands started to fly. And she fought like a bitch. Open hands pawing at me like a cat with a ball of yarn. I closed my hand to a fist, pulled it back, and thrust it downward into her face. Specks of blood splattered from her lips as she stumbled backward.

I don't know how many times I hit her. I just kept punching. Once she was on the ground, I started kicking and kept kicking. My wrists were aching as they began to swell, and my knuckles were bleeding but I just couldn't stop.

It all came back. Every time I was powerless inside that prison was because of her. When I had a bullet wound healing in my thigh and that motherfucker spread my shackled legs and forced himself inside of me, that cunt couldn't have been more than a room away. She heard me begging him to stop and she *helped him.*

She was on the other side of that glass every time they slashed that whip against my back. She was there when he sliced my arms, and wrists, and throat, and she listened to me scream.

She stole my fucking baby. She got to hold him. She got to kiss his doughy cheeks and cuddle him after his first shots. She got to comb his hair and smell his soft, velvety head. She got to hold his hands as he took his first steps. She got to watch him grow from an infant to a toddler. She got every moment with my son that I was meant to.

That wasn't the kind of woman I felt guilty for beating to a pulp.

Honestly, I have no idea what Jeremy was doing while I continued to thrust my fists into Amy's sobbing body. All I saw was red. I heard her begging me to stop but I didn't. Not until I felt a tase knock me off my feet.

"I expected more from you, Laila," Chris said.

My body fell to the ground in electrified contortions. I writhed on the ground in paralysis.

He walked toward Amy and helped her to her feet. The expression on his face as he dusted sand off of Amy's back made it abundantly clear that it wasn't my brother-in-law in there. "I thought you'd have found them by now."

He smiled down at me with a shake of his head.

Then they disappeared.

The electrocution stopped suddenly. I gasped and struggled to my feet. Jeremy staggered to his feet, teleported to me, and took my hand in his. "Are you okay?"

I nodded, and we teleported again.

We landed in wet, dew covered grass at the crest of a hillside. Gray clouds hung above us dropping angry beads of water to our hot skin. I heard violent waves crashing behind me.

At the top of the hill, Amy stood confidently beside Chris. Behind them loomed the infamous witch.

Nastya's long black hair was swept into an elegant bun. She wore a red blouse over a pair of neat black slacks with a pair of modest dress shoes. She looked softer than I'd anticipated from the photos.

Once I saw her, I realized what this game of tag was leading us to. Not Micah. Her.

She was their arsenal.

And I was ours.

"Where is he?!" I screamed, starting toward them.

Chris smiled. Nastya began murmuring in Latin. My stomach clenched and a groan left my lips. I brought a flame to my hand and began to thrust it toward Nastya. But then she raised hers. The pain in my stomach spread to my extremities and I began to lose my balance. Then my legs melted to a gelatin like substance. I dropped to my knees.

"Somewhere safe," Peterson said from Chris's lips. "We can take you to him, if you'd like."

"Fuck you." I made out, struggling to pull air into my lungs.

Jeremy collapsed to the ground beside me.

"You aren't ready for him, Laila. If Nastya can still incapacitate you, then you aren't ready. I wish you were, but you aren't. Trust that all things are going just as they need to. I assure you that this is the best course of action available."

"Killing him?!" I screamed, blood pouring from my lips and I struggled to keep myself on all fours. "Killing my son is the best course of action?"

"All great things come at a price. You know that as much as I do," he said.

No, fuck that. I'd paid plenty. It was time I got back what was always mine.

Using every ounce of energy I had in me, I staggered to my feet. I spun the wind toward them. Then a stabbing pain radiated through my abdomen. I fell back to the damp grass. I clenched my stomach, and his voice drew a tad closer.

"See, that's where you're getting it all wrong. You got it right the first time. You were willing to make the greatest sacrifice imaginable. Your own child for a cause greater than yourself. But now, when his sacrifice is truly needed, you couldn't possibly allow it. I suppose that could be my doing. Having to suffer his loss once, the thought of doing it again is probably unbearable. I thought that it would prepare you, but I think there was a fault to that logic."

That wasn't true. I hadn't sacrificed my son. I believed I could end them. I was egotistical, but I would never willingly sacrifice my baby. Never. That's not what I was doing that day.

He sighed as I stumbled to my feet. "You will be reunited with your son, Laila. But now isn't the time. Back down."

"Fuck you." I began taking pain filled steps toward them.

He laughed—loudly, and obnoxiously. "Haven't you realized yet? I know this story better than you do." I tried to summon fire to my fingertips but instead, only sparks left my skin. "Back down, Laila. Our epic battle's still in the distance."

"Where is he?" Warm lines of crimson clouded my vision and began to race from my eyes. "Where is my son?!"

"Aren't you worried about the one inside of you?" He gestured toward my stomach. "Wouldn't want to lose another one, would we?"

I lunged toward him. Then I fell face first.

He kneeled beside me. "I don't need this one. You do. Leave before she's wiped from history."

If he hadn't been wearing Chris's face like a costume, I'd have ripped his throat out with my bare hand. But I couldn't. I could barely bring air into my lungs.

She was killing me. She was killing Jeremy. She was killing Milly.

"Just give me my son." I coughed up blood. I looked up to him. "Please. Please just give me my son."

He reached out to wipe blood from my cheek. Still, I don't know how he saw me to know where I was. But somehow, he did. Somehow, it was like he was staring straight into my soul with those empty eyes.

"I won't give him to you, but I promise that one day, you will have him back. And you will have him until eternity ends," he murmured. "But for now, think of the others as a peace offering. Whether you see it yet or not, we're on the same side here. I know you think I'm your enemy. In many ways, in this time, I suppose that I am. But in the end, I'm fighting for *you*. And for your son. I know you won't see it until my part of the story comes to a close, but that will be when your story truly begins."

"I don't want a story, Peterson." I made out between coughs. "I just want my baby. I want to be his mom."

His lips curved down at the ends. "You'll always be his mother, Laila. He knows who you are. He smiles at your pictures and calls you Mommy." I furrowed my brows in confusion. A smile pulled at his lips. "He loves you. He loves us all. He loves everyone and everything."

"Take me to them." Jeremy staggered to his feet. I turned to look at him as he blinked through the blood pouring from his blue eyes. He struggled to stand, but his hand holding the gun toward them was steady.

Peterson laughed. He stood back up. "Oh, come on, Jeremy. We both know you aren't going to shoot your brother."

Wake up, Chris. I projected into his mind as the pain surged around my body. *You can make this stop. Wake up and come home.*

Peterson laughed. He turned his empty gaze to me then back to Jeremy. "Sorry, Chris isn't available at the moment. Can I take a message?"

I saw Jeremy's teeth grit to a hard line through his grimace. He looked between me, Chris, Amy and Nastya. He was clenching his stomach, but he wasn't dropping that gun.

"I won't kill my brother," Jeremy said. "But I'll kill your army."

He quickly shifted the gun toward the women. I didn't see him pull the trigger, but I saw that bullet in slow motion. It was headed straight for Nastya. Then, Amy jumped in front of her.

I watched as that piece of metal sliced into her chest. I watched the look of awe on her face as the blood began to pour. I watched Nastya's chanting stop. I heard her gasp.

Then I watched Peterson teleport beside her just before she fell to the ground. Her cool blue eyes held mine as she fell into his chest. Nastya cried out. The pain in my body stopped and I rushed to my feet.

Jeremy raised the gun back to eye level. He had a perfect shot at her. Just as he was about to pull the trigger, she began chanting again and the gun flung from his hand to hers.

I tried to teleport to Jeremy, but it wouldn't work. My body didn't even vibrate. He must have been trying to do the same with no success.

I didn't expect her to be able to do anything close to that. I didn't expect a pain so crippling to exist. It was worse than the beatings or childbirth combined. I didn't expect her to be able to have the ability to physically disable me the way that she could. But somehow, at least at that proximity, she was capable of a hell of a lot more than I could have imagined.

Jeremy darted across the grass to me and took my hand.

474

She continued chanting, drawing closer, and the pain all over my body picked back up. He squeezed my hand. The rain fell down harder and lightning cracked across the gray sky, hues of bright blue vibrating through it like a firework.

Then bullets began to fly.

I don't know how the bitch missed; we were wide open targets. We stood a few meters from the edge of a cliff on a grassy hilltop with almost no vegetation. There was no reason she should have missed.

But the bullets aren't what made us start running.

Pale blue smoke began to fly from Nastya's fingertips, eye sockets, lips, and nostrils. Her expression was furious as the smoke billowed toward us. Through the writhing pain, I managed to bring a small flame to my hand. I sent it toward her in a steady stream, but the blue smoke acted like water. As soon as the two made contact, my fire was extinguished.

Chris pulled his and Amy's shirts over their mouths as she began clearing the distance between us. The smoke was faster, licking my outstretched arm and hand. I wafted it away. As it touched my skin, it began to burn and boil as if splashed with battery acid.

I took off running with Jeremy's hand locked in mine.

"*Go,*" I said as we ran. He glanced at her over his shoulder and then to me. The only place to go was the edge of that cliff.

I was trying to teleport, but I could barely bring a flame to my hand. Jeremy must have been trying too.

"Where?!" he yelled as I kept my gaze on the precipice in the distance.

I didn't have time to think. I didn't have the resources to stop Nastya. I didn't have the opportunity to end any of it.

All I knew was that proximities were what created the barriers that prevent us from using our powers. If we jumped, they'd be back before we hit the bottom.

Or so I hoped.

Jumping is the only way we make it out, I said into his mind. *We have to take the leap.*

He squeezed my hand tighter, still sprinting the ledge.

Don't let go, his voice whispered into my mind.

Then, we jumped.

CHAPTER EIGHTY-EIGHT

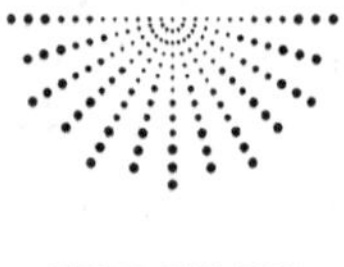

JEREMY

Falling from that cliff side was the worst moment of my life. All I saw below me was a giant protruding rock. It was tall and angled to a near point.

It reminded me of a church steeple in town we used to walk past as kids. I remember having this odd, meandering thought as a child that if someone were skydiving and they went off course a little, landing on that at just the right angle could turn them into a human shish kabob.

As I plummeted toward it desperately attempting to teleport, that's all I kept thinking. Laila and I were about to be human shish kabobs. Although, I guessed it was more exciting to go as a human shish kabob than a needle in your vein on the toilet.

But as we drew closer, a swift wind rushed beside us and flung us to the water a few dozen feet away.

As we hit the waves, the impact rushed between our hands. And I let go.

The tides pulled me down. I tried to swim against them but just as I thought I'd moved through one, another came and ripped me under. The salt stung my eyes as I opened them, but I could barely see already from the blood. I didn't see her.

Fuck, I didn't see her.

Then I felt a heavy smack against the back of my head. Or hers. No, I felt it against the back of *her* head. But it left me disoriented for a second. Just long enough to send a deep gasp into my closed nostrils.

Fuck.

Bright light blinded my vision. "Don't let her fuck this up," a familiar voice said. I coughed, struggling to see through the water and debris.

"You have to make sure she keeps Milly safe," he continued as I gasped for air. "She has to be born. She has to live. Laila can't lose her. *You* can't lose her. Peterson doesn't want her because he can't use her like he can use Micah. Milly has a part to play in this too, it's just different than his. You have to keep her safe. You have to make sure she's born."

I crab crawled backward.

His hair was short. The top half was pulled into a wet, top-knot, trendy man bun. The sides were no more than an inch long. Water dripped down his forehead in long beads past his blue eyes down to his short, well maintained beard.

But every other detail was identical. The jaw, the complexion, the eyes, the nose. Every detail.

He was me. But he wasn't me.

"Who are you?"

"You know who I am." His gaze locked with mine and he studied me hard.

His expression reminded me of the few memories I had of my dad. Parental, but compassionate. The one time when I ran into the street and almost got hit by a car while we were walking into the supermarket. That terrified, loving gaze as he gripped my shoulders and assertively told me to never do it again.

"But that doesn't matter. What matters is that you understand how important your daughter is. Milly and Micah are the biggest pieces to this puzzle. But Laila's reckless. She will lose this baby if she isn't careful. She won't be able to live with herself if she does and Micah will die because she won't be there to save him. You will kill yourself afterward and *the cycle will repeat*. You'll be born again, and you will find each other in the next life and you'll have to start over. The cycle repeats and repeats and the only way you break it is if you listen to me and keep your daughter safe."

I struggled to find words. "I don't understand."

"I've already said too much. Just keep our girls safe. Micah's okay for now. Just keep them safe, Jeremy."

Then black.

My eyes flung open.

I bolted forward gasping for air on the cool, wet sand.

My heart hammered against my chest. I looked around the empty, rocky beach. A sharp, ninety-degree incline to a grassy plateau rested behind me. I struggled to bring myself back to reality from my dream.

"Laila." I staggered to my feet. I wiped water from my eyes, looking around. Rain poured down around me as it had minutes before, but she was nowhere in sight.

"Fuck." I focused on her.

I felt her. But then, I felt pain.

Healing.

Someone was healing her. Leah must have tracked us through those chips and sent someone to heal her.

She was close. I started running, then teleporting every ten feet or so, and calling her name.

I made it about a hundred feet in ten seconds until I rounded a large cliff side. As I made it around the bend, I saw them in the distance.

At first, I thought it was Leah and Adam. They were leaning over her body. White light radiated around them. I only saw the back of them. They wore wet black hoodies tucked over their heads and dark blue jeans with soggy black converse. Typical attire for everyone in our family, I guess.

Relief washed over me as I drew closer and knew she was alive.

"How'd you guys get here so quick?" I called, jogging toward them.

Then they disappeared.

CHAPTER EIGHTY-NINE

JEREMY

The forms vanished. Why would they leave? I was here now, but... why did they vanish? Maybe they were needed back at the rendezvous.

Laila shot forward crying out. She clutched her stomach with one hand and her head with the other. My heart raced and I teleported beside her.

Her pain filled cry turned to a tragic sob. She looked down.

A growing splotch of crimson spread over the crotch of her gray pants.

The shaking hand in her hair moved to cover her mouth. "No. No, no no."

"Come here." I put an arm behind her shoulders and the other beneath her knees. My heart hammered against my chest. I watched her shaking hands in slow motion while I lifted her to my torso.

We spun through the air until we landed at our underground hospital back home.

"I need help," I called as we landed. I spun around toward the check-in center. A nurse sprinted from her desk and began wheeling a gurney toward us. "She's pregnant." I teleported to the gurney. Laila tried to stifle her cries as I sat her down on the bed and looked up to the nurse. "She's fourteen weeks pregnant."

"What hurts, sweetie?" the nurse asked, wheeling the gurney down the hallway.

"It's like labor pains." Tears raced down her cheeks. "It's not as bad but it hurts. It really hurts."

"Someone was healing her when I got to her." I gripped Laila's hand, sprinting down the hall as more nurses approached us. They spoke with the one wheeling the gurney before turning to me.

"We're going to do an exam and an ultrasound," she began. "It's probably best if you wait here."

"No." Laila shook her head. "No, I want him to stay."

"I'll go get Kai." I squeezed her hand as we rushed down the hallway. My gaze shifted from the path in front of me back down to her. I touched her cheek. "I'll be right back. Just take care of that baby 'til I get back, alright?"

Her teeth began to chatter. Water overflowed her eyes.

I forced a smile as a nurse clicked the elevator button. "You're gonna be okay. Just hang on for a few minutes."

She pressed her trembling lips together and nodded.

"Can I borrow someone's phone?" My gaze shifted between the nurses.

One beside me pulled a phone from his pocket. He opened the locked screen, went to the call app, and handed it to me. I hurriedly typed Leah's number and held the phone to my ear.

After two rings, Leah answered. "Shit, hello?"

"Where'd you go?" I said quickly.

"What?" she asked. "Jeremy?"

"Yeah. It doesn't matter, where are you? One of you needs to heal Laila," I said quickly.

"We're at that store across the street from the hotel," Leah said. "Nothing's happened, just meet Kai at the hotel. He's going now. We got the GPS from the car. It's password encrypted but I can get into it. Kai's a better healer anyway."

"Got it." I glanced down at Laila's shaking hand in mine as the elevator door opened. The peeling flesh on her hand was healed but it looked like the blood on her pants was growing. "Tell him to run. And send Hannah."

I ended the call and handed the nurse his phone. I pulled a smile on, quickly kissed Laila's knuckles, and let them go. "I'll be right back."

She pressed her trembling lips together.

I landed in the shit hole hotel room just as Kai opened the door panting with Hannah at his tail. I rushed toward them, pushed the door shut, grasped their shoulders, and landed back in the elevator.

It shifted downward as our weight suddenly landed. "Jesus Christ," one of the nurses said, grasping her chest.

Kai braced himself on the wall. I grasped the gurney's frame. Hannah grabbed the other side. Laila looked up at me with wide eyes and slow, uneven breaths.

"I told you I'd be right back." I smiled and touched her cheek.

Once Kai regained his balance, he rushed his hand over Laila. Her eyes closed.

Her thoughts opened to Hannah and pulled me along.

Is the baby alive?

Hannah nodded, looking at me.

A sigh of relief left my lips. Laila did the same, despite the pain of being healed. She nodded through the pain and Kai went on healing.

I squeezed her shaking hand and lowered my lips to her forehead.

I couldn't let her lose that baby too. I couldn't. I couldn't let it happen again.

As the elevator door opened, Kai continued to heal her while the nurses wheeled her out into the hallway. I released her hand as they pulled her through the doorway that was too small for me to stay beside her. My feet pedaled close beside them, next to Hannah, while the nurses wheeled her down another hallway.

"Do you have your phone?" I asked Hannah. She pulled it from her back pocket and passed it to me. "Can I borrow it 'til things settle down? Me and Laila's are either broke or lost."

As they wheeled Laila into a room on the left, she said, "Just buy me a new one if you break it."

"Deal." I followed them into the pink room.

Kai continued healing her. I joined Laila on the right side of the bed. The nurses waited for Kai to finish. I took her hand. She opened her closed, grimacing eyes, and met my gaze with tears pearling down her cheeks.

I raised my hand to wipe her tears and forced a smile. The lump forming in my throat was getting thicker by the second.

"It's okay." I lowered myself to her eye level. My fingers pushed messy wet hair behind her ears. I kissed her forehead. "It's okay, she's okay."

CHAPTER NINETY

JEREMY

"It looks like the healers took care of whatever caused all that blood," the doctor said, moving the scope around on Laila's stomach.

My gaze stayed locked with the image of the tiny baby on the black screen. I took slow, short breaths as I squeezed her hand.

She looked like a baby. Not a little peanut or tadpole. Her legs were tiny in proportion to the top half of her body and her big head, but she was very much a baby. A tiny, beautiful little baby. *My* tiny, beautiful little baby.

My daughter. My baby girl. My Milly.

"The heart rate's a little high. Probably from all of that excitement, but everything looks great." She moved the mouse and clicked things on the screen. "You're measuring between fifteen and sixteen weeks from what I see here but everything looks perfect. Kidney development looks to be coming along smoothly. Organ function seems to be developing normally, I like the size of baby's head. Still, I'd like to keep you for an hour or two until we get your bloodwork back."

"Sure," Laila murmured, staring up at the screen.

"Why don't you go get Mom some clean clothes, Dad?" The doctor smiled as she turned her gaze to me.

I blinked hard for a second.

Dad. I was going to be a dad.

That was the first time anyone ever referred to me as 'Dad.'

And dads do things that don't make sense to keep their family safe. We make mistakes. We fail. But we try. And that's what I had to do. I had to do everything in my power to keep that little girl safe.

"Maybe some for you too." She gave a smile and moved the tool from Laila's stomach back to the machine.

I turned my gaze to Laila. "Yeah. Yeah, sure. Do you need anything else?"

"Could you grab me a pair of tennis shoes? These one's are kinda ruined."

I cleared my throat. "Alright, I'll be back."

She forced a smile. I leaned down and kissed her forehead. As I went to pull away, she grabbed either side of my face and yanked my lips to hers. Her mouth molded into mine for a moment. I raised my hand to her cheek. After a few seconds, she pulled back and met my gaze.

"I'm going to shower while we wait to hear back about my blood work. You should probably get one real quick too. Hannah's here, I'll be fine for a little bit." She rubbed her thumb against the back of mine.

"Yeah, probably not a bad idea. Just give me a minute, okay?"

The doctor started to the door. I held her gaze. I didn't want to leave her. I knew Hannah was right outside, but I didn't want to leave her.

I lowered myself to the bed beside her and twined my fingers with hers. She looked down at them and then back up to me. Her eyes filled with tears and her teeth began to tighten.

"Come here." I leaned forward and wrapped my arms around her shoulders. She locked hers around my upper back. Her head nuzzled into the nape of my neck as I felt warm water fall to my damp shirt.

I squeezed harder, looking at the printed ultrasound on the table beside her. My hands trembled as I wrapped them tighter around her damp shirt. I closed my eyes and saw that blood pouring from her orifices. I watched her clutch her stomach when I fell to the ground beside her. Then the blood on her pants.

I opened them and looked back at that ultrasound. Milly. My little girl.

And my wife.

I had to keep them safe. I couldn't let this happen again. I couldn't lose them. I couldn't.

CHAPTER NINETY-ONE

LAILA

I held my hand over my trembling lips, staring at myself in the mirror. My teeth gritted together. I moved my hand from my mouth to my little belly.

Most of the blood Nastya forced from my orifices had been washed away in the waves of the ocean. But it still crusted in the corners of my eyes. Pieces of seaweed and small branches stuck out of my partially dried, damp ponytail.

Moisture began to fog the mirror. I stared at the scars. I covered them up with those flowers and butterflies like it took them away. But covering something didn't change what was underneath. Maybe it drew more attention to what I was trying to hide.

I looked at the one between my ribs. That one may have hurt the worst. The one at the base of my throat was pretty rough too. But it wasn't as painful as the others. It was more of the idea. Watching that scalpel heading to my throat was terrifying.

The only defense I had was lying still as he cut. If I squirmed, the scalpel would slice too deep. I'd bleed out before he had time to save me.

The one at my ribs was like a horror movie. While my neck was still oozing, he ran that scalpel down my chest like a seductive BDSM porn. Then it carefully sliced an inch or two into my skin. I remember shaking my torso against the metal and it shifting inside of me, creating an even more agonizing stab.

484

Those tattoos didn't change the scars. They didn't change that I was still a victim to that man's lunacy. They didn't change that he was still hurting me.

I pressed my trembling lips together. I turned away from the mirror and took a few steps into the small hospital shower. The warm water began rushing against my skin.

And the tears erupted from my eyes.

I gripped the wall and lowered myself to the ground. My hand moved to the heart that raced in my chest. Heavy cries began to leave my lips.

I lost him again.

If I could have grabbed Chris instead of beating the shit out of Amy, maybe we could have forced Peterson from his head. Maybe he could have led us to Micah.

I almost lost Milly too.

My heart hammered against my ribs and my teeth chattered. My hands shook. I could barely get an even breath into my lungs.

I hadn't had a panic attack in a long time, but I couldn't breathe through it after the day I'd had. I couldn't even stand.

My gaze met the scar on my thigh. I pulled my knees to my chest so I didn't have to look at the personification of my failure.

Chris was there. He was *right* there. His skin touched mine, and I lost him too.

He told me they were using him. That's what he meant. They didn't need to synthesize his abilities. They could throw his body on like a costume.

He points to your pictures and calls you Mommy.

The words repeating inside my mind sent heaving sobs from my lips.

CHAPTER NINETY-TWO

JEREMY

JEREMY

I sat in my boxers on the bed with my hand propped beneath my face. My fingertips rubbed my eyes. I breathed out slow, uneven sighs.

We weren't getting Micah back. Not today. We lost. If that bullet would have gone through Nastya's head the way it was supposed to, I'd be wrapping my arms around my brother's chest at that moment. Maybe my son's a moment later.

But we lost. We weren't strong enough.

In twenty-four to twenty-five weeks, I'd be holding my daughter in my arms. But she had to make it those twenty-four more weeks. Laila had to stay away from flesh melting smoke and cliff edges.

Hannah's phone buzzed on the bed beside me. Leah's name across the screen. I answered it and clicked the speaker button.

"Please tell me you have good news." I stood.

"For the first time in forever, I do." Leah laughed. "I do. I have the compound."

"You found it?" I rushed into a pair of clean pants.

"I think so," she continued. "I guess it could be a trap, but we definitely got the compound. Heavily guarded, two points of entry. Only guards and a couple cars have been in and out in the past seventy-two hours. I got into their cameras."

"Yeah, that's too easy. It's got to be a trap." I pulled on a t-shirt. "But maybe not. He said something. Something to Laila. 'Think of the others as a peace offering,' I think."

"Who? Peterson? You saw him and you didn't kill him?" Leah blurted.

"I couldn't or I would have," I muttered. "Technically, I didn't see Peterson. I saw Chris. But Peterson was inside of him."

"Son of a bitch," Leah murmured.

"Yeah. I have a lot to tell you. But I don't think Chris and Micah are going to be there." I raised my hand to my head. I summed it up quickly, ending with, "Laila was knocked out cold in the water, no way in hell she just washed up on the shore. Hell, I don't know how I did either. But someone was healing her when I got to her. I thought it was you and Adam or you and Brody but then they disappeared."

"Someone was helping you?" Leah asked.

"Someone saved our asses." I gathered some things into a bag for Laila.

"What did they look like?" she asked quickly.

"I don't know. I only saw them from behind. It looked like a girl and a guy judging by the size. They were wearing hoodies and converse. The girl was healing her, I saw the light. That's why I thought it was you guys. But when I said something, they disappeared."

"That's fucking weird," Leah murmured.

"Yeah, tell me about it." I zipped her bag shut. "Laila's hand was healed when I got to her, but she was losing the baby. That's why I came to get Kai. Milly's okay though. They're keeping Laila for a little while to run some tests."

"She'll be out in a few hours, right?" Leah asked. "We'll need her to get the others out."

Uh. No.

I gritted my teeth together. "I don't think she can handle anything else today, Leah. She almost lost another kid."

"Yeah, but—"

"But nothing. She has to recoup. This isn't about Micah; this is about the other survivors. We can handle it. She's sitting this out."

Leah laughed. "Does *she* know she's sitting this out?"

"I'll meet you at the hotel in an hour. Start a call list, get as many people together as you can and give them a gun." I quickly ended the call.

She was right. Laila would want to be there. But I couldn't. I couldn't let her live through what we just lived through an hour before. I had to keep them safe.

I knew she was going to hate me for what I was about to do. But I had to do it. I had to keep them safe.

———

"Helena," I yelled, walking through her front door. "Helena, where are you?"

"I'm with a customer, just a minute!" she called.

I huffed and walked past the formal dining room to her office. I pushed open the door. "I don't have time to wait."

She sat across from a middle-aged man with tarot cards laid out in front of her. "I'm with a customer, Jeremy. Be seated in the waiting area and I'll be with you shortly—"

"I've given you almost fifteen thousand dollars in the last six months. No, I'm not waiting for shit. This is more important than some stupid tarot. No offense." I gestured to the man.

"Boy, I don't know who the hell you think you're talking to—"

"They didn't work." I gritted my teeth together. "We almost died. Laila, me, the baby. We all nearly died because you had us banking on Laila."

She turned to her customer. "I'm sorry, Phil. This session's on the house. Please give me a call to reschedule."

He grumbled something under his breath. Then he shoulder-checked me on his way out the door.

"What didn't work?" Helena asked.

"Laila couldn't do much of anything and I damn well couldn't teleport," I said quickly. "Nastya cast something on us. It made us bleed everywhere, made us feel like we were being stabbed all over at once."

"She must have been blocking Laila's powers somehow," she murmured. "If Laila's wouldn't work, neither would yours.

"Do you know how to do that?" I asked. "Block Laila's powers?"

She furrowed her brows and cocked her head to the side.

"Just for a few hours. Maybe a day," I said.

"What are you talking about, kid?" Helena asked. "You want me to take away your best defense?"

"No," I said. "No. I just need to keep her back home until we get the other survivors out. Micah isn't there. Chris isn't there. I still want to get them out, and I'll die to get it done, but I won't let her. I can't save Micah, but she can. I know she can. But not if she dies first. Not if she loses this baby because I don't think she'll have a reason to live if she does. And getting him home can't be done without her. But it can be done without me. I don't want to die, and I don't think I will, but we both will if she loses this baby. I have to keep her safe, Helena."

She was quiet for a moment. "It's her name on the checks I get, you know."

"And if she dies, you'll lose a lot of income." I desperately looked between her eyes. "Please. Give me something here."

"She's going to hate you." Helena ran her hand against her mouth. "She's going to hate us both."

"She can hate me all she wants as long as she's alive," I said.

She was quiet for a moment. "I can't block her powers. Binding Laila is damn near impossible. Nastya did that, you said?"

"Kind of," I said. "Not for long. The whole thing happened in less than two minutes. But yeah, she had her. She could still do some things. I felt the air gust like she was trying to use it. She brought a small flame to her hand."

"See, even Nastya can't control her," Helena murmured. "But I could trap her."

"What do you mean?"

"I could create an area that she couldn't teleport out of. Block off her Angel powers. It won't stick long. Twelve hours tops. Her energy will devour mine. But it'll buy you some time." She paused, eyes growing concerned. "Are you sure you want to do this?"

"No." I shook my head. "If I don't die getting the others out, she'll kill me when I get back."

Helena let out a slow sigh.

"But I have to keep them safe. If she hates me for it, then she hates me for it," I murmured. "As long as at least one of my kids are safe."

"This is very anti-feminist of me, you know," Helena began. "Taking away her choice and everything."

"She doesn't want to lose this baby," I said. "She's traumatized. She's hormonal. She isn't thinking straight."

"I don't think we are either."

"No, probably not."

CHAPTER NINETY-THREE

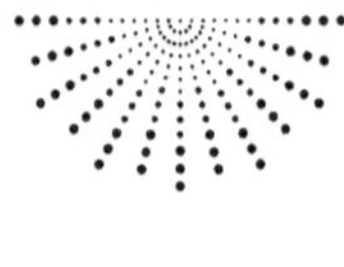

LAILA

"Th he babe's all right, ye said?" Kai asked.

I stared down at the ultrasound in my hands. I nodded, running my finger along the image of her head. "Yeah. Yeah, she's okay."

"Good," Kai said. "Is she movin' yet? Kickin' and whatnot?"

"Not yet," I murmured. "It wasn't until around eighteen weeks with Micah."

"How 'bout you? How're ye doing?"

Shitty. I was doing really fucking shitty. "I've seen better days."

"What happened back there?"

After a few calming breaths, I explained. Once I was finished, he said, "Well, at least ye're all right now."

"Right."

All right. I was not all right. I was all but losing my damn mind.

I needed to get up. I needed to clean something, or eat something, or kill something. My heart was still thumping in my brain. My hands still trembled. My stomach was spinning.

Jeremy made it through the doorway with my overnight bag. "Hey."

"Hey." I started to my feet and summoned a smile.

Kai stood. "I ought to get back out there with Hannah."

"Sure." I held the hospital gown closed behind me. "Thanks for healing me."

"Don't mention it." He smiled over his shoulder. I smiled back. He patted Jeremy's and continued through the doorway.

Jeremy shut the door and headed toward me. He dropped the bag to the bed and wrapped his arms around my waist. His hands on my back pulled my body close to him. I laid my head against his chest. I twisted my arms around him and listened to his racing heart behind my ear.

He kissed my wet hair and held me firmly for a moment. "Are you okay?"

I tightened my arms around him. "Yeah, I'm okay. Are you?"

He shook his head and rested it on top of mine.

I closed my eyes. "It's gonna be okay."

I didn't believe that. But that's what he told me when I was losing Milly on that gurney, and for some reason, it'd helped. Maybe hearing me say it helped him too.

His open hands moved along my back. "I brought you a pair of sweatpants, a t-shirt, and a hoodie. I couldn't find your tennis shoes, so I grabbed your slippers. I figured you'd want to be comfy anyway."

I pulled back. "They're in the shoebox by the front door."

"Oh, sorry, I looked in your closet," he murmured. I turned to the bag on the bed. "Did you get your blood work back?"

"Yeah, everything's good." I pulled the pants from the bag. Stepping into them, I said, "My HCG levels are higher than they were last week. Everything came back normal on the ultrasound. Everything looks good."

"Good." He lowered himself to the bed. I pulled the hospital gown off and threw on the T-shirt. "Do you remember who was healing you?"

"Kai?" I dropped the moccasins to the ground and stepped into them. "Who else?"

"No," he said. "No, right before I got to you on the beach. We lost each other in the waves, remember? Somebody else pulled you out. Somebody pulled me out too. But when I got to you, someone was healing you. I thought it was Leah and Adam or Brody but it wasn't. They teleported when they heard me."

"The last thing I remember is hitting my head. Then you running toward me. If someone was healing me, I wasn't conscious to process it."

His blue eyes were heavy. "Did you have any dreams while you were unconscious?"

"No. No, it was just black."

He gazed at the floor and thought hard for a moment.

"Did you?" I sat beside him.

"It doesn't matter. Leah... She got into the car's GPS system. She found the compound."

My eyes widened. A smile came to my lips. "Really?"

Jeremy gave a slight smile. His fingers twined between mine. "We're going in about half an hour. She got some others together. Celena found some time in her very busy schedule, Wyatt's gonna be there. Liam, I guess. Two others I haven't met. She got into their cameras too, so we have inside eyes."

"Well, let's go get something to eat real quick then. We're going to need our strength. We're both running on little sleep so—"

"Baby," Jeremy whispered. His eyes softened. "Micah and Chris aren't going to be there."

I knew that. I heard what Peterson said. One day, but not today.

"Either way. It's still a lead. We find where they've been keeping him, we learn things about him. Maybe—Maybe he has something laying around that'll point us to where they are. Or, or maybe we can get enough of Micah's blood somewhere to cast a locator spell. Or maybe even to bind one of us to him. Maybe—"

"Laila." He took my face in his hands. "I want you to stay home."

I swatted his hand away. "We've already had this conversation, Jeremy—"

"You almost lost her." His eyes filled with tears. His hand travelled from my face to my stomach. "I understand fighting to find Micah, but we know he isn't there. Peterson's smart. He was stashed somewhere else by the time we made it to the country. I want to help these people too, but Milly almost died a few hours ago."

I put my hand over his. "Everything came back normal, baby. She's okay—"

"Because some stranger saved you," he said with wide, scared eyes. "We weren't ready for that, Laila. We jumped in and we had to jump right back out. Literally."

"But we're okay." I smiled. I squeezed my hand around his. "We're okay."

"You might not be if you do this," he said softly. His hand found my jaw. "That smoke nearly melted your skin to the bone, Lai. And our baby, she's... She's inside of you. It's one thing to gamble her life for her brother, but we can't gamble it for anyone else."

I pushed his hand away. "I'm not *gambling* my daughter's life."

"Please just sit this one out. You almost miscarried—"

"But I didn't—"

"But what did it do to you for those seconds that you thought it did?" he said.

I gritted my teeth together. "I'm not fighting with you about this, Jeremy. If we're not getting something to eat, let's just go. We can go over the plans and figure out our best point of entry."

He looked between my eyes for a moment. His hand lifted to mine. "I don't want to fight either."

I twined my fingers through his.

Of course, I understood his concern. But Nastya and Amy were my concern. Not guards. I could handle a thousand guards. There was no reason for me not to go.

He leaned forward and pressed our lips together. His hand on my lap moved to my neck. He pulled me into him. His lips parted along mine. His thumb brushed against my jaw. I relaxed into his gentle yet firm touch for a moment. Then he pulled back and rested his forehead against mine.

"I'm sorry," he murmured. "I know you're going to hate me for this and I'm so sorry."

I pulled back. "What?"

He nervously licked his lips. Then we spun through the air.

We landed in the basement of the Skoulda home. My gaze shifted around.

A mattress from the guest room was set up in the corner with clean pillows and blankets. A few bags of snacks and drinks laid in bags beside it. One of the TVs from upstairs was set up across from it with Netflix open to our account.

My forehead creased. I looked back up to him. "What is this?"

"You have to sit this one out, baby."

"I'm going, Jeremy. You can't tell me that I'm not."

"I just need you to stay here for a few hours. We can get these people out. But I need you to stay safe while we do. I need you to keep our baby safe."

"Baby, I know that you're scared but—"

"Laila, if you lose this baby, neither of us will forgive ourselves. Milly is just as important as Micah. She's our baby too. If you lose her, I know you won't be able to live with yourself. What it did to you when we lost Micah, I know that you can't live through that again." His eyes were soft as they looked between mine. "If you die, I won't be able to find Micah without you. They'll kill him. And if the two of us aren't dead already, we won't have a reason to live. When we get a chance at Micah, you're our only shot and if you're dead by then..." His voice shook and tears formed in his eyes. "You can bring him home without me. But I can't bring him home without you."

I reached out to wipe his cheek. He dusted them away with his knuckles, leaned forward, and kissed my head. "I know you're scared, but I can handle this, baby." I leaned onto the tips of my toes to press my lips to his. He kissed me again. Then I pulled back. A smile came to my lips. I tried to teleport.

But just as I thought I'd land in the hotel, I landed back where I stood. I tried again only to have the same result.

"Why can't I teleport?" I looked up with furrowed brows.

He gazed down at me gently. "It'll only last for a few hours. We should be back by then."

"You're blocking my powers?" My eyes glowed, creasing at either end.

"No. But they're confined to the basement."

"What?" My heart raced as I looked around the room. "Jeremy, what is this? What are you doing?"

He looked at me with a heartbroken gaze. A tear began to dribble from the corner of his eye. "I don't want to do this, baby. I just—I have to keep you safe."

"You're..." I took a step back and looked around. My hand cupped over my mouth. Tears welled in my eyes. "You're... You can't just lock me in here. You—You can't do this to me. I'm your wife, you can't just—You can't force me to be your prisoner. This isn't—"

"You aren't a prisoner," he said.

I ran past him. My hand reached for the heavy-duty lock at the top of the steps but I was shocked the moment I made contact with it.

My breathing got heavy. I raised a flame to the hinges. But the fire couldn't break through the electrified barrier.

"It's only going to last a few hours." Jeremy came up the steps behind me.

"So I'm your prisoner for the next few hours?!" I screamed. Anxious tears began to bead down my cheeks. He reached out to touch my face, but I sent a gust of wind toward him that left him stumbling backward. "Let me out of here. Right now, Jeremy. Let me out."

He brought himself back to his feet a few steps below me. Tears filled his eyes. He looked between mine. "I can't, Lai. You have to stay here. You have to keep Milly safe—"

"You sound like him." The tears bubbling down my cheeks turned to sobs. "You sound just like him."

"Please don't say that." He took a step toward me. "I'd never hurt you, you know that."

"Then don't do this," I said between chattering teeth. "I—I was trapped inside a box for months. You—You can't trap me in a box too, baby. You can't. Please. Please don't do this. Don't do this to me."

"I don't want to." Tears pearled his cheeks. "I just want you to stay home and keep our baby safe. But I know that you won't and I—I know you're going to hate me for this, and I'm so sorry, baby—"

"No." I took his face in my hands. "No, I understand, baby. I do, I know you love Milly and I know you love me, but I can do this. I'm stronger than you think and I—I won't hate you, just let me out of here. Let me save those people. Let me find our son. We—We can forget this. I don't hate you, I get it, baby, please just..." Violent sobs erupted from me as I held his crying face. "Please don't lock me in here. Please don't do what he did to me. Please just, just take me with you. Please."

Tears overflowed from his eyes. He looked between mine. "If I don't come back, please don't hate me. I did this because I love you."

"Baby—"

He was gone.

I was alone.

Locked behind a cold door with no way out.

I got it.

I understood his perspective.

But man, was I fucking pissed.

CHAPTER NINETY-FOUR

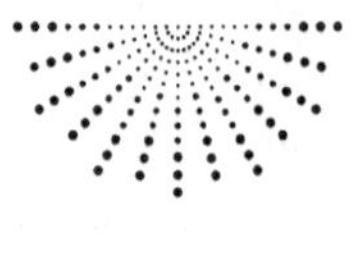

JEREMY

I splashed my red, burning eyes with some water in the bathroom sink. Leah and Brody argued outside the door about which entrance would be better to go in through.

You sound just like him.

That was the worst thing anyone could ever tell me. But to hear the words leave her lips felt like a dagger to the heart.

She was right though. I took away her freedom. I locked her inside my sister's basement.

My intentions were good. But it's true what they say. The path to hell is paved with good intentions.

I started from the bathroom as I dried my hands on my jeans. "We should go in through the back. The entrance is smaller but there's less guards. Smaller is better anyway. We stick close in our large group and pick them off as they come at us."

"Thank you," Leah agreed.

"Where's Lai?" Brody asked.

"Yeah, idn't she coming?" Kai stood from the bed.

"She's back home." I leaned down to tighten my shoelaces. "She's been through a lot today; she needs a breather."

"Really?" Brody asked. "She was pretty adamant about being here."

"Things changed. She almost lost the baby." I stood. "She needs to rest. And Micah and Chris aren't here."

I couldn't tell them what I'd just done. They'd kill me. Maybe not literally, but they'd at least punch me in the face and that wasn't ideal. We needed to hurry before they had the chance to move again.

He gave a slow, unsure nod. "Well, grab a couple guns. If we don't have Lai, we're gonna need them."

"Yeah, congrats, by the way." Celena smiled as she entered from the adjoining room with Wyatt close behind. "We just found out."

I forced a smile. "Yeah, thanks. We're really excited."

"I bet." She smiled.

"A girl this time, Adam said." Wyatt grinned. "You're naming her Milly?"

"Malina, Milly for short."

"Hey, it rhymes with Celena." Celena smiled. "That was intentional, I'm sure."

"Oh, yeah," I said. "Totally planned."

God, they'd all kill me if they knew what I just did. Hell, I'd kill me if I were in their shoes. But maybe I wouldn't. Maybe I'd understand if Kai locked Hannah in the basement for a few hours.

Then again, I didn't really do it to protect Laila. I did it to protect Milly. Although, I guess that was protecting Laila. It was also protecting me.

Fuck, I could feel her crying. The tightness in her chest as she struggled to breathe. Her tongue ached, clamping it between her chattering teeth.

She was having a panic attack. Of course she was, I fucking locked her in the basement. She was held captive for months and I locked her in the basement. I was forcing her to relive one of her worst nightmares.

But I was preventing another nightmare. That's what I had to keep telling myself. She was angry, and hurt, and afraid, and that was my fault. But she was *alive.*

Milly was alive. Laila and Milly were alive. And they were going to stay alive. Even if she hated me for it, she'd be alive.

"Stay low," Adam murmured, crouching beside me in the bushes near the large, circular door carved into the hillside.

I kept my eyes on the thick piece of metal. Kai narrowed his gaze at the large chain linked fence a few yards in the distance. "I can take it down, but when I do, they'll ken we're here."

"How long do you think it'll take you?" Brody asked.

"Least five ticks," Kai muttered. "Our flame won't be strong enough. We'll have to use wind."

I looked at the guard standing beside the large door. "Leah can't hack into it?"

"No," Adam murmured. "Something about a firewall, I don't know."

"If we use our air together, we could get it down quicker. I'm better with water but if you guys can handle the guards, Kai and I can get the door," Celena murmured beside Brody.

I pulled a swirling ball of energy to my hand to make sure it still worked. "Brody, Adam and I handle the guards. Just get the door down."

It seemed like a good plan. Not full proof but it made sense. Laila did the same all by herself. We had five people there and another six standing guard at the front door to get any stragglers.

There were eleven of us total. If Laila could handle an entire compound on her own, the eleven of us could handle this. Two of us were her siblings with similar abilities. We had this.

Or so I thought.

"Let Leah know, Celena," Adam murmured. "She gives us the clear, we teleport past that fence and we storm the door. I'll get the guard. You guys take anyone else who comes out."

"I'll get the left," I muttered. "You get the right."

Brody nodded.

Celena looked between us. "Ready when you are."

"On your go, Kai." I glanced his way.

He took Celena's hand and met her gaze. "On three."

Brody and Adam grabbed ahold of either of their shoulders as they began to count.

On three, the five of us almost simultaneously landed about twenty feet from the large cement door. Adam teleported behind the guard and had a knife through his throat before Celena and Kai even caught their balance.

The moment blood began to pour from the slit in the guard's neck, red lights flashed. Loud alarms blared. Bullets began to rain down from above.

They must have had watch towers tucked away in the trees. Celena and Kai began manipulating the air. I body blocked them, looking for the source of the bullets. I pulled a ball of energy to either hand and outstretched it around the five of us. I held it upward toward the direction of the bullets.

"Nice." Adam laughed, nodding up to it.

"Thanks." I held it in place and the air around us rushed faster and harder.

"Shit," Celena murmured behind me.

"What?" I glanced at her over my shoulder.

She plummeted to the ground. The air's spinning stopped swirling and Kai grasped her body. "Wyatt's hurt." She gasped.

"Leah's with him—"

"They got swarmed. Everyone's hurt," Kai said fast. "Adam, take Celena. She can heal them; I'll work on the door."

Adam said, "Work fast." They disappeared.

I held the orb above us as the wind picked back up. Facing the opposite way beside me, Brody quickly called, "Incoming," and raised his gun.

It was almost simultaneous.

Suddenly, the wind stopped. Kai cried out in agony behind me. A stabbing, burning hot pained slice through my chest.

I looked down at the blood pouring from my ribs. My hands holding the shield began to fumble.

"Fuck. Fuck, fuck." Brody grasped our shoulders.

Then we were stumbling to the ground in the bushes we'd been in a moment earlier. "Shit, man. Shit. We're two healers down, we need Laila. She's coming, right?"

Fuck.

I shook my head as I tried to heave a gasp into my lungs. Brody grasped my shoulders. "What did you do, Jeremy?"

I gasped again as blood gurgled from my lips.

His furrowed eyes grew wide. "Where is she?"

"Basement," I coughed out.

He lowered me back into the bushes. "She's going to fucking kill you if you don't die."

He disappeared.

CHAPTER NINETY-FIVE

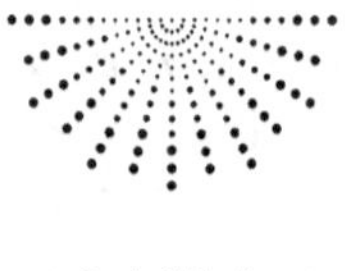

LAILA

It couldn't have been more than half an hour when the bullet sliced through Jeremy's chest. I nearly fell to the ground as the surge violently erupted through my body. Once the gasp had finished its way from my lips, I looked around for an escape.

The bathroom. A small glass block window in the shower. I wasn't going to destroy my sister in law's home before, but I could replace the window. I couldn't replace my soulmate. My stupid, idiotic, dickhead fucking soulmate.

I darted to the armoire and grabbed a large axe from inside. Then I teleported to the small wet room. I raised the axe and began thrusting it into the glass. The first smack didn't do anything, but the second hit shattered a block in the middle. I kept whacking it, terrified that his stupid ass got himself killed because he just *had* to be the hero.

"Laila," Brody's voice called from the main room. "Damn it. Laila!"

I teleported back to the large room still carrying the axe. "I'm gonna kill him. I'm gonna save him, then I'm gonna fucking kill him."

He laughed. He grabbed ahold of my shoulder.

Then we landed in some mosquito infested grass. Jeremy lay gurgling in the low brush grasping his chest. Blood dripped from his mouth. Kai was beside him grasping his upper pectoral. I teleported between them and held a glowing hand above either wound. Kai squirmed a bit. Brody firmly grasped his shoulders to hold him down.

It was hurting Jeremy, I felt it, but he fought the urge to show it. It took everything in me not to stop healing and smack him across his stupid face. But I saw the pain in his eyes. He knew I was pissed. I'm sure it was all over my face.

As the wound sealed shut, Jeremy began to say something. But I couldn't fight the urge. My open hand slammed across his cheek. His head fell to the side and his hand raised to his lip.

I lowered myself above him to meet his gaze. My finger wagged in his face, eyes glowing. "Don't fucking tell me what to do. Lock me up again, Jeremy, and I swear to God, you will wake up to a baseball bat to your kneecaps."

He painfully, yet fearfully looked between my eyes. "I'm sorry—"

"Not a fucking word unless 'it's okay, baby.'" I wagged my finger in his face. "We will fight about this later, but I need your dumb ass to listen to me so that we all make it out of this alive. Got it?"

He swallowed. "Okay, baby."

I narrowed my gaze. Then I teleported to my feet. "Where is everyone?"

"Front door," Brody said.

"You bring Kai," I said to Jeremy. Then I turned back to Brody. "Take me to them."

Brody grabbed ahold of my shoulder. And we landed in the middle of a gun fight. A bullet sliced through his ankle. He stumbled. I teleported to the outskirts of where we stood. "Shit, you alright?"

"Just a graze. Handle the guards. I'll start moving our people."

I gazed out over the gunfire ahead. I saw Adam tucked behind a tree to my right. He craned his head around the edge and fired his gun.

I teleported just to the outside of where the enemy bullets were flying. Without much effort, I sent flames from both hands in fast, steady streams of deep purple.

I couldn't see much through the thick foliage, there wasn't enough time to hear their screams, but I cleared a good thirty-foot span of trees in less than five seconds. I don't know how many guards were in the brush casting bullets at my family. I have no idea how many I killed on sight.

I didn't care regardless.

Kai was approaching a few feet behind me. Water poured over the still burning trees to prevent the flames from spreading.

"We need a healer over here!" Adam called.

I teleported to him and collapsed to the ground.

Hannah. Adam kneeled with his hand around hers. She pressed a wad of cloth to her lower abdomen.

"Ever been healed, Han?" I pushed hair behind her ear.

Her head shook and her lip quivered.

"Well, it hurts like a son of a bitch. Try biting down on the rolled-up edge of your hoodie." I turned up to Adam. "Let Kai know I got her. He's gonna hear her scream."

Adam stood. "Celena's healing Leah and Wyatt. They're in bad shape. Get Hannah healed quick. They might need her."

My chest tightened as I started healing. Hannah erupted in violent squeals as I looked at Adam. "Get Kai over there. We can put the fire out after everyone's healed."

Her body convulsed against the light. I climbed over top of her shifting legs to hold her down.

She wasn't begging me to stop, but her body was involuntarily pulling from the pain. For a first timer being healed, she was actually doing pretty well.

After a while, the skin molded shut, and I climbed off of her. "Feeling better?"

"Holy shit." Hannah made out between pants. "And you guys just do that every time you get hurt?"

"It's not so bad after a while." I started to my feet, extended my hand to her, and she stumbled to stand.

Celena let out a long, heavy cry.

"Hannah!" Adam screamed.

I tightened my hand on hers and teleported to them.

It wasn't Celena that cried. It was Haley. She was grasping Leah's bleeding face in the mud as her cold, empty green eyes stared up at us. A gaping hole of crimson pooled at her chest.

My mouth fell agape. Hannah released my hand and ran toward her. Jeremy stood a few feet away with his hand cupped over his mouth. Tears poured from his eyes.

I couldn't help the fury that flooded through me as I looked at him.

His sister died. Because of him. Had Brody not come for me, our key to the afterlife would've been gone and she'd have stayed that way.

I darted toward them. Hannah grabbed ahold of Leah's face. I held my hands over her chest.

It was littered with bullet holes. Like that of Bonnie and Clyde's 1934 Ford Deluxe the day they were gunned down in Louisiana. I could see where Celena tried to heal the wounds before she inevitably bled out. She was probably able to keep her alive in agony for a few short seconds, maybe a minute, but the only way to survive that kind of damage was doing exactly what we began. A necromancer holding the soul to their body while a Fae heals their agonizing organ damage.

After a moment or two of my healing and Hannah's shaking hands holding her sister's dead face, the wounds began to close, and Leah's body convulsed.

Her eyes rolled to her head. Her back and neck arched in an inhuman contortion. "Hold her down, Haley." I pushed my glowing hands into Leah's oozing chest.

Haley swiveled around us until she was at Leah's head. She grasped her shoulders.

Then the crack of one more gunshot.

Before I had the chance to defend us, Jeremy flung a blue force field of electricity above us.

I didn't so much as glance at him as I screamed for someone to take care of them. Celena stood beside me and erupted into a giant flame. She took off outside of the blue shield. With her keen hearing and scent, in addition to her ability to selfheal and melt bullets, she was the best chance we had at killing whoever was in those woods until Hannah and I got Leah back. Then I could stop healing and start killing.

CHAPTER NINETY-SIX

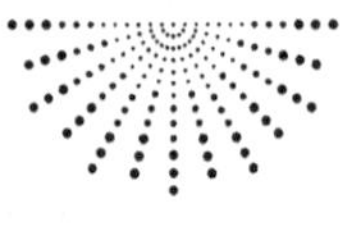

LAILA

Once Leah's wounds were closed, I told everyone to teleport back to the house. We all needed a second to recoup. We also needed somewhere to discuss without bullets raining down around us.

Truthfully, I didn't want Leah nor Hannah out in the field either. They were both near defenseless and too valuable in other ways to lose. Hannah was every one of our lifelines. Leah was our tech expert. They needed to stay close, but not that close.

We stood in the kitchen. Leah grasped her blood-drenched chest with trembling hands. Haley stood close behind her with a gentle hand on her upper arm. Hannah wrapped her arm around Kai's waist. Brody and Adam were chugging bottles of water. Celena was pulling a hoodie over her naked body as Wyatt struggled to shield her. Jeremy held his hand over his mouth as he looked around at the damage.

That's when I noticed the three others. Two people I hadn't met but one I knew pretty well. Liam. He stood against the breakfast nook wiping sweat from his forehead. A woman with a blond pixie cut stood to his left and an older gentleman in jeans with suspenders over a white shirt stood on his other side.

"Why would you set yourself up in an open field?" I looked between Jeremy, Kai and Celena. "The only one of you that's close to bullet proof is Celena."

"We had to get the door down. You weren't there, we had to work with what we had." Celena stepped into a pair of sweatpants.

"Yeah, who's fault is that?" I barked with a darting gaze at Jeremy.

He hung his head.

"What?" Leah asked.

"He had Helena cast a spell to lock me in the basement," I snapped, looking between his eyes.

"You what?" Adam blurted.

Kai released Hannah's waist and took a step toward him. "You locked my sister in a basement?"

"I was trying to keep you safe," he said with bloodshot red eyes.

"And you almost got all of us killed because of it," Leah yelled. "I died, Jeremy. I fucking died. And if Laila wouldn't have shown up—"

"Don't you think I know that?" Jeremy barked.

"It doesn't matter. We're all here, we're alive, we can argue later. They're either locking down or evacuating as we speak. We need to get inside. Leah, Hannah, I want you to stay here. Or at least on the outskirts. You're both too valuable to lose aside from your lack of ability to defend yourself."

"I'll stay back at the hotel," Leah said.

"You stay with her, Han," Brody said. "Our healers go down, we come to you guys."

"Liam." I gestured toward him "Can you spread your invisibility to others?"

He grabbed the shoulders of the man and woman beside him. As they disappeared, I gave a nod and they reappeared. "You stay at the back door with Kai. You stay invisible, and Kai, you kill anyone who walks out that isn't in scrubs. Only try to capture someone if they look important. Guards won't do us any good, they don't know anything important. Anyone wearing normal clothes we need. They might have powers so knock them out and tie them up. We have tranquilizers, right?" I looked around. Brody nodded. I turned my gaze between the boys. "Take them back to the basement. That'll be your job, Adam. You stay out back with them and move people out. Your powers work outside but they probably won't inside. You're a good shot but you're stronger than Brody. You'll have better luck subduing someone and he'll have better luck with a gun."

"Sounds good to me," Adam said.

I turned to the other two. "What are you?"

The man opened his mouth. Long, sharp fangs protruded from above his canines. Thin though, not thick like Celena and Wyatt's. A vamp. "Good, you stay with me. You'll be able to withstand my heat if I ignite."

I turned to the woman. "Demon," she said.

"Fallen or hybrid?" I asked.

"Oh, definitely fallen, love." She smiled.

"You probably know her." Brody gestured her way.

She rolled her eyes. "I go by Lily. But you'd probably know me as Lilith."

"No shit," I murmured. "Why do you care about all this?"

"We're both survivors." The vamp gestured between them.

"Nathaniel and I were cellmates for a good decade," Lily said.

"Well, thanks for your help. We'll have to meet up for lunch when the dust settles. For what it's worth, I don't think you should have been kicked out of Eden. Fuck bowing to a man." I glanced at Jeremy before looking back to her. "Your powers will work in there then?"

"They did last time. Unless that Witch is there and can confine me to a room, my powers can't be bound," Lily said.

"Good, you go with Celena and Wyatt then. They get hurt, you teleport them out. Bring them to Kai outside, me, or Leah back here. Celena can heal either of you so you keep her safe," I said.

Lily said, "I'm getting sick of this skin anyway. I'll hop in another patrol if it gets damaged. Don't worry about trying to heal me."

"Gross," Liam murmured.

"Jeremy and Brody, the two of you stick close. You're the only pair without a healer but we each have a teleporter and a telepath. Brody, you have Jeremy's back. He teleports you to me or Celena if you get hurt." I took in a deep breath. "Otherwise, we do what we did last time. We open doors. We get our people into groups and keep them safe until we can move them to the closest hospital. Once everyone's out and every guard is killed, we investigate every inch of the place. We take any piece of evidence they have. We clear every inch. Then we call Tina Davis."

"Where do you want me?" Haley took a step away from Leah.

"You aren't staying?" I asked.

"You need as many hands as you can get," Haley said. "If you can use me, I want to help."

"Then you go with Brody and Jeremy." I looked around the room. "If you see purple fire, you grab your team and you teleport out. We're going to be underground—my fire will eat the oxygen in that space before you have time to blink. None of our people need to go down in friendly fire. I'll try to control myself, but I'm pissed so we'll see what happens."

"How do we get in?" Brody asked. "Kai and Celena couldn't get the door to budge."

"Because you can't take the door *down*, you have to create your own." I huffed. "Everybody wait in the brush. I'll make us an opening. But have me a set of clothes ready."

CHAPTER NINETY-SEVEN

LAILA

As we landed in the grass outside of the large metal door, I took in my surroundings. There were now ten large, almost military grade SUVs blocking the entrance in a semicircle. I saw a few guards in each, not to mention the line of them just behind the vehicles. I leaned down and began tugging at the back of my moccasins. I pulled them from my feet and handed them to Jeremy.

"Laila, are you—" he began.

"Not a word, Jeremy." I lifted off my hoodie. "They're humans. I can handle this."

"I love you," he whispered.

I huffed, narrowing my gaze. "You're fucking lucky I love you too."

A sad smile pulled at his lips. And I gritted my teeth.

Then I teleported a good twenty feet into the brush behind me and brought flames to my skin. I closed my eyes and let them grow. When I opened them, I was engulfed in a violent eruption of purplish white light.

And I teleported just in front of the line of cars.

I heard the guns begin to fire but any bullet that got within five feet of me melted to small puddles on the ground. My arms outstretched toward the vehicles. The same white-purple light flew toward them in large streams. The flames consumed the oxygen around them and grew larger as they contacted vehicles. In a second or two, flames were all that remained.

It probably took me about five seconds total to turn all ten cars to dust.

I could have flown them away; it may have been easier. But I had to clear the area. Every guard dead was one less bullet flying toward us.

As the cluster of men in bullet proof vests became clear in the smoke where the vehicles stood, more gun fire cracked toward me. My hand traveled over them through the distance. Fire danced off of my outstretched fingers like water from a garden hose. Only instead of a refreshing cool mist, the fire left nothing but dust behind.

They didn't even have time to scream. Although, I suppose most people I wanted to kill never did. They were just gone. At least fifty people in less than thirty seconds. Simply wiped from existence.

Once the area was full of smoke and the smell of burned flesh and plastic, I made my way through the ash and smog to the door. I closed my eyes as the silence drew in. Then I felt the earth begin to quake beneath me.

A small, localized earthquake cracked beneath the door. Then I summoned air from behind it, violently siphoning it into a tornado behind the thick, circular opening.

It flung above my head as if a giant flying saucer. Like a Frisbee to a dog the size of Clifford.

More gunfire cracked toward me. I wasn't sure why they had yet to realize that a bullet couldn't take me down when I was glowing the hottest flame known to earth. I poured more fire from my hands like a reversed firefighter.

I didn't stop the flames until there was silence yet again. All that I heard was the roar and crackling of flames as I looked out at the damage I'd done. There wasn't even a way to count the bodies.

Not even a minute, and I was inside. Exactly why I knew I could handle this.

Stay back. I'll tell you when the coast is clear. Send Kai's group to the back. Tell them to let me know if they need me, I murmured into Jeremy's thoughts as I started into the wreckage.

Okay, baby, he whispered into my mind. *Be careful, okay?*

When I continued ahead, I heard his voice again.

I'm so sorry, Laila. I—I shouldn't have done that, but I just didn't want anything to happen to you and I—

Please just shut the fuck up.

His voice fell silent as I continued inside.

All that remained as my bare feet pressed into the glowing ashes was an opening in a hillside. As I drew further inside, I slid my hand along the warm cement. My gaze shifted down the long hall.

Of course, there laid another door. Charred and burning red. I summoned the air behind it toward me. That door then flew past me the way the first had. Although, it was far less dramatic than the first. It crashed to the ground near my feet.

I stared into the dark doorway ahead.

I knew this scary movie. I'd go through that doorway and get slammed by fifty guards at once. They'd all try to kill me.

The scene ends two ways. I kill them all. Or they kill me.

But I couldn't use fire that time. I didn't know how close the survivor's rooms were. I didn't know how sturdy they were. I didn't know if they could withstand the flame without killing them too.

I held my flames as a shield and started inside. But once I crossed the threshold, I closed my eyes and let another kind of light radiate from my skin. Bullets rushed toward me. My nearly white flames began to seep sparkling flakes of gold and violet smoke outward in every direction.

The gunfire ceased. I opened my eyes. I didn't take time to note the nearly fifty guards standing around me as I gazed out over the hallway. I projected the image into Jeremy's mind as I started down the hall siphoning air from the guard's lungs.

One by one, their gasping bodies fell to the ground with a thud.

Metal doors. One-way handles. Small glass rectangles in each.

A smile pulled at my lips. I looked into the first window. Tears welled in my eyes as I gazed at the young boy behind the door. He wore blue scrubs. His hair was buzzed to his scalp. He had the scar on his neck.

I pulled a thrust of wind to knock the door down. He rushed toward it. He began speaking in some foreign language I didn't understand. He laughed and grasped my shoulders. I smiled as tears began to pearl from my eyes.

We did it.

Most of it, anyway.

After I opened each of these doors, there were only two people left who needed rescued.

And I'd be damned before I gave up on them.

We've got our first survivor, I sent to Jeremy's mind. *Storm the door and help me get the rest of them out.*

The story continues in *Land of Light*. Turn the page for a sneak peek, or click the link below to download now:
https://www.amazon.com/gp/product/B094KZT5SP/

Sign up for Charlie's newsletter and receive a free copy of the Eluding Destiny prequel, *Blood Bar*:
https://liquidmind.media/eluding-destiny-prequel/

If you enjoyed this story, please consider leaving a rating or review on Amazon:
https://www.amazon.com/dp/B091YSK6X9/

Join Charlie's private reader group on Facebook and discuss all things Eluding Destiny and Charlie Nottingham:
https://www.facebook.com/groups/661440911724435/

LAND OF LIGHT CHAPTER ONE

MARCH 2022 - CHRIS

"What happened, Micah?" I grasped his tiny shoulders. My wrist throbbed as the disgusting stench of charred flesh burned my nostrils.

"Is you okay?" Micah whispered. Of course. Changing the subject. As he often did when he didn't like the topic of discussion.

I clutched the electrical burn at my wrist. "Yeah, buddy. I'm okay."

His hand at my shoulder moved to my forearm. The white-hot pain pulsed through me, and I struggled to ignore the agony. I took long, heavy whiffs of the smoky, awful smelling air as it healed and tried to forget how badly I wanted to scream.

"I didn't mean to," he murmured. The wound closed and his hand pulled back.

"It's okay, buddy." I drew closer, following the sound of his voice, and took his face in my hands. He tugged my palm from his cheek and cupped it together with his. He sniffled. "It's okay, I'm not mad."

"I didn't mean to," he whispered.

Fuck, I hoped he was only apologizing for the burn he'd given me. I hoped he didn't realize what he'd just done. I prayed he kept his eyes closed like he was supposed to.

I smiled. "I'm not mad, kiddo. It's okay."

"Pwomise?" he asked softly.

I nodded, holding my smile. "I promise, buddy. I promise."

He reached his little arms out and wrapped them around my neck. His head rested against my shoulder. I raised my hand to the back of his hair. "Is he wight? Awe we leaving?"

"If that's what he said," I said. "If that's what he said, then... Then, yeah. He wouldn't have said it if he didn't mean it."

"Can I open my eyes yet?" he asked.

I fought the urge to gag at the smoking body behind me. "Not yet. Not yet, kiddo. Just hang in there."

He nodded against my chest, squeezing my back. The wind whirled outside the window. Silence crept in for a moment while I tried to retain my composure.

Fuck, I prayed he was right. I prayed they were coming. I prayed he didn't fill Micah with empty hope.

I could take the pain and misery, but my nephew couldn't. He needed out of here. Even if it was without me, he needed out of here. He needed his parents. I loved him with everything I had, but he needed what my brothers and sisters and I never had. He needed a mom and a dad.

I knew they were doing everything they could, but they needed to hurry.

Micah's tears warmed my shirt. "I'm scawd."

"Are you hurt?" I held his body tighter against my chest.

His tiny hands trembled at my back. "You has to stay 'til they get hewe."

I tucked my lips together to keep them from trembling. "I'll try, buddy. I'll try."

He nodded and squeezed me tighter.

Maybe he'd seen. Maybe he knew. Fuck, I hoped he didn't. But I had to ask.

"What did you do, Micah?" I whispered. "What happened?"

He shook his head, and his arms tightened around me. His quiet tears turned to gentle, silent sobs as his body quivered.

"Okay, it's okay," I said. "It's okay, you don't have to talk about it."

"It's almost ovew, wight?" Micah asked quietly.

I swallowed hard, nodding fast. "I think so. I think so, buddy."

"He said it was," he murmured.

A bang pounded at the door. My heart thudded in my chest, hands going clammy. But I had to stay steady. I had to keep it together for him.

His arms tightened around my body. "You can't go. You has to stay."

"I have an idea. Hold my hand, okay?"

He nodded against my shoulder and leaned back. His fingers found mine. That nails on a chalkboard sensation vibrated in my brain.

They were trying to get inside of me. I'd held them off a few times, but it was harder than ever tonight. But I held onto myself with every fiber of my being. My hands trembled as I squeezed them around his.

He was the only chance we had. He was the only reason we could get messages to them in the first place. I had to piggyback onto his abilities just to keep control of my own body, rarely even to my success.

Then, the earth beneath my feet began to quake. I gripped the cold cement for stability. Micah moved back to my lap with a gasp.

The last time I felt something that strong was when Laila blew the roof off of our cells.

"What was that?" Micah's body curled into me. "I'm scawd. I'm weally scawd."

Chris?

My stomach nearly hit the floor.

Jeremy. Jeremy's voice inside my head.

"Is it them?" Micah's hand touched my face.

Thank god. A quiet laugh left my lips.

Are you okay? Is Micah okay?

Yeah, we're okay. We're okay. I think someone's trying to get the door down, you have to hurry.

That might be one of us. Be ready to run, alright? You hear a guy with a weird Irish accent, listen to him. But we're coming. We're taking care of Peterson and Nastya then we'll be there. But if they get there first, do what they say.

I laughed. *You've got a real plan this time, huh?*

I'll see you soon.

"Uncle Chwis, I'm scawd." Micah's quiet, gentle voice shook. "I—I'm weally scawd."

"Don't be." A smile came to my lips. The ground quaked again. He grasped my shoulders and buried his head into my chest. "Don't be, buddy. Remember what we talked about? About going home? Remember those places we've shown you with the huge house and the little fountain and all the trees and the big blue sky?" He nodded against my chest. "That's where we're going. We're going home, buddy."

"You said that befowe," he whispered.

"This time's different."

A loud crack sounded outside—a gun. Micah quivered and pushed himself further into my chest as his teeth began to chatter. His shaking hand wrapped around mine, and I squeezed his body closer.

"It's almost over, buddy. We're going home." Screams erupted behind the metal wall. His little body trembled, but I held him tighter. "He wouldn't have said it if he wasn't sure."

LAND OF LIGHT CHAPTER TWO

DECEMBER 23, 2020 - LAILA

Once we got inside, we did exactly as we'd done last time. We divided into our groups. We killed guards. We opened doors. We led the survivors outside where Brody began teleporting them to our closest hospital.

I should have been happy as I gazed out over the clusters of supernaturals standing around in small huddles. I should have had some remnant of pride or joy or accomplishment.

But all I felt was pain.

Micah wasn't here. Chris wasn't here. And I knew it was awful, but I would have left the rest of them there for all of eternity if it meant that I brought my son and brother-in-law home.

I wasn't sure how many people I killed that day. I know it was well over a couple hundred, but I couldn't say an exact number for certain. It's not like there were bodies left to count.

That made it easier to detach. Aside from the fact that they were the ones firing their guns at me and that I had every right to shoot back, the reality of living with the fact that I'd killed well past a hundred people is something that's difficult to accept. Tack on all the others I'd killed up until that point and you're looking at the largest serial killer the United States had ever seen besides Harry Truman when he gave notice to drop the atom bomb.

I killed more people than Ted Bundy and Jeffrey Dahmer combined in less than the time it takes most people to tie their shoes. It was as easy as blinking. It didn't feel any more difficult either.

As I watched their bodies turn to ash, I felt no remorse. I felt relieved.

After losing to Nastya, all I wanted to do was kill. I wanted to fucking end them. But I couldn't. So I took my pain out on the next available outlet that deserved it just as much.

Once upon a time, I thought that murder was always bad. That statement alone is somewhat comical. There was a time that I didn't even believe in the death penalty. But somewhere along the way, I realized that the line between death and life isn't as finite as I once believed it to be.

I once viewed living as a right. But at some point, I realized that being alive is a privilege. With a good enough reason, that privilege can—and should—be taken away.

***

"Here." Jeremy draped his jacket around my bare shoulders, handed me a pair of pants, and met my gaze. "I saw some steps a few halls over. No one's come up, but we've got Celena and Wyatt standing watch by them just in case."

I stepped into the sweatpants. "Sounds good. Any idea how many we got out?"

"Shit, I don't even know," he muttered. "Last I heard was around two-fifty. The closest hospital's at max capacity so we had to start moving people to another."

"Grand total's around five hundred so far then, right?" I asked. "If you count everyone I got out last time."

He gave a gentle smile. "Something like that."

I fixed the sweatpants around my hips. He handed me a shirt. I quickly threw it over my head. "Did we get any captors?"

"One," he said. "A young kid. Eighteen or nineteen, maybe twenty, I think. He's tied up in the basement."

"Sounds familiar."

"I didn't tie you up," he muttered.

"May as well have."

"That's not fair," he said quietly. "I was just trying to keep—"

"Me safe. Yeah, I know. You've said it a thousand times." I rolled my eyes. "We'll talk about this later. We aren't done here. Show me these stairs."

He pulled a ball of energy to his fingertips and started down the hallway. I walked silently beside him and took the place in for the first time.

It almost reminded me of a subway. Cement block walls curved into a semicircle above us. Mice scurried through small puddles of water beneath our feet. The area was lit only by the light we produced. There were lights on the ceiling, but they must have been shut off during the lockdown. Maybe the guards had been wearing night vision goggles. If they were, I hadn't noticed.

As I looked around, I found myself feeling somewhat relieved that I had been at the other facility. This one would have been far worse. At least I had a window in my cell. These prisoners had nothing.

The cells were slightly different than mine had been. There was still a spigot sticking out of the wall beside the toilet sink combination, there were still metal tables as beds, the floors were still concrete. But instead of steel walls, they were composed of thick concrete block. I doubted they could even communicate with other prisoners through them.

"You didn't get hit by any bullets, did you?" Jeremy asked as we turned right down a hallway.

"No, I'm fine," I muttered. "And you?"

"Yeah, I'm good," he said quietly. "I guess Wyatt got hit in the leg, but Celena took care of it."

As we continued down the hall, I said, "Why didn't I know that Lilith was a captor?"

"I thought you did."

"No, I didn't," I said. "I guess I don't know that many of them. Survivors, I mean. I want to though. After that bomb, I wasn't... Well, you know."

He gave what he could of a smile. "We can go to the hospitals tomorrow and make some rounds, if you want."

"Maybe we should go to the store and get everyone a Christmas gift. It's been a long time since they had one, and their families won't have enough time to get them any," I said. "Just something to open, you know?"

"Yeah, that sounds nice," he said.

"Oh, do you remember that little boy? The one Janis and Elijah have? I can't remember his name."

"Cage." He smiled. "His name was Cage."

"Cage," I said. "I wonder if his Dad's at the hospital. Maybe they'll get to spend Christmas together."

His smile lifted slightly. "Maybe."

Suddenly, another thought dawned on me. "Do you think Daniel's mom or dad was here?"

He nearly held his breath. "Maybe."

"I don't know what I'll say to them if they are."

"We'll tell them the truth. Peterson used him to trap you. Then you gave yourself over to him to keep Daniel safe."

The memory flashed through my mind. That look of terror in his eyes as his neck broke. As if it were happening in front of me, I instinctively pressed my eyelids together.

My head shook slightly, like shaking off the instant replay. It hit too close to home. Another little boy thrusted into a life that made no sense, tortured for some maniac's cause, then murdered for nothing.

"And then they snapped his neck," I murmured.

He was quiet for a moment. "Maybe they're already gone too."

"Maybe," I muttered. "Do you know if Liam found his brother?"

He smiled. "They're at the hospital together now."

I tried to smile. At least someone had their family back. I supposed a lot of someones would have their family back by the day's end. It did give me a touch of relief. Not really joy, but relief.

We rounded the corner to the cranny beside a narrow, metal set of steps. "Leah said she needs us to help organize people outside. You got this?" Celena called as we closed the distance between each other. Wyatt stood next to her, rolling his neck from side to side.

"Yeah, you're good," I said. "Tell anyone available to come inside and start looking. There's got to be something here that'll help us."

"Sure." Celena smiled and put her arms around me. "Congratulations, by the way. I'm so happy for you guys."

"Yeah, thanks." I forced a smile as my hand coasted over my bump. "We're really excited. But quit being such a stranger. Come visit your sister once in a while."

And I was. Truly, having my little girl meant the world to me. But I wanted my son too. I wanted the four of us to be a family. Micah, Milly, Jeremy, me. I wanted us all together. I wanted the family we'd been planning for more than two years. I wanted what was mine.

Peterson's words pulsed through my mind.

I promise that one day, you'll have him back.

Jesus fuck, why were his words my only sense of hope?

She laughed. "Yeah, coming from the one that can teleport. It's a two-hour drive for me, ya know."

"More like hour and a half." I smiled. "But you're right. It'd be easier for me than you. You guys are still coming for Christmas dinner, right?"

Wyatt's lips flapped in a trill. "Nowhere else to go."

"Oh yeah, I meant to ask," Celena said. "Is it alright if my mom comes?"

"Yeah, of course," I said. "Hey, at least our moms can bond over their exceptionally gifted daughters now."

A laugh left her lips. "Yeah, I guess so. But let us know if you need us. We're going to go outside before Leah bites our heads off."

Captivated by *The Quiet Army*? Click the link below to download now!

https://www.amazon.com/gp/product/B094KZT5SP/

ALSO BY CHARLIE NOTTINGHAM

The Eluding Destiny Series

Eluding Destiny

The Horrors That Created Us

Aftershocks

The Precipice

Land of Light

The Quiet Army

Sacred Sins

Flash Back

The Shift

Lost to Time

Gods Among Us

The Cover Up

Blank Slate

Eluding Destiny Prequels

The Last Beginning

Blood Bar

Raven's Cry Series

(MMFM Paranormal Romance)

Raven's Cry

Raven's Song

Celena's Story Duology

(Completed—paranormal romance, urban fantasy)

New Normal: Celena's Story Part 1

Reprisal: Celena's Story Part 2

Origins of the Gods

(Completed Trilogy—fantasy romance, more information on the origins of the Fae and Angels, how life began on earth, where Guardians came from, and—most importantly—a badass forbidden romance)

Origins

The Thrones of Ore and Ice

Creation

Stand Alone Novels

Curse of the Gods: The Bridge Between Origins of the Gods and the Eluding Destiny Series

Sign up for Charlie's newsletter and receive a free copy of the Eluding Destiny prequel, Blood Bar:

https://liquidmind.media/eluding-destiny-prequel/

ABOUT THE AUTHOR

Charlie is a... Okay, talking about myself in third person is weird.

Nice to meet you! My name's Charlie Nottingham, and my whole world revolves around fantasy. When I'm not writing a new book, I'm either hanging out with my dogs, talking with my fans online, or reading some amazing urban fantasy, paranormal romance, or fantasy romance series (always a series, never a stand-alone, because I hate to fall for a character and never see them again). Or re-watching some Buffy or Supernatural. (They never get old!)